THE WENDIGO AND OTHER STORIES

ALGERNON BLACKWOOD was born in 1869 at Wood Lodge, Shooter's Hill, Kent, into a family with aristocratic connections and strongly evangelical Christian beliefs. After a spotty education at a succession of schools, followed by a year at the University of Edinburgh, he lived for nine years in Canada and the United States, much of it spent in extreme poverty. Upon his return to Britain, Blackwood began writing horror stories, with his first collection, *The Empty House and Other Ghost Stories*, appearing in 1906 to positive reviews. Other collections, as well as novels, followed in rapid order; between 1906 and the outbreak of the Great War, Blackwood published five novels and something like ninety stories and novellas. Several of these, including 'The Willows', 'Ancient Sorceries', and 'The Wendigo', are acknowledged classics of the weird tale. Many of Blackwood's best and most characteristic stories are less conventionally supernatural than 'Super-Natural', concerned with the relationship between humans and non-human systems and environments. Late in life he reinvented himself as a media star of sorts, appearing regularly on BBC radio and television broadcasts. It was at this time that Blackwood became popularly known as 'The Ghost Man', an epithet he himself resisted, insisting that his real theme had always been 'the Extension of Human Faculty'. Blackwood died in London in 1951, aged 82.

AARON WORTH is Associate Professor of Rhetoric at Boston University. He has edited Arthur Machen's *The Great God Pan and Other Horror Stories*, Sheridan Le Fanu's *Green Tea and Other Weird Stories*, and Vernon Lee's *The Virgin of the Seven Daggers and Other Stories* for Oxford World's Classics.

T0130607

OXFORD WORLD'S CLASSICS

ALGERNON BLACKWOOD

The Wendigo and Other Stories

Edited with an Introduction and Notes by
AARON WORTH

OXFORD
UNIVERSITY PRESS

OXFORD
UNIVERSITY PRESS

Great Clarendon Street, Oxford, OX2 6DP,
United Kingdom

Oxford University Press is a department of the University of Oxford.
It furthers the University's objective of excellence in research, scholarship,
and education by publishing worldwide. Oxford is a registered trade mark of
Oxford University Press in the UK and in certain other countries

Published in the United States of America by Oxford University Press
198 Madison Avenue, New York, NY 10016, United States of America

British Library Cataloguing in Publication Data
Data available

Library of Congress Control Number: 2023935768

ISBN 978-0-19-884888-2

Printed and bound in the UK by
Clays Ltd, Elcograf S.p.A.

MIX
Paper | Supporting
responsible forestry
FSC
www.fsc.org
FSC® C018072

ACKNOWLEDGEMENTS

ONCE again I am deeply grateful to my editor, Luciana O'Flaherty, as well as to Emma Varley, Phoebe Aldridge, and many others at Oxford University Press who worked on the book; thanks also to Vasuki Ravichandran at Straive and my copy-editor Rowena Anketell; Rhoda Bilansky at Boston University; and Hajnalka Kovacs, Katherine Bishop, Dennis Denisoff, and Dawn Keetley for information and/or help along the way. Finally, my heartfelt thanks to Mike Ashley, who not only knows more about Blackwood than anyone living but was generously willing to share some of his knowledge with me.

CONTENTS

Introduction   ix

Note on the Text   xxxvii

Select Bibliography   xxxviii

A Chronology of Algernon Blackwood   xl

THE WENDIGO AND OTHER STORIES   1

A Haunted Island   3

The Empty House   18

The Listener   33

The Willows   58

Secret Worship   103

Ancient Sorceries   134

The Kit-Bag   177

The Man Who Found Out   188

The Face of the Earth   203

The Wendigo   212

The Man Whom the Trees Loved   256

A Descent into Egypt   318

Onanonanon   382

The Land of Green Ginger   388

The Doll   395

Explanatory Notes   425

INTRODUCTION

*Readers who are unfamiliar with the stories may prefer to
treat the Introduction as an Afterword.*

ON Halloween night in 1947, before the wondering eyes of tens of
thousands of television viewers, the storyteller popularly known in
Britain as the 'Ghost Man' magically disappeared. One moment, the
gaunt figure with the hypnotic eyes had been sitting there in the BBC
studio, holding his far-flung audience spellbound with a tale of
a stockbroker who vanishes after an uncanny summons from another
dimension; the next, the speaker had himself vanished, leaving behind
an empty chair and a disembodied voice which lingered on for a few
moments, like an aural version of the Cheshire Cat's grin. This pioneering use of special effects on live television astonished all who
witnessed it: 'Even staff at the BBC wondered what had happened.
The switchboard was jammed with callers saying they had seen
Mr Blackwood disappear.'[1] The 78-year-old storyteller was himself
dissatisfied with his own performance that evening, though it had
nothing to do with age: Algernon Blackwood at his best could still
electrify an audience, and he knew it. No, it was the camera trick—
getting it just right had meant an unusual amount of preparation
beforehand, and over-rehearsal, Blackwood felt, always took the fizz
out of his delivery (though all the evidence suggests that viewers on
this occasion found him quite chillingly effervescent).

It is tempting to read this episode in facilely symbolic or allegorical
terms, with Blackwood—one of the twentieth century's great idol-
aters of Nature capitalized—chafing at the restricting shackles
imposed by modernity's rival god, Technology. To be sure, even such
a simplistic reading generates complicating ironies aplenty, none less
glaring than the fact that Blackwood had achieved his greatest fame
late in life as a multimedia celebrity, and there is no indication that he
did not relish the role (and the fame). After a lifetime spent working
in different writerly forms and genres—his first stories and essays

[1] Mike Ashley, *Starlight Man: The Extraordinary Life of Algernon Blackwood* (Eureka,
CA, 2019), 408.

appeared in late Victorian periodicals, followed by a steady flow of
story collections and novels—in the 1930s Blackwood made a successful transition to the new broadcast media of the twentieth century. In fact, he cuts a significant figure in the early history of those
media, appearing in the first BBC television broadcast (in November
1936, on the programme *Picture Page*). By this time Blackwood had
already established himself as a media star of sorts, having appeared
regularly on radio broadcasts for the previous two years (the BBC had
tried to get him into the studio nearly a decade earlier, but his wan-
derlust kept him away from the microphone until 1934, when he
appeared on the programme *In Town Tonight*). The year 1949—in
which Blackwood received the medal of the British Television Society,
which recognized him 'as creator of the most outstanding contribution to television entertainment'[2]—saw him appearing on cinema
screens as well, in the first of a series of short films he would make
with Twentieth Century Fox's Rayant Pictures. It would be wrong to
say that Blackwood wholeheartedly embraced the brave new world of
twentieth-century media technologies. In an essay published in the
BBC's own listings magazine, he claimed that, given the listener's
awareness, at some level, of the medium's rational, scientific under-
pinnings, radio radically undermined the effectiveness of 'the ghost
story proper', which was 'a heritage of animistic days, when thunder
was a great god roaring, and a mountain stream a lovely, visible
Naiad—other-worldly'.[3] On balance, however, and despite the apparently Luddite note of pantheistic longing in evidence here, the 'Ghost
Man' was not really hostile to technology per se, at least not intransi-
gently; in an essay of 1929 Blackwood, while noting the superstition-
destroying potential of modern inventions, was able to recognize, if
a shade grudgingly, the possibility of relocating wonder in twentieth-
century science and technology: 'The poet turns nowadays to machinery, speed, electricity and electrons . . . The magi of today are physicists,
the fairies rays, the magic carpet is space-time. . . .'[4] Certainly if he
lived today (given his third-act self-reinvention as a household name
in the broadcast era), it is easy to imagine Blackwood's promiscuous

    [2] Kenneth Baily (ed.), *The Television Annual 1950/51* (London, 1951), 93.
    [3] Algernon Blackwood, 'You Can't Tell Ghost Stories on the Radio', *Radio Times*
(11 Dec. 1936), 11.
    [4] Algernon Blackwood, 'Dreams and Fairies', in *The Lure of the Unknown: Essays on
the Strange* (Dublin, 2022), 127.

presence on podcasts, YouTube videos, and other digital platforms (one imagines him lending his sepulchral voice to a character in a North Woods adventure video game based on 'The Wendigo' for Xbox or PlayStation).

Rather, what Blackwood rebelled against in the BBC studio, as he had done throughout his long life, was anything and everything that smacked of constraint or confinement of any kind. He disliked and resisted categorial capture as well, objecting even to the 'Ghost Man' label, which he called 'almost a derogatory classification'.[5] To be sure, this epithet is purely an artefact of Blackwood's BBC career; only a relatively small portion of his prodigious fictional output features conventional spectres or revenants, while his most characteristic—and celebrated—tales, such as 'The Willows' and 'The Wendigo', are more likely to fall under such aegises as 'Nature Gothic' or 'Cosmic Horror' (this, of course, is just more categorizing; Blackwood would undoubtedly have bristled equally at being called 'the Nature Man', or 'Mr Cosmic-Fear'). Still other fiction by Blackwood is better classed as fantasy, evoking wonder and awe rather than terror, or even science fiction. Beyond questions of genre, readers of Blackwood have always differed widely in assessing his gifts—and faults—as a writer, with even his most devoted admirers often finding very different things to admire. To many readers, during his lifetime and since, he was a nonpareil maker of classic ghost stories, and should (some of these have irritably added) have stuck to that honourable craft. Others have always been drawn less to his supernatural tales than to his 'Super-Natural' ones; in the rapturous words of his editor Maude ffoulkes, what made Blackwood truly exceptional was his role as an 'Interpreter of Nature in the primitive, poetic-animistic sense; and as the boldest Interpreter of what I may call Super-Nature among any writers of the day in any country'.[6] Among those unimpressed by

[5] In his introduction to a 1938 collection of his stories, reproduced in Algernon Blackwood, *Tales of Terror and the Unknown* (New York, 1964), 8. On another occasion Blackwood wrote, 'I am called the "ghost man"; editors want "ghost stories" from me. Yet my chief interest I should describe as an interest in the Extension of Human Faculty: in other words, latent powers that suggest we are all potentially much greater and more wonderful than we suspect' (Blackwood, 'Looking Back at Christmas', in *The Lure of the Unknown*, 8).

[6] She rounded out this assessment by calling him also an 'Interpreter of Children, in the Wordsworthian sense'; this, presumably, with novels such as *Jimbo* in mind (Maude M. C. ffoulkes, *My Own Past* (London, 1915), 201).

Blackwood the visionary 'Interpreter' was fellow weird writer (and fellow member of the Hermetic Order of the Golden Dawn) Arthur Machen, who remarked to the American writer Vincent Starrett: 'Tennyson, you remember, says "the cedars sigh for Lebanon", and that is exquisite poetry; but Blackwood believes the cedars really *do* sigh for Lebanon and that, Starrett, is damned nonsense!'[7] Yet it may be in Blackwood's conception of our relation to Nature and other non-human systems—his willingness, indeed, to imagine the post-human—that he speaks to us most urgently today, well into the pro-posed geological epoch that has been termed the 'Anthropocene'.

Life and Work

Algernon Henry Blackwood was born on 14 March 1869 at Wood Lodge, Shooter's Hill, Kent. It could be argued, however, that the event which would most decisively shape the course of his life and the character of his writing (and the two would always be closely inter-twined) had taken place on a June evening some thirteen years earlier, at a high-society ball in London's famous Willis's Rooms in King Street. There a young Stevenson Arthur Blackwood, who appears in his son's memoir as a kind of belated Regency beau ('a man of fash-ion', known by the soubriquet 'Beauty Blackwood'[8]), experienced the powerful consummation of a process of religious conversion whose first stirrings had been felt amid the horrors of war in the Crimea, where he had recently served as a volunteer:

Standing and looking on at the Quadrilles which were being danced, and putting—why I know not—my fingers in my ears, so that no sound of music reached me, the thought forced itself upon me, 'What folly! . . . and all these people have immortal souls to be saved!' . . . That was the last ball to which I ever went. The next time I entered Willis's Rooms, six years later, was to preach the Gospel.[9]

---

[7] Ashley, *Starlight Man*, 153–4. Blackwood's own feelings about Machen's writing are more difficult to assess, or perhaps they simply changed over the years: in 1943 he wrote, 'I read all his books some forty years ago but they left no special mark on me', but Maude ffoulkes wrote in 1915 that Blackwood 'revealed to me the genius of Arthur Machen' (*My Own Past*, 189).

[8] Algernon Blackwood, *Episodes before Thirty* (London, 1923), 24.

[9] H. S. D. Montagu, Lady Blackwood (ed.), *Some Records of the Life of Stevenson Arthur Blackwood, K.C.B.* (London, 1896), 133.

Henceforth 'renounc[ing] the world, the flesh, the devil and all their works' as Algernon would somewhat archly put it, Arthur married a woman of like mind (Harriet Sydney Montagu, the young widow of the sixth Duke of Manchester) and worked to become 'a leader in the evangelical movement, then approaching its height',[10] even while rising to the top of his worldly profession (an important official in the Post Office, he was knighted in 1887).

It is revealing that Blackwood would later liken his father's faith to that of Victorian naturalist Philip Gosse (1810–88), whose son Edmund rejected his own strict upbringing in the fundamentalist Plymouth Brethren, rather witheringly anatomizing them in the autobiographical novel *Father and Son* (1907). Young Algernon's own rebellion against his parents' evangelical Christianity—they seem not to have belonged to any particular sect[11]—was, as he himself recognized, complicated. On the one hand, any belief in the divinity of Christ, or in, as he put it, 'a Deity . . . specially active on Sundays only',[12] if he had ever truly had them, had been quite extinguished before he was out of his teens. It was not so easy, however, to root out the spiritual yearning, and the shaping patterns of thought, which he inherited from the familial brand of Victorian evangelism: 'Without wholeheartedly sharing my father's faith . . . his religious and emotional temperament, with its imperious need of believing *something*, he certainly bequeathed to me.'[13] Nor, indeed, did he want to root them out, as these were precisely the things which, mutatis mutandis, would help to give shape and purpose to his life. Like many a 'New Ager' in the century to come, the young Blackwood had been bequeathed a particular set of affective and conceptual bottles, into which he would experimentally pour a succession of novel vintages as he grew older. Among the alternatives to conventional religious faith which he pursued (these included a keen interest in the occult investigations of the Society for Psychical Research and a period of membership in the esoteric Order of the Golden Dawn), and towering far above them all, was a form of animistic or pantheistic Nature worship:

[10] Algernon Blackwood, *Episodes*, 24.

[11] E. F. Bleiler links them with the Sandemanians, the Church in which the English scientist Michael Faraday was raised, but there is no evidence for this claim (Algernon Blackwood, *Best Ghost Stories* (New York, 1973), p. v).

[12] Blackwood, *Episodes*, 29.   [13] Blackwood, *Episodes*, 26.

By far the strongest influence in my life, however, was Nature; it betrayed itself early, growing in intensity with every year. Bringing comfort, companionship, inspiration, joy, the spell of Nature has remained dominant, a truly magical spell. The early feeling that everything was alive, a dim sense that some kind of consciousness struggled through every form, even that a sort of inarticulate communion with this 'other life' was possible, could I but discover the way—these moods coloured its opening wonder. Nature, at any rate, produced effects in me that only something living could produce.[14]

This belief in a numinous, living universe best filled the god-shaped—and god-sized—hole in his heart; and just as he had been taught that 'People were sharply divided into souls that were saved and those that were—not saved', the young Blackwood soon transferred a similar sense of spiritual election to the context of his new quasi-faith:

I thought of all the people asleep in their silent rooms, and wondered how they could be so dull and unenterprising, when out here they could see these sweeping branches and hear the wind sighing so beautifully among the needles. These people, it seemed to me at such moments, belonged to a different race. I had nothing in common with them.[15]

The adolescent Blackwood was sent to a succession of 'horrible private school[s]—I went to four or five', acquiring his share of emotional scars along the way. At Sevenoaks in Kent he was accused of taking a book of poetry from a schoolmate, and was hauled before a 'fiendish' red-whiskered headmaster to be threatened with criminal prosecution (the episode, as recorded by Blackwood, sounds like a scene from Dickens or Pink Floyd's *The Wall*). The fact that the 'Satan[ic]' father figure was 'a clergyman of evangelical persuasion' was another nail in the coffin of Blackwood's Christian faith. More positive were the memories Blackwood retained from the year he spent at a Moravian school in Königsfeld im Schwarzwald, Germany: the masters there were strict, but something in their almost monastic asceticism appealed to the 16-year-old Algernon, as did the sense of fellowship he experienced there, and the simplicity of forms of worship which he saw as harmonious with the natural environment: 'Those leagues of Black Forest rolling over distant mountains, velvet-coloured, leaping to the sky in grey cliffs, or passing quietly like the

[14] Blackwood, *Episodes*, 36–7.   [15] Blackwood, *Episodes*, 38.

sea in immense waves . . . the whole setting of this Moravian school was so beautifully simple that it lent just the proper atmosphere for lives consecrated without flourish of trumpets to God.'[16] Still, Blackwood notes that life at the school 'did not wholly obliterate my fear of hell', and we may make what we will of his story 'Secret Worship', in which the Brothers are reimagined as undead Satan-worshippers, eager to deliver him up to their demonic *Hauptbruder* Asmodelius as an 'Opfer' (sacrifice).

At any rate, it should have been abundantly clear by now that Blackwood did not thrive within institutional structures. Sir Arthur, beginning to be seriously alarmed at his son's lack of direction, made one last effort, sending him up to Edinburgh in October 1888 to pursue a degree in agriculture (the pair had gone out to Canada the previous year to explore a possible career in farming). This was Blackwood's final experience with formal education and, even with his older brother's supervisory presence hovering over him, it was an abject failure: 'The year spent at Edinburgh University to learn the agricultural trade had been wasted, for, instead, I attended what interested me far more—the post-mortems, operations, lectures on pathology, and the dissecting room.'[17]

There was evidently nothing more—or perhaps more accurately, nothing at all—that formal schooling could do for Blackwood, and so, in the spring of 1890, he boarded a passenger ship in Liverpool, alone, bound for New York. He would spend the next nine years in America—Canada and the United States—ostensibly a young man in search of a career (while still nurturing vague plans of an agricultural career, he also carried letters of introduction from his father to Canadian railway 'bigwigs'), though his own account of these years suggests nothing so much as a fixed period of self-imposed punishment—a kind of exile or excommunication, perhaps, for having strayed, mentally and spiritually, from the evangelical fold in which he had been raised (he would finally return to England in 1899, by which time his father was dead). It is significant that the only autobiography Blackwood ever wrote focuses exclusively on this decade; part *Inferno*, part *Pilgrim's Progress*, *Episodes before Thirty* (1923) tells a tale of almost constant suffering and struggle, starring a naïf picaro who stumbles into a succession of adventures and misadventures,

---

[16] Blackwood, *Episodes*, 28–9.   [17] Blackwood, *Episodes*, 16.

gradually losing some of his innocence along the ways with respect to the world and its, well, worldliness. When not being preyed upon by charming conmen (a disproportionate number of pages are devoted to a parasitic, and erotically ambiguous, relationship with a socio-pathic Englishman), or drawn into dubious investment schemes, Blackwood worked variously as a journalist, a teacher of 'violin, French, German, and shorthand', and a model, posing for artists including the American illustrator Charles Dana Gibson, remem-bered today for his depictions of the iconic 'Gibson girl'.

What stick most firmly in the mind, however, are the book's vivid tableaux of (frequently extreme) poverty in New York City: we see Blackwood suffering 'physical and mental anguish' in a wretched boarding house, with 'loathsome vermin running over my body night after night'; one night, all but paralysed with terror, he watches 'a tall man pass the end of [my bedroom], one eye on me and another on the door, opening a razor slowly as he went'.[18] On other occasions we find him stretched out on a bench in Central Park, a Chaplinesque tramp subsisting on dried apples and boiled water ('I never see apple rings in a grocer's window without getting their taste and feeling them rise and swell within me like some troublesome emotion').[19] One word that recurs again and again in the memoir is 'horror', and some years later Blackwood, writing in the wake of Freud, came to credit, or blame, these experiences for turning him into a writer of horror fic-tion upon his return to Britain in the spring of 1899:

I recall . . . that these tales poured from me spontaneously, as though a tap were turned on, and I have often since leaned to the suggestion that many of them derived from buried, unresolved shocks—shocks to the emotions; and by 'unresolved', I mean, of course, unexpressed. These 'shocks' had come to an exceptionally ignorant youth of twenty who had drifted into the life of a newspaper reporter in New York after a disastrous cattle-farm and a hotel in Canada, and the drifting had included the stress of extreme pov-erty and starvation . . . the New York experiences in a world of crime and vice had bruised and bludgeoned a sensitive nature that swallowed the hor-rors without being able to digest them, and that the seeds thus sown, dormant and unresolved in the subconscious, possibly emerged later—and, since the subconscious always dramatises, emerged in story form.[20]

---

[18] Blackwood, *Episodes*, 3.   [19] Blackwood, *Episodes*, 332.
[20] Blackwood, *Tales of Terror and the Unknown*, 8.

And so, over the next few years, Blackwood spent his spare time filling a cupboard with the 'queer stories' which his exposure to American 'horrors' had thus stirred up from the depths of his subconscious ('It had been my habit and delight to spend my evenings composing yarns on my typewriter, finding more pleasure in this than in any dinner engagement, theatre or concert'[21]). While Manhattan traumas may (or may not) have catalysed his decision to write these first stories, they are more or less evenly divided between the Old and New Worlds, with both urban and rural settings represented on both sides of the Atlantic. Blackwood sent a pair of these to *Pall Mall Magazine*—'A Haunted Island' appeared there in 1899, 'A Case of Eavesdropping' the following year—but otherwise he seems to have had little thought of publishing these early efforts. Then a journalist friend from his New York days, Angus Hamilton, came to visit Blackwood in his room in Chelsea:

He reminded me of the stories I used to tell in the New York boarding house. I had written some of these, a couple of dozen perhaps, and they lay in a cupboard. Could he see them? Might he take them away and read them? . . . Hamilton took a dozen or so away with him, but forgot to send them back as promised. . . . It didn't matter much, I went on writing others, the stories were no good to anybody, the important thing being the relief and keen pleasure I found in their expression. But some weeks later a letter came from a publisher: 'I have read your book . . . My reader tells me . . .' this and that 'about your stories . . . I shall be glad to publish them for you.'[22]

The publisher was Eveleigh Nash, to whom Hamilton had sent the stories without their author's permission. Blackwood expressed, or affected, irritation at the liberty his friend had taken, though a sceptic might suspect him of having secretly hoped for some such outcome (one often wonders whether Blackwood is quite the ingenuous, naïf figure he sometimes makes himself out to be; there is a certain obliqueness to his character, like that of the cat people in 'Ancient Sorceries').

In any event, Nash promptly snapped up the stories, and *The Empty House and Other Ghost Stories* was published shortly before

[21] Blackwood, *Episodes*, 255. [22] Blackwood, *Episodes*, 255–6.

Christmastime in 1906.[23] The book garnered positive reviews and established Blackwood, greatly to his surprise, as a professional writer. *The Spectator*'s reviewer, while grumpily dismissive of the overall state of the genre since the heyday of Dickens and Sheridan Le Fanu ('the exploits of mid-Victorian authors need fear no comparison with modern exponents of the *macabre* and the cadaverous'), was nonetheless able, with a few reservations, to 'cordially commend' *The Empty House* 'to those who may wish for once in a way to sup full of horrors'.[24] More unequivocally enthusiastic was Hilaire Belloc, writing anonymously in the *Morning Post*. First declaring polemically that 'The English Ghost Story (by which we mean the Anglo-Welsh-Cornish-Irish-Scotch ghost story) is a thing the like of which does not exist in Europe', Belloc went on to characterize Blackwood's tales as a triumph of the race—a kind of litmus test, indeed, for British identity on the part of the reader:

Here on the table is a book of such a sort as does from time to time appear, making, one supposes, no particular pretence to fame, and yet exceedingly well done, because it is instinct with this national power, and everyone who has a shelf for the horrible in his library will welcome it and give it its place. It is called 'The Empty House'. No one will read this book without dread—at least if he does he is a foreigner, and much more truly a foreigner than the man who neglects to slap his chest and talk about command of the sea.[25]

The Bookman warned, enticingly: 'Persons of weak nerves would do well not to read the stories in "The Empty House" just before going to bed; there is a brood of weird and grisly nightmares in each one of them. . . . No book of ghost stories so cunningly and so powerfully written has appeared for a very long time'; *The Academy* declared, 'Mr Algernon Blackwood is to be congratulated on having produced one of the best books of "horrors" since the appearance of Mr Bram Stoker's "Dracula". . . . it is the convincing manner in which [these stories] are told which compels admiration'.[26] In the wake of this maiden collection's success, Blackwood was asked to raid his cupboard

[23] Nash's reader, Maude ffoulkes, 'was in the throes of a violent influenza cold' when she received the MS., but this was soon forgotten in her admiration for the unknown author's stories; the following day she told Nash, 'Here is a "find" worth keeping. . . . For Heaven's sake, don't miss this book, because it will be a long time before you will ever meet with another Algernon Blackwood' (*My Own Past*, 179).

[24] *The Spectator* (26 Jan. 1907), 145.   [25] *Morning Post* (3 Jan. 1907), 2.

[26] *The Bookman* (Feb. 1907), 232; *The Academy* (15 Dec. 1906), 612.

again, and a second book, *The Listener and Other Stories*, appeared in late 1907. In addition to the title story, whose protagonist, a 'dreadfully nervous' figure in the Edgar Allan Poe tradition, finds himself sharing a Marylebone flat with a spectral leper, the book included what has always been one of Blackwood's most celebrated tales, 'The Willows'. Like most of his best work, this story draws much of its power from its peerless evocation of a sense of place—in this case, a setting recollected from a voyage Blackwood had made in 1900 with a friend 'down the Danube in a Canadian canoe'.[27] With its harrowing account of two men trapped on a vanishing island with a host of hostile, elemental forces which can only be perceived through symbols or as highly subjective mental constructions, 'The Willows' is a masterpiece of both description and the tactical withholding of description. When one of the extra-dimensional entities finally comes into view, it can only be represented as a succession of imperfect conceptual blends, through a process resembling nothing so much as one of the ink-blot tests the Swiss psychologist Hermann Rorschach was developing at around the same time:

I saw it through a veil that hung before my eyes like the gauze drop-curtain used at the back of a theatre—hazily a little. It was neither a human figure nor an animal. To me it gave the strange impression of being as large as several animals grouped together, like horses, two or three, moving slowly. The Swede, too, got a similar result, though expressing it differently, for he thought it was shaped and sized like a clump of willow bushes, rounded at the top, and moving all over upon its surface—'coiling upon itself like smoke', he said afterwards. (p. 97)

The reviewer for *The Academy* saw *The Listener* as an advance on *The Empty House*, writing, 'in the present volume Mr Blackwood has gone far towards fulfilling the promise of his earlier work . . . when Mr Blackwood rises to his full height he is likely to be positively spine-chilling'.[28]

For his next collection, the cupboard being now bare, or nearly so,[29] new stories were needed—as was, in his publisher's opinion, a unifying

---

[27] This was the title of an essay which Blackwood wrote for *Macmillan's Magazine* in 1901.

[28] *The Academy* (28 Dec. 1907), 297.

[29] Two of the five stories included in *John Silence*, probably 'Secret Worship' and 'Ancient Sorceries', had likely been written previously. There is less of John Silence himself in both of these stories—a good thing, in the opinion of many readers.

conceit. And so was born Blackwood's contribution to the 'supernatural sleuth' subgenre of weird literature, the 'psychic doctor' John
Silence—heir to Sheridan Le Fanu's Dr Hesselius, whose occult
inquiries had been featured in the 1872 collection *In a Glass Darkly*.
The new book sold well, aided by an intensive publicity campaign in
which posters were slapped up all over London showing a slender,
bearded man in profile, with a high intellectual brow, gazing out
a window; below this figure appeared the words: 'JOHN
SILENCE—The Most Mysterious Character of Modern Fiction'.
Belloc, whose praise of *The Empty House* Blackwood had found so
encouraging, was even more enthusiastic about *John Silence*, calling it
'a considerable and lasting addition to the literature of our time'.[30]
Three story collections in three years, with another four to follow
between 1910 and 1914; the first of these, *The Lost Valley and Other
Stories*, included the masterful tale of Northwoods horror 'The
Wendigo', a story drawing again upon Blackwood's Canadian experience (as had the earlier 'A Haunted Island' and 'Skeleton Lake',
included in *The Empty House*) and pointing the way to a greater
emphasis on fiction exploring man's fraught relationship with Nature.
    This relationship was yet more fully explored in his next collec-
tion. As with John Silence, Blackwood had in mind a book held
together by a unifying concept—though this time thematic rather
than structural—writing of the proposed collection to his publisher
(now Macmillan) in October 1911,

Although composed of separate pieces, varying from 26,000 words to 2,000
words it is a coherent whole, the same idea running throughout, and it
illustrates that characteristic belief, present in all my work, that there exists
a definite relationship between Human Beings and Nature. I have been
steadily adding to this book for some years, taking in turn different aspects
of Nature—Sea, Mountains, Snow, Fire etc.[31]

Provisionally titled *The Man Whom the Trees Loved*, the collection was
published in 1912 as *Pan's Garden: A Volume of Nature Stories*. Two
further collections, *Ten Minute Stories* and *Incredible Adventures*,
appeared in 1914, with three of the five stories from the latter book,
including the remarkable 'A Descent into Egypt', sprawling to novella

[30] Hilaire Belloc, 'On Algernon Blackwood', in Clive Bloom (ed.), *Gothic Horror:
A Reader's Guide from Poe to King and Beyond* (London, 1998), 52–3.
[31] Ashley, *Starlight Man*, 223–4.

length. Maude ffoulkes noted at this point in his career that Blackwood had largely moved away from 'studies of fear and horror', adding, 'his outlook has widened and deepened to interpret the universe via mystical dreams on more majestic lines'.[32] Meanwhile, Blackwood had begun publishing novels as well, beginning with *Jimbo* (a fantasy written some years earlier under the title *A Flying Boy*) and *The Education of Uncle Paul* (both 1909). There followed the strikingly original *The Human Chord* (1910), in which a musical clergyman named Skale (!) attempts to recreate the true name of God by means of mystical vibrations; *The Centaur* (1911); and *A Prisoner in Fairyland* (1913), which would eventually become the basis for the children's play *The Starlight Express*, with music by the great English composer Edward Elgar (it bears no relation to the Andrew Lloyd Webber musical of the same name).

An astonishing burst of production, in terms of both quality and quantity: between 1906 and 1914 Blackwood published five novels and something like ninety stories and novellas, several of which would take their places among the most-anthologized weird tales of the twentieth century. At this point the Great War, in which Blackwood served for a time as an intelligence agent and a Red Cross volunteer, stamped a semicolon upon Blackwood's writing career (and a grim full stop to so many others'). During and after the war his writing pace, while never stopping altogether, slowed appreciably; fewer and further between, too, were the high points; this is, then, perhaps a good time to pause and look more closely at some of the themes and obsessions which characterize so much of Blackwood's most compelling fiction.

'Indians', Trees, and other Monsters

The Blackwood children (there were five of them) were not allowed to read fiction—an inauspicious beginning, one would think, if not a serious handicap, for a future master of the fantastic and the macabre.[33] Novels in particular were 'strictly forbidden' on his evangelical parents' watch—and this was the heyday, as Blackwood later recalled, of the

---

[32] ffoulkes, *My Own Past*, 188.

[33] With the exception of Lewis Carroll, and of certain unspecified 'goody-goody stories'; the young Blackwood's mind was otherwise 'fed upon insipid stuff, such as Longfellow, Mrs Hemans . . . and thousands of religious tracts' (Blackwood, *Episodes*, 30).

sensation novel, first cousin to the Gothic tale: '[i]t was the days of Yellow-backs in three volumes, of Ouida especially, of Miss Braddon, and Wilkie Collins'. Presumably the young Blackwood was never exposed to such nineteenth-century masters of nightmare as Mary Shelley, Edgar Allan Poe, or Sheridan Le Fanu. Nevertheless, he seems to have persisted in seeking out the weird, the fantastic, and the monstrous wherever he could, often finding it in the unlikeliest places (even in the 'insipid' Longfellow, as we shall see, there lurks the Wendigo).

One such unexpected source was the English theologian George Hawkins Pember (1837–1910), a member of the Plymouth Brethren who wrote popular books breathlessly connecting the dots between biblical prophecies and current events (a genre still very much alive today). Blackwood considered Pember a fantastic writer manqué, calling him 'an evangelical, but an imaginative evangelical' and adding, 'As a novelist of fantastic kind—an evangelical Wells, a "converted" Dunsany—he might have become a bestseller'.[34] The work which particularly captured his adolescent imagination was *Earth's Earliest Ages*, one of many nineteenth-century attempts to reconcile deep geological time with an anti-Darwinian position by positing a second creation. Pember was particularly obsessed with that apocryphal race of 'mongrel giants',[35] the Nephilim. This original, pre-Adamic race, described in the apocalyptic Book of Enoch as cannibalistic, was the product of miscegenation between fallen angels and human women, whose 'progeny', as Blackwood later recalled, 'formed a race apart from humans . . . Pember was convinced that this unlawful procreation was being resumed in modern days'.[36]

If for no other reason, *Earth's Earliest Ages* was important to Blackwood's creative development by sending him off in eager search of the occult doctrines which Pember warned his readers to shun at all costs ('Signs the Nephilim brought with them were spiritualism, theosophy, the development of secret powers latent in man, a new and awful type of consciousness'). But this biblical monster also emblematizes Blackwood's tendency to seek out unconventional monsters outside the literary mainstream. Perhaps it is not too

---

[34] Blackwood, *Episodes*, 34.

[35] Stephen T. Asma, *On Monsters: An Unnatural History of Our Worst Fears* (Oxford, 2011), 72.

[36] Blackwood, *Episodes*, 34.

fanciful, as well, to see conceptual traces of the Nephilim distributed throughout much of his later fiction, including themes involving racial indigenousness, monstrosity, and hybridity. One might consider, for instance, Blackwood's first notable story to appear in print, 'A Haunted Island', as well as one of his very last, 'The Doll'.[37] These two stories share a dubious characteristic; both, namely, contain 'Indian' monsters, with the inverted commas here signifying (if nothing else) the slipperiness of the racial label: the 1890s tale features a pair of bloodthirsty First Nations revenants—one a 'giant' ('immense . . . the largest figure of a man I have ever seen outside of a circus hall', p. 11), while the 'devil[ish]' 'black man' with 'eyes of fire' in the 1940s story (p. 395) has come all the way from India, in the final days of the British Raj, to seek a grim occult vengeance in a quiet London suburb. Interestingly, however, in the latter tale the real monster—to judge by the number of times the epithet is applied to it—is the doll itself, which seems to be associated with figures of racial and/or cultural hybridity (the story is maddeningly oblique,[38] but circles doggedly around vexed issues of biological and cultural reproduction; one possible reading is that the Colonel's daughter Monica is of mixed race, being raised 'English', with the 'fair . . . pallid, white . . . flaxen[-]hair[ed]' doll (p. 400) speaking 'Hindustani' serving as her uncanny counterpart, a counterfactual white child raised in India).

This brings us to Blackwood's adaptation of the Windigo or Wendigo,[39] the terrible Northwoods monster of Algonquian legend. Belief in the creature was historically widespread, its territory correspondingly

[37] 'A Haunted Island', published in *Pall Mall Magazine* in 1899, was the first of Blackwood's stories which he himself evidently thought worthy of preservation, as it was the earliest which he subsequently included in a story collection (*The Empty House*, 1906); a pair of earlier, rather slight, tales, both originally published in 1889, have since been unearthed: 'A Mysterious House' (*Belgravia*) and 'A Strange Adventure in the Black Forest' (*Blackfriars Magazine*). 'The Doll', while likely written in 1839, first appeared in the (slim) final collection of new stories by Blackwood to appear during his lifetime (*The Doll, and One Other* (Sauk City, WI, 1946)). These two tales are, in other words, very close to forming bookends for Blackwood's career as a writer of fiction.

[38] In its obliqueness, its depiction of a relationship between a governess and her haunted or corrupted charge, and its writing style, I strongly suspect the story of having been influenced by Henry James's novella *The Turn of the Screw*, in relation to which, at times, it almost approaches a quality of pastiche or even parody.

[39] Or Windego, or Wetikoo, or Windagoo, or Wentiko, or Wihtikow, or Windigoag, or Wiijigoo . . . there are countless variations of the name.

immense.[40] The Wendigo (to use the spelling favoured by Blackwood), while morphologically elusive, is most often described as a cannibal giant with a heart of ice. It craves—and of course prefers—human flesh when it can get it; otherwise it subsists on 'mushrooms, rotten wood, moss, lichen, and other forest effluvia'.[41] Moss in particular is closely associated with the creature in folklore, with 'Moss Eater' being a common epithet,[42] one utilized several times in Blackwood's story:

'An' its food, of all the muck in the whole bush is—moss!' And he laughed a short, unnatural laugh. 'It's a moss-eater, is the Wendigo,' he added, looking up excitedly into the faces of his companions, 'moss-eater,' he repeated, with a string of the most outlandish oaths he could invent. (p. 246)

Often the creature is described as having chewed its own lips away, revealing horrible broken teeth; often, too, its eyeballs are seen to be bleeding, or 'swimming' in blood. It is associated with winter and the great North Wind, depicted as 'traveling, or flying, on the Arctic winds from the North'.[43] Moreover, the creature represents both an external and an internal threat, in that one can *become* a Wendigo for a number of reasons ('go wendigo' is the common expression, eating human flesh the most common catalyst). Supernatural manifestations aside, cases of 'going wendigo', at least to the extent of developing a compulsive craving for human flesh, were at one time common enough to merit the coining of a diagnostic term, 'Windigo psychosis'.[44] The Wendigo thus represents a double horror: it might *eat* you, or it might *transform* you, turning you into a monster like itself. In Algonquian legend, while always truly monstrous in the sense of imaginatively blending the human with the non-human, it has been depicted variously as beast-man, cannibal giant, spirit, elemental,

---

[40] 'The haunt of the Windigo', according to John Colombo, 'is . . . the vast triangular domain marked off by the Atlantic Ocean to the east, the Arctic Ocean to the north, and the Rocky Mountains . . . to the west' (Colombo (ed.), *Windigo: An Anthology of Fact and Fantastic Fiction* (Saskatoon, 1982), 1).

[41] David D. Gilmore, *Monsters: Evil Beings, Mythical Beasts, and All Manner of Imaginary Terrors* (Philadelphia, 2003), 80.

[42] Howard A. Norman, *Where the Chill Came From: Cree Windigo Tales and Journeys* (San Francisco, 1982), 28–9.

[43] Chad Lewis and Kevin Lee Nelson, *Wendigo Lore: Monsters, Myths, and Madness* (Eau Claire, WI, 2020), 37.

[44] Albeit one not recognized by the American Psychological Association's *Diagnostic and Statistical Manual of Mental Disorders*.

skeleton, and walking dead. By contrast, the first European accounts of the monster tended to conceptualize it simply in the more familiar language of lycanthropy.[45] (The French Jesuit missionary Paul Le Jeune, for example, described the creature in 1636 as 'a sort of were-wolf', writing in 1661 of a contagious form of 'canine hunger' that was turning his indigenous deputies into 'veritable werewolves', 'so raven-ous for human flesh that they pounce upon women, children, and even upon men . . . and devour them voraciously'.[46]) Later non-native interpretations of the creature have similarly tended to merge the Wendigo with other, extraneous monster-figures: nowadays a pair of antlers are often grafted onto the creature's head, for example, bring-ing it into closer alignment with archetypal European therianthropes, while in popular media (as in the Marvel Comics version), the Wendigo is often depicted simply as a Sasquatch or Bigfoot figure with white fur.

Blackwood's own conception of the entity, while original in many respects, suggests substantial acquaintance with Algonquian lore. His story preserves, as we have seen, the monster's association with moss, while after Défago's aerial frolic with the creature, the exact nature of which is left to the reader's imagination, there are 'faint indications of recent bleeding' under his eyes (p. 255). 'The Wendigo', while actu-ally written in Switzerland in 1907 ('there was a touch of goose-flesh down my back', Blackwood recalled, 'as I watched my "Wendigo" in a mountain inn above Champéry'[47]), has its origins in a moose-hunting trip near Garden Lake, Ontario, some ten years earlier. For whatever reason—a simple memory lapse, or a perhaps unconscious desire to magnify his own myth-making powers—Blackwood, writ-ing later about the genesis of the tale, played down his familiarity with the legend:

[45] One of the more conventional monsters one does often encounter in Blackwood is the lycanthrope, though he does usually put his own personal stamp on the archetype. Two of the five stories in *John Silence*, for instance, fall into this category: 'The Camp of the Dog' is a werewolf story, while 'Ancient Sorceries' features shape-shifting cat people. There is also a were-tiger in 'The Man-Eater', more werewolves in 'The Empty Sleeve' and, arguably, 'Running Wolf', as well as a strong suspicion of lycanthropy, which proves merely to be a case of homicidal mania, in 'The Strange Adventures of a Private Secretary in New York'.

[46] Colombo (ed.), *Wendigo*, 7–8. The Algonquian word Le Jeune uses in the first instance is 'Atchen', but this is almost certainly yet another name for the Wendigo.

[47] Blackwood, *Tales of Terror and the Unknown*, 11–12. The name Défago (the Wendigo's victim in Blackwood's tale) is taken from a family surname in the Champéry region.

Then the awful 'Wendigo' comes shouldering up over a hill of memory, a name I remembered vividly in *Hiawatha* ('Wendigos and giants' runs the line), yet hardly thought of again till a friend, just back from Labrador, told me honest tales about mysterious evacuations of a whole family from a lonely valley because the 'Wendigo had come blundering in' and 'scared them stiff'. . .[48]

It is most unlikely, however, that Blackwood drew solely upon one friend's account of a single family's travails in writing his story (let alone a fleeting reference in Longfellow), particularly as one of his companions on the earlier hunting trip had been the American ethnographer and linguist John Dyneley Prince (1868–1945). Prince was (among many other things) a collector and translator of Algonquian legends and stories, collaborating with American folklorist Charles Godfrey Leland (1824–1903) on the collection *Kulóskap the Master and Other Algonkin Poems* (1904); Leland had previously compiled the classic *Algonquin Legends of New England; or Myths and Folk Lore of the Micmac, Passamaquoddy, and Penobscot Tribes* (1884), while Prince's own *Passamaquoddy Texts* appeared in 1921 in a series edited by the celebrated anthropologist Franz Boas. All these collections contain tales of the Wendigo under different names: 'Cheenoo', 'Kiwa'kwa', 'Muttóntoe'.[49] It is quite possible, too, that Blackwood heard Wendigo legends in Ontario not only from Prince but alongside him, directly from indigenous storytellers; in a two-part review of *Kulóskap the Master*, Blackwood wrote: 'I well remember hunting moose with Prince, and how his interest in the Redskins was so keen that he would turn aside, forgetting the game altogether, and hold conversations with Indians encountered on the way.'[50] Moreover, in the 1880s and 1890s both Canadian and American newspapers were

---

[48] Blackwood, *Tales of Terror and the Unknown*, 11.

[49] Chenoo and Kiwakwa are widely accepted as equivalent avatars of the Wendigo. ('The concept [of the Kiwakwa] corresponds with that of the windigo of the far northern Algonkian, for a Ki-wá'kwe is simply an ordinary man who only assumes the hideous role of man-eater when angry. He has a piece of ice in his heart'; Frank G. Speck, 'Penobscot Tales and Religious Beliefs', *Journal of American Folk-Lore*, 48/187 (Mar. 1935), 14.) 'Muttóntoe' is clearly 'Matantu' or 'Matanto', an evil spirit in Delaware (Lenape) folklore, but from the description of the 'cannibal monster' in the tale as retold by Prince and Leland (in their collection *Kulóskap the Master*) I suspect they may have confused or conflated this figure with the Delaware monster Mhuwe, a cannibal and Wendigo counterpart.

[50] Algernon Blackwood, 'Algonquin Songs and Legends', *Country Life* (23 Nov. 1912), 705.

full of accounts of Native Americans either 'going Wendigo' or killing others whom they suspected of becoming Wendigos. Such sensational reports appear to have reached a peak during Blackwood's years in Canada and the USA. One case, leading to a trial and conviction, took place shortly before his hunting trip, near Rat Portage (today Kenora, Ontario), which features in Blackwood's story; here one Mackekequonabe, 'a pagan Indian, was indicted for manslaughter. The evidence showed that he had shot a man, believing him to be a "Wendigo", or evil spirit'.[51]

In one glaring respect, however, 'The Wendigo' departs radically from the legend in all its multifarious forms—namely, in its omission of any mention whatever of cannibalism, which, it is fair to say, is *the* defining feature of the Wendigo myth. It is like writing a vampire story which carefully elides any hint of blood-drinking. It is possible, of course, that one is simply expected to read between the lines; certainly the story's atmosphere of oppressive dread is further intensified if one imagines this knot of isolated, terrified men trying desperately *not* to refer to the elephant—or cannibal—in the room. (For that matter, it may be even more frightening to interpret *all* the events of the story as a study in group psychosis—'Collective Hallucination' is, after all, the title of Dr Cathcart's book.[52]) Or perhaps Blackwood deliberately elides the cannibal theme in order to liberate the potent emotional charge of the taboo, allowing it to attach itself to other fears, particularly that of transformation itself—the prospect of becoming non-human, becoming monstrous.

One particularly troubling vector of transformation seems to be racial in nature. It is suggestive that it is Défago's already suspect hereditary make-up that puts him at greatest risk of transformation: he is a 'Canuck' whose French blood places him objectively, as it were, within the same category as the Native American of the party. This is Punk, 'an Indian . . . [who] dressed in the worn-out clothes bequeathed to him by former patrons, and, except for his coarse black hair and dark skin . . . looked in these city garments no more like a real redskin than a stage negro looks like a real African' (p. 213). Blackwood's

---

[51] 'Reg. v. Mackekequonabe', *The Barrister*, 3/1 (Jan. 1897), 61.

[52] Blackwood perhaps opens the door—if only a crack—to the possibility of such a reading: 'This particular story . . . found no mention in [Cathcart's] book . . . for the simple reason (so he confided once to a fellow colleague) that he himself played too intimate a part in it to form a competent judgment of the affair as a whole' (p. 212).

conception of 'race' in the story is thus both essentialized and disconcertingly slippery. On the one hand, Blackwood resorts here as elsewhere to conventional stereotypes: his conception of the Native
American tended to oscillate between the poles of 'savage, murderous, noble' (as in 'The Haunted Island') and 'pathetic, emasculated,
on the verge of extinction'. In an essay for *The Boy's Own Paper* titled
'The Vanishing Redskins', Blackwood wrote with a certain longing of
the bygone days of 'scalping raids and midnight attacks . . . [and]
dreaded war-whoops', before confessing, 'The first time I saw a Red
Indian I experienced a dreadful shock—of disappointment . . . The
man was undersized and walked with a shuffling gait. He was
dressed—I hardly like to tell you—in a faded old frock-coat and
a top-hat, with baggy striped trousers and brown boots.'[53] Punk
seems to be cut from the same cloth as this 'disappointing' figure,
though he is fortunate in possessing 'still the instincts of his dying
race; his taciturn silence and his endurance survived; also his superstition' (p. 213). It is precisely these traits which give him sense
enough to flee the camp altogether, 'cover[ing] the entire journey of
three days as only Indian blood could have' done ('The terror of
a whole race drove him') (p. 255). But Défago is equally racialized in
the story—he is 'true to type, Latin type'—and equally vulnerable to
the Wendigo's call, equally sensitive to its domain. The two things are
related: with the approach of the Wendigo's inhuman scent, the narrator notes that both, and only, '[t]he French Canadian and the man
of Indian blood each stirred uneasily in his sleep just about this time'
(p. 217). Blackwood thus hybridizes Défago—inarguably white in
other contexts, he shares a kinship with the 'Indian' in the realm of
the Wendigo. The creature singles out Défago for 'interpellation' (as
the French philosopher Louis Althusser would put it), defamiliarizing his European surname by breaking it up into primal, hyphenated
syllables, so that it resembles nothing so much as Native American
proper names as they were rendered in English-language collections
of indigenous tales (such as Prince's and Leland's): 'It rang out . . . in
three separate and distinct notes, or cries, that bore in some odd fashion a resemblance, far-fetched yet recognizable, to the name of the
guide: "*Dé—fa—go!*"' (p. 230). The Wendigo is an 'Indian' monster

---

[53] Algernon Blackwood, 'The Vanishing Redskins', in Philip Warner (ed.), *The Best of
British Pluck: The Boy's Own Paper* (London, 1976), 165.

that might be, so to speak, contagious. Perhaps this is one of the dangers of colonial expansion, particularly as the Wendigo could symbolize selfishness, greed, and the improper exploitation of natural resources—including, in some post-contact versions of the legend, by Europeans.[54] And even the hard-headed Scotsmen in the hunting party may not be immune.

Monsters, broadly speaking, cross conceptual wires. According to philosopher Noël Carroll's influential discussion of horror in art, a monster is a categorial hybrid which unsettles because it threatens culturally accepted systems of classification. Blending that which is ordinarily distinct—whether man and animal, living and dead, organic and inorganic, or some other normative binary opposition— monsters 'are not only physically threatening; they are cognitively threatening'.[55] As we have seen, much of Blackwood's fiction explores transgressions involving the first of these oppositions, though these may themselves announce or figure other forms of monstrous mixing, such as racial confusion.[56] Many other Blackwood stories, however, rove beyond the bounds of the animal kingdom altogether in search of 'others' that are even more . . . other. And plants have long stood as a kind of final frontier of radical otherness in the human imagination.[57] In his pioneering exploration of such topics as plant consciousness and agency, ecological catastrophe (even when the prospect is ironized, as in 'The Face of the Earth'), and monstrous human entanglements within natural systems, Blackwood

[54] According to folklorist Howard Norman, who collected and translated Wendigo stories from indigenous storytellers, 'It is said that sometimes a Windigo appears as a white trapper, often one who poaches food animals with no regard for the environment' (Norman, *Where the Chill Came From*, 5).

[55] Noël Carroll, *The Philosophy of Horror, or Paradoxes of the Heart* (New York, 1990), 34. Carroll's definition, itself indebted to the thought of anthropologist Mary Douglas, has been influential in later theoretical accounts of the monstrous.

[56] Carroll mentions the were-cats in Blackwood's 'Ancient Sorceries' as a paradigmatic example of 'temporal fission' (i.e. the sort of monster that takes different forms at different times), adding, '[b]ut this division—between cat and human—heralds other oppositions . . . sensual versus staid . . . female versus male, and maybe even French versus British' (Carroll, *The Nature of Horror*, 48).

[57] 'Plants', Dawn Keetley notes, 'exist on (and beyond) the outer limits of what we know (and what we have wanted to know): they are the utterly and ineffably strange, embodying an *absolute alterity*' (Dawn Keetley, 'Introduction: Six Theses on Plant Horror; or, Why Are Plants Horrifying?', in Dawn Keetley and Angela Tenga (eds.), *Plant Horror: Approaches to the Monstrous Vegetal in Literature and Film* (London, 2016), 1–30, at 6; emphasis in the original).

emerges in retrospect as an indispensable figure in the history, or pre-history, of such genre categories as 'plant horror', 'ecohorror', and 'EcoGothic'—categories which are themselves of recent coinage, coalescing conceptually only with the growing awareness of ecological and environmental crises in the late twentieth and early twenty-first centuries.

There is not space here to consider in any depth Blackwood's many imaginative engagements with the vegetal other—his most famous such work, certainly, is 'The Willows', whose titular growths, catego-rially promiscuous and actively hostile to human life, are both utterly alien and disconcertingly threatening to the very taxonomies which allow us to declare something to be 'utterly alien'.[58] A less well-known story, though one beginning to attract critical attention, is 'The Man Whom the Trees Loved' (1912), one of several Blackwood stories centring upon a man who is interpellated by a rival, non-human sym-bolic order, and is, after a half-hearted struggle (or simply an unduly protracted surrender), lost in the end, to the human world at least. The victim in this case (if that is the right word) is one David Bittacy, who has, like Blackwood's own father, been honoured with member-ship in the Order of the Bath for services rendered to the Empire. Their respective forms of civil service might seem to be very different in kind: Stevenson Blackwood was an important Post Office official, while Bittacy served for years in the Department of Woods and Forests in colonial India (also called the Imperial Forest Service, later the Indian Forest Service). There are certainly points of contact between the two, however, one of the most intriguing being their shared connection with Britain's colonial railway systems: it was on behalf of the Post Office that Blackwood first travelled with his son to Canada, to inspect the new Canadian Pacific Railway,[59] while it was massive deforestation, caused chiefly by the building of the railway network in India, which had led to the founding of the Forest Service

[58] The story 'create[s] a frightening sense of the radical alterity of nonhuman, non-animal nature, but it also begins to draw attention to the possibility that this alterity exists *within* the human'. Jessica George, 'Weird Flora: Plant Life in the Classic Weird Tale', in Katherine E. Bishop, David Higgins, and Jerry Määttä (eds.), *Plants in Science Fiction: Speculative Vegetation* (Cardiff, 2020), 11–31, at 13.

[59] For more information about Arthur Blackwood's importance to the Post Office and its networks (rail, telegraphic, telephonic), see Duncan Campbell-Smith, *Masters of the Post: The Authorized History of the Royal Mail* (London, 2011).

there (Bittacy's connection with the trees may be emotional, but they are very much a material resource of Empire). Furthermore, Blackwood's story imagines the trees of the world as forming a global telecommunications network (they are likened to a transnational postal network 'linking dropped messages and meanings' and to a 'vast [radio] Emitter', pp. 272 and 301), a kind of uncanny vegetal— and colonial—counterpart to the worldwide web of Empire of which the Post Office was such a crucial part.[60] A figure, perhaps, of a potential global unity among colonized peoples[61]—and, if so, one of many suggestions in Blackwood's fiction of the fragility of an imperial system, then at its height, whose dissolution he would live to see and, apparently, to regret (in 1948, upon receiving the CBE medal, he wrote in his diary, 'Odd to be a Commander of an Empire which the bestowers of the honour have destroyed!'[62]).

The story may have roots (so to speak) in Blackwood's one year at Edinburgh University where, as we have seen, he was to have acquired a practical education in farming, only to emerge no more adept in the 'agricultural trade' than when he matriculated: 'I knew nothing about farming', he admits in his memoir; 'My notebooks of Professor Wallace's lectures'—this would have been Robert Wallace's Agricultural and Rural Economy course—'crammed as they were, with entries about soil, rotation of crops, and drainage, represented no genuine practical knowledge'.[63] No 'practical knowledge', perhaps—but it is interesting to speculate what other ideas Blackwood's 'crammed' notebooks might have contained, in that Wallace, soon to be named Garton Lecturer on Colonial and Indian Agriculture, had just returned from a year travelling in India on an agricultural research tour. His book, *India in 1887 as Seen by Robert Wallace*, which appeared in 1888—the same year Blackwood attended his lectures—contains an extensive discussion of the role of the colonial forestry service in balancing 'their [the Government's] duties as regards the protection of forests', the welfare of 'the native population', and

---

[60] The trees' communication is also likened to a drum-language—a familiar conduit of hostile and/or uncanny 'native' communications in imperial fiction set (especially) in Africa.

[61] Katherine Bishop makes a similar case; see 'The Botanical Ekphrastic and Ecological Relocation', in Katherine E. Bishop, David Higgins, and Jerry Määttä (eds.), *Plants in Science Fiction: Speculative Vegetation* (Cardiff, 2020), 214–31.

[62] Ashley, *Starlight Man*, 410.   [63] Blackwood, *Episodes*, 16.

'the best interests of the Empire'.[64] Whatever its particular origins in Blackwood's imagination, however, the political and historical contexts of his haunting story very clearly include the colonial as well as the environmental.

Matters of Scale

Such contingent entanglements aside, what else do ecological and imperial (particularly, as in the case of the British Empire, global-imperial) systems have in common? Both, surely, are paradigmatic examples of what have been called 'hyperobjects'—non-human entities and processes so vast in scale that they are literally incomprehensible to us, 'massively distributed' as they are 'in time and space relative to humans'.[65] Examples of hyperobjects given by philosopher Timothy Morton include planets, black holes, the Florida Everglades (just imagine the story Blackwood might have written had he ever visited there!), capitalism, climate change, and global pandemics. Although Morton invokes H. P. Lovecraft's tentacled monster Cthulhu, lurking in its 'non-Euclidean' home beneath the waves, as an early twentieth-century harbinger or symbol of modern attempts to think beyond human scale, Blackwood (who strongly influenced Lovecraft) has perhaps the better claim to be considered the first, and possibly greatest, weird writer of the hyperobject, one who probed persistently at the interactions between, on the one hand, human powers of perception and conceptualization and, on the other, the vast non-human systems that stubbornly resist capture within them. In this encounter fear can certainly be generated, but so can wonder, awe, and a powerful sense of longing; very often in Blackwood, contact with the hyperobject, even—or especially—if it means personal annihilation, is a consummation devoutly to be wished.

Questions of scale, perspective, and proportion seem always to have fascinated Blackwood; he often conjured with tropes of magnification and distortion, exploring the effects that could be generated by merging human and non-human perspectives and spatio-temporal scales. It is perhaps significant that the one fiction writer mentioned

[64] Robert Wallace, *India in 1887 as Seen by Robert Wallace* (Edinburgh, 1888), 294, 297.

[65] Timothy Morton, *Hyperobjects: Philosophy and Ecology after the End of the World* (Minneapolis, 2013), 1.

by name as having been permitted in the Blackwood home was the mathematician-fantasist Lewis Carroll, who took such delight in disorienting, defamiliarizing changes in size. We also know that one of Blackwood's most treasured books which he carried throughout his American sojourn was Thomas De Quincey's *Confessions of an Opium Eater*, with its memorably horrific scenes of drug-induced distortions of both time and space. Blackwood himself, seeking—one suspects—to emulate De Quincey by opening the doors of his own perception, experimented in New York with both morphine and hashish or cannabis, turning the latter experience into a piece which ran in the *Evening Sun*. Titled 'He Tried Hasheesh', and prudently couched as both a third-person narrative and a cautionary tale, it describes a sequence of terrifying magnifications and distortions, violent shifts of scale: while being shaved at the barber shop, the Blackwood-protagonist suddenly sees the ceiling fly 'up in the air at an astonishing rate. The door receded hundreds of feet in the distance, the barber increased in proportion to a colossus', and so on.[66] Many of Blackwood's stories are premised upon such unsettling effects. In 'The Face of the Earth', Arthur Spinrobin experiences an 'unpleasant sense of alarm and disgust' (p. 205) upon beholding that monstrous Gaian countenance; he has difficulties, too, absorbing the vertiginous implications of the panpsychist thought of Gustave Fechner, to whose work the sinister Professor Finkelstein has introduced him. Similarly, in 'Perspective' (1910), an English clergyman, already staggered by the sublimity of the Alps ('the scale of the surrounding mountains rose appallingly with him'), is suddenly confronted by 'a Face . . . so stupendous in scale that he never understood to this day how he could have perceived that it was—a Face'.[67] 'Proportion' (1916) features a soldier shaken to his core by the sheer 'scale' of the cosmos ('There's horror in magnitude of that kind . . . You lose proportion'[68]), while another war story, 'Wireless Confusion' (1919), centres upon a dizzying series of hallucinations involving grotesque magnification and diminution, supernaturally induced by a pair of binoculars.

[66] 'He Tried Hasheesh', *Evening Sun* (11 June 1893). Perhaps some dim memory of this episode helped spawn the hallucinatory vision in 'A Descent into Egypt' in which Moleson and Isley are transformed into the 'twin Colossi' of Memnon.

[67] Algernon Blackwood, *The Lost Valley and Other Stories* (London, 1910), 181, 187.

[68] Algernon Blackwood, *The Face of the Earth and Other Imaginings* (Eureka, CA, 2015), 195.

Blackwood's masterpiece of scale-induced disorientation, however, is surely 'A Descent into Egypt'. While Blackwood wrote a number of Egyptian tales, including the earlier 'The Nemesis of Fire', actually visiting Egypt was a revelatory experience for him,[69] resulting in two hypnotic and thought-provoking novellas written close together (the other, 'Sand', appeared in *Pan's Garden*). The 'descent' of the story's title refers to the Englishman George Isley's slow 'withdr[awal] from the present . . . back into a mighty Past where he belonged' (p. 318). Isley was once a vital, vibrant individual; now, contact with what is perhaps Blackwood's ultimate hyperobject, an essentialized and reified Egypt, has transformed him into a zombified 'simulacrum' of a man, 'a dummy', a 'well-trained automaton' whose 'soul' has gone . . . elsewhere (p. 319). The narrator can only watch helplessly as Isley becomes at once artificially inflated, rather like the bladder-blown Défago ('he grew within—gigantic. The size of Egypt entered into him', p. 343), yet at the same time 'shrunken into the proportions of some minuter scale' (p. 332). This transformation is not the result, however, of any common or garden Egyptian curse: Blackwood's narrator pointedly notes that Isley 'told no mummy stories, nor ever hinted at the supernatural quality [of Egypt] that leaps to the mind of the majority' (p. 342)—there will be, in other words, no human-scale narratives involving tomb robbery or ambulatory mummies *here*. Rather, Isley's fate, not unlike Bittacy's or even Défago's, is the result of the encounter between human subjectivity and an object intolerably vastly distributed in space and time. Egypt, the narrator repeatedly tells us, 'stuns' the mind:[70]

I recalled its first effect upon myself, and how my mind had been unable to cope with the memory of it afterwards . . . a colossal medley, a gigantic, coloured blur that merely bewildered . . . a chaotic vision: sands drenched in dazzling light, vast granite aisles, stupendous figures that stared unblinking at the sun, a shining river and a shadowy desert, both endless as the sky, mountainous pyramids and gigantic monoliths, armies of heads, of paws,

---

[69] 'Blackwood's vision of Egypt and its place in his cosmic imaginary was transformed by the visits he took to Egypt in successive winters between 1912 and 1914' (Roger Luckhurst, *The Mummy's Curse: The True History of a Dark Fantasy* (Oxford, 2012), 178).

[70] One recalls the repeated 'shocks' visited upon Blackwood's brain by his experiences in that most modern of urban hyperobjects, Manhattan.

of faces—all set to a scale of size that was prodigious. The items stunned; the composite effect was too unwieldy to be grasped. (p. 337)

Much of the story is taken up with attempts to represent this unrepresentable entity through analogy with other hyperobjects, such as the cosmos ('My mind grasped it as little as the fact that our solar system . . . rushes annually many million miles towards a star in Hercules, while yet that constellation appears no closer than it did six thousand years ago', p. 339), or through invocation of Egypt's own metonyms, themselves, through vastness or monstrous hybridity, resistant to human apprehension, such as the 'Gizeh monsters', the Colossi of Memnon, and the Sphinx—'a being of non-human lineage' possessing a 'countenance that is too huge to focus as a face . . . [an] alien, uncomfortable thing' (p. 341; shades, once again, of 'The Face of the Earth'). At other times Egypt is figured as what psychoanalyst Jacques Lacan called a 'Big Other'—an immense, unknowable system, described as a 'web' or network whose 'call' unerringly targets its victim (like the Wendigo, again, or the trees in 'The Man Whom the Trees Loved'). Egypt is 'monstrous', too, in temporal as well as spatial extension: here, in contradistinction to so much of Blackwood's fiction, there is an apparent encounter with the properly historical; yet Egypt's deep history is here rendered as, paradoxically, ahistorical—an essentialized, unchanging, and inhuman thing.

Perhaps most interesting is the way the story's form mirrors its content. As a narrative, 'A Descent into Egypt' is calculatedly disproportionate, with a high degree of redundancy awkwardly outweighing what is really rather a meagre plot in terms of actual incident. We know the bones of the story almost from the outset: like an undergraduate dutifully placing the thesis statement as early as possible in an essay, the narrator provides a précis within the first couple of paragraphs; the rest is gradual elaboration, circling in place, repetition with variation. There are no surprises here, no suspense in the conventional sense. The story, in the terms of structural linguistics, favours paradigm over syntagm; it must seem, to an unsympathetic reader, too long by an order of magnitude at least; it is the very opposite of the kind of 'well-made tale' which Blackwood the professional storyteller crafted to fit into fixed broadcasting slots. To a sympathetic reader, however, it is apparent that Blackwood is attempting to reproduce something like the *experience* of Isley's absorption into the

Egypt-object, since mere description, one feels, could never do it justice. Vast and immobile as one of the Colossi of Memnon, the novella 'draws' the reader 'down' into itself—and, perhaps, into the deep core of one's own subjectivity.

Though in the end Blackwood's narrator pulls away from the abyss in horror, he is clearly not by any means immune to the 'call' of Egypt, allowing himself to be drawn some way into its fatal web alongside Isley. This ambivalence in the face of individual destruction clearly reflects Blackwood's own: he seems always to have understood the attraction of personal annihilation: not necessarily suicide, though he did write quite a few stories about that, but the disappearance of the self. And this brings us back to that BBC broadcast, and to all of those television viewers across Britain gaping at their screens as the gaunt storyteller in the leather armchair seemingly vanished into oblivion. It is easy to imagine Blackwood welcoming the prospect of vanishing. And yet Blackwood—whose stories have remained perennially essential to any serious discussion of twentieth-century weird and supernatural fiction—has never vanished. Nor (though he might well have found the idea perplexing and upsetting) does there seem to be any danger of his fading away anytime soon—particularly as so many of his own abiding preoccupations seem to be coming into sharp alignment with our own twenty-first century concerns.

NOTE ON THE TEXT

MOST of these stories appeared first in collections, from which they are here reprinted ('An Empty House', 'The Listener', 'The Willows', 'Secret Worship', 'Ancient Sorceries', 'The Wendigo', 'A Descent into Egypt', and 'The Doll'). 'The Haunted Island', 'The Man Who Found Out', and 'The Land of Green Ginger' first appeared in periodicals (*Pall Mall Magazine*, 1899; *Lady's Realm*, 1909; and *Radio Times*, 1927 respectively), but are here reproduced from the earliest collections in which they appear. 'The Man Whom the Trees Loved' appeared in 1912 in both the *London Magazine* and *Pan's Garden*; the latter has been consulted here. 'The Kit-Bag', 'The Face of the Earth', and 'Onanonanon' have been taken from their original periodical publications (for more information see the Explanatory Notes).

SELECT BIBLIOGRAPHY

Biography and Bio-Bibliography

Ashley, Mike, *Starlight Man: The Extraordinary Life of Algernon Blackwood* (London, 2001; rev. edn. Eureka, CA, 2019). The revised edition, which adds new information and restores material cut from the biography as originally published, will be of interest to Blackwood scholars; others will prefer the tighter and far better-edited 2001 edition.

Ashley, Mike, *Algernon Blackwood: A Bio-Bibliography* (New York, 1987). (An updated bibliographical listing of Blackwood's stories, novels, essays, and plays can be found at the end of *The Face of the Earth and Other Imaginings* by Algernon Blackwood, ed. Mike Ashley (Eureka, CA, 2015).)

Colombo, John Robert, *Blackwood's Books: A Bibliography Devoted to Algernon Blackwood* (Toronto, 1981).

Criticism

Bishop, Katherine E., 'The Botanical Ekphrastic and Ecological Relocation', in Katherine E. Bishop, David Higgins, and Jerry Määttä (eds.), *Plants in Science Fiction: Speculative Vegetation* (Cardiff, 2020), 214–31.

Camara, Anthony, 'Nature Unbound: Cosmic Horror in Algernon Blackwood's "The Willows"', *Horror Studies*, 4/1 (2013), 43–62.

Conley, Greg, 'The Uncrossable Evolutionary Gulfs of Algernon Blackwood', *Journal of the Fantastic in the Arts*, 24/3 (2014), 426–45.

De Cicco, Mark, '"More than Human": The Queer Occult Explorer of the Fin-de-Siècle', *Journal of the Fantastic in the Arts*, 23/1 (2012), 4–24.

Denisoff, Dennis, 'The Lie of the Land: Decadence, Ecology, and Arboreal Communications', *Victorian Literature and Culture*, 49/4 (2021), 621–41.

George, Jessica, 'Weird Flora: Plant Life in the Classic Weird Tale', in Katherine E. Bishop, David Higgins, and Jerry Määttä (eds.), *Plants in Science Fiction: Speculative Vegetation* (Cardiff, 2020), 11–31.

Graf, Susan Johnston, *Talking to the Gods: Occultism in the Work of W. B. Yeats, Arthur Machen, Algernon Blackwood, and Dion Fortune* (Albany, NY, 2015).

Joshi, S. T., *The Weird Tale* (Austin, TX, 1990).

Keetley, Dawn, 'Tentacular Ecohorror and the Agency of Trees in Algernon Blackwood's "The Man Whom the Trees Loved" and Lorcan Finnegan's "Without Name"', in Christy Tidwell and Carter Soles (eds.), *Fear and Nature: Ecohorror Studies in the Anthropocene* (University Park, PA, 2021), 23–41.

Miller, John MacNeill, 'Weird beyond Description: Weird Fiction and the Suspicion of Scenery', *Victorian Studies: An Interdisciplinary Journal of Social, Political, and Cultural Studies*, 62/2 (2020), 244–52.

Penzoldt, Peter, *The Supernatural in Fiction* (New York, 1965).

Punter, David, 'Algernon Blackwood: Nature and Spirit', in Andrew Smith and William Hughes (eds.), *EcoGothic* (Manchester, 2013), 44–57.

Scarborough, Dorothy, *The Supernatural in Modern English Fiction* (New York, 1917).

Sullivan, Jack, *Elegant Nightmares: The English Ghost Story from Le Fanu to Blackwood* (Athens, OH, 1978).

Wagenknecht, Edward, *Seven Masters of Supernatural Fiction* (New York, 1991).

Further Reading in Oxford World's Classics

James, M. R., *Collected Ghost Stories*, ed. Darryl Jones.

Jones, Darryl (ed.), *Horror Stories: Classic Tales from Hoffmann to Hodgson*.

Lee, Vernon, *The Virgin of the Seven Daggers and Other Stories*, ed. Aaron Worth.

Le Fanu, Sheridan, *Green Tea and Other Weird Stories*, ed. Aaron Worth.

Lovecraft, H. P., *The Classic Horror Stories*, ed. Roger Luckhurst.

Machen, Arthur, *The Great God Pan and Other Horror Stories*, ed. Aaron Worth.

A CHRONOLOGY OF ALGERNON BLACKWOOD

1869   (14 Mar.) Algernon Blackwood born at Wood Lodge, Shooter's Hill, Kent, into a family of strong evangelical bent.

1880s   Joins members of the SPR (Society for Psychical Research) in investigating purportedly haunted houses (though he is not himself a member).

1880   AB's father, Stevenson Arthur Blackwood, becomes secretary to the Post Office.

1885–6   Studies for one year at a Moravian school in Königsfeld im Schwarzwald, Germany; his experiences there are largely positive, though he will later imagine the schoolmasters as demonic revenants in the story 'Secret Worship'.

1887   Travels to United States and Canada with his father, who is sent to evaluate the potential of the new Canadian Pacific Railway line for postal delivery.

1888–9   Studies for a single year at Edinburgh University (with his older brother Stevenson transferring there from Cambridge as well); takes Robert Wallace's course in Agriculture and Rural Economy, Wallace having recently returned from a tour of India investigating the state of colonial forestry among other subjects (a possible influence on 'The Man Whom the Trees Loved').

1889   Blackwood's first story, 'A Mysterious House', published in *Belgravia*.

1890   Sails alone for New York; he will spend the next nine years in Canada and Manhattan, experiencing significant poverty while working as a reporter, among other miscellaneous jobs.

1892   Spends the summer on an island in Lake Rosseau, Ontario (inspires 'A Haunted Island').

1892–3   Given injections of morphine by his friend Dr Otto Huebner; also experiments with cannabis, writing an article titled 'He Tried Hasheesh' for a New York newspaper.

1893   Death of Stevenson Arthur Blackwood.

1898   (Oct.) Moose-hunting trip in northern Canada in the company of linguist John Dyneley Prince (inspires 'The Wendigo' as well as other Canadian stories).

1899   Returns to England and begins to write horror stories; 'A Haunted Island' published in the *Pall Mall Magazine*. AB is accepted into the London Lodge of the Theosophical Society.

1900   Journeys down the Danube River by canoe with Wilfrid Wilson; in October, AB is initiated into the Hermetic Order of the Golden Dawn.

1906   Eveleigh Nash publishes AB's first collection of stories, *The Empty House and Other Ghost Stories* to favourable reviews.

1907   Publishes *The Listener and Other Stories*, containing 'The Willows', which will become one of AB's most celebrated tales. Death of AB's mother.

1908   *John Silence—Physician Extraordinary* published by Eveleigh Nash.

1909   Publication of AB's first two novels, *Jimbo* (written some time earlier, originally titled *A Flying Boy*) and *The Education of Uncle Paul*.

1910   Publishes *The Lost Valley and Other Stories* (which includes 'The Wendigo') and the novel *The Human Chord*.

1911   Publishes *The Centaur*, a novel based on the panpsychist ideas of Gustave Fechner, to widespread acclaim.

1912   Visits Egypt for the first time; the experience makes a deep impact upon AB, inspiring essays and stories including 'Sand' and 'A Descent into Egypt'. Macmillan publishes *Pan's Garden: A Volume of Nature Stories*, which includes 'The Man Whom the Trees Loved', illustrating AB's belief 'that there exists a definite relationship between Human Beings and Nature'.

1913   Publishes the novel *A Prisoner in Fairyland* (later the basis for the children's play *The Starlight Express*, adapted by Violet Pearn, with music by Edward Elgar).

1914   Publication of two new collections, *Ten Minute Stories* (John Murray) and *Incredible Adventures* (Macmillan), with the latter including 'A Descent into Egypt'.

1914   Outbreak of First World War; AB tries unsuccessfully to volunteer as an interpreter; later he tries to get involved with propaganda work.

1916   Recruited by the War Office for secret service work (which he dislikes intensely) in Switzerland; the experience partly inspires his story 'Onanonanon'.

1918   Volunteers as a searcher for the Red Cross, tracking down information about missing men.

1923   Cassell's publishes AB's autobiographical *Episodes Before Thirty*, focusing primarily on his experiences in New York and Canada.

1927   AB's story 'The Land of Green Ginger' appears in *Radio Times*, the BBC's listings magazine.

1929   Ernest Benn publishes AB's novel *Dudley & Gilderoy: A Nonsense*.

1934   AB's first appearance on the radio, as part of the BBC programme *In Town Tonight*.

1936   (Nov.) AB appears on the first BBC television broadcast, on the programme *Picture Page*.

1940   (13 Oct.) German bomb destroys AB's home (he and his nephew Patrick are safe in garden air-raid shelter).

1946   (Aug.) Derleth's Arkham House publishes *The Doll and One Other*, containing 'The Doll' and 'The Trod'; last original collection of AB's stories to appear during his lifetime.

1949   Awarded the medal of the British Television Society, recognizing him 'as creator of the most outstanding contribution to television entertainment', as well as the CBE (Commander of the British Empire) medal.

1951   (10 Dec.) Dies at 15 Sheffield Terrace, London, aged 82.

THE WENDIGO
AND OTHER STORIES

A HAUNTED ISLAND

THE following events occurred on a small island of isolated position in a large Canadian lake* to whose cool waters the inhabitants of Montreal and Toronto flee for rest and recreation in the hot months. It is only to be regretted that events of such peculiar interest to the genuine student of the psychical should be entirely uncorroborated. Such unfortunately, however, is the case.

Our own party of nearly twenty had returned to Montreal that very day, and I was left in solitary possession for a week or two longer, in order to accomplish some important 'reading'* for the law which I had foolishly neglected during the summer.

It was late in September, and the big trout and maskinonge* were stirring themselves in the depths of the lake, and beginning slowly to move up to the surface waters as the north winds and early frosts lowered their temperature. Already the maples were crimson and gold, and the wild laughter of the loons echoed in sheltered bays that never knew their strange cry in the summer.

With a whole island to oneself, a two-storey cottage, a canoe, and only the chipmunks, and the farmer's weekly visit with eggs and bread, to disturb one, the opportunities for hard reading might be very great. It all depends!

The rest of the party had gone off with many warnings to beware of Indians, and not to stay late enough to be the victim of a frost that thinks nothing of forty below zero. After they had gone, the loneliness of the situation made itself unpleasantly felt. There were no other islands within six or seven miles, and though the mainland forests lay a couple of miles behind me, they stretched for a very great distance unbroken by any signs of human habitation. But, though the island was completely deserted and silent, the rocks and trees that had echoed human laughter and voices almost every hour of the day for two months could not fail to retain some memories of it all; and I was not surprised to fancy I heard a shout or a cry as I passed from rock to rock, and more than once to imagine that I heard my own name called aloud.

In the cottage there were six tiny little bedrooms divided from one another by plain unvarnished partitions of pine. A wooden bedstead, a mattress, and a chair, stood in each room, but I only found two mirrors, and one of these was broken.

The boards creaked a good deal as I moved about, and the signs of occupation were so recent that I could hardly believe I was alone. I half expected to find someone left behind, still trying to crowd into a box more than it would hold. The door of one room was stiff, and refused for a moment to open, and it required very little persuasion to imagine someone was holding the handle on the inside, and that when it opened I should meet a pair of human eyes.

A thorough search of the floor led me to select as my own sleeping quarters a little room with a diminutive balcony over the verandah roof. The room was very small, but the bed was large, and had the best mattress of them all. It was situated directly over the sitting-room where I should live and do my 'reading,' and the miniature window looked out to the rising sun. With the exception of a narrow path which led from the front door and verandah through the trees to the boat-landing, the island was densely covered with maples, hemlocks, and cedars. The trees gathered in round the cottage so closely that the slightest wind made the branches scrape the roof and tap the wooden walls. A few moments after sunset the darkness became impenetrable, and ten yards beyond the glare of the lamps that shone through the sitting-room windows—of which there were four—you could not see an inch before your nose, nor move a step without running up against a tree.

The rest of that day I spent moving my belongings from my tent to the sitting-room, taking stock of the contents of the larder, and chopping enough wood for the stove to last me for a week. After that, just before sunset, I went round the island a couple of times in my canoe for precaution's sake. I had never dreamed of doing this before, but when a man is alone he does things that never occur to him when he is one of a large party.

How lonely the island seemed when I landed again! The sun was down, and twilight is unknown in these northern regions. The darkness comes up at once. The canoe safely pulled up and turned over on her face, I groped my way up the little narrow pathway to the verandah. The six lamps were soon burning merrily in the front room; but in the kitchen, where I 'dined,' the shadows were so gloomy, and the lamplight was so inadequate, that the stars could be seen peeping through the cracks between the rafters.

I turned in early that night. Though it was calm and there was no wind, the creaking of my bedstead and the musical gurgle of the water over the rocks below were not the only sounds that reached my ears. As I lay awake, the appalling emptiness of the house grew upon me. The corridors and vacant rooms seemed to echo innumerable foot-steps, shufflings, the rustle of skirts, and a constant undertone of whispering. When sleep at length overtook me, the breathings and noises, however, passed gently to mingle with the voices of my dreams.

A week passed by, and the 'reading' progressed favourably. On the tenth day of my solitude, a strange thing happened. I awoke after a good night's sleep to find myself possessed with a marked repugnance for my room. The air seemed to stifle me. The more I tried to define the cause of this dislike, the more unreasonable it appeared. There was something about the room that made me afraid. Absurd as it seems, this feeling clung to me obstinately while dressing, and more than once I caught myself shivering, and conscious of an inclination to get out of the room as quickly as possible. The more I tried to laugh it away, the more real it became; and when at last I was dressed, and went out into the passage, and downstairs into the kitchen, it was with feelings of relief, such as I might imagine would accompany one's escape from the presence of a dangerous contagious disease.

While cooking my breakfast, I carefully recalled every night spent in the room, in the hope that I might in some way connect the dislike I now felt with some disagreeable incident that had occurred in it. But the only thing I could recall was one stormy night when I suddenly awoke and heard the boards creaking so loudly in the corridor that I was convinced there were people in the house. So certain was I of this, that I had descended the stairs, gun in hand, only to find the doors and windows securely fastened, and the mice and black-beetles in sole possession of the floor. This was certainly not sufficient to account for the strength of my feelings.

The morning hours I spent in steady reading; and when I broke off in the middle of the day for a swim and luncheon, I was very much surprised, if not a little alarmed, to find that my dislike for the room had, if anything, grown stronger. Going upstairs to get a book, I experienced the most marked aversion to entering the room, and while within I was conscious all the time of an uncomfortable feeling that was half uneasiness and half apprehension. The result of it was that, instead of reading, I spent the afternoon on the water paddling and fishing, and when I got home about sundown, brought with me half a dozen delicious black bass for the supper-table and the larder.

As sleep was an important matter to me at this time, I had decided that if my aversion to the room was so strongly marked on my return as it had been before, I would move my bed down into the sitting-room, and sleep there. This was, I argued, in no sense a concession to an absurd and fanciful fear, but simply a precaution to ensure a good night's sleep. A bad night involved the loss of the next day's reading,—a loss I was not prepared to incur.

I accordingly moved my bed downstairs into a corner of the sitting-room facing the door, and was moreover uncommonly glad when the operation was completed, and the door of the bedroom closed finally upon the shadows, the silence, and the strange *fear* that shared the room with them.

The croaking stroke of the kitchen clock sounded the hour of eight as I finished washing up my few dishes, and closing the kitchen door behind me, passed into the front room. All the lamps were lit, and their reflectors, which I had polished up during the day, threw a blaze of light into the room.

Outside the night was still and warm. Not a breath of air was stirring; the waves were silent, the trees motionless, and heavy clouds hung like an oppressive curtain over the heavens. The darkness seemed to have rolled up with unusual swiftness, and not the faintest glow of colour remained to show where the sun had set. There was present in the atmosphere that ominous and overwhelming silence which so often precedes the most violent storms.

I sat down to my books with my brain unusually clear, and in my heart the pleasant satisfaction of knowing that five black bass were lying in the ice-house, and that to-morrow morning the old farmer would arrive with fresh bread and eggs. I was soon absorbed in my books.

As the night wore on the silence deepened. Even the chipmunks were still; and the boards of the floors and walls ceased creaking. I read on steadily till, from the gloomy shadows of the kitchen, came the hoarse sound of the clock striking nine. How loud the strokes sounded! They were like blows of a big hammer. I closed one book and opened another, feeling that I was just warming up to my work.

This, however, did not last long. I presently found that I was reading the same paragraphs over twice, simple paragraphs that did not require such effort. Then I noticed that my mind began to wander to other things, and the effort to recall my thoughts became harder with each digression. Concentration was growing momentarily more difficult. Presently I discovered that I had turned over two pages instead of one, and had not noticed my mistake until I was well down the page. This was becoming serious. What was the disturbing influence? It could not be physical fatigue. On the contrary, my mind was unusually alert, and in a more receptive condition than usual I made a new and determined effort to read, and for a short time succeeded in giving my whole attention to my subject. But in a very few moments again I found myself leaning back in my chair, staring vacantly into space.

Something was evidently at work in my sub-consciousness. There was something I had neglected to do. Perhaps the kitchen door and windows were not fastened. I accordingly went to see, and found that they were! The fire perhaps needed attention. I went in to see, and found that it was all right! I looked at the lamps, went upstairs into every bedroom in turn, and then went round the house, and even into the ice-house. Nothing was wrong; everything was in its place. Yet something *was* wrong! The conviction grew stronger and stronger within me.

When I at length settled down to my books again and tried to read, I became aware, for the first time, that the room seemed growing cold. Yet the day had been oppressively warm, and evening had brought no relief. The six big lamps, moreover, gave out heat enough to warm the room pleasantly. But a chilliness, that perhaps crept up from the lake, made itself felt in the room, and caused me to get up to close the glass door opening on to the verandah.

For a brief moment I stood looking out at the shaft of light that fell from the windows and shone some little distance down the pathway, and out for a few feet into the lake.

As I looked, I saw a canoe glide into the pathway of light, and immediately crossing it, pass out of sight again into the darkness. It was perhaps a hundred feet from the shore, and it moved swiftly.

I was surprised that a canoe should pass the island at that time of night, for all the summer visitors from the other side of the lake had gone home weeks before, and the island was a long way out of any line of water traffic.

My reading from this moment did not make very good progress, for somehow the picture of that canoe, gliding so dimly and swiftly across the narrow track of light on the black waters, silhouetted itself against the background of my mind with singular vividness. It kept coming between my eyes and the printed page. The more I thought about it the more surprised I became. It was of larger build than any I had seen during the past summer months, and was more like the old Indian war canoes with the high curving bows and stern and wide beam. The more I tried to read, the less success attended my efforts; and finally I closed my books and went out on the verandah to walk up and down a bit, and shake the chilliness out of my bones.

The night was perfectly still, and as dark as imaginable. I stumbled down the path to the little landing wharf, where the water made the very faintest of gurgling under the timbers. The sound of a big tree falling in the mainland forest, far across the lake, stirred echoes in the heavy air, like the first guns of a distant night attack. No other sound disturbed the stillness that reigned supreme.

As I stood upon the wharf in the broad splash of light that followed me from the sitting-room windows, I saw another canoe cross the pathway of uncertain light upon the water, and disappear at once into the impenetrable gloom that lay beyond. This time I saw more distinctly than before. It was like the former canoe, a big birch-bark, with high-crested bows and stern and broad beam. It was paddled by two Indians, of whom the one in the stern—the steerer—appeared to be a very large man. I could see this very plainly; and though the second canoe was much nearer the island than the first, I judged that they were both on their way home to the Government Reservation, which was situated some fifteen miles away upon the mainland.

I was wondering in my mind what could possibly bring any Indians down to this part of the lake at such an hour of the night, when a third canoe, of precisely similar build, and also occupied by two Indians, passed silently round the end of the wharf. This time the canoe was very much nearer shore, and it suddenly flashed into my mind that the three canoes were in reality one and the same, and that only one canoe was circling the island!

This was by no means a pleasant reflection, because, if it were the correct solution of the unusual appearance of the three canoes in this lonely part of the lake at so late an hour, the purpose of the two men could only reasonably be considered to be in some way connected with myself. I had never known of the Indians attempting any violence upon the settlers who shared the wild, inhospitable country with them; at the same time, it was not beyond the region of possibility to suppose . . . But then I did not care even to think of such hideous possibilities, and my imagination immediately sought relief in all manner of other solutions to the problem, which indeed came readily enough to my mind, but did not succeed in recommending themselves to my reason.

Meanwhile, by a sort of instinct, I stepped back out of the bright light in which I had hitherto been standing, and waited in the deep shadow of a rock to see if the canoe would again make its appearance. Here I could see, without being seen, and the precaution seemed a wise one.

After less than five minutes the canoe, as I had anticipated, made its fourth appearance. This time it was not twenty yards from the wharf, and I saw that the Indians meant to land. I recognised the two men as those who had passed before, and the steerer was certainly an immense fellow. It was unquestionably the same canoe. There could be no longer any doubt that for some purpose of their own the men had been going round and round the island for some time, waiting for an opportunity to land. I strained my eyes to follow them in the darkness, but the night had completely swallowed them up, and not even the faintest swish of the paddles reached my ears as the Indians plied their long and powerful strokes. The canoe would be round again in a few moments, and this time it was possible that the men might land. It was well to be prepared. I knew nothing of their intentions, and two to one (when the two are big Indians!) late at night on a lonely island was not exactly my idea of pleasant intercourse.

In a corner of the sitting-room, leaning up against the back wall, stood my Marlin rifle, with ten cartridges in the magazine and one lying snugly in the greased breech. There was just time to get up to the house and take up a position of defence in that corner. Without an instant's hesitation I ran up to the verandah, carefully picking my way among the trees, so as to avoid being seen in the light. Entering the room, I shut the door leading to the verandah, and as quickly as possible turned out every one of the six lamps. To be in a room so brilliantly lighted, where my every movement could be observed from outside, while I could see nothing but impenetrable darkness at every window, was by all laws of warfare an unnecessary concession to the enemy. And this enemy, if enemy it was to be, was far too wily and dangerous to be granted any such advantages.

I stood in the corner of the room with my back against the wall, and my hand on the cold rifle-barrel. The table, covered with my books, lay between me and the door, but for the first few minutes after the lights were out the darkness was so intense that nothing could be discerned at all. Then, very gradually, the outline of the room became visible, and the framework of the windows began to shape itself dimly before my eyes.

After a few minutes the door (its upper half of glass), and the two windows that looked out upon the front verandah, became specially distinct; and I was glad that this was so, because if the Indians came up to the house I should be able to see their approach, and gather something of their plans. Nor was I mistaken, for there presently came to my ears the peculiar hollow sound of a canoe landing and being carefully dragged up over the rocks. The paddles I distinctly heard being placed underneath, and the silence that ensued thereupon I rightly interpreted to mean that the Indians were stealthily approaching the house. . . .

While it would be absurd to claim that I was not alarmed—even frightened—at the gravity of the situation and its possible outcome, I speak the whole truth when I say that I was not overwhelmingly afraid for myself. I was conscious that even at this stage of the night I was passing into a psychical condition in which my sensations seemed no longer normal. Physical fear at no time entered into the nature of my feelings; and though I kept my hand upon my rifle the greater part of the night, I was all the time conscious that its assistance could be of little avail against the terrors that I had to face. More than once I seemed to feel most curiously that I was in no real sense a part of the proceedings, nor actually involved in them, but that I was playing the part of a spectator—a spectator, moreover, on a psychic rather than on a material plane. Many of my sensations that night were too vague for definite description and analysis, but the main feeling that will stay with me to the end of my days is the awful horror of it all, and the miserable sensation that if the strain had lasted a little longer than was actually the case my mind must inevitably have given way.

Meanwhile I stood still in my corner, and waited patiently for what was to come. The house was as still as the grave, but the inarticulate voices of the night sang in my ears, and I seemed to hear the blood running in my veins and dancing in my pulses.

If the Indians came to the back of the house, they would find the kitchen door and window securely fastened. They could not get in there without making considerable noise, which I was bound to hear. The only mode of getting in was by means of the door that faced me, and I kept my eyes glued on that door without taking them off for the smallest fraction of a second.

My sight adapted itself every minute better to the darkness. I saw the table that nearly filled the room, and left only a narrow passage on each side. I could also make out the straight backs of the wooden chairs pressed up against it, and could even distinguish my papers and inkstand lying on the white oilcloth covering. I thought of the gay faces that had gathered round that table during the summer, and I longed for the sunlight as I had never longed for it before.

Less than three feet to my left the passage-way led to the kitchen, and the stairs leading to the bedrooms above commenced in this passage-way, but almost in the sitting-room itself. Through the windows I could see the dim motionless outlines of the trees: not a leaf stirred, not a branch moved.

A few moments of this awful silence, and then I was aware of a soft tread on the boards of the verandah, so stealthy that it seemed an impression directly on my brain rather than upon the nerves of hearing. Immediately afterwards a black figure darkened the glass door, and I perceived that a face was pressed against the upper panes. A shiver ran down my back, and my hair was conscious of a tendency to rise and stand at right angles to my head.

It was the figure of an Indian, broad-shouldered and immense; indeed, the largest figure of a man I have ever seen outside of a circus hall. By some power of light that seemed to generate itself in the brain, I saw the strong dark face with the aquiline nose and high cheek-bones flattened against the glass. The direction of the gaze I could not determine; but faint gleams of light as the big eyes rolled round and showed their whites, told me plainly that no corner of the room escaped their searching.

For what seemed fully five minutes the dark figure stood there, with the huge shoulders bent forward so as to bring the head down to the level of the glass; while behind him, though not nearly so large, the shadowy form of the other Indian swayed to and fro like a bent tree. While I waited in an agony of suspense and agitation for their next movement little currents of icy sensation ran up and down my

spine and my heart seemed alternately to stop beating and then start
off again with terrifying rapidity. They must have heard its thumping
and the singing of the blood in my head! Moreover, I was conscious,
as I felt a cold stream of perspiration trickle down my face, of a desire
to scream, to shout, to bang the walls like a child, to make a noise,
or do anything that would relieve the suspense and bring things to
a speedy climax.

It was probably this inclination that led me to another discovery,
for when I tried to bring my rifle from behind my back to raise it and
have it pointed at the door ready to fire, I found that I was powerless
to move. The muscles, paralysed by this strange fear, refused to obey
the will. Here indeed was a terrifying complication!

* * *

There was a faint sound of rattling at the brass knob, and the door was
pushed open a couple of inches. A pause of a few seconds, and it was
pushed open still further. Without a sound of footsteps that was
appreciable to my ears, the two figures glided into the room, and the
man behind gently closed the door after him.

They were alone with me between the four walls. Could they see
me standing there, so still and straight in my corner? Had they, perhaps, already seen me? My blood surged and sang like the roll of drums
in an orchestra; and though I did my best to suppress my breathing,
it sounded like the rushing of wind through a pneumatic tube.*

My suspense as to the next move was soon at an end—only, however, to give place to a new and keener alarm. The men had hitherto
exchanged no words and no signs, but there were general indications
of a movement across the room, and whichever way they went they
would have to pass round the table. If they came my way they would
have to pass within six inches of my person. While I was considering
this very disagreeable possibility, I perceived that the smaller Indian
(smaller by comparison) suddenly raised his arm and pointed to the
ceiling. The other fellow raised his head and followed the direction of
his companion's arm. I began to understand at last. They were going
upstairs, and the room directly overhead to which they pointed had
been until this night my bedroom. It was the room in which I had
experienced that very morning so strange a sensation of fear, and but
for which I should then have been lying asleep in the narrow bed
against the window.

The Indians then began to move silently around the room; they were going upstairs, and they were coming round my side of the table. So stealthy were their movements that, but for the abnormally sensitive state of the nerves, I should never have heard them. As it was, their cat-like tread was distinctly audible. Like two monstrous black cats they came round the table toward me, and for the first time I perceived that the smaller of the two dragged something along the floor behind him. As it trailed along over the floor with a soft, sweeping sound, I somehow got the impression that it was a large dead thing with outstretched wings, or a large, spreading cedar branch. Whatever it was, I was unable to see it even in outline, and I was too terrified, even had I possessed the power over my muscles, to move my neck forward in the effort to determine its nature.

Nearer and nearer they came. The leader rested a giant hand upon the table as he moved. My lips were glued together, and the air seemed to burn in my nostrils. I tried to close my eyes, so that I might not see as they passed me; but my eyelids had stiffened, and refused to obey. Would they never get by me? Sensation seemed also to have left my legs, and it was as if I were standing on mere supports of wood or stone. Worse still, I was conscious that I was losing the power of balance, the power to stand upright, or even to lean backwards against the wall. Some force was drawing me forward, and a dizzy terror seized me that I should lose my balance, and topple forward against the Indians just as they were in the act of passing me.

Even moments drawn out into hours must come to an end some time, and almost before I knew it the figures had passed me and had their feet upon the lower step of the stairs leading to the upper bedrooms. There could not have been six inches between us, and yet I was conscious only of a current of cold air that followed them. They had not touched me, and I was convinced that they had not seen me. Even the trailing thing on the floor behind them had not touched my feet, as I had dreaded it would, and on such an occasion as this I was grateful even for the smallest mercies.

The absence of the Indians from my immediate neighbourhood brought little sense of relief. I stood shivering and shuddering in my corner, and, beyond being able to breathe more freely, I felt no whit less uncomfortable. Also, I was aware that a certain light, which, without apparent source or rays, had enabled me to follow their every gesture and movement, had gone out of the room with their departure. An unnatural darkness now filled the room, and pervaded its every corner so that I could barely make out the positions of the windows and the glass doors.

As I said before, my condition was evidently an abnormal one. The capacity for feeling surprise seemed, as in dreams, to be wholly absent. My senses recorded with unusual accuracy every smallest occurrence, but I was able to draw only the simplest deductions.

The Indians soon reached the top of the stairs, and there they halted for a moment. I had not the faintest clue as to their next movement. They appeared to hesitate. They were listening attentively. Then I heard one of them, who by the weight of his soft tread must have been the giant, cross the narrow corridor and enter the room directly overhead—my own little bedroom. But for the insistence of that unaccountable dread I had experienced there in the morning, I should at that very moment have been lying in the bed with the big Indian in the room standing beside me.

For the space of a hundred seconds there was silence, such as might have existed before the birth of sound. It was followed by a long quivering shriek of terror, which rang out into the night, and ended in a short gulp before it had run its full course. At the same moment the other Indian left his place at the head of the stairs, and joined his companion in the bedroom. I heard the 'thing' trailing behind him along the floor. A thud followed, as of something heavy falling, and then all became as still and silent as before.

It was at this point that the atmosphere, surcharged all day with the electricity of a fierce storm, found relief in a dancing flash of brilliant lightning simultaneously with a crash of loudest thunder. For five seconds every article in the room was visible to me with amazing distinctness, and through the windows I saw the tree trunks standing in solemn rows. The thunder pealed and echoed across the lake and among the distant islands, and the flood-gates of heaven then opened and let out their rain in streaming torrents.

The drops fell with a swift rushing sound upon the still waters of the lake, which leaped up to meet them, and pattered with the rattle of shot on the leaves of the maples and the roof of the cottage. A moment later and another flash, even more brilliant and of longer duration than the first, lit up the sky from zenith to horizon, and bathed the room momentarily in dazzling whiteness. I could see the rain glistening on the leaves and branches outside. The wind rose suddenly, and in less than a minute the storm that had been gathering all day burst forth in its full fury.

Above all the noisy voices of the elements, the slightest sounds in the room overhead made themselves heard, and in the few seconds of deep silence that followed the shriek of terror and pain I was aware that the movements had commenced again. The men were leaving the room and approaching the top of the stairs. A short pause, and they began to descend. Behind them, tumbling from step to step, I could hear that trailing 'thing' being dragged along. It had become ponderous!

I awaited their approach with a degree of calmness, almost of apathy, which was only explicable on the ground that after a certain point Nature applies her own anaesthetic, and a merciful condition of numbness supervenes. On they came, step by step, nearer and nearer, with the shuffling sound of the burden behind growing louder as they approached.

They were already half-way down the stairs when I was galvanised afresh into a condition of terror by the consideration of a new and horrible possibility. It was the reflection that if another vivid flash of lightning were to come when the shadowy procession was in the room, perhaps when it was actually passing in front of me, I should see everything in detail, and worse, be seen myself! I could only hold my breath and wait—wait while the minutes lengthened into hours, and the procession made its slow progress round the room.

The Indians had reached the foot of the staircase. The form of the huge leader loomed in the doorway of the passage, and the burden with an ominous thud had dropped from the last step to the floor. There was a moment's pause while I saw the Indian turn and stoop to assist his companion. Then the procession moved forward again, entered the room close on my left, and began to move slowly round my side of the table. The leader was already beyond me, and his companion, dragging on the floor behind him the burden, whose confused outline I could dimly make out, was exactly in front of me, when the cavalcade came to a dead halt. At the same moment, with the strange suddenness of thunderstorms, the splash of the rain ceased altogether, and the wind died away into utter silence.

For the space of five seconds my heart seemed to stop beating, and then the worst came. A double flash of lightning lit up the room and its contents with merciless vividness.

The huge Indian leader stood a few feet past me on my right. One leg was stretched forward in the act of taking a step. His immense shoulders were turned toward his companion, and in all their magnificent fierceness I saw the outline of his features. His gaze was directed upon the burden his companion was dragging along the floor; but his profile, with the big aquiline nose, high cheekbone, straight black hair and bold chin, burnt itself in that brief instant into my brain, never again to fade.

Dwarfish, compared with this gigantic figure, appeared the proportions of the other Indian, who, within twelve inches of my face, was stooping over the thing he was dragging in a position that lent to his person the additional horror of deformity. And the burden, lying upon a sweeping cedar branch which he held and dragged by a long stem, was the body of a white man. The scalp had been neatly lifted, and blood lay in a broad smear upon the cheeks and forehead.

Then, for the first time that night, the terror that had paralysed my muscles and my will lifted its unholy spell from my soul. With a loud cry I stretched out my arms to seize the big Indian by the throat, and, grasping only air, tumbled forward unconscious upon the ground.

I had recognised the body, and *the face was my own!* . . .

It was bright daylight when a man's voice recalled me to consciousness. I was lying where I had fallen, and the farmer was standing in the room with the loaves of bread in his hands. The horror of the night was still in my heart, and as the bluff settler helped me to my feet and picked up the rifle which had fallen with me, with many questions and expressions of condolence, I imagine my brief replies were neither self-explanatory nor even intelligible.

That day, after a thorough and fruitless search of the house, I left the island, and went over to spend my last ten days with the farmer; and when the time came for me to leave, the necessary reading had been accomplished, and my nerves had completely recovered their balance.

On the day of my departure the farmer started early in his big boat with my belongings to row to the point, twelve miles distant, where a little steamer ran twice a week for the accommodation of hunters. Late in the afternoon I went off in another direction in my canoe, wishing to see the island once again, where I had been the victim of so strange an experience.

In due course I arrived there, and made a tour of the island. I also made a search of the little house, and it was not without a curious sensation in my heart that I entered the little upstairs bedroom. There seemed nothing unusual.

Just after I re-embarked, I saw a canoe gliding ahead of me around the curve of the island. A canoe was an unusual sight at this time of the year, and this one seemed to have sprung from nowhere. Altering my course a little, I watched it disappear around the next projecting point of rock. It had high curving bows, and there were two Indians in it. I lingered with some excitement, to see if it would appear again round the other side of the island; and in less than five minutes it came into view. There were less than two hundred yards between us, and the Indians, sitting on their haunches, were paddling swiftly in my direction.

I never paddled faster in my life than I did in those next few minutes. When I turned to look again, the Indians had altered their course, and were again circling the island.

The sun was sinking behind the forests on the mainland, and the crimson-coloured clouds of sunset were reflected in the waters of the lake, when I looked round for the last time, and saw the big bark canoe and its two dusky occupants still going round the island. Then the shadows deepened rapidly; the lake grew black, and the night wind blew its first breath in my face as I turned a corner, and a projecting bluff of rock hid from my view both island and canoe.

THE EMPTY HOUSE

CERTAIN houses, like certain persons, manage somehow to proclaim at once their character for evil. In the case of the latter, no particular feature need betray them; they may boast an open countenance and an ingenuous smile; and yet a little of their company leaves the unalterable conviction that there is something radically amiss with their being: that they are evil. Willy nilly, they seem to communicate an atmosphere of secret and wicked thoughts which makes those in their immediate neighbourhood shrink from them as from a thing diseased.

And, perhaps, with houses the same principle is operative, and it is the aroma of evil deeds committed under a particular roof, long after the actual doers have passed away, that makes the gooseflesh come and the hair rise. Something of the original passion of the evil-doer, and of the horror felt by his victim, enters the heart of the innocent watcher, and he becomes suddenly conscious of tingling nerves, creeping skin, and a chilling of the blood. He is terror-stricken without apparent cause.

There was manifestly nothing in the external appearance of this particular house to bear out the tales of the horror that was said to reign within. It was neither lonely nor unkempt. It stood, crowded into a corner of the square, and looked exactly like the houses on either side of it. It had the same number of windows as its neighbours; the same balcony overlooking the gardens; the same white steps leading up to the heavy black front door; and, in the rear, there was the same narrow strip of green, with neat box borders, running up to the wall that divided it from the backs of the adjoining houses. Apparently, too, the number of chimney pots on the roof was the same; the breadth and angle of the eaves; and even the height of the dirty area railings.

And yet this house in the square, that seemed precisely similar to its fifty ugly neighbours, was as a matter of fact entirely different—horribly different.

Wherein lay this marked, invisible difference is impossible to say. It cannot be ascribed wholly to the imagination, because persons who had spent some time in the house, knowing nothing of the facts, had declared positively that certain rooms were so disagreeable they would rather die than enter them again, and that the atmosphere of the whole house produced in them symptoms of a genuine terror; while the series of innocent tenants who had tried to live in it and been forced to decamp at the shortest possible notice, was indeed little less than a scandal in the town.

When Shorthouse arrived to pay a 'week-end' visit to his Aunt Julia in her little house on the sea-front at the other end of the town,* he found her charged to the brim with mystery and excitement. He had only received her telegram that morning, and he had come anticipating boredom; but the moment he touched her hand and kissed her apple-skin wrinkled cheek, he caught the first wave of her electrical condition. The impression deepened when he learned that there were to be no other visitors, and that he had been telegraphed for with a very special object.

Something was in the wind, and the 'something' would doubtless bear fruit; for this elderly spinster aunt, with a mania for psychical research,* had brains as well as will power, and by hook or by crook she usually managed to accomplish her ends. The revelation was made soon after tea, when she sidled close up to him as they paced slowly along the sea-front in the dusk.

'I've got the keys,' she announced in a delighted, yet half awesome voice. 'Got them till Monday!'

'The keys of the bathing-machine,* or——?' he asked innocently, looking from the sea to the town. Nothing brought her so quickly to the point as feigning stupidity.

'Neither,' she whispered. 'I've got the keys of the haunted house in the square*—and I'm going there to-night.'

Shorthouse was conscious of the slightest possible tremor down his back. He dropped his teasing tone. Something in her voice and manner thrilled him. She was in earnest.

'But you can't go alone——' he began.

'That's why I wired for you,' she said with decision.

He turned to look at her. The ugly, lined, enigmatical face was alive with excitement. There was the glow of genuine enthusiasm round it like a halo. The eyes shone. He caught another wave of her excitement, and a second tremor, more marked than the first, accompanied it.

'Thanks, Aunt Julia,' he said politely; 'thanks awfully.'

'I should not dare to go quite alone,' she went on, raising her voice; 'but with you I should enjoy it immensely. You're afraid of nothing, I know.'

'Thanks so much,' he said again. 'Er—is anything likely to happen?'

'A great deal *has* happened,' she whispered, 'though it's been most cleverly hushed up. Three tenants have come and gone in the last few months, and the house is said to be empty for good now.'

In spite of himself Shorthouse became interested. His aunt was so very much in earnest.

'The house is very old indeed,' she went on, 'and the story—an unpleasant one—dates a long way back. It has to do with a murder committed by a jealous stableman who had some affair with a servant in the house. One night he managed to secrete himself in the cellar, and when everyone was asleep, he crept upstairs to the servants' quarters, chased the girl down to the next landing, and before anyone could come to the rescue threw her bodily over the banisters into the hall below.'

'And the stableman——?'

'Was caught, I believe, and hanged for murder; but it all happened a century ago, and I've not been able to get more details of the story.'

Shorthouse now felt his interest thoroughly aroused; but, though he was not particularly nervous for himself, he hesitated a little on his aunt's account.

'On one condition,' he said at length.

'Nothing will prevent my going,' she said firmly; 'but I may as well hear your condition.'

'That you guarantee your power of self-control if anything really horrible happens. I mean—that you are sure you won't get too frightened.'

'Jim,' she said scornfully, 'I'm not young, I know, nor are my nerves; but *with you* I should be afraid of nothing in the world!'

This, of course, settled it, for Shorthouse had no pretensions to being other than a very ordinary young man, and an appeal to his vanity was irresistible. He agreed to go.

Instinctively, by a sort of sub-conscious preparation, he kept himself and his forces well in hand the whole evening, compelling an accumulative reserve of control by that nameless inward process of gradually putting all the emotions away and turning the key upon them—a process difficult to describe, but wonderfully effective, as all men who have lived through severe trials of the inner man well understand. Later, it stood him in good stead.

But it was not until half-past ten, when they stood in the hall, well in the glare of friendly lamps and still surrounded by comforting human influences, that he had to make the first call upon this store of collected strength. For, once the door was closed, and he saw the deserted silent street stretching away white in the moonlight before them, it came to him clearly that the real test that night would be in dealing with *two fears* instead of one. He would have to carry his aunt's fear as well as his own. And, as he glanced down at her Sphinx-like countenance and realised that it might assume no pleasant aspect in a rush of real terror, he felt satisfied with only one thing in the whole adventure—that he had confidence in his own will and power to stand against any shock that might come.

Slowly they walked along the empty streets of the town; a bright autumn moon silvered the roofs, casting deep shadows; there was no breath of wind; and the trees in the formal gardens by the sea-front watched them silently as they passed along. To his aunt's occasional remarks Shorthouse made no reply, realising that she was simply surrounding herself with mental buffers—saying ordinary things to prevent herself thinking of extra-ordinary things. Few windows showed lights, and from scarcely a single chimney came smoke or sparks. Shorthouse had already begun to notice everything, even the smallest details. Presently they stopped at the street corner and looked up at the name on the side of the house full in the moonlight, and with one accord, but without remark, turned into the square and crossed over to the side of it that lay in shadow.

'The number of the house is thirteen,' whispered a voice at his side; and neither of them made the obvious reference, but passed across the broad sheet of moonlight and began to march up the pavement in silence.

It was about half-way up the square that Shorthouse felt an arm slipped quietly but significantly into his own, and knew then that their adventure had begun in earnest, and that his companion was already yielding imperceptibly to the influences against them. She needed support.

A few minutes later they stopped before a tall, narrow house that rose before them into the night, ugly in shape and painted a dingy white. Shutterless windows, without blinds, stared down upon them, shining here and there in the moonlight. There were weather streaks in the wall and cracks in the paint, and the balcony bulged out from the first floor a little unnaturally. But, beyond this generally forlorn appearance of an unoccupied house, there was nothing at first sight to single out this particular mansion for the evil character it had most certainly acquired.

Taking a look over their shoulders to make sure they had not been followed, they went boldly up the steps and stood against the huge black door that fronted them forbiddingly. But the first wave of nervousness was now upon them, and Shorthouse fumbled a long time with the key before he could fit it into the lock at all. For a moment, if truth were told, they both hoped it would not open, for they were a prey to various unpleasant emotions as they stood there on the threshold of their ghostly adventure. Shorthouse, shuffling with the key and hampered by the steady weight on his arm, certainly felt the solemnity of the moment. It was as if the whole world—for all experience seemed at that instant concentrated in his own consciousness—were listening to the grating noise of that key. A stray puff of wind wandering down the empty street woke a momentary rustling in the trees behind them, but otherwise this rattling of the key was the only sound audible; and at last it turned in the lock and the heavy door swung open and revealed a yawning gulf of darkness beyond.

With a last glance at the moonlit square, they passed quickly in, and the door slammed behind them with a roar that echoed prodigiously through empty halls and passages. But, instantly, with the echoes, another sound made itself heard, and Aunt Julia leaned suddenly so heavily upon him that he had to take a step backwards to save himself from falling.

A man had coughed close beside them—so close that it seemed they must have been actually by his side in the darkness.

With the possibility of practical jokes in his mind, Shorthouse at once swung his heavy stick in the direction of the sound; but it met nothing more solid than air. He heard his aunt give a little gasp beside him.

'There's someone here,' she whispered; 'I heard him.'

'Be quiet!' he said sternly. 'It was nothing but the noise of the front door.'

'Oh! get a light—quick!' she added, as her nephew, fumbling with a box of matches, opened it upside down and let them all fall with a rattle on to the stone floor.

The sound, however, was not repeated; and there was no evidence of retreating footsteps. In another minute they had a candle burning, using an empty end of a cigar case as a holder; and when the first flare had died down he held the impromptu lamp aloft and surveyed the scene. And it was dreary enough in all conscience, for there in nothing more desolate in all the abodes of men than an unfurnished house dimly lit, silent, and forsaken, and yet tenanted by rumour with the memories of evil and violent histories.

They were standing in a wide hall-way; on their left was the open door of a spacious dining-room, and in front the hall ran, ever narrowing, into a long, dark passage that led apparently to the top of the kitchen stairs. The broad uncarpeted staircase rose in a sweep before them, everywhere draped in shadows, except for a single spot about half-way up where the moonlight came in through the window and fell on a bright patch on the boards. This shaft of light shed a faint radiance above and below it, lending to the objects within its reach a misty outline that was infinitely more suggestive and ghostly than complete darkness. Filtered moonlight always seems to paint faces on the surrounding gloom, and as Shorthouse peered up into the well of darkness and thought of the countless empty rooms and passages in the upper part of the old house, he caught himself longing again for the safety of the moonlit square, or the cosy, bright drawing-room they had left an hour before. Then realising that these thoughts were dangerous, he thrust them away again and summoned all his energy for concentration on the present.

'Aunt Julia,' he said aloud, severely, 'we must now go through the house from top to bottom and make a thorough search.'

The echoes of his voice died away slowly all over the building, and in the intense silence that followed he turned to look at her. In the candle-light he saw that her face was already ghastly pale; but she dropped his arm for a moment and said in a whisper, stepping close in front of him—

'I agree. We must be sure there's no one hiding. That's the first thing.'

She spoke with evident effort, and he looked at her with admiration.

'You feel quite sure of yourself? It's not too late——'

'I think so,' she whispered, her eyes shifting nervously toward the shadows behind. 'Quite sure, only one thing——'

'What's that?'

'You must never leave me alone for an instant.'

'As long as you understand that any sound or appearance must be investigated at once, for to hesitate means to admit fear. That is fatal.'

'Agreed,' she said, a little shakily, after a moment's hesitation. 'I'll try——'

Arm in arm, Shorthouse holding the dripping candle and the stick, while his aunt carried the cloak over her shoulders, figures of utter comedy to all but themselves, they began a systematic search.

Stealthily, walking on tip-toe and shading the candle lest it should betray their presence through the shutterless windows, they went first into the big dining-room. There was not a stick of furniture to be seen. Bare walls, ugly mantel-pieces and empty grates stared at them. Everything, they felt, resented their intrusion, watching them, as it were, with veiled eyes; whispers followed them; shadows flitted noiselessly to right and left; something seemed ever at their back, watching, waiting an opportunity to do them injury. There was the inevitable sense that operations which went on when the room was empty had been temporarily suspended till they were well out of the way again. The whole dark interior of the old building seemed to become a malignant Presence that rose up, warning them to desist and mind their own business; every moment the strain on the nerves increased.

Out of the gloomy dining-room they passed through large folding doors into a sort of library or smoking-room, wrapt equally in silence, darkness, and dust; and from this they regained the hall near the top of the back stairs.

Here a pitch black tunnel opened before them into the lower regions, and—it must be confessed—they hesitated. But only for a minute. With the worst of the night still to come it was essential to turn from nothing. Aunt Julia stumbled at the top step of the dark descent, ill lit by the flickering candle, and even Shorthouse felt at least half the decision go out of his legs.

'Come on!' he said peremptorily, and his voice ran on and lost itself in the dark, empty spaces below.

'I'm coming,' she faltered, catching his arm with unnecessary violence.

They went a little unsteadily down the stone steps, a cold, damp air meeting them in the face, close and malodorous. The kitchen, into which the stairs led along a narrow passage, was large, with a lofty ceiling. Several doors opened out of it—some into cupboards with empty jars still standing on the shelves, and others into horrible little ghostly back offices, each colder and less inviting than the last. Black beetles scurried over the floor, and once, when they knocked against a deal table standing in a corner, something about the size of a cat jumped down with a rush and fled, scampering across the stone floor into the darkness. Everywhere there was a sense of recent occupation, an impression of sadness and gloom.

Leaving the main kitchen, they next went towards the scullery. The door was standing ajar, and as they pushed it open to its full extent Aunt Julia uttered a piercing scream, which she instantly tried to stifle by placing her hand over her mouth. For a second Shorthouse stood stock-still, catching his breath. He felt as if his spine had suddenly become hollow and someone had filled it with particles of ice.

Facing them, directly in their way between the doorposts, stood the figure of a woman. She had dishevelled hair and wildly staring eyes, and her face was terrified and white as death.

She stood there motionless for the space of a single second. Then the candle flickered and she was gone—gone utterly—and the door framed nothing but empty darkness.

'Only the beastly jumping candle-light,' he said quickly, in a voice that sounded like someone else's and was only half under control. 'Come on, aunt. There's nothing there.'

He dragged her forward. With a clattering of feet and a great appearance of boldness they went on, but over his body the skin moved as if crawling ants covered it, and he knew by the weight on his arm that he was supplying the force of locomotion for two. The scullery was cold, bare, and empty; more like a large prison cell than anything else. They went round it, tried the door into the yard, and the windows, but found them all fastened securely, His aunt moved beside him like a person in a dream. Her eyes were tightly shut, and she seemed merely to follow the pressure of his arm. Her courage filled him with amazement. At the same time he noticed that a certain odd change had come over her face, a change which somehow evaded his power of analysis.

'There's nothing here, aunty,' he repeated aloud quickly. 'Let's go upstairs and see the rest of the house. Then we'll choose a room to wait up in.'

She followed him obediently, keeping close to his side, and they locked the kitchen door behind them. It was a relief to get up again.

In the hall there was more light than before, for the moon had travelled a little further down the stairs. Cautiously they began to go up into the dark vault of the upper house, the boards creaking under their weight.

On the first floor they found the large double drawing-rooms, a search of which revealed nothing. Here also was no sign of furniture or recent occupancy; nothing but dust and neglect and shadows. They opened the big folding doors between front and back drawing-rooms and then came out again to the landing and went on upstairs.

They had not gone up more than a dozen steps when they both simultaneously stopped to listen, looking into each other's eyes with a new apprehension across the flickering candle flame. From the room they had left hardly ten seconds before came the sound of doors quietly closing. It was beyond all question; they heard the booming noise that accompanies the shutting of heavy doors, followed by the sharp catching of the latch.

'We must go back and see,' said Shorthouse briefly, in a low tone, and turning to go downstairs again.

Somehow she managed to drag after him, her feet catching in her dress, her face livid.

When they entered the front drawing-room it was plain that the folding doors had been closed—half a minute before. Without hesitation Shorthouse opened them. He almost expected to see someone facing him in the back room; but only darkness and cold air met him. They went through both rooms, finding nothing unusual. They tried in every way to make the doors close of themselves, but there was not wind enough even to set the candle flame flickering. The doors would not move without strong pressure. All was silent as the grave. Undeniably the rooms were utterly empty, and the house utterly still.

'It's beginning,' whispered a voice at his elbow which he hardly recognised as his aunt's.

He nodded acquiescence, taking out his watch to note the time. It was fifteen minutes before midnight; he made the entry of exactly what had occurred in his notebook, setting the candle in its case upon the floor in order to do so. It took a moment or two to balance it safely against the wall.

Aunt Julia always declared that at this moment she was not actually watching him, but had turned her head towards the inner room, where she fancied she heard something moving; but, at any rate, both positively agreed that there came a sound of rushing feet, heavy and very swift—and the next instant the candle was out!

But to Shorthouse himself had come more than this, and he has always thanked his fortunate stars that it came to him alone and not to his aunt too. For, as he rose from the stooping position of balancing the candle, and before it was actually extinguished, a face thrust itself forward so close to his own that he could almost have touched it with his lips. It was a face working with passion; a man's face, dark, with thick features, and angry, savage eyes. It belonged to a common man, and it was evil in its ordinary normal expression, no doubt, but as he saw it, alive with intense, aggressive emotion, it was a malignant and terrible human countenance.

There was no movement of the air; nothing but the sound of rushing feet—stockinged or muffled feet; the apparition of the face; and the almost simultaneous extinguishing of the candle.

In spite of himself, Shorthouse uttered a little cry, nearly losing his balance as his aunt clung to him with her whole weight in one moment of real, uncontrollable terror. She made no sound, but simply seized him bodily. Fortunately, however, she had seen nothing, but had only heard the rushing feet, for her control returned almost at once, and he was able to disentangle himself and strike a match.

The shadows ran away on all sides before the glare, and his aunt stooped down and groped for the cigar case with the precious candle. Then they discovered that the candle had not been *blown* out at all; it had been *crushed* out. The wick was pressed down into the wax, which was flattened as if by some smooth, heavy instrument.

How his companion so quickly overcame her terror, Shorthouse never properly understood; but his admiration for her self-control increased tenfold, and at the same time served to feed his own dying flame—for which he was undeniably grateful. Equally inexplicable to him was the evidence of physical force they had just witnessed. He at once suppressed the memory of stories he had heard of 'physical mediums'* and their dangerous phenomena; for if these were true, and either his aunt or himself was unwittingly a physical medium, it meant that they were simply aiding to focus the forces of a haunted house already charged to the brim. It was like walking with unprotected lamps among uncovered stores of gunpowder.

So, with as little reflection as possible, he simply relit the candle and went up to the next floor. The arm in his trembled, it is true, and his own tread was often uncertain, but they went on with thoroughness, and after a search revealing nothing they climbed the last flight of stairs to the top floor of all.

Here they found a perfect nest of small servants' rooms, with broken pieces of furniture, dirty cane-bottomed chairs, chests of drawers, cracked mirrors, and decrepit bedsteads. The rooms had low sloping ceilings already hung here and there with cobwebs, small windows, and badly plastered walls—a depressing and dismal region which they were glad to leave behind.

It was on the stroke of midnight when they entered a small room on the third floor, close to the top of the stairs, and arranged to make themselves comfortable for the remainder of their adventure. It was absolutely bare, and was said to be the room—then used as a clothes closet—into which the infuriated groom had chased his victim and finally caught her. Outside, across the narrow landing, began the stairs leading up to the floor above, and the servants' quarters where they had just searched.

In spite of the chilliness of the night there was something in the air of this room that cried for an open window. But there was more than this. Shorthouse could only describe it by saying that he felt less master of himself here than in any other part of the house. There was something that acted directly on the nerves, tiring the resolution, enfeebling the will. He was conscious of this result before he had been in the room five minutes, and it was in the short time they stayed there that he suffered the wholesale depletion of his vital forces, which was, for himself, the chief horror of the whole experience.

They put the candle on the floor of the cupboard, leaving the door a few inches ajar, so that there was no glare to confuse the eyes, and no shadow to shift about on walls and ceiling. Then they spread the cloak on the floor and sat down to wait, with their backs against the wall.

Shorthouse was within two feet of the door on to the landing; his position commanded a good view of the main staircase leading down into the darkness, and also of the beginning of the servants' stairs going to the floor above; the heavy stick lay beside him within easy reach.

The moon was now high above the house. Through the open window they could see the comforting stars like friendly eyes watching in the sky. One by one the clocks of the town struck midnight, and when the sounds died away the deep silence of a windless night fell again over everything. Only the boom of the sea, far away and lugubrious, filled the air with hollow murmurs.

Inside the house the silence became awful; awful, he thought, because any minute now it might be broken by sounds portending terror. The strain of waiting told more and more severely on the nerves; they talked in whispers when they talked at all, for their voices aloud sounded queer and unnatural. A chilliness, not altogether due to the night air, invaded the room, and made them cold. The influences against them, whatever these might be, were slowly robbing them of self-confidence, and the power of decisive action; their forces were on the wane, and the possibility of real fear took on a new and terrible meaning. He began to tremble for the elderly woman by his side, whose pluck could hardly save her beyond a certain extent.

He heard the blood singing in his veins. It sometimes seemed so loud that he fancied it prevented his hearing properly certain other sounds that were beginning very faintly to make themselves audible in the depths of the house. Every time he fastened his attention on these sounds, they instantly ceased. They certainly came no nearer. Yet he could not rid himself of the idea that movement was going on somewhere in the lower regions of the house. The drawing-room floor, where the doors had been so strangely closed, seemed too near; the sounds were further off than that. He thought of the great kitchen, with the scurrying black-beetles, and of the dismal little scullery; but, somehow or other, they did not seem to come from there either. Surely they were not *outside* the house!

Then, suddenly, the truth flashed into his mind, and for the space of a minute he felt as if his blood had stopped flowing and turned to ice.

The sounds were not downstairs at all; they were *upstairs*—upstairs, somewhere among those horrid gloomy little servants' rooms with their bits of broken furniture, low ceilings, and cramped windows— upstairs where the victim had first been disturbed and stalked to her death.

And the moment he discovered where the sounds were, he began to hear them more clearly. It was the sound of feet, moving stealthily along the passage overhead, in and out among the rooms, and past the furniture.

He turned quickly to steal a glance at the motionless figure seated beside him, to note whether she had shared his discovery. The faint candle-light coming through the crack in the cupboard door, threw her strongly-marked face into vivid relief against the white of the wall. But it was something else that made him catch his breath and stare again. An extraordinary something had come into her face and seemed to spread over her features like a mask; it smoothed out the deep lines and drew the skin everywhere a little tighter so that the wrinkles disappeared; it brought into the face—with the sole exception of the old eyes—an appearance of youth and almost of childhood.

He stared in speechless amazement—amazement that was dangerously near to horror. It was his aunt's face indeed, but it was her face of forty years ago, the vacant innocent face of a girl. He had heard stories of that strange effect of terror which could wipe a human countenance clean of other emotions, obliterating all previous expressions; but he had never realised that it could be literally true, or could mean anything so simply horrible as what he now saw. For the dreadful signature of overmastering fear was written plainly in that utter vacancy of the girlish face beside him; and when, feeling his intense gaze, she turned to look at him, he instinctively closed his eyes tightly to shut out the sight.

Yet, when he turned a minute later, his feelings well in hand, he saw to his intense relief another expression; his aunt was smiling, and though the face was deathly white, the awful veil had lifted and the normal look was returning.

'Anything wrong?' was all he could think of to say at the moment. And the answer was eloquent, coming from such a woman.

'I feel cold—and a little frightened,' she whispered.

He offered to close the window, but she seized hold of him and begged him not to leave her side even for an instant.

'It's upstairs, I know,' she whispered, with an odd half laugh; 'but I can't possibly go up.'

But Shorthouse thought otherwise, knowing that in action lay their best hope of self-control.

He took the brandy flask and poured out a glass of neat spirit, stiff enough to help anybody over anything. She swallowed it with a little shiver. His only idea now was to get out of the house before her collapse became inevitable; but this could not safely be done by turning tail and running from the enemy. Inaction was no longer possible; every minute he was growing less master of himself and desperate, aggressive measures were imperative without further delay. Moreover, the action must be taken *towards* the enemy, not away from it; the climax, if necessary and unavoidable, would have to be faced boldly. He could do it now; but in ten minutes he might not have the force left to act for himself, much less for both!

Upstairs, the sounds were meanwhile becoming louder and closer, accompanied by occasional creaking of the boards. Someone was moving stealthily about, stumbling now and then awkwardly against the furniture.

Waiting a few moments to allow the tremendous dose of spirits to produce its effect, and knowing this would last but a short time under the circumstances, Shorthouse then quietly got on his feet, saying in a determined voice—

'Now, Aunt Julia, we'll go upstairs, and find out what all this noise is about. You must come too. It's what we agreed.'

He picked up his stick and went to the cupboard for the candle. A limp form rose shakily beside him breathing hard, and he heard a voice say very faintly something about being 'ready to come.' The woman's courage amazed him; it was so much greater than his own; and, as they advanced, holding aloft the dripping candle, some subtle force exhaled from this trembling, white-faced old woman at his side that was the true source of his inspiration. It held something really great that shamed him and gave him the support without which he would have proved far less equal to the occasion.

They crossed the dark landing, avoiding with their eyes the deep black space over the banisters. Then they began to mount the narrow staircase to meet the sounds which, minute by minute, grew louder and nearer. About half-way up the stairs Aunt Julia stumbled and Shorthouse turned to catch her by the arm, and just at that moment there came a terrific crash in the servants' corridor overhead. It was instantly followed by a shrill, agonised scream that was a cry of terror and a cry for help melted into one.

Before they could move aside, or go down a single step, someone came rushing along the passage overhead, blundering horribly, racing madly, at full speed, three steps at a time, down the very staircase where they stood. The steps were light and uncertain; but close behind them sounded the heavier tread of another person, and the staircase seemed to shake.

Shorthouse and his companion just had time to flatten themselves against the wall when the jumble of flying steps was upon them, and two persons, with the slightest possible interval between them, dashed past at full speed. It was a perfect whirlwind of sound breaking in upon the midnight silence of the empty building.

The two runners, pursuer and pursued, had passed clean through them where they stood, and already with a thud the boards below had received first one, then the other. Yet they had seen absolutely nothing—not a hand, or arm, or face, or even a shred of flying clothing.

There came a second's pause. Then the first one, the lighter of the two, obviously the pursued one, ran with uncertain footsteps into the little room which Shorthouse and his aunt had just left. The heavier one followed. There was a sound of scuffling, gasping, and smothered screaming; and then out on to the landing came the step—of a single person *treading weightily.*

A dead silence followed for the space of half a minute, and then was heard a rushing sound through the air. It was followed by a dull, crashing thud in the depths of the house below—on the stone floor of the hall.

Utter silence reigned after. Nothing moved. The flame of the candle was steady. It had been steady the whole time, and the air had been undisturbed by any movement whatsoever. Palsied with terror, Aunt Julia, without waiting for her companion, began fumbling her way downstairs; she was crying gently to herself, and when Shorthouse put his arm round her and half carried her he felt that she was trembling like a leaf. He went into the little room and picked up the cloak from the floor, and, arm in arm, walking very slowly, without speaking a word or looking once behind them, they marched down the three flights into the hall.

In the hall they saw nothing, but the whole way down the stairs they were conscious that someone followed them; step by step; when they went faster IT was left behind, and when they went more slowly IT caught them up. But never once did they look behind to see; and at each turning of the staircase they lowered their eyes for fear of the following horror they might see upon the stairs above.

With trembling hands Shorthouse opened the front door, and they walked out into the moonlight and drew a deep breath of the cool night air blowing in from the sea.

SEPT. 4.—I have hunted all over London for rooms suited to my income—£120 a year—and have at last found them. Two rooms, without modern conveniences, it is true, and in an old, ramshackle building, but within a stone's throw of P——Place* and in an eminently respectable street. The rent is only £25 a year. I had begun to despair when at last I found them by chance. The chance was a mere chance, and unworthy of record. I had to sign a lease for a year, and I did so willingly. The furniture from our old place in H——shire* which has been stored so long, will just suit them.

Oct. 1.—Here I am in my two rooms, in the centre of London, and not far from the offices of the periodicals where occasionally I dispose of an article or two. The building is at the end of a *cul-de-sac.* The alley is well paved and clean, and lined chiefly with the backs of sedate and institutional-looking buildings. There is a stable in it. My own house is dignified with the title of 'Chambers.' I feel as if one day the honour must prove too much for it, and it will swell with pride—and fall asunder. It is very old. The floor of my sitting-room has valleys and low hills on it, and the top of the door slants away from the ceiling with a glorious disregard of what is usual. They must have quarrelled—fifty years ago—and have been going apart ever since.

Oct. 2.—My landlady is old and thin, with a faded, dusty face. She is uncommunicative. The few words she utters seem to cost her pain. Probably her lungs are half choked with dust. She keeps my rooms as free from this commodity as possible, and has the assistance of a strong girl who brings up the breakfast and lights the fire. As I have said already, she is not communicative. In reply to pleasant efforts on my part she informed me briefly that I was the only occupant of the house at present. My rooms had not been occupied for some years. There had been other gentlemen upstairs, but they had left.

She never looks straight at me when she speaks, but fixes her dim eyes on my middle waistcoat button, till I get nervous and begin to think it isn't on straight, or is the wrong sort of button altogether.

Oct. 8.—My week's book is nicely kept, and so far is reasonable. Milk and sugar 7d., bread 6d., butter 8d., marmalade 6d., eggs 1s. 8d., laundress 2s. 9d., oil 6d., attendance 5s.; total 12s. 2d.

The landlady has a son who, she told me, is 'somethink on a hom-nibus.' He comes occasionally to see her. I think he drinks, for he talks very loud, regardless of the hour of the day or night, and tumbles about over the furniture downstairs.

All the morning I sit indoors writing—articles; verses for the comic papers; a novel I've been 'at' for three years, and concerning which I have dreams; a children's book, in which the imagination has free rein; and another book which is to last as long as myself; as myself, since it is an honest record of my soul's advance or retreat in the struggle of life.* Besides these, I keep a book of poems which I use as a safety valve, and concerning which I have no dreams whatsoever. Between the lot I am always occupied. In the afternoons I generally try to take a walk for my health's sake, through Regent's Park, into Kensington Gardens, or farther afield to Hampstead Heath.

Oct. 10.—Everything went wrong to-day. I have two eggs for breakfast. This morning one of them was bad. I rang the bell for Emily. When she came in I was reading the paper, and, without look-ing up, I said, 'Egg's bad.' 'Oh, is it, sir?' she said; 'I'll get another one,' and went out, taking the egg with her. I waited my breakfast for her return, which was in five minutes. She put the new egg on the table and went away. But, when I looked down, I saw that she had taken away the good egg and left the bad one—all green and yel-low—in the slop basin. I rang again.

'You've taken the wrong egg,' I said.

'Oh!' she exclaimed; 'I thought the one I took down didn't smell so *very* bad.' In due time she returned with the good egg, and returned my breakfast with two eggs, but less appetite. It was all very trivial, to be sure, but so stupid that I felt annoyed. The character of that egg influenced everything I did. I wrote a bad article, and tore it up. I got a bad headache. I used bad words—to myself. Everything was bad, so I 'chucked' work and went for a long walk.

I dined at a cheap chop-house on my way back, and reached home about nine o'clock.

Rain was just beginning to fall as I came in, and the wind was ris-ing. It promised an ugly night. The alley looked dismal and dreary, and the hall of the house, as I passed through it, felt chilly as a tomb. It was the first stormy night I had experienced in my new quarters. The draughts were awful. They came criss-cross, met in the middle of the room, and formed eddies and whirlpools and cold silent currents that almost lifted the hair of my head. I stuffed up the sashes of the windows with neckties and odd socks, and sat over the smoky fire to keep warm. First I tried to write, but found it too cold. My hand turned to ice on the paper.

What tricks the wind did play with the old place! It came rushing up the forsaken alley with a sound like the feet of a hurrying crowd of people who stopped suddenly at the door. I felt as if a lot of curious folk had arranged themselves just outside and were staring up at my windows. Then they took to their heels again and fled whispering and laughing down the lane, only, however, to return with the next gust of wind and repeat their impertinence. On the other side of my room a single square window opens into a sort of shaft, or well, that measures about six feet across to the back wall of another house. Down this funnel the wind dropped, and puffed and shouted. Such noises I never heard before. Between these two entertainments I sat over the fire in a great-coat, listening to the deep booming in the chimney. It was like being in a ship at sea, and I almost looked for the floor to rise in undulations and rock to and fro.

Oct. 12.—I wish I were not quite so lonely—and so poor. And yet I love both my loneliness and my poverty. The former makes me appreciate the companionship of the wind and rain, while the latter preserves my liver and prevents me wasting time in dancing attendance upon women. Poor, ill-dressed men are not acceptable 'attendants.'

My parents are dead, and my only sister is—no, not dead exactly, but married to a very rich man. They travel most of the time, he to find his health, she to lose herself. Through sheer neglect on her part she has long passed out of my life. The door closed when, after an absolute silence of five years, she sent me a cheque for £50 at Christmas. It was signed by her husband! I returned it to her in a thousand pieces and in an unstamped envelope. So at least I had the satisfaction of knowing that it cost her something! She wrote back with a broad quill pen that covered a whole page with three lines, 'You are evidently as cracked as ever, and rude and ungrateful into the bargain.' It had always been my special terror lest the insanity in my father's family should leap across the generations and appear in me. This thought haunted me, and she knew it. So after this little exchange of civilities the door slammed, never to open again. I heard the crash it made, and, with it, the falling from the walls of my heart of many little bits of china with their own peculiar value—rare china, some of it, that only needed dusting.

The same walls, too, carried mirrors in which I used sometimes to see reflected the misty lawns of childhood, the daisy chains, the wind-torn blossoms scattered through the orchard by warm rains, the robbers' cave in the long walk, and the hidden store of apples in the hay-loft. She was my inseparable companion then—but, when the door slammed, the mirrors cracked across their entire length, and the visions they held vanished for ever. Now I am quite alone. At forty one cannot begin all over again to build up careful friendships, and all others are comparatively worthless.

Oct. 14.—My bedroom is 10 by 10. It is below the level of the front room, and a step leads down into it. Both rooms are very quiet on calm nights, for there is no traffic down this forsaken alley-way. In spite of the occasional larks of the wind, it is a most sheltered strip. At its upper end, below my windows, all the cats of the neighbourhood congregate as soon as darkness gathers. They lie undisturbed on the long ledge of a blind window of the opposite building, for after the postman has come and gone at 9.30, no footsteps ever dare to interrupt their sinister conclave, no step but my own, or sometimes the unsteady footfall of the son who 'is somethink on a homnibus.'

Oct. 15.—I dined at an 'A.B.C.' shop* on poached eggs and coffee, and then went for a stroll round the outer edge of Regent's Park It was ten o'clock when I got home. I counted no less than thirteen cats, all of a dark colour, crouching under the lee side of the alley walls. It was a cold night, and the stars shone like points of ice in a blue-black sky. The cats turned their heads and stared at me in silence as I passed. An odd sensation of shyness took possession of me under the glare of so many pairs of unblinking eyes. As I fumbled with the latch-key they jumped noiselessly down and pressed against my legs, as if anxious to be let in. But I slammed the door in their faces and ran quickly upstairs. The front room, as I entered to grope for the matches, felt as cold as a stone vault, and the air held an unusual dampness.

Oct. 17.—For several days I have been working on a ponderous article that allows no play for the fancy. My imagination requires a judicious rein; I am afraid to let it loose, for it carries me sometimes into appalling places beyond the stars and beneath the world. No one realises the danger more than I do. But what a foolish thing to write here—for there is no one to know, no one to realise! My mind of late has held unusual thoughts. thoughts I have never had before, about medicines and drugs and the treatment of strange illnesses. I cannot imagine their source. At no time in my life have I dwelt upon such ideas as now constantly throng my brain. I have had no exercise lately, for the weather has been shocking; and all my afternoons have been spent in the reading-room of the British Museum, where I have a reader's ticket.

I have made an unpleasant discovery: there are rats in the house. At night from my bed I have heard them scampering across the hills and valleys of the front room, and my sleep has been a good deal disturbed in consequence.

Oct. 19.—The landlady, I find, has a little boy with her, probably her son's child. In fine weather he plays in the alley, and draws a wooden cart over the cobbles. One of the wheels is off, and it makes a most distracting noise. After putting up with it as long as possible, I found it was getting on my nerves, and I could not write. So I rang the bell. Emily answered it.

'Emily, will you ask the little fellow to make less noise? It's impossible to work.'

The girl went downstairs, and soon afterwards the child was called in by the kitchen door. I felt rather a brute for spoiling his play. In a few minutes, however, the noise began again, and I felt that he was the brute. He dragged the broken toy with a string over the stones till the rattling noise jarred every nerve in my body. It became unbearable, and I rang the bell a second time.

'That noise *must* be put a stop to!' I said to the girl, with decision.

'Yes, sir,' she grinned, 'I know; but one of the wheels is hoff. The men in the stable offered to mend it for 'im, but he wouldn't let them. He says he likes it that way.'

'I can't help what he likes. The noise must stop. I can't write.'

'Yes, sir; I'll tell Mrs Monson.'

The noise stopped for the day then.

Oct. 23.—Every day for the past week that cart has rattled over the stones, till I have come to think of it as a huge carrier's van with four wheels and two horses; and every morning I have been obliged to ring the bell and have it stopped. The last time Mrs Monson herself came up, and said she was sorry I had been annoyed; the sounds should not occur again. With rare discursiveness she went on to ask if I was comfortable, and how I liked the rooms. I replied cautiously. I mentioned the rats. She said they were mice. I spoke of the draughts. She said, 'Yes, it were a draughty 'ouse.' I referred to the cats, and she said they had been

as long as she could remember. By way of conclusion, she informed me
that the house was over two hundred years old, and that the last gentleman who had occupied my rooms was a painter who ''ad real Jimmy
Bueys and Raffles 'anging all hover the walls.' It took me some moments
to discern that Cimabue and Raphael* were in the woman's mind.

Oct. 24.—Last night the son who is 'somethink on a homnibus'
came in. He had evidently been drinking, for I heard loud and angry
voices below in the kitchen long after I had gone to bed. Once, too,
I caught the singular words rising up to me through the floor, 'Burning
from top to bottom is the only thing that'll ever make this 'ouse right.'
I knocked on the floor, and the voices ceased suddenly, though later
I again heard their clamour in my dreams.

These rooms are very quiet, almost too quiet sometimes. On windless nights they are silent as the grave, and the house might be miles
in the country. The roar of London's traffic reaches me only in heavy,
distant vibrations. It holds an ominous note sometimes, like that of an
approaching army, or an immense tidal-wave very far away thundering in the night.

Oct. 27.—Mrs Monson, though admirably silent, is a foolish, fussy
woman. She does such stupid things. In dusting the room she puts all
my things in the wrong places. The ash-trays, which should be on the
writing-table, she sets in a silly row on the mantelpiece. The pen-tray,
which should be beside the inkstand, she hides away cleverly among
the books on my reading-desk. My gloves she arranges daily in idiotic
array upon a half-filled book-shelf, and I always have to rearrange
them on the low table by the door. She places my armchair at impossible
angles between the fire and the light, and the tablecloth—the one with
Trinity Hall* stains—she puts on the table in such a fashion that when
I look at it I feel as if my tie and all my clothes were on crooked and
awry. She exasperates me. Her very silence and meekness are irritating. Sometimes I feel inclined to throw the inkstand at her, just to
bring an expression into her watery eyes and a squeak from those
colourless lips. Dear me! What violent expressions I am making use
of! How very foolish of me! And yet it almost seems as if the words
were not my own, but had been spoken into my ear—I mean, I never
make use of such terms naturally.

Oct. 30.—I have been here a month. The place does not agree with
me, I think. My headaches are more frequent and violent, and my
nerves are a perpetual source of discomfort and annoyance.

I have conceived a great dislike for Mrs Monson, a feeling I am certain she reciprocates. Somehow, the impression comes frequently to me that there are goings on in this house of which I know nothing, and which she is careful to hide from me.

Last night her son slept in the house, and this morning as I was standing at the window I saw him go out. He glanced up and caught my eye. It was a loutish figure and a singularly repulsive face that I saw, and he gave me the benefit of a very unpleasant leer. At least, so I imagined.

Evidently I am getting absurdly sensitive to trifles, and I suppose it is my disordered nerves making themselves felt. In the British Museum this afternoon I noticed several people at the readers' table staring at me and watching every movement I made. Whenever I looked up from my books I found their eyes upon me. It seemed to me unnecessary and unpleasant, and I left earlier than was my custom. When I reached the door I threw back a last look into the room, and saw every head at the table turned in my direction. It annoyed me very much, and yet I know it is foolish to take note of such things. When I am well they pass me by. I must get more regular exercise. Of late I have had next to none.

Nov. 2.—The utter stillness of this house is beginning to oppress me. I wish there were other fellows living upstairs. No footsteps ever sound overhead, and no tread ever passes my door to go up the next flight of stairs. I am beginning to feel some curiosity to go up myself and see what the upper rooms are like. I feel lonely here and isolated, swept into a deserted corner of the world and forgotten. . . . Once I actually caught myself gazing into the long, cracked mirrors, trying to see the sunlight dancing beneath the trees in the orchard. But only deep shadows seemed to congregate there now, and I soon desisted.

It has been very dark all day, and no wind stirring. The fogs have begun. I had to use a reading-lamp all this morning. There was no cart to be heard to-day. I actually missed it. This morning, in the gloom and silence, I think I could almost have welcomed it. After all, the sound is a very human one, and this empty house at the end of the alley holds other noises that are not quite so satisfactory.

I have never once seen a policeman in the lane, and the postmen always hurry out with no evidence of a desire to loiter.

10 p.m.—As I write this I hear no sound but the deep murmur of the distant traffic and the low sighing of the wind. The two sounds

melt into one another. Now and again a cat raises its shrill, uncanny cry upon the darkness. The cats are always there under my windows when the darkness falls. The wind is dropping into the funnel with a noise like the sudden sweeping of immense distant wings. It is a dreary night. I feel lost and forgotten.

Nov. 3.—From my windows I can see arrivals. When any one comes to the door I can just see the hat and shoulders and the hand on the bell. Only two fellows have been to see me since I came here two months ago. Both of them I saw from the window before they came up, and heard their voices asking if I was in. Neither of them ever came back.

I have finished the ponderous article. On reading it through, how-ever, I was dissatisfied with it, and drew my pencil through almost every page. There were strange expressions and ideas in it that I could not explain, and viewed with amazement, not to say alarm. They did not sound like my *very own*, and I could not remember having written them. Can it be that my memory is beginning to be affected?

My pens are never to be found. That stupid old woman puts them in a different place each day. I must give her due credit for finding so many new hiding places; such ingenuity is wonderful. I have told her repeatedly, but she always says, 'I'll speak to Emily, sir.' Emily always says, 'I'll tell Mrs Monson, sir.' Their foolishness makes me irritable and scatters all my thoughts. I should like to stick the lost pens into them and turn them out, blind-eyed, to be scratched and mauled by those thousand hungry cats. Whew! What a ghastly thought! Where in the world did it come from? Such an idea is no more my own than it is the policeman's. Yet I felt I *had* to write it. It was like a voice singing in my head, and my pen wouldn't stop till the last word was finished. What ridiculous nonsense! I must and will restrain myself. I must take more regular exercise; my nerves and liver plague me horribly.

Nov. 4.—I attended a curious lecture in the French quarter on 'Death,' but the room was so hot and I was so weary that I fell asleep. The only part I heard, however, touched my imagination vividly. Speaking of suicides, the lecturer said that self-murder was no escape from the miseries of the present, but only a preparation of greater sorrow for the future. Suicides, he declared, cannot shirk their responsibilities so easily. They must return to take up life exactly where they laid it so violently down, but with the added pain and punishment of their weakness. Many of them wander the earth in unspeakable misery till they can *reclothe* themselves in the body of some one else—generally a lunatic, or weak-minded person, who cannot resist the hideous obsession. This is their only means of escape. Surely a weird and horrible idea! I wish I had slept all the time and not heard it at all. My mind is morbid enough without such ghastly fancies. Such mischievous propaganda should be stopped by the police. I'll write to the *Times* and suggest it. Good idea.

I walked home through Greek Street, Soho, and imagined that a hundred years had slipped back into place and De Quincey was still there, haunting the night with invocations to his 'just, subtle, and mighty' drug. His vast dreams seemed to hover not very far away. Once started in my brain, the pictures refused to go away; and I saw him sleeping in that cold, tenantless mansion with the strange little waif who was afraid of its ghosts, both together in the shadows under a single horseman's cloak; or wandering in the companionship of the spectral Anne; or, later still, on his way to the eternal rendezvous at the foot of Great Titchfield Street, the rendezvous she never was able to keep.* What an unutterable gloom, what an untold horror of sorrow and suffering comes over me as I try to realise something of what that man—boy he then was—must have taken into his lonely heart.

As I came up the alley I saw a light in the top window, and a head and shoulders thrown in an exaggerated shadow upon the blind. I wondered what the son could be doing up there at such an hour.

Nov. 5.—This morning, while writing, some one came up the creaking stairs and knocked cautiously at my door. Thinking it was the landlady, I said, 'Come in!' The knock was repeated, and I cried louder, 'Come in, come in!' But no one turned the handle, and I continued my writing with a vexed 'Well, stay out, then!' under my breath. Went on writing? I tried to, but my thoughts had suddenly dried up at their source. I could not set down a single word. It was a dark, yellow-fog morning, and there was little enough inspiration in the air as it was, but that stupid woman standing just outside my door waiting to be told again to come in roused a spirit of vexation that filled my head to the exclusion of all else. At last I jumped up and opened the door myself.

'What do you want, and why in the world don't you come in?' I cried out. But the words dropped into empty air. There was no one there. The fog poured up the dingy staircase in deep yellow coils, but there was no sign of a human being anywhere.

I slammed the door, with imprecations upon the house and its noises, and went back to my work. A few minutes later Emily came in with a letter.

'Were you or Mrs Monson outside a few minutes ago knocking at my door?'

'No, sir.'

'Are you sure?'

'Mrs Monson's gone to market, and there's no one but me and the child in the 'ole 'ouse, and I've been washing the dishes for the last hour, sir.'

I fancied the girl's face turned a shade paler. She fidgeted towards the door with a glance over her shoulder.

'Wait, Emily,' I said, and then told her what I had heard. She stared stupidly at me, though her eyes shifted now and then over the articles in the room.

'Who was it?' I asked when I had come to the end.

'Mrs Monson says it's honly mice,' she said, as if repeating a learned lesson.

'Mice!' I exclaimed; 'it's nothing of the sort. Some one was feeling about outside my door. Who was it? Is the son in the house?'

Her whole manner changed suddenly, and she became earnest instead of evasive. She seemed anxious to tell the truth.

'Oh no, sir; there's no one in the house at all but you and me and the child, and there couldn't 'ave been nobody at your door. As for them knocks——' She stopped abruptly, as though she had said too much.

'Well, what about the knocks?' I said more gently.

'Of course,' she stammered, 'the knocks isn't mice, nor the foot-steps neither, but then——' Again she came to a full halt.

'Anything wrong with the house?'

'Lor', no, sir; the drains is splendid!'

'I don't mean drains, girl. I mean, did anything—anything bad ever happen here?'

She flushed up to the roots of her hair, and then turned suddenly pale again. She was obviously in considerable distress, and there was something she was anxious, yet afraid to tell—some forbidden thing she was not allowed to mention.

'I don't mind what it was, only I should like to know,' I said encouragingly.

Raising her frightened eyes to my face, she began to blurt out something about 'that which 'appened once to a gentleman that lived hupstairs,' when a shrill voice calling her name sounded below.

'Emily, Emily!' It was the returning landlady, and the girl tumbled downstairs as if pulled backward by a rope, leaving me full of conjectures as to what in the world could have happened to a gentleman *upstairs* that could in so curious a manner affect my ears *downstairs*.

Nov. 10.—I have done capital work; have finished the ponderous article and had it accepted for the *Review*, and another one ordered. I feel well and cheerful, and have had regular exercise and good sleep; no headaches, no nerves, no liver! Those pills the chemist recommended are wonderful. I can watch the child playing with his cart and feel no annoyance; sometimes I almost feel inclined to join him. Even the grey-faced landlady rouses pity in me; I am sorry for her: so worn, so weary, so oddly put together, just like the building. She looks as if she had once suffered some shock of terror, and was momentarily dreading another. When I spoke to her to-day very gently about not putting the pens in the ash-tray and the gloves on the book-shelf she raised her faint eyes to mine for the first time, and said with the ghost of a smile, 'I'll try and remember, sir,' I felt inclined to pat her on the back and say, 'Come, cheer up and be jolly. Life's not so bad after all.' Oh! I am much better. There's nothing like open air and success and good sleep. They build up as if by magic the portions of the heart eaten down by despair and unsatisfied yearnings. Even to the cats I feel friendly. When I came in at eleven o'clock to-night they followed me to the door in a stream, and I stooped down to stroke the one nearest to me. Bah! The brute hissed and spat, and struck at me with her paws. The claw caught my hand and drew blood in a thin line. The others danced sideways into the darkness, screeching, as though I had done them an injury. I believe these cats really hate me. Perhaps they are only waiting to be reinforced. Then they will attack me. Ha, ha! In spite of the momentary annoyance, this fancy sent me laughing upstairs to my room.

The fire was out, and the room seemed unusually cold. As I groped my way over to the mantelpiece to find the matches I realised all at once that there was another person standing beside me in the darkness. I could, of course, see nothing, but my fingers, feeling along the ledge, came into forcible contact with something that was at once with-drawn. It was cold and moist. I could have sworn it was somebody's hand. My flesh began to creep instantly.

'Who's that?' I exclaimed in a loud voice.

My voice dropped into the silence like a pebble into a deep well. There was no answer, but at the same moment I heard some one moving away from me across the room in the direction of the door. It was a confused sort of footstep, and the sound of garments brushing the furniture on the way. The same second my hand stumbled upon the match-box, and I struck a light. I expected to see Mrs Monson, or Emily, or perhaps the son who is something on an omnibus. But the flare of the gas jet illumined an empty room; there was not a sign of a person anywhere. I felt the hair stir upon my head, and instinctively I backed up against the wall, lest something should approach me from behind. I was distinctly alarmed. But the next minute I recovered myself. The door was open on to the landing, and I crossed the room, not without some inward trepidation, and went out. The light from the room fell upon the stairs, but there was no one to be seen any-where, nor was there any sound on the creaking wooden staircase to indicate a departing creature.

I was in the act of turning to go in again when a sound overhead caught my ear. It was a very faint sound, not unlike the sigh of wind; yet it could not have been the wind, for the night was still as the grave. Though it was not repeated, I resolved to go upstairs and see for myself what it all meant. Two senses had been affected—touch and hearing—and I could not believe that I had been deceived. So, with a lighted candle, I went stealthily forth on my unpleasant journey into the upper regions of this queer little old house.

On the first landing there was only one door, and it was locked. On the second there was also only one door, but when I turned the handle it opened. There came forth to meet me the chill musty air that is characteristic of a long unoccupied room. With it there came an indescribable odour. I use the adjective advisedly. Though very faint, diluted as it were, it was nevertheless an odour that made my gorge rise. I had never smelt anything like it before, and I cannot describe it.

The room was small and square, close under the roof, with a slop-ing ceiling and two tiny windows. It was cold as the grave, without a shred of carpet or a stick of furniture. The icy atmosphere and the nameless odour combined to make the room abominable to me, and, after lingering a moment to see that it contained no cupboards or corners into which a person might have crept for concealment, I made haste to shut the door, and went downstairs again to bed. Evidently I had been deceived after all as to the noise.

In the night I had a foolish but very vivid dream. I dreamed that the landlady and another person, dark and not properly visible, entered my room on all fours, followed by a horde of immense cats. They attacked me as I lay in bed, and murdered me, and then dragged my body upstairs and deposited it on the floor of that cold little square room under the roof.

Nov. 11.—Since my talk with Emily—the unfinished talk—I have hardly once set eyes on her. Mrs Monson now attends wholly to my wants. As usual, she does everything exactly as I don't like it done. It is all too utterly trivial to mention, but it is exceedingly irritating. Like small doses of morphine often repeated, she has finally a cumulative effect.

Nov. 12.—This morning I woke early, and came into the front room to get a book, meaning to read in bed till it was time to get up. Emily was laying the fire.

'Good morning!' I said cheerfully. 'Mind you make a good fire. It's very cold.'

The girl turned and showed me a startled face. It was not Emily at all!

'Where's Emily?' I exclaimed.

'You mean the girl as was 'ere before me?'

'Has Emily left?'

'I came on the 6th,' she replied sullenly, 'and she'd gone then.' I got my book and went back to bed. Emily must have been sent away almost immediately after our conversation. This reflection kept coming between me and the printed page. I was glad when it was time to get up. Such prompt energy, such merciless decision, seemed to argue something of importance—to somebody.

Nov. 13.—The wound inflicted by the cat's claw has swollen, and causes me annoyance and some pain. It throbs and itches. I'm afraid my blood must be in poor condition, or it would have healed by now. I opened it with a penknife soaked in an antiseptic solution, and cleansed it thoroughly. I have heard unpleasant stories of the results of wounds inflicted by cats.

Nov. 14.—In spite of the curious effect this house certainly exercises upon my nerves, I like it. It is lonely and deserted in the very heart of London, but it is also for that reason quiet to work in. I wonder why it is so cheap. Some people might be suspicious, but I did not even ask the reason. No answer is better than a lie. If only I could remove the cats from the outside and the rats from the inside. I feel that I shall grow accustomed more and more to its peculiarities, and shall die here. Ah, that expression reads queerly and gives a wrong impression: I meant *live and die* here. I shall renew the lease from year to year till one of us crumbles to pieces. From present indications the building will be the first to go.

Nov. 16.—It is abominable the way my nerves go up and down with me—and rather discouraging. This morning I woke to find my clothes scattered about the room, and a cane chair overturned beside the bed. My coat and waistcoat looked just as if they had been *tried on* by some one in the night. I had horribly vivid dreams, too, in which some one covering his face with his hands kept coming close up to me, crying out as if in pain, 'Where can I find covering? Oh, who will clothe me?' How silly, and yet it frightened me a little. It was so dreadfully real. It is now over a year since I last walked in my sleep and woke up with such a shock on the cold pavement of Earl's Court Road,* where I then lived. I thought I was cured, but evidently not. This discovery has rather a disquieting effect upon me. To-night I shall resort to the old trick of tying my toe to the bed-post.

Nov. 17.—Last night I was again troubled by most oppressive dreams. Some one seemed to be moving in the night up and down my room, sometimes passing into the front room, and then returning to stand beside the bed and stare intently down upon me. I was being watched by this person all night long. I never actually awoke, though I was often very near it. I suppose it was a nightmare from indigestion, for this morning I have one of my old vile headaches. Yet all my clothes lay about the floor when I awoke, where they had evidently been flung (had I so tossed them?) during the dark hours, and my trousers trailed over the step into the front room.

Worse than this, though—I fancied I noticed about the room in the morning that strange, fetid odour. Though very faint, its mere suggestion is foul and nauseating. What in the world can it be, I wonder? . . . In future I shall lock my door.

Nov. 26.—I have accomplished a lot of good work during this past week, and have also managed to get regular exercise. I have felt well and in an equable state of mind. Only two things have occurred to disturb my equanimity. The first is trivial in itself, and no doubt to be easily explained. The upper window where I saw the light on the night of November 4, with the shadow of a large head and shoulders upon the blind, is one of the windows in the square room under the roof. In reality it has *no blind at all!*

Here is the other thing. I was coming home last night in a fresh fall of snow about eleven o'clock, my umbrella low down over my head. Half way up the alley, where the snow was wholly untrodden, I saw a man's legs in front of me. The umbrella hid the rest of his figure, but on raising it I saw that he was tall and broad and was walking, as I was, towards the door of my house. He could not have been four feet ahead of me. I had thought the alley was empty when I entered it, but might of course have been mistaken very easily.

A sudden gust of wind compelled me to lower the umbrella, and when I raised it again, not half a minute later, there was no longer any man to be seen. With a few more steps I reached the door. It was closed as usual. I then noticed with a sudden sensation of dismay that the surface of the freshly fallen snow was *unbroken*. My own footmarks were the only ones to be seen anywhere, and though I retraced my way to the point where I had first seen the man, I could find no slightest impression of any other boots. Feeling creepy and uncomfortable, I went upstairs, and was glad to get into bed.

Nov. 28.—With the fastening of my bedroom door the disturbances ceased. I am convinced that I walked in my sleep. Probably I untied my toe and then tied it up again. The fancied security of the locked door would alone have been enough to restore sleep to my troubled spirit and enable me to rest quietly.

Last night, however, the annoyance was suddenly renewed in another and more aggressive form. I woke in the darkness with the impression that some one was standing outside my bedroom door *listening*. As I became more awake the impression grew into positive knowledge. Though there was no appreciable sound of moving or breathing, I was so convinced of the propinquity of a listener that I crept out of bed and approached the door. As I did so there came faintly from the next room the unmistakable sound of some one retreating stealthily across the floor. Yet, as I heard it, it was neither the tread of a man nor a regular footstep, but rather, it seemed to me, a confused sort of crawling, almost as of some one on his hands and knees.

I unlocked the door in less than a second, and passed quickly into the front room, and I could feel, as by the subtlest imaginable vibrations upon my nerves, that the spot I was standing in had just that instant been vacated! The Listener had moved; he was now behind the other door, standing in the passage. Yet this door was also closed. I moved swiftly, and as silently as possible, across the floor, and turned the handle. A cold rush of air met me from the passage and sent shiver after shiver down my back. There was no one in the doorway; there was no one on the little landing; there was no one moving down the staircase. Yet I had been so quick that this midnight Listener could not be very far away, and I felt that if I persevered I should eventually come face to face with him. And the courage that came so opportunely to overcome my nervousness and horror seemed born of the unwelcome conviction that it was somehow necessary for my safety as well as my sanity that I should find this intruder and force his secret from him. For was it not the intent action of his mind upon my own, in concentrated listening, that had awakened me with such a vivid realisation of his presence?

Advancing across the narrow landing, I peered down into the well of the little house. There was nothing to be seen; no one was moving in the darkness. How cold the oilcloth was to my bare feet.

I cannot say what it was that suddenly drew my eyes upwards. I only know that, without apparent reason, I looked up and saw a person about half-way up the next turn of the stairs, leaning forward over the balustrade and staring straight into my face. It was a man. He appeared to be clinging to the rail rather than standing on the stairs. The gloom made it impossible to see much beyond the general outline, but the head and shoulders were seemingly enormous, and stood sharply silhouetted against the skylight in the roof immediately above. The idea flashed into my brain in a moment that I was looking into the visage of something monstrous. The huge skull, the mane-like hair, the wide-humped shoulders, suggested, in a way I did not pause to analyse, that which was scarcely human; and for some seconds, fascinated by horror, I returned the gaze and stared into the dark, inscrutable countenance above me, without knowing exactly where I was or what I was doing,

Then I realised in quite a new way that I was face to face with the secret midnight Listener, and I steeled myself as best I could for what was about to come.

The source of the rash courage that came to me at this awful moment will ever be to me an inexplicable mystery. Though shivering with fear, and my forehead wet with an unholy dew, I resolved to advance. Twenty questions leaped to my lips: What are you? What do you want? Why do you listen and watch? Why do you come into my room? But none of them found articulate utterance.

I began forthwith to climb the stairs, and with the first signs of my advance *he* drew himself back into the shadows and began to move too. He retreated as swiftly as I advanced. I heard the sound of his crawling motion a few steps ahead of me, ever maintaining the same distance. When I reached the landing he was half-way up the next flight, and when I was half-way up the next flight he had already arrived at the top landing. I then heard him open the door of the little square room under the roof and go in. Immediately, though the door did not close after him, the sound of his moving entirely ceased.

At this moment I longed for a light, or a stick, or any weapon whatsoever; but I had none of these things, and it was impossible to go back. So I marched steadily up the rest of the stairs, and in less than a minute found myself standing in the gloom face to face with the door through which this creature had just entered.

For a moment I hesitated. The door was about half way open, and the Listener was standing evidently in his favourite attitude just behind it—listening. To search through that dark room for him seemed hopeless; to enter the same small space where he was seemed horrible. The very idea filled me with loathing, and I almost decided to turn back.

It is strange at such times how trivial things impinge on the consciousness with a shock as of something important and immense. Something—it may have been a beetle or a mouse—scuttled over the bare boards behind me. The door moved quarter of an inch, closing. My decision came back with a sudden rush, as it were, and thrusting out a foot, I kicked the door so that it swung sharply back to its full extent, and permitted me to walk forward slowly into the aperture of profound blackness beyond. What a queer soft sound my bare feet made on the boards! How the blood sang and buzzed in my head!

I was inside. The darkness closed over me, hiding even the windows. I began to grope my way round the walls in a thorough search; but in order to prevent all possibility of the other's escape, I first of all *closed the door*.

There we were, we two, shut in together between four walls, within a few feet of one another. But with what, with whom, was I thus momentarily imprisoned? A new light flashed suddenly over the affair with a swift, illuminating brilliance—and I knew I was a fool, an utter fool! I was wide awake at last, and the horror was evaporating. My cursed nerves again; a dream, a nightmare, and the old result— walking in my sleep. The figure was a dream-figure. Many a time before had the actors in my dreams stood before me for some moments after I was awake. . . . There was a chance match in my pyjamas' pocket, and I struck it on the wall. The room was utterly empty. It held not even a shadow. I went quickly down to bed, cursing my wretched nerves and my foolish, vivid dreams. But as soon as ever I was asleep again, the same uncouth figure of a man crept back to my bedside, and bending over me with his immense head close to my ear, whispered repeatedly in my dreams, 'I want your body; I want its covering. I'm waiting for it, and listening always.' Words scarcely less foolish than the dream.

But I wonder what that queer odour was up in the square room. I noticed it again, and stronger than ever before, and it seemed to be also in my bedroom when I woke this morning.

Nov. 29.—Slowly, as moonbeams rise over a misty sea in June, the thought is entering my mind that my nerves and somnambulistic dreams do not adequately account for the influence this house exercises upon me. It holds me as with a fine, invisible net. I cannot escape if I would. It draws me, and it means to keep me.

Nov. 30.—The post this morning brought me a letter from Aden, forwarded from my old rooms in Earl's Court. It was from Chapter, my former Trinity chum, who is on his way home from the East, and asks for my address. I sent it to him at the hotel he mentioned, 'to await arrival.'

As I have already said, my windows command a view of the alley, and I can see an arrival without difficulty. This morning, while I was busy writing, the sound of footsteps coming up the alley filled me with a sense of vague alarm that I could in no way account for. I went over to the window, and saw a man standing below waiting for the door to be opened. His shoulders were broad, his top-hat glossy, and his overcoat fitted beautifully round the collar. All this I could see, but no more. Presently the door was opened, and the shock to my nerves was unmistakable when I heard a man's voice ask, 'Is Mr——still here?' mentioning my name. I could not catch the answer, but it could only have been in the affirmative, for the man entered the hall and the door shut to behind him. But I waited in vain for the sound of his steps on the stairs. There was no sound of any kind. It seemed to me so strange that I opened my door and looked out. No one was anywhere to be seen. I walked across the narrow landing, and looked through the window that commands the whole length of the alley. There was no sign of a human being, coming or going. The lane was deserted. Then I deliberately walked downstairs into the kitchen, and asked the grey-faced landlady if a gentleman had just that minute called for me.

The answer, given with an odd, weary sort of smile, was '*No!*'

Dec. 1.—I feel genuinely alarmed and uneasy over the state of my nerves. Dreams are dreams, but never before have I had dreams in broad daylight.

I am looking forward very much to Chapter's arrival. He is a capital fellow, vigorous, healthy, with no nerves, and even less imagination; and he has £2000 a year into the bargain. Periodically he makes me offers—the last was to travel round the world with him as secretary, which was a delicate way of paying my expenses and giving me some pocket-money—offers, however, which I invariably decline. I prefer to keep his friendship. Women could not come between us; money might—therefore I give it no opportunity. Chapter always laughed at what he called my 'fancies,' being himself possessed only of that thin-blooded quality of imagination which is ever associated with the prosaic-minded man. Yet, if taunted with this obvious lack, his wrath is deeply stirred. His psychology is that of the crass materialist—always a rather funny article. It will afford me genuine relief, none the less, to hear the cold judgment his mind will have to pass upon the story of this house as I shall have it to tell.

Dec. 2.—The strangest part of it all I have not referred to in this brief diary. Truth to tell, I have been afraid to set it down in black and white. I have kept it in the background of my thoughts, preventing it as far as possible from taking shape. In spite of my efforts, however, it has continued to grow stronger.

Now that I come to face the issue squarely, it is harder to express than I imagined. Like a half-remembered melody that trips in the head but vanishes the moment you try to sing it, these thoughts form a group in the background of my mind, *behind* my mind, as it were, and refuse to come forward. They are crouching ready to spring, but the actual leap never takes place.

In these rooms, except when my mind is strongly concentrated on my own work, I find myself suddenly dealing in thoughts and ideas that are not my own! New, strange conceptions, wholly foreign to my temperament, are for ever cropping up in my head. What precisely they are is of no particular importance. The point is that they are entirely apart from the channel in which my thoughts have hitherto been accustomed to flow. Especially they come when my mind is at rest, unoccupied; when I'm dreaming over the fire, or sitting with a book which fails to hold my attention. Then these thoughts which are not mine spring into life and make me feel exceedingly uncomfortable. Sometimes they are so strong that I almost feel as if some one were in the room beside me, thinking aloud.

Evidently my nerves and liver are shockingly out of order. I must work harder and take more vigorous exercise. The horrid thoughts never come when my mind is much occupied. But they are always there—waiting and as it were *alive*.

What I have attempted to describe above came first upon me gradually after I had been some days in the house, and then grew steadily in strength. The other strange thing has come to me only twice in all these weeks. *It appals me.* It is the consciousness of the propinquity of some deadly and loathsome disease. It comes over me like a wave of fever heat, and then passes off, leaving me cold and trembling. The air seems for a few seconds to become tainted. So penetrating and convincing is the thought of this sickness, that on both occasions my brain has turned momentarily dizzy, and through my mind, like flames of white heat, have flashed the ominous names of all the dangerous illnesses I know. I can no more explain these visitations than I can fly, yet I know there is no dreaming about the clammy skin and palpitating heart which they always leave as witnesses of their brief visit.

Most strongly of all was I aware of this nearness of a mortal sickness when, on the night of the 28th, I went upstairs in pursuit of the listening figure. When we were shut in together in that little square room under the roof, I felt that I was face to face with the actual essence of this invisible and malignant disease. Such a feeling never entered my heart before, and I pray to God it never may again.

There! Now I have confessed. I have given some expression at least to the feelings that so far I have been afraid to see in my own writing.

For—since I can no longer deceive myself—the experiences of that night (28th) were no more a dream than my daily breakfast is a dream; and the trivial entry in this diary by which I sought to explain away an occurrence that caused me unutterable horror was due solely to my desire not to acknowledge in words what I really felt and believed to be true. The increase that would have accrued to my horror by so doing might have been more than I could stand.

Dec. 3.—I wish Chapter would come. My facts are all ready marshalled, and I can see his cool, grey eyes fixed incredulously on my face as I relate them: the knocking at my door, the well-dressed caller, the light in the upper window and the shadow upon the blind, the man who preceded me in the snow, the scattering of my clothes at night, Emily's arrested confession, the landlady's suspicious reticence, the midnight listener on the stairs, and those awful subsequent words in my sleep; and above all, and hardest to tell, the presence of the abominable sickness, and the stream of thoughts and ideas that are not my own.

I can see Chapter's face, and I can almost hear his deliberate words, 'You've been at the tea again, and underfeeding, I expect, as usual. Better see my nerve doctor, and then come with me to the south of France.' For this fellow, who knows nothing of disordered liver or high-strung nerves, goes regularly to a great nerve specialist with the periodical belief that his nervous system is beginning to decay.

Dec. 5.—Ever since the incident of the Listener, I have kept a night-light burning in my bedroom, and my sleep has been undisturbed. Last night, however, I was subjected to a far worse annoyance. I woke suddenly, and saw a man in front of the dressing-table regarding himself in the mirror. The door was locked, as usual. I knew at once it was the Listener, and the blood turned to ice in my veins. Such a wave of horror and dread swept over me that it seemed to turn me rigid in the bed, and I could neither move nor speak. I noted, however, that the odour I so abhorred was strong in the room.

The man seemed to be tall and broad. He was stooping forward over the mirror. His back was turned to me, but in the glass I saw the reflection of a huge head and face illumined fitfully by the flicker of the night-light. The spectral grey of very early morning stealing in round the edges of the curtains lent an additional horror to the picture, for it fell upon hair that was tawny and mane-like, hanging loosely about a face whose swollen, rugose features bore the once seen never forgotten leonine expression of——I dare not write down that awful word. But, by way of corroborative proof, I saw in the faint mingling of the two lights that there were several bronze-coloured blotches on the cheeks which the man was evidently examining with great care in the glass. The lips were pale and very thick and large. One hand I could not see, but the other rested on the ivory back of my hair-brush. Its muscles were strangely contracted, the fingers thin to emaciation, the back of the hand closely puckered up. It was like a big grey spider crouching to spring, or the claw of a great bird.

The full realisation that I was alone in the room with this nameless creature, almost within arm's reach of him, overcame me to such a degree that, when he suddenly turned and regarded me with small beady eyes, wholly out of proportion to the grandeur of their massive setting, I sat bolt upright in bed, uttered a loud cry, and then fell back in a dead swoon of terror upon the bed.

Dec. 6.—. . . When I came to this morning, the first thing I noticed was that my clothes were strewn all over the floor . . . I find it difficult to put my thoughts together, and have sudden accesses of violent trembling. I determined that I would go at once to Chapter's hotel and find out when he is expected. I cannot refer to what happened in the night; it is too awful, and I have to keep my thoughts rigorously away from it. I feel light-headed and queer, couldn't eat any breakfast, and have twice vomited with blood. While dressing to go out, a hansom rattled up noisily over the cobbles, and a minute later the door opened, and to my great joy in walked the very subject of my thoughts.

The sight of his strong face and quiet eyes had an immediate effect upon me, and I grew calmer again. His very handshake was a sort of tonic. But, as I listened eagerly to the deep tones of his reassuring voice, and the visions of the night time paled a little, I began to realise how very hard it was going to be to tell him my wild, intangible tale. Some men radiate an animal vigour that destroys the delicate woof of a vision and effectually prevents its reconstruction. Chapter was one of these men.

We talked of incidents that had filled the interval since we last met, and he told me something of his travels. He talked and I listened. But, so full was I of the horrid thing I had to tell, that I made a poor listener. I was for ever watching my opportunity to leap in and explode it all under his nose.

Before very long, however, it was borne in upon me that he too was merely talking for time. He too held something of importance in the background of his mind, something too weighty to let fall till the right moment presented itself. So that during the whole of the first half-hour we were both waiting for the psychological moment in which properly to release our respective bombs; and the intensity of our minds' action set up opposing forces that merely sufficed to hold one another in check—and nothing more. As soon as I realised this, therefore, I resolved to yield. I renounced for the time my purpose of telling my story, and had the satisfaction of seeing that his mind, released from the restraint of my own, at once began to make preparations for the discharge of its momentous burden. The talk grew less and less magnetic; the interest waned; the descriptions of his travels became less alive. There were pauses between his sentences. Presently he repeated himself. His words clothed no living thoughts. The pauses grew longer. Then the interest dwindled altogether and went out like a candle in the wind. His voice ceased, and he looked up squarely into my face with serious and anxious eyes.

The psychological moment had come at last!

'I say——' he began, and then stopped short.

I made an unconscious gesture of encouragement, but said no word. I dreaded the impending disclosure exceedingly. A dark shadow seemed to precede it.

'I say,' he blurted out at last, 'what in the world made you ever come to this place—to these rooms, I mean?'

'They're cheap, for one thing,' I began, 'and central and——'

'They're too cheap,' he interrupted. 'Didn't you ask what made 'em so cheap?'

'It never occurred to me at the time.'

There was a pause in which he avoided my eyes.

'For God's sake, go on, man, and tell it!' I cried, for the suspense was getting more than I could stand in my nervous condition.

'This was where Blount lived so long,' he said quietly, 'and where he—died. You know, in the old days I often used to come here and see him, and do what I could to alleviate his——' He stuck fast again.

'Well!' I said with a great effort. '*Please* go on—faster.'

'But,' Chapter went on, turning his face to the window with a perceptible shiver, 'he finally got so terrible I simply couldn't stand it, though I always thought I could stand anything. It got on my nerves and made me dream, and haunted me day and night.'

I stared at him, and said nothing. I had never heard of Blount in my life, and didn't know what he was talking about. But, all the same, I was trembling, and my mouth had become strangely dry.

'This is the first time I've been back here since,' he said almost in a whisper, 'and, 'pon my word, it gives me the creeps. I swear it isn't fit for a man to live in. I never saw you look so bad, old man.'

'I've got it for a year,' I jerked out, with a forced laugh; 'signed the lease and all. I thought it was rather a bargain.'

Chapter shuddered, and buttoned his overcoat up to his neck Then he spoke in a low voice, looking occasionally behind him as though he thought some one was listening. I too could have sworn some one else was in the room with us.

'He did it himself, you know, and no one blamed him a bit; his sufferings were awful. For the last two years he used to wear a veil when he went out, and even then it was always in a closed carriage. Even the attendant who had nursed him for so long was at length obliged to leave. The extremities of both the lower limbs were gone, dropped off, and he moved about the ground on all fours with a sort of crawling motion. The odour, too, was——'

I was obliged to interrupt him here. I could hear no more details of that sort. My skin was moist, I felt hot and cold by turns, for at last I was beginning to understand.

'Poor devil,' Chapter went on; '*I* used to keep my eyes closed as much as possible. He always begged to be allowed to take his veil off, and asked if I minded very much. I used to stand by the open window. He never touched me, though. He rented the whole house. Nothing would induce him to leave it.'

'Did he occupy—these very rooms?'

'No. He had the little room on the top floor, the square one just under the roof. He preferred it because it was dark. These rooms were too near the ground, and he was afraid people might see him through the windows. A crowd had been known to follow him up to the very door, and then stand below the windows in the hope of catching a glimpse of his face.'

'But there were hospitals.'

'He wouldn't go near one, and they didn't like to force him. You know, they say it's *not* contagious, so there was nothing to prevent his staying here if he wanted to. He spent all his time reading medical books, about drugs and so on. His head and face were something appalling, just like a lion's.'

I held up my hand to arrest further description.

'He was a burden to the world, and he knew it. One night I suppose he realised it too keenly to wish to live. He had the free use of drugs—and in the morning he was found dead on the floor. Two years ago, that was, and they said then he had still several years to live.'

'Then, in Heaven's name!' I cried, unable to bear the suspense any longer, 'tell me what it was he had, and be quick about it.'

'I thought you knew!' he exclaimed, with genuine surprise. 'I thought you knew!'

He leaned forward and our eyes met. In a scarcely audible whisper I caught the words his lips seemed almost afraid to utter:

'He was a leper!'*

THE WILLOWS

AFTER leaving Vienna, and long before you come to Buda-Pesth, the Danube enters a region of singular loneliness and desolation, where its waters spread away on all sides regardless of a main channel, and the country becomes a swamp for miles upon miles, covered by a vast sea of low willow-bushes. On the big maps this deserted area is painted in a fluffy blue, growing fainter in colour as it leaves the banks, and across it may be seen in large straggling letters the word *Sümpfe*, meaning marshes.

In high flood this great acreage of sand, shingle-beds, and willow-grown islands is almost topped by the water, but in normal seasons the bushes bend and rustle in the free winds, showing their silver leaves to the sunshine in an ever-moving plain of bewildering beauty. These willows never attain to the dignity of trees; they have no rigid trunks; they remain humble bushes, with rounded tops and soft out-line, swaying on slender stems that answer to the least pressure of the wind; supple as grasses, and so continually shifting that they some-how give the impression that the entire plain is moving and *alive*. For the wind sends waves rising and falling over the whole surface, waves of leaves instead of waves of water, green swells like the sea, too, until the branches turn and lift, and then silvery white as their under-side turns to the sun.

Happy to slip beyond the control of stern banks, the Danube here wanders about at will among the intricate network of channels inter-secting the islands everywhere with broad avenues down which the waters pour with a shouting sound; making whirlpools, eddies, and foaming rapids; tearing at the sandy banks; carrying away masses of shore and willow-clumps; and forming new islands innumerable which shift daily in size and shape and possess at best an imperman-ent life, since the flood-time obliterates their very existence.

Properly speaking, this fascinating part of the river's life begins soon after leaving Pressburg, and we, in our Canadian canoe, with gipsy tent* and frying-pan on board, reached it on the crest of a ris-ing flood about mid-July. That very same morning, when the sky was reddening before sunrise, we had slipped swiftly through still-sleeping Vienna, leaving it a couple of hours later a mere patch of smoke against the blue hills of the Wienerwald on the horizon; we had break-fasted below Fischeramend under a grove of birch trees roaring in the wind; and had then swept on the tearing current past Orth, Hainburg, Petronell (the old Roman Carnuntum of Marcus Aurelius), and so under the frowning heights of Theben on a spur of the Carpathians, where the March steals in quietly from the left and the frontier is crossed between Austria and Hungary.*

Racing along at twelve kilometres an hour soon took us well into Hungary, and the muddy waters—sure sign of flood—sent us aground on many a shingle-bed, and twisted us like a cork in many a sudden belching whirlpool before the towers of Pressburg (Hungarian, Poszony) showed against the sky; and then the canoe, leaping like a spirited horse, flew at top speed under the grey walls, negotiated safely the sunken chain of the Fliegende Brücke ferry, turned the corner sharply to the left, and plunged on yellow foam into the wilderness of islands, sand-banks, and swamp-land beyond—the land of the willows.

The change came suddenly, as when a series of bioscope pictures* snaps down on the streets of a town and shifts without warning into the scenery of lake and forest. We entered the land of desolation on wings, and in less than half an hour there was neither boat nor fishing-hut nor red roof, nor any single sign of human habitation and civilisation within sight. The sense of remoteness from the world of human kind, the utter isolation, the fascination of this singular world of willows, winds, and waters, instantly laid its spell upon us both, so that we allowed laughingly to one another that we ought by rights to have held some special kind of passport to admit us, and that we had, somewhat audaciously, come without asking leave into a separate little kingdom of wonder and magic—a kingdom that was reserved for the use of others who had a right to it, with everywhere unwritten warnings to trespassers for those who had the imagination to discover them.

Though still early in the afternoon, the ceaseless buffetings of a most tempestuous wind made us feel weary, and we at once began casting about for a suitable camping-ground for the night. But the bewildering character of the islands made landing difficult; the swirling flood carried us in-shore and then swept us out again; the willow branches tore our hands as we seized them to stop the canoe, and we pulled many a yard of sandy bank into the water before at length we shot with a great sideways blow from the wind into a backwater and managed to beach the bows in a cloud of spray. Then we lay panting and laughing after our exertions on hot yellow sand, sheltered from the wind, and in the full blaze of a scorching sun, a cloudless blue sky above, and an immense army of dancing, shouting willow bushes, closing in from all sides, shining with spray and clapping their thousand little hands as though to applaud the success of our efforts.

'What a river!' I said to my companion, thinking of all the way we had travelled from the source in the Black Forest, and how we had often been obliged to wade and push in the upper shallows at the beginning of June.

'Won't stand much nonsense now, will it?' he said, pulling the canoe a little farther into safety up the sand, and then composing himself for a nap.

I lay by his side, happy and peaceful in the bath of the elements—water, wind, sand, and the great fire of the sun—thinking of the long journey that lay behind us, and of the great stretch before us to the Black Sea, and how lucky I was to have such a delightful and charming travelling companion as my friend, the Swede.

We had made many similar journeys together, but the Danube, more than any other river I knew, impressed us from the very beginning with its *aliveness*. From its tiny bubbling entry into the world among the pinewood gardens of Donaueschingen* until this moment when it began to play the great river-game of losing itself among the deserted swamps, unobserved, unrestrained, it had seemed to us like following the growth of some living creature. Sleepy at first, but later developing violent desires as it became conscious of its deep soul, it rolled, like some huge fluid being, through all the countries we had passed, holding our little craft on its mighty shoulders, playing roughly with us sometimes, yet always friendly and well-meaning, till at length we had come inevitably to regard it as a Great Personage.

How, indeed, could it be otherwise, since it told us so much of its secret life? At night we heard it singing to the moon as we lay in our tent, uttering that odd sibilant note peculiar to itself and said to be caused by the rapid tearing of the pebbles along its bed, so great is its hurrying speed. We knew, too, the voice of its gurgling whirlpools, suddenly bubbling up on a surface previously quite calm; the roar of its shallows and swift rapids; its constant steady thundering below all mere surface sounds; and that ceaseless tearing of its icy waters at the banks. How it stood up and shouted when the rains fell flat upon its face! And how its laughter roared out when the wind blew upstream and tried to stop its growing speed! We knew all its sounds and voices, its tumblings and foamings, its unnecessary splashing against the bridges; that self-conscious chatter when there were hills to look on; the affected dignity of its speech when it passed through the little towns, far too important to laugh; and all these faint, sweet whisperings when the sun caught it fairly in some slow curve and poured down upon it till the steam rose.

It was full of tricks, too, in its early life before the great world knew it. There were places in the upper reaches among the Swabian forests, when yet the first whispers of its destiny had not reached it, where it elected to disappear through holes in the ground, to appear again on the other side of the porous limestone hills and start a new river with another name; leaving, too, so little water in its own bed that we had to climb out and wade and push the canoe through miles of shallows!

And a chief pleasure, in those early days of its irresponsible youth, was to lie low, like Brer Fox,* just before the little turbulent tributaries came to join it from the Alps, and to refuse to acknowledge them when in, but to run for miles side by side, the dividing line well marked, the very levels different, the Danube utterly declining to recognise the newcomer. Below Passau, however, it gave up this particular trick, for there the Inn comes in with a thundering power impossible to ignore, and so pushes and incommodes the parent river that there is hardly room for them in the long twisting gorge that follows, and the Danube is shoved this way and that against the cliffs, and forced to hurry itself with great waves and much dashing to and fro in order to get through in time. And during the fight our canoe slipped down from its shoulder to its breast, and had the time of its life among the struggling waves. But the Inn taught the old river a lesson, and after Passau it no longer pretended to ignore new arrivals.

This was many days back, of course, and since then we had come to know other aspects of the great creature, and across the Bavarian wheat plain of Straubing she wandered so slowly under the blazing June sun that we could well imagine only the surface inches were water, while below there moved, concealed as by a silken mantle, a whole army of Undines,* passing silently and unseen down to the sea, and very leisurely too, lest they be discovered.

Much, too, we forgave her because of her friendliness to the birds and animals that haunted the shores. Cormorants lined the banks in lonely places in rows like short black palings; grey crows crowded the shingle beds; storks stood fishing in the vistas of shallower water that opened up between the islands, and hawks, swans, and marsh birds of all sorts filled the air with glinting wings and singing, petulant cries. It was impossible to feel annoyed with the river's vagaries after seeing a deer leap with a splash into the water at sunrise and swim past the bows of the canoe; and often we saw fawns peering at us from the underbrush, or looked straight into the brown eyes of a stag as we charged full tilt round a corner and entered another reach of the river. Foxes, too, everywhere haunted the banks, tripping daintily among the driftwood and disappearing so suddenly that it was impossible to see how they managed it.

But now, after leaving Pressburg, everything changed a little, and the Danube became more serious. It ceased trifling. It was half-way to the Black Sea, within scenting distance almost of other, stranger countries where no tricks would be permitted or understood. It became suddenly grown up, and claimed our respect and even our awe. It broke out into three arms, for one thing, that only met again a hundred kilometres farther down, and for a canoe there were no indications which one was intended to be followed.

'If you take a side channel,' said the Hungarian officer we met in the Pressburg shop while buying provisions, 'you may find yourselves, when the flood subsides, forty miles from anywhere, high and dry, and you may easily starve. There are no people, no farms, no fishermen. I warn you not to continue. The river, too, is still rising, and this wind will increase.'

The rising river did not alarm us in the least, but the matter of being left high and dry by a sudden subsidence of the waters might be serious, and we had consequently laid in an extra stock of provisions. For the rest, the officer's prophecy held true, and the wind, blowing down a perfectly clear sky, increased steadily till it reached the dignity of a westerly gale.

It was earlier than usual when we camped, for the sun was a good hour or two from the horizon, and leaving my friend still asleep on the hot sand, I wandered about in desultory examination of our hotel. The island, I found, was less than an acre in extent, a mere sandy bank standing some two or three feet above the level of the river. The far end, pointing into the sunset, was covered with flying spray which the tremendous wind drove off the crests of the broken waves. It was triangular in shape, with the apex up stream.

I stood there for several minutes, watching the impetuous crimson flood bearing down with a shouting roar, dashing in waves against the bank as though to sweep it bodily away, and then swirling by in two foaming streams on either side. The ground seemed to shake with the shock and rush, while the furious movement of the willow bushes as the wind poured over them increased the curious illusion that the island itself actually moved. Above, for a mile or two, I could see the great river descending upon me: it was like looking up the slope of a sliding hill, white with foam, and leaping up everywhere to show itself to the sun.

The rest of the island was too thickly grown with willows to make walking pleasant, but I made the tour, nevertheless. From the lower end the light, of course, changed, and the river looked dark and angry. Only the backs of the flying waves were visible, streaked with foam, and pushed forcibly by the great puffs of wind that fell upon them from behind. For a short mile it was visible, pouring in and out among the islands, and then disappearing with a huge sweep into the willows, which closed about it like a herd of monstrous antediluvian creatures crowding down to drink. They made me think of gigantic sponge-like growths that sucked the river up into themselves. They caused it to vanish from sight. They herded there together in such overpowering numbers.

Altogether it was an impressive scene, with its utter loneliness, its bizarre suggestion; and as I gazed, long and curiously, a singular emotion began to stir somewhere in the depths of me. Midway in my delight of the wild beauty, there crept, unbidden and unexplained, a curious feeling of disquietude, almost of alarm.

A rising river, perhaps, always suggests something of the ominous: many of the little islands I saw before me would probably have been swept away by the morning; this resistless, thundering flood of water touched the sense of awe. Yet I was aware that my uneasiness lay deeper far than the emotions of awe and wonder. It was not that I felt. Nor had it directly to do with the power of the driving wind—this shouting hurricane that might almost carry up a few acres of willows into the air and scatter them like so much chaff over the landscape. The wind was simply enjoying itself, for nothing rose out of the flat landscape to stop it, and I was conscious of sharing its great game with a kind of pleasurable excitement. Yet this novel emotion had nothing to do with the wind. Indeed, so vague was the sense of distress

I experienced, that it was impossible to trace it to its source and deal with it accordingly, though I was aware somehow that it had to do with my realisation of our utter insignificance before this unrestrained power of the elements about me. The huge-grown river had something to do with it too—a vague, unpleasant idea that we had somehow trifled with these great elemental forces in whose power we lay helpless every hour of the day and night. For here, indeed, they were gigantically at play together, and the sight appealed to the imagination.

But my emotion, so far as I could understand it, seemed to attach itself more particularly to the willow bushes, to these acres and acres of willows, crowding, so thickly growing there, swarming everywhere the eye could reach, pressing upon the river as though to suffocate it, standing in dense array mile after mile beneath the sky, watching, waiting, listening. And, apart quite from the elements, the willows connected themselves subtly with my malaise, attacking the mind insidiously somehow by reason of their vast numbers, and contriving in some way or other to represent to the imagination a new and mighty power, a power, moreover, not altogether friendly to us.

Great revelations of nature, of course, never fail to impress in one way or another, and I was no stranger to moods of the kind. Mountains overawe and oceans terrify, while the mystery of great forests exercises a spell peculiarly its own. But all these, at one point or another, somewhere link on intimately with human life and human experience. They stir comprehensible, even if alarming, emotions. They tend on the whole to exalt.

With this multitude of willows, however, it was something far different, I felt. Some essence emanated from them that besieged the heart. A sense of awe awakened, true, but of awe touched somewhere by a vague terror. Their serried ranks, growing everywhere darker about me as the shadows deepened, moving furiously yet softly in the wind, woke in me the curious and unwelcome suggestion that we had trespassed here upon the borders of an alien world, a world where we were intruders, a world where we were not wanted or invited to remain—where we ran grave risks perhaps!

The feeling, however, though it refused to yield its meaning entirely to analysis, did not at the time trouble me by passing into menace. Yet it never left me quite, even during the very practical business of putting up the tent in a hurricane of wind and building a fire for the stew-pot. It remained, just enough to bother and perplex, and to rob a most delightful camping-ground of a good portion of its charm. To my companion, however, I said nothing, for he was a man I considered devoid of imagination. In the first place, I could never have explained to him what I meant, and in the second, he would have laughed stupidly at me if I had.

There was a slight depression in the centre of the island, and here we pitched the tent. The surrounding willows broke the wind a bit.

'A poor camp,' observed the imperturbable Swede when at last the tent stood upright; 'no stones and precious little firewood. I'm for moving on early to-morrow—eh? This sand won't hold anything.'

But the experience of a collapsing tent at midnight had taught us many devices, and we made the cosy gipsy house as safe as possible, and then set about collecting a store of wood to last till bedtime. Willow bushes drop no branches, and driftwood was our only source of supply. We hunted the shores pretty thoroughly. Everywhere the banks were crumbling as the rising flood tore at them and carried away great portions with a splash and a gurgle.

'The island's much smaller than when we landed,' said the accurate Swede. 'It won't last long at this rate. We'd better drag the canoe close to the tent, and be ready to start a moment's notice. *I* shall sleep in my clothes.'

He was a little distance off, climbing along the bank, and I heard his rather jolly laugh as he spoke.

'By Jove!' I heard him call, a moment later, and turned to see what had caused his exclamation. But for the moment he was hidden by the willows, and I could not find him.

'What in the world's this?' I heard him cry again, and this time his voice had become serious.

I ran up quickly and joined him on the bank. He was looking over the river, pointing at something in the water.

'Good Heavens, it's a man's body!' he cried excitedly. 'Look!'

A black thing, turning over and over in the foaming waves, swept rapidly past. It kept disappearing and coming up to the surface again. It was about twenty feet from the shore, and just as it was opposite to where we stood it lurched round and looked straight at us. We saw its eyes reflecting the sunset, and gleaming an odd yellow as the body turned over. Then it gave a swift, gulping plunge, and dived out of sight in a flash.

'An otter, by gad!' we exclaimed in the same breath, laughing.

It *was* an otter, alive, and out on the hunt; yet it had looked exactly like the body of a drowned man turning helplessly in the current. Far below it came to the surface once again, and we saw its black skin, wet and shining in the sunlight.

Then, too, just as we turned back, our arms full of driftwood, another thing happened to recall us to the river bank. This time it really was a man, and what was more, a man in a boat. Now a small boat on the Danube was an unusual sight at any time, but here in this deserted region, and at flood time, it was so unexpected as to constitute a real event. We stood and stared.

Whether it was due to the slanting sunlight, or the refraction from the wonderfully illumined water, I cannot say, but, whatever the cause, I found it difficult to focus my sight properly upon the flying apparition. It seemed, however, to be a man standing upright in a sort of flat-bottomed boat, steering with a long oar, and being carried down the opposite shore at a tremendous pace. He apparently was looking across in our direction, but the distance was too great and the light too uncertain for us to make out very plainly what he was about. It seemed to me that he was gesticulating and making signs at us. His voice came across the water to us shouting something furiously, but the wind drowned it so that no single word was audible. There was something curious about the whole appearance—man, boat, signs, voice—that made an impression on me out of all proportion to its cause.

'He's crossing himself!' I cried. 'Look, he's making the sign of the Cross!'

'I believe you're right,' the Swede said, shading his eyes with his hand and watching the man out of sight. He seemed to be gone in a moment, melting away down there into the sea of willows where the sun caught them in the bend of the river and turned them into a great crimson wall of beauty. Mist, too, had begun to rise, so that the air was hazy.

'But what in the world is he doing at night-fall on this flooded river?' I said, half to myself. 'Where is he going at such a time, and what did he mean by his signs and shouting? D'you think he wished to warn us about something?'

'He saw our smoke, and thought we were spirits probably,' laughed my companion. 'These Hungarians believe in all sorts of rubbish: you remember the shopwoman at Pressburg warning us that no one ever landed here because it belonged to some sort of beings outside man's world! I suppose they believe in fairies and elementals, possibly demons too. That peasant in the boat saw people on the islands for the first time in his life,' he added, after a slight pause, 'and it scared him, that's all.'

The Swede's tone of voice was not convincing, and his manner lacked something that was usually there. I noted the change instantly while he talked, though without being able to label it precisely.

'If they had enough imagination,' I laughed loudly—I remember trying to make as much *noise* as I could—'they might well people a place like this with the old gods of antiquity. The Romans must have haunted all this region more or less with their shrines and sacred groves and elemental deities.'

The subject dropped and we returned to our stew pot, for my friend was not given to imaginative conversation as a rule. Moreover, just then I remember feeling distinctly glad that he was not imaginative; his stolid, practical nature suddenly seemed to me welcome and comforting. It was an admirable temperament, I felt: he could steer down rapids like a red Indian, shoot dangerous bridges and whirlpools better than any white man I ever saw in a canoe. He was a grand fellow for an adventurous trip, a tower of strength when untoward things happened. I looked at his strong face and light curly hair as he staggered along under his pile of driftwood (twice the size of mine!), and I experienced a feeling of relief. Yes, I was distinctly glad just then that the Swede was—what he was, and that he never made remarks that suggested more than they said.

'The river's still rising, though,' he added, as if following out some thoughts of his own, and dropping his load with a gasp. 'This island will be under water in two days if it goes on.'

'I wish the *wind* would go down,' I said. 'I don't care a fig for the river.'

The flood, indeed, had no terrors for us; we could get off at ten minutes notice, and the more water the better we liked it. It meant an increasing current and the obliteration of the treacherous shingle-beds that so often threatened to tear the bottom out of our canoe.

Contrary to our expectations, the wind did not go down with the sun. It seemed to increase with the darkness, howling overhead and shaking the willows round us like straws. Curious sounds accompanied it sometimes, like the explosion of heavy guns, and it fell upon the water and the island in great flat blows of immense power. It made me think of the sounds a planet must make, could we only hear it, driving along through space.

But the sky kept wholly clear of clouds, and soon after supper the full moon rose up in the east and covered the river and the plain of shouting willows with a light like the day.

We lay on the sandy patch beside the fire, smoking, listening to the noises of the night round us, and talking happily of the journey we had already made, and of our plans ahead. The map lay spread in the door of the tent, but the high wind made it hard to study, and presently we lowered the curtain and extinguished the lantern. The firelight was enough to smoke and see each other's faces by, and the sparks flew about overhead like fireworks. A few yards beyond, the river gurgled and hissed, and from time to time a heavy splash announced the falling away of further portions of the bank.

Our talk, I noticed, had to do with the far-away scenes and incidents of our first camps in the Black Forest, or of other subjects altogether remote from the present setting, for neither of us spoke of the actual moment more than was necessary—almost as though we had agreed tacitly to avoid discussion of the camp and its incidents. Neither the otter nor the boatman, for instance, received the honour of a single mention, though ordinarily these would have furnished discussion for the greater part of the evening. They were, of course, distinct events in such a place.

The scarcity of wood made it a business to keep the fire going, for the wind, that drove the smoke in our faces wherever we sat, helped at the same time to make a forced draught. We took it in turn to make foraging expeditions into the darkness, and the quantity the Swede brought back always made me feel that he took an absurdly long time finding it; for the fact was I did not care much about being left alone, and yet it always seemed to be my turn to grub about among the bushes or scramble along the slippery banks in the moonlight. The long day's battle with wind and water—such wind and such water!—had tired us both, and an early bed was the obvious programme. Yet neither of us made the move for the tent. We lay there, tending the fire, talking in desultory fashion, peering about us into the dense willow bushes, and listening to the thunder of wind and river. The loneliness of the place had entered our very bones, and silence seemed natural, for after a bit the sound of our voices became a trifle unreal and forced; whispering would have been the fitting mode of communication, I felt, and the human voice, always rather absurd amid the roar of the elements, now carried with it something almost illegitimate. It was like talking out loud in church, or in some place where it was not lawful, perhaps not quite *safe*, to be overheard.

The eeriness of this lonely island, set among a million willows, swept by a hurricane, and surrounded by hurrying deep waters, touched us both, I fancy. Untrodden by man, almost unknown to man, it lay there beneath the moon, remote from human influence, on the frontier of another world, an alien world, a world tenanted by willows only and the souls of willows. And we, in our rashness, had dared to invade it, even to make use of it! Something more than the power of its mystery stirred in me as I lay on the sand, feet to fire, and peered up through the leaves at the stars. For the last time I rose to get firewood.

'When this has burnt up,' I said firmly, 'I shall turn in,' and my companion watched me lazily as I moved off into the surrounding shadows.

For an unimaginative man I thought he seemed unusually receptive that night, unusually open to suggestion of things other than sensory. He too was touched by the beauty and loneliness of the place. I was not altogether pleased, I remember, to recognise this slight change in him, and instead of immediately collecting sticks, I made my way to the far point of the island where the moonlight on plain and river could be seen to better advantage. The desire to be alone had come suddenly upon me; my former dread returned in force; there was a vague feeling in me I wished to face and probe to the bottom.

When I reached the point of sand jutting out among the waves, the spell of the place descended upon me with a positive shock. No mere 'scenery' could have produced such an effect. There was something more here, something to alarm.

I gazed across the waste of wild waters; I watched the whispering willows; I heard the ceaseless beating of the tireless wind; and, one and all, each in its own way, stirred in me this sensation of a strange distress. But the *willows* especially: for ever they went on chattering and talking among themselves, laughing a little, shrilly crying out, sometimes sighing—but what it was they made so much to-do about belonged to the secret life of the great plain they inhabited. And it was utterly alien to the world I knew, or to that of the wild yet kindly elements.

They made me think of a host of beings from another plane of life, another evolution altogether, perhaps, all discussing a mystery known only to themselves. I watched them moving busily together, oddly shaking their big bushy heads, twirling their myriad leaves even when there was no wind. They moved of their own will as though alive, and they touched, by some incalculable method, my own keen sense of the *horrible*.

There they stood in the moonlight, like a vast army surrounding our camp, shaking their innumerable silver spears defiantly, formed all ready for an attack.

The psychology of places,* for some imaginations at least, is very vivid; for the wanderer, especially, camps have their 'note' either of welcome or rejection. At first it may not always be apparent, because the busy preparations of tent and cooking prevent, but with the first pause—after supper usually—it comes and announces itself. And the note of this willow-camp now became unmistakably plain to me: we were interlopers, trespassers; we were not welcomed. The sense of unfamiliarity grew upon me as I stood there watching. We touched the frontier of a region where our presence was resented. For a night's lodging we might perhaps be tolerated; but for a prolonged and inquisitive stay—No! by all the gods of the trees and the wilderness, no! We were the first human influences upon this island, and we were not wanted. *The willows were against us.*

Strange thoughts like these, bizarre fancies, borne I know not whence, found lodgment in my mind as I stood listening. What, I thought, if, after all, these crouching willows proved to be alive; if suddenly they should rise up, like a swarm of living creatures, marshalled by the gods whose territory we had invaded, sweep towards us off the vast swamps, booming overhead in the night—and then *settle down!* As I looked it was so easy to imagine they actually moved, crept nearer, retreated a little, huddled together in masses, hostile, waiting for the great wind that should finally start them a-running. I could have sworn their aspect changed a little, and their ranks deepened and pressed more closely together.

The melancholy shrill cry of a night-bird sounded overhead, and suddenly I nearly lost my balance as the piece of bank I stood upon fell with a great splash into the river, undermined by the flood. I stepped back just in time, and went on hunting for firewood again, half laughing at the odd fancies that crowded so thickly into my mind and cast their spell upon me. I recalled the Swede's remark about moving on next day, and I was just thinking that I fully agreed with him, when I turned with a start and saw the subject of my thoughts standing immediately in front of me. He was quite close. The roar of the elements had covered his approach.

'You've been gone so long,' he shouted above the wind, 'I thought something must have happened to you.'

But there was that in his tone, and a certain look in his face as well, that conveyed to me more than his actual words, and in a flash I understood the real reason for his coming. It was because the spell of the place had entered his soul too, and he did not like being alone.

'River still rising,' he cried, pointing to the flood in the moonlight, 'and the wind's simply awful.'

He always said the same things, but it was the cry for companionship that gave the real importance to his words.

'Lucky,' I cried back, 'our tent's in the hollow. I think it'll hold all right.' I added something about the difficulty of finding wood, in order to explain my absence, but the wind caught my words and flung them across the river, so that he did not hear, but just looked at me through the branches, nodding his head.

'Lucky if we get away without disaster!' he shouted, or words to that effect; and I remember feeling half angry with him for putting the thought into words, for it was exactly what I felt myself. There was disaster impending somewhere, and the sense of presentiment lay unpleasantly upon me.

We went back to the fire and made a final blaze, poking it up with our feet. We took a last look round. But for the wind the heat would have been unpleasant. I put this thought into words, and I remember my friend's reply struck me oddly: that he would rather have the heat, the ordinary July weather, than this 'diabolical wind.'

Everything was snug for the night; the canoe lying turned over beside the tent, with both yellow paddles beneath her; the provision sack hanging from a willow-stem, and the washed-up dishes removed to a safe distance from the fire, all ready for the morning meal.

We smothered the embers of the fire with sand, and then turned in. The flap of the tent door was up, and I saw the branches and the stars and the white moonlight. The shaking willows and the heavy buffetings of the wind against our taut little house were the last things I remembered as sleep came down and covered all with its soft and delicious forgetfulness.

II

SUDDENLY I found myself lying awake, peering from my sandy mattress through the door of the tent. I looked at my watch pinned against the canvas, and saw by the bright moonlight that it was past twelve o'clock—the threshold of a new day— and I had therefore slept a couple of hours. The Swede was asleep still beside me; the wind howled as before; something plucked at my heart and made me feel afraid. There was a sense of disturbance in my immediate neighbourhood.

I sat up quickly and looked out. The trees were swaying violently to and fro as the gusts smote them, but our little bit of green canvas lay snugly safe in the hollow, for the wind passed over it without meeting enough resistance to make it vicious. The feeling of disquietude did not pass, however, and I crawled quietly out of the tent to see if our belongings were safe. I moved carefully so as not to waken my companion. A curious excitement was on me.

I was half-way out, kneeling on all fours, when my eye first took in that the tops of the bushes opposite, with their moving tracery of leaves, made shapes against the sky. I sat back on my haunches and stared. It was incredible, surely, but there, opposite and slightly above me, were shapes of some indeterminate sort among the willows, and as the branches swayed in the wind they seemed to group themselves about these shapes, forming a series of monstrous outlines that shifted rapidly beneath the moon. Close, about fifty feet in front of me, I saw these things.

My first instinct was to waken my companion, that he too might see them, but something made me hesitate—the sudden realisation, probably, that I should not welcome corroboration; and meanwhile I crouched there staring in amazement with smarting eyes. I was wide awake. I remember saying to myself that I was *not* dreaming.

They first became properly visible, these huge figures, just within the tops of the bushes—immense, bronze-coloured, moving, and wholly independent of the swaying of the branches. I saw them plainly and noted, now I came to examine them more calmly, that they were very much larger than human, and indeed that something in their appearance proclaimed them to be *not human* at all. Certainly they were not merely the moving tracery of the branches against the moonlight. They shifted independently. They rose upwards in a continuous stream from earth to sky, vanishing utterly as soon as they reached the dark of the sky. They were interlaced one with another, making a great column, and I saw their limbs and huge bodies melting in and out of each other, forming this serpentine line that bent and swayed and twisted spirally with the contortions of the wind-tossed trees. They were nude, fluid shapes, passing up the bushes, *within* the leaves almost—rising up in a living column into the heavens. Their faces I never could see. Unceasingly they poured upwards, swaying in great bending curves, with a hue of dull bronze upon their skins.

I stared, trying to force every atom of vision from my eyes. For a long time I thought they *must* every moment disappear and resolve themselves into the movements of the branches and prove to be an optical illusion. I searched everywhere for a proof of reality, when all the while I understood quite well that the standard of reality had changed. For the longer I looked the more certain I became that these figures were real and living, though perhaps not according to the standards that the camera and the biologist would insist upon.

Far from feeling fear, I was possessed with a sense of awe and wonder such as I have never known. I seemed to be gazing at the personified elemental forces of this haunted and primeval region. Our intrusion had stirred the powers of the place into activity. It was we who were the cause of the disturbance, and my brain filled to bursting with stories and legends of the spirits and deities of places that have been acknowledged and worshipped by men in all ages of the world's history. But, before I could arrive at any possible explanation, something impelled me to go farther out, and I crept forward on to the sand and stood upright. I felt the ground still warm under my bare feet; the wind tore at my hair and face; and the sound of the river burst upon my ears with a sudden roar. These things, I knew, were real, and proved that my senses were acting normally. Yet the figures still rose from earth to heaven, silent, majestically, in a great spiral of grace and strength that overwhelmed me at length with a genuine deep emotion of worship. I felt that I must fall down and worship—absolutely worship.

Perhaps in another minute I might have done so, when a gust of wind swept against me with such force that it blew me sideways, and I nearly stumbled and fell. It seemed to shake the dream violently out of me. At least it gave me another point of view somehow. The figures still remained, still ascended into heaven from the heart of the night, but my reason at last began to assert itself. It must be a subjective experience, I argued—none the less real for that, but still subjective. The moonlight and the branches combined to work out these pictures upon the mirror of my imagination, and for some reason I projected them outwards and made them appear objective. I knew this must be the case, of course. I was the subject of a vivid and interesting hallucination. I took courage, and began to move forward across the open patches of sand. By Jove, though, was it all hallucination? Was it merely subjective? Did not my reason argue in the old futile way from the little standard of the known?

I only know that great column of figures ascended darkly into the sky for what seemed a very long period of time, and with a very complete measure of reality as most men are accustomed to gauge reality. Then suddenly they were gone!

And, once they were gone and the immediate wonder of their great presence had passed, fear came down upon me with a cold rush. The esoteric meaning of this lonely and haunted region suddenly flamed up within me, and I began to tremble dreadfully. I took a quick look round— a look of horror that came near to panic—calculating vainly ways of escape; and then, realising how helpless I was to achieve anything really effective, I crept back silently into the tent and lay down again upon my sandy mattress, first lowering the door-curtain to shut out the sight of the willows in the moonlight, and then burying my head as deeply as possibly beneath the blankets to deaden the sound of the terrifying wind.

III

As though further to convince me that I had not been dreaming, I remember that it was a long time before I fell again into a troubled and restless sleep; and even then only the upper crust of me slept, and underneath there was something that never quite lost consciousness, but lay alert and on the watch.

But this second time I jumped up with a genuine start of terror. It was neither the wind nor the river that woke me, but the slow approach of something that caused the sleeping portion of me to grow smaller and smaller till at last it vanished altogether, and I found myself sitting bolt upright—listening.

Outside there was a sound of multitudinous little patterings. They had been coming, I was aware, for a long time, and in my sleep they had first become audible. I sat there nervously wide awake as though I had not slept at all. It seemed to me that my breathing came with difficulty, and that there was a great weight upon the surface of my body. In spite of the hot night, I felt clammy with cold and shivered. Something surely was pressing steadily against the sides of the tent and weighing down upon it from above. Was it the body of the wind? Was this the pattering rain, the dripping of the leaves? The spray blown from the river by the wind and gathering in big drops? I thought quickly of a dozen things.

Then suddenly the explanation leaped into my mind: a bough from the poplar, the only large tree on the island, had fallen with the wind. Still half caught by the other branches, it would fall with the next gust and crush us, and meanwhile its leaves brushed and tapped upon the tight canvas surface of the tent. I raised the loose flap and rushed out, calling to the Swede to follow.

But when I got out and stood upright I saw that the tent was free. There was no hanging bough; there was no rain or spray; nothing approached.

A cold, grey light filtered down through the bushes and lay on the faintly gleaming sand. Stars still crowded the sky directly overhead, and the wind howled magnificently, but the fire no longer gave out any glow, and I saw the east reddening in streaks through the trees. Several hours must have passed since I stood there before watching the ascending figures, and the memory of it now came back to me horribly, like an evil dream. Oh, how tired it made me feel, that ceaseless raging wind! Yet, though the deep lassitude of a sleepless night was on me, my nerves were tingling with the activity of an equally tireless apprehension, and all idea of repose was out of the question. The river I saw had risen further. Its thunder filled the air, and a fine spray made itself felt through my thin sleeping shirt.

Yet nowhere did I discover the slightest evidences of anything to cause alarm. This deep, prolonged disturbance in my heart remained wholly unaccounted for.

My companion had not stirred when I called him, and there was no need to waken him now. I looked about me carefully, noting everything: the turned-over canoe; the yellow paddles—two of them, I'm certain; the provision sack and the extra lantern hanging together from the tree; and, crowding everywhere about me, enveloping all, the willows, those endless, shaking willows. A bird uttered its morning cry, and a string of duck passed with whirring flight overhead in the twilight. The sand whirled, dry and stinging, about my bare feet in the wind.

I walked round the tent and then went out a little way into the bush, so that I could see across the river to the farther landscape, and the same profound yet indefinable emotion of distress seized upon me again as I saw the interminable sea of bushes stretching to the horizon, looking ghostly and unreal in the wan light of dawn. I walked softly here and there, still puzzling over that odd sound of infinite pattering, and of that pressure upon the tent that had wakened me. It *must* have been the wind, I reflected—the wind beating upon the loose, hot sand, driving the dry particles smartly against the taut canvas—the wind dropping heavily upon our fragile roof.

Yet all the time my nervousness and malaise increased appreciably.

I crossed over to the farther shore and noted how the coast-line had altered in the night, and what masses of sand the river had torn away. I dipped my hands and feet into the cool current, and bathed my forehead. Already there was a glow of sunrise in the sky and the exquisite freshness of coming day. On my way back I passed purposely beneath the very bushes where I had seen the column of figures rising into the air, and midway among the clumps I suddenly found myself overtaken by a sense of vast terror. From the shadows a large figure went swiftly by. Some one passed me, as sure as ever man did. . . .

It was a great staggering blow from the wind that helped me forward again, and once out in the more open space, the sense of terror diminished strangely. The winds were about and walking, I remember saying to myself; for the winds often move like great presences under the trees. And altogether the fear that hovered about me was such an unknown and immense kind of fear, so unlike anything I had ever felt before, that it woke a sense of awe and wonder in me that did much to counteract its worst effects; and when I reached a high point in the middle of the island from which I could see the wide stretch of river, crimson in the sunrise, the whole magical beauty of it all was so overpowering that a sort of wild yearning woke in me and almost brought a cry up into the throat.

But this cry found no expression, for as my eyes wandered from the plain beyond to the island round me and noted our little tent half hidden among the willows, a dreadful discovery leaped out at me, compared to which my terror of the walking winds seemed as nothing at all.

For a change, I thought, had somehow come about in the arrangement of the landscape. It was not that my point of vantage gave me a different view, but that an alteration had apparently been effected in the relation of the tent to the willows, and of the willows to the tent. Surely the bushes now crowded much closer—unnecessarily, unpleasantly close. *They had moved nearer.*

Creeping with silent feet over the shifting sands, drawing imperceptibly nearer by soft, unhurried movements, the willows had come closer during the night. But had the wind moved them, or had they moved of themselves? I recalled the sound of infinite small patterings and the pressure upon the tent and upon my own heart that caused me to wake in terror. I swayed for a moment in the wind like a tree, finding it hard to keep my upright position on the sandy hillock. There was a suggestion here of personal agency, of deliberate intention, of aggressive hostility, and it terrified me into a sort of rigidity.

Then the reaction followed quickly. The idea was so bizarre, so absurd, that I felt inclined to laugh. But the laughter came no more readily than the cry, for the knowledge that my mind was so respective to such dangerous imaginings brought the additional terror that it was through our minds and not through our physical bodies that the attack would come, and was coming.

The wind buffeted me about, and, very quickly it seemed, the sun came up over the horizon, for it was after four o'clock, and I must have stood on that little pinnacle of sand longer than I knew, afraid to come down at close quarters with the willows. I returned quietly, creepily, to the tent, first taking another exhaustive look round and—yes, I confess it—making a few measurements. I paced out on the warm sand the distances between the willows and the tent, making a note of the shortest distance particularly.

I crawled stealthily into my blankets. My companion, to all appearances, still slept soundly, and I was glad that this was so. Provided my experiences were not corroborated, I could find strength somehow to deny them, perhaps. With the daylight I could persuade myself that it was all a subjective hallucination, a fantasy of the night, a projection of the excited imagination.

Nothing further came to disturb me, and I fell asleep almost at once, utterly exhausted, yet still in dread of hearing again that weird sound of multitudinous pattering, or of feeling the pressure upon my heart that had made it difficult to breathe.

IV

THE sun was high in the heavens when my companion woke me from a heavy sleep and announced that the porridge was cooked and there was just time to bathe. The grateful smell of frizzling bacon entered the tent door.

'River still rising,' he said, 'and several islands out in mid-stream have disappeared altogether. Our own island's much smaller.'

'Any wood left?' I asked sleepily.

'The wood and the island will finish to-morrow in a dead heat,' he laughed, 'but there's enough to last us till then.'

I plunged in from the point of the island, which had indeed altered a lot in size and shape during the night, and was swept down in a moment to the landing place opposite the tent. The water was icy, and the banks flew by like the country from an express train. Bathing under such conditions was an exhilarating operation, and the terror of the night seemed cleansed out of me by a process of evaporation in the brain. The sun was blazing hot; not a cloud showed itself anywhere; the wind, however, had not abated one little jot.

Quite suddenly then the implied meaning of the Swede's words flashed across me, showing that he no longer wished to leave post-haste, and had changed his mind. 'Enough to last till to-morrow'—he assumed we should stay on the island another night. It struck me as odd. The night before he was so positive the other way. How had the change come about?

Great crumblings of the banks occurred at breakfast, with heavy splashings and clouds of spray which the wind brought into our frying-pan, and my fellow-traveller talked incessantly about the difficulty the Vienna-Pesth steamers must have to find the channel in flood. But the state of his mind interested and impressed me far more than the state of the river or the difficulties of the steamers. He had changed somehow since the evening before. His manner was different—a trifle excited, a trifle shy, with a sort of suspicion about his voice and gestures. I hardly know how to describe it now in cold blood, but at the time I remember being quite certain of one thing, viz., that he had become frightened!

He ate very little breakfast, and for once omitted to smoke his pipe. He had the map spread open beside him, and kept studying its markings.

'We'd better get off sharp in an hour,' I said presently, feeling for an opening that must bring him indirectly to a partial confession at any rate. And his answer puzzled me uncomfortably: 'Rather! If they'll let us.'

'Who'll let us? The elements?' I asked quickly, with affected indifference.

'The powers of this awful place, whoever they are,' he replied, keeping his eyes on the map. 'The gods are here, if they are anywhere at all in the world.'

'The elements are always the true immortals,' I replied, laughing as naturally as I could manage, yet knowing quite well that my face reflected my true feelings when he looked up gravely at me and spoke across the smoke:

'We shall be fortunate if we get away without further disaster.'

This was exactly what I had dreaded, and I screwed myself up to the point of the direct question. It was like agreeing to allow the dentist to extract the tooth; it *had* to come anyhow in the long run, and the rest was all pretence.

'Further disaster! Why, what's happened?'

'For one thing—the steering paddle's gone,' he said quietly.

'The steering paddle gone!' I repeated, greatly excited, for this was our rudder, and the Danube in flood without a rudder was suicide. 'But what——'

'And there's a tear in the bottom of the canoe,' he added, with a genuine little tremor in his voice.

I continued staring at him, able only to repeat the words in his face somewhat foolishly. There, in the heat of the sun, and on this burning sand, I was aware of a freezing atmosphere descending round us I got up to follow him, for he merely nodded his head gravely and led the way towards the tent a few yards on the other side of the fire-place. The canoe still lay there as I had last seen her in the night, ribs uppermost, the paddles, or rather, *the* paddle, on the sand beside her.

'There's only one,' he said, stooping to pick it up. 'And here's the rent in the base-board.'

It was on the tip of my tongue to tell him that I had clearly noticed *two* paddles a few hours before, but a second impulse made me think better of it, and I said nothing. I approached to see.

There was a long, finely-made tear in the bottom of the canoe where a little slither of wood had been neatly taken clean out; it looked as if the tooth of a sharp rock or snag had eaten down her length, and investigation showed that the hole went through. Had we launched out in her without observing it we must inevitably have foundered. At first the water would have made the wood swell so as to close the hole, but once out in mid-stream the water must have poured in, and the canoe, never more than two inches above the surface, would have filled and sunk very rapidly.

'There, you see, an attempt to prepare a victim for the sacrifice,' I heard him saying, more to himself than to me, 'two victims rather,' he added as he bent over and ran his fingers along the slit.

I began to whistle—a thing I always do unconsciously when utterly nonplussed—and purposely paid no attention to his words. I was determined to consider them foolish.

'It wasn't there last night,' he said presently, straightening up from his examination and looking anywhere but at me.

'We must have scratched her in landing, of course,' I stopped whistling to say, 'The stones are very sharp——'

I stopped abruptly, for at that moment he turned round and met my eye squarely. I knew just as well as he did how impossible my explanation was. There were no stones, to begin with.

'And then there's this to explain too,' he added quietly, handling me the paddle and pointing to the blade.

A new and curious emotion spread freezingly over me as I took and examined it. The blade was scraped down all over, beautifully scraped, as though some one had sand-papered it with care, making it so thin that the first vigorous stroke must have snapped it off at the elbow.

'One of us walked in his sleep and did this thing,' I said feebly, 'or—or it has been filed by the constant stream of sand particles blown against it by the wind, perhaps.'

'Ah,' said the Swede, turning away, laughing a little, 'you can explain everything!'

'The same wind that caught the steering paddle and flung it so near the bank that it fell in with the next lump that crumbled,' I called out after him, absolutely determined to find an explanation for everything he showed me.

'I see,' he shouted back, turning his head to look at me before disappearing among the willow bushes.

Once alone with these perplexing evidences of personal agency, I think my first thought took the form of 'One of us must have done this thing, and it certainly was not I.' But my second thought decided how impossible it was to suppose, under all the circumstances, that either of us had done it. That my companion, the trusted friend of a dozen similar expeditions, could have knowingly had a hand in it, was a suggestion not to be entertained for a moment. Equally absurd seemed the explanation that this imperturbable and densely practical nature had suddenly become insane and was busied with insane purposes.

Yet the fact remained that what disturbed me most, and kept my fear actively alive even in this blaze of sunshine and wild beauty, was the clear certainty that some curious alteration had come about in his *mind*—that he was nervous, timid, suspicious, aware of goings on he did not speak about, watching a series of secret and hitherto unmentionable events—waiting, in a word, for a climax that he expected, and, I thought, expected very soon. This grew up in my mind intuitively—I hardly knew how.

I made a hurried examination of the tent and its surroundings, but the measurements of the night remained the same. There were deep hollows formed in the sand, I now noticed for the first time, basin-shaped and of various depths and sizes, varying from that of a tea-cup to a large bowl. The wind, no doubt, was responsible for these mini-ature craters, just as it was for lifting the paddle and tossing it towards the water. The rent in the canoe was the only thing that seemed quite inexplicable and, after all, it *was* conceivable that a sharp point had caught it when we landed. The examination I made of the shore did not assist this theory, but all the same I clung to it with that diminishing portion of my intelligence which I called my 'reason.' An explanation of some kind was an absolute necessity, just as some working explanation of the universe is necessary— however absurd—to the happiness of every individual who seeks to do his duty in the world and face the problems of life. The simile seemed to me at the time an exact parallel.

I at once set the pitch melting, and presently the Swede joined me at the work, though under the best conditions in the world the canoe could not be safe for travelling till the following day. I drew his attention casually to the hollows in the sand.

'Yes,' he said, 'I know. They're all over the island. But *you* can explain them, no doubt!'

'Wind, of course,' I answered without hesitation. 'Have you never watched those little whirlwinds in the street that twist and twirl everything into a circle? This sand's loose enough to yield, that's all.'

He made no reply, and we worked on in silence for a bit. I watched him surreptitiously all the time, and I had an idea he was watching me. He seemed, too, to be always listening attentively to something I could not hear, or perhaps for something that he expected to hear, for he kept turning about and staring into the bushes, and up into the sky, and out across the water where it was visible through the openings among the willows. Sometimes he even put his hand to his ear and held it there for several minutes. He said nothing to me, however, about it, and I asked no questions. And meanwhile, as he mended that torn canoe with the skill and address of a red Indian, I was glad to notice his absorption in the work, for there was a vague dread in my heart that he would speak of the changed aspect of the willows. And, if he had noticed *that*, my imagination could no longer be held a sufficient explanation of it.

At length, after a long pause, he began to talk.

'Queer thing,' he added in a hurried sort of voice, as though he wanted to say something and get it over. 'Queer thing, I mean, about that otter last night.'

I had expected something so totally different that he caught me with surprise, and I looked up sharply.

'Shows how lonely this place is. Otters are awfully shy things——'

'I don't mean that, of course,' he interrupted. 'I mean—do you think—did you think it really *was* an otter? '

'What else, in the name of Heaven, what else?'

'You know, I saw it before you did, and at first it seemed—so *much* bigger than an otter.'

'The sunset as you looked up-stream magnified it, or something,' I replied.

He looked at me absently a moment, as though his mind were busy with other thoughts.

'It had such extraordinary yellow eyes,' he went on half to himself.

'That was the sun too,' I laughed, a trifle boisterously. 'I suppose you'll wonder next if that fellow in the boat——'

I suddenly decided not to finish the sentence. He was in the act again of listening, turning his head to the wind, and something in the expression of his face made me halt. The subject dropped, and we went on with our caulking. Apparently he had not noticed my unfinished sentence. Five minutes later, however, he looked at me across the canoe, the smoking pitch in his hand, his face exceedingly grave.

'I *did* rather wonder, if you want to know,' he said slowly, 'what that thing in the boat was. I remember thinking at the time it was not a man. The whole business seemed to rise quite suddenly out of the water.'

I laughed again boisterously in his face, but this time there was impatience, and a strain of anger too, in my feeling.

'Look here now,' I cried; 'this place is quite queer enough without going out of our way to imagine things! That boat was an ordinary boat, and the man in it was an ordinary man, and they were both going down stream as fast as they could lick. And that otter *was* an otter, so don't let's play the fool about it!'

He looked steadily at me with the same grave expression. He was not in the least annoyed. I took courage from his silence.

'And, for Heaven's sake,' I went on, 'don't keep pretending you hear things, because it only gives me the jumps, and there's nothing to hear but the river and this cursed old thundering wind.'

'You *fool!*' he answered in a low, shocked voice, 'you utter fool. That's just the way all victims talk. As if you didn't understand just as well as I do!' he sneered with scorn in his voice, and a sort of resignation. 'The best thing you can do is to keep quiet and try to hold your mind as firm as possible. This feeble attempt at self-deception only makes the truth harder when you're forced to meet it.'

My little effort was over, and I found nothing more to said, for I knew quite well his words were true, and that *I* was the fool, not *he*. Up to a certain stage in the adventure he kept ahead of me easily, and I think I felt annoyed to be out of it, to be thus proved less psychic, less sensitive than himself to these extraordinary happenings, and half ignorant all the time of what was going on under my very nose. *He knew* from the very beginning, apparently. But at the moment I wholly missed the point of his words about the necessity of there being a victim, and that we ourselves were destined to satisfy the want. I dropped all pretence thenceforward, but thenceforward likewise my fear increased steadily to the climax.

'But you're quite right about one thing,' he added, before the subject passed, 'and that is that we're wiser not to talk about it, or even to think about it, because what one *thinks* finds expression in words, and what one *says*, happens.'

That afternoon, while the canoe dried and hardened, we spent trying to fish, testing the leak, collecting wood, and watching the enormous

flood of rising water. Masses of driftwood swept near our shores
sometimes, and we fished for them with long willow branches. The
island grew perceptibly smaller as the banks were torn away with
great gulps and splashes. The weather kept brilliantly fine till about
four o'clock, and then for the first time for three days the wind showed
signs of abating. Clouds began to gather in the south-west, spreading
thence slowly over the sky.

This lessening of the wind came as a great relief, for the incessant
roaring, banging, and thundering had irritated our nerves. Yet the
silence that came about five o'clock with its sudden cessation was in
a manner quite as oppressive. The booming of the river had everything
its own way then: it filled the air with deep murmurs, more musical
than the wind noises, but infinitely more monotonous. The wind held
many notes, rising, falling, always beating out some sort of great
elemental tune; whereas the river's song lay between three notes at
most—dull pedal notes, that held a lugubrious quality foreign to the
wind, and somehow seemed to me, in my then nervous state, to sound
wonderfully well the music of doom.

It was extraordinary, too, how the withdrawal suddenly of bright
sunlight took everything out of the landscape that made for cheerfulness; and since this particular landscape had already managed to convey the suggestion of something sinister, the change of course was all
the more unwelcome and noticeable. For me, I know, the darkening
outlook became distinctly more alarming, and I found myself more
than once calculating how soon after sunset the full moon would get
up in the east, and whether the gathering clouds would greatly interfere with her lighting of the little island.

With this general hush of the wind—though it still indulged in
occasional brief gusts—the river seemed to me to grow blacker, the
willows to stand more densely together. The latter, too, kept up a sort
of independent movement of their own, rustling among themselves
when no wind stirred, and shaking oddly from the roots upwards.
When common objects in this way become charged with the suggestion of horror, they stimulate the imagination far more than things of
unusual appearance; and these bushes, crowding huddled about us,
assumed for me in the darkness a bizarre *grotesquerie* of appearance
that lent to them somehow the aspect of purposeful and living creatures. Their very ordinariness, I felt, masked what was malignant and
hostile to us. The forces of the region drew nearer with the coming of

night. They were focussing upon our island, and more particularly upon ourselves. For thus, somehow, in the terms of the imagination, did my really indescribable sensations in this extraordinary place present themselves.

I had slept a good deal in the early afternoon, and had thus recovered somewhat from the exhaustion of a disturbed night, but this only served apparently to render me more susceptible than before to the obsessing spell of the haunting. I fought against it, laughing at my feelings as absurd and childish, with very obvious physiological explanations, yet, in spite of every effort, they gained in strength upon me so that I dreaded the night as a child lost in a forest must dread the approach of darkness.

The canoe we had carefully covered with a waterproof sheet during the day, and the one remaining paddle had been securely tied by the Swede to the base of a tree, lest the wind should rob us of that too. From five o'clock onwards I busied myself with the stew-pot and preparations for dinner, it being my turn to cook that night. We had potatoes, onions, bits of bacon fat to add flavour, and a general thick residue from former stews at the bottom of the pot; with black bread broken up into it the result was most excellent, and it was followed by a stew of plums with sugar and a brew of strong tea with dried milk. A good pile of wood lay close at hand, and the absence of wind made my duties easy. My companion sat lazily watching me, dividing his attentions between cleaning his pipe and giving useless advice—an admitted privilege of the off-duty man. He had been very quiet all the afternoon, engaged in re-caulking the canoe, strengthening the tent ropes, and fishing for driftwood while I slept. No more talk about undesirable things had passed between us, and I think his only remarks had to do with the gradual destruction of the island, which he declared was now fully a third smaller than when we first landed.

The pot had just begun to bubble when I heard his voice calling to me from the bank, where he had wandered away without my noticing. I ran up.

'Come and listen,' he said, 'and see what you make of it.' He held his hand cupwise to his ear, as so often before.

'*Now* do you hear anything?' he asked, watching me curiously.

We stood there, listening attentively together. At first I heard only the deep note of the water and the hissings rising from its turbulent surface. The willows, for once, were motionless and silent. Then a sound began to reach my ears faintly, a peculiar sound—something like the humming of a distant gong. It seemed to come across to us in the darkness from the waste of swamps and willows opposite. It was repeated at regular intervals, but it was certainly neither the sound of a bell nor the hooting of a distant steamer. I can liken it to nothing so much as to the sound of an immense gong, suspended far up in the sky, repeating incessantly its muffled metallic note, soft and musical, as it was repeatedly struck. My heart quickened as I listened.

'I've heard it all day,' said my companion. 'While you slept this afternoon it came all round the island. I hunted it down, but could never get near enough to see—to localise it correctly. Sometimes it was overhead, and sometimes it seemed under the water. Once or twice, too, I could have sworn it was not outside at all, but *within myself*—you know—the way a sound in the fourth dimension* is supposed to come.'

I was too much puzzled to pay much attention to his words. I listened carefully, striving to associate it with any known familiar sound I could think of, but without success. It changed in direction, too, coming nearer, and then sinking utterly away into remote distance. I cannot say that it was ominous in quality, because to me it seemed distinctly musical, yet I must admit it set going a distressing feeling that made me wish I had never heard it,

'The wind blowing in those sand-funnels,' I said, determined to find an explanation, 'or the bushes rubbing together after the storm perhaps.'

'It comes off the whole swamp,' my friend answered. 'It comes from everywhere at once.' He ignored my explanations. 'It comes from the willow bushes somehow——'

'But now the wind has dropped,' I objected. 'The willows can hardly make a noise by themselves, can they?'

His answer frightened me, first because I had dreaded it, and secondly, because I knew intuitively it was true.

'It is *because* the wind has dropped we now hear it. It was drowned before. It is the cry, I believe, of the——'

I dashed back to my fire, warned by a sound of bubbling that the stew was in danger, but determined at the same time to escape from further conversation. I was resolute, if possible, to avoid the exchanging of views. I dreaded, too, that he would begin again about the gods, or the elemental forces, or something else disquieting, and I wanted to keep myself well in hand for what might happen later.

There was another night to be faced before we escaped from this distressing place, and there was no knowing yet what it might bring forth.

'Come and cut up bread for the pot,' I called to him, vigorously stirring the appetising mixture. That stew-pot held sanity for us both, and the thought made me laugh.

He came over slowly and took the provision sack from the tree, fumbling in its mysterious depths, and then emptying the entire contents upon the ground-sheet at his feet

'Hurry up!' I cried; 'it's boiling.'

The Swede burst out into a roar of laughter that startled me. It was forced laughter, not artificial exactly, but mirthless.

'There's nothing here!' he shouted, holding his sides.

'Bread, I mean.'

'It's gone. There is no bread. They've taken it!'

I dropped the long spoon and ran up. Everything the sack had contained lay upon the groundsheet, but there was no loaf.

The whole dead weight of my growing fear fell upon me and shook me. Then I burst out laughing too. It was the only thing to do: and the sound of my own laughter also made me understand his. The strain of psychical pressure caused it—this explosion of unnatural laughter in both of us; it was an effort of repressed forces to seek relief; it was a temporary safety valve. And with both of us it ceased quite suddenly.

'How criminally stupid of me!' I cried, still determined to be consistent and find an explanation. 'I clean forgot to buy a loaf at Pressburg. That chattering woman put everything out of my head, and I must have left it lying on the counter or——'

'The oatmeal, too, is much less than it was this morning,' the Swede interrupted.

Why in the world need he draw attention to it? I thought angrily.

'There's enough for to-morrow,' I said, stirring vigorously, 'and we can get lots more at Komorn or Gran.* In twenty-four hours we shall be miles from here.'

'I hope so—to God,' he muttered, putting the things back into the sack, 'unless we're claimed first as victims for the sacrifice,' he added with a foolish laugh. He dragged the sack into the tent, for safety's sake, I suppose, and I heard him mumbling on to himself, but so indistinctly that it seemed quite natural for me to ignore his words.

Our meal was beyond question a gloomy one, and we ate it almost in silence, avoiding one another's eyes, and keeping the fire bright. Then we washed up and prepared for the night, and, once smoking, our minds unoccupied with any definite duties, the apprehension I had felt all day long became more and more acute. It was not then active fear, I think, but the very vagueness of its origin distressed me far more than if I had been able to ticket and face it squarely. The curious sound I have likened to the note of a gong became now almost incessant, and filled the stillness of the night with a faint, continuous ringing rather than a series of distinct notes. At one time it was behind and at another time in front of us. Sometimes I fancied it came from the bushes on our left, and then again from the clumps on our right. More often it hovered directly overhead like the whirring of wings. It was really everywhere at once, behind, in front, at our sides and over our heads, completely surrounding us. The sound really defies description. But nothing within my knowledge is like that ceaseless muffled humming rising off the deserted world of swamps and willows.

We sat smoking in comparative silence, the strain growing every minute greater. The worst feature of the situation seemed to me that we did not know what to expect, and could therefore make no sort of preparation by way of defence. We could anticipate nothing. My explanations made in the sunshine, moreover, now came to haunt me with their foolish and wholly unsatisfactory nature, and it was more and more clear to us that some kind of plain talk with my companion was inevitable, whether I liked it or not. After all, we had to spend the night together, and to sleep in the same tent side by side. I saw that I could not get along much longer without the support of his mind, and for that, of course, plain talk was imperative. As long as possible, however, I postponed this little climax, and tried to ignore or laugh at the occasional sentences he flung into the emptiness.

Some of these sentences, moreover, were confoundedly disquieting to me, coming as they did to corroborate much that I felt myself: corroboration, too—which made it so much more convincing—from a totally different point of view. He composed such curious sentences, and hurled them at me in such an inconsequential sort of way, as though his main line of thought was secret to himself, and these fragments were the bits he found it impossible to digest. He got rid of them by uttering them. Speech relieved him. It was like being sick.

'There are things about us, I'm sure, that make for disorder, disintegration, destruction, *our* destruction,' he said once, while the fire blazed between us. 'We've strayed out of a safe line somewhere.'

And another time, when the gong sounds had come nearer, ringing much louder than before, and directly over our heads, he said, as though talking to himself:

'I don't think a phonograph would show any record of that. The sound doesn't come to me by the ears at all. The vibrations reach me in another manner altogether, and seem to be within me, which is precisely how a fourth dimensional sound might be supposed to make itself heard.'

I purposely made no reply to this, but I sat up a little closer to the fire and peered about me into the darkness. The clouds were massed all over the sky and no trace of moonlight came through. Very still, too, everything was, so that the river and the frogs had things all their own way.

'It has that about it,' he went on, 'which is utterly out of common experience. It is *unknown*. Only one thing describes it really: it is a nonhuman sound; I mean a sound outside humanity.'

Having rid himself of this indigestible morsel, he lay quiet for a time; but he had so admirably expressed my own feeling that it was a relief to have the thought out, and to have confined it by the limitation of words from dangerous wandering to and fro in the mind.

The solitude of that Danube camping-place, can I ever forget it? The feeling of being utterly alone on an empty planet! My thoughts ran incessantly upon cities and the haunts of men. I would have given my soul, as the saying is, for the 'feel' of those Bavarian villages we had passed through by the score; for the normal, human commonplaces: peasants drinking beer, tables beneath the trees, hot sunshine, and a ruined castle on the rocks behind the red-roofed church. Even the tourists would have been welcome.

Yet what I felt of dread was no ordinary ghostly fear. It was infinitely greater, stranger, and seemed to arise from some dim ancestral sense of terror more profoundly disturbing than anything I had known or dreamed of. We had 'strayed,' as the Swede put it, into some region or some set of conditions where the risks were great, yet unintelligible to us; where the frontiers of some unknown world lay close about us. It was a spot held by the dwellers in some outer space, a sort of peep-hole whence they could spy upon the earth, themselves unseen, a point where the veil between had worn a little thin. As the final result of too long a sojourn here, we should be carried over the border and deprived of what we called 'our lives,' yet by mental, not physical, processes. In that sense, as he said, we should be the victims of our adventure—a sacrifice.

It took us in different fashion, each according to the measure of his sensitiveness and powers of resistance. I translated it vaguely into a personification of the mightily disturbed elements, investing them with the horror of a deliberate and malefic purpose, resentful of our audacious intrusion into their breeding-place; whereas my friend threw it into the unoriginal form at first of a trespass on some ancient shrine, some place where the old gods still held sway, where the emotional forces of former worshippers still clung, and the ancestral portion of him yielded to the old pagan spell.

At any rate, here was a place unpolluted by men, kept clean by the winds from coarsening human influences, a place where spiritual agencies were within reach and aggressive. Never, before or since, have I been so attacked by indescribable suggestions of a 'beyond region,' of another scheme of life, another evolution not parallel to the human. And in the end our minds would succumb under the weight of the awful spell, and we should be drawn across the frontier into *their* world.

Small things testified to this amazing influence of the place, and now in the silence round the fire they allowed themselves to be noted by the mind. The very atmosphere had proved itself a magnifying medium to distort every indication: the otter rolling in the current, the hurrying boatman making signs, the shifting willows, one and all had been robbed of its natural character, and revealed in something of its other aspect—as it existed across the border in that other region. And this changed aspect I felt was new not merely to me, but to the race. The whole experience whose verge we touched was unknown to humanity at all. It was a new order of experience, and in the true sense of the word *unearthly*.

'It's the deliberate, calculating purpose that reduces one's courage to zero,' the Swede said suddenly, as if he had been actually following my thoughts. 'Otherwise imagination might count for much. But the paddle, the canoe, the lessening food——'

'Haven't I explained all that once?' I interrupted viciously.

'You have,' he answered dryly; 'you have indeed.'

He made other remarks too, as usual, about what be called the 'plain determination to provide a victim'; but, having now arranged my thoughts better, I recognised that this was simply the cry of his frightened soul against the knowledge that he was being attacked in a vital part, and that he would be somehow taken or destroyed. The situation called for a courage and calmness of reasoning that neither of us could compass, and I have never before been so clearly conscious of two persons in me—the one that explained everything, and the other that laughed at such foolish explanations, yet was horribly afraid.

Meanwhile, in the pitchy night the fire died down and the wood pile grew small. Neither of us moved to replenish the stock, and the darkness consequently came up very close to our faces. A few feet beyond the circle of firelight it was inky black. Occasionally a stray puff of wind set the willows shivering about us, but apart from this not very welcome sound a deep and depressing silence reigned, broken only by the gurgling of the river and the humming in the air overhead.

We both missed, I think, the shouting company of the winds.

At length, at a moment when a stray puff prolonged itself as though the wind were about to rise again, I reached the point for me of saturation, the point where it was absolutely necessary to find relief in plain speech, or else to betray myself by some hysterical extravagance that must have been far worse in its effect upon both of us. I kicked the fire into a blaze, and turned to my companion abruptly. He looked up with a start.

'I can't disguise it any longer,' I said; 'I don't like this place, and the darkness, and the noises, and the awful feelings I get. There's something here that beats me utterly. I'm in a blue funk, and that's the plain truth. If the other shore was—different, I swear I'd be inclined to swim for it!'

The Swede's face turned very white beneath the deep tan of sun and wind. He stared straight at me and answered quietly, but his voice betrayed his huge excitement by its unnatural calmness. For the moment, at any rate, he was the strong man of the two. He was more phlegmatic, for one thing.

'It's not a physical condition we can escape from by running away,' he replied, in the tone of a doctor diagnosing some grave disease; 'we must sit tight and wait. There are forces close here that could kill a herd of elephants in a second as easily as you or I could squash a fly.

Our only chance is to keep perfectly still. Our insignificance perhaps
may save us.'

I put a dozen questions into my expression of face, but found no
words. It was precisely like listening to an accurate description of
a disease whose symptoms had puzzled me.

'I mean that so far, although aware of our disturbing presence, they
have not *found* us—not "located" us, as the Americans say,* he went
on. 'They're blundering about like men hunting for a leak of gas. The
paddle and canoe and provisions prove that. I think they *feel* us, but
cannot actually see us. We must keep our minds quiet—it's our minds
they feel. We must control our thoughts, or it's all up with us.'

'Death you mean?' I stammered, icy with the horror of his suggestion.

'Worse—by far,' he said. 'Death, according to one's belief, means
either annihilation or release from the limitations of the senses, but it
involves no change of character. *You* don't suddenly alter just because
the body's gone. But this means a radical alteration, a complete
change, a horrible loss of oneself by substitution—far worse than
death, and not even annihilation. We happen to have camped in a spot
where their region touches ours, where the veil between has worn
thin'—horrors! he was using my very own phrase, my actual
words—'so that they are aware of our being in their neighbourhood.'

'But *who* are aware?' I asked.

I forgot the shaking of the willows in the windless calm, the humming overhead, everything except that I was waiting for an answer
that I dreaded more than I can possibly explain.

He lowered his voice at once to reply, leaning forward a little over
the fire, an indefinable change in his face that made me avoid his eyes
and look down upon the ground.

'All my life,' he said, 'I have been strangely, vividly conscious of
another region—not far removed from our own world in one sense,
yet wholly different in kind—where great things go on unceasingly,
where immense and terrible personalities hurry by, intent on vast
purposes compared to which earthly affairs, the rise and fall of
nations, the destinies of empires, the fate of armies and continents,
are all as dust in the balance; vast purposes, I mean, that deal directly
with the soul, and not indirectly with mere expressions of the soul—'

'I suggest just now——' I began, seeking to stop him, feeling as
though I was face to face with a madman. But he instantly overbore
me with his torrent that *had* to come.

'You think,' he said, 'it is the spirits of the elements, and I thought perhaps it was the old gods. But I tell you now it is—*neither*. These would be comprehensible entities, for they have relations with men, depending upon them for worship or sacrifice, whereas these beings who are now about us have absolutely nothing to do with mankind, and it is mere chance that their space happens just at this spot to touch our own.'

The mere conception, which his words somehow made so convincing, as I listened to them there in the dark stillness of that lonely island, set me shaking a little all over. I found it impossible to control my movements.

'And what do you propose?' I began again.

'A sacrifice, a victim, might save us by distracting them until we could get away,' he went on, 'just as the wolves stop to devour the dogs and give the sleigh another start. But—I see no chance of any other victim now.'

I stared blankly at him. The gleam in his eyes was dreadful. Presently he continued.

'It's the willows, of course. The willows *mask* the others, but the others are feeling about for us. If we let our minds betray our fear, we're lost, lost utterly.' He looked at me with an expression so calm, so determined, so sincere, that I no longer had any doubts as to his sanity. He was as sane as any man ever was. 'If we can hold out through the night,' he added, 'we may get off in the daylight unnoticed, or rather, *undiscovered*.'

'But you really think a sacrifice would——'

That gong-like humming came down very close over our heads as I spoke, but it was my friend's scared face that really stopped my mouth.

'Hush!' he whispered, holding up his hand. 'Do not mention them more than you can help. Do not refer to them *by name*. To name is to reveal: it is the inevitable clue, and our only hope lies in ignoring them, in order that they may ignore us.'

'Even in thought?' He was extraordinarily agitated.

'Especially in thought. Our thoughts make spirals in their world. We must keep them *out of our minds* at all costs if possible.'

I raked the fire together to prevent the darkness having everything its own way. I never longed for the sun as I longed for it then in the awful blackness of that summer night.

'Were you awake all last night?' he went on suddenly.

'I slept badly a little after dawn,' I replied evasively, trying to follow his instructions, which I knew instinctively were true, 'but the wind, of course——'

'I know. But the wind won't account for all the noises.'

'Then you heard it too?'

'The multiplying countless little footsteps I heard,' he said, adding, after a moment's hesitation, 'and that other sound——'

'You mean above the tent, and the pressing down upon us of something tremendous, gigantic?' He nodded significantly.

'It was like the beginning of a sort of inner suffocation?' I said.

'Partly, yes. It seemed to me that the weight of the atmosphere had been altered—had increased enormously, so that we should be crushed.'

'And *that*,' I went on, determined to have it all out, pointing upwards where the gong-like note hummed ceaselessly, rising and falling like wind. 'What do you make of that?'

'It's *their* sound,' he whispered gravely. 'It's the sound of their world, the humming in their region. The division here is so thin that it leaks through somehow. But, if you listen carefully, you'll find it's not above so much as around us. It's in the willows. It's the willows themselves humming, because here the willows have been made symbols of the forces that are against us.'

I could not follow exactly what he meant by this, yet the thought and idea in my mind were beyond question the thought and idea in his. I realised what he realised, only with less power of analysis than his. It was on the tip of my tongue to tell him at last about my hallucination of the ascending figures and the moving bushes, when he suddenly thrust his face again close into mine across the firelight and began to speak in a very earnest whisper. He amazed me by his calmness and pluck, his apparent control of the situation. This man I had for years deemed unimaginative, stolid!

'Now listen,' he said. 'The only thing for us to do is to go on as though nothing had happened, follow our usual habits, go to bed, and so forth; pretend we feel nothing and notice nothing. It is a question wholly of the mind, and the less we think about them the better our chance of escape. Above all, don't *think*, for what you think happens!'

'All right,' I managed to reply, simply breathless with his words and the strangeness of it all; 'all right, I'll try, but tell me one thing more first. Tell me what you make of those hollows in the ground all about us, those sand-funnels?'

'No!' he cried, forgetting to whisper in his excitement. 'I dare not, simply dare not, put the thought into words. If you have not guessed I am glad. Don't try to. *They* have put it into my mind; try your hardest to prevent their putting it into yours.'

He sank his voice again to a whisper before he finished, and I did not press him to explain. There was already just about as much horror in me as I could hold. The conversation came to an end, and we smoked our pipes busily in silence.

Then something happened, something unimportant apparently, as the way is when the nerves are in a very great state of tension, and this small thing for a brief space gave me an entirely different point of view. I chanced to look down at my sandshoe—the sort we used for the canoe—and something to do with the hole at the toe suddenly recalled to me the London shop where I had bought them, the difficulty the man had in fitting me, and other details of the uninteresting but practical operation. At once, in its train, followed a wholesome view of the modern sceptical world I was accustomed to move in at home. I thought of roast beef and ale, motor-cars, policemen, brass bands, and a dozen other things that proclaimed the soul of ordinariness or utility. The effect was immediate and astonishing even to myself. Psychologically, I suppose, it was simply a sudden and violent reaction after the strain of living in an atmosphere of things that to the normal consciousness must seem impossible and incredible. But, whatever the cause, it momentarily lifted the spell from my heart, and left me for the short space of a minute feeling free and utterly unafraid. I looked up at my friend opposite.

'You damned old pagan!' I cried, laughing aloud in his face. 'You imaginative idiot! You superstitious idolator! You——'

I stopped in the middle, seized anew by the old horror. I tried to smother the sound of my voice as something sacrilegious. The Swede, of course, heard it too—that strange cry overhead in the darkness—and that sudden drop in the air as though something had come nearer.

He had turned ashen white under the tan. He stood bolt upright in front of the fire, stiff as a rod, staring at me.

'After that,' he said in a sort of helpless, frantic way, 'we must go! We can't stay now; we must strike camp this very instant and go on—down the river.'

He was talking, I saw, quite wildly, his word dictated by abject terror—the terror he had resisted so long, but which had caught him at last.

'In the dark?' I exclaimed, shaking with fear after my hysterical outburst, but still realising our position better than he did. 'Sheer madness! The river's in flood, and we've only got a single paddle. Besides, we only go deeper into their country! There's nothing ahead for fifty miles but willows, willows, willows!'

He sat down again in a state of semi-collapse. The positions, by one of those kaleidoscopic changes nature loves, were suddenly reversed, and the control of our forces passed over into my hands. His mind at last had reached the point where it was beginning to weaken.

'What on earth possessed you to do such a thing?' he whispered, with the awe of genuine terror in his voice and face.

I crossed round to his side of the fire. I took both his hands in mine, kneeling down beside him and looking straight into his frightened eyes.

'We'll make one more blaze,' I said firmly, 'and then turn in for the night. At sunrise we'll be off full speed for Komorn. Now, pull yourself together a bit, and remember your own advice about *not thinking fear!*'

He said no more, and I saw that he would agree and obey. In some measure, too, it was a sort of relief to get up and make an excursion into the darkness for more wood. We kept close together, almost touching, groping among the bushes and along the bank. The humming overhead never ceased, but seemed to me to grow louder as we increased our distance from the fire. It was shivery work!

We were grubbing away in the middle of a thickish clump of willows where some driftwood from a former flood had caught high among the branches, when my body was seized in a grip that made me half drop upon the sand. It was the Swede. He had fallen against me, and was clutching me for support. I heard his breath coming and going in short gasps.

'Look! By my soul!' he whispered, and for the first time in my experience I knew what it was to hear tears of terror in a human voice. He was pointing to the fire, some fifty feet away. I followed the direction of his finger, and I swear my heart missed a beat.

There, in front of the dim glow, *something was moving.*

I saw it through a veil that hung before my eyes like the gauze drop-curtain used at the back of a theatre—hazily a little. It was neither a human figure nor an animal. To me it gave the strange impression of being as large as several animals grouped together, like horses, two or three, moving slowly. The Swede, too, got a similar result, though expressing it differently, for he thought it was shaped and sized like a clump of willow bushes, rounded at the top, and moving all over upon its surface—'coiling upon itself like smoke,' he said afterwards.

'I watched it settle downwards through the bushes,' he sobbed at me. 'Look, by God! It's coming this way! Oh, oh!'—he gave a kind of whistling cry. *'They've found us.'*

I gave one terrified glance, which just enabled me to see that the shadowy form was swinging towards us through the bushes, and then I collapsed backwards with a crash into the branches. These failed, of course, to support my weight, so that with the Swede on the top of me we fell in a struggling heap upon the sand. I really hardly knew what was happening. I was conscious only of a sort of enveloping sensation of icy fear that plucked the nerves out of their fleshly covering, twisted them this way and that, and replaced them quivering. My eyes were tightly shut; something in my throat choked me; a feeling that my consciousness was expanding, extending out into space, swiftly gave way to another feeling that I was losing it altogether, and about to die.

An acute spasm of pain passed through me, and I was aware that the Swede had hold of me in such a way that he hurt me abominably. It was the way he caught at me in falling.

But it was this pain, he declared afterwards, that saved me: it caused me to *forget them* and think of something else at the very instant when they were about to find me. It concealed my mind from them at the moment of discovery, yet just in time to evade their terrible seizing of me. He himself, he says, actually swooned at the same moment, and that was what saved him.

I only know that at a later time, how long or short is impossible to say, I found myself scrambling up out of the slippery network of willow branches, and saw my companion standing in front of me holding out a hand to assist me. I stared at him in a dazed way, rubbing the arm he had twisted for me. Nothing came to me to say, somehow.

'I lost consciousness for a moment or two,' I heard him say. 'That's what saved me. It made me stop thinking about them.'

'You nearly broke my arm in two,' I said, uttering my only connected thought at the moment. A numbness came over me.

'That's what saved *you!*' he replied. 'Between us, we've managed to set them off on a false tack somewhere. The humming has ceased. Its gone—for the moment at any rate!'

A wave of hysterical laughter seized me again, and this time spread to my friend too—great healing gusts of shaking laughter that brought a tremendous sense of relief in their train. We made our way back to the fire and put the wood on so that it blazed at once. Then we saw that the tent had fallen over and lay in a tangled heap upon the ground.

We picked it up, and during the process tripped more than once and caught our feet in sand.

'It's those sand-funnels,' exclaimed the Swede, when the tent was up again and the firelight lit up the ground for several yards about us. 'And look at the size of them!'

All round the tent and about the fireplace where we had seen the moving shadows there were deep funnel-shaped hollows in the sand, exactly similar to the ones we had already found over the island, only far bigger and deeper, beautifully formed, and wide enough in some instances to admit the whole of my foot and leg.

Neither of us said a word. We both knew that sleep was the safest thing we could do, and to bed we went accordingly without further delay, having first thrown sand on the fire and taken the provision sack and the paddle inside the tent with us. The canoe, too, we propped in such a way at the end of the tent that our feet touched it, and the least motion would disturb and wake us.

In case of emergency, too, we again went to bed in our clothes, ready for a sudden start.

V

IT was my firm intention to lie awake all night and watch, but the exhaustion of nerves and body decreed otherwise, and sleep after a while came over me with a welcome blanket of oblivion. The fact that my companion also slept quickened its approach. At first he fidgeted and constantly sat up, asking me if I 'heard this' or 'heard that.' He tossed about on his cork mattress, and said the tent was moving and the river had risen over the point of the island; but each time I went out to look I returned with the report that all was well, and finally he grew calmer and lay still. Then at length his breathing became regular and I heard unmistakable sounds of snoring—the first and only time in my life when snoring has been a welcome and calming influence.

This, I remember, was the last thought in my mind before dozing off.

A difficulty in breathing woke me, and I found the blanket over my face. But something else besides the blanket was pressing upon me, and my first thought was that my companion had rolled off his mattress on to my own in his sleep. I called to him and sat up, and at the same moment it came to me that the tent was *surrounded*. That sound of multitudinous soft pattering was again audible outside, filling the night with horror.

I called again to him, louder than before. He did not answer, but I missed the sound of his snoring, and also noticed that the flap of the tent door was down. This was the unpardonable sin. I crawled out in the darkness to hook it back securely, and it was then for the first time I realised positively that the Swede was not there. He had gone.

I dashed out in a mad run, seized by a dreadful agitation, and the moment I was out I plunged into a sort of torrent of humming that surrounded me completely and came out of every quarter of the heavens at once. It was that same familiar humming—gone mad! A swarm of great invisible bees might have been about me in the air. The sound seemed to thicken the very atmosphere, and I felt that my lungs worked with difficulty.

But my friend was in danger, and I could not hesitate.

The dawn was just about to break, and a faint whitish light spread upwards over the clouds from a thin strip of clear horizon. No wind stirred. I could just make out the bushes and river beyond, and the pale sandy patches. In my excitement I ran frantically to and fro about the island, calling him by name, shouting at the top of my voice the first words that came into my head. But the willows smothered my voice, and the humming muffled it, so that the sound only travelled a few feet round me. I plunged among the bushes, tripping headlong, tumbling over roots, and scraping my face as I tore this way and that among the preventing branches.

Then, quite unexpectedly, I came out upon the island's point and saw a dark figure outlined between the water and the sky. It was the Swede. And already he had one foot in the river! A moment more and he would have taken the plunge.

I threw myself upon him, flinging my arms about his waist and dragging him shorewards with all my strength. Of course he struggled furiously, making a noise all the time just like that cursed humming, and using the most outlandish phrases in his anger about 'going *inside* to Them,' and 'taking the way of the water and the wind,' and God only knows what more besides, that I tried in vain to recall afterwards, but which turned me sick with horror and amazement as I listened. But in the end I managed to get him into the comparative safety of the tent, and flung him breathless and cursing upon the mattress, where I held him until the fit had passed.

I think the suddenness with which it all went and he grew calm, coinciding as it did with the equally abrupt cessation of the humming and pattering outside—I think this was almost the strangest part of the whole business perhaps. For he just opened his eyes and turned his tired face up to me so that the dawn threw a pale light upon it through the doorway, and said, for all the world just like a frightened child:

'My life, old man—it's my life I owe you. But it's all over now anyhow. They've found a victim in our place!'

Then he dropped back upon his blankets and went to sleep literally under my eyes. He simply collapsed, and began to snore again as healthily as though nothing had happened and he had never tried to offer his own life as a Sacrifice by drowning. And when the sunlight woke him three hours later—hours of ceaseless vigil for me—it became so clear to me that he remembered absolutely nothing of what he had attempted to do, that I deemed it wise to hold my peace and ask no dangerous questions.

He woke naturally and easily, as I have said, when the sun was already high in a windless hot sky, and he at once got up and set about the preparation of the fire for breakfast. I followed him anxiously at bathing, but he did not attempt to plunge in, merely dipping his head and making some remark about the extra coldness of the water.

'River's falling at last,' he said, 'and I'm glad of it.'

'The humming has stopped too,' I said.

He looked up at me quietly with his normal expression. Evidently he remembered everything except his own attempt at suicide.

'Everything has stopped,' he said, 'because——'

He hesitated. But I knew some reference to that remark he had made just before he fainted was in his mind, and I was determined to know it.

'Because "They've found another victim"?' I said, forcing a little laugh.

'Exactly,' he answered, 'exactly! I feel as positive of it as though—as though—I feel quite safe again, I mean,' he finished.

He began to look curiously about him. The sunlight lay in hot patches on the sand. There was no wind. The willows were motionless. He slowly rose to feet.

'Come,' he said; 'I think if we look, we shall find it.'

He started off on a run, and I followed him. He kept to the banks, poking with a stick among the sandy bays and caves and little backwaters, myself always close on his heels.

'Ah!' he exclaimed presently, 'ah!'

The tone of his voice somehow brought back to me a vivid sense of the horror of the last twenty-four hours, and I turned up to join him. He was pointing with his stick at a large black object that lay half in the water and half on the sand. It appeared to be caught by some twisted willow roots so that the river could not sweep it away. A few hours before the spot must have been under water.

'See,' he said quietly, 'the victim that made our escape possible!'

And when I peered across his shoulder I saw that his stick rested on the body of a man. He turned it over. It was the corpse of a peasant, and the face was hidden in the sand. Clearly the man had been drowned but a few hours before, and his body must have been swept down upon our island somewhere about the hour of the dawn—at the very time the fit had passed.

'We must give it a decent burial, you know.'

'I suppose so,' I replied. I shuddered a little in spite of myself, for there was something about the appearance of that poor drowned man that turned me cold.

The Swede glanced up sharply at me, an undecipherable expression on his face, and began clambering down the bank. I followed him more leisurely. The current, I noticed, had torn away much of the clothing from the body, so that the neck and part of the chest lay bare.

Half-way down the bank my companion suddenly stopped and held up his hand in warning; but either my foot slipped, or I had gained too much momentum to bring myself quickly to a halt, for I bumped into him and sent him forward with a sort of leap to save himself. We tumbled together on to the hard sand so that our feet splashed into the water. And, before anything could be done, we had collided a little heavily against the corpse.

The Swede uttered a sharp cry. And I sprang back as if I had been shot.

At the moment we touched the body there rose from its surface the loud sound of humming—the sound of several hummings—which passed with a vast commotion as of winged things in the air about us and disappeared upwards into the sky, growing fainter and fainter till they finally ceased in the distance. It was exactly as though we had disturbed some living yet invisible creatures at work,

My companion clutched me, and I think I clutched him, but before either of us had time properly to recover from the unexpected shock, we saw that a movement of the current was turning the corpse round so that it became released from the grip of the willow roots. A moment later it had turned completely over, the dead face uppermost, staring at the sky. It lay on the edge of the main stream. In another moment it would be swept away.

The Swede started to save it, shouting again something I did not catch about a 'proper burial'—and then abruptly dropped upon his knees on the sand and covered his eyes with his hands. I was beside him in an instant.

I saw what he had seen.

For just as the body swung round to the current the face and the exposed chest turned full towards us, and showed plainly how the skin and flesh were indented with small hollows, beautifully formed, and exactly similar in shape and kind to the sand-funnels that we had found all over the island.

'Their mark!' I heard my companion mutter under his breath. 'Their awful mark.'

And when I turned my eyes again from his ghastly face to the river, the current had done its work, and the body had been swept away into midstream and was already beyond our reach and almost out of sight, turning over and over on the waves like an otter.

SECRET WORSHIP

HARRIS, the silk merchant, was in South Germany on his way home from a business trip when the idea came to him suddenly that he would take the mountain railway from Strassbourg and run down to revisit his old school after an interval of something more than thirty years. And it was to this chance impulse of the junior partner in Harris Brothers of St Paul's Churchyard that John Silence owed one of the most curious cases of his whole experience, for at that very moment he happened to be tramping these same mountains with a holiday knapsack, and from different points of the compass the two men were actually converging towards the same inn.

Now, deep down in the heart that for thirty years had been concerned chiefly with the profitable buying and selling of silk, this school had left the imprint of its peculiar influence, and, though perhaps unknown to Harris, had strongly coloured the whole of his subsequent existence. It belonged to the deeply religious life of a small Protestant community (which it is unnecessary to specify), and his father had sent him there at the age of fifteen, partly because he would learn the German requisite for the conduct of the silk business, and partly because the discipline was strict, and discipline was what his soul and body needed just then more than anything else.

The life, indeed, had proved exceedingly severe, and young Harris benefited accordingly; for though corporal punishment was unknown, there was a system of mental and spiritual correction which somehow made the soul stand proudly erect to receive it, while it struck at the very root of the fault and taught the boy that his character was being cleaned and strengthened, and that he was not merely being tortured in a kind of personal revenge.

That was over thirty years ago, when he was a dreamy and impressionable youth of fifteen; and now, as the train climbed slowly up the winding mountain gorges, his mind travelled back somewhat lovingly over the intervening period, and forgotten details rose vividly again before him out of the shadows. The life there had been very wonderful, it seemed to him, in that remote mountain village, protected from the tumults of the world by the love and worship of the devout Brotherhood that ministered to the needs of some hundred boys from every country in Europe. Sharply the scenes came back to him. He smelt again the long stone corridors, the hot pinewood rooms, where the sultry hours of summer study were passed with bees droning through open windows in the sunshine, and German characters struggling in the mind with dreams of English lawns—and then the sudden awful cry of the master in German—

'Harris, stand up! You sleep!'

And he recalled the dreadful standing motionless for an hour, book in hand, while the knees felt like wax and the head grew heavier than a cannon-ball.

The very smell of the cooking came back to him—the daily *Sauerkraut*, the watery chocolate on Sundays, the flavour of the stringy meat served twice a week at *Mittagessen*;* and he smiled to think again of the half-rations that was the punishment for speaking English. The very odour of the milk-bowls,—the hot sweet aroma that rose from the soaking peasant-bread at the six-o'clock break-fast,—came back to him pungently, and he saw the huge *Speisesaal** with the hundred boys in their school uniform, all eating sleepily in silence, gulping down the coarse bread and scalding milk in terror of the bell that would presently cut them short—and, at the far end where the masters sat, he saw the narrow slit windows with the vistas of enticing field and forest beyond.

And this, in turn, made him think of the great barn-like room on the top floor where all slept together in wooden cots, and he heard in memory the clamour of the cruel bell that woke them on winter mornings at five o'clock and summoned them to the stone-flagged *Waschkammer*,* where boys and masters alike, after scanty and icy washing, dressed in complete silence.

From this his mind passed swiftly, with vivid picture-thoughts, to other things, and with a passing shiver he remembered how the loneli-ness of never being alone had eaten into him, and how everything—work, meals, sleep, walks, leisure—was done with his 'division' of twenty other boys and under the eyes of at least two masters. The only solitude possible was by asking for half an hour's practice in the cell-like music rooms, and Harris smiled to himself as he recalled the zeal of his violin studies.*

Then, as the train puffed laboriously through the great pine forests that cover these mountains with a giant carpet of velvet, he found the pleasanter layers of memory giving up their dead, and he recalled with admiration the kindness of the masters, whom all addressed as Brother, and marvelled afresh at their devotion in burying themselves for years in such a place, only to leave it, in most cases, for the still rougher life of missionaries in the wild places of the world.

He thought once more of the still, religious atmosphere that hung over the little forest community like a veil, barring the distressful world; of the picturesque ceremonies at Easter, Christmas, and New Year; of the numerous feast-days and charming little festivals. The *Beschehr-Fest*, in particular, came back to him,—the feast of gifts at Christmas,—when the entire community paired off and gave presents, many of which had taken weeks to make or the savings of many days to purchase. And then he saw the midnight ceremony in the church at New Year, with the shining face of the *Prediger* in the pulpit,—the village preacher who, on the last night of the old year, saw in the empty gallery beyond the organ loft the faces of all who were to die in the ensuing twelve months, and who at last recognised himself among them, and, in the very middle of his sermon, passed into a state of rapt ecstasy and burst into a torrent of praise.

Thickly the memories crowded upon him. The picture of the small village dreaming its unselfish life on the mountain-tops, clean, wholesome, simple, searching vigorously for its God, and training hundreds of boys in the grand way, rose up in his mind with all the power of an obsession. He felt once more the old mystical enthusiasm, deeper than the sea and more wonderful than the stars; he heard again the winds sighing from leagues of forest over the red roofs in the moonlight; he heard the Brothers' voices talking of the things beyond this life as though they had actually experienced them in the body; and, as he sat in the jolting train, a spirit of unutterable longing passed over his seared and tired soul, stirring in the depths of him a sea of emotions that he thought had long since frozen into immobility.

And the contrast pained him,—the idealistic dreamer then, the man of business now,—so that a spirit of unworldly peace and beauty known only to the soul in meditation laid its feathered finger upon his heart, moving strangely the surface of the waters.

Harris shivered a little and looked out of the window of his empty carriage. The train had long passed Hornberg, and far below the streams tumbled in white foam down the limestone rocks. In front of him, dome upon dome of wooded mountain stood against the sky. It was October, and the air was cool and sharp, wood-smoke and damp moss exquisitely mingled in it with the subtle odours of the pines. Overhead, between the tips of the highest firs, he saw the first stars peeping, and the sky was a clean, pale amethyst that seemed exactly the colour all these memories clothed themselves with in his mind.

He leaned back in his corner and sighed. He was a heavy man, and he had not known sentiment for years; he was a big man, and it took much to move him, literally and figuratively; he was a man in whom the dreams of God that haunt the soul in youth, though overlaid by the scum that gathers in the fight for money, had not, as with the majority, utterly died the death.

He came back into this little neglected pocket of the years, where so much fine gold had collected and lain undisturbed, with all his semi-spiritual emotions aquiver; and, as he watched the mountain-tops come nearer, and smelt the forgotten odours of his boyhood, something melted on the surface of his soul and left him sensitive to a degree he had not known since, thirty years before, he had lived here with his dreams, his conflicts, and his youthful suffering.

A thrill ran through him as the train stopped with a jolt at a tiny station and he saw the name in large black lettering on the grey stone building, and below it, the number of metres it stood above the level of the sea.

'The highest point on the line!' he exclaimed. 'How well I remember it—Sommerau—Summer Meadow. The very next station is mine!'

And, as the train ran downhill with brakes on and steam shut off, he put his head out of the window and one by one saw the old familiar landmarks in the dusk. They stared at him like dead faces in a dream. Queer, sharp feelings, half poignant, half sweet, stirred in his heart.

'There's the hot, white road we walked along so often with the two Brüder always at our heels,' he thought; 'and there, by Jove, is the turn through the forest to "*Die Galgen*", the stone gallows where they hanged the witches in olden days!'

He smiled a little as the train slid past.

'And there's the copse where the Lilies of the Valley powdered the ground in spring; and, I swear,'—he put his head out with a sudden impulse,—'if that's not the very clearing where Calame, the French boy, chased the swallow-tail with me, and Bruder Pagel gave us half-rations for leaving the road without permission, and for shouting in our mother tongues!' And he laughed again as the memories came back with a rush, flooding his mind with vivid detail.

The train stopped, and he stood on the grey gravel platform like a man in a dream. It seemed half a century since he last waited there with corded wooden boxes, and got into the train for Strassbourg and home after the two years' exile. Time dropped from him like an old garment and he felt a boy again. Only, things looked so much smaller than his memory of them; shrunk and dwindled they looked, and the distances seemed on a curiously smaller scale.

He made his way across the road to the little Gasthaus, and, as he went, faces and figures of former schoolfellows,—German, Swiss, Italian, French, Russian,—slipped out of the shadowy woods and silently accompanied him. They flitted by his side, raising their eyes questioningly, sadly, to his. But their names he had forgotten. Some of the Brothers, too, came with them, and most of these he remembered by name—Bruder Röst, Bruder Pagel, Bruder Schliemann, and the bearded face of the old preacher who had seen himself in the haunted gallery of those about to die—Bruder Gysin. The dark forest lay all about him like a sea that any moment might rush with velvet waves upon the scene and sweep all the faces away. The air was cool and wonderfully fragrant, but with every perfumed breath came also a pallid memory. . . .

Yet, in spite of the underlying sadness inseparable from such an experience, it was all very interesting, and held a pleasure peculiarly its own, so that Harris engaged his room and ordered supper feeling well pleased with himself, and intending to walk up to the old school that very evening. It stood in the centre of the community's village, some four miles distant through the forest, and he now recollected for the first time that this little Protestant settlement dwelt isolated in a section of the country that was otherwise Catholic. Crucifixes and shrines surrounded the clearing like the sentries of a beleaguring army. Once beyond the square of the village, with its few acres of field and orchard, the forest crowded up in solid phalanxes, and beyond the rim of trees began the country that was ruled by the priests of another faith. He vaguely remembered, too, that the Catholics had showed sometimes a certain hostility towards the little Protestant oasis that flourished so quietly and benignly in their midst. He had quite forgotten this. How trumpery it all seemed now with his wide experience of life and his knowledge of other countries and the great outside world. It was like stepping back, not thirty years, but three hundred.

There were only two others besides himself at supper. One of them, a bearded, middle-aged man in tweeds, sat by himself at the far end, and Harris kept out of his way because he was English. He feared he might be in business, possibly even in the silk business, and that he would perhaps talk on the subject. The other traveller, however, was a Catholic priest. He was a little man who ate his salad with a knife, yet so gently that it was almost inoffensive, and it was the sight of 'the cloth' that recalled his memory of the old antagonism. Harris mentioned by way of conversation the object of his sentimental journey, and the priest looked up sharply at him with raised eyebrows and an expression of surprise and suspicion that somehow piqued him. He ascribed it to his difference of belief.

'Yes,' went on the silk merchant, pleased to talk of what his mind was so full, 'and it was a curious experience for an English boy to be dropped down into a school of a hundred foreigners. I well remember the loneliness and intolerable Heimweh* of it at first.' His German was very fluent.

The priest opposite looked up from his cold veal and potato salad and smiled. It was a nice face. He explained quietly that he did not belong here, but was making a tour of the parishes of Württemberg and Baden.

'It was a strict life,' added Harris. 'We English, I remember, used to call it *Gefängnisleben*—prison life!'

The face of the other, for some unaccountable reason, darkened. After a slight pause, and more by way of politeness than because he wished to continue the subject, he said quietly—

'It was a flourishing school in those days, of course. Afterwards, I have heard——' He shrugged his shoulders slightly, and the odd look—it almost seemed a look of alarm—came back into his eyes. The sentence remained unfinished.

Something in the tone of the man seemed to his listener uncalled for—in a sense reproachful, singular. Harris bridled in spite of himself.

'It has changed?' he asked. 'I can hardly believe——'

'You have not heard, then?' observed the priest gently, making a gesture as though to cross himself, yet not actually completing it. 'You have not heard what happened there before it was abandoned?'

It was very childish, of course, and perhaps he was overtired and overwrought in some way, but the words and manner of the little priest seemed to him so offensive—so disproportionately offensive—that he hardly noticed the concluding sentence. He recalled the old bitterness and the old antagonism, and for a moment he almost lost his temper.

'Nonsense,' he interrupted with a forced laugh, '*Unsinn!** You must forgive me, sir, for contradicting you. But I was a pupil there myself. I was at school there. There was no place like it. I cannot believe that anything serious could have happened to—to take away its character. The devotion of the Brothers would be difficult to equal anywhere.'

He broke off suddenly, realising that his voice had been raised unduly and that the man at the far end of the table might understand German; and at the same moment he looked up and saw that this individual's eyes were fixed upon his face intently. They were peculiarly bright. Also they were rather wonderful eyes, and the way they met his own served in some way he could not understand to convey both a reproach and a warning. The whole face of the stranger, indeed, made a vivid impression upon him, for it was a face, he now noticed for the first time, in whose presence one would not willingly have said or done anything unworthy. Harris could not explain to himself how it was he had not become conscious sooner of its presence.

But he could have bitten off his tongue for having so far forgotten himself. The little priest lapsed into silence. Only once he said, looking up and speaking in a low voice that was not intended to be overheard, but that evidently *was* overheard, 'You will find it different.' Presently he rose and left the table with a polite bow that included both the others.

And, after him, from the far end rose also the figure in the tweed suit, leaving Harris by himself.

He sat on for a bit in the darkening room, sipping his coffee and smoking his fifteen-pfennig cigar, till the girl came in to light the oil lamps. He felt vexed with himself for his lapse from good manners, yet hardly able to account for it. Most likely, he reflected, he had been annoyed because the priest had unintentionally changed the pleasant character of his dream by introducing a jarring note. Later he must seek an opportunity to make amends. At present, however, he was too impatient for his walk to the school, and he took his stick and hat and passed out into the open air.

And, as he crossed before the Gasthaus, he noticed that the priest and the man in the tweed suit were engaged already in such deep conversation that they hardly noticed him as he passed and raised his hat.

He started off briskly, well remembering the way, and hoping to reach the village in time to have a word with one of the Brüder. They might even ask him in for a cup of coffee. He felt sure of his welcome, and the old memories were in full possession once more. The hour of return was a matter of no consequence whatever.

It was then just after seven o'clock, and the October evening was drawing in with chill airs from the recesses of the forest. The road plunged straight from the railway clearing into its depths, and in a very few minutes the trees engulfed him and the clack of his boots fell dead and echoless against the serried stems of a million firs. It was very black; one trunk was hardly distinguishable from another. He walked smartly, swinging his holly stick. Once or twice he passed a peasant on his way to bed, and the guttural 'Gruss Got,'* unheard for so long, emphasised the passage of time, while yet making it seem as nothing. A fresh group of pictures crowded his mind. Again the figures of former schoolfellows flitted out of the forest and kept pace by his side, whispering of the doings of long ago. One reverie stepped hard upon the heels of another. Every turn in the road, every clearing of the forest, he knew, and each in turn brought forgotten associations to life. He enjoyed himself thoroughly.

He marched on and on. There was powdered gold in the sky till the moon rose, and then a wind of faint silver spread silently between the earth and stars. He saw the tips of the fir trees shimmer, and heard them whisper as the breeze turned their needles towards the light. The mountain air was indescribably sweet. The road shone like the foam of a river through the gloom. White moths flitted here and there like silent thoughts across his path, and a hundred smells greeted him from the forest caverns across the years.

Then, when he least expected it, the trees fell away abruptly on both sides, and he stood on the edge of the village-clearing.

He walked faster. There lay the familiar outlines of the houses, sheeted with silver; there stood the trees in the little central square with the fountain and small green lawns; there loomed the shape of the church next to the Gasthof der Brüdergemeinde;* and just beyond, dimly rising into the sky, he saw with a sudden thrill the mass of the huge school building, blocked castle-like with deep shadows in the moonlight, standing square and formidable to face him after the silences of more than a quarter of a century.

He passed quickly down the deserted village street and stopped close beneath its shadow, staring up at the walls that had once held him prisoner for two years—two unbroken years of discipline and homesickness. Memories and emotions surged through his mind; for the most vivid sensations of his youth had focused about this spot, and it was here he had first begun to live and learn values. Not a single footstep broke the silence, though lights glimmered here and there through cottage windows; but when he looked up at the high walls of the school, draped now in shadow, he easily imagined that well-known faces crowded to the windows to greet him—closed windows that really reflected only moonlight and the gleam of stars.

This, then, was the old school building, standing foursquare to the world, with its shuttered windows, its lofty, tiled roof, and the spiked lightning-conductors pointing like black and taloned fingers from the corners. For a long time he stood and stared. Then, presently, he came to himself again, and realised to his joy that a light still shone in the windows of the *Bruderstube.**

He turned from the road and passed through the iron railings; then climbed the twelve stone steps and stood facing the black wooden door with the heavy bars of iron, a door he had once loathed and dreaded with the hatred and passion of an imprisoned soul, but now looked upon tenderly with a sort of boyish delight.

Almost timorously he pulled the rope and listened with a tremor of excitement to the clanging of the bell deep within the building. And the long-forgotten sound brought the past before him with such a vivid sense of reality that he positively shivered. It was like the magic bell in the fairy-tale that rolls back the curtain of Time and summons the figures from the shadows of the dead. He had never felt so sentimental in his life. It was like being young again. And, at the same time, he began to bulk rather large in his own eyes with a certain spurious importance. He was a big man from the world of strife and action. In this little place of peaceful dreams would he, perhaps, not cut something of a figure?

'I'll try once more,' he thought after a long pause, seizing the iron bell-rope, and was just about to pull it when a step sounded on the stone passage within, and the huge door slowly swung open.

A tall man with a rather severe cast of countenance stood facing him in silence.

'I must apologise—it is somewhat late,' he began a trifle pompously, 'but the fact is I am an old pupil. I have only just arrived and really could not restrain myself.' His German seemed not quite so fluent as usual. 'My interest is so great. I was here in '70.'

The other opened the door wider and at once bowed him in with a smile of genuine welcome.

'I am Bruder Kalkmann,' he said quietly in a deep voice. 'I myself was a master here about that time. It is a great pleasure always to welcome a former pupil.' He looked at him very keenly for a few seconds, and then added, 'I think, too, it is splendid of you to come—very splendid.'

'It is a very great pleasure,' Harris replied, delighted with his reception.

The dimly-lighted corridor with its flooring of grey stone, and the familiar sound of a German voice echoing through it,—with the peculiar intonation the Brothers always used in speaking,—all combined to lift him bodily, as it were, into the dream-atmosphere of long-forgotten days. He stepped gladly into the building and the door shut with the familiar thunder that completed the reconstruction of the past. He almost felt the old sense of imprisonment, of aching nostalgia, of having lost his liberty.

Harris sighed involuntarily and turned towards his host, who returned his smile faintly and then led the way down the corridor.

'The boys have retired,' he explained, 'and, as you remember, we keep early hours here. But, at least, you will join us for a little while in the *Bruderstube* and enjoy a cup of coffee.' This was precisely what the silk merchant had hoped, and he accepted with an alacrity that he intended to be tempered by graciousness. 'And tomorrow,' continued the Bruder, 'you must come and spend a whole day with us. You may even find acquaintances, for several pupils of your day have come back here as masters.'

For one brief second there passed into the man's eyes a look that made the visitor start. But it vanished as quickly as it came. It was impossible to define. Harris convinced himself it was the effect of a shadow cast by the lamp they had just passed on the wall. He dismissed it from his mind.

'You are very kind, I'm sure,' he said politely. 'It is perhaps a greater pleasure to me than you can imagine to see the place again. Ah,'—he stopped short opposite a door with the upper half of glass and peered in—'surely there is one of the music rooms where I used to practise the violin. How it comes back to me after all these years!'

Bruder Kalkmann stopped indulgently, smiling, to allow his guest a moment's inspection.

'You still have the boys' orchestra? I remember I used to play "*zweite Geige*"* in it. Bruder Schliemann conducted at the piano. Dear me, I can see him now with his long black hair and—and——'

He stopped abruptly. Again the odd, dark look passed over the stern face of his companion. For an instant it seemed curiously familiar.

'We still keep up the pupils' orchestra,' he said, 'but Bruder Schliemann, I am sorry to say——'

He hesitated an instant, and then added, 'Bruder Schliemann is dead.'

'Indeed, indeed,' said Harris quickly. 'I am sorry to hear it.' He was conscious of a faint feeling of distress, but whether it arose from the news of his old music teacher's death, or—from something else—he could not quite determine. He gazed down the corridor that lost itself among shadows. In the street and village everything had seemed so much smaller than he remembered, but here, inside the school building, everything seemed so much bigger. The corridor was loftier and longer, more spacious and vast, than the mental picture he had preserved. His thoughts wandered dreamily for an instant.

He glanced up and saw the face of the Bruder watching him with a smile of patient indulgence.

'Your memories possess you,' he observed gently, and the stern look passed into something almost pitying.

'You are right,' returned the man of silk, 'they do. This was the most wonderful period of my whole life in a sense. At the time I hated it——'

He hesitated, not wishing to hurt the Brother's feelings.

'According to English ideas it seemed strict, of course,' the other said persuasively, so that he went on.

'——Yes, partly that; and partly the ceaseless nostalgia, and the solitude which came from never being really alone. In English schools the boys enjoy peculiar freedom, you know.'

Bruder Kalkmann, he saw, was listening intently.

'But it produced one result that I have never wholly lost,' he continued self-consciously, 'and am grateful for.'

'*Ach! Wie so, denn?*'*

'The constant inner pain threw me headlong into your religious life, so that the whole force of my being seemed to project itself towards the search for a deeper satisfaction—a real resting-place for the soul. During my two years here I yearned for God in my boyish way as perhaps I have never yearned for anything since. Moreover, I have never quite lost that sense of peace and inward joy which accompanied the search. I can never quite forget this school and the deep things it taught me.'

He paused at the end of his long speech, and a brief silence fell between them. He feared he had said too much, or expressed himself clumsily in the foreign language, and when Bruder Kalkmann laid a hand upon his shoulder, he gave a little involuntary start.

'So that my memories perhaps do possess me rather strongly,' he added apologetically; 'and this long corridor, these rooms, that barred and gloomy front door, all touch chords that—that——' His German failed him and he glanced at his companion with an explanatory smile and gesture. But the brother had removed the hand from his shoulder and was standing with his back to him, looking down the passage.

'Naturally, naturally so,' he said hastily without turning round. '*Es ist doch Selbstverständlich.*'* We shall all understand.'

Then he turned suddenly, and Harris saw that his face had turned most oddly and disagreeably sinister. It may only have been the shadows again playing their tricks with the wretched oil lamps on the wall, for the dark expression passed instantly as they retraced their steps down the corridor, but the Englishman somehow got the impression that he had said something to give offence, something that was not quite to the other's taste. Opposite the door of the *Bruderstube* they stopped. Harris realised that it was late and he had possibly stayed talking too long. He made a tentative effort to leave, but his companion would not hear of it.

'You must have a cup of coffee with us,' he said firmly as though he meant it, 'and my colleagues will be delighted to see you. Some of them will remember you, perhaps.'

The sound of voices came pleasantly through the door, men's voices talking together. Bruder Kalkmann turned the handle and they entered a room ablaze with light and full of people.

'Ah,—but your name?' he whispered, bending down to catch the reply; 'you have not told me your name yet.'

'Harris,' said the Englishman quickly as they went in. He felt nervous as he crossed the threshold, but ascribed the momentary trepidation to the fact that he was breaking the strictest rule of the whole establishment, which forbade a boy under severest penalties to come near this holy of holies where the masters took their brief leisure.

'Ah, yes, of course—Harris,' repeated the other as though he remembered it. 'Come in, Herr Harris, come in, please. Your visit will be immensely appreciated. It is really very fine, very wonderful of you to have come in this way.'

The door closed behind them and, in the sudden light which made his sight swim for a moment, the exaggeration of the language escaped his attention. He heard the voice of Bruder Kalkmann introducing him. He spoke very loud, indeed, unnecessarily,—absurdly loud, Harris thought.

'Brothers,' he announced, 'it is my pleasure and privilege to introduce to you Herr Harris from England. He has just arrived to make us a little visit, and I have already expressed to him on behalf of us all the satisfaction we feel that he is here. He was, as you remember, a pupil in the year '70.'

It was a very formal, a very German introduction, but Harris rather liked it. It made him feel important and he appreciated the tact that made it almost seem as though he had been expected.

The black forms rose and bowed; Harris bowed; Kalkmann bowed. Every one was very polite and very courtly. The room swam with moving figures; the light dazzled him after the gloom of the corridor; there was thick cigar smoke in the atmosphere. He took the chair that was offered to him between two of the Brothers, and sat down, feeling vaguely that his perceptions were not quite as keen and accurate as usual. He felt a trifle dazed perhaps, and the spell of the past came strongly over him, confusing the immediate present and making everything dwindle oddly to the dimensions of long ago. He seemed to pass under the mastery of a great mood that was a composite reproduction of all the moods of his forgotten boyhood.

Then he pulled himself together with a sharp effort and entered into the conversation that had begun again to buzz round him. Moreover, he entered into it with keen pleasure, for the Brothers—there were perhaps a dozen of them in the little room—treated him with a charm of manner that speedily made him feel one of themselves. This, again, was a very subtle delight to him. He felt that he had stepped out of the greedy, vulgar, self-seeking world, the world of silk and markets and profit-making—stepped into the cleaner atmosphere where spiritual ideals were paramount and life was simple and devoted. It all charmed him inexpressibly, so that he realised—yes, in a sense—the degradation of his twenty years' absorption in business. This keen atmosphere under the stars where men thought only of their souls, and of the souls of others, was too rarefied for the world he was now associated with. He found himself making comparisons to his own disadvantage.—comparisons with the mystical little dreamer that had stepped thirty years before from the stern peace of this devout community, and the man of the world that he had since become,—and the contrast made him shiver with a keen regret and something like self-contempt.

He glanced round at the other faces floating towards him through tobacco smoke—this acrid cigar smoke he remembered so well: how keen they were, how strong, placid, touched with the nobility of great aims and unselfish purposes. At one or two he looked particularly. He hardly knew why. They rather fascinated him. There was something so very stern and uncompromising about them, and something, too, oddly, subtly, familiar, that yet just eluded him. But whenever their eyes met his own they held undeniable welcome in them; and some held more—a kind of perplexed admiration, he thought, something that was between esteem and deference. This note of respect in all the faces was very flattering to his vanity.

Coffee was served presently, made by a black-haired Brother who sat in the corner by the piano and bore a marked resemblance to Bruder Schliemann, the musical director of thirty years ago. Harris exchanged bows with him when he took the cup from his white hands, which he noticed were like the hands of a woman. He lit a cigar, offered to him by his neighbour, with whom he was chatting delightfully, and who, in the glare of the lighted match, reminded him sharply for a moment of Bruder Pagel, his former room-master.

'*Es ist wirklich merkwürdig*,'* he said, 'how many resemblances I see, or imagine. It is really *very* curious!'

'Yes,' replied the other, peering at him over his coffee cup, 'the spell of the place is wonderfully strong. I can well understand that the old faces rise before your mind's eye—almost to the exclusion of ourselves perhaps.'

They both laughed pleasantly. It was soothing to find his mood understood and appreciated. And they passed on to talk of the mountain village, its isolation its remoteness from worldly life, its peculiar fitness for meditation and worship, and for spiritual development—of a certain kind.

'And your coming back in this way, Herr Harris, has pleased us all so much,' joined in the Bruder on his left. 'We esteem you for it most highly. We honour you for it.'

Harris made a deprecating gesture. 'I fear, for my part, it is only a very selfish pleasure,' he said a trifle unctuously.

'Not all would have had the courage,' added the one who resembled Bruder Pagel.

'You mean,' said Harris, a little puzzled, 'the disturbing memories——?'

Bruder Pagel looked at him steadily, with unmistakable admiration and respect. 'I mean that most men hold so strongly to life, and can give up so little for their beliefs,' he said gravely.

The Englishman felt slightly uncomfortable. These worthy men really made too much of his sentimental journey. Besides, the talk was getting a little out of his depth. He hardly followed it.

'The worldly life still has *some* charms for me,' he replied smilingly, as though to indicate that sainthood was not yet quite within his grasp.

'All the more, then, must we honour you for so freely coming,' said the Brother on his left; 'so unconditionally!'

A pause followed, and the silk merchant felt relieved when the conversation took a more general turn, although he noted that it never travelled very far from the subject of his visit and the wonderful situation of the lonely village for men who wished to develop their spiritual powers and practise the rites of a high worship. Others joined in, complimenting him on his knowledge of the language, making him feel utterly at his ease, yet at the same time a little uncomfortable by the excess of their admiration. After all, it was such a very small thing to do, this sentimental journey.

The time passed along quickly; the coffee was excellent, the cigars soft and of the nutty flavour he loved. At length, fearing to outstay his welcome, he rose reluctantly to take his leave. But the others would not hear of it. It was not often a former pupil returned to visit them in this simple, unaffected way. The night was young. If necessary they could even find him a corner in the great *Schlafzimmer** upstairs.

He was easily persuaded to stay a little longer. Somehow he had become the centre of the little party. He felt pleased, flattered, honoured.

'And perhaps Bruder Schliemann will play something for us—now.'

It was Kalkmann speaking, and Harris started visibly as he heard the name, and saw the black-haired man by the piano turn with a smile. For Schliemann was the name of his old music director, who was dead. Could this be his son? They were so exactly alike.

'If Bruder Meyer has not put his Amati* to bed, I will accompany him,' said the musician suggestively, looking across at a man whom Harris had not yet noticed, and who, he now saw, was the very image of a former master of that name.

Meyer rose and excused himself with a little bow, and the Englishman quickly observed that he had a peculiar gesture as though his neck had a false join on to the body just below the collar and feared it might break. Meyer of old had this trick of movement. He remembered how the boys used to copy it.

He glanced sharply from face to face, feeling as though some silent, unseen process were changing everything about him. All the faces seemed oddly familiar. Pagel, the Brother he had been talking with, was of course the image of Pagel, his former room-master; and Kalkmann, he now realised for the first time, was the very twin of another master whose name he had quite forgotten, but whom he used to dislike intensely in the old days. And, through the smoke, peering at him from the corners of the room, he saw that all the Brothers about him had the faces he had known and lived with long ago—Röst, Fluheim, Meinert, Rigel, Gysin.

He stared hard, suddenly grown more alert, and everywhere saw, or fancied he saw, strange likenesses, ghostly resemblances,—more, the identical faces of years ago. There was something queer about it all, something not quite right, something that made him feel uneasy. He shook himself, mentally and actually, blowing the smoke from before his eyes with a long breath, and as he did so he noticed to his dismay that every one was fixedly staring. They were watching him.

This brought him to his senses. As an Englishman, and a foreigner, he did not wish to be rude, or to do anything to make himself foolishly conspicuous and spoil the harmony of the evening. He was a guest, and a privileged guest at that. Besides, the music had already begun.

Bruder Schliemann's long white fingers were caressing the keys to some purpose.

He subsided into his chair and smoked with half-closed eyes that yet saw everything.

But the shudder had established itself in his being, and, whether he would or not, it kept repeating itself. As a town, far up some inland river, feels the pressure of the distant sea, so he became aware that mighty forces from somewhere beyond his ken were urging themselves up against his soul in this smoky little room. He began to feel exceedingly ill at ease.

And as the music filled the air his mind began to clear. Like a lifted veil there rose up something that had hitherto obscured his vision. The words of the priest at the railway inn flashed across his brain unbidden: 'You will find it different.' And also, though why he could not tell, he saw mentally the strong, rather wonderful eyes of that other guest at the supper-table, the man who had overhead his conversation, and had later got into earnest talk with the priest. He took out his watch and stole a glance at it. Two hours had slipped by. It was already eleven o'clock.

Schliemann, meanwhile, utterly absorbed in his music, was playing a solemn measure. The piano sang marvellously. The power of a great conviction, the simplicity of great art, the vital spiritual message of a soul that had found itself—all this, and more, were in the chords, and yet somehow the music was what can only be described as impure—atrociously and diabolically impure. And the piece itself, although Harris did not recognise it as anything familiar, was surely the music of a Mass—huge, majestic, sombre? It stalked through the smoky room with slow power, like the passage of something that was mighty, yet profoundly intimate, and as it went there stirred into each and every face about him the signature of the enormous forces of which it was the audible symbol. The countenances round him turned sinister, but not idly, negatively sinister: they grew dark with purpose. He suddenly recalled the face of Bruder Kalkmann in the corridor earlier in the evening. The motives of their secret souls rose to the eyes, and mouths, and foreheads, and hung there for all to see like the black banners of an assembly of ill-starred and fallen creatures. Demons—was the horrible word that flashed through his brain like a sheet of fire.

When this sudden discovery leaped out upon him, for a moment he lost his self-control. Without waiting to think and weigh his extraordinary impression, he did a very foolish but a very natural thing. Feeling himself irresistibly driven by the sudden stress to some kind of action, he sprang to his feet—and screamed! To his own utter amazement he stood up and shrieked aloud!

But no one stirred. No one, apparently, took the slightest notice of his absurdly wild behaviour. It was almost as if no one but himself had heard the scream at all—as though the music had drowned it and swallowed it up—as though after all perhaps he had not really screamed as loudly as he imagined, or had not screamed at all.

Then, as he glanced at the motionless, dark faces before him, something of utter cold passed into his being, touching his very soul. . . . All emotion cooled suddenly, leaving him like a receding tide. He sat down again, ashamed, mortified, angry with himself for behaving like a fool and a boy. And the music, meanwhile, continued to issue from the white and snake-like fingers of Bruder Schliemann, as poisoned wine might issue from the weirdly-fashioned necks of antique phials.

And, with the rest of them, Harris drank it in.

Forcing himself to believe that he had been the victim of some kind of illusory perception, he vigorously restrained his feelings. Then the music presently ceased, and every one applauded and began to talk at once, laughing, changing seats, complimenting the player, and behaving naturally and easily as though nothing out of the way had happened. The faces appeared normal once more. The Brothers crowded round their visitor, and he joined in their talk and even heard himself thanking the gifted musician.

But, at the same time, he found himself edging towards the door, nearer and nearer, changing his chair when possible, and joining the groups that stood closest to the way of escape.

'I must thank you all *tausendmal** for my little reception and the great pleasure—the very great honour you have done me,' he began in decided tones at length, 'but I fear I have trespassed far too long already on your hospitality. Moreover, I have some distance to walk to my inn.'

A chorus of voices greeted his words. They would not hear of his going,—at least not without first partaking of refreshment. They produced pumpernickel from one cupboard, and rye-bread and sausage from another, and all began to talk again and eat. More coffee was made, fresh cigars lighted, and Bruder Meyer took out his violin and began to tune it softly.

'There is always a bed upstairs if Herr Harris will accept it,' said one.

'And it is difficult to find the way out now, for all the doors are locked,' laughed another loudly.

'Let us take our simple pleasures as they come,' cried a third. 'Bruder Harris will understand how we appreciate the honour of this last visit of his.'

They made a dozen excuses. They all laughed, as though the politeness of their words was but formal, and veiled thinly—more and more thinly—a very different meaning.

'And the hour of midnight draws near,' added Bruder Kalkmann with a charming smile, but in a voice that sounded to the Englishman like the grating of iron hinges.

Their German seemed to him more and more difficult to understand. He noted that they called him 'Bruder' too, classing him as one of themselves.

And then suddenly he had a flash of keener perception, and realised with a creeping of his flesh that he had all along misinterpreted—grossly misinterpreted all they had been saying. They had talked about the beauty of the place, its isolation and remoteness from the world, its peculiar fitness for certain kinds of spiritual development and worship—yet hardly, he now grasped, in the sense in which he had taken the words. They had meant something different. Their spiritual powers, their desire for loneliness, their passion for worship, were not the powers, the solitude, or the worship that *he* meant and understood. He was playing a part in some horrible masquerade; he was among men who cloaked their lives with religion in order to follow their real purposes unseen of men.

What did it all mean? How had he blundered into so equivocal a situation? Had he blundered into it at all? Had he not rather been led into it, deliberately led? His thoughts grew dreadfully confused, and his confidence in himself began to fade. And why, he suddenly thought again, were they so impressed by the mere fact of his coming to revisit his old school? What was it they so admired and wondered at in his simple act? Why did they set such store upon his having the courage to come, to 'give himself so freely,' 'unconditionally' as one of them had expressed it with such a mockery of exaggeration?

Fear stirred in his heart most horribly, and he found no answer to any of his questionings. Only one thing he now understood quite clearly: it was their purpose to keep him here. They did not intend that he should go. And from this moment he realised that they were sinister, formidable and, in some way he had yet to discover, inimical to himself, inimical to his life. And the phrase one of them had used a moment ago—'this *last* visit of his'—rose before his eyes in letters of flame.

Harris was not a man of action, and had never known in all the course of his career what it meant to be in a situation of real danger. He was not necessarily a coward, though, perhaps, a man of untried nerve. He realised at last plainly that he was in a very awkward predicament indeed, and that he had to deal with men who were utterly in earnest. What their intentions were he only vaguely guessed. His mind, indeed, was too confused for definite ratiocination, and he was only able to follow blindly the strongest instincts that moved in him. It never occurred to him that the Brothers might all be mad, or that he himself might have temporarily lost his senses and be suffering under some terrible delusion. In fact, nothing occurred to him—he realised nothing—except that he meant to escape—and the quicker the better. A tremendous revulsion of feeling set in and overpowered him.

Accordingly, without further protest for the moment, he ate his pumpernickel and drank his coffee, talking meanwhile as naturally and pleasantly as he could, and when a suitable interval had passed, he rose to his feet and announced once more that he must now take his leave. He spoke very quietly, but very decidedly. No one hearing him could doubt that he meant what he said. He had got very close to the door by this time.

'I regret,' he said, using his best German, and speaking to a hushed room, 'that our pleasant evening must come to an end, but it is now time for me to wish you all good-night.' And then, as no one said anything, he added, though with a trifle less assurance, 'And I thank you all most sincerely for your hospitality.'

'On the contrary,' replied Kalkmann instantly, rising from his chair and ignoring the hand the Englishman had stretched out to him, 'it is we who have to thank you; and we do so most gratefully and sincerely.'

And at the same moment at least half a dozen of the Brothers took up their position between himself and the door.

'You are very good to say so,' Harris replied as firmly as he could manage, noticing this movement out of the corner of his eye, 'but really I had no conception that—my little chance visit could have afforded you so much pleasure.' He moved another step nearer the door, but Bruder Schliemann came across the room quickly and stood in front of him. His attitude was uncompromising. A dark and terrible expression had come into his face.

'But it was *not* by chance that you came, Bruder Harris,' he said so that all the room could hear; 'surely we have not misunderstood your presence here?' He raised his black eyebrows.

'No, no,' the Englishman hastened to reply, 'I was—I am delighted to be here. I told you what pleasure it gave me to find myself among you. Do not misunderstand me, I beg.' His voice faltered a little, and he had difficulty in finding the words. More and more, too, he had difficulty in understanding *their* words.

'Of course,' interposed Bruder Kalkmann in his iron bass, '*we* have not misunderstood. You have come back in the spirit of true and unselfish devotion. You offer yourself freely, and we all appreciate it. It is your willingness and nobility that have so completely won our veneration and respect.' A faint murmur of applause ran round the room. 'What we all delight in—what our great Master will especially delight in—is the value of your spontaneous and voluntary——'

He used a word Harris did not understand. He said '*Opfer.*' The bewildered Englishman searched his brain for the translation, and searched in vain. For the life of him he could not remember what it meant. But the word, for all his inability to translate it, touched his soul with ice. It was worse, far worse, than anything he had imagined. He felt like a lost, helpless creature, and all power to fight sank out of him from that moment.

'It is magnificent to be such a willing——' added Schliemann, sidling up to him with a dreadful leer on his face. He made use of the same word—'*Opfer.*'

God! What could it all mean? 'Offer himself!' 'True spirit of devotion!' 'Willing,' 'unselfish,' 'magnificent!' *Opfer, Opfer, Opfer!* What in the name of heaven did it mean, that strange, mysterious word that struck such terror into his heart?

He made a valiant effort to keep his presence of mind and hold his nerves steady. Turning, he saw that Kalkmann's face was a dead white. Kalkmann! He understood that well enough. *Kalkmann* meant 'Man of Chalk'; he knew that. But what did '*Opfer*' mean? That was the real key to the situation. Words poured through his disordered mind in an endless stream—unusual, rare words he had perhaps heard but once in his life—while '*Opfer*' a word in common use, entirely escaped him. What an extraordinary mockery it all was!

Then Kalkmann, pale as death, but his face hard as iron, spoke a few low words that he did not catch, and the Brothers standing by the walls at once turned the lamps down so that the room became dim. In the half light he could only just discern their faces and movements.

'It is time,' he heard Kalkmann's remorseless voice continue just behind him. 'The hour of midnight is at hand. Let us prepare. He comes! He comes; Bruder Asmodelius* comes!' His voice rose to a chant.

And the sound of that name, for some extraordinary reason, was terrible—utterly terrible; so that Harris shook from head to foot as he heard it. Its utterance filled the air like soft thunder, and a hush came over the whole room. Forces rose all about him, transforming the normal into the horrible, and the spirit of craven fear ran through all his being, bringing him to the verge of collapse.

Asmodelius! Asmodelius! The name was appalling. For he understood at last to whom it referred and the meaning that lay between its great syllables. At the same instant, too, he suddenly understood the meaning of that unremembered word. The import of the word '*Opfer*' flashed upon his soul* like a message of death.

He thought of making a wild effort to reach the door, but the weakness of his trembling knees, and the row of black figures that stood between, dissuaded him at once. He would have screamed for help, but remembering the emptiness of the vast building, and the loneliness of the situation, he understood that no help could come that way, and he kept his lips closed. He stood still and did nothing. But he knew now what was coming.

Two of the brothers approached and took him gently by the arm.

'Bruder Asmodelius accepts you,' they whispered; 'are you ready?'

Then he found his tongue and tried to speak. 'But what have I to do with this Bruder Asm—Asmo——?' he stammered, a desperate rush of words crowding vainly behind the halting tongue.

The name refused to pass his lips. He could not pronounce it as they did. He could not pronounce it at all. His sense of helplessness then entered the acute stage, for this inability to speak the name produced a fresh sense of quite horrible confusion in his mind, and he became extraordinarily agitated.

'I came here for a friendly visit,' he tried to say with a great effort, but, to his intense dismay, he heard his voice saying something quite different, and actually making use of that very word they had all used: 'I came here as a willing *Opfer*,' he heard his own voice say, 'and *I am quite ready*.'

He was lost beyond all recall now! Not alone his mind, but the very muscles of his body had passed out of control. He felt that he was hovering on the confines of a phantom or demonworld,—a world in which the name they had spoken constituted the Master-name, the word of ultimate power.

What followed he heard and saw as in a night mare.

'In the half light that veils all truth, let us prepare to worship and adore,' chanted Schliemann, who had preceded him to the end of the room.

'In the mists that protect our faces before the Black Throne, let us make ready the willing victim,' echoed Kalkmann in his great bass.

They raised their faces, listening expectantly, as a roaring sound, like the passing of mighty projectiles, filled the air, far, far away, very wonderful, very forbidding. The walls of the room trembled.

'He comes! He comes! He comes!' chanted the Brothers in chorus.

The sound of roaring died away, and an atmosphere of still and utter cold established itself over all. Then Kalkmann, dark and unutterably stern, turned in the dim light and faced the rest.

'Asmodelius, our *Hauptbruder*,* is about us,' he cried in a voice that even while it shook was yet a voice of iron; 'Asmodelius is about us. Make ready.'

There followed a pause in which no one stirred or spoke. A tall Brother approached the Englishman; but Kalkmann held up his hand.

'Let the eyes remain uncovered,' he said, 'in honour of so freely giving himself.' And to his horror Harris then realised for the first time that his hands were already fastened to his sides.

The Brother retreated again silently, and in the pause that followed all the figures about him dropped to their knees, leaving him standing alone, and as they dropped, in voices hushed with mingled reverence and awe, they cried softly, odiously, appallingly, the name of the Being whom they momentarily expected to appear.

Then, at the end of the room, where the windows seemed to have disappeared so that he saw the stars, there rose into view far up against the night sky, grand and terrible, the outline of a man. A kind of grey glory enveloped it so that it resembled a steel-cased statue, immense, imposing, horrific in its distant splendour; while, at the same time, the face was so spiritually mighty, yet so proudly, so austerely sad, that Harris felt as he stared, that the sight was more than his eyes could meet, and that in another moment the power of vision would fail him altogether, and he must sink into utter nothingness.

So remote and inaccessible hung this figure that it was impossible to gauge anything as to its size, yet at the same time so strangely close, that when the grey radiance from its mightily broken visage, august and mournful, beat down upon his soul, pulsing like some dark star with the powers of spiritual evil, he felt almost as though he were looking into a face no farther removed from him in space than the face of any one of the Brothers who stood by his side.

And then the room filled and trembled with sounds that Harris understood full well were the failing voices of others who had preceded him in a long series down the years. There came first a plain, sharp cry, as of a man in the last anguish, choking for his breath, and yet, with the very final expiration of it, breathing the name of the Worship—of the dark Being who rejoiced to hear it. The cries of the strangled; the short, running gasp of the suffocated; and the smothered gurgling of the tightened throat, all these, and more, echoed back and forth between the walls, the very walls in which he now stood a prisoner, a sacrificial victim. The cries, too, not alone of the broken bodies, but—far worse—of beaten, broken souls. And as the ghastly chorus rose and fell, there came also the faces of the lost and unhappy creatures to whom they belonged, and, against that curtain of pale grey light, he saw float past him in the air, an array of white and piteous human countenances that seemed to beckon and gibber at him as though he were already one of themselves.

Slowly, too, as the voices rose, and the pallid crew sailed past, that giant form of grey descended from the sky and approached the room that contained the worshippers and their prisoner. Hands rose and sank about him in the darkness, and he felt that he was being draped in other garments than his own; a circlet of ice seemed to run about his head, while round the waist, enclosing the fastened arms, he felt a girdle tightly drawn. At last, about his very throat, there ran a soft and silken touch which, better than if there had been full light, and a mirror held to his face, he understood to be the cord of sacrifice—and of death.

At this moment the Brothers, still prostrate upon the floor, began again their mournful, yet impassioned chanting, and as they did so a strange thing happened. For, apparently without moving or altering its position, the huge Figure seemed, at once and suddenly, to be inside the room, almost beside him, and to fill the space around him to the exclusion of all else.

He was now beyond all ordinary sensations of fear, only a drab feeling as of death—the death of the soul—stirred in his heart. His thoughts no longer even beat vainly for escape. The end was near, and he knew it.

The dreadfully chanting voices rose about him in a wave: 'We worship! We adore! We offer!' The sounds filled his ears and hammered, almost meaningless, upon his brain.

Then the majestic grey face turned slowly downwards upon him, and his very soul passed outwards and seemed to become absorbed in the sea of those anguished eyes. At the same moment a dozen hands forced him to his knees, and in the air before him he saw the arm of Kalkmann upraised, and felt the pressure about his throat grow strong.

It was in this awful moment, when he had given up all hope, and the help of gods or men seemed beyond question, that a strange thing happened. For before his fading and terrified vision there slid, as in a dream of light,—yet without apparent rhyme or reason—wholly unbidden and unexplained,—the face of that other man at the supper table of the railway inn. And the sight, even mentally, of that strong, wholesome, vigorous English face, inspired him suddenly with a new courage.

It was but a flash of fading vision before he sank into a dark and terrible death, yet, in some inexplicable way, the sight of that face stirred in him unconquerable hope and the certainty of deliverance. It was a face of power, a face, he now realised, of simple goodness such as might have been seen by men of old on the shores of Galilee; a face, by heaven, that could conquer even the devils of outer space.

And, in his despair and abandonment, he called upon it, and called with no uncertain accents. He found his voice in this overwhelming moment to some purpose; though the words he actually used, and whether they were in German or English, he could never remember. Their effect, nevertheless, was instantaneous. The Brothers understood, and that grey Figure of evil understood.

For a second the confusion was terrific. There came a great shattering sound. It seemed that the very earth trembled. But all Harris remembered afterwards was that voices rose about him in the clamour of terrified alarm—

'A man of power is among us! A man of God!'

The vast sound was repeated—the rushing through space as of huge projectiles—and he sank to the floor of the room, unconscious. The entire scene had vanished, vanished like smoke over the roof of a cottage when the wind blows.

And, by his side, sat down a slight, un-German figure,—the figure of the stranger at the inn,—the man who had the 'rather wonderful eyes.'

When Harris came to himself he felt cold. He was lying under the open sky, and the cool air of field and forest was blowing upon his face. He sat up and looked about him. The memory of the late scene was still horribly in his mind, but no vestige of it remained. No walls or ceiling enclosed him; he was no longer in a room at all. There were no lamps turned low, no cigar smoke, no black forms of sinister worshippers, no tremendous grey Figure hovering beyond the windows.

Open space was about him, and he was lying on a pile of bricks and mortar, his clothes soaked with dew, and the kind stars shining brightly overhead.

He was lying, bruised and shaken, among the heaped-up debris of a ruined building.

He stood up and stared about him. There, in the shadowy distance, lay the surrounding forest, and here, close at hand, stood the outline of the village buildings. But, underfoot, beyond question, lay nothing but the broken heaps of stones that betokened a building long since crumbled to dust. Then he saw that the stones were blackened, and that great wooden beams, half burnt, half rotten, made lines through the general débris. He stood, then, among the ruins of a burnt and shattered building, the weeds and nettles proving conclusively that it had lain thus for many years.

The moon had already set behind the encircling forest, but the stars that spangled the heavens threw enough light to enable him to make quite sure of what he saw. Harris, the silk merchant, stood among these broken and burnt stones and shivered.

Then he suddenly became aware that out of the gloom a figure had risen and stood beside him. Peering at him, he thought he recognised the face of the stranger at the railway inn.

'Are *you* real?' he asked in a voice he hardly recognised as his own.

'More than real—I'm friendly,' replied the stranger; 'I followed you up here from the inn.'

Harris stood and stared for several minutes without adding anything. His teeth chattered. The least sound made him start; but the simple words in his own language, and the tone in which they were uttered, comforted him inconceivably.

'You're English too, thank God,' he said inconsequently. 'These German devils——'

He broke off and put a hand to his eyes. 'But what's become of them all—and the room—and—and——'

The hand travelled down to his throat and moved nervously round his neck. He drew a long, long breath of relief. 'Did I dream everything—everything?' he said distractedly.

He stared wildly about him, and the stranger moved forward and took his arm. '*Come,*' he said soothingly, yet with a trace of command in the voice, 'we will move away from here. The high-road, or even the woods will be more to your taste, for we are standing now on one of the most haunted—and most terribly haunted—spots of the whole world.'

He guided his companion's stumbling footsteps over the broken masonry until they reached the path, the nettles stinging their hands, and Harris feeling his way like a man in a dream. Passing through the twisted iron railing they reached the path, and thence made their way to the road, shining white in the night. Once safely out of the ruins, Harris collected himself and turned to look back.

'But, how is it possible?' he exclaimed, his voice still shaking. 'How can it be possible? When I came in here I saw the building in the moonlight. They opened the door. I saw the figures and heard the voices and touched, yes touched their very hands, and saw their damned black faces, saw them far more plainly than I see you now.' He was deeply bewildered. The glamour was still upon his eyes with a degree of reality stronger than the reality even of normal life. 'Was I so utterly deluded?'

Then suddenly the words of the stranger, which he had only half heard or understood, returned to him.

'Haunted?' he asked, looking hard at him; 'haunted, did you say?' He paused in the roadway and stared into the darkness where the building of the old school had first appeared to him. But the stranger hurried him forward.

'We shall talk more safely farther on,' he said. 'I followed you from the inn the moment I realised where you had gone. When I found you it was eleven o'clock.'

'Eleven o'clock,' said Harris, remembering with a shudder.

'——I saw you drop. I watched over you till you recovered consciousness of your own accord, and now—now I am here to guide you safely back to the inn. I have broken the spell—the glamour——'

'I owe you a great deal, sir,' interrupted Harris again, beginning to understand something of the stranger's kindness, 'but I don't understand it all. I feel dazed and shaken.' His teeth still chattered, and spells of violent shivering passed over him from head to foot. He found that he was clinging to the other's arm. In this way they passed beyond the deserted and crumbling village and gained the highroad that led homewards through the forest.

'That school building has long been in ruins,' said the man at his side presently; 'it was burnt down by order of the Elders of the community at least ten years ago. The village has been uninhabited ever since. But the simulacra of certain ghastly events that took place under that roof in past days still continue. And the "shells" of the chief participants still enact there the dreadful deeds that led to its final destruction, and to the desertion of the whole settlement. They were devil-worshippers!'

Harris listened with beads of perspiration on his forehead that did not come alone from their leisurely pace through the cool night. Although he had seen this man but once before in his life, and had never before exchanged so much as a word with him, he felt a degree of confidence and a subtle sense of safety and well-being in his presence that were the most healing influences he could possibly have wished after the experience he had been through. For all that, he still felt as if he were walking in a dream, and though he heard every word that fell from his companion's lips, it was only the next day that the full import of all he said became fully clear to him. The presence of this quiet stranger, the man with the wonderful eyes which he felt now, rather than saw, applied a soothing anodyne to his shattered spirit that healed him through and through. And this healing influence, distilled from the dark figure at his side, satisfied his first imperative need, so that he almost forgot to realise how strange and opportune it was that the man should be there at all.

It somehow never occurred to him to ask his name, or to feel any undue wonder that one passing tourist should take so much trouble on behalf of another. He just walked by his side, listening to his quiet words, and allowing himself to enjoy the very wonderful experience after his recent ordeal, of being helped, strengthened, blessed. Only once, remembering vaguely something of his reading of years ago, he turned to the man beside him, after some more than usually remarkable words, and heard himself, almost involuntarily it seemed, putting the question: 'Then are you a Rosicrucian,* sir, perhaps?' But the stranger had ignored the words, or possibly not heard them, for he continued with his talk as though unconscious of any interruption, and Harris became aware that another somewhat unusual picture had taken possession of his mind, as they walked there side by side through the cool reaches of the forest, and that he had found his imagination suddenly charged with the childhood memory of Jacob wrestling with an angel,* wrestling all night with a being of superior quality whose strength eventually became his own.

'It was your abrupt conversation with the priest at supper that first put me upon the track of this remarkable occurrence,' he heard the man's quiet voice beside him in the darkness, 'and it was from him I learned after you left the story of the devil-worship that became secretly established in the heart of this simple and devout little community.'

'Devil-worship! Here——'!' Harris stammered, aghast.

'Yes—here;—conducted secretly for years by a group of Brothers before unexplained disappearances in the neighbourhood led to its discovery. For where could they have found a safer place in the whole wide world for their ghastly traffic and perverted powers than here, in the very precincts—under cover of the very shadow of saintliness and holy living?'

'Awful, awful!' whispered the silk merchant, 'and when I tell you the words they used to me——'

'I know it all,' the stranger said quietly. 'I saw and heard everything. My plan first was to wait till the end and then to take steps for their destruction, but in the interest of your personal safety,'—he spoke with the utmost gravity and conviction,—'in the interest of the safety of your soul, I made my presence known when I did, and before the conclusion had been reached——'

'My safety! The danger, then, was real. They were alive and——' Words failed him. He stopped in the road and turned towards his

companion, the shining of whose eyes he could just make out in
the gloom.

'It was a concourse of the shells of violent men, spiritually-
developed but evil men, seeking after death—the death of the
body—to prolong their vile and unnatural existence. And had they
accomplished their object you, in turn, at the death of your body,
would have passed into their power and helped to swell their dreadful
purposes.'

Harris made no reply. He was trying hard to concentrate his mind
upon the sweet and common things of life. He even thought of silk
and St Paul's Churchyard and the faces of his partners in business.

'For you came all prepared to be caught,' he heard the other's
voice like some one talking to him from a distance; 'your deeply
introspective mood had already reconstructed the past so vividly, so
intensely, that you were *en rapport* at once with any forces of those
days that chanced still to be lingering. And they swept you up all
unresistingly.'

Harris tightened his hold upon the stranger's arm as he heard. At
the moment he had room for one emotion only. It did not seem to him
odd that this stranger should have such intimate knowledge of his
mind.

'It is, alas, chiefly the evil emotions that are able to leave their
photographs upon surrounding scenes and objects,' the other added,
'and who ever heard of a place haunted by a noble deed, or of beautiful and lovely ghosts revisiting the glimpses of the moon? It is unfortunate. But the wicked passions of men's hearts alone seem strong
enough to leave pictures that persist; the good are ever too lukewarm.'

The stranger sighed as he spoke. But Harris, exhausted and shaken
as he was to the very core, paced by his side, only half listening. He
moved as in a dream still. It was very wonderful to him, this walk
home under the stars in the early hours of the October morning,
the peaceful forest all about them, mist rising here and there over the
small clearings, and the sound of water from a hundred little invisible
streams filling in the pauses of the talk. In after life he always looked
back to it as something magical and impossible, something that had
seemed too beautiful, too curiously beautiful, to have been quite true.
And, though at the time he heard and understood but a quarter of
what the stranger said, it came back to him afterwards, staying with
him till the end of his days, and always with a curious, haunting sense

of unreality, as though he had enjoyed a wonderful dream of which he could recall only faint and exquisite portions.

But the horror of the earlier experience was effectually dispelled; and when they reached the railway inn, somewhere about three o'clock in the morning, Harris shook the stranger's hand gratefully, effusively, meeting the look of those rather wonderful eyes with a full heart, and went up to his room, thinking in a hazy, dream-like way of the words with which the stranger had brought their conversation to an end as they left the confines of the forest—

'And if thought and emotion can persist in this way so long after the brain that sent them forth has crumbled into dust, how vitally important it must be to control their very birth in the heart, and guard them with the keenest possible restraint.'

But Harris, the silk merchant, slept better than might have been expected, and with a soundness that carried him half-way through the day. And when he came downstairs and learned that the stranger had already taken his departure, he realised with keen regret that he had never once thought of asking his name.

'Yes, he signed in the visitors' book,' said the girl in reply to his question.

And he turned over the blotted pages and found there, the last entry, in a very delicate and individual handwriting—

'*John Silence*, London.'

ANCIENT SORCERIES

I

THERE are, it would appear, certain wholly unremarkable persons, with none of the characteristics that invite adventure, who yet once or twice in the course of their smooth lives undergo an experience so strange that the world catches its breath—and looks the other way! And it was cases of this kind, perhaps, more than any other, that fell into the widespread net of John Silence, the psychic doctor, and, appealing to his deep humanity, to his patience, and to his great qualities of spiritual sympathy, led often to the revelation of problems of the strangest complexity, and of the profoundest possible human interest.

Matters that seemed almost too curious and fantastic for belief he loved to trace to their hidden sources. To unravel a tangle in the very soul of things—and to release a suffering human soul in the process—was with him a veritable passion. And the knots he untied were, indeed, often passing strange.

The world, of course, asks for some plausible basis to which it can attach credence—something it can, at least, pretend to explain. The adventurous type it can understand: such people carry about with them an adequate explanation of their exciting lives, and their characters obviously drive them into the circumstances which produce the adventures. It expects nothing else from them, and is satisfied. But dull, ordinary folk have no right to out-of-the-way experiences, and the world having been led to expect otherwise, is disappointed with them, not to say shocked. Its complacent judgment has been rudely disturbed.

'Such a thing happen to *that* man!' it cries—'a commonplace person like that! It is too absurd! There must be something wrong!'

Yet there could be no question that something did actually happen to little Arthur Vezin, something of the curious nature he described to Dr Silence. Outwardly, or inwardly, it happened beyond a doubt, and in spite of the jeers of his few friends who heard the tale, and observed wisely that 'such a thing might perhaps have come to Iszard, that crack-brained Iszard, or to that odd fish Minski, but it could never have happened to commonplace little Vezin, who was fore-ordained to live and die according to scale.'

But, whatever his method of death was, Vezin certainly did not 'live according to scale' so far as this particular event in his otherwise uneventful life was concerned; and to hear him recount it, and watch his pale delicate features change, and hear his voice grow softer and more hushed as he proceeded, was to know the conviction that his halting words perhaps failed sometimes to convey. He lived the thing over again each time he told it. His whole personality became muffled in the recital. It subdued him more than ever, so that the tale became a lengthy apology for an experience that he deprecated. He appeared to excuse himself and ask your pardon for having dared to take part in so fantastic an episode. For little Vezin was a timid, gentle, sensitive soul, rarely able to assert himself, tender to man and beast, and almost constitutionally unable to say No, or to claim many things that should rightly have been his. His whole scheme of life seemed utterly remote from anything more exciting than missing a train or losing an umbrella on an omnibus. And when this curious event came upon him he was already more years beyond forty than his friends suspected or he cared to admit.

John Silence, who heard him speak of his experience more than once, said that he sometimes left out certain details and put in others; yet they were all obviously true. The whole scene was unforgettably cinematographed on to his mind. None of the details were imagined or invented. And when he told the story with them all complete, the effect was undeniable. His appealing brown eyes shone, and much of the charming personality, usually so carefully repressed, came forward and revealed itself. His modesty was always there, of course, but in the telling he forgot the present and allowed himself to appear almost vividly as he lived again in the past of his adventure.

He was on the way home when it happened, crossing northern France from some mountain trip or other where he buried himself solitary-wise every summer. He had nothing but an unregistered bag in the rack, and the train was jammed to suffocation, most of the passengers being unredeemed holiday English. He disliked them, not because they were his fellow-countrymen, but because they were noisy and obtrusive, obliterating with their big limbs and tweed clothing all the quieter tints of the day that brought him satisfaction and enabled him to melt into insignificance and forget that he was anybody. These English clashed about him like a brass band, making him feel vaguely that he ought to be more self-assertive and obstreperous, and that he did not claim insistently enough all kinds of things that he didn't want and that were really valueless, such as corner seats, windows up or down, and so forth.

So that he felt uncomfortable in the train, and wished the journey were over and he was back again living with his unmarried sister in Surbiton.*

And when the train stopped for ten panting minutes at the little station in northern France, and he got out to stretch his legs on the platform, and saw to his dismay a further batch of the British Isles debouching from another train, it suddenly seemed impossible to him to continue the journey. Even *his* flabby soul revolted, and the idea of staying a night in the little town and going on next day by a slower, emptier train, flashed into his mind. The guard was already shouting '*en voiture*' and the corridor of his compartment was already packed when the thought came to him. And, for once, he acted with decision and rushed to snatch his bag.

Finding the corridor and steps impassable, he tapped at the window (for he had a corner seat) and begged the Frenchman who sat opposite to hand his luggage out to him, explaining in his wretched French that he intended to break the journey there. And this elderly Frenchman, he declared, gave him a look, half of warning, half of reproach, that to his dying day he could never forget; handed the bag through the window of the moving train; and at the same time poured into his ears a long sentence, spoken rapidly and low, of which he was able to comprehend only the last few words: '*à cause du sommeil et à cause des chats.*'

In reply to Dr Silence, whose singular psychic acuteness at once seized upon this Frenchman as a vital point in the adventure, Vezin admitted that the man had impressed him favourably from the beginning, though without being able to explain why. They had sat facing one another during the four hours of the journey, and though no conversation had passed between them—Vezin was timid about his stuttering French—he confessed that his eyes were being continually drawn to his face, almost, he felt, to rudeness, and that each, by a dozen nameless little politenesses and attentions, had evinced the desire to be kind. The men liked each other and their personalities did not clash, or would not have clashed had they chanced to come to terms of acquaintance. The Frenchman, indeed, seemed to have exercised a silent protective influence over the insignificant little

Englishman, and without words or gestures betrayed that he wished him well and would gladly have been of service to him.

'And this sentence that he hurled at you after the bag?' asked John Silence, smiling that peculiarly sympathetic smile that always melted the prejudices of his patient, 'were you unable to follow it exactly?'

'It was so quick and low and vehement,' explained Vezin, in his small voice, 'that I missed practically the whole of it. I only caught the few words at the very end, because he spoke them so clearly, and his face was bent down out of the carriage window so near to mine.'

' "*À cause du sommeil et à cause des chats*"?' repeated Dr Silence, as though half speaking to himself.

'That's it exactly,' said Vezin; 'which, I take it, means something like "because of sleep and because of the cats," doesn't it?'

'Certainly, that's how I should translate it,' the doctor observed shortly, evidently not wishing to interrupt more than necessary.

'And the rest of the sentence—all the first part I couldn't understand, I mean—was a warning not to do something—not to stop in the town, or at some particular place in the town, perhaps. That was the impression it made on me.'

Then, of course, the train rushed off, and left Vezin standing on the platform alone and rather forlorn.

The little town climbed in straggling fashion up a sharp hill rising out of the plain at the back of the station, and was crowned by the twin towers of the ruined cathedral peeping over the summit.* From the station itself it looked uninteresting and modern, but the fact was that the mediæval position lay out of sight just beyond the crest. And once he reached the top and entered the old streets, he stepped clean out of modern life into a bygone century. The noise and bustle of the crowded train seemed days away. The spirit of this silent hill-town, remote from tourists and motor-cars, dreaming its own quiet life under the autumn sun, rose up and cast its spell upon him. Long before he recognised this spell he acted under it. He walked softly, almost on tiptoe down the winding narrow streets where the gables all but met over his head, and he entered the doorway of the solitary inn with a deprecating and modest demeanour that was in itself an apology for intruding upon the place and disturbing its dream.

At first, however, Vezin said, he noticed very little of all this. The attempt at analysis came much later. What struck him then was only the delightful contrast of the silence and peace after the dust and noisy rattle of the train. He felt soothed and stroked like a cat.

'Like a cat, you said?' interrupted John Silence, quickly catching him up.

'Yes. At the very start I felt that.' He laughed apologetically. 'I felt as though the warmth and the stillness and the comfort made me purr. It seemed to be the general mood of the whole place—then.'

The inn, a rambling ancient house, the atmosphere of the old coaching days still about it, apparently did not welcome him too warmly. He felt he was only tolerated, he said. But it was cheap and comfortable, and the delicious cup of afternoon tea he ordered at once made him feel really very pleased with himself for leaving the train in this bold, original way. For to him it had seemed bold and original. He felt something of a dog. His room, too, soothed him with its dark panelling and low irregular ceiling, and the long sloping passage that led to it seemed the natural pathway to a real Chamber of Sleep— a little dim cubby hole out of the world where noise could not enter. It looked upon the courtyard at the back. It was all very charming, and made him think of himself as dressed in very soft velvet somehow, and the floors seemed padded, the walls provided with cushions. The sounds of the streets could not penetrate there. It was an atmosphere of absolute rest that surrounded him.

On engaging the two-franc room he had interviewed the only person who seemed to be about that sleepy afternoon, an elderly waiter with Dundreary whiskers* and a drowsy courtesy, who had ambled lazily towards him across the stone yard; but on coming downstairs again for a little promenade in the town before dinner he encountered the proprietress herself. She was a large woman whose hands, feet, and features seemed to swim towards him out of a sea of person. They emerged, so to speak. But she had great dark, vivacious eyes that counteracted the bulk of her body, and betrayed the fact that in reality she was both vigorous and alert. When he first caught sight of her she was knitting in a low chair against the sunlight of the wall, and something at once made him see her as a great tabby cat, dozing, yet awake, heavily sleepy, and yet at the same time prepared for instantaneous action. A great mouser on the watch occurred to him.

She took him in with a single comprehensive glance that was polite without being cordial. Her neck, he noticed, was extraordinarily supple in spite of its proportions, for it turned so easily to follow him, and the head it carried bowed so very flexibly.

'But when she looked at me, you know,' said Vezin, with that little apologetic smile in his brown eyes, and that faintly deprecating gesture of the shoulders that was characteristic of him, 'the odd notion came to me that really she had intended to make quite a different movement, and that with a single bound she could have leaped at me across the width of that stone yard and pounced upon me like some huge cat upon a mouse.'

He laughed a little soft laugh, and Dr Silence made a note in his book without interrupting, while Vezin proceeded in a tone as though he feared he had already told too much and more than we could believe.

'Very soft, yet very active she was, for all her size and mass, and I felt she knew what I was doing even after I had passed and was behind her back. She spoke to me, and her voice was smooth and running. She asked if I had my luggage, and was comfortable in my room, and then added that dinner was at seven o'clock, and that they were very early people in this little country town. Clearly, she intended to convey that late hours were not encouraged.'

Evidently, she contrived by voice and manner to give him the impression that here he would be 'managed,' that everything would be arranged and planned for him, and that he had nothing to do but fall into the groove and obey. No decided action or sharp personal effort would be looked for from him. It was the very reverse of the train. He walked quietly out into the street feeling soothed and peaceful. He realised that he was in a *milieu* that suited him and stroked him the right way. It was so much easier to be obedient. He began to purr again, and to feel that all the town purred with him.

About the streets of that little town he meandered gently, falling deeper and deeper into the spirit of repose that characterised it. With no special aim he wandered up and down, and to and fro. The September sunshine fell slantingly over the roofs. Down winding alleyways, fringed with tumbling gables and open casements, he caught fairylike glimpses of the great plain below, and of the meadows and yellow copses lying like a dream-map in the haze. The spell of the past held very potently here, he felt.

The streets were full of picturesquely garbed men and women, all busy enough, going their respective ways; but no one took any notice of him or turned to stare at his obviously English appearance. He was even able to forget that with his tourist appearance he was a false note in a charming picture, and he melted more and more into the scene, feeling delightfully insignificant and unimportant and unself-conscious. It was like becoming part of a softly-coloured dream which he did not even realise to be a dream.

On the eastern side the hill fell away more sharply, and the plain below ran off rather suddenly into a sea of gathering shadows in which the little patches of woodland looked like islands and the stubble fields like deep water. Here he strolled along the old ramparts of ancient fortifications that once had been formidable, but now were only vision-like with their charming mingling of broken grey walls and wayward vine and ivy. From the broad coping on which he sat for a moment, level with the rounded tops of clipped plane trees, he saw the esplanade far below lying in shadow. Here and there a yellow sun-beam crept in and lay upon the fallen yellow leaves, and from the height he looked down and saw that the townsfolk were walking to and fro in the cool of the evening. He could just hear the sound of their slow footfalls, and the murmur of their voices floated up to him through the gaps between the trees. The figures looked like shadows as he caught glimpses of their quiet movements far below.

He sat there for some time pondering, bathed in the waves of mur-murs and half-lost echoes that rose to his ears, muffled by the leaves of the plane trees. The whole town, and the little hill out of which it grew as naturally as an ancient wood, seemed to him like a being lying there half asleep on the plain and crooning to itself as it dozed.

And, presently, as he sat lazily melting into its dream, a sound of horns and strings and wood instruments rose to his ears, and the town band began to play at the far end of the crowded terrace below to the accompaniment of a very soft, deep-throated drum. Vezin was very sensitive to music, knew about it intelligently, and had even ventured, unknown to his friends, upon the composition of quiet melodies with low-running chords which he played to himself with the soft pedal when no one was about. And this music floating up through the trees from an invisible and doubtless very picturesque band of the towns-people wholly charmed him. He recognised nothing that they played, and it sounded as though they were simply improvising without a conductor. No definitely marked time ran through the pieces, which ended and began oddly after the fashion of wind through an Æolian harp.* It was part of the place and scene, just as the dying sunlight and faintly-breathing wind were part of the scene and hour, and the mellow notes of old-fashioned plaintive horns, pierced here and there by the sharper strings, all half smothered by the continuous booming of the deep drum, touched his soul with a curiously potent spell that was almost too engrossing to be quite pleasant.

There was a certain queer sense of bewitchment in it all. The music seemed to him oddly unartificial. It made him think of trees swept by the wind, of night breezes singing among wires and chimney-stacks, or in the rigging of invisible ships; or—and the simile leaped up in his thoughts with a sudden sharpness of suggestion—a chorus of animals, of wild creatures, somewhere in desolate places of the world, crying and singing as animals will, to the moon. He could fancy he heard the wailing, half-human cries of cats upon the tiles at night, rising and falling with weird intervals of sound, and this music, muffled by distance and the trees, made him think of a queer company of these creatures on some roof far away in the sky, uttering their solemn music to one another and the moon in chorus.

It was, he felt at the time, a singular image to occur to him, yet it expressed his sensation pictorially better than anything else. The instruments played such impossibly odd intervals, and the crescendos and diminuendos were so very suggestive of cat-land on the tiles at night, rising swiftly, dropping without warning to deep notes again, and all in such strange confusion of discords and accords. But, at the same time a plaintive sweetness resulted on the whole, and the discords of these half-broken instruments were so singular that they did not distress his musical soul like fiddles out of tune.

He listened a long time, wholly surrendering himself as his character was, and then strolled homewards in the dusk as the air grew chilly.

'There was nothing to alarm?' put in Dr Silence briefly.

'Absolutely nothing,' said Vezin; 'but you know it was all so fantastical and charming that my imagination was profoundly impressed. Perhaps, too,' he continued, gently explanatory, 'it was this stirring of my imagination that caused other impressions; for, as I walked back, the spell of the place began to steal over me in a dozen ways, though all intelligible ways. But there were other things I could not account for in the least, even then.'

'Incidents, you mean?'

'Hardly incidents, I think. A lot of vivid sensations crowded themselves upon my mind and I could trace them to no causes. It was just after sunset and the tumbled old buildings traced magical outlines against an opalescent sky of gold and red. The dusk was running down the twisted streets. All round the hill the plain pressed in like a dim sea, its level rising with the darkness. The spell of this kind of scene, you know, can be very moving, and it was so that night. Yet I felt that what came to me had nothing directly to do with the mystery and wonder of the scene.'

'Not merely the subtle transformations of the spirit that come with beauty,' put in the doctor, noticing his hesitation.

'Exactly,' Vezin went on, duly encouraged and no longer so fearful of our smiles at his expense. 'The impressions came from somewhere else. For instance, down the busy main street where men and women were bustling home from work, shopping at stalls and barrows, idly gossiping in groups, and all the rest of it, I saw that I aroused no interest and that no one turned to stare at me as a foreigner and stranger. I was utterly ignored, and my presence among them excited no special interest or attention.

'And then, quite suddenly, it dawned upon me with conviction that all the time this indifference and inattention were merely feigned. Everybody as a matter of fact was watching me closely. Every movement I made was known and observed. Ignoring me was all a pretence—an elaborate pretence.'

He paused a moment and looked at us to see if we were smiling, and then continued, reassured—

'It is useless to ask me how I noticed this, because I simply cannot explain it. But the discovery gave me something of a shock. Before I got back to the inn, however, another curious thing rose up strongly in my mind and forced my recognition of it as true. And this, too, I may as well say at once, was equally inexplicable to me. I mean I can only give you the fact, as fact it was to me.'

The little man left his chair and stood on the mat before the fire. His diffidence lessened from now onwards, as he lost himself again in the magic of the old adventure. His eyes shone a little already as he talked.

'Well,' he went on, his soft voice rising somewhat with his excitement, 'I was in a shop when it came to me first—though the idea must have been at work for a long time subconsciously to appear in so complete

a form all at once. I was buying socks, I think,' he laughed, 'and struggling with my dreadful French, when it struck me that the woman in the
shop did not care two pins whether I bought anything or not. She was
indifferent whether she made a sale or did not make a sale. She was only
pretending to sell.

'This sounds a very small and fanciful incident to build upon what
follows. But really it was not small. I mean it was the spark that lit the
line of powder and ran along to the big blaze in my mind.

'For the whole town, I suddenly realised, was something other than
I so far saw it. The real activities and interests of the people were elsewhere and otherwise than appeared. Their true lives lay somewhere
out of sight behind the scenes. Their busy-ness was but the outward
semblance that masked their actual purposes. They bought and sold,
and ate and drank, and walked about the streets, yet all the while the
main stream of their existence lay somewhere beyond my ken, underground, in secret places. In the shops and at the stalls they did not care
whether I purchased their articles or not; at the inn, they were indifferent to my staying or going; their life lay remote from my own,
springing from hidden, mysterious sources, coursing out of sight,
unknown. It was all a great elaborate pretence, assumed possibly for
my benefit, or possibly for purposes of their own. But the main current
of their energies ran elsewhere. I almost felt as an unwelcome foreign
substance might be expected to feel when it has found its way into the
human system and the whole body organises itself to eject it or to
absorb it. The town was doing this very thing to me.

'This bizarre notion presented itself forcibly to my mind as
I walked home to the inn, and I began busily to wonder wherein the
true life of this town could lie and what were the actual interests and
activities of its hidden life.

'And, now that my eyes were partly opened, I noticed other things
too that puzzled me, first of which, I think, was the extraordinary
silence of the whole place. Positively, the town was muffled. Although
the streets were paved with cobbles the people moved about silently,
softly, with padded feet, like cats. Nothing made noise. All was
hushed, subdued, muted. The very voices were quiet, low-pitched
like purring. Nothing clamorous, vehement or emphatic seemed able
to live in the drowsy atmosphere of soft dreaming that soothed this
little hill-town into its sleep. It was like the woman at the inn—an
outward repose screening intense inner activity and purpose.

'Yet there was no sign of lethargy or sluggishness anywhere about it. The people were active and alert. Only a magical and uncanny softness lay over them all like a spell.'

Vezin passed his hand across his eyes for a moment as though the memory had become very vivid. His voice had run off into a whisper so that we heard the last part with difficulty. He was telling a true thing obviously, yet something that he both liked and hated telling.

'I went back to the inn,' he continued presently in a louder voice, 'and dined. I felt a new strange world about me. My old world of reality receded. Here, whether I liked it or no, was something new and incomprehensible. I regretted having left the train so impulsively. An adventure was upon me, and I loathed adventures as foreign to my nature. Moreover, this was the beginning apparently of an adventure somewhere deep within me, in a region I could not check or measure, and a feeling of alarm mingled itself with my wonder—alarm for the stability of what I had for forty years recognised as my "personality."

'I went upstairs to bed, my mind teeming with thoughts that were unusual to me, and of rather a haunting description. By way of relief I kept thinking of that nice, prosaic noisy train and all those wholesome, blustering passengers. I almost wished I were with them again. But my dreams took me elsewhere. I dreamed of cats, and soft-moving creatures, and the silence of life in a dim muffled world beyond the senses.'

II

VEZIN stayed on from day to day, indefinitely, much longer than he had intended. He felt in a kind of dazed, somnolent condition. He did nothing in particular, but the place fascinated him and he could not decide to leave. Decisions were always very difficult for him and he sometimes wondered how he had ever brought himself to the point of leaving the train. It seemed as though some one else must have arranged it for him, and once or twice his thoughts ran to the swarthy Frenchman who had sat opposite. If only he could have understood that long sentence ending so strangely with '*à cause du sommeil et à cause des chats.*' He wondered what it all meant.

Meanwhile the hushed softness of the town held him prisoner and he sought in his muddling, gentle way to find out where the mystery lay, and what it was all about. But his limited French and his constitutional hatred of active investigation made it hard for him to buttonhole any-body and ask questions. He was content to observe, and watch, and remain negative.

The weather held on calm and hazy, and this just suited him. He wandered about the town till he knew every street and alley. The people suffered him to come and go without let or hindrance, though it became clearer to him every day that he was never free himself from observation. The town watched him as a cat watches a mouse. And he got no nearer to finding out what they were all so busy with or where the main stream of their activities lay. This remained hidden. The people were as soft and mysterious as cats.

But that he was continually under observation became more evident from day to day.

For instance, when he strolled to the end of the town and entered a lit-tle green public garden beneath the ramparts and seated himself upon one of the empty benches in the sun, he was quite alone—at first. Not another seat was occupied; the little park was empty, the paths deserted. Yet, within ten minutes of his coming, there must have been fully twenty persons scattered about him, some strolling aimlessly along the gravel walks, staring at the flowers, and others seated on the wooden benches enjoying the sun like himself. None of them appeared to take any notice of him; yet he understood quite well they had all come there to watch. They kept him under close observation. In the street they had seemed busy enough, hurrying upon various errands; yet these were suddenly all forgotten and they had nothing to do but loll and laze in the sun, their duties unremembered. Five minutes after he left, the garden was again deserted, the seats vacant. But in the crowded street it was the same thing again; he was never alone. He was ever in their thoughts.

By degrees, too, he began to see how it was he was so cleverly watched, yet without the appearance of it. The people did nothing *directly*. They behaved *obliquely*. He laughed in his mind as the thought thus clothed itself in words, but the phrase exactly described it. They looked at him from angles which naturally should have led their sight in another direction altogether. Their movements were oblique, too, so far as these concerned himself. The straight, direct thing was not their way evidently. They did nothing obviously. If he entered a shop to buy, the woman walked instantly away and busied herself with something at the farther end of the counter, though answering at once when he spoke, showing that she knew he was there and that this was only her way of attending to him. It was the fashion of the cat she followed. Even in the dining-room of the inn, the be-whiskered and courteous waiter, lithe and silent in all his movements, never seemed able to come straight to his table for an order or a dish. He came by zigzags, indirectly, vaguely, so that he appeared to be going to another table altogether, and only turned suddenly at the last moment, and was there beside him.

Vezin smiled curiously to himself as he described how he began to realise these things. Other tourists there were none in the hostel, but he recalled the figures of one or two old men, inhabitants, who took their *déjeuner* and dinner there, and remembered how fantastically they entered the room in similar fashion. First, they paused in the doorway, peering about the room, and then, after a temporary inspection, they came in, as it were, sideways, keeping close to the walls so that he wondered which table they were making for, and at the last minute making almost a little quick run to their particular seats. And again he thought of the ways and methods of cats.

Other small incidents, too, impressed him as all part of this queer, soft town with its muffled, indirect life, for the way some of the people appeared and disappeared with extraordinary swiftness puzzled him exceedingly. It may have been all perfectly natural, he knew, yet he could not make it out how the alleys swallowed them up and shot them forth in a second of time when there were no visible doorways or openings near enough to explain the phenomenon. Once he fol-lowed two elderly women who, he felt, had been particularly examin-ing him from across the street—quite near the inn this was—and saw them turn the corner a few feet only in front of him. Yet when he sharply followed on their heels he saw nothing but an utterly deserted alley stretching in front of him with no sign of a living thing. And the only opening through which they could have escaped was a porch some fifty yards away, which not the swiftest human runner could have reached in time.

And in just such sudden fashion people appeared when he never expected them. Once when he heard a great noise of fighting going on behind a low wall, and hurried up to see what was going on, what should he see but a group of girls and women engaged in vociferous conversation which instantly hushed itself to the normal whispering note of the town when his head appeared over the wall. And even then none of them turned to look at him directly, but slunk off with the most unaccountable rapidity into doors and sheds across the yard. And their voices, he thought, had sounded so like, so strangely like, the angry snarling of fighting animals, almost of cats.

The whole spirit of the town, however, continued to evade him as something elusive, protean, screened from the outer world, and at the same time intensely, genuinely vital; and, since he now formed part of its life, this concealment puzzled and irritated him; more—it began rather to frighten him.

Out of the mists that slowly gathered about his ordinary surface thoughts, there rose again the idea that the inhabitants were waiting for him to declare himself, to take an attitude, to do this, or to do that; and that when he had done so they in their turn would at length make some direct response, accepting or rejecting him. Yet the vital matter concerning which his decision was awaited came no nearer to him.

Once or twice he purposely followed little processions or groups of the citizens in order to find out, if possible, on what purpose they were bent; but they always discovered him in time and dwindled away, each individual going his or her own way. It was always the same: he never could learn what their main interest was. The cathedral was ever empty, the old church of St Martin,* at the other end of the town, deserted. They shopped because they had to, and not because they wished to. The booths stood neglected, the stalls unvisited, the little cafés desolate. Yet the streets were always full, the townsfolk ever on the bustle.

'Can it be,' he thought to himself, yet with a deprecating laugh that he should have dared to think anything so odd, 'can it be that these people are people of the twilight, that they live only at night their real life, and come out honestly only with the dusk? That during the day they make a sham though brave pretence, and after the sun is down their true life begins? Have they the souls of night-things, and is the whole blessed town in the hands of the cats?'

The fancy somehow electrified him with little shocks of shrinking and dismay. Yet, though he affected to laugh, he knew that he was beginning to feel more than uneasy, and that strange forces were tugging with a thousand invisible cords at the very centre of his being. Something utterly remote from his ordinary life, something that had not waked for years, began faintly to stir in his soul, sending feelers abroad into his brain and heart, shaping queer thoughts and penetrating even into certain of his minor actions. Something exceedingly vital to himself, to his soul, hung in the balance.

And, always when he returned to the inn about the hour of sunset, he saw the figures of the townsfolk stealing through the dusk from their shop doors, moving sentry-wise to and fro at the corners of the streets, yet always vanishing silently like shadows at his near approach. And as the inn invariably closed its doors at ten o'clock he had never yet found the opportunity he rather half-heartedly sought to see for himself what account the town could give of itself at night.

'——*à cause du sommeil et à cause des chats*'—the words now rang in his ears more and more often, though still as yet without any definite meaning.

Moreover, something made him sleep like the dead.

III

IT was, I think, on the fifth day—though in this detail his story sometimes varied—that he made a definite discovery which increased his alarm and brought him up to a rather sharp climax. Before that he had already noticed that a change was going forward and certain subtle transformations being brought about in his character which modified several of his minor habits. And he had affected to ignore them. Here, however, was something he could no longer ignore; and it startled him.

At the best of times he was never very positive, always negative rather, compliant and acquiescent; yet, when necessity arose he was capable of reasonably vigorous action and could take a strongish decision. The discovery he now made that brought him up with such a sharp turn was that this power had positively dwindled to nothing. He found it impossible to make up his mind. For, on this fifth day, he realised that he had stayed long enough in the town and that for reasons he could only vaguely define to himself it was wiser *and safer* that he should leave.

And he found that he could not leave!

This is difficult to describe in words, and it was more by gesture and the expression of his face that he conveyed to Dr Silence the state of impotence he had reached. All this spying and watching, he said, had as it were spun a net about his feet so that he was trapped and powerless to escape; he felt like a fly that had blundered into the intricacies of a great web; he was caught, imprisoned, and could not get away. It was a distressing sensation. A numbness had crept over his will till it had become almost incapable of decision. The mere thought of vigorous action—action towards escape—began to terrify him. All the currents of his life had turned inwards upon himself, striving to bring to the surface something that lay buried almost beyond reach, determined to force his recognition of something he had long forgotten—forgotten years upon years, centuries almost ago. It seemed as though a window deep within his being would presently open and reveal an entirely new world, yet somehow a world that was not unfamiliar. Beyond that, again, he fancied a great curtain hung; and when that too rolled up he would see still farther into this region and at last understand something of the secret life of these extraordinary people.

'Is this why they wait and watch?' he asked himself with rather a shaking heart, 'for the time when I shall join them—or refuse to join them? Does the decision rest with me after all, and not with them?'

And it was at this point that the sinister character of the adventure first really declared itself, and he became genuinely alarmed. The stability of his rather fluid little personality was at stake, he felt, and something in his heart turned coward.

Why otherwise should he have suddenly taken to walking stealthily, silently, making as little sound as possible, for ever looking behind him? Why else should he have moved almost on tiptoe about the passages of the practically deserted inn, and when he was abroad have found himself deliberately taking advantage of what cover presented itself? And why, if he was not afraid, should the wisdom of staying indoors after sundown have suddenly occurred to him as eminently desirable? Why, indeed?

And, when John Silence gently pressed him for an explanation of these things, he admitted apologetically that he had none to give.

'It was simply that I feared something might happen to me unless I kept a sharp look-out. I felt afraid. It was instinctive,' was all he could say. 'I got the impression that the whole town was after me—wanted me for something; and that if it got me I should lose myself, or at least the Self I knew, in some unfamiliar state of consciousness. But I am not a psychologist, you know,' he added meekly, 'and I cannot define it better than that.'

It was while lounging in the courtyard half an hour before the evening meal that Vezin made this discovery, and he at once went upstairs to his quiet room at the end of the winding passage to think it over alone. In the yard it was empty enough, true, but there was always the possibility that the big woman whom he dreaded would come out of some door, with her pretence of knitting, to sit and watch him. This had happened several times, and he could not endure the sight of her. He still remembered his original fancy, bizarre though it was, that she would spring upon him the moment his back was turned and land with one single crushing leap upon his neck. Of course it was nonsense, but then it haunted him, and once an idea begins to do that it ceases to be nonsense. It has clothed itself in reality.

He went upstairs accordingly. It was dusk, and the oil lamps had not yet been lit in the passages. He stumbled over the uneven surface of the ancient flooring, passing the dim outlines of doors along the corridor—doors that he had never once seen opened—rooms that seemed never occupied. He moved, as his habit now was, stealthily and on tiptoe.

Half-way down the last passage to his own chamber there was a sharp turn, and it was just here, while groping round the walls with outstretched hands, that his fingers touched something that was not wall—something that moved. It was soft and warm in texture, indescribably fragrant, and about the height of his shoulder; and he immediately thought of a furry, sweet-smelling kitten. The next minute he knew it was something quite different.

Instead of investigating, however,—his nerves must have been too overwrought for that, he said,—he shrank back as closely as possible against the wall on the other side. The thing, whatever it was, slipped past him with a sound of rustling, and retreating with light footsteps down the passage behind him, was gone. A breath of warm, scented air was wafted to his nostrils.

Vezin caught his breath for an instant and paused, stockstill, half leaning against the wall—and then almost ran down the remaining distance and entered his room with a rush, locking the door hurriedly behind him. Yet it was not fear that made him run: it was excitement, pleasurable excitement. His nerves were tingling, and a delicious glow made itself felt all over his body. In a flash it came to him that this was just what he had felt twenty-five years ago as a boy when he was in love for the first time. Warm currents of life ran all over him and mounted to his brain in a whirl of soft delight. His mood was suddenly become tender, melting, loving.

The room was quite dark, and he collapsed upon the sofa by the window, wondering what had happened to him and what it all meant.

But the only thing he understood clearly in that instant was that something in him had swiftly, magically changed: he no longer wished to leave, or to argue with himself about leaving. The encounter in the passage-way had changed all that. The strange perfume of it still hung about him, bemusing his heart and mind. For he knew that it was a girl who had passed him, a girl's face that his fingers had brushed in the darkness, and he felt in some extraordinary way as though he had been actually kissed by her, kissed full upon the lips.

Trembling, he sat upon the sofa by the window and struggled to collect his thoughts. He was utterly unable to understand how the mere passing of a girl in the darkness of a narrow passage-way could communicate so electric a thrill to his whole being that he still shook with the sweetness of it. Yet, there it was! And he found it as useless to deny as to attempt analysis. Some ancient fire had entered his veins, and now ran coursing through his blood; and that he was forty-five instead of twenty did not matter one little jot. Out of all the inner turmoil and confusion emerged the one salient fact that the mere atmosphere, the merest casual touch, of this girl, unseen, unknown in the darkness, had been sufficient to stir dormant fires in the centre of his heart, and rouse his whole being from a state of feeble sluggishness to one of tearing and tumultuous excitement.

After a time, however, the number of Vezin's years began to assert their cumulative power; he grew calmer; and when a knock came at length upon his door and he heard the waiter's voice suggesting that dinner was nearly over, he pulled himself together and slowly made his way downstairs into the dining-room.

Every one looked up as he entered, for he was very late, but he took his customary seat in the far corner and began to eat. The trepidation was still in his nerves, but the fact that he had passed through the courtyard and hall without catching sight of a petticoat served to calm him a little. He ate so fast that he had almost caught up with the current stage of the table d'hôte, when a slight commotion in the room drew his attention.

His chair was so placed that the door and the greater portion of the long *salle à manger* were behind him, yet it was not necessary to turn round to know that the same person he had passed in the dark passage had now come into the room. He felt the presence long before he heard or saw any one. Then he became aware that the old men, the only other guests, were rising one by one in their places, and exchanging greetings with some one who passed among them from table to table. And when at length he turned with his heart beating furiously to ascertain for himself, he saw the form of a young girl, lithe and slim, moving down the centre of the room and making straight for his own table in the corner. She moved wonderfully, with sinuous grace, like a young panther, and her approach filled him with such delicious bewilderment that he was utterly unable to tell at first what her face was like, or discover what it was about the whole presentment of the creature that filled him anew with trepidation and delight.

'Ah, Ma'mselle est de retour!'* he heard the old waiter murmur at his side, and he was just able to take in that she was the daughter of the proprietress, when she was upon him, and he heard her voice. She was addressing him. Something of red lips he saw and laughing white teeth, and stray wisps of fine dark hair about the temples; but all the rest was a dream in which his own emotion rose like a thick cloud before his eyes and prevented his seeing accurately, or knowing exactly what he did. He was aware that she greeted him with a charming little bow; that her beautiful large eyes looked searchingly into his own; that the perfume he had noticed in the dark passage again assailed his nostrils, and that she was bending a little towards him and leaning with one hand on the table at his side. She was quite close to him—that was the chief thing he knew—explaining that she had been asking after the comfort of her mother's guests, and was now introducing herself to the latest arrival—himself.

'M'sieur has already been here a few days,' he heard the waiter say; and then her own voice, sweet as singing, replied—

'Ah, but M'sieur is not going to leave us just yet, I hope. My mother is too old to look after the comfort of our guests properly, but now I am here I will remedy all that.' She laughed deliciously. 'M'sieur shall be well looked after.'

Vezin, struggling with his emotion and desire to be polite, half rose to acknowledge the pretty speech, and to stammer some sort of reply, but as he did so his hand by chance touched her own that was resting upon the table, and a shock that was for all the world like a shock of electricity, passed from her skin into his body. His soul wavered and shook deep within him. He caught her eyes fixed upon his own with look of most curious intentness, and the next moment he knew that he had sat down wordless again on his chair, that the girl was already half-way across the room, and that he was trying to eat his salad with a dessert-spoon and a knife.

Longing for her return, and yet dreading it, he gulped down the remainder of his dinner, and then went at once to his bedroom to be alone with his thoughts. This time the passages were lighted, and he suffered no exciting contretemps; yet the winding corridor was dim with shadows, and the last portion, from the bend of the walls onwards, seemed longer than he had ever known it. It ran downhill like the pathway on a mountain side, and as he tiptoed softly down it he felt that by rights it ought to have led him clean out of the house into the heart of a great forest. The world was singing with him. Strange fancies filled his brain, and once in the room, with the door securely locked, he did not light the candles, but sat by the open window thinking long, long thoughts that came unbidden in troops to his mind.

IV

THIS part of the story he told to Dr Silence, without special coaxing, it is true, yet with much stammering embarrassment. He could not in the least understand, he said, how the girl had managed to affect him so profoundly, and even before he had set eyes upon her. For her mere proximity in the darkness had been sufficient to set him on fire. He knew nothing of enchantments, and for years had been a stranger to anything approaching tender relations with any member of the opposite sex, for he was encased in shyness, and realised his overwhelming defects only too well. Yet this bewitching young creature came to him deliberately. Her manner was unmistakable, and she sought him out on every possible occasion. Chaste and sweet she was undoubtedly, yet frankly inviting; and she won him utterly with the first glance of her shining eyes, even if she had not already done so in the dark merely by the magic of her invisible presence.

'You felt she was altogether wholesome and good?' queried the doctor. 'You had no reaction of any sort—for instance, of alarm?'

Vezin looked up sharply with one of his inimitable little apologetic smiles. It was some time before he replied. The mere memory of the adventure had suffused his shy face with blushes, and his brown eyes sought the floor again before he answered.

'I don't think I can quite say that,' he explained presently. 'I acknowledged certain qualms, sitting up in my room afterwards.

A conviction grew upon me that there was something about her—how shall I express it?—well, something unholy. It is not impurity in any sense, physical or mental, that I mean, but something quite indefinable that gave me a vague sensation of the creeps. She drew me, and at the same time repelled me, more than—than——'

He hesitated, blushing furiously, and unable to finish the sentence.

'Nothing like it has ever come to me before or since,' he concluded, with lame confusion. 'I suppose it was, as you suggested just now, something of an enchantment. At any rate, it was strong enough to make me feel that I would stay in that awful little haunted town for years if only I could see her every day, hear her voice, watch her wonderful movements, and sometimes, perhaps, touch her hand.'

'Can you explain to me what you felt was the source of her power?' John Silence asked, looking purposely anywhere but at the narrator.

'I am surprised that *you* should ask me such a question,' answered Vezin, with the nearest approach to dignity he could manage, 'I think no man can describe to another convincingly wherein lies the magic of the woman who ensnares him. I certainly cannot. I can only say this slip of a girl bewitched me, and the mere knowledge that she was living and sleeping in the same house filled me with an extraordinary sense of delight.

'But there's one thing I can tell you,' he went on earnestly, his eyes aglow, 'namely, that she seemed to sum up and synthesise in herself all the strange hidden forces that operated so mysteriously in the town and its inhabitants. She had the silken movements of the panther, going smoothly, silently to and fro, and the same indirect, oblique methods as the townsfolk, screening, like them, secret purposes of her own—purposes that I was sure had *me* for their objective. She kept me, to my terror and delight, ceaselessly under observation, yet so carelessly, so consummately, that another man less sensitive, if I may say so'—he made a deprecating gesture—'or less prepared by what had gone before, would never have noticed it at all. She was always still, always reposeful, yet she seemed to be everywhere at once, so that I never could escape from her. I was continually meeting the stare and laughter of her great eyes, in the corners of the rooms, in the passages, calmly looking at me through the windows, or in the busiest parts of the public streets.'

Their intimacy, it seems, grew very rapidly after this first encounter which had so violently disturbed the little man's equilibrium.

He was naturally very prim, and prim folk live mostly in so small a world that anything violently unusual may shake them clean out of it, and they therefore instinctively distrust originality. But Vezin began to forget his primness after a while. The girl was always modestly behaved, and as her mother's representative she naturally had to do with the guests in the hotel. It was not out of the way that a spirit of camaraderie should spring up. Besides, she was young, she was charmingly pretty, she was French, and—she obviously liked him.

At the same time, there was something indescribable—a certain indefinable atmosphere of other places, other times—that made him try hard to remain on his guard, and sometimes made him catch his breath with a sudden start. It was all rather like a delirious dream, half delight, half dread, he confided in a whisper to Dr Silence; and more than once he hardly knew quite what he was doing or saying, as though he were driven forward by impulses he scarcely recognised as his own.

And though the thought of leaving presented itself again and again to his mind, it was each time with less insistence, so that he stayed on from day to day, becoming more and more a part of the sleepy life of this dreamy mediaeval town, losing more and more of his recognisable personality. Soon, he felt, the Curtain within would roll up with an awful rush, and he would find himself suddenly admitted into the secret purposes of the hidden life that lay behind it all. Only, by that time, he would have become transformed into an entirely different being.

And, meanwhile, he noticed various little signs of the intention to make his stay attractive to him: flowers in his bedroom, a more comfortable arm-chair in the corner, and even special little extra dishes on his private table in the dining-room. Conversations, too, with 'Mademoiselle Ilsé' became more and more frequent and pleasant, and although they seldom travelled beyond the weather, or the details of the town, the girl, he noticed, was never in a hurry to bring them to an end, and often contrived to interject little odd sentences that he never properly understood, yet felt to be significant.

And it was these stray remarks, full of a meaning that evaded him, that pointed to some hidden purpose of her own and made him feel uneasy. They all had to do, he felt sure, with reasons for his staying on in the town indefinitely.

'And has M'sieur not even yet come to a decision?' she said softly in his ear, sitting beside him in the sunny yard before *déjeuner*, the acquaintance having progressed with significant rapidity. 'Because, if it's so difficult, we must all try together to help him!'

The question startled him, following upon his own thoughts. It was spoken with a pretty laugh, and a stray bit of hair across one eye, as she turned and peered at him half roguishly. Possibly he did not quite understand the French of it, for her near presence always confused his small knowledge of the language distressingly. Yet the words, and her manner, and something else that lay behind it all in her mind, frightened him. It gave such point to his feeling that the town was waiting for him to make his mind up on some important matter.

At the same time, her voice, and the fact that she was there so close beside him in her soft dark dress, thrilled him inexpressibly.

'It is true I find it difficult to leave,' he stammered, losing his way deliciously in the depths of her eyes, 'and especially now that Mademoiselle Ilsé has come.'

He was surprised at the success of his sentence, and quite delighted with the little gallantry of it. But at the same time he could have bitten his tongue off for having said it.

'Then after all you like our little town, or you would not be pleased to stay on,' she said, ignoring the compliment.

'I am enchanted with it, and enchanted with you,' he cried, feeling that his tongue was somehow slipping beyond the control of his brain. And he was on the verge of saying all manner of other things of the wildest description, when the girl sprang lightly up from her chair beside him, and made to go.

'It is *soupe à l'oignon** to-day!' she cried, laughing back at him through the sunlight, 'and I must go and see about it. Otherwise, you know, M'sieur will not enjoy his dinner, and then, perhaps, he will leave us!'

He watched her cross the courtyard, moving with all the grace and lightness of the feline race, and her simple black dress clothed her, he thought, exactly like the fur of the same supple species. She turned once to laugh at him from the porch with the glass door, and then stopped a moment to speak to her mother, who sat knitting as usual in her corner seat just inside the hall-way.

But how was it, then, that the moment his eye fell upon this ungainly woman, the pair of them appeared suddenly as other than they were? Whence came that transforming dignity and sense of power that enveloped them both as by magic? What was it about that massive woman that made her appear instantly regal, and set her on a throne in some dark and dreadful scenery, wielding a sceptre over the red glare of some tempestuous orgy? And why did this slender stripling of a girl, graceful as a willow, lithe as a young leopard, assume suddenly an air of sinister majesty, and move with flame and smoke about her head, and the darkness of night beneath her feet?

Vezin caught his breath and sat there transfixed. Then, almost simultaneously with its appearance, the queer notion vanished again, and the sunlight of day caught them both, and he heard her laughing to her mother about the *soupe à l'onion*, and saw her glancing back at him over her dear little shoulder with a smile that made him think of a dew-kissed rose bending lightly before summer airs.

And, indeed, the onion soup was particularly excellent that day, because he saw another cover laid at his small table and, with fluttering heart, heard the waiter murmur by way of explanation that 'Ma'mselle Ilsé would honour M'sieur to-day at *déjeuner*, as her custom sometimes is with her mother's guests.'

So actually she sat by him all through that delirious meal, talking quietly to him in easy French, seeing that he was well looked after, mixing the salad-dressing, and even helping him with her own hand.

And, later in the afternoon, while he was smoking in the courtyard, longing for a sight of her as soon as her duties were done, she came again to his side, and when he rose to meet her, she stood facing him a moment, full of a perplexing sweet shyness before she spoke—

'My mother thinks you ought to know more of the beauties of our little town, and *I* think so too! Would M'sieur like me to be his guide, perhaps? I can show him everything, for our family has lived here for many generations.'

She had him by the hand, indeed, before he could find a single word to express his pleasure, and led him, all unresisting, out into the street, yet in such a way that it seemed perfectly natural she should do so, and without the faintest suggestion of boldness or immodesty. Her face glowed with the pleasure and interest of it, and with her short dress and tumbled hair she looked every bit the charming child of seventeen that she was, innocent and playful, proud of her native town, and alive beyond her years to the sense of its ancient beauty.

So they went over the town together, and she showed him what she considered its chief interest: the tumble-down old house where her forebears had lived; the sombre, aristocratic-looking mansion where her mother's family dwelt for centuries, and the ancient market-place where several hundred years before the witches had been burnt by the score.* She kept up a lively running stream of talk about it all, of which he understood not a fiftieth part as he trudged along by her side, cursing his forty-five years and feeling all the yearnings of his early manhood revive and jeer at him. And, as she talked, England and Surbiton seemed very far away indeed, almost in another age of the world's history. Her voice touched something immeasurably old in him, something that slept deep. It lulled the surface parts of his consciousness to sleep, allowing what was far more ancient to awaken. Like the town, with its elaborate pretence of modern active life, the upper layers of his being became dulled, soothed, muffled, and what lay underneath began to stir in its sleep. That big Curtain swayed a little to and fro. Presently it might lift altogether. . . .

He began to understand a little better at last. The mood of the town was reproducing itself in him. In proportion as his ordinary external self became muffled, that inner secret life, that was far more real and vital, asserted itself. And this girl was surely the high-priestess of it all, the chief instrument of its accomplishment. New thoughts, with new interpretations, flooded his mind as she walked beside him through the winding streets, while the picturesque old gabled town, softly coloured in the sunset, had never appeared to him so wholly wonderful and seductive.

And only one curious incident came to disturb and puzzle him, slight in itself, but utterly inexplicable, bringing white terror into the child's face and a scream to her laughing lips. He had merely pointed to a column of blue smoke that rose from the burning autumn leaves and made a picture against the red roofs, and had then run to the wall and called her to his side to watch the flames shooting here and there through the heap of rubbish. Yet, at the sight of it, as though taken by surprise, her face had altered dreadfully, and she had turned and run like the wind, calling out wild sentences to him as she ran, of which he had not understood a single word, except that the fire apparently frightened her, and she wanted to get quickly away from it, and to get him away too.

Yet five minutes later she was as calm and happy again as though nothing had happened to alarm or waken troubled thoughts in her, and they had both forgotten the incident.

They were leaning over the ruined ramparts together listening to the weird music of the band as he had heard it the first day of his arrival. It moved him again profoundly as it had done before, and somehow he managed to find his tongue and his best French. The girl leaned across the stones close beside him. No one was about. Driven by some remorseless engine within he began to stammer something—he hardly knew what—of his strange admiration for her. Almost at the first word she sprang lightly off the wall and came up smiling in front of him, just touching his knees as he sat there. She was hatless as usual, and the sun caught her hair and one side of her cheek and throat.

'Oh, I'm *so* glad!' she cried, clapping her little hands softly in his face, 'so very glad, because that means that if you like me you must also like what I do, and what I belong to.'

Already he regretted bitterly having lost control of himself. Something in the phrasing of her sentence chilled him. He knew the fear of embarking upon an unknown and dangerous sea.

'You will take part in our real life, I mean,' she added softly, with an indescribable coaxing of manner, as though she noticed his shrinking. 'You will come back to us.'

Already this slip of a child seemed to dominate him; he felt her power coming over him more and more; something emanated from her that stole over his senses and made him aware that her personality, for all its simple grace, held forces that were stately, imposing, august. He saw her again moving through smoke and flame amid broken and tempestuous scenery, alarmingly strong, her terrible mother by her side. Dimly this shone through her smile and appearance of charming innocence.

'You will, I know,' she repeated, holding him with her eyes.

They were quite alone up there on the ramparts, and the sensation that she was overmastering him stirred a wild sensuousness in his blood. The mingled abandon and reserve in her attracted him furiously, and all of him that was man rose up and resisted the creeping influence, at the same time acclaiming it with the full delight of his forgotten youth. An irresistible desire came to him to question her, to summon what still remained to him of his own little personality in an effort to retain the right to his normal self.

The girl had grown quiet again, and was now leaning on the broad wall close beside him, gazing out across the darkening plain, her elbows on the coping, motionless as a figure carved in stone. He took his courage in both hands.

'Tell me, Ilsé,' he said, unconsciously imitating her own purring softness of voice, yet aware that he was utterly in earnest, 'what is the meaning of this town, and what is this real life you speak of? And why is it that the people watch me from morning to night? Tell me what it all means? And, tell me,' he added more quickly with passion in his voice, 'what you really are—yourself?'

She turned her head and looked at him through half-closed eyelids, her growing inner excitement betraying itself by the faint colour that ran like a shadow across her face.

'It seems to me,'—he faltered oddly under her gaze—'that I have some right to know——'

Suddenly she opened her eyes to the full. 'You love me, then?' she asked softly.

'I swear,' he cried impetuously, moved as by the force of a rising tide, 'I never felt before—I have never known any other girl who——'

'Then you *have* the right to know,' she calmly interrupted his confused confession; 'for love shares all secrets.'

She paused, and a thrill like fire ran swiftly through him. Her words lifted him off the earth, and he felt a radiant happiness, followed almost the same instant in horrible contrast by the thought of death. He became aware that she had turned her eyes upon his own and was speaking again.

'The real life I speak of,' she whispered, 'is the old, old life within, the life of long ago, the life to which you, too, once belonged, and to which you still belong.'

A faint wave of memory troubled the deeps of his soul as her low voice sank into him. What she was saying he knew instinctively to be true, even though he could not as yet understand its full purport. His present life seemed slipping from him as he listened, merging his personality in one that was far older and greater. It was this loss of his present self that brought to him the thought of death.

'You came here,' she went on, 'with the purpose of seeking it, and the people felt your presence and are waiting to know what you decide, whether you will leave them without having found it, or whether——'

Her eyes remained fixed upon his own, but her face began to change, growing larger and darker with an expression of age.

'It is their thoughts constantly playing about your soul that makes you feel they watch you. They do not watch you with their eyes. The purposes of their inner life are calling to you, seeking to claim you.

You were all part of the same life long, long ago, and now they want you back again among them.'

Vezin's timid heart sank with dread as he listened; but the girl's eyes held him with a net of joy so that he had no wish to escape. She fascinated him, as it were, clean out of his normal self.

'Alone, however, the people could never have caught and held you,' she resumed. 'The motive force was not strong enough; it has faded through all these years. But I'—she paused a moment and looked at him with complete confidence in her splendid eyes—'I possess the spell to conquer you and hold you: the spell of old love. I can win you back again and make you live the old life with me, for the force of the ancient tie between us, if I choose to use it, is irresistible. And I do choose to use it I still want you. And you, dear soul of my dim past'—she pressed closer to him so that her breath passed across his eyes, and her voice positively sang—'I mean to have you, for you love me and are utterly at my mercy.'

Vezin heard, and yet did not hear; understood, yet did not understand. He had passed into a condition of exaltation. The world was beneath his feet, made of music and flowers, and he was flying somewhere far above it through the sunshine of pure delight. He was breathless and giddy with the wonder of her words. They intoxicated him. And, still, the terror of it all, the dreadful thought of death, pressed ever behind her sentences. For flames shot through her voice out of black smoke and licked at his soul.

And they communicated with one another, it seemed to him, by a process of swift telepathy, for his French could never have compassed all he said to her. Yet she understood perfectly, and what she said to him was like the recital of verses long since known. And the mingled pain and sweetness of it as he listened were almost more than his little soul could hold.

'Yet I came here wholly by chance——' he heard himself saying.

'No,' she cried with passion, 'you came here because I called to you. I have called to you for years, and you came with the whole force of the past behind you. You had to come, for I own you, and I claim you.'

She rose again and moved closer, looking at him with a certain insolence in the face—the insolence of power.

The sun had set behind the towers of the old cathedral and the darkness rose up from the plain and enveloped them. The music of the band had ceased. The leaves of the plane trees hung motionless, but the chill of the autumn evening rose about them and made Vezin shiver. There was no sound but the sound of their voices and the occasional soft rustle of the girl's dress. He could hear the blood rushing in his ears. He scarcely realised where he was or what he was doing. Some terrible magic of the imagination drew him deeply down into the tombs of his own being, telling him in no unfaltering voice that her words shadowed forth the truth. And this simple little French maid, speaking beside him with so strange authority, he saw curiously alter into quite another being. As he stared into her eyes, the picture in his mind grew and lived, dressing itself vividly to his inner vision with a degree of reality he was compelled to acknowledge. As once before, he saw her tall and stately, moving through wild and broken scenery of forests and mountain caverns, the glare of flames behind her head and clouds of shifting smoke about her feet. Dark leaves encircled her hair, flying loosely in the wind, and her limbs shone through the merest rags of clothing. Others were about her too, and ardent eyes on all sides cast delirious glances upon her, but her own eyes were always for One only, one whom she held by the hand. For she was leading the dance in some tempestuous orgy to the music of chanting voices, and the dance she led circled about a great and awful Figure on a throne, brooding over the scene through lurid vapours, while innumerable other wild faces and forms crowded furiously about her in the dance. But the one she held by the hand he knew to be himself, and the monstrous shape upon the throne he knew to be her mother.

The vision rose within him, rushing to him down the long years of buried time, crying aloud to him with the voice of memory reawakened. And then the scene faded away and he saw the clear circle of the girl's eyes gazing steadfastly into his own, and she became once more the pretty little daughter of the innkeeper, and he found his voice again.

'And you,' he whispered tremblingly—'you child of visions and enchantment, how is it that you so bewitch me that I loved you even before I saw?'

She drew herself up beside him with an air of rare dignity.

'The call of the Past,' she said; 'and besides,' she added proudly, 'in the real life I am a princess——'

'A princess!' he cried.

'——and my mother is a queen!'

At this, little Vezin utterly lost his head. Delight tore at his heart and swept him into sheer ecstasy. To hear that sweet singing voice, and to see those adorable little lips utter such things, upset his balance beyond all hope of control. He took her in his arms and covered her unresisting face with kisses.

But even while he did so, and while the hot passion swept him, he felt that she was soft and loathsome, and that her answering kisses stained his very soul. . . . And when, presently, she had freed herself and vanished into the darkness, he stood there, leaning against the wall in a state of collapse, creeping with horror from the touch of her yielding body, and inwardly raging at the weakness that he already dimly realised must prove his undoing.

And from the shadows of the old buildings into which she disappeared there rose in the stillness of the night a singular, long-drawn cry, which at first he took for laughter, but which later he was sure he recognised as the almost human wailing of a cat.

V

For a long time Vezin leant there against the wall, alone with his surging thoughts and emotions. He understood at length that he had done the one thing necessary to call down upon him the whole force of this ancient Past. For in those passionate kisses he had acknowledged the tie of olden days, and had revived it. And the memory of that soft impalpable caress in the darkness of the inn corridor came back to him with a shudder. The girl had first mastered him, and then led him to the one act that was necessary for her purpose. He had been waylaid, after the lapse of centuries—caught, and conquered.

Dimly he realised this, and sought to make plans for his escape. But, for the moment at any rate, he was powerless to manage his thoughts or will, for the sweet, fantastic madness of the whole adventure mounted to his brain like a spell, and he gloried in the feeling that he was utterly enchanted and moving in a world so much larger and wilder than the one he had ever been accustomed to.

The moon, pale and enormous, was just rising over the sea-like plain, when at last he rose to go. Her slanting rays drew all the houses into new perspective, so that their roofs, already glistening with dew, seemed to stretch much higher into the sky than usual, and their gables and quaint old towers lay far away in its purple reaches.

The cathedral appeared unreal in a silver mist. He moved softly, keeping to the shadows; but the streets were all deserted and very silent; the doors were closed, the shutters fastened. Not a soul was astir. The hush of night lay over everything; it was like a town of the dead, a churchyard with gigantic and grotesque tombstones.

Wondering where all the busy life of the day had so utterly disappeared to, he made his way to a back door that entered the inn by means of the stables, thinking thus to reach his room unobserved. He reached the courtyard safely and crossed it by keeping close to the shadow of the wall. He sidled down it, mincing along on tiptoe, just as the old men did when they entered the *salle à manger.* He was horrified to find himself doing this instinctively. A strange impulse came to him, catching him somehow in the centre of his body—an impulse to drop upon all fours and run swiftly and silently. He glanced upwards and the idea came to him to leap up upon his window-sill overhead instead of going round by the stairs. This occurred to him as the easiest, and most natural way. It was like the beginning of some horrible transformation of himself into something else. He was fearfully strung up.

The moon was higher now, and the shadows very dark along the side of the street where he moved. He kept among the deepest of them, and reached the porch with the glass doors.

But here there was light; the inmates, unfortunately, were still about. Hoping to slip across the hall unobserved and reach the stairs, he opened the door carefully and stole in. Then he saw that the hall was not empty. A large dark thing lay against the wall on his left. At first he thought it must be household articles. Then it moved, and he thought it was an immense cat, distorted in some way by the play of light and shadow. Then it rose straight up before him and he saw that it was the proprietress.

What she had been doing in this position he could only venture a dreadful guess, but the moment she stood up and faced him he was aware of some terrible dignity clothing her about that instantly recalled the girl's strange saying that she was a queen. Huge and sinister she stood there under the little oil lamp; alone with him in the empty hall. Awe stirred in his heart, and the roots of some ancient fear. He felt that he must bow to her and make some kind of obeisance. The impulse was fierce and irresistible, as of long habit. He glanced quickly about him. There was no one there. Then he deliberately inclined his head towards her. He bowed.

'Enfin! M'sieur s'est donc décidé. C'est bien alors. J'en suis contente.'*

Her words came to him sonorously as through a great open space.

Then the great figure came suddenly across the flagged hall at him and seized his trembling hands. Some overpowering force moved with her and caught him.

'On pourrait faire un p'tit tour ensemble, n'est-ce pas? Nous y allons cette nuit et il faut s'exercer un peu d'avance pour cela. Ilsé, Ilsé, viens donc ici. Viens vite!'*

And she whirled him round in the opening steps of some dance that seemed oddly and horribly familiar. They made no sound on the stones, this strangely assorted couple. It was all soft and stealthy. And presently, when the air seemed to thicken like smoke, and a red glare as of flame shot through it, he was aware that some one else had joined them and that his hand the mother had released was now tightly held by the daughter. Ilsé had come in answer to the call, and he saw her with leaves of vervain* twined in her dark, hair, clothed in tattered vestiges of some curious garment, beautiful as the night, and horribly, odiously, loathsomely seductive.

'To the Sabbath! to the Sabbath!' they cried. 'On to the Witches' Sabbath!'

Up and down that narrow hall they danced, the women on each side of him, to the wildest measure he had ever imagined, yet which he dimly, dreadfully remembered, till the lamp on the wall flickered and went out, and they were left in total darkness. And the devil woke in his heart with a thousand vile suggestions and made him afraid.

Suddenly they released his hands and he heard the voice of the mother cry that it was time, and they must go. Which way they went he did not pause to see. He only realised that he was free, and he blundered through the darkness till he found the stairs and then tore up them to his room as though all hell was at his heels.

He flung himself on the sofa, with his face in his hands, and groaned. Swiftly reviewing a dozen ways of immediate escape, all equally impossible, he finally decided that the only thing to do for the moment was to sit quiet and wait. He must see what was going to happen. At least in the privacy of his own bedroom he would be fairly safe. The door was locked. He crossed over and softly opened the window which gave upon the courtyard and also permitted a partial view of the hall through the glass doors.

As he did so the hum and murmur of a great activity reached his ears from the streets beyond—the sound of footsteps and voices muffled by distance. He leaned out cautiously and listened. The moonlight was clear and strong now, but his own window was in shadow, the silver disc being still behind the house. It came to him irresistibly that the inhabitants of the town, who a little while before had all been invisible behind closed doors, were now issuing forth, busy upon some secret and unholy errand. He listened intently.

At first everything about him was silent, but soon he became aware of movements going on in the house itself. Rustlings and cheepings came to him across that still, moonlit yard. A concourse of living beings sent the hum of their activity into the night. Things were on the move everywhere. A biting, pungent odour rose through the air, coming he knew not whence. Presently his eyes became glued to the windows of the opposite wall where the moonshine fell in a soft blaze. The roof overhead, and behind him, was reflected clearly in the panes of glass, and he saw the outlines of dark bodies moving with long footsteps over the tiles and along the coping. They passed swiftly and silently, shaped like immense cats, in an endless procession across the pictured glass, and then appeared to leap down to a lower level where he lost sight of them. He just caught the soft thudding of their leaps. Sometimes their shadows fell upon the white wall opposite, and then he could not make out whether they were the shadows of human beings or of cats. They seemed to change swiftly from one to the other. The transformation looked horribly real, for they leaped like human beings, yet changed swiftly in the air immediately afterwards, and dropped like animals.

The yard, too, beneath him, was now alive with the creeping movements of dark forms all stealthily drawing towards the porch with the glass doors. They kept so closely to the wall that he could not determine their actual shape, but when he saw that they passed on to the great congregation that was gathering in the hall, he understood that these were the creatures whose leaping shadows he had first seen reflected in the window-panes opposite. They were coming from all parts of the town, reaching the appointed meeting-place across the roofs and tiles, and springing from level to level till they came to the yard.

Then a new sound caught his ear, and he saw that the windows all about him were being softly opened, and that to each window came a face. A moment later figures began dropping hurriedly down into the yard. And these figures, as they lowered themselves down from the windows, were human, he saw; but once safely in the yard they fell upon all fours and changed in the swiftest possible second into—cats—huge, silent cats. They ran in streams to join the main body in the hall beyond.

So, after all, the rooms in the house had not been empty and unoccupied.

Moreover, what he saw no longer filled him with amazement. For he remembered it all. It was familiar. It had all happened before just so, hundreds of times, and he himself had taken part in it and known the wild madness of it all. The outline of the old building changed, the yard grew larger, and he seemed to be staring down upon it from a much greater height through smoky vapours. And, as he looked, half remembering, the old pains of long ago, fierce and sweet, furiously assailed him, and the blood stirred horribly as he heard the Call of the Dance again in his heart and tasted the ancient magic of Ilsé whirling by his side.

Suddenly he started back. A great lithe cat had leaped softly up from the shadows below on to the sill close to his face, and was staring fixedly at him with the eyes of a human. 'Come,' it seemed to say, 'come with us to the Dance! Change as of old! Transform yourself swiftly and come!' Only too well he understood the creature's soundless call.

It was gone again in a flash with scarcely a sound of its padded feet on the stones, and then others dropped by the score down the side of the house, past his very eyes, all changing as they fell and darting away rapidly, softly, towards the gathering point. And again he felt the dreadful desire to do likewise; to murmur the old incantation, and then drop upon hands and knees and run swiftly for the great flying leap into the air. Oh, how the passion of it rose within him like a flood, twisting his very entrails, sending his heart's desire flaming forth into the night for the old, old Dance of the Sorcerers at the Witches' Sabbath! The whirl of the stars was about him; once more he met the magic of the moon. The power of the wind, rushing from precipice and forest, leaping from cliff to cliff across the valleys, tore him away. . . . He heard the cries of the dancers and their wild laughter, and with this savage girl in his embrace he danced furiously about the dim Throne where sate the Figure with the sceptre of majesty. . . .

Then, suddenly, all became hushed and still, and the fever died down a little in his heart. The calm moonlight flooded a courtyard empty and deserted. They had started. The procession was off into the sky. And he was left behind—alone.

Vezin tiptoed softly across the room and unlocked the door. The murmur from the streets, growing momentarily as he advanced, met his ears. He made his way with the utmost caution down the corridor. At the head of the stairs he paused and listened. Below him, the hall where they had gathered was dark and still, but through opened doors and windows on the far side of the building came the sound of a great throng moving farther and farther into the distance.

He made his way down the creaking wooden stairs, dreading yet longing to meet some straggler who should point the way, but finding no one; across the dark hall, so lately thronged with living, moving things, and out through the opened front doors into the street. He could not believe that he was really left behind, really forgotten, that he had been purposely permitted to escape. It perplexed him.

Nervously he peered about him, and up and down the street; then, seeing nothing, advanced slowly down the pavement.

The whole town, as he went, showed itself empty and deserted, as though a great wind had blown everything alive out of it. The doors and windows of the houses stood open to the night; nothing stirred; moonlight and silence lay over all. The night lay about him like a cloak. The air, soft and cool, caressed his cheek like the touch of a great furry paw. He gained confidence and began to walk quickly, though still keeping to the shadowed side. Nowhere could he discover the faintest sign of the great unholy exodus he knew had just taken place. The moon sailed high over all in a sky, cloudless and serene.

Hardly realising where he was going, he crossed the open market-place and so came to the ramparts, whence he knew a pathway descended to the high road and along which he could make good his escape to one of the other little towns that lay to the northward, and so to the railway.

But first he paused and gazed out over the scene at his feet where the great plain lay like a silver map of some dream country. The still beauty of it entered his heart, increasing his sense of bewilderment and unreality. No air stirred, the leaves of the plane trees stood motionless, the near details were defined with the sharpness of day against dark shadows, and in the distance the fields and woods melted away into haze and shimmering mistiness.

But the breath caught in his throat and he stood stockstill as though transfixed when his gaze passed from the horizon and fell upon the near prospect in the depth of the valley at his feet. The whole lower slopes of the hill, that lay hid from the brightness of the moon, were aglow, and through the glare he saw countless moving forms, shifting thick and fast between the openings of the trees; while overhead, like leaves driven by the wind, he discerned flying shapes that hovered darkly one moment against the sky and then settled down with cries and weird singing through the branches into the region that was aflame.

Spellbound, he stood and stared for a time that he could not measure. And then, moved by one of the terrible impulses that seemed to control the whole adventure, he climbed swiftly upon the top of the broad coping, and balanced a moment where the valley gaped at his feet. But in that very instant, as he stood hovering, a sudden movement among the shadows of the houses caught his eye, and he turned to see the outline of a large animal dart swiftly across the open space behind him, and land with a flying leap upon the top of the wall a little lower down. It ran like the wind to his feet and then rose up beside him upon the ramparts. A shiver seemed to run through the moonlight, and his sight trembled for a second. His heart pulsed fearfully. Ilsé stood beside him, peering into his face.

Some dark substance, he saw, stained the girl's face and skin, shining in the moonlight as she stretched her hands towards him; she was dressed in wretched tattered garments that yet became her mightily; rue and vervain twined about her temples; her eyes glittered with unholy light. He only just controlled the wild impulse to take her in his arms and leap with her from their giddy perch into the valley below.

'See!' she cried, pointing with an arm on which the rags fluttered in the rising wind towards the forest aglow in the distance. 'See where they await us! The woods are alive! Already the Great Ones are there, and the dance will soon begin! The salve is here! Anoint yourself and come!'*

Though a moment before the sky was clear and cloudless, yet even while she spoke the face of the moon grew dark and the wind began to toss in the crests of the plane trees at his feet. Stray gusts brought the sounds of hoarse singing and crying from the lower slopes of the hill, and the pungent odour he had already noticed about the courtyard of the inn rose about him in the air.

'Transform, transform!' she cried again, her voice rising like a song. 'Rub well your skin before you fly. Come! Come with me to the Sabbath, to the madness of its furious delight, to the sweet abandonment of its evil worship! See! the Great Ones are there, and the terrible Sacraments prepared. The Throne is occupied. Anoint and come! Anoint and come!'

She grew to the height of a tree beside him, leaping upon the wall with flaming eyes and hair strewn upon the night. He too began to change swiftly. Her hands touched the skin of his face and neck, streaking him with the burning salve that sent the old magic into his blood with the power before which fades all that is good.

A wild roar came up to his ears from the heart of the wood, and the girl, when she heard it, leaped upon the wall in the frenzy of her wicked joy.

'Satan is there!' she screamed, rushing upon him and striving to draw him with her to the edge of the wall. 'Satan has come! The Sacraments call us! Come, with your dear apostate soul, and we will worship and dance till the moon dies and the world is forgotten!'

Just saving himself from the dreadful plunge, Vezin struggled to release himself from her grasp, while the passion tore at his reins and all but mastered him. He shrieked aloud, not knowing what he said, and then he shrieked again. It was the old impulses, the old awful habits instinctively finding voice; for though it seemed to him that he merely shrieked nonsense, the words he uttered really had meaning in them, and were intelligible. It was the ancient call. And it was heard below. It was answered.

The wind whistled at the skirts of his coat as the air round him darkened with many flying forms crowding upwards out of the valley. The crying of hoarse voices smote upon his ears, coming closer. Strokes of wind buffeted him, tearing him this way and that along the crumbling top of the stone wall; and Ilsé clung to him with her long shining arms, smooth and bare, holding him fast about the neck. But not Ilsé alone, for a dozen of them surrounded him, dropping out of the air. The pungent odour of the anointed bodies stifled him, exciting him to the old madness of the Sabbath, the dance of the witches and sorcerers doing honour to the personified Evil of the world.

'Anoint and away! Anoint and away!' they cried in wild chorus about him. 'To the Dance that never dies! To the sweet and fearful fantasy of evil!'

Another moment and he would have yielded and gone, for his will turned soft and the flood of passionate memory all but overwhelmed him, when—so can a small thing alter the whole course of an adventure—he caught his foot upon a loose stone in the edge of the wall, and then fell with a sudden crash on to the ground below. But he fell towards the houses, in the open space of dust and cobble stones, and fortunately not into the gaping depth of the valley on the farther side.

And they, too, came in a tumbling heap about him, like flies upon a piece of food, but as they fell he was released for a moment from the power of their touch, and in that brief instant of freedom there flashed into his mind the sudden intuition that saved him. Before he could regain his feet he saw them scrabbling awkwardly back upon the wall, as though bat-like they could only fly by dropping from a height, and had no hold upon him in the open. Then, seeing them perched there in a row like cats upon a roof, all dark and singularly shapeless, their eyes like lamps, the sudden memory came back to him of Ilsé's terror at the sight of fire.

Quick as a flash he found his matches and lit the dead leaves that lay under the wall.

Dry and withered, they caught fire at once, and the wind carried the flame in a long line down the length of the wall, licking upwards as it ran; and with shrieks and wailings, the crowded row of forms upon the top melted away into the air on the other side, and were gone with a great rush and whirring of their bodies down into the heart of the haunted valley, leaving Vezin breathless and shaken in the middle of the deserted ground.

'Ilsé!' he called feebly; 'Ilsé!' for his heart ached to think that she was really gone to the great Dance without him, and that he had lost the opportunity of its fearful joy. Yet at the same time his relief was so great, and he was so dazed and troubled in mind with the whole thing, that he hardly knew what he was saying, and only cried aloud in the fierce storm of his emotion. . . .

The fire under the wall ran its course, and the moonlight came out again, soft and clear, from its temporary eclipse. With one last shuddering look at the ruined ramparts, and a feeling of horrid wonder for the haunted valley beyond, where the shapes still crowded and flew, he turned his face towards the town and slowly made his way in the direction of the hotel.

And as he went, a great wailing of cries, and a sound of howling, followed him from the gleaming forest below, growing fainter and fainter with the bursts of wind as he disappeared between the houses.

VI

'IT may seem rather abrupt to you, this sudden tame ending,' said Arthur Vezin, glancing with flushed face and timid eyes at Dr Silence sitting there with his notebook, 'but the fact is—er—from that moment my memory seems to have failed rather. I have no distinct recollection of how I got home or what precisely I did.

'It appears I never went back to the inn at all. I only dimly recollect racing down a long white road in the moonlight, past woods and villages, still and deserted, and then the dawn came up, and I saw the towers of a biggish town and so came to a station.

'But, long before that, I remember pausing somewhere on the road and looking back to where the hill-town of my adventure stood up in the moonlight, and thinking how exactly like a great monstrous cat it lay there upon the plain, its huge front paws lying down the two main streets, and the twin and broken towers of the cathedral marking its torn ears against the sky. That picture stays in my mind with the utmost vividness to this day.

'Another thing remains in my mind from that escape—namely, the sudden sharp reminder that I had not paid my bill, and the decision I made, standing there on the dusty highroad, that the small baggage I had left behind would more than settle for my indebtedness.

'For the rest, I can only tell you that I got coffee and bread at a café on the outskirts of this town I had come to, and soon after found my way to the station and caught a train later in the day. That same evening I reached London.'

'And how long altogether,' asked John Silence quietly, 'do you think you stayed in the town of the adventure?'

Vezin looked up sheepishly.

'I was coming to that,' he resumed, with apologetic wrigglings of his body. 'In London I found that I was a whole week out in my reckoning of time. I had stayed over a week in the town, and it ought to have been September 15th,—instead of which it was only September 10th!'

'So that, in reality, you had only stayed a night or two in the inn?' queried the doctor.

Vezin hesitated before replying. He shuffled upon the mat.

'I must have gained time somewhere,' he said at length—'somewhere or somehow. I certainly had a week to my credit. I can't explain it. I can only give you the fact.'

'And this happened to you last year, since when you have never been back to the place?'

'Last autumn, yes,' murmured Vezin; 'and I have never dared to go back. I think I never want to.'

'And, tell me,' asked Dr Silence at length, when he saw that the little man had evidently come to the end of his words and had nothing more to say, 'had you ever read up the subject of the old witchcraft practices during the Middle Ages, or been at all interested in the subject?'

'Never!' declared Vezin emphatically. 'I had never given a thought to such matters so far as I know——'

'Or to the question of reincarnation, perhaps?'

'Never—before my adventure; but I have since,' he replied significantly.

There was, however, something still on the man's mind that he wished to relieve himself of by confession, yet could with difficulty bring himself to mention; and it was only after the sympathetic tactfulness of the doctor had provided numerous openings that he at length availed himself of one of them, and stammered that he would like to show him the marks he still had on his neck where, he said, the girl had touched him with her anointed hands.

He took off his collar after infinite fumbling hesitation, and lowered his shirt a little for the doctor to see. And there, on the surface of the skin, lay a faint reddish line across the shoulder and extending a little way down the back towards the spine. It certainly indicated exactly the position an arm might have taken in the act of embracing. And on the other side of the neck, slightly higher up, was a similar mark, though not quite so clearly defined.

'That was where she held me that night on the ramparts,' he whispered, a strange light coming and going in his eyes.

It was some weeks later when I again found occasion to consult John Silence concerning another extraordinary case that had come under my notice, and we fell to discussing Vezin's story. Since hearing it, the doctor had made investigations on his own account, and one of his secretaries had discovered that Vezin's ancestors had actually lived for generations in the very town where the adventure came to him. Two of them, both women, had been tried and convicted as witches, and had been burned alive at the stake. Moreover, it had not been difficult to prove that the very inn where Vezin stayed was built about 1700 upon the spot where the funeral pyres stood and the executions took place. The town was a sort of headquarters for all the sorcerers and witches of the entire region, and after conviction they were burnt there literally by scores.

'It seems strange,' continued the doctor, 'that Vezin should have remained ignorant of all this; but, on the other hand, it was not the kind of history that successive generations would have been anxious to keep alive, or to repeat to their children. Therefore I am inclined to think he still knows nothing about it.

'The whole adventure seems to have been a very vivid revival of the memories of an earlier life, caused by coming directly into contact with the living forces still intense enough to hang about the place, and, by a most singular chance too, with the very souls who had taken part with him in the events of that particular life. For the mother and daughter who impressed him so strangely must have been leading actors, with himself, in the scenes and practices of witchcraft which at that period dominated the imaginations of the whole country.

'One has only to read the histories of the times to know that these witches claimed the power of transforming themselves into various animals, both for the purposes of disguise and also to convey themselves swiftly to the scenes of their imaginary orgies. Lycanthropy, or the power to change themselves into wolves, was everywhere believed in, and the ability to transform themselves into cats by rubbing their bodies with a special salve or ointment provided by Satan himself, found equal credence. The witchcraft trials abound in evidences of such universal beliefs.'

Dr Silence quoted chapter and verse from many writers on the subject, and showed how every detail of Vezin's adventure had a basis in the practices of those dark days.

'But that the entire affair took place subjectively in the man's own consciousness, I have no doubt,' he went on, in reply to my questions; 'for my secretary who has been to the town to investigate, discovered his signature in the visitors' book, and proved by it that he had arrived on September 8th, and left suddenly without paying his bill. He left two days later, and they still were in possession of his dirty brown bag and some tourist clothes. I paid a few francs in settlement of his debt, and have sent his luggage on to him. The daughter was absent from home, but the proprietress, a large woman very much as he described her, told my secretary that he had seemed a very strange, absent-minded kind of gentleman, and after his disappearance she had feared for a long time that he had met with a violent end in the neighbouring forest where he used to roam about alone.

'I should like to have obtained a personal interview with the daughter so as to ascertain how much was subjective and how much actually took place with her as Vezin told it. For her dread of fire and the sight of burning must, of course, have been the intuitive memory of her former painful death at the stake, and have thus explained why he fancied more than once that he saw her through smoke and flame.'

'And that mark on his skin, for instance?' I inquired.

'Merely the marks produced by hysterical brooding,' he replied, 'like the stigmata of the *religieuses*,* and the bruises which appear on the bodies of hypnotised subjects who have been told to expect them. This is very common and easily explained. Only it seems curious that these marks should have remained so long in Vezin's case. Usually they disappear quickly.'

'Obviously he is still thinking about it all, brooding, and living it all over again,' I ventured.

'Probably. And this makes me fear that the end of his trouble is not yet. We shall hear of him again. It is a case, alas! I can do little to alleviate.'

Dr Silence spoke gravely and with sadness in his voice.

'And what do you make of the Frenchman in the train?' I asked further—'the man who warned him against the place, *à cause du sommeil et à cause des chats*? Surely a very singular incident?'

'A *very* singular incident indeed,' he made answer slowly, 'and one I can only explain on the basis of a highly improbable coincidence——'

'Namely?'

'That the man was one who had himself stayed in the town and undergone there a similar experience. I should like to find this man and ask him. But the crystal is useless here, for I have no slightest clue to go upon, and I can only conclude that some singular psychic affinity, some force still active in his being out of the same past life, drew him thus to the personality of Vezin, and enabled him to fear what might happen to him, and thus to warn him as he did.

'Yes,' he presently continued, half talking to himself, 'I suspect in this case that Vezin was swept into the vortex of forces arising out of the intense activities of a past life, and that he lived over again a scene in which he had often played a leading part centuries before. For strong actions set up forces that are so slow to exhaust themselves, they may be said in a sense never to die. In this case they were not vital enough to render the illusion complete, so that the little man found himself caught in a very distressing confusion of the present and the past; yet he was sufficiently sensitive to recognise that it was true, and to fight against the degradation of returning, even in memory, to a former and lower state of development.

'Ah yes!' he continued, crossing the floor to gaze at the darkening sky, and seemingly quite oblivious of my presence, 'subliminal up-rushes of memory like this can be exceedingly painful, and sometimes exceedingly dangerous. I only trust that this gentle soul may soon escape from this obsession of a passionate and tempestuous past. But I doubt it, I doubt it.'

His voice was hushed with sadness as he spoke, and when he turned back into the room again there was an expression of profound yearning upon his face, the yearning of a soul whose desire to help is sometimes greater than his power.

THE KIT-BAG*

WHEN the words 'Not Guilty' sounded through the crowded court-room that dark December afternoon, Arthur Wilbraham, the great criminal K.C.* and leader for the triumphant defence, was represented by his junior; but Johnson, his private secretary, carried the verdict across to his chambers like lightning.

'It's what we expected, I think,' said the barrister, without emotion; 'and, personally, I am glad the case is over.' There was no particular sign of pleasure that his defence of John Turk, the murderer, on a plea of insanity, had been successful, for no doubt he felt, as everybody who had watched the case felt, that no man had ever better deserved the gallows.

'I'm glad too,' said Johnson. He had sat in the court for ten days watching the face of the man who had carried out with callous detail one of the most brutal and cold-blooded murders of recent years.

The counsel glanced up at his secretary. They were more than employer and employed; for family and other reasons, they were friends. 'Ah, I remember; yes,' he said with a kind smile, 'and you want to get away for Christmas? You're going to skate and ski in the Alps,* aren't you? If I was your age I'd come with you.'

Johnson laughed shortly. He was a young man of twenty-six, with a delicate face like a girl's. 'I can catch the morning boat now,' he said; 'but that's not the reason I'm glad the trial is over. I'm glad it's over because I've seen the last of that man's dreadful face. It positively haunted me. That white skin, with the black hair brushed low over the forehead, is a thing I shall never forget, and the description of the way the dismembered body was crammed and packed with lime into that——'

'Don't dwell on it, my dear fellow,' interrupted the other, looking at him curiously out of his keen eyes, 'don't think about it. Such pictures have a trick of coming back when one least wants them.' He paused a moment. 'Now go,' he added presently, 'and enjoy your holiday. I shall want all your energy for my Parliamentary work when you get back. And don't break your neck ski-ing.'

Johnson shook hands and took his leave. At the door he turned suddenly.

'I knew there was something I wanted to ask you,' he said. 'Would you mind lending me one of your kit-bags? It's too late to get one to-night, and I leave in the morning before the shops are open.'

'Of course; I'll send Henry over with it to your rooms, You shall have it the moment I get home.'

'I promise to take great care of it,' said Johnson gratefully, delighted to think that within thirty hours he would be nearing the brilliant sunshine of the high Alps in winter. The thought of that criminal court was like an evil dream in his mind.

He dined at his club and went on to Bloomsbury, where he occupied the top floor in one of those old, gaunt houses in which the rooms are large and lofty. The floor below his own was vacant and unfurnished, and below that were other lodgers whom he did not know. It was cheerless, and he looked forward heartily to a change. The night was even more cheerless: it was miserable, and few people were about. A cold, sleety rain was driving down the streets before the keenest east wind he had ever felt. It howled dismally among the big, gloomy houses of the great squares, and when he reached his rooms he heard it whistling and shouting over the world of black roofs beyond his windows,

In the hall he met his landlady, shading a candle from the draughts with her thin band. 'This come by a man from Mr Wilbr'im's, sir.'

She pointed to what was evidently the kit-bag, and Johnson thanked her. and took it upstairs with him. 'I shall be going abroad in the morning for ten days, Mrs Monks,' he said. 'I'll leave an address for letters.'

'And I hope you'll have a merry Christmas, sir,' she said, in a raucous, wheezy voice that suggested spirits, 'and better weather than this.'

'I hope so too,' replied her lodger, shuddering a little as the wind went roaring down the street outside.

When he got upstairs he heard the sleet volleying against the window-panes. He put his kettle on to make a cup of hot coffee, and then set about putting a few things in order for his absence. 'And now I must pack—such as my packing is,' he laughed to himself, and set to work at once.

He liked the packing, for it brought the snow mountains so vividly before him, and made him forget the unpleasant scenes of the past ten days. Besides, it was not elaborate in nature. His friend had lent him the very thing—a stout canvas kit-bag, sack-shaped, with holes round the neck for the brass bar and padlock. It was a bit shapeless, true, and not much to look at, but its capacity was unlimited, and there was no need to pack carefully. He shoved in his waterproof coat, his fur cap and gloves, his skates and climbing boots, his sweaters, snow-boots, and ear-caps; and then on the top of these he piled his woollen shirts and underwear, his thick socks, puttees,* and knickerbockers. The dress suit came next, in case the hotel people dressed for dinner, and then, thinking of the best way to pack his white shirts, he paused a moment to reflect. 'That's the worst of these kit-bags,' he mused vaguely, standing in the centre of the sitting-room, where he had come to fetch some string.

It was after ten o'clock. A furious gust of wind rattled the windows as though to hurry him up, and he thought with pity of the poor Londoners whose Christmas would be spent in such a climate, whilst he was skimming over snowy slopes in bright sunshine, and dancing in the evening with rosy-cheeked girls——Ah! that reminded him; he must put in his dancing-pumps and evening socks. He crossed over from his sitting-room to the cupboard on the landing where he kept his linen.

And as he did so he heard some one coming softly up the stairs.

He stood still a moment on the landing to listen. It was Mrs Monks's step, he thought; she must be coming up with the last post. But then the steps ceased suddenly, and he heard no more. They were at least two flights down, and he came to the conclusion they were too heavy to be those of his bibulous landlady. No doubt they belonged to a late lodger who had mistaken his floor. He went into his bedroom and packed his pumps and dress-shirts as best he could.

The kit-bag by this time was two-thirds full, and stood upright on its own base like a sack of flour. For the first time he noticed that it was old and dirty, the canvas faded and worn, and that it had obviously been subjected to rather rough treatment. It was not a very nice bag to have sent him—certainly not a new one, or one that his chief valued. He gave the matter a passing thought, and went on with his packing. Once or twice, however, he caught himself wondering who it could have been wandering down below, for Mrs Monks had not come up with letters, and the floor was empty and unfurnished. From time to time, moreover, he was almost certain he heard a soft tread of some one padding about over the bare boards—cautiously, stealthily, as silently as possible—and, further, that the sounds had been lately coming distinctly nearer.

For the first time in his life he began to feel a little creepy. Then, as though to emphasise this feeling, an odd thing happened: as he left the bedroom, having just packed his recalcitrant white shirts, he noticed that the top of the kit-bag lopped over towards him with an extraordinary resemblance to a human face. The canvas fell into a fold like a nose and forehead, and the brass rings for the padlock just filled the position of the eyes. A shadow—or was it a travel stain? for he could not tell exactly—looked like hair. It gave him rather a turn, for it was so absurdly, so outrageously, like the face of John Turk, the murderer.

He laughed, and went into the front room, where the light was stronger.

'That horrid case has got on my mind,' he thought; 'I shall be glad of a change of scene and air.' In the sitting-room, however, he was not pleased to hear again that stealthy tread upon the stairs, and to realise that it was much closer than before, as well as unmistakably real. And this time he got up and went out to see who it could be creeping about on the upper staircase at so late an hour.

But the sound ceased; there was no one visible on the stairs. He went to the floor below, not without trepidation, and turned on the electric light to make sure that no one was hiding in the empty rooms of the unoccupied suite. There was not a stick of furniture large enough to hide a dog. Then he called over the banisters to Mrs Monks, but there was no answer, and his voice echoed down into the dark vault of the house, and was lost in the roar of the gale that howled outside. Every one was in bed and asleep—every one except himself and the owner of this soft and stealthy tread.

'My absurd imagination, I suppose,' he thought. 'It must have been the wind after all, although—it seemed so *very* real and close, I thought.' He went back to his packing. It was by this time getting on towards midnight. He drank his coffee up and lit another pipe—the last before turning in.

It is difficult to say exactly at what point fear begins, when the causes of that fear are not plainly before the eyes. Impressions gather on the surface of the mind, film by film, as ice gathers upon the surface of still water, but often so lightly that they claim no definite recognition from the consciousness. Then a point is reached where the accumulated impressions become a definite emotion, and the mind realises that something has happened. With something of a start, Johnson suddenly recognised that he felt nervous—oddly nervous; also, that for some time past the causes of this feeling had been gathering slowly in his mind, but that he had only just reached the point where he was forced to acknowledge them.

It was a singular and curious malaise that had come over him, and he hardly knew what to make of it. He felt as though he were doing something that was strongly objected to by another person, another person, moreover, who had some right to object. It was a most disturbing and disagreeable feeling, not unlike the persistent promptings of conscience: almost, in fact, as if he were doing something he knew to be wrong. Yet, though he searched vigorously and honestly in his mind, he could nowhere lay his finger upon the secret of this growing uneasiness, and it perplexed him. More, it distressed and frightened him.

'Pure nerves, I suppose,' he said aloud with a forced laugh. 'Mountain air will cure all that! Ah,' he added, still speaking to himself, 'and that reminds me—my snow-glasses.'*

He was standing by the door of the bedroom during this brief soliloquy, and as he passed quickly towards the sitting-room to fetch them from the cupboard he saw out of the corner of his eye the indistinct outline of a figure standing on the stairs, a few feet from the top. It was some one in a stooping position, with one hand on the banisters, and the face peering up towards the landing. And at the same moment he heard a shuffling footstep. The person who had been creeping about below all this time had at last come up to his own floor. Who in the world could it be? And what in the name of Heaven did he want?

Johnson caught his breath sharply and stood stock still. Then, after a few seconds' hesitation, he found his courage, and turned to investigate. The stairs, he saw to his utter amazement, were empty; there was no one. He felt a series of cold shivers run over him, and something about the muscles of his legs gave a little and grew weak. For the space of several minutes he peered steadily into the shadows that congregated about the top of the staircase where he had seen the figure, and then he walked fast—almost ran, in fact—into the light of the front room; but hardly had he passed inside the doorway when he heard some one come up the stairs behind him with a quick bound and go swiftly into his bedroom. It was a heavy, but at the same time a stealthy footstep—the tread of somebody who did not wish to be seen. And it was at this precise moment that the nervousness he had hitherto experienced leaped the boundary line, and entered the state of fear, almost of acute, unreasoning fear. Before it turned into terror there was a further boundary to cross, and beyond that again lay the region of pure horror. Johnson's position was an unenviable one.

'By Jove! That *was* some one on the stairs, then,' he muttered, his flesh crawling all over; 'and whoever it was has now gone into my bedroom.' His delicate, pale face turned absolutely white, and for some minutes he hardly knew what to think or do. Then he realised intuitively that delay only set a premium upon fear; and he crossed the landing boldly and went straight into the other room, where, a few seconds before, the steps had disappeared.

'Who's there? Is that you, Mrs Monks?' he called aloud, as he went, and heard the first half of his words echo down the empty stairs, while the second half fell dead against the curtains in a room that apparently held no other human figure than his own.

'Who's there?' he called again, in a voice unnecessarily loud and that only just held firm. 'What do you want here?'

The curtains swayed very slightly, and, as he saw it, his heart felt as if it almost missed a beat; yet he dashed forward and drew them aside with a rush, A window, streaming with rain, was all that met his gaze. He continued his search, but in vain; the cupboards held nothing but rows of clothes, hanging motionless; and under the bed there was no sign of any one hiding. He stepped backwards into the middle of the room, and, as he did so, something all but tripped him up. Turning with a sudden spring of alarm he saw—the kit-bag.

'Odd!' he thought. 'That's not where I left it!' A few moments before it had surely been on his right, between the bed and the bath; he did not remember having moved it. It was very curious. What in the world was the matter with everything? Were all his senses gone queer? A terrific gust of wind tore at the windows, dashing the sleet against the glass with the force of small gun-shot, and then fled away howling dismally over the waste of Bloomsbury roofs. A sudden vision of the Channel next day rose in his mind and recalled him sharply to realities.

'There's no one here at any rate; that's quite clear!' he exclaimed aloud. Yet at the time he uttered them he knew perfectly well that his words were not true and that he did not believe them himself. He felt exactly as though some one was hiding close about him, watching all his movements, trying to hinder his packing in some way. 'And two of my senses,' he added, keeping up the pretence, 'have played me the most absurd tricks: the steps I heard and the figure I saw were both entirely imaginary.'

He went back to the front room, poked the fire into a blaze, and sat down before it to think. What impressed him more than anything else was the fact that the kit-bag was no longer where he had left it. It had been dragged nearer to the door.

What happened afterwards that night happened, of course, to a man already excited by fear, and was perceived by a mind that had not the full and proper control, therefore, of the senses. Outwardly, Johnson remained calm and master of himself to the end, pretending to the very last that everything he witnessed had a natural explanation, or was merely delusions of his tired nerves. But inwardly, in his very heart, he knew all along that some one had been hiding downstairs in the empty suite when he came in, that this person had watched his opportunity and then stealthily made his way up to the bedroom, and that all he saw and heard afterwards, from the moving of the kit-bag to—well, to the other things this story has to tell—were caused directly by the presence of this invisible person.

And it was here, just when he most desired to keep his mind and thoughts controlled, that the vivid pictures received day after day upon the mental plates exposed in the court-room of the Old Bailey,* came strongly to light and developed themselves in the dark room of his inner vision. Unpleasant, haunting memories have a way of coming to life again just when the mind least desires them—in the silent watches of the night, on sleepless pillows, during the lonely hours spent by sick and dying beds. And so now, in the same way, Johnson saw nothing but the dreadful face of John Turk, the murderer, lowering at him from every corner of his mental field of vision; the white skin, the evil eyes, and the fringe of black hair low over the forehead. All the pictures of those ten days in court crowded back into his mind unbidden, and very vivid.

'This is all rubbish and nerves,' he exclaimed at length, springing with sudden energy from his chair. 'I shall finish my packing and go to bed, I'm overwrought, overtired. No doubt, at this rate I shall hear steps and things all night!'

But his face was deadly while all the same. He snatched up his field-glasses and walked across to the bedroom, humming a music-hall song as he went—a trifle too loud to be natural; and the instant he crossed the threshold and stood within the room something turned cold about his heart, and he felt that every hair on his head stood up.

The kit-bag lay close in front of him, several feet nearer to the door than he had left it, and just over its crumpled top he saw a head and face slowly sinking down out of sight as though some one were crouching behind it to hide, and at the same moment a sound like a long-drawn sigh was distinctly audible in the still air about him between the gusts of the storm outside.

Johnson had more courage and willpower than the girlish indecision of his face indicated; but at first such a wave of terror came over him that for some seconds he could do nothing but stand and stare. A violent trembling ran down his back and legs, and he was conscious of a foolish, almost a hysterical, impulse to scream aloud. That sigh seemed in his very ear, and the air still quivered with it. It was unmistakably a human sigh.

'Who's there?' he said at length, finding his voice; but though he meant to speak with loud decision, the tones come out instead in a faint whisper, for he had partly lost the control of his tongue and lips.

He stepped forward, so that he could see all round and over the kit-bag. Of course there was nothing there, nothing but the faded carpet and the bulging canvas sides. He put out his hands and threw open the mouth of the sack where it had fallen over, being only three parts full, and then he saw for the first time that round the inside, some six inches from the top, there ran a broad smear of dull crimson. It was an old and faded blood stain. He uttered a scream, and drew back his hands as if they had been burnt. At the same moment the kit-bag gave a faint, but unmistakable, lurch forward towards the door,

Johnson collapsed backwards, searching with his hands for the support of something solid, and the door, being farther behind him than he realised, received his weight just in time to prevent his falling, and shut to with a resounding bang. At the same moment the swinging of his left arm accidentally touched the electric switch, and the light in the room went out.

It was an awkward and disagreeable predicament, and if Johnson had not been possessed of real pluck he might have done all manner of foolish things. As it was, however, he pulled himself together, and groped furiously for the little brass knob to turn the light on again. But the rapid closing of the door had set the coats hanging on it a-swinging, and his fingers became entangled in a confusion of sleeves and pockets, so that it was some moments before he found the switch. And in those few moments of bewilderment and terror two things happened that sent him beyond recall over the boundary into the region of genuine horror—he distinctly heard the kit-bag shuffling heavily across the floor in jerks, and close in front of his face sounded once again the sigh of a human being.

In his anguished efforts to find the brass button on the wall he nearly scraped the nails from his fingers, but even then, in those frenzied moments of alarm—so swift and alert are the impressions of a mind keyed up by a vivid emotion—he had time to realise that he dreaded the return of the light, and that it might be better for him to stay hidden in the merciful screen of darkness. It was but the impulse of a moment, however, and before he had time to act upon it he had yielded automatically to the original desire, and the room was flooded again with light.

But the second instinct had been right. It would have been better for him to have stayed in the shelter of the kind darkness. For there, close before him, bending over the half-packed kit-bag, clear as life in the merciless glare of the electric light, stood the figure of John Turk, the murderer. Not three feet from him the man stood, the fringe of black hair marked plainly against the pallor of the forehead, the whole horrible presentment of the scoundrel, as vivid as he had seen him day after day in the Old Bailey when he stood there in the dock, cynical and callous, under the very shadow of the gallows.

In a flash Johnson realised what it all meant: the dirty and much-used bag; the smear of crimson within the top; the dreadful stretched condition of the bulging sides. He remembered how the victim's body had been stuffed into a canvas bag for burial, the ghastly, dismembered fragments forced with lime into this very bag; and the bag itself produced as evidence——It all came back to him as clear as day. . . .

Very softly and stealthily his hand groped behind him for the handle of the door, but before he could actually turn it the very thing that he most of all dreaded came about, and John Turk lifted his devil's face and looked at him. At the same moment that heavy sigh passed through the air of the room, formulated somehow into words: 'It's my bag. And I want it.'

Johnson just remembered clawing the door open, and then falling in a heap upon the floor of the landing, as he tried frantically to make his way into the front room.

He remained unconscious for a long time, and it was still dark when he opened his eyes and realised that he was lying, stiff and bruised, on the cold boards. Then the memory of what he had seen rushed back into his mind, and he promptly fainted again. When he woke the second time the wintry dawn was just beginning to peep in at the windows, painting the stairs a cheerless, dismal grey, and he managed to crawl into the front room, and cover himself with an overcoat in the armchair, where at length he fell asleep.

A great clamour woke him, He recognised Mrs Monks's voice, loud and voluble.

'What! You ain't been to bed, sir! Are you ill, or has anything 'appened? And there's an urgent gentleman to see you, though it ain't seven o'clock yet, and——'

'Who is it?' he stammered. 'I'm all right, thanks. Fell asleep in my chair, I suppose.'

'Some one from Mr Wilb'rim's, and he says he ought to see you quick before you go abroad, and I told him——'

'Show him up, please, at once,' said Johnson, whose head was whirling, and his mind was still full of dreadful visions.

Mr Wilbraham's man came in with many apologies, and explained briefly and quickly that an absurd mistake had been made, and that the wrong kit-bag had been sent over the night before.

'Henry somehow got hold of the one that came over from the court-room, and Mr Wilbraham only discovered it when he saw his own lying in his room, and asked why it had not gone to you,' the man said.

'Oh! said Johnson stupidly.

'And he must have brought you the one from the murder case instead, sir, I'm afraid,' the man continued, without the ghost of an expression on his face. 'The one John Turk packed the dead body in, Mr Wilbraham's awful upset about it, sir, and told me to come over first thing this morning with the right one, as you were leaving by the boat.'

He pointed to a clean-looking kit-bag on the floor, which he had just brought, 'And I was to bring the other one back, sir,' he added casually.

For some minutes Johnson could not find his voice. At last he pointed in the direction of his bedroom. 'Perhaps you would kindly unpack it for me. Just empty the things out on the floor.'

The man disappeared into the other room, and was gone for five minutes. Johnson heard the shifting to and fro of the bag, and the rattle of the skates and boots being unpacked.

'Thank you, sir,' the man said, returning with the bag folded over his arm. 'And can I do anything more to help you, sir.'

'What is it?' asked Johnson, seeing that he still had something he wished to say.

The man shuffled and looked mysterious. 'Beg pardon, sir, but knowing your interest in the Turk case, I thought you'd maybe like to know what's happened——'

'Yes.'

'John Turk killed hisself last night with poison immediately on getting his release, and he left a note for Mr Wilbraham saying as he'd be much obliged if they'd have him put away, same as the woman he murdered, in the old kit-bag.'

'What time—did he do it?' asked Johnson.

'Ten o'clock last night, sir, the warder says.'

THE MAN WHO FOUND OUT

(A NIGHTMARE)

I

PROFESSOR MARK EBOR, the scientist, led a double life, and the only persons who knew it were his assistant, Dr Laidlaw, and his publishers. But a double life need not always be a bad one, and, as Dr Laidlaw and the gratified publishers well knew, the parallel lives of this particular man were equally good, and indefinitely produced would certainly have ended in a heaven somewhere that can suitably contain such strangely opposite characteristics as his remarkable personality combined.

For Mark Ebor, F.R.S.,* etc., etc., was that unique combination hardly ever met with in actual life, a man of science and a mystic.

As the first, his name stood in the gallery of the great, and as the second—but there came the mystery! For under the pseudonym of 'Pilgrim' (the author of that brilliant series of books that appealed to so many), his identity was as well concealed as that of the anonymous writer of the weather reports in a daily newspaper. Thousands read the sanguine, optimistic, stimulating little books that issued annually from the pen of 'Pilgrim,' and thousands bore their daily burdens better for having read; while the Press generally agreed that the author, besides being an incorrigible enthusiast and optimist, was also—a woman; but no one ever succeeded in penetrating the veil of anonymity and discovering that 'Pilgrim' and the biologist were one and the same person.

Mark Ebor, as Dr Laidlaw knew him in his laboratory, was one man; but Mark Ebor, as he sometimes saw him after work was over, with rapt eyes and ecstatic face, discussing the possibilities of 'union with God' and the future of the human race, was quite another.

'I have always held, as you know,' he was saying one evening as he sat in the little study beyond the laboratory with his assistant and intimate, 'that Vision should play a large part in the life of the awakened man—not to be regarded as infallible, of course, but to be observed and made use of as a guide-post to possibilities——'

'I am aware of your peculiar views, sir,' the young doctor put in deferentially, yet with a certain impatience.

'For Visions come from a region of the consciousness where observation and experiment are out of the question,' pursued the other with enthusiasm, not noticing the interruption, 'and, while they should be checked by reason afterwards, they should not be laughed at or ignored. All inspiration, I hold, is of the nature of interior Vision, and all our best knowledge has come—such is my confirmed belief—as a sudden revelation to the brain prepared to receive it——'

'Prepared by hard work first, by concentration, by the closest possible study of ordinary phenomena,' Dr Laidlaw allowed himself to observe.

'Perhaps,' sighed the other; 'but by a process, none the less, of spiritual illumination. The best match in the world will not light a candle unless the wick be first suitably prepared.'

It was Laidlaw's turn to sigh. He knew so well the impossibility of arguing with his chief when he was in the regions of the mystic, but at the same time the respect he felt for his tremendous attainments was so sincere that he always listened with attention and deference, wondering how far the great man would go and to what end this curious combination of logic and 'illumination' would eventually lead him.

'Only last night,' continued the elder man, a sort of light coming into his rugged features, 'the vision came to me again—the one that has haunted me at intervals ever since my youth, and that will not be denied.'

Dr Laidlaw fidgeted in his chair.

'About the Tablets of the Gods, you mean—and that they lie somewhere hidden in the sands,' he said patiently. A sudden gleam of interest came into his face as he turned to catch the professor's reply.

'And that I am to be the one to find them, to decipher them, and to give the great knowledge to the world——'

'Who will not believe,' laughed Laidlaw shortly, yet interested in spite of his thinly-veiled contempt.

'Because even the keenest minds, in the right sense of the word, are hopelessly—unscientific,' replied the other gently, his face positively aglow with the memory of his vision. 'Yet what is more likely,' he continued after a moment's pause, peering into space with rapt eyes that saw things too wonderful for exact language to describe, 'than that there should have been given to man in the first ages of the world some record of the purpose and problem that had been set him to solve? In a word,' he cried, fixing his shining eyes upon the face of his perplexed assistant, 'that God's messengers in the far-off ages should have given to His creatures some full statement of the secret of the world, of the secret of the soul, of the meaning of life and death—the explanation of our being here, and to what great end we are destined in the ultimate fullness of things?'

Dr Laidlaw sat speechless. These outbursts of mystical enthusiasm he had witnessed before. With any other man he would not have listened to a single sentence, but to Professor Ebor, man of knowledge and profound investigator, he listened with respect, because he regarded this condition as temporary and pathological, and in some sense a reaction from the intense strain of the prolonged mental concentration of many days.

He smiled, with something between sympathy and resignation as he met the other's rapt gaze.

'But you have said, sir, at other times, that you consider the ultimate secrets to be screened from all possible——'

'The *ultimate* secrets, yes,' came the unperturbed reply; 'but that there lies buried somewhere an indestructible record of the secret meaning of life, originally known to men in the days of their pristine innocence, I am convinced. And, by this strange vision so often vouchsafed to me, I am equally sure that one day it shall be given to me to announce to a weary world this glorious and terrific message.'

And he continued at great length and in glowing language to describe the species of vivid dream that had come to him at intervals since earliest childhood, showing in detail how he discovered these very Tablets of the Gods, and proclaimed their splendid contents—whose precise nature was always, however, withheld from him in the vision—to a patient and suffering humanity.

'The *Scrutator*,* sir, well described "Pilgrim" as the Apostle of Hope,' said the young doctor gently, when he had finished; 'and now, if that reviewer could hear you speak and realize from what strange depths comes your simple faith——'

The professor held up his hand, and the smile of a little child broke over his face like sunshine in the morning.

'Half the good my books do would be instantly destroyed,' he said sadly; 'they would say that I wrote with my tongue in my cheek. But wait!' he added significantly; 'wait till I find these Tablets of the Gods! Wait till I hold the solutions of the old world-problems in my hands! Wait till the light of this new revelation breaks upon confused humanity, and it wakes to find its bravest hopes justified! Ah, then, my dear Laidlaw——'

He broke off suddenly; but the doctor, cleverly guessing the thought in his mind, caught him up immediately.

'Perhaps this very summer,' he said, trying hard to make the suggestion keep pace with honesty; 'in your explorations in Assyria—your digging in the remote civilization of what was once Chaldea, you may find—what you dream of——'

The professor looked up with a delighted smile on his fine old face.

'Perhaps,' he murmured softly, 'perhaps!'

And the young doctor, thanking the gods of science that his leader's aberrations were of so harmless a character, went home strong in the certitude of his knowledge of externals, proud that he was able to refer his visions to self-suggestion, and wondering complaisantly whether in his old age he might not after all suffer himself from visitations of the very kind that afflicted his respected chief.

And as he got into bed and thought again of his master's rugged face, and finely shaped head, and the deep lines traced by years of work and self-discipline, he turned over on his pillow and fell asleep with a sigh that was half of wonder, half of regret.

II

IT was in February, nine months later, when Dr Laidlaw made his way to Charing Cross to meet his chief after his long absence of travel and exploration. The vision about the so-called Tablets of the Gods had meanwhile passed almost entirely from his memory.

There were few people in the train, for the stream of traffic was now running the other way, and he had no difficulty in finding the man he had come to meet. The shock of white hair beneath the low-crowned felt hat was alone enough to distinguish him by easily.

'Here I am at last!' exclaimed the professor, somewhat wearily, clasping his friend's hand as he listened to the young doctor's warm greetings and questions. 'Here I am—a little older, and *much* dirtier than when you last saw me!' He glanced down laughingly at his travel-stained garments.

'And *much* wiser,' said Laidlaw, with a smile, as he bustled about the platform for porters and gave his chief the latest scientific news.

At last they came down to practical considerations.

'And your luggage—where is that? You must have tons of it, I suppose?' said Laidlaw.

'Hardly anything,' Professor Ebor answered. 'Nothing, in fact, but what you see.'

'Nothing but this hand-bag?' laughed the other, thinking he was joking.

'And a small portmanteau in the van,' was the quiet reply. 'I have no other luggage.'

'You have no other luggage?' repeated Laidlaw, turning sharply to see if he were in earnest.

'Why should I need more?' the professor added simply.

Something in the man's face, or voice, or manner—the doctor hardly knew which—suddenly struck him as strange. There was a change in him, a change so profound—so little on the surface, that is—that at first he had not become aware of it. For a moment it was as though an utterly alien personality stood before him in that noisy, bustling throng. Here, in all the homely, friendly turmoil of a Charing Cross crowd, a curious feeling of cold passed over his heart, touching his life with icy finger, so that he actually trembled and felt afraid.

He looked up quickly at his friend, his mind working with startled and unwelcome thoughts.

'Only this?' he repeated, indicating the bag. 'But where's all the stuff you went away with? And—have you brought nothing home—no treasures?'

'This is all I have,' the other said briefly. The pale smile that went with the words caused the doctor a second indescribable sensation of uneasiness. Something was very wrong, something was very queer; he wondered now that he had not noticed it sooner.

'The rest follows, of course, by slow freight,' he added tactfully, and as naturally as possible. 'But come, sir, you must be tired and in want of food after your long journey. I'll get a taxi at once, and we can see about the other luggage afterwards.'

It seemed to him he hardly knew quite what he was saying; the change in his friend had come upon him so suddenly and now grew upon him more and more distressingly. Yet he could not make out exactly in what it consisted. A terrible suspicion began to take shape in his mind, troubling him dreadfully.

'I am neither very tired, nor in need of food, thank you,' the professor said quietly. 'And this is all I have. There is no luggage to follow. I have brought home nothing—nothing but what you see.'

His words conveyed finality. They got into a taxi, tipped the porter, who had been staring in amazement at the venerable figure of the scientist, and were conveyed slowly and noisily to the house in the north of London where the laboratory was, the scene of their labours of years.

And the whole way Professor Ebor uttered no word, nor did Dr Laidlaw find the courage to ask a single question.

It was only late that night, before he took his departure, as the two men were standing before the fire in the study—that study where they had discussed so many problems of vital and absorbing interest—that Dr Laidlaw at last found strength to come to the point with direct questions. The professor had been giving him a superficial and desultory account of his travels, of his journeys by camel, of his encampments among the mountains and in the desert, and of his explorations among the buried temples, and, deeper, into the waste of the pre-historic sands, when suddenly the doctor came to the desired point with a kind of nervous rush, almost like a frightened boy.

'And you found——' he began stammering, looking hard at the other's dreadfully altered face, from which every line of hope and cheerfulness seemed to have been obliterated as a sponge wipes markings from a slate—'you found——'

'I found,' replied the other, in a solemn voice, and it was the voice of the mystic rather than the man of science—'I found what I went to seek. The vision never once failed me. It led me straight to the place like a star in the heavens. I found—the Tablets of the Gods.'

Dr Laidlaw caught his breath, and steadied himself on the back of a chair. The words fell like particles of ice upon his heart. For the first time the professor had uttered the well-known phrase without the glow of light and wonder in his face that always accompanied it.

'You have—brought them?' he faltered.

'I have brought them home,' said the other, in a voice with a ring like iron; 'and I have—deciphered them.'

Profound despair, the gloom of outer darkness, the dead sound of a hopeless soul freezing in the utter cold of space seemed to fill in the pauses between the brief sentences. A silence followed, during which Dr Laidlaw saw nothing but the white face before him alternately fade and return. And it was like the face of a dead man.

'They are, alas, indestructible,' he heard the voice continue, with its even, metallic ring.

'Indestructible,' Laidlaw repeated mechanically, hardly knowing what he was saying.

Again a silence of several minutes passed, during which, with a creeping cold about his heart, he stood and stared into the eyes of the man he had known and loved so long—aye, and worshipped, too; the man who had first opened his own eyes when they were blind, and had led him to the gates of knowledge, and no little distance along the difficult path beyond; the man who, in another direction, had passed on the strength of his faith into the hearts of thousands by his books.

'I may see them?' he asked at last, in a low voice he hardly recognized as his own. 'You will let me know—their message?'

Professor Ebor kept his eyes fixedly upon his assistant's face as he answered, with a smile that was more like the grin of death than a living human smile.

'When I am gone,' he whispered; 'when I have passed away. Then you shall find them and read the translation I have made. And then, too, in your turn, you must try, with the latest resources of science at your disposal to aid you, to compass their utter destruction.' He paused a moment, and his face grew pale as the face of a corpse. 'Until that time,' he added presently, without looking up, 'I must ask you not to refer to the subject again—and to keep my confidence meanwhile—*ab—so—lute—ly.*'

III

A YEAR passed slowly by, and at the end of it Dr Laidlaw had found it necessary to sever his working connexion with his friend and one-time leader. Professor Ebor was no longer the same man. The light had gone out of his life; the laboratory was closed; he no longer put pen to paper or applied his mind to a single problem. In the short space of a few months he had passed from a hale and hearty man of late middle life to the condition of old age—a man collapsed and on the edge of dissolution. Death, it was plain, lay waiting for him in the shadows of any day—and he knew it.

To describe faithfully the nature of this profound alteration in his character and temperament is not easy, but Dr Laidlaw summed it up to himself in three words: *Loss of Hope.* The splendid mental powers remained indeed undimmed, but the incentive to use them—to use them, for the help of others—had gone. The character still held to its fine and unselfish habits of years, but the far goal to which they had been the leading strings had faded away. The desire for knowledge—knowledge for its own sake—had died, and the passionate hope which hitherto had animated with tireless energy the heart and brain of this splendidly equipped intellect had suffered total eclipse. The central fires had gone out. Nothing was worth doing, thinking, working for. There *was* nothing to work for any longer!

The professor's first step was to recall as many of his books as possible; his second to close his laboratory and stop all research. He gave no explanation, he invited no questions. His whole personality crumbled away, so to speak, till his daily life became a mere mechanical process of clothing the body, feeding the body, keeping it in good health so as to avoid physical discomfort, and, above all, doing nothing that could interfere with sleep. The professor did everything he could to lengthen the hours of sleep, and therefore of forgetfulness.

It was all clear enough to Dr Laidlaw. A weaker man, he knew, would have sought to lose himself in one form or another of sensual indulgence—sleeping-draughts, drink, the first pleasures that came to hand. Self-destruction would have been the method of a little bolder type; and deliberate evil-doing, poisoning with his awful knowledge all he could, the means of still another kind of man. Mark Ebor was none of these. He held himself under fine control, facing silently and without complaint the terrible facts he honestly believed himself to have been unfortunate enough to discover. Even to his intimate friend and assistant, Dr Laidlaw, he vouchsafed no word of true explanation or lament. He went straight forward to the end, knowing well that the end was not very far away.

And death came very quietly one day to him, as he was sitting in the arm-chair of the study, directly facing the doors of the laboratory—the doors that no longer opened. Dr Laidlaw, by happy chance, was with him at the time, and was just able to reach his side in response to the sudden painful efforts for breath; just in time, too, to catch the murmured words that fell from the pallid lips like a message from the other side of the grave.

'Read them, if you must; and, if you can—destroy. But'—his voice sank so low that Dr Laidlaw only just caught the dying syllables—'but—never, never—give them to the world.'

And like a grey bundle of dust loosely gathered up in an old garment the professor sank back into his chair and expired.

But this was only the death of the body. His spirit had died two years before.

IV

THE estate of the dead man was small and uncomplicated, and Dr Laidlaw, as sole executor and residuary legatee, had no difficulty in settling it up. A month after the funeral he was sitting alone in his upstairs library, the last sad duties completed, and his mind full of poignant memories and regrets for the loss of a friend he had revered and loved, and to whom his debt was so incalculably great. The last two years, indeed, had been for him terrible. To watch the swift decay of the greatest combination of heart and brain he had ever known, and to realize he was powerless to help, was a source of profound grief to him that would remain to the end of his days.

At the same time an insatiable curiosity possessed him. The study of dementia was, of course, outside his special province as a specialist, but he knew enough of it to understand how small a matter might be the actual cause of how great an illusion, and he had been devoured from the very beginning by a ceaseless and increasing anxiety to know what the professor had found in the sands of 'Chaldea,' what these precious Tablets of the Gods might be, and particularly—for this was the real cause that had sapped the man's sanity and hope—what the inscription was that he had believed to have deciphered thereon.

The curious feature of it all to his own mind was, that whereas his friend had dreamed of finding a message of glorious hope and comfort, he had apparently found (so far as he had found anything intelligible at all, and not invented the whole thing in his dementia) that the secret of the world, and the meaning of life and death, was of so terrible a nature that it robbed the heart of courage and the soul of hope. What, then, could be the contents of the little brown parcel the professor had bequeathed to him with his pregnant dying sentences?

Actually his hand was trembling as he turned to the writing-table and began slowly to unfasten a small old-fashioned desk on which the small gilt initials 'M.E.' stood forth as a melancholy memento. He put the key into the lock and half turned it. Then, suddenly, he stopped and looked about him. Was that a sound at the back of the room? It was just as though someone had laughed and then tried to smother the laugh with a cough. A slight shiver ran over him as he stood listening.

'This is absurd,' he said aloud; 'too absurd for belief—that I should be so nervous! It's the effect of curiosity unduly prolonged.' He smiled a little sadly and his eyes wandered to the blue summer sky and the plane trees swaying in the wind below his window. 'It's the reaction,' he continued. 'The curiosity of two years to be quenched in a single moment! The nervous tension, of course, must be considerable.'

He turned back to the brown desk and opened it without further delay. His hand was firm now, and he took out the paper parcel that lay inside without a tremor. It was heavy. A moment later there lay on the table before him a couple of weather-worn plaques of grey stone—they looked like stone, although they felt like metal—on which he saw markings of a curious character that might have been the mere tracings of natural forces through the ages, or, equally well, the half-obliterated hieroglyphics cut upon their surface in past centuries by the more or less untutored hand of a common scribe.

He lifted each stone in turn and examined it carefully. It seemed to him that a faint glow of heat passed from the substance into his skin, and he put them down again suddenly, as with a gesture of uneasiness.

'A very clever, or a very imaginative man,' he said to himself, 'who could squeeze the secrets of life and death from such broken lines as those!'

Then he turned to a yellow envelope lying beside them in the desk, with the single word on the outside in the writing of the professor—the word *Translation*.

'Now,' he thought, taking it up with a sudden violence to conceal his nervousness, 'now for the great solution. Now to learn the meaning of the worlds, and why mankind was made, and why discipline is worth while, and sacrifice and pain the true law of advancement.'

There was the shadow of a sneer in his voice, and yet something in him shivered at the same time. He held the envelope as though weighing it in his hand, his mind pondering many things. Then curiosity won the day, and he suddenly tore it open with the gesture of an actor who tears open a letter on the stage, knowing there is no real writing inside at all.

A page of finely written script in the late scientist's handwriting lay before him. He read it through from beginning to end, missing no word, uttering each syllable distinctly under his breath as he read.

The pallor of his face grew ghastly as he neared the end. He began to shake all over as with ague. His breath came heavily in gasps. He still gripped the sheet of paper, however, and deliberately, as by an intense effort of will, read it through a second time from beginning to end. And this time, as the last syllable dropped from his lips, the whole face of the man flamed with a sudden and terrible anger. His skin became deep, deep red, and he clenched his teeth. With all the strength of his vigorous soul he was struggling to keep control of himself.

For perhaps five minutes he stood there beside the table without stirring a muscle. He might have been carved out of stone. His eyes were shut, and only the heaving of the chest betrayed the fact that he was a living being. Then, with a strange quietness, he lit a match and applied it to the sheet of paper he held in his hand. The ashes fell slowly about him, piece by piece, and he blew them from the window-sill into the air, his eyes following them as they floated away on the summer wind that breathed so warmly over the world.

He turned back slowly into the room. Although his actions and movements were absolutely steady and controlled, it was clear that he was on the edge of violent action. A hurricane might burst upon the still room any moment. His muscles were tense and rigid. Then, suddenly, he whitened, collapsed, and sank backwards into a chair, like a tumbled bundle of inert matter. He had fainted.

In less than half an hour he recovered consciousness and sat up. As before, he made no sound. Not a syllable passed his lips. He rose quietly and looked about the room.

Then he did a curious thing.

Taking a heavy stick from the rack in the corner he approached the mantelpiece, and with a heavy shattering blow he smashed the clock to pieces. The glass fell in shivering atoms.

'Cease your lying voice for ever,' he said, in a curiously still, even tone. 'There is no such thing as *time!*'

He took the watch from his pocket, swung it round several times by the long gold chain, smashed it into smithereens against the wall with a single blow, and then walked into his laboratory next door, and hung its broken body on the bones of the skeleton in the corner of the room.

'Let one damned mockery hang upon another,' he said, smiling oddly. 'Delusions, both of you, and cruel as false!'

He slowly moved back to the front room. He stopped opposite the bookcase where stood in a row the 'Scriptures of the World,' choicely bound and exquisitely printed, the late professor's most treasured possession, and next to them several books signed 'Pilgrim.'

One by one he took them from the shelf and hurled them through the open window.

'A devil's dreams! A devil's foolish dreams!' he cried, with a vicious laugh.

Presently he stopped from sheer exhaustion. He turned his eyes slowly to the wall opposite, where hung a weird array of Eastern swords and daggers, scimitars and spears, the collections of many journeys. He crossed the room and ran his finger along the edge. His mind seemed to waver.

'No,' he muttered presently; 'not that way. There are easier and better ways than that.'

He took his hat and passed downstairs into the street.

V

IT was five o'clock, and the June sun lay hot upon the pavement. He felt the metal door-knob burn the palm of his hand.

'Ah, Laidlaw, this is well met,' cried a voice at his elbow; 'I was in the act of coming to see you. I've a case that will interest you, and besides, I remembered that you flavoured your tea with orange leaves!—and I admit——'

It was Alexis Stephen, the great hypnotic doctor.*

'I've had no tea to-day,' Laidlaw said, in a dazed manner, after staring for a moment as though the other had struck him in the face. A new idea had entered his mind.

'What's the matter?' asked Dr Stephen quickly. 'Something's wrong with you. It's this sudden heat, or overwork. Come, man, let's go inside.'

A sudden light broke upon the face of the younger man, the light of a heaven-sent inspiration. He looked into his friend's face, and told a direct lie.

'Odd,' he said, 'I myself was just coming to see you. I have something of great importance to test your confidence with. But in *your* house, please,' as Stephen urged him towards his own door—'in your house. It's only round the corner, and I—I cannot go back there—to my rooms—till I have told you.'

'I'm your patient—for the moment,' he added stammeringly as soon as they were seated in the privacy of the hypnotist's sanctum, 'and I want—er——'

'My dear Laidlaw,' interrupted the other, in that soothing voice of command which had suggested to many a suffering soul that the cure for its pain lay in the powers of its own reawakened will, 'I am always at your service, as you know. You have only to tell me what I can do for you, and I will do it.' He showed every desire to help him out. His manner was indescribably tactful and direct.

Dr Laidlaw looked up into his face.

'I surrender my will to you,' he said, already calmed by the other's healing presence, 'and I want you to treat me hypnotically—and at once. I want you to suggest to me'—his voice became very tense—'that I shall forget—forget till I die—everything that has occurred to me during the last two hours; till I die, mind,' he added, with solemn emphasis, 'till I die.'

He floundered and stammered like a frightened boy. Alexis Stephen looked at him fixedly without speaking.

'And further,' Laidlaw continued, 'I want you to ask me no questions. I wish to forget for ever something I have recently discovered—something so terrible and yet so obvious that I can hardly understand why it is not patent to every mind in the world—for I have had a moment of absolute *clear vision*—of merciless clairvoyance. But I want no one else in the whole world to know what it is—least of all, old friend, yourself.'

He talked in utter confusion, and hardly knew what he was saying. But the pain on his face and the anguish in his voice were an instant passport to the other's heart.

'Nothing is easier,' replied Dr Stephen, after a hesitation so slight that the other probably did not even notice it. 'Come into my other room where we shall not be disturbed. I can heal you. Your memory of the last two hours shall be wiped out as though it had never been. You can trust me absolutely.'

'I know I can,' Laidlaw said simply, as he followed him in.

VI

AN hour later they passed back into the front room again. The sun was already behind the houses opposite, and the shadows began to gather.

'I went off easily?' Laidlaw asked.

'You were a little obstinate at first. But though you came in like a lion, you went out like a lamb. I let you sleep a bit afterwards.'

Dr Stephen kept his eyes rather steadily upon his friend's face.

'What were you doing by the fire before you came here?' he asked, pausing, in a casual tone, as he lit a cigarette and handed the case to his patient.

'I? Let me see. Oh, I know; I was worrying my way through poor old Ebor's papers and things. I'm his executor, you know. Then I got weary and came out for a whiff of air.' He spoke lightly and with perfect naturalness. Obviously he was telling the truth. 'I prefer specimens to papers,' he laughed cheerily.

'I know, I know,' said Dr Stephen, holding a lighted match for the cigarette. His face wore an expression of content. The experiment had been a complete success. The memory of the last two hours was wiped out utterly. Laidlaw was already chatting gaily and easily about a dozen other things that interested him. Together they went out into the street, and at his door Dr Stephen left him with a joke and a wry face that made his friend laugh heartily.

'Don't dine on the professor's old papers by mistake,' he cried, as he vanished down the street.

Dr Laidlaw went up to his study at the top of the house. Half way down he met his housekeeper, Mrs Fewings. She was flustered and excited, and her face was very red and perspiring.

'There've been burglars here,' she cried excitedly, 'or something funny! All your things is just any'ow, sir. I found everything all about everywhere!' She was very confused. In this orderly and very precise establishment it was unusual to find a thing out of place.

'Oh, my specimens!' cried the doctor, dashing up the rest of the stairs at top speed. 'Have they been touched or——'

He flew to the door of the laboratory. Mrs Fewings panted up heavily behind him.

'The labatry ain't been touched,' she explained, breathlessly, 'but they smashed the libry clock and they've 'ung your gold watch, sir, on the skelinton's hands. And the books that weren't no value they flung out er the window just like so much rubbish. They must have been wild drunk, Dr Laidlaw, sir!'

The young scientist made a hurried examination of the rooms. Nothing of value was missing. He began to wonder what kind of burglars they were. He looked up sharply at Mrs Fewings standing in the doorway. For a moment he seemed to cast about in his mind for something.

'Odd,' he said at length. 'I only left here an hour ago and everything was all right then.'

'Was it, sir? Yes, sir.' She glanced sharply at him. Her room looked out upon the courtyard, and she must have seen the books come crashing down, and also have heard her master leave the house a few minutes later.

'And what's this rubbish the brutes have left?' he cried, taking up two slabs of worn gray stone, on the writing-table. 'Bath brick* or something, I do declare.'

He looked very sharply again at the confused and troubled housekeeper.

'Throw them on the dust heap, Mrs Fewings, and—and let me know if anything is missing in the house, and I will notify the police this evening.'

When she left the room he went into the laboratory and took his watch off the skeleton's fingers. His face wore a troubled expression, but after a moment's thought it cleared again. His memory was a complete blank.

'I suppose I left it on the writing-table when I went out to take the air,' he said. And there was no one present to contradict him.

He crossed to the window and blew carelessly some ashes of burned paper from the sill, and stood watching them as they floated away lazily over the tops of the trees.

THE FACE OF THE EARTH

FINKELSTEIN, like many another German, resembled a weak edition of Bismarck.* A little way off the appearance was remarkable. Closer, of course, one saw the softness of eye and indecision of jaw that destroyed the illusion.

'I want you to fearful be—of nozzing,' he said, looking the young man up and down.

'I am afraid of nothing,' said Arthur Spinrobin,* believing that the secretaryship was already his.

'Goot,' said the old professor. 'I take you on!'

And thus Arthur Spinrobin, orphan, penniless, the money provided for his Cambridge education just exhausted, began the high adventure of his life by a three months' engagement to Professor Adolf Finkelstein. The only qualification was that he should know German, have some knowledge of surveying, and be 'afraid of nothing.' Finkelstein, for reasons best known to himself, lived at the time in a little farmhouse of greystone among the folds of the Dorsetshire hills; and thither Spinrobin, small, round, and active, with cheerful face and sanguine heart, betook himself, as agreed, on September 1.

'It may lead to something,' he said to himself at the end of the first week, 'but it's all jolly queer. I wonder if the old boy is a spy—or merely a lunatic.' He remembered that he was expected to be afraid of nothing. Arrest, high treason, and other ominous words occurred to him; but in the end he rejected them all. 'He's one of these Teutonic dreamers—transcendentalist and all that—gone a little bit cracky.' Only the map-making puzzled him—uneasily.

For the life they led was not quite ordinary. They had a big sitting-room and a bedroom each in the farm house that was glad enough to take in a couple of boarders. The mornings they spent translating various German passages, beginning with authors like Novalis and Schlegel,* and ending with more modern writers that Spinrobin had never heard of. While Finkelstein translated into French, Spinrobin did likewise into English—apparently with a view to simultaneous publication in both languages of some big Essay the German professor was at work on. This Essay was to include these passages, but Finkelstein did not take the secretary into his confidence concerning it.

There was an air of mystery about the whole thing. And the translated passages always had to do with one subject, viz., that the Earth was the body of a great Being—living, conscious; that it had organs and a physiognomy; that the beauty of nature was merely a revelation of its personality; and that human beings could no more realise this than a fly on an elephant could realise that it walked upon a living body differing from its own merely in size and habits.

'Some faces are too big to be seen as faces,' Finkelstein said one morning to him. Then leaning forward through the tobacco smoke above their work-table he suddenly touched Spinrobin's little turn-up nose with his thick finger. 'The ten million microbes there dwelling,' he said with an earnestness that made the secretary start, 'do not know they are on a human face, *was?*' For he talked German and English indiscriminately. The afternoons they walked together upon the hills, Spinrobin in normal shooting costume, and Finkelstein in baggy, grey knickerbockers, elastic side boots with nails, a loose jacket of Austrian Loden cloth, and a Tyrolese hat. A camera was swung round his shoulder, for he took frequent photographs, which he developed himself.

'Look,' he said, pointing to the smooth, rounded hill-tops about them, treeless, with sheep and cattle feeding in groups. 'The cheeks of a great face I see. I photograph it now, and later show you somezing your own little sight cannot take in. *Ach!* The camera is fine for that. *Wer weisst? Wer weisst?*'*

But the chalk pits drew him most, and he was forever taking photographs or making sketches of them, and asking his secretary to draw accurate plans showing the exact relation they bore to one another; and poring over the results on paper, at home till the smoke got too thick to see, and he would put them away with a sigh and discuss plans for the morrow. In particular there were two pits about a mile apart that interested him, with a third some hundreds of feet below them, very deep, with a ragged edge where gorse and furze bushes grew in a fringe along the lips.

'There we have it, I think,' he used to say in German, after wandering for hours from one to the other, and studying endless photographs and plans of them at home, 'there we have it. Wait und see if I am not right.' All of which bewildered the secretary hopelessly until one day, in his chief's absence, he peeped into his bedroom, and saw on the walls his own series of maps, distorted out of all truth or accuracy, with the pits marked in red, and the whole presenting different aspects of a mighty and very dreadful countenance. The two smaller pits were eyes, and the lower deep one with the bushes fringing it like hair, was a mouth, a huge, open, gaping mouth. The sight produced in him an unpleasant sense of alarm and disgust he was at a loss to account for.

'Ach, not here! Do not stumble here!' the German cried one day when Spinrobin slipped near the edge of the bigger pit, and his face was so white that for a moment it seemed almost as if the depths of chalk below had shot up some curious message of reflected light upon his skin. And for some reason he never could explain quite to himself, the secretary always avoided that particular pit afterwards. A certain sense of personality pervaded it; and when the Professor told him the stories (corroborated in some measure, too, by the farmer) about the number of sheep and cattle it devoured yearly, the sense of dread—though he laughed at it—increased. One evening, too, coming home alone, he heard the wind whistling and booming round its white sides, polishing them to smoothness, and the sudden fancy leaped into his brain of a great purring throat. 'Absurd!' he laughed, turning with a run in a safer direction; 'this old Finkelstein with his crazy anthropomorphism has got into my imagination.'

And that very night they translated long passages from Fechner*—told with a bold power and originality that made it all unpleasantly real to the ordinarily cheerful, healthy-minded little secretary. 'Like your own visionary, ze great Blake,'* exclaimed Finkelstein. In the middle, curiously excited (and using a vigorous English phrase utterly incongruous to the professional type, and picked up heaven knows where!) 'zis Fechner has a great Imagination that bangs straight through into Reality!'

Thus there gradually grew up about the innocent Spinrobin a queer sense that the world was no longer quite the same as he had hitherto seen it. This Fechner, whom the Professor studied, laid a new spell upon him. The water for fish; the air for birds; the ether—well, the ether, too, in turn had its own denizens: worlds! The stars were alive; the planets great spiritual Beings; the earth on which he lived was the physical body of some vast Intelligence that boomed its mighty way through space just as he himself pattered with quick little footsteps across a field. Moreover, Finkelstein elaborated the theory of his fellow countryman with singular conviction.

'Ze worlds are ze true angels,' he said, 'and not imachination is ze music of the spheres.* Ach! I will proof it to everypody when I gif out zis great book I write.' Then, puffing his pipe voluminously into his secretary's face, he would become enthusiastic and more confidential. The worlds, he declared, were some kind of Beings superior to men and animals, but alive and conscious in the same sense. He dwelt upon the analogy till water came into his soft eyes, and his gesticulations threatened the crockery as well as Spinrobin's own astonished features. Arms and legs, he said, after all, are only crutches to enable ill-constructed creatures to get about—whereas the worlds have no need for them, being round. Eyes are equally unnecessary, for they find their way through the ether without them infallibly. For lungs—their whole surface is in continual commerce with the winds; and for circulation, the rivers, springs, and rains are unceasing. Also all the worlds are in most delicate touch with one another, keenly sensitive to the last variation; and where they grow cold—they die.

'*Ach*! *Donnenwetter!** They starve!' he would cry with something between anger and laughter, as though his uncouth imaginations were really true. And Spinrobin, hearing all this from morning till night, and having practical explanations given to him during their walks among the hills, reached a point before long where he became exceedingly uncomfortable. Those maps and tortured photographs haunted his dreams with their suggestions of Races that it is not good for man to look upon. . . .

He kept incessant watch upon Finkelstein. It came to him somehow or other that the work, and the walks, and all the rest of it were a laboured pretence. The German dreamer had some very practical, matter-of-fact purpose behind all his imaginative writing and talking. It made him uneasy. Once or twice on the hills he caught Finkelstein looking at him with a singular expression in his eyes—an expression that made him inclined to run or to cry for help, or do something to draw attention to themselves; and on more than one occasion he was certain he heard something treading softly in the night about the door of his bedroom. And Spinrobin, though not a coward, was decidedly of the timid order. He did not like it! It bewildered his respectable and commonplace soul.

'There,' exclaimed Finkelstein, in his native tongue, one November evening, when a first spray of snow had whitened the hills, 'there you see it well. The snow helps to bring it out—the great whitened face with glorious features! *Ach*! *Ach*! In these desolate places where men have done little to obliterate or disturb, you can see more plainly.' He indicated the curious configuration of the hills about them. From the high point on which they stood, Spinrobin's awakened imagination easily permitted him to trace the 'great whitened face' the enthusiastic German referred to. The pits marked the two eyes, now closed by the shadows of the dusk; and he saw the large, deep, capacious mouth, gaping wide open beneath its fringe of hair-like trees and bushes. It certainly bore a curious resemblance to a vast Face thrust up from below, the features outlined by the powdered snow.

The man came close to his side, and began to talk very rapidly. The secretary's knowledge of German was good, but the other talked so quickly, using such strange phrases and dipping his words with such guttural gymnastics that he found it difficult to follow.

The only thing he gathered generally was that Finkelstein was indulging his imagination, aided by a grotesque humour, in describing the Death of the Earth. The snow and cold made him forecast the time when the body of the earth would be finally dead; and the cause, he declared—here came in the grotesque humour—was that she could no longer feed her internal fires. Mouths, channels, monstrous funnels to act as feeding pipes should be constructed, and the old earth should be kept alive for ever. Or she might even be fed through smaller holes like these very pits—he pointed to them, catching Spinrobin suddenly by the arm—just as human beings might be fed through the pores of the skin!

Spinrobin jumped away from his side in the middle of the strange outburst. They had approached nearer to the edge of the big pit than he cared about.

'My imachination runs me away!' cried the Professor. 'Come let us get home to supper. For it is our duty to feed our own bodies before we feed the earth'; and he laughed aloud as he followed his startled secretary down the stony hillpath back to the farm. During the next few days he made frequent reference, however, to this bizarre notion of feeding the dying earth through holes in her surface—pores in her skin. Spinrobin watched him more carefully than before.

Apparently he was not the only person who watched him, for one afternoon that same week the farmer came abruptly into the secretary's room, and asked for a private word with him. Finkelstein was out. Briefly the man came with a warning. 'You seem innocent like,' explained he, 'but you ain't the first secretary he's had down here, nor the first that's disappeared.'

'But I've not disappeared,' gasped Spinrobin.

'You may do, though—in the cold weather.'

The old man was cryptic and mysterious. He received a big price for his rooms, he explained, but—well, he could not help giving a warning to such a nice young fellow as Spinrobin.

The secretary felt his flesh begin to crawl, and a sudden light dawned upon him. The step of the German already sounded in the hall below, and he turned with a quick question to the friendly farmer. It was guess work, but apparently it hit the bull's-eye.

'The sheep and cattle, then, that disappear—?'

Oh! But he pays me big prices for them—?

The approaching steps of Finkelstein sent the farmer about his business, but Spinrobin went into his room and locked the door. He began to understand things better. His first quarter was up that week. He came to an abrupt decision. Finkelstein could get a new secretary! . . . and next day when he chose a discreet opportunity to announce his decision with plausible excuses, the Professor merely fixed his watery eyes on his face with the remark in German, 'I regret it. You have been a patient and admirable secretary—just the material I want for my great—my great purpose.' But the phrase 'just the material' was ominous and stuck in Spinrobin's mind. Somehow he had come now to loathe the man, his voice, eyes, and gestures. His speculations no longer interested him as before. They touched secret springs of abhorrence and alarm in the depths of him. The figure with Tyrolese hat, baggy knickerbockers and shapeless legs ending in the ridiculous elastic side boots became cloaked with suggestions of a strange horror he could not in the least explain to himself.

And it was a week later—his last day in fact—when a sound woke him at two in the morning, and he peeped out of his window and saw Finkelstein in the moonlight standing with the Loden cloak about his shoulders and throwing up small stones to attract his attention. The moon was reflected in his big spectacles. He carried a long stick. Grotesquely forbidding he looked.

'Come out,' he whispered gutturally, holding up a finger to enjoin silence, 'come out and see. It is too wonderful! *Ach*! It is too wonderful!' He was greatly excited it seemed.

'What?' stammered little Spinrobin, half-frightened. It was like a figure in a nightmare he felt, a figure he was compelled to obey, for his unlined young soul was very sensitive to suggestion, and this German undoubtedly exercised unconscious hypnotic influence over him.

'The pits are working!' continued the thick German voice. 'Only once in a lifetime you see such a thing, perhaps. *Ach*, but quick; come, quick. It is the feeding-time. I show you! *Was?* The feeding-time . . . !'

A crowd of conflicting emotions in the breast of the shivering Spinrobin—curiosity, fear, wonder, and a rash courage of youth that urged him to see this extraordinary adventure to its end—found their resultant expression (to this day he cannot quite explain how!) and brought him in a few minutes to the side of the German outside. They moved rapidly up the hill.

Moonlight lay over the whole tossed landscape of mountain and valley, and a gusty south-west wind from the sea boomed and echoed in the hollows. He heard it swish through the patches of long grass about their feet, and past his ears. The German, wrapped in his cloak, and holding his long stick partly concealed, led the way. His calves, thought Spinrobin, looked just like sausages. At any other time he could have laughed. . . . Instead, he pattered behind, shivering.

'Hark!' whispered Finkelstein, stopping a moment for breath, after a mile of silent climbing. 'Now, you hear it.'

And the secretary heard in the distance that booming sound of the wind as it rushed like mighty breathing about the mouth of the big pit. The same intense curiosity that had brought him out on this mad expedition overcame the instinct to turn and run—for his life. Finkelstein, he saw, was making sudden awkward movements under cover of his cloak. They were standing some fifty yards from the edge now. The great opening gaped there in the moonlight down the steep slope in front.

'It is the great cold,' the German was crying, half to himself, 'the cold that means death! She cries for food! Listen.' He was very excited. '*Ach*! The great service you shall perhaps render!'

The wind rose with a wild roar about them, freezingly cold; it shouted horribly in the depths of the capacious opening in the hill-side. It cried with shrill swishing sounds as it rushed through the fringe of bushes that grew along the dizzy edge.

'She cried for you, for you, for you! *Ach*! You are so privileged as that!' called out Finkelstein, the crisis of his mania full upon him, and fairly dancing with excitement. 'It is only young food she wants. She refuses me again . . . !' And a lot more that Spinrobin did not understand.

The whole thing, and the ghastly dementia of this crazy German was very clear to him now! He was an active, nimble-footed little fellow, but somehow or other he stumbled at the first step. The German's arm shot out, and the rope at the end of the long stick whistled dreadfully in the air as it flew towards him, and entangled itself about his legs. It flashed in the moonlight—death in its coils.

Spinrobin yelled and struggled. Finkelstein, breathing hard, came up along the shortening rope hand over hand towards him, pulling him nearer and nearer to the edge. They rolled and bumped down the precipitous slope, the German just managing to keep out of reach, and the mingled shouting of the two voices rose in wild clamour through the night.

'But why struggle?' cried the lunatic. 'There will be no pain, no pain. And you are worth fifty sheep or cattle . . . !' The spectacled eyes shone like little lamps of silver.

'You shall come too, you brute!' shrieked Spinrobin, at last catching him by an elastic boot and dragging him down upon the ground with a crash. They rolled a bit. Close to the brink, caught by the fringe of gorse bushes which tore and scratched him (though he only knew it afterwards when he saw the scars), they stopped. The rope was hopelessly entangled about their feet. For a second the struggle ceased. Spinrobin heard a loosened stone drop past them, and land with a distant clatter far below. He made a tremendous effort. But the German wriggled free, and stood over him.

Spinrobin, dizzy and exhausted, closed his eyes. The wind rose with a booming roar, and to his terrified imagination, it seemed like great arms that spread out a net to catch him as he fell.

'You feed her! You feed her! *Ach*, it is fine . . . !' The wind tore away with his words.

A moment later he would have toppled over to his death, when one of the gorse bushes, to his utter amazement, stood upright, struck the figure of the German a resounding blow in the chest that sent him spinning backwards to the ground, and at the same instant clutched Spinrobin's feet, and dragged him up into comparative safety.

It was the farmer, who had been disturbed by their leaving the house, and had followed them up the hill. But Spinrobin never knew quite how it happened. He fairly spun—mind and body. . . .

How they managed between them to truss the maniac with the rope and stick and carry him back was not without humour; but the full meaning of the 'secretaryship' (for which Spinrobin never received his salary) was only apparent some weeks later when the advertisement caused by the adventure drew out the whole facts.

For Finkelstein, it appeared, with his singular form of homicidal mania, was proved by the joint investigations of the English and German police to have been the author of at least three mysterious 'disappearances' of young men who had acted as his secretaries; and his remarkable lunacy that imagined the Earth to be a living Being who required human sustenance to keep her alive (he, Finkelstein, being High Priest of the Ceremony), is now minutely recorded for all who care to read, in the Proceedings of the Psychological Societies of both countries.

THE WENDIGO*

I

A CONSIDERABLE number of hunting parties were out that year without finding so much as a fresh trail; for the moose were uncommonly shy, and the various Nimrods* returned to the bosoms of their respective families with the best excuses the facts or their imaginations could suggest. Dr Cathcart, among others, came back without a trophy; but he brought instead the memory of an experience which he declares was worth all the bull-moose that had ever been shot. But then Cathcart, of Aberdeen, was interested in other things besides moose—amongst them the vagaries of the human mind. This particular story, however, found no mention in his book on *Collective Hallucination* for the simple reason (so he confided once to a fellow colleague) that he himself played too intimate a part in it to form a competent judgment of the affair as a whole. . . .

Besides himself and his guide, Hank Davis, there was young Simpson, his nephew, a divinity student destined for the 'Wee Kirk'* (then on his first visit to Canadian backwoods), and the latter's guide, Défago.* Joseph Défago was a French 'Canuck,' who had strayed from his native Province of Quebec years before, and had got caught in Rat Portage when the Canadian Pacific Railway was a-building;* a man who, in addition to his unparalleled knowledge of woodcraft and bush-lore, could also sing the old *voyageur* songs* and tell a capital hunting yarn into the bargain. He was deeply susceptible, moreover, to that singular spell which the wilderness lays upon certain lonely natures, and he loved the wild solitudes with a kind of romantic passion that amounted almost to an obsession. The life of the backwoods fascinated him—whence, doubtless, his surpassing efficiency in dealing with their mysteries.

On this particular expedition he was Hank's choice. Hank knew him and swore by him. He also swore at him, 'jest as a pal might,' and since he had a vocabulary of picturesque, if utterly meaningless, oaths, the conversation between the two stalwart and hardy woodsmen was often of a rather lively description. This river of expletives, however, Hank agreed to dam a little out of respect for his old 'hunting boss,' Dr Cathcart, whom of course he addressed after the fashion of the country as 'Doc'; and also because he understood that young Simpson was already a 'bit of a parson.' He had, however, one objection to Défago, and one only—which was, that the French Canadian sometimes exhibited what Hank described as 'the output of a cursed and dismal mind,' meaning apparently that he sometimes was true to type, Latin type, and suffered fits of a kind of silent moroseness when nothing could induce him to utter speech. Défago, that is to say, was imaginative and melancholy. And, as a rule, it was too long a spell of 'civilization' that induced the attacks, for a few days of the wilderness invariably cured them.

This, then, was the party of four that found themselves in camp the last week in October of that 'shy moose year' 'way up in the wilderness north of Rat Portage—a forsaken and desolate country. There was also Punk, an Indian, who had accompanied Dr Cathcart and Hank on their hunting trips in previous years, and who acted as cook. His duty was merely to stay in camp, catch fish, and prepare venison steaks and coffee at a few minutes' notice. He dressed in the worn-out clothes bequeathed to him by former patrons, and, except for his coarse black hair and dark skin, he looked in these city garments no more like a real redskin than a stage negro looks like a real African. For all that, however, Punk had in him still the instincts of his dying race; his taciturn silence and his endurance survived; also his superstition.

The party round the blazing fire that night were despondent, for a week had passed without a single sign of recent moose discovering itself. Défago had sung his song and plunged into a story, but Hank, in bad humour, reminded him so often that 'he kep' mussing-up the fac's so, that it was 'most all nothin' but a petred-out lie,' that the Frenchman had finally subsided into a sulky silence which nothing seemed likely to break. Dr Cathcart and his nephew were fairly done after an exhausting day. Punk was washing up the dishes, grunting to himself under the lean-to of branches, where he later also slept. No one troubled to stir the slowly dying fire. Overhead the stars were brilliant in a sky quite wintry, and there was so little wind that ice was already forming stealthily along the shores of the still lake behind them. The silence of the vast listening forest stole forward and enveloped them.

Hank broke in suddenly with his nasal voice.

'I'm in favour of breaking new ground tomorrow, Doc,' he observed with energy, looking across at his employer. 'We don't stand a dead Dago's chance about here.'

'Agreed,' said Cathcart, always a man of few words. 'Think the idea's good.'

'Sure pop, it's good,' Hank resumed with confidence. 'S'pose, now, you and I strike west, up Garden Lake* way for a change! None of us ain't touched that quiet bit o' land yet——'

'I'm with you.'

'And you, Défago, take Mr Simpson along in the small canoe, skip across the lake, portage over* into Fifty Island Water, and take a good squint down that thar southern shore. The moose "yarded" there like hell last year, and for all we know they may be doin' it agin this year jest to spite us.'

Défago, keeping his eyes on the fire, said nothing by way of reply. He was still offended, possibly, about his interrupted story.

'No one's been up that way this year, an' I'll lay my bottom dollar on *that!*' Hank added with emphasis, as though he had a reason for knowing. He looked over at his partner sharply. 'Better take the little silk tent and stay away a couple o' nights,' he concluded, as though the matter were definitely settled. For Hank was recognized as general organizer of the hunt, and in charge of the party.

It was obvious to any one that Défago did not jump at the plan, but his silence seemed to convey something more than ordinary disapproval, and across his sensitive dark face there passed a curious expression like a flash of firelight—not so quickly, however, that the three men had not time to catch it. 'He funked* for some reason, *I* thought,' Simpson said afterwards in the tent he shared with his uncle. Dr Cathcart made no immediate reply, although the look had interested him enough at the time for him to make a mental note of it. The expression had caused him a passing uneasiness he could not quite account for at the moment.

But Hank, of course, had been the first to notice it, and the odd thing was that instead of becoming explosive or angry over the other's reluctance, he at once began to humour him a bit.

'But there ain't no *speshul* reason why no one's been up there this year,' he said, with a perceptible hush in his tone; 'not the reason *you* mean, anyway! Las' year it was the fires that kep' folks out, and this year I guess—I guess it jest happened so, that's all!' His manner was clearly meant to be encouraging.

Joseph Défago raised his eyes a moment, then dropped them again. A breath of wind stole out of the forest and stirred the embers into a passing blaze. Dr Cathcart again noticed the expression in the guide's face, and again he did not like it. But this time the nature of the look betrayed itself. In those eyes, for an instant, he caught the gleam of a man scared in his very soul. It disquieted him more than he cared to admit.

'Bad Indians up that way?' he asked, with a laugh to ease matters a little, while Simpson, too sleepy to notice this subtle by-play, moved off to bed with a prodigious yawn; 'or—or anything wrong with the country?' he added, when his nephew was out of hearing.

Hank met his eye with something less than his usual frankness.

'He's jest skeered,' he replied good-humouredly, 'skeered stiff about some ole feery tale! That's all, ain't it, ole pard?' And he gave Défago a friendly kick on the moccasined foot that lay nearest the fire.

Défago looked up quickly, as from an interrupted reverie, a reverie, however, that had not prevented his seeing all that went on about him.

'Skeered—*nuthin'*!' he answered, with a flush of defiance. 'There's nuthin' in the Bush that can skeer Joseph Défago, and don't you forget it!' And the natural energy with which he spoke made it impossible to know whether he told the whole truth or only a part of it.

Hank turned towards the doctor. He was just going to add something when he stopped abruptly and looked round. A sound close behind them in the darkness made all three start. It was old Punk, who had moved up from his lean-to while they talked and now stood there just beyond the circle of firelight—listening.

''Nother time, Doc!' Hank whispered, with a wink, 'when the gallery ain't stepped down into the stalls!' And, springing to his feet, he slapped the Indian on the back and cried noisily, 'Come up t' the fire an' warm yer dirty red skin a bit.' He dragged him towards the blaze and threw more wood on. 'That was a mighty good feed you give us an hour or two back,' he continued heartily, as though to set the man's thoughts on another scent, 'and it ain't Christian to let you stand out there freezin' yer ole soul to hell while we're gettin' all good an' toasted!' Punk moved in and warmed his feet, smiling darkly at the other's volubility which he only half understood, but saying nothing. And presently Dr Cathcart, seeing that further conversation was impossible, followed his nephew's example and moved off to the tent, leaving the three men smoking over the now blazing fire.

It is not easy to undress in a small tent without waking one's companion, and Cathcart, hardened and warm-blooded as he was in spite of his fifty odd years, did what Hank would have described as 'considerable of his twilight' in the open. He noticed, during the process, that Punk had meanwhile gone back to his lean-to, and that Hank and Défago were at it hammer and tongs, or, rather, hammer and anvil, the little French Canadian being the anvil. It was all very like the conventional stage picture of Western melodrama: the fire lighting up their faces with patches of alternate red and black; Défago, in slouch hat and moccasins in the part of the 'badlands'' villain; Hank, open-faced and hatless, with that reckless fling of his shoulders, the honest and deceived hero; and old Punk, eavesdropping in the background, supplying the atmosphere of mystery. The doctor smiled as he noticed the details; but at the same time something deep within him—he hardly knew what—shrank a little, as though an almost imperceptible breath of warning had touched the surface of his soul and was gone again before he could seize it. Probably it was traceable to that 'scared expression' he had seen in the eyes of Défago; 'probably'—for this hint of fugitive emotion otherwise escaped his usually so keen analysis. Défago, he was vaguely aware, might cause trouble somehow. . . . He was not as steady a guide as Hank, for instance. . . . Further than that he could not get . . .

He watched the men a moment longer before diving into the stuffy tent where Simpson already slept soundly. Hank, he saw, was swearing like a mad African in a New York nigger saloon; but it was the swearing of 'affection.' The ridiculous oaths flew freely now that the cause of their obstruction was asleep. Presently he put his arm almost tenderly upon his comrade's shoulder, and they moved off together into the shadows where their tent stood faintly glimmering. Punk, too, a moment later followed their example and disappeared between his odorous blankets in the opposite direction.

Dr Cathcart then likewise turned in, weariness and sleep still fighting in his mind with an obscure curiosity to know what it was had scared Défago about the country up Fifty Island Water way,— wondering, too, why Punk's presence had prevented the completion of what Hank had to say. Then sleep overtook him. He would know tomorrow. Hank would tell him the story while they trudged after the elusive moose.

Deep silence fell about the little camp, planted there so audaciously in the jaws of the wilderness. The lake gleamed like a sheet of black glass beneath the stars. The cold air pricked. In the draughts of night that poured their silent tide from the depths of the forest, with messages from distant ridges and from lakes just beginning to freeze, there lay already the faint, bleak odours of coming winter. White men, with their dull scent, might never have divined them; the fragrance of the wood-fire would have concealed from them these almost electrical hints of moss and bark and hardening swamp a hundred miles away. Even Hank and Défago, subtly in league with the soul of the woods as they were, would probably have spread their delicate nostrils in vain . . .

But an hour later, when all slept like the dead, old Punk crept from his blankets and went down to the shore of the lake like a shadow—silently, as only Indian blood can move. He raised his head and looked about him. The thick darkness rendered sight of small avail, but, like the animals, he possessed other senses that darkness could not mute. He listened—then sniffed the air. Motionless as a hemlock-stem he stood there. After five minutes again he lifted his head and sniffed, and yet once again. A tingling of the wonderful nerves that betrayed itself by no outer sign, ran through him as he tasted the keen air. Then, merging his figure into the surrounding blackness in a way that only wild men and animals understand, he turned, still moving like a shadow, and went stealthily back to his lean-to and his bed.

And soon after he slept, the change of wind he had divined stirred gently the reflection of the stars within the lake. Rising among the far ridges of the country beyond Fifty Island Water, it came from the direction in which he had stared, and it passed over the sleeping camp with a faint and sighing murmur through the tops of the big trees that was almost too delicate to be audible. With it, down the desert paths of night, though too faint, too high even for the Indian's hair-like nerves, there passed a curious, thin odour, strangely disquieting, an odour of something that seemed unfamiliar—utterly unknown.

The French Canadian and the man of Indian blood each stirred uneasily in his sleep just about this time, though neither of them woke. Then the ghost of that unforgettably strange odour passed away and was lost among the leagues of tenantless forest beyond.

II

IN the morning the camp was astir before the sun. There had been a light fall of snow during the night and the air was sharp. Punk had done his duty betimes, for the odours of coffee and fried bacon reached every tent. All were in good spirits.

'Wind's shifted!' cried Hank vigorously, watching Simpson and his guide already loading the small canoe. 'It's across the lake—dead right for you fellers. And the snow'll make bully trails! If there's any moose mussing around up thar, they'll not get so much as a tail-end scent of you with the wind as it is. Good luck, Monsieur Défago!' he added, facetiously giving the name its French pronunciation for once, '*bonne chance!*'

Défago returned the good wishes, apparently in the best of spirits, the silent mood gone. Before eight o'clock old Punk had the camp to himself, Cathcart and Hank were far along the trail that led westwards, while the canoe that carried Défago and Simpson, with silk tent and grub for two days, was already a dark speck bobbing on the bosom of the lake, going due east.

The wintry sharpness of the air was tempered now by a sun that topped the wooded ridges and blazed with a luxurious warmth upon the world of lake and forest below; loons flew skimming through the sparkling spray that the wind lifted; divers shook their dripping heads to the sun and popped smartly out of sight again; and as far as eye could reach rose the leagues of endless, crowding Bush, desolate in its lonely sweep and grandeur, untrodden by foot of man, and stretching its mighty and unbroken carpet right up to the frozen shores of Hudson Bay.

Simpson, who saw it all for the first time as he paddled hard in the bows of the dancing canoe, was enchanted by its austere beauty. His heart drank in the sense of freedom and great spaces just as his lungs drank in the cool and perfumed wind. Behind him in the stern seat, singing fragments of his native chanties, Défago steered the craft of birchbark like a thing of life, answering cheerfully all his companion's questions. Both were gay and light-hearted. On such occasions men lose the superficial, worldly distinctions; they become human beings working together for a common end. Simpson, the employer, and Défago the employed, among these primitive forces, were simply—two men, the 'guider' and the 'guided.' Superior knowledge, of course, assumed control, and the younger man fell without a second thought into the quasi-subordinate position. He never dreamed of objecting when Défago dropped the 'Mr,' and addressed him as 'Say, Simpson,' or 'Simpson, boss,' which was invariably the case before they reached the farther shore after a stiff paddle of twelve miles against a head wind. He only laughed, and liked it; then ceased to notice it at all.

For this 'divinity student' was a young man of parts and character, though as yet, of course, untravelled; and on this trip—the first time he had seen any country but his own and little Switzerland—the huge scale of things somewhat bewildered him. It was one thing, he realized, to hear about primeval forests, but quite another to see them. While to dwell in them and seek acquaintance with their wild life was, again, an initiation that no intelligent man could undergo without a certain shifting of personal values hitherto held for permanent and sacred.

Simpson knew the first faint indication of this emotion when he held the new '303 rifle in his hands and looked along its pair of faultless, gleaming barrels. The three days' journey to their headquarters, by lake and portage, had carried the process a stage farther. And now that he was about to plunge beyond even the fringe of wilderness where they were camped into the virgin heart of uninhabited regions as vast as Europe itself, the true nature of the situation stole upon him with an effect of delight and awe that his imagination was fully capable of appreciating. It was himself and Défago against a multitude—at least, against a Titan!*

The bleak splendours of these remote and lonely forests rather overwhelmed him with the sense of his own littleness. That stern quality of the tangled backwoods which can only be described as merciless and terrible, rose out of these far blue woods swimming upon the horizon, and revealed itself. He understood the silent warning. He realized his own utter helplessness. Only Défago, as a symbol of a distant civilization where man was master, stood between him and a pitiless death by exhaustion and starvation.

It was thrilling to him, therefore, to watch Défago turn over the canoe upon the shore, pack the paddles carefully underneath, and then proceed to 'blaze'* the spruce stems for some distance on either side of an almost invisible trail, with the careless remark thrown in, 'Say, Simpson, if anything happens to me, you'll find the canoe all correc' by these marks;—then strike doo west into the sun to hit the home camp agin, see?'

It was the most natural thing in the world to say, and he said it without any noticeable inflexion of the voice, only it happened to express the youth's emotions at the moment with an utterance that was symbolic of the situation and of his own helplessness as a factor in it. He was alone with Défago in a primitive world: that was all. The canoe, another symbol of man's ascendancy, was now to be left behind. Those small yellow patches, made on the trees by the axe, were the only indications of its hiding-place.

Meanwhile, shouldering the packs between them, each man carrying his own rifle, they followed the slender trail over rocks and fallen trunks and across half-frozen swamps; skirting numerous lakes that fairly gemmed the forest, their borders fringed with mist; and towards five o'clock found themselves suddenly on the edge of the woods, looking out across a large sheet of water in front of them, dotted with pine-clad islands of all describable shapes and sizes.

'Fifty Island Water,' announced Défago wearily, 'and the sun jest goin' to dip his bald old head into it!' he added, with unconscious poetry; and immediately they set about pitching camp for the night.

In a very few minutes, under those skilful hands that never made a movement too much or a movement too little, the silk tent stood taut and cosy, the beds of balsam boughs ready laid, and a brisk cooking-fire burned with the minimum of smoke. While the young Scotchman cleaned the fish they had caught trolling behind the canoe, Défago 'guessed' he would 'jest as soon' take a turn through the Bush for indications of moose. '*May* come across a trunk where they bin and rubbed horns,' he said, as he moved off, 'or feedin' on the last of the maple leaves,'—and he was gone.

His small figure melted away like a shadow in the dusk, while Simpson noted with a kind of admiration how easily the forest absorbed him into herself. A few steps, it seemed, and he was no longer visible.

Yet there was little underbrush hereabouts; the trees stood somewhat apart, well spaced; and in the clearings grew silver-birch and maple, spear-like and slender, against the immense stems of spruce and hemlock. But for occasional prostrate monsters, and the boulders of grey rock that thrust uncouth shoulders here and there out of the ground, it might well have been a bit of park in the Old Country. Almost, one might have seen in it the hand of man. A little to the right, however, began the great burnt section, miles in extent, proclaiming its real character—*brulé*, as it is called, where the fires of the previous year had raged for weeks, and the blackened stumps now rose gaunt and ugly, bereft of branches, like gigantic match-heads stuck into the ground, savage and desolate beyond words. The perfume of charcoal and rain-soaked ashes still hung faintly about it.

The dusk rapidly deepened; the glades grew dark; the crackling of the fire and the wash of little waves along the rocky lake shore were the only sounds audible. The wind had dropped with the sun, and in all that vast world of branches nothing stirred. Any moment, it seemed, the woodland gods, who are to be worshipped in silence and loneliness, might sketch their mighty and terrific outlines among the trees. In front, through doorways pillared by huge straight stems, lay the stretch of Fifty Island Water, a crescent-shaped lake some fifteen miles from tip to tip, and perhaps five miles across where they were camped. A sky of rose and saffron, more clear than any atmosphere Simpson had ever known, still dropped its pale streaming fires across the waves, where the islands—a hundred, surely, rather than fifty—floated like the fairy barques of some enchanted fleet. Fringed with pines, whose crests fingered most delicately the sky, they almost seemed to move upwards as the light faded—about to weigh anchor and navigate the pathways of the heavens instead of the currents of their native and desolate lake.

And strips of coloured cloud, like flaunting pennons, signalled their departure to the stars. . . .

The beauty of the scene was strangely uplifting. Simpson smoked the fish and burnt his fingers into the bargain in his efforts to enjoy it and at the same time tend the frying-pan and the fire. Yet, ever at the back of his thoughts, lay that other aspect of the wilderness: the indifference to human life, the merciless spirit of desolation which took no note of man. The sense of his utter loneliness, now that even Défago had gone, came close as he looked about him and listened for the sound of his companion's returning footsteps.

There was pleasure in the sensation, yet with it a perfectly comprehensible alarm. And instinctively the thought stirred in him: 'What should I—*could* I, do—if anything happened and he did not come back——?'

They enjoyed their well-earned supper, eating untold quantities of fish, and drinking unmilked tea strong enough to kill men who had not covered thirty miles of hard 'going,' eating little on the way. And when it was over, they smoked and told stories round the blazing fire, laughing, stretching weary limbs, and discussing plans for the morrow. Défago was in excellent spirits, though disappointed at having no signs of moose to report. But it was dark and he had not gone far. The *brulé*, too, was bad. His clothes and hands were smeared with charcoal. Simpson, watching him, realized with renewed vividness their position—alone together in the wilderness.

'Défago,' he said presently, 'these woods, you know, are a bit too big to feel quite at home in—to feel comfortable in, I mean! . . . Eh?' He merely gave expression to the mood of the moment; he was hardly prepared for the earnestness, the solemnity even, with which the guide took him up.

'You've hit it right, Simpson, boss,' he replied, fixing his searching brown eyes on his face, 'and that's the truth, sure. There's no end to 'em—no end at all.' Then he added in a lowered tone as if to himself, 'There's lots found out *that*, and gone plumb to pieces!'

But the man's gravity of manner was not quite to the other's liking; it was a little too suggestive for this scenery and setting; he was sorry he had broached the subject. He remembered suddenly how his uncle had told him that men were sometimes stricken with a strange fever of the wilderness, when the seduction of the uninhabited wastes caught them so fiercely that they went forth, half fascinated, half deluded, to their death. And he had a shrewd idea that his companion held something in sympathy with that queer type. He led the conversation on to other topics, on to Hank and the doctor, for instance, and the natural rivalry as to who should get the first sight of moose.

'If they went doo west,' observed Défago carelessly, 'there's sixty miles between us now—with ole Punk at halfway house eatin' himself full to bustin' with fish and corfee.' They laughed together over the picture. But the casual mention of those sixty miles again made Simpson realize the prodigious scale of this land where they hunted; sixty miles was a mere step; two hundred little more than a step. Stories of lost hunters rose persistently before his memory. The passion and mystery of homeless and wandering men, seduced by the beauty of great forests, swept his soul in a way too vivid to be quite pleasant. He wondered vaguely whether it was the mood of his companion that invited the unwelcome suggestion with such persistence.

'Sing us a song, Défago, if you're not too tired,' he asked; 'one of those old *voyageur* songs you sang the other night.' He handed his tobacco pouch to the guide and then filled his own pipe, while the Canadian, nothing loth, sent his light voice across the lake in one of those plaintive, almost melancholy chanties with which lumbermen and trappers lessen the burden of their labour. There was an appealing and romantic flavour about it, something that recalled the atmosphere of the old pioneer days when Indians and wilderness were leagued together, battles frequent, and the Old Country farther off than it is to–day. The sound travelled pleasantly over the water, but the forest at their backs seemed to swallow it down with a single gulp that permitted neither echo nor resonance.

It was in the middle of the third verse that Simpson noticed something unusual—something that brought his thoughts back with a rush from far-away scenes. A curious change had come into the man's voice. Even before he knew what it was, uneasiness caught him, and looking up quickly, he saw that Défago, though still singing, was peering about him into the Bush, as though he heard or saw something. His voice grew fainter—dropped to a hush—then ceased altogether. The same instant, with a movement amazingly alert, he started to his feet and stood upright—*sniffing the air.* Like a dog scenting game, he drew the air into his nostrils in short, sharp breaths, turning quickly as he did so in all directions, and finally 'pointing' down the lake shore, eastwards. It was a performance unpleasantly suggestive and at the same time singularly dramatic. Simpson's heart fluttered disagreeably as he watched it.

'Lord, man! How you made me jump!' he exclaimed, on his feet beside him the same instant, and peering over his shoulder into the sea of darkness. 'What's up? Are you frightened——?'

Even before the question was out of his mouth he knew it was foolish, for any man with a pair of eyes in his head could see that the Canadian had turned white down to his very gills. Not even sunburn and the glare of the fire could hide that.

The student felt himself trembling a little, weakish in the knees. 'What's up?' he repeated quickly. 'D'you smell moose? Or anything queer, anything—wrong?' He lowered his voice instinctively.

The forest pressed round them with its encircling wall; the nearer tree-stems gleamed like bronze in the firelight; beyond that—blackness, and, so far as he could tell, a silence of death. Just behind them a passing puff of wind lifted a single leaf, looked at it, then laid it softly down again without disturbing the rest of the covey. It seemed as if a million invisible causes had combined just to produce that single visible effect. *Other* life pulsed about them—and was gone.

Défago turned abruptly; the livid hue of his face had turned to a dirty grey.

'I never said I heered—or smelt—nuthin',' he said slowly and emphatically, in an oddly altered voice that conveyed somehow a touch of defiance. 'I was only—takin' a look round—so to speak. It's always a mistake to be too previous with yer questions.' Then he added suddenly with obvious effort, in his more natural voice, 'Have you got the matches, Boss Simpson?' and proceeded to light the pipe he had half filled just before he began to sing.

Without speaking another word they sat down again by the fire, Défago changing his side so that he could face the direction the wind came from. For even a tenderfoot could tell that. Délago changed his position in order to hear and smell—all there was to be heard and smelt. And, since he now faced the lake with his back to the trees it was evidently nothing in the forest that had sent so strange and sudden a warning to his marvellously trained nerves.

'Guess now I don't feel like singing any,' he explained presently of his own accord. 'That song kinder brings back memories that's troublesome to me; I never oughter've begun it. It sets me on t' imagining things, see?'

Clearly the man was still fighting with some profoundly moving emotion. He wished to excuse himself in the eyes of the other. But the explanation, in that it was only a part of the truth, was a lie, and he knew perfectly well that Simpson was not deceived by it. For nothing could explain away the livid terror that had dropped over his face while he stood there sniffing the air. And nothing—no amount of blazing fire, or chatting on ordinary subjects—could make that camp exactly as it had been before. The shadow of an unknown horror, naked if unguessed, that had flashed for an instant in the face and gestures of the guide, had also communicated itself, vaguely and therefore more potently, to his companion. The guide's visible efforts to dissemble the truth only made things worse. Moreover, to add to the younger man's uneasiness, was the difficulty, nay, the impossibility he felt of asking questions, and also his complete ignorance as to the cause. . . . Indians, wild animals, forest fires—all these, he knew, were wholly out of the question. His imagination searched vigorously, but in vain. . . .

Yet, somehow or other, after another long spell of smoking, talking and roasting themselves before the great fire, the shadow that had so suddenly invaded their peaceful camp began to lift. Perhaps Défago's efforts, or the return of his quiet and normal attitude accomplished this; perhaps Simpson himself had exaggerated the affair out of all proportion to the truth; or possibly the vigorous air of the wilderness brought its own powers of healing. Whatever the cause, the feeling of immediate horror seemed to have passed away as mysteriously as it had come, for nothing occurred to feed it. Simpson began to feel that he had permitted himself the unreasoning terror of a child. He put it down partly to a certain subconscious excitement that this wild and immense scenery generated in his blood, partly to the spell of solitude, and partly to over fatigue. That pallor in the guide's face was, of course, uncommonly hard to explain, yet it *might* have been due in some way to an effect of firelight, or his own imagination. . . . He gave it the benefit of the doubt; he was Scotch.

When a somewhat unordinary emotion has disappeared, the mind always finds a dozen ways of explaining away its causes. . . . Simpson lit a last pipe and tried to laugh to himself. On getting home to Scotland it would make quite a good story. He did not realize that this laughter was a sign that terror still lurked in the recesses of his soul—that, in fact, it was merely one of the conventional signs by which a man, seriously alarmed, tries to persuade himself that he is *not* so.

Défago, however, heard that low laughter and looked up with surprise on his face. The two men stood, side by side, kicking the embers about before going to bed. It was ten o'clock—a late hour for hunters to be still awake.

'What's ticklin' yer?' he asked in his ordinary tone, yet gravely.

'I—I was thinking of our little toy woods at home, just at that moment,' stammered Simpson, coming back to what really dominated his mind, and startled by the question, 'and comparing them to—to all this,' and he swept his arm round to indicate the Bush.

A pause followed in which neither of them said anything.

'All the same I wouldn't laugh about it, if I was you,' Défago added, looking over Simpson's shoulder into the shadows. 'There's places in there nobody won't never see into—nobody knows what lives in there either.'

'Too big—too far off?' The suggestion in the guide's manner was immense and horrible.

Défago nodded. The expression on his face was dark. He, too, felt uneasy. The younger man understood that in a *hinterland* of this size there might well be depths of wood that would never in the life of the world be known or trodden. The thought was not exactly the sort he welcomed. In a loud voice, cheerfully, he suggested that it was time for bed. But the guide lingered, tinkering with the fire, arranging the stones needlessly, doing a dozen things that did not really need doing. Evidently there was something he wanted to say, yet found it difficult to 'get at.'

'Say, you, Boss Simpson,' he began suddenly, as the last shower of sparks went up into the air, 'you don't—smell nothing, do you— nothing pertickler, I mean?' The commonplace question, Simpson realized, veiled a dreadfully serious thought in his mind. A shiver ran down his back.

'Nothing but this burning wood,' he replied firmly, kicking again at the embers. The sound of his own foot made him start.

'And all the evenin' you ain't smelt—nothing?' persisted the guide, peering at him through the gloom; 'nothing extrordiny, and different to anything else you ever smelt before?'

'No, no, man; nothing at all!' he replied aggressively, half angrily.

Défago's face cleared. 'That's good!' he exclaimed, with evident relief. 'That's good to hear.'

'Have *you?*' asked Simpson sharply, and the same instant regretted the question.

The Canadian came closer in the darkness. He shook his head. 'I guess not,' he said, though without overwhelming conviction. 'It must 've been jest that song of mine that did it. It's the song they sing in lumber-camps and god-forsaken places like that, when they're skeered the Wendigo's somewheres around, doin' a bit of swift travellin'——'

'And what's the Wendigo, pray?' Simpson asked quickly, irritated because again he could not prevent that sudden shiver of the nerves. He knew that he was close upon the man's terror and the cause of it. Yet a rushing passionate curiosity overcame his better judgment, *and* his fear.

Défago turned swiftly and looked at him as though he were suddenly about to shriek. His eyes shone, his mouth was wide open. Yet all he said, or whispered rather, for his voice sank very low, was—

'It's nuthin'—nuthin' but what those lousy fellers believe when they've bin hittin' the bottle too long—a sort of great animal that lives up yonder,' he jerked his head northwards, 'quick as lightning in its tracks, an' bigger'n anything else in the Bush, an' ain't supposed to be very good to look at—*that's all!*'

'A backwoods superstition——' began Simpson, moving hastily towards the tent in order to shake off the hand of the guide that clutched his arm. 'Come, come, hurry up for God's sake, and get the lantern going! It's time we were in bed and asleep if we're to be up with the sun tomorrow. . . .'

The guide was close on his heels. 'I'm coming,' he answered out of the darkness, 'I'm coming.' And after a slight delay he appeared with the lantern and hung it from a nail in the front pole of the tent. The shadows of a hundred trees shifted their places quickly as he did so, and when he stumbled over the rope, diving swiftly inside, the whole tent trembled as though a gust of wind struck it.

The two men lay down, without undressing, upon their beds of soft balsam boughs, cunningly arranged.

Inside, all was warm and cosy, but outside the world of crowding trees pressed close about them, marshalling their million shadows, and smothering the little tent that stood there like a wee white shell facing the ocean of tremendous forest.

Between the two lonely figures within, however, there pressed another shadow that was *not* a shadow from the night. It was the Shadow cast by the strange Fear, never wholly exorcised, that had leaped suddenly upon Défago in the middle of his singing. And Simpson, as he lay there, watching the darkness through the open flap of the tent, ready to plunge into the fragrant abyss of sleep, knew first that unique and profound stillness of a primeval forest when no wind stirs . . . and when the night has weight and substance that enters into the soul to bind a veil about it. . . . Then sleep took him. . . .

III

THUS it seemed to him, at least. Yet it was true that the lap of the water, just beyond the tent door, still beat time with his lessening pulses when he realized that he was lying with his eyes open and that another sound had recently introduced itself with cunning softness between the splash and murmur of the little waves.

And, long before he understood what this sound was, it had stirred in him the centres of pity and alarm. He listened intently, though at first in vain, for the running blood beat all its drums too noisily in his ears. Did it come, he wondered, from the lake, or from the woods? . . .

Then, suddenly, with a rush and a flutter of the heart, he knew that it was close beside him in the tent; and, when he turned over for a better hearing, it focussed itself unmistakably not two feet away. It was a sound of weeping: Défago upon his bed of branches was sobbing in the darkness as though his heart would break, the blankets evidently stuffed against his mouth to stifle it.

And his first feeling, before he could think or reflect, was the rush of a poignant and searching tenderness. This intimate, human sound, heard amid the desolation about them, woke pity. It was so incongruous, so pitifully incongruous—and so vain! Tears—in this vast and cruel wilderness: of what avail? He thought of a little child crying in mid-Atlantic. . . . Then, of course, with fuller realization, and the memory of what had gone before, came the descent of the terror upon him, and his blood ran cold.

'Défago,' he whispered quickly, 'what's the matter?' He tried to make his voice very gentle. 'Are you in pain—unhappy?' There was no reply, but the sounds ceased abruptly. He stretched his hand out and touched him. The body did not stir.

'Are you awake?' for it occurred to him that the man was crying in his sleep. 'Are you cold?' He noticed that his feet, which were uncovered, projected beyond the mouth of the tent. He spread an extra fold of his own blankets over them. The guide had slipped down in his bed, and the branches seemed to have been dragged with him. He was afraid to pull the body back again, for fear of waking him.

One or two tentative questions he ventured softly, but though he waited for several minutes there came no reply, nor any sign of movement. Presently he heard his regular and quiet breathing, and putting his hand again gently on the breast, felt the steady rise and fall beneath.

'Let me know if anything's wrong,' he whispered, 'or if I can do anything. Wake me at once if you feel—queer.'

He hardly knew quite what to say. He lay down again, thinking and wondering what it all meant. Défago, of course, had been crying in his sleep. Some dream or other had afflicted him. Yet never in his life would he forget that pitiful sound of sobbing, and the feeling that the whole awful wilderness of woods listened. . . .

His own mind busied itself for a long time with the recent events, of which *this* took its mysterious place as one, and though his reason successfully argued away all unwelcome suggestions, a sensation of uneasiness remained, resisting ejection, very deep-seated—peculiar beyond ordinary.

IV

BUT sleep, in the long run, proves greater than all emotions. His thoughts soon wandered again; he lay there, warm as a toast, exceedingly weary; the night soothed and comforted, blunting the edges of memory and alarm. Half-an-hour later he was oblivious of everything in the outer world about him.

Yet sleep, in this case, was his great enemy, concealing all approaches, smothering the warning of his nerves.

As, sometimes, in a nightmare events crowd upon each others' heels with a conviction of dreadfullest reality, yet some inconsistent detail accuses the whole display of incompleteness and disguise, so the events that now followed, though they actually happened, persuaded the mind somehow that the detail which could explain them had been overlooked in the confusion, and that therefore they were but partly true, the rest delusion. At the back of the sleeper's mind something remains awake, ready to let slip the judgment, 'All this is not *quite* real; when you wake up you'll understand.'

And thus, in a way, it was with Simpson. The events, not wholly inexplicable or incredible in themselves, yet remain for the man who saw and heard them a sequence of separate acts of cold horror, because the little piece that might have made the puzzle clear lay concealed or overlooked.

So far as he can recall, it was a violent movement, running downwards through the tent towards the door, that first woke him and made him aware that his companion was sitting bolt upright beside him—quivering. Hours must have passed, for it was the pale gleam of the dawn that revealed his outline against the canvas. This time the man was not crying; he was quaking like a leaf; the trembling he felt plainly through the blankets down the entire length of his own body.

Défago had huddled down against him for protection, shrinking away from something that apparently concealed itself near the doorflaps of the little tent.

Simpson thereupon called out in a loud voice some question or other—in the first bewilderment of waking he does not remember exactly what—and the man made no reply. The atmosphere and feeling of true nightmare lay horribly about him, making movement and speech both difficult. At first, indeed, he was not sure where he was—whether in one of the earlier camps, or at home in his bed at Aberdeen. The sense of confusion was very troubling.

And next—almost simultaneous with his waking, it seemed—the profound stillness of the dawn outside was shattered by a most uncommon sound. It came without warning, or audible approach; and it was unspeakably dreadful. It was a voice, Simpson declares, possibly a human voice; hoarse yet plaintive—a soft, roaring voice close outside the tent, overhead rather than upon the ground, of immense volume, while in some strange way most penetratingly and seductively sweet. It rang out, too, in three separate and distinct notes, or cries, that bore in some odd fashion a resemblance, far-fetched yet recognizable, to the name of the guide: '*Dé—fa—go!*'

The student admits he is unable to describe it quite intelligently, for it was unlike any sound he had ever heard in his life, and combined a blending of such contrary qualities. 'A sort of windy, crying voice,' he calls it, 'as of something lonely and untamed, wild and of abominable power. . . .'

And, even before it ceased, dropping back into the great gulfs of silence, the guide beside him had sprung to his feet with an answering though unintelligible cry. He blundered against the tent-pole with violence, shaking the whole structure, spreading his arms out frantically for more room, and kicking his legs impetuously free of the clinging blankets. For a second, perhaps two, he stood upright by the door, his outline dark against the pallor of the dawn; then, with a furious, rushing speed, before his companion could move a hand to stop him, he shot with a plunge through the flaps of canvas—and was gone. And as he went—so astonishingly fast that the voice could actually be heard dying in the distance—he called aloud in tones of anguished terror that at the same time held something strangely like the frenzied exultation of delight—

'Oh! oh! My feet of fire! My burning feet of fire! Oh! oh! This height and fiery speed!'

And then the distance quickly buried it, and the deep silence of very early morning descended upon the forest as before.

It had all come about with such rapidity that, but for the evidence of the empty bed beside him, Simpson could almost have believed it to have been the memory of a nightmare carried over from sleep. He still felt the warm pressure of that vanished body against his side; there lay the twisted blankets in a heap; the very tent yet trembled with the vehemence of the impetuous departure. The strange words rang in his ears, as though he still heard them in the distance—wild language of a suddenly stricken mind. Moreover, it was not only the senses of sight and hearing that reported uncommon things to his brain, for even while the man cried and ran, he had become aware that a strange perfume, faint yet pungent, pervaded the interior of the tent. And it was at this point, it seems, brought to himself by the consciousness that his nostrils were taking this distressing odour down into his throat, that he found his courage, sprang quickly to his feet—and went out.

The grey light of dawn that dropped, cold and glimmering, between the trees revealed the scene tolerably well. There stood the tent behind him, soaked with dew; the dark ashes of the fire, still warm; the lake, white beneath a coating of mist, the islands rising darkly out of it like objects packed in wool; and patches of snow beyond among the clearer spaces of the Bush—everything cold, still, waiting for the sun. But nowhere a sign of the vanished guide—still, doubtless, flying at frantic speed through the frozen woods. There was not even the sound of disappearing footsteps, nor the echoes of the dying voice. He had gone—utterly.

There was nothing; nothing but the sense of his recent presence, so strongly left behind about the camp; *and*—this penetrating, all-pervading odour.

And even this was now rapidly disappearing in its turn. In spite of his exceeding mental perturbation, Simpson struggled hard to detect its nature, and define it, but the ascertaining of an elusive scent, not recognized subconsciously and at once, is a very subtle operation of the mind. And he failed. It was gone before he could properly seize or name it. Approximate description, even, seems to have been difficult, for it was unlike any smell he knew. Acrid rather, not unlike the odour of a lion, he thinks, yet softer and not wholly unpleasing, with something almost sweet in it that reminded him of the scent of decaying garden leaves, earth, and the myriad, nameless perfumes that make up the odour of a big forest. Yet the 'odour of lions' is the phrase with which he usually sums it all up.

Then—it was wholly gone, and he found himself standing by the ashes of the fire in a state of amazement and stupid terror that left him the helpless prey of anything that chose to happen. Had a musk-rat poked its pointed muzzle over a rock, or a squirrel scuttled in that instant down the bark of a tree, he would most likely have collapsed without more ado and fainted. For he felt about the whole affair the touch somewhere of a great Outer Horror. . . . and his scattered powers had not as yet had time to collect themselves into a definite attitude of fighting self-control.

Nothing did happen, however. A great kiss of wind ran softly through the awakening forest, and a few maple leaves here and there rustled tremblingly to earth. The sky seemed to grow suddenly much lighter. Simpson felt the cool air upon his cheek and uncovered head; realized that he was shivering with the cold; and, making a great effort, realized next that he was alone in the Bush—and that he was called upon to take immediate steps to find and succour his vanished companion.

Make an effort, accordingly, he did, though an ill-calculated and futile one. With that wilderness of trees about him, the sheet of water cutting him off behind, and the horror of that wild cry in his blood, he did what any other inexperienced man would have done in similar bewilderment: he ran about, without any sense of direction, like a frantic child, and called. loudly without ceasing the name of the guide—

' Défago! Défago! Défago!' he yelled, and the trees gave him back the name as often as he shouted, only a little softened—'Défago! Défago! Défago!'

He followed the trail that lay for a short distance across the patches of snow, and then lost it again where the trees grew too thickly for snow to lie. He shouted till he was hoarse, and till the sound of his own voice in all that unanswering and listening world began to frighten him. His confusion increased in direct ratio to the violence of his efforts. His distress became formidably acute, till at length his exertions defeated their own object, and from sheer exhaustion he headed back to the camp again. It remains a wonder that he ever found his way. It was with great difficulty, and only after numberless false clues, that he at last saw the white tent between the trees, and so reached safety.

Exhaustion then applied its own remedy, and he grew calmer. He made the fire and breakfasted. Hot coffee and bacon put a little sense and judgment into him again, and he realized that he had been behaving like a boy. He now made another, and more successful attempt to face the situation collectedly, and, a nature naturally plucky coming to his assistance, he decided that he must first make as thorough a search as possible, failing success in which, he must find his way to the home camp as best he could and bring help.

And this was what he did. Taking food, matches and rifle with him, and a small axe to blaze the trees against his return journey, he set forth. It was eight o'clock when he started, the sun shining over the tops of the trees in a sky without clouds. Pinned to a stake by the fire he left a note in case Defago returned while he was away.

This time, according to a careful plan, he took a new direction, intending to make a wide sweep that must sooner or later cut into indications of the guide's trail; and, before he had gone a quarter of a mile he came across the tracks of a large animal in the snow, and beside it the light and smaller tracks of what were beyond question human feet—the feet of Défago. The relief he at once experienced was natural, though brief; for at first sight he saw in these tracks a simple explanation of the whole matter: these big marks had surely been left by a bull moose that, wind against it, had blundered upon the camp, and uttered its singular cry of warning and alarm the moment its mistake was apparent. Défago, in whom the hunting instinct was developed to the point of uncanny perfection, had scented the brute coming down the wind hours before. His excitement and disappearance were due, of course, to—to his——

Then the impossible explanation at which he grasped faded, as common sense showed him mercilessly that none of this was true. No guide, much less a guide like Défago, could have acted in so irrational a way, going off even without his rifle. . . . ! The whole affair demanded a far more complicated elucidation, when he remembered the details of it all—the cry of terror, the amazing language, the grey face of horror when his nostrils first caught the new odour; that muffled sobbing in the darkness, and—for this, too, now came back to him dimly—the man's original aversion for this particular bit of country. . . .

Besides, now that he examined them closer, these were not the tracks of a moose at all! Hank had explained to him the outline of a bull's hoofs, of a cow's or calf's, too, for that matter; he had drawn them clearly on a strip of birch bark. And these were wholly different. They were big, round, ample, and with no pointed outline as of sharp hoofs. He wondered for a moment whether bear-tracks were like that. There was no other animal he could think of, for caribou did not come so far south at this season, and, even if they did, would leave hoof-marks.

They were ominous signs—these mysterious writings left in the snow by the unknown creature that had lured a human being away from safety—and when he coupled them in his imagination with that haunting sound that broke the stillness of the dawn, a momentary dizziness shook his mind, distressing him again beyond belief. He felt the *threatening* aspect of it all. And, stooping down to examine the marks more closely, he caught a faint whiff of that sweet yet pungent odour that made him instantly straighten up again, fighting a sensation almost of nausea.

Then his memory played him another evil trick. He suddenly recalled those uncovered feet projecting beyond the edge of the tent, and the body's appearance of having been dragged towards the opening; the man's shrinking from something by the door when he woke later. The details now beat against his trembling mind with concerted attack. They seemed to gather in those deep spaces of the silent forest about him, where the host of trees stood waiting, listening, watching to see what he would do. The woods were closing round him.

With the persistence of true pluck, however, Simpson went forward, following the tracks as best he could, smothering these ugly emotions that sought to weaken his will. He blazed innumerable trees as he went, ever fearful of being unable to find the way back, and calling aloud at intervals of a few seconds the name of the guide. The dull tapping of the axe upon the massive trunks, and the unnatural accents of his own voice became at length sounds that he even dreaded to make, dreaded to hear. For they drew attention without ceasing to his presence and exact whereabouts, and if it were really the case that something was hunting himself down in the same way that he was hunting down another——

With a strong effort, he crushed the thought out the instant it rose. It was the beginning, he realized, of a bewilderment utterly diabolical in kind that would speedily destroy him.

Although the snow was not continuous, lying merely in shallow flurries over the more open spaces, he found no difficulty in following the tracks for the first few miles. They went straight as a ruled line wherever the trees permitted. The stride soon began to increase in length, till it finally assumed proportions that seemed absolutely impossible for any ordinary animal to have made. Like huge flying leaps they became. One of these he measured, and though he knew that 'stretch' of eighteen feet must be somehow wrong, he was at a complete loss to understand why, he found no signs on the snow between the extreme points. But what perplexed him even more, making him feel his vision had gone utterly awry, was that Défago's stride increased in the same manner, and finally covered the same incredible distances. It looked as if the great beast had lifted him with it and carried him across these astonishing intervals. Simpson, who was much longer in the limb, found that he could not compass even half the stretch by taking a running jump.

And the sight of these huge tracks, running side by side, silent evidence of a dreadful journey in which terror or madness had urged to impossible results, was profoundly moving. It shocked him in the secret depths of his soul. It was the most horrible thing his eyes had ever looked upon. He began to follow them mechanically, absent-mindedly almost, ever peering over his shoulder to see if he, too, were being followed by something with a gigantic tread. . . . And soon it came about that he no longer quite realized what it was they signified— these impressions left upon the snow by something nameless and untamed, always accompanied by the footmarks of the little French Canadian, his guide, his comrade, the man who had shared his tent a few hours before, chatting, laughing, even singing by his side. . . .

V

FOR a man of his years and inexperience, only a canny Scot, perhaps, grounded in common sense and established in logic, could have preserved even that measure of balance that this youth somehow or other did manage to preserve through the whole adventure. Otherwise, two things he presently noticed, while forging pluckily ahead, must have sent him headlong back to the comparative safety of his tent, instead of only making his hands close more tightly upon the rifle-stock, while his heart, trained for the Wee Kirk, sent a wordless prayer winging its way to heaven. Both tracks, he saw, had undergone a change, and this change, so far as it concerned the footsteps of the man, was in some undecipherable manner—appalling.

It was in the bigger tracks he first noticed this, and for a long time he could not quite believe his eyes. Was it the blown leaves that produced odd effects of light and shade, or that the dry snow, drifting like finely-ground rice about the edges, cast shadows and high lights? Or was it actually the fact that the great marks had become faintly coloured? For round about the deep, plunging holes of the animal there now appeared a mysterious, reddish tinge that was more like an effect of light than of anything that dyed the substance of the snow itself. Every mark had it, and had it increasingly—this indistinct fiery tinge that painted a new touch of ghastliness into the picture.

But when, wholly unable to explain or credit it, he turned his attention to the other tracks to discover if they, too, bore similar witness, he noticed that these had meanwhile undergone a change that was infinitely worse, and charged with far more horrible suggestion. For, in the last hundred yards or so, he saw that they had grown gradually into the semblance of the parent tread. Imperceptibly the change had come about, yet unmistakably. It was hard to see where the change first began. The result, however, was beyond question. Smaller, neater, more cleanly modelled, they formed now an exact and careful duplicate of the larger tracks beside them. The feet that produced them had, therefore, also changed. And something in his mind reared up with loathing and with terror as he saw it.

Simpson, for the first time, hesitated; then, ashamed of his alarm and indecision, took a few hurried steps ahead; the next instant stopped dead in his tracks. Immediately in front of him all signs of the trail ceased; both tracks came to an abrupt end. On all sides, for a hundred yards and more, he searched in vain for the least indication of their continuance. There was—nothing.

The trees were very thick just there, big trees all of them, spruce, cedar, hemlock; there was no underbrush. He stood, looking about him, all distraught; bereft of any power of judgment. Then he set to work to search again, and again, and yet again, but always with the same result: *nothing*. The feet that printed the surface of the snow thus far had now, apparently, left the ground!

And it was in that moment of distress and confusion that the whip of terror laid its most nicely calculated lash about his heart. It dropped with deadly effect upon the sorest spot of all, completely unnerving him. He had been secretly dreading all the time that it would come—and come it did.

Far overhead, muted by great height and distance, strangely thinned and wailing, he heard the crying voice of Défago, the guide.

The sound dropped upon him out of that still, wintry sky with an effect of dismay and terror unsurpassed. The rifle fell to his feet. He stood motionless an instant, listening as it were with his whole body, then staggered back against the nearest tree for support, disorganized hopelessly in mind and spirit. To him, in that moment, it seemed the most shattering and dislocating experience he had ever known, so that his heart emptied itself of all feeling whatsoever as by a sudden draught.

'Oh! oh! This fiery height! Oh, my feet of fire! My burning feet of fire. . . . !' ran in far, beseeching accents of indescribable appeal this voice of anguish down the sky. Once it called—then silence through all the listening wilderness of trees.

And Simpson, scarcely knowing what he did, presently found himself running wildly to and fro, searching, calling, tripping over roots and boulders, and flinging himself in a frenzy of undirected pursuit after the Caller. Behind the screen of memory and emotion with which experience veils events, he plunged, distracted and half-deranged, picking up false lights like a ship at sea, terror in his eyes and heart and soul. For the Panic of the Wilderness had called to him in that far voice—the Power of untamed Distance—the Enticement of the Desolation that destroys. He knew in that moment all the pains of some one hopelessly and irretrievably lost, suffering the lust and travail of a soul in the final Loneliness. A vision of Défago, eternally hunted, driven and pursued across the skiey vastness of those ancient forests, fled like a flame across the dark ruin of his thoughts. . . .

It seemed ages before he could find anything in the chaos of his disorganized sensations to which he could anchor himself steady for a moment, and think. . . .

The cry was not repeated; his own hoarse calling brought no response; the inscrutable forces of the Wild had summoned their victim beyond recall—and held him fast.

Yet he searched and called, it seems, for hours afterwards, for it was late in the afternoon when at length he decided to abandon a useless pursuit and return to his camp on the shores of Fifty Island Water. Even then he went with reluctance, that crying voice still echoing in his ears. With difficulty he found his rifle and the homeward trail. The concentration necessary to follow the badly blazed trees, and a biting hunger that gnawed, helped to keep his mind steady. Otherwise, he admits, the temporary aberration he had suffered might have been prolonged to the point of positive disaster. Gradually the ballast shifted back again, and he regained something that approached his normal equilibrium.

But for all that the journey through the gathering dusk was miserably haunted. He heard innumerable following footsteps; voices that laughed and whispered; and saw figures crouching behind trees and boulders, making signs to one another for a concerted attack the moment he had passed. The creeping murmur of the wind made him start and listen. He went stealthily, trying to hide where possible, and making as little sound as he could. The shadows of the woods, hitherto protective or covering merely, had now become menacing, challenging; and the pageantry in his frightened mind masked a host of possibilities that were all the more ominous for being obscure. The presentiment of a nameless doom lurked ill-concealed behind every detail of what had happened.

It was really admirable how he emerged victor in the end; men of riper powers and experience might have come through the ordeal with less success. He had himself tolerably well in hand, all things considered, and his plan of action proves it. Sleep being absolutely out of the question, and travelling an unknown trail in the darkness equally impracticable, he sat up the whole of that night, rifle in hand, before a fire he never for a single moment allowed to die down. The severity of the haunted vigil marked his soul for life; but it was successfully accomplished; and with the very first signs of dawn he set forth upon the long return journey to the home-camp to get help. As before, he left a written note to explain his absence, and to indicate where he had left a plentiful *cache* of food and matches—though he had no expectation that any human hands would find them!

How Simpson found his way alone by lake and forest might well make a story in itself, for to hear him tell it is to *know* the passionate loneliness of soul that a man can feel when the Wilderness holds him in the hollow of its illimitable hand—and laughs. It is also to admire his indomitable pluck.

He claims no skill, declaring that he followed the almost invisible trail mechanically, and without thinking. And this, doubtless, is the truth. He relied upon the guiding of the unconscious mind, which is instinct. Perhaps, too, some sense of orientation, known to animals and primitive men, may have helped as well, for through all that tangled region he succeeded in reaching the exact spot where Défago had hidden the canoe nearly three days before with the remark, 'Strike doo west across the lake into the sun to find the camp.'

There was not much sun left to guide him, but he used his compass to the best of his ability, embarking in the frail craft for the last twelve miles of his journey with a sensation of immense relief that the forest was at last behind him. And, fortunately, the water was calm; he took his line across the centre of the lake instead of coasting round the shores for another twenty miles. Fortunately, too, the other hunters were back. The light of their fires furnished a steering-point without which he might have searched all night long for the actual position of the camp.

It was close upon midnight all the same when his canoe grated on the sandy cove, and Hank, Punk and his uncle, disturbed in their sleep by his cries, ran quickly down and helped a very exhausted and broken specimen of Scotch humanity over the rocks towards a dying fire.

VI

THE sudden entrance of his prosaic uncle into this world of wizardry and horror that had haunted him without interruption now for two days and two nights, had the immediate effect of giving to the affair an entirely new aspect. The sound of that crisp 'Hulloa, my boy! And what's up *now?*' and the grasp of that dry and vigorous hand introduced another standard of judgment. A revulsion of feeling washed through him. He realized that he had let himself 'go' rather badly. He even felt vaguely ashamed of himself. The native hard-headedness of his race reclaimed him.

And this doubtless explains why he found it so hard to tell that group round the fire—everything. He told enough, however, for the immediate decision to be arrived at that a relief party must start at the earliest possible moment, and that Simpson, in order to guide it capably, must first have food and, above all, sleep. Dr Cathcart observing the lad's condition more shrewdly than his patient knew, gave him a very slight injection of morphine. For six hours he slept like the dead.

From the description carefully written out afterwards by this student of divinity, it appears that the account he gave to the astonished group omitted sundry vital and important details. He declares that, with his uncle's wholesome, matter-of-fact countenance staring him in the face, he simply had not the courage to mention them. Thus, all the search-party gathered, it would seem, was that Défago had suffered in the night an acute and inexplicable attack of mania, had imagined himself 'called' by some one or something, and had plunged into the bush after it without food or rifle, where he must die a horrible and lingering death by cold and starvation unless he could be found and rescued in time. 'In time,' moreover, meant 'at once.'

In the course of the following day, however—they were off by seven, leaving Punk in charge with instructions to have food and fire always ready—Simpson found it possible to tell his uncle a good deal more of the story's true inwardness, without divining that it was drawn out of him as a matter of fact by a very subtle form of cross-examination. By the time they reached the beginning of the trail, where the canoe was laid up against the return journey, he had mentioned how Défago spoke vaguely of 'something he called a "Wendigo"'; how he cried in his sleep; how he imagined an unusual scent about the camp; and had betrayed other symptoms of mental excitement. He also admitted the bewildering effect of 'that extraordinary odour' upon himself, 'pungent and acrid like the odour of lions.' And by the time they were within an easy hour of Fifty Island Water he had let slip the further fact—a foolish avowal of his own hysterical condition, as he felt afterwards—that he had heard the vanished guide call 'for help.' He omitted the singular phrases used, for he simply could not bring himself to repeat the preposterous language. Also, while describing how the man's footsteps in the snow had gradually assumed an exact miniature likeness of the animal's plunging tracks, he left out the fact that they measured a *wholly* incredible distance. It seemed a question, nicely balanced between individual pride and honesty, what he should reveal and what suppress. He mentioned the fiery tinge in the snow, for instance, yet shrank from telling that body and bed had been partly dragged out of the tent. . . .

With the net result that Dr Cathcart, adroit psychologist that he fancied himself to be, had assured him clearly enough exactly where his mind, influenced by loneliness, bewilderment and terror, had yielded to the strain and invited delusion. While praising his conduct, he managed at the same time to point out where, when, and how his mind had gone astray. He made his nephew think himself finer than he was by judicious praise, yet more foolish than he was by minimizing the value of his evidence. Like many another materialist, that is, he lied cleverly on the basis of insufficient knowledge, *because* the knowledge supplied seemed to his own particular intelligence inadmissible.

'The spell of these terrible solitudes,' he said, 'cannot leave any mind untouched, any mind, that is, possessed of the higher imaginative qualities. It has worked upon yours exactly as it worked upon my own when I was your age. The animal that haunted your little camp was undoubtedly a moose, for the "belling" of a moose may have, sometimes, a very peculiar quality of sound. The coloured appearance of the big tracks was obviously a defect of vision in your own eyes produced by excitement. The size and stretch of the tracks we shall prove when we come to them. But the hallucination of an audible voice, of course, is one of the commonest forms of delusion due to mental excitement—an excitement, my dear boy, perfectly excusable, and, let me add, wonderfully controlled by you under the circumstances. For the rest, I am bound to say, you have acted with a splendid courage, for the terror of feeling oneself lost in this wilderness is nothing short of awful, and, had I been in your place, I don't for a moment believe I could have behaved with one quarter of your wisdom and decision. The only thing I find it uncommonly difficult to explain is—that—damned odour.'

'It made me feel sick, I assure you,' declared his nephew, 'positively dizzy!' His uncle's attitude of calm omniscience, merely because he knew more psychological formulae, made him slightly defiant. It was so easy to be wise in the explanation of an experience one has not personally witnessed. 'A kind of desolate and terrible odour is the only way I can describe it,' he concluded, glancing at the features of the quiet, unemotional man beside him.

'I can only marvel,' was the reply, 'that under the circumstances it did not seem to you even worse.' The dry words, Simpson knew, hovered between the truth, and his uncle's interpretation of 'the truth.'

And so at last they came to the little camp and found the tent still standing, the remains of the fire, and the piece of paper pinned to a stake beside it—untouched. The *cache*, poorly contrived by inexperienced hands, however, had been discovered and opened—by musk rats, mink and squirrel. The matches lay scattered about the opening, but the food had been taken to the last crumb.

'Well, fellers, he ain't here,' exclaimed Hank loudly after his fashion, 'and that's as sartain as the coal supply down below! But whar he's got to by this time is 'bout as onsartain as the trade in crowns in t'other place.' The presence of a divinity student was no barrier to his language at such a time, though for the reader's sake it may be severely edited. 'I propose,' he added, 'that we start out at once an' hunt for'm like hell!'

The gloom of Défago's probable fate oppressed the whole party with a sense of dreadful gravity the moment they saw the familiar signs of recent occupancy. Especially the tent, with the bed of balsam branches still smoothed and flattened by the pressure of his body, seemed to bring his presence near to them. Simpson, feeling vaguely as if his word were somehow at stake, went about explaining particulars in a hushed tone. He was much calmer now, though overwearied with the strain of his many journeys. His uncle's method of explaining—'explaining away,' rather—the details still fresh in his haunted memory helped, too, to put ice upon his emotions.

'And that's the direction he ran off in,' he said to his two companions, pointing in the direction where the guide had vanished that morning in the grey dawn. 'Straight down there he ran like a deer, in between the birch and the hemlock. . . .'

Hank and Dr Cathcart exchanged glances.

'And it was about two miles down there, in a straight line,' continued the other, speaking with something of the former terror in his voice, 'that I followed his trail to the place where—it stopped—dead!'

'And where you heered him callin' an' caught the stench, an' all the rest of the wicked entertainment,' cried Hank, with a volubility that betrayed his keen distress.

'And where your excitement overcame you to the point of producing illusions,' added Dr Cathcart, under his breath, yet not so low that his nephew did not hear it.

It was early in the afternoon, for they had travelled quickly, and there were still a good two hours of daylight left. Dr Cathcart and Hank lost no time in beginning the search, but Simpson was too exhausted to accompany them. They would follow the blazed marks on the trees, and where possible, his footsteps. Meanwhile the best thing he could do was to keep a good fire going, and rest.

But after something like three hours' search, the darkness already down, the two men returned to camp with nothing to report. Fresh snow had covered all signs, and though they had followed the blazed trees to the spot where Simpson had turned back, they had not discovered the smallest indications of a human being—or, for that matter, of an animal. There were no fresh tracks of any kind; the snow lay undisturbed.

It was difficult to know what was best to do, though in reality there was nothing more they *could* do. They might stay and search for weeks without much chance of success. The fresh snow destroyed their only hope, and they gathered round the fire for supper, a gloomy and despondent party. The facts, indeed, were sad enough, for Défago had a wife at Rat Portage, and his earnings were the family's sole means of support.

Now that the whole truth in all its ugliness was out, it seemed useless to deal in further disguise or pretence. They talked openly of the facts and probabilities. It was not the first time, even in the experience of Dr Cathcart, that a man had yielded to the singular seduction of the Solitudes and gone out of his mind; Défago, moreover, was predisposed to something of the sort, for he already had the touch of melancholia in his blood, and his fibre was weakened by bouts of drinking that often lasted for weeks at a time. Something on this trip—one might never know precisely what—had sufficed to push him over the line, that was all. And he had gone, gone off into the great wilderness of trees and lakes to die by starvation and exhaustion. The chances against his finding camp again were overwhelming; the delirium that was upon him would also doubtless have increased, and it was quite likely he might do violence to himself and so hasten his cruel fate. Even while they talked, indeed, the end had probably come. On the suggestion of Hank, his old pal, however, they proposed to wait a little longer and devote the whole of the following day, from dawn to darkness, to the most systematic search they could devise. They would divide the territory between them. They discussed their plan in great detail. All that men could do they would do.

And, meanwhile, they talked about the particular form in which the singular Panic of the Wilderness had made its attack upon the mind of the unfortunate guide. Hank, though familiar with the legend in its general outline, obviously did not welcome the turn the conversation had taken. He contributed little, though that little was illuminating. For he admitted that a story ran over all this section of country to the effect that several Indians had 'seen the Wendigo' along the shores of Fifty Island Water in the 'fall' of last year, and that this was the true reason of Défago's disinclination to hunt there. Hank doubtless felt that he had in a sense helped his old pal to death by over-persuading him. 'When an Indian goes crazy,' he explained, talking to himself more than to the others, it seemed, 'it's always put that he's "seen the Wendigo." An' pore old Défaygo was superstitious down to his very heels . . . !'

And then Simpson, feeling the atmosphere more sympathetic, told over again the full story of his astonishing tale; he left out no details this time; he mentioned his own sensations and gripping fears. He only omitted the strange language used.

'But Défago surely had already told you all these details of the Wendigo legend, my dear fellow,' insisted the doctor. 'I mean, he had talked about it, and thus put into your mind the ideas which your own excitement afterwards developed?'

Whereupon Simpson again repeated the facts. Défago, he declared, had barely mentioned the beast. He, Simpson, knew nothing of the story, and, so far as he remembered, had never even read about it. Even the word was unfamiliar.

Of course he was telling the truth, and Dr Cathcart was reluctantly compelled to admit the singular character of the whole affair. He did not do this in words so much as in manner, however. He kept his back against a good, stout tree; he poked the fire into a blaze the moment it showed signs of dying down; he was quicker than any of them to notice the least sound in the night about them—a fish jumping in the lake, a twig snapping in the bush, the dropping of occasional fragments of frozen snow from the branches overhead where the heat loosened them. His voice, too, changed a little in quality, becoming a shade less confident, lower also in tone. Fear, to put it plainly, hovered close about that little camp, and though all three would have been glad to speak of other matters, the only thing they seemed able to discuss was this—the source of their fear. They tried other subjects in vain; there was nothing to say about them. Hank was the most honest of the group; he said next to nothing. He never once, however, turned his back to the darkness. His face was always to the forest, and when wood was needed he didn't go farther than was necessary to get it.

VII

A WALL of silence wrapped them in, for the snow, though not thick, was sufficient to deaden any noise, and the frost held things pretty tight besides. No sound but their voices and the soft roar of the flames made itself heard. Only, from time to time, something soft as the flutter of a pine-moth's wings went past them through the air. No one seemed anxious to go to bed. The hours slipped towards midnight.

'The legend is picturesque enough,' observed the doctor after one of the longer pauses, speaking to break it rather than because he had anything to say, 'for the Wendigo is simply the Call of the Wild personified, which some natures hear to their own destruction.'

'That's about it,' Hank said presently. 'An' there's no misunderstandin' when you hear it. It calls you by name right 'nough.'

Another pause followed. Then Dr Cathcart came back to the forbidden subject with a rush that made the others jump.

'The allegory *is* significant,' he remarked, looking about him into the darkness, 'for the Voice, they say, resembles all the minor sounds of the Bush—wind, falling water, cries of animals, and so forth. And, once the victim hears *that*—he's off for good, of course! His most vulnerable points, moreover, are said to be the feet and the eyes; the feet, you see, for the lust of wandering, and the eyes for the lust of beauty. The poor beggar goes at such a dreadful speed that he bleeds beneath the eyes, and his feet burn.'

Dr Cathcart, as he spoke, continued to peer uneasily into the surrounding gloom. His voice sank to a hushed tone.

'The Wendigo,' he added, 'is said to burn his feet—owing to the friction, apparently caused by its tremendous velocity—till they drop off, and new ones form exactly like its own.'

Simpson listened in horrified amazement; but it was the pallor on Hank's face that fascinated him most. He would willingly have stopped his ears and closed his eyes, had he dared.

'It don't always keep to the ground neither,' came in Hank's slow, heavy drawl, 'for it goes so high that he thinks the stars have set him all a-fire. An' it'll take great thumpin' jumps sometimes, an' run along the tops of the trees, carrying its partner with it, an' then droppin' him jest as a fish-hawk 'll drop a pickerel to kill it before eatin'. An' its food, of all the muck in the whole Bush is—moss!' And he laughed a short, unnatural laugh. 'It's a moss-eater, is the Wendigo,' he added, looking up excitedly into the faces of his companions, 'moss-eater,' he repeated, with a string of the most outlandish oaths he could invent.

But Simpson now understood the true purpose of all this talk. What these two men, each strong and 'experienced' in his own way, dreaded more than anything else was—silence. They were talking against time. They were also talking against darkness, against the invasion of panic, against the admission reflection might bring that they were in an enemy's country—against anything, in fact, rather than allow their inmost thoughts to assume control. He himself, already initiated by the awful vigil with terror, was beyond both of them in this respect. He had reached the stage where he was immune. But these two, the scoffing, analytical doctor, and the honest, dogged backwoodsman, each sat trembling in the depths of his being.

Thus the hours passed; and thus, with lowered voices and a kind of taut inner resistance of spirit, this little group of humanity sat in the jaws of the wilderness and talked foolishly of the terrible and haunting legend. It was an unequal contest, all things considered, for the wilderness had already the advantage of first attack—and of a hostage. The fate of their comrade hung over them with a steadily increasing weight of oppression that finally became insupportable.

It was Hank, after a pause longer than the preceding ones that no one seemed able to break, who first let loose all this pent-up emotion in very unexpected fashion, by springing suddenly to his feet and letting out the most ear-shattering yell imaginable into the night. He could not contain himself any longer, it seemed. To make it carry even beyond an ordinary cry he interrupted its rhythm by shaking the palm of his hand before his mouth.

'That's for Défago,' he said, looking down at the other two with a queer, defiant laugh, 'for it's my belief'—the sandwiched oaths may be omitted—'that my ole partner's not far from us at this very minute.'

There was a vehemence and recklessness about his performance that made Simpson, too, start to his feet in amazement, and betrayed even the doctor into letting the pipe slip from between his lips. Hank's face was ghastly, but Cathcart's showed a sudden weakness—

a loosening of all his faculties, as it were. Then a momentary anger blazed into his eyes, and he too, though with deliberation born of habitual self-control, got upon his feet and faced the excited guide. For this was unpermissible, foolish, dangerous, and he meant to stop it in the bud.

What might have happened in the next minute or two one may speculate about, yet never definitely know, for in the instant of profound silence that followed Hank's roaring voice, and as though in answer to it, something went past through the darkness of the sky overhead at terrific speed—something of necessity very large, for it displaced much air, while down between the trees there fell a faint and windy cry of a human voice, calling in tones of indescribable anguish and appeal—

'Oh, oh! this fiery height! Oh, oh! My feet of fire! My burning feet of fire!'

White to the very edge of his shirt, Hank looked stupidly about him like a child. Dr Cathcart uttered some kind of unintelligible cry, turning as he did so with an instinctive movement of blind terror towards the protection of the tent, then halting in the act as though frozen. Simpson, alone of the three, retained his presence of mind a little. His own horror was too deep to allow of any immediate reaction. He had heard that cry before.

Turning to his stricken companions, he said almost calmly—

'That's exactly the cry I heard—the very words he used!'

Then, lifting his face to the sky, he cried aloud, ' Défago, Défago! Come down here to us! Come down——!'

And before there was time for anybody to take definite action one way or another, there came the sound of something dropping heavily between the trees, striking the branches on the way down, and landing with a dreadful thud upon the frozen earth below. The crash and thunder of it was really terrific.

'That's him, s'help me the good Gawd!' came from Hank in a whispering cry half choked, his hand going automatically towards the hunting-knife in his belt. 'And he's coming! He's coming!' he added, with an irrational laugh of terror, as the sounds of heavy footsteps crunching over the snow became distinctly audible, approaching through the blackness towards the circle of light.

And while the steps, with their stumbling motion, moved nearer and nearer upon them, the three men stood round that fire, motionless and dumb. Dr Cathcart had the appearance as of a man suddenly withered; even his eyes did not move. Hank, suffering shockingly, seemed on the verge again of violent action; yet did nothing. He, too, was hewn of stone. Like stricken children they seemed. The picture was hideous. And, meanwhile, their owner still invisible, the footsteps came closer, crunching the frozen snow. It was endless—too prolonged to be quite real—this measured and pitiless approach. It was accursed.

VIII

THEN at length the darkness, having thus laboriously conceived, brought forth—a figure. It drew forward into the zone of uncertain light where fire and shadows mingled, not ten feet away; then halted, staring at them fixedly. The same instant it started forward again with the spasmodic motion as of a thing moved by wires, and coming up closer to them, full into the glare of the fire, they perceived then that—it was a man; and apparently that this man was—Défago.

Something like a skin of horror almost perceptibly drew down in that moment over every face, and three pairs of eyes shone through it as though they saw across the frontiers of normal vision into the Unknown.

Défago advanced, his tread faltering and uncertain; he made his way straight up to them as a group first, then turned sharply and peered close into the face of Simpson. The sound of a voice issued from his lips—

'Here I am, Boss Simpson. I heered some one calling me.' It was a faint, dried-up voice, made wheezy and breathless as by immense exertion. 'I'm havin' a reg'lar hell-fire kind of a trip, I am.' And he laughed, thrusting his head forward into the other's face.

But that laugh started the machinery of the group of wax-work figures with the wax-white skins. Hank immediately sprang forward with a stream of oaths so far-fetched that Simpson did not recognize them as English at all, but thought he had lapsed into Indian or some other lingo. He only realized that Hank's presence, thrust thus between them, was welcome—uncommonly welcome. Dr Cathcart, though more calmly and leisurely, advanced behind him, heavily stumbling.

Simpson seems hazy as to what was actually said and done in those next few seconds, for the eyes of that detestable and blasted visage peering at such close quarters into his own utterly bewildered his senses at first. He merely stood still. He said nothing. He had not the trained will of the older men that forced them into action in defiance of all emotional stress. He watched them moving as behind a glass, that half destroyed their reality: it was dream-like, perverted. Yet, through the torrent of Hank's meaningless phrases, he remembers hearing his uncle's tone of authority—hard and forced—saying several things about food and warmth, blankets, whisky and the rest; . . . and, further, that whiffs of that penetrating, unaccustomed odour, vile, yet sweetly bewildering, assailed his nostrils during all that followed.

It was no less a person than himself, however—less experienced and adroit than the others though he was—who gave instinctive utterance to the sentence that brought a measure of relief into the ghastly situation by expressing the doubt and thought in each one's heart.

'It *is*—YOU, isn't it, Défago?' he asked under his breath, horror breaking his speech.

And at once Cathcart burst out with the loud answer before the other had time to move his lips. 'Of course it is! Of course it is! Only—can't you see—he's nearly dead with exhaustion, cold and terror? Isn't *that* enough to change a man beyond all recognition?' It was said in order to convince himself as much as to convince the others. The overemphasis alone proved that. And continually, while he spoke and acted, he held a handkerchief to his nose. That odour pervaded the whole camp.

For the 'Défago' who sat huddled by the big fire, wrapped in blankets, drinking hot whisky and holding food in wasted hands, was no more like the guide they had last seen alive than the picture of a man of sixty is like the daguerreotype of his early youth in the costume of another generation. Nothing really can describe that ghastly caricature, that parody, masquerading there in the firelight as Défago. From the ruins of the dark and awful memories he still retains, Simpson declares that the face was more animal than human, the features drawn about into wrong proportions, the skin loose and hanging, as though he had been subjected to extraordinary pressures and tensions. It made him think vaguely of those bladderfaces blown up by the hawkers on Ludgate Hill, that change their expression as they swell, and as they collapse emit a faint and wailing imitation of a voice. Both face and voice suggested some such abominable resemblance. But Cathcart long afterwards, seeking to describe the indescribable, asserts that thus might have looked a face and body that had been in air so rarified that, the weight of atmosphere being removed, the entire structure threatened to fly asunder and become—*incoherent*. . . .

It was Hank, though all distraught and shaking with a tearing volume of emotion he could neither handle nor understand, who brought things to a head without more ado. He went off to a little distance from the fire, apparently so that the light should not dazzle him too much, and shading his eyes for a moment with both hands, shouted in a loud voice that held anger and affection dreadfully mingled—

'You ain't Défaygo! You ain't Défaygo at all! I don't give a——damn, but that ain't you, my ole pal of twenty years!' He glared upon the huddled figure as though he would destroy him with his eyes. 'An' if it is I'll swab the floor of hell with a wad of cotton-wool on a toothpick, s'help me the good Gawd!' he added, with a violent fling of horror and disgust.

It was impossible to silence him. He stood there shouting like one possessed, horrible to see, horrible to hear—*because it was the truth*. He repeated himself in fifty different ways, each more outlandish than the last. The woods rang with echoes. At one time it looked as if he meant to fling himself upon 'the intruder,' for his hand continually jerked towards the long hunting-knife in his belt.

But in the end he did nothing, and the whole tempest completed itself very nearly with tears. Hank's voice suddenly broke, he collapsed on the ground, and Cathcart somehow or other persuaded him at last to go into the tent and lie quiet. The remainder of the affair, indeed, was witnessed by him from behind the canvas, his white and terrified face peeping through the crack of the tent door-flap.

Then Dr Cathcart, closely followed by his nephew who so far had kept his courage better than all of them, went up with a determined air and stood opposite to the figure of Défago huddled over the fire. He looked him squarely in the face and spoke. At first his voice was firm.

'Défago, tell us what's happened—just a little, so that we can know how best to help you?' he asked in a tone of authority, almost of command. And at that point, it *was* command. At once afterwards, however, it changed in quality, for the figure turned up to him a face so piteous, so terrible and so little like humanity, that the doctor shrank back from him as from something spiritually unclean. Simpson, watching close behind him, says he got the impression of a mask that was on the verge of dropping off, and that underneath they would discover something black and diabolical, revealed in utter nakedness. 'Out with it, man, out with it!' Cathcart cried, terror running neck and neck with entreaty. 'None of us can stand this much longer . . . !' It was the cry of instinct over reason.

And then 'Défago,' smiling *whitely*, answered in that thin and fading voice that already seemed passing over into a sound of quite another character—

'I seen that great Wendigo thing,' he whispered, sniffing the air about him exactly like an animal. 'I been with it too——'

Whether the poor devil would have said more, or whether Dr Cathcart would have continued the impossible cross-examination cannot be known, for at that moment the voice of Hank was heard yelling at the top of his shout from behind the canvas that concealed all but his terrified eyes. Such a howling was never heard.

'His feet! Oh, Gawd, his feet! Look at his great changed—feet!'

Défago, shuffling where he sat, had moved in such a way that for the first time his legs were in full light and his feet were visible. Yet Simpson had no time, himself, to see properly what Hank had seen. And Hank has never seen fit to tell. That same instant, with a leap like that of a frightened tiger, Cathcart was upon him, bundling the folds of blanket about his legs with such speed that the young student caught little more than a passing glimpse of something dark and oddly massed where moccasined feet ought to have been, and saw even that but with uncertain vision.

Then, before the doctor had time to do more, or Simpson time to even think a question, much less ask it, Défago was standing upright in front of them, balancing with pain and difficulty, and upon his shapeless and twisted visage an expression so dark and so malicious that it was, in the true sense, monstrous.

'Now *you* seen it too,' he wheezed, 'you seen my fiery, burning feet! And now—that is, unless you kin save me an' prevent—it's 'bout time for——'

His piteous and beseeching voice was interrupted by a sound that was like the roar of wind coming across the lake. The trees overhead shook their tangled branches. The blazing fire bent its flames as before a blast. And something swept with a terrific, rushing noise about the little camp and seemed to surround it entirely in a single moment of time. Défago shook the clinging blankets from his body, turned towards the woods behind, and with the same stumbling motion that had brought him—was gone: gone, before any one could move muscle to prevent him, gone with an amazing, blundering swiftness that left no time to act. The darkness positively swallowed him; and less than a dozen seconds later, above the roar of the swaying trees and the shout of the sudden wind, all three men, watching and listening with stricken hearts, heard a cry that seemed to drop down upon them from a great height of sky and distance—

'Oh, oh! This fiery height! Oh, oh! My feet of fire! My burning feet of fire . . . !' then died away, into untold space and silence.

Dr Cathcart—suddenly master of himself, and therefore of the others—was just able to seize Hank violently by the arm as he tried to dash headlong into the Bush.

'But I want ter know,——you!' shrieked the guide. 'I want ter see! That ain't him at all, but some——devil that's shunted into his place . . . !'

Somehow or other—he admits he never quite knew how he accomplished it—he managed to keep him in the tent and pacify him. The doctor, apparently, had reached the stage where reaction had set in and allowed his own innate force to conquer. Certainly he 'managed' Hank admirably. It was his nephew, however, hitherto so wonderfully controlled, who gave him most cause for anxiety, for the cumulative strain had now produced a condition of lachrymose hysteria which made it necessary to isolate him upon a bed of boughs and blankets as far removed from Hank as was possible under the circumstances.

And there he lay, as the watches of that haunted night passed over the lonely camp, crying startled sentences, and fragments of sentences, into the folds of his blankets. A quantity of gibberish about speed and height and fire mingled oddly with biblical memories of the class-room. 'People with broken faces all on fire are coming at a most awful, awful, pace towards the camp!' he would moan one minute; and the next would sit up and stare into the woods, intently listening, and whisper, 'How terrible in the wilderness are—are the feet of them that——'* until his uncle came across to change the direction of his thoughts and comfort him.

The hysteria, fortunately, proved but temporary. Sleep cured him, just as it cured Hank.

Till the first signs of daylight came, soon after five o'clock, Dr Cathcart kept his vigil. His face was the colour of chalk, and there were strange flushes beneath the eyes. An appalling terror of the soul battled with his will all through those silent hours. These were some of the outer signs. . . .

At dawn he lit the fire himself, made breakfast, and woke the others, and by seven they were well on their way back to the home camp—three perplexed and afflicted men, but each in his own way having reduced his inner turmoil to a condition of more or less systematized order again.

IX

THEY talked little, and then only of the most wholesome and common things, for their minds were charged with painful thoughts that clamoured for explanation, though no one dared refer to them. Hank, being nearest to primitive conditions, was the first to find himself, for he was also less complex. In Dr Cathcart 'civilization' championed his forces against an attack singular enough. To this day, perhaps, he is not *quite* sure of certain things. Anyhow, he took longer to 'find himself.'

Simpson, the student of divinity, it was who arranged his conclusions probably with the best, though not most scientific, appearance of order. Out there, in the heart of unreclaimed wilderness, they had surely witnessed something crudely and essentially primitive. Something that had survived somehow the advance of humanity had emerged terrifically, betraying a scale of life still monstrous and immature. He envisaged it rather as a glimpse into prehistoric ages, when superstitions, gigantic and uncouth, still oppressed the hearts of men; when the forces of nature were still untamed, the Powers that may have haunted a primeval universe not yet withdrawn. To this day he thinks of what he termed years later in a sermon 'savage and formidable Potencies lurking behind the souls of men, not evil perhaps in themselves, yet instinctively hostile to humanity as it exists.'

With his uncle he never discussed the matter in detail, for the barrier between the two types of mind made it difficult. Only once, years later, something led them to the frontier of the subject—of a single detail of the subject, rather—

'Can't you even tell me what—*they* were like?' he asked; and the reply, though conceived in wisdom, was not encouraging, ' It is far better you should not try to know, or to find out.'

'Well—that odour . . . ?' persisted the nephew.

'What do you make of that?'

Dr Cathcart looked at him and raised his eyebrows.

'Odours,' he replied, 'are not so easy as sounds and sights of telepathic communication. I make as much, or as little, probably, as you do yourself.'

He was not quite so glib as usual with his explanations. That was all.

At the fall of day, cold, exhausted, famished, the party came to the end of the long portage and dragged themselves into a camp that at first glimpse seemed empty. Fire there was none, and no Punk came forward to welcome them. The emotional capacity of all three was too over-spent to recognize either surprise or annoyance; but the cry of spontaneous affection that burst from the lips of Hank, as he rushed ahead of them towards the fire-place, came probably as a warning that the end of the amazing affair was not quite yet. And both Cathcart and his nephew confessed afterwards that when they saw him kneel down in his excitement and embrace something that reclined, gently moving, beside the extinguished ashes, they felt in their very bones that this 'something' would prove to be Défago—the true Défago, returned.

And so, indeed, it was.

It is soon told. Exhausted to the point of emaciation, the French Canadian—what was left of him, that is—fumbled among the ashes, trying to make a fire. His body crouched there, the weak fingers obeying feebly the instinctive habit of a lifetime with twigs and matches. But there was no longer any mind to direct the simple operation. The mind had fled beyond recall. And with it, too, had fled memory. Not only recent events, but all previous life was a blank.

This time it was the real man, though incredibly and horribly shrunken. On his face was no expression of any kind whatever—fear, welcome, or recognition. He did not seem to know who it was that embraced him, or who it was that fed, warmed and spoke to him the words of comfort and relief. Forlorn and broken beyond all reach of human aid, the little man did meekly as he was bidden. The 'something' that had constituted him 'individual' had vanished for ever.

In some ways it was more terribly moving than anything they had yet seen—that idiot smile as he drew wads of coarse moss from his swollen cheeks and told them that he was 'a damned moss eater'; the continued vomiting of even the simplest food; and, worst of all, the piteous and childish voice of complaint in which he told them that his feet pained him—'burn like fire'—which was natural enough when Dr Cathcart examined them and found that both were dreadfully frozen. Beneath the eyes there were faint indications of recent bleeding.

The details of how he survived the prolonged exposure, of where he had been, or of how he covered the great distance from one camp to the other, including an immense detour of the lake on foot since he had no canoe—all this remains unknown. His memory had vanished completely. And before the end of the winter whose beginning witnessed this strange occurrence, Défago, bereft of mind, memory and soul, had gone with it. He lingered only a few weeks.

And what Punk was able to contribute to the story throws no further light upon it. He was cleaning fish by the take shore about five o'clock in the evening—an hour, that is, before the search party returned—when he saw this shadow of the guide picking its way weakly into camp. In advance of him, he declares, came the faint whiff of a certain singular odour.

That same instant old Punk started for home. He covered the entire journey of three days as only Indian blood could have covered it. The terror of a whole race drove him. He knew what it all meant. Défago had 'seen the Wendigo.'

THE MAN WHOM THE TREES LOVED

I

HE painted trees as by some special divining instinct of their essential qualities. He understood them. He knew why in an oak forest, for instance, each individual was utterly distinct from its fellows, and why no two beeches in the whole world were alike. People asked him down to paint a favourite lime or silver birch, for he caught the individuality of a tree as some catch the individuality of a horse. How he managed it was something of a puzzle, for he never had painting lessons, his drawing was often wildly inaccurate, and, while his perception of a Tree Personality was true and vivid, his rendering of it might almost approach the ludicrous. Yet the character and personality of that particular tree stood there alive beneath his brush—shining, frowning, dreaming, as the case might be, friendly or hostile, good or evil. It emerged.

There was nothing else in the wide world that he could paint; flowers and landscapes he only muddled away into a smudge; with people he was helpless and hopeless; also with animals. Skies he could sometimes manage, or effects of wind in foliage, but as a rule he left these all severely alone. He kept to trees, wisely following an instinct that was guided by love. It was quite arresting, this way he had of making a tree look almost like a being—alive. It approached the uncanny.

'Yes, Sanderson* knows what he's doing when he paints a tree!' thought old David Bittacy, C.B., late of the Woods and Forests.* 'Why, you can almost hear it rustle. You can smell the thing. You can hear the rain drip through its leaves. You can almost see the branches move. It grows.' For in this way somewhat he expressed his satisfaction, half to persuade himself that the twenty guineas were well spent (since his wife thought otherwise), and half to explain this uncanny reality of life that lay in the fine old cedar framed above his study table.

Yet in the general view the mind of Mr Bittacy was held to be austere, not to say morose. Few divined in him the secretly tenacious love of nature that had been fostered by years spent in the forests and jungles of the eastern world. It was odd for an Englishman, due possibly to that Eurasian ancestor. Surreptitiously, as though half ashamed of it, he had kept alive a sense of beauty that hardly belonged to his type, and was unusual for its vitality. Trees, in particular, nourished it. He, also, understood trees, felt a subtle sense of communion with them, born perhaps of those years he had lived in caring for them, guarding, protecting, nursing, years of solitude among their great shadowy presences. He kept it largely to himself, of course, because he knew the world he lived in. He also kept it from his wife—to some extent. He knew it came between them, knew that she feared it, was opposed. But what he did not know, or realise at any rate, was the extent to which she grasped the power which they wielded over his life. Her fear, he judged, was simply due to those years in India, when for weeks at a time his calling took him away from her into the jungle forests, while she remained at home dreading all manner of evils that might befall him. This, of course, explained her instinctive opposition to the passion for woods that still influenced and clung to him. It was a natural survival of those anxious days of waiting in solitude for his safe return.

For Mrs Bittacy, daughter of an evangelical clergyman,* was a self-sacrificing woman, who in most things found a happy duty in sharing her husband's joys and sorrows to the point of self-obliteration. Only in this matter of the trees she was less successful than in others. It remained a problem difficult of compromise.

He knew, for instance, that what she objected to in this portrait of the cedar on their lawn was really not the price he had given for it, but the unpleasant way in which the transaction emphasised this breach between their common interests—the only one they had, but deep.

Sanderson, the artist, earned little enough money by his strange talent; such cheques were few and far between. The owners of fine or interesting trees who cared to have them painted singly were rare indeed; and the 'studies' that he made for his own delight he also kept for his own delight. Even were there buyers, he would not sell them. Only a few, and these peculiarly intimate friends, might even see them, for he disliked to hear the undiscerning criticisms of those who did not understand. Not that he minded laughter at his craftmanship—he admitted it with scorn—but that remarks about the personality of the tree itself could easily wound or anger him. He resented slighting observations concerning them, as though insults offered to personal friends who could not answer for themselves. He was instantly up in arms.

'It really *is* extraordinary,' said a Woman who Understood, 'that you can make that cypress seem an individual, when in reality all cypresses are so *exactly* alike.'

And though the bit of calculated flattery had come so near to saying the right, true thing, Sanderson flushed as though she had slighted a friend beneath his very nose. Abruptly he passed in front of her and turned the picture to the wall.

'Almost as queer,' he answered rudely, copying her silly emphasis, 'as that *you* should have imagined individuality in your husband, Madame, when in reality all men are so *exactly* alike!'

Since the only thing that differentiated her husband from the mob was the money for which she had married him, Sanderson's relations with that particular family terminated on the spot, chance of prospective 'orders' with it. His sensitiveness, perhaps, was morbid. At any rate the way to reach his heart lay through his trees. He might be said to love trees. He certainly drew a splendid inspiration from them, and the source of a man's inspiration, be it music, religion, or a woman, is never a safe thing to criticise.

'I do think, perhaps, it was just a little extravagant, dear,' said Mrs Bittacy, referring to the cedar cheque, 'when we want a lawn-mower so badly too. But, as it gives you such pleasure——'

'It reminds me of a certain day, Sophia,' replied the old gentleman, looking first proudly at herself, then fondly at the picture, 'now long gone by. It reminds me of another tree—that Kentish lawn in the spring, birds singing in the lilacs, and some one in a muslin frock waiting patiently beneath a certain cedar—not the one in the picture, I know, but——'

'I was not waiting,' she said indignantly, 'I was picking fir-cones for the schoolroom fire——'

'Fir-cones, my dear, do not grow on cedars, and schoolroom fires were not made in June in my young days.'

'And anyhow it isn't the same cedar.'

'It has made me fond of all cedars for its sake,' he answered, 'and it reminds me that you are the same young girl still——'

She crossed the room to his side, and together they looked out of the window where, upon the lawn of their Hampshire cottage, a ragged Lebanon stood in solitary state.

'You're as full of dreams as ever,' she said gently, 'and I don't regret the cheque a bit—really. Only it would have been more real if it had been the original tree, wouldn't it?'

'That was blown down long ago. I passed the place last year, and there's not a sign of it left,' he replied tenderly. And presently, when he released her from his side, she went up to the wall and carefully dusted the picture Sanderson had made of the cedar on their present lawn. She went all round the frame with her tiny handkerchief, standing on tiptoe to reach the top rim.

'What I like about it,' said the old fellow to himself when his wife had left the room, 'is the way he has made it live. All trees have it, of course, but a cedar taught it to me first—the "something" trees possess that make them know I'm there when I stand close and watch. I suppose I felt it then because I was in love, and love reveals life everywhere.' He glanced a moment at the Lebanon looming gaunt and sombre through the gathering dusk. A curious wistful expression danced a moment through his eyes. 'Yes, Sanderson has seen it as it is,' he murmured, 'solemnly dreaming there its dim hidden life against the Forest edge, and as different from that other tree in Kent as I am from—from the vicar, say. It's quite a stranger, too. I don't know anything about it really. That other cedar I loved; this old fellow I respect. Friendly though—yes, on the whole quite friendly. He's painted the friendliness right enough. He saw that. I'd like to know that man better,' he added. 'I'd like to ask him how he saw so clearly that it stands there between this cottage and the Forest—yet somehow more in sympathy with us than with the mass of woods behind—a sort of go-between. *That* I never noticed before. I see it now—through his eyes. It stands there like a sentinel—protective rather.'

He turned away abruptly to look through the window. He saw the great encircling mass of gloom that was the Forest, fringing their little lawn. It pressed up closer in the darkness. The prim garden with its formal beds of flowers seemed an impertinence almost—some little coloured insect that sought to settle on a sleeping monster—some gaudy fly that danced impudently down the edge of a great river that could engulf it with a toss of its smallest wave. That Forest with its thousand years of growth and its deep spreading being was some such slumbering monster, yes. Their cottage and garden stood too near its running lip. When the winds were strong and lifted its shadowy skirts

of black and purple. . . . He loved this feeling of the Forest Personality;
he had always loved it.

'Queer,' he reflected, 'awfully queer, that trees should bring me
such a sense of dim, vast living! I used to feel it particularly, I remember, in India; in Canadian woods as well; but never in little English
woods till here. And Sanderson's the only man I ever knew who felt it
too. He's never said so, but there's the proof,' and he turned again to
the picture that he loved. A thrill of unaccustomed life ran through
him as he looked. 'I wonder, by Jove, I wonder,' his thoughts ran on,
'whether a tree—er—in any lawful meaning of the term can
be—alive. I remember some writing fellow telling me long ago that
trees had once been moving things, animal organisms of some sort,
that had stood so long feeding, sleeping, dreaming, or something, in
the same place, that they had lost the power to get away. . . !'

Fancies flew pell-mell about his mind, and, lighting a cheroot, he
dropped into an armchair beside the open window and let them play.
Outside the blackbirds whistled in the shrubberies across the lawn.
He smelt the earth and trees and flowers, the perfume of mown grass,
and the bits of open heath-land far away in the heart of the woods.
The summer wind stirred very faintly through the leaves. But the
great New Forest* hardly raised her sweeping skirts of black and purple shadow.

Mr Bittacy, however, knew intimately every detail of that wilderness of trees within. He knew all the purple coombs splashed with
yellow waves of gorse; sweet with juniper and myrtle, and gleaming
with clear and dark-eyed pools that watched the sky. There hawks
hovered, circling hour by hour, and the flicker of the peewit's flight
with its melancholy, petulant cry, deepened the sense of stillness. He
knew the solitary pines, dwarfed, tufted, vigorous, that sang to every
lost wind, travellers like the gipsies who pitched their bush-like tents
beneath them; he knew the shaggy ponies, with foals like baby cen-
taurs; the chattering jays, the milky call of cuckoos in the spring,
and the boom of the bittern from the lonely marshes. The under-
growth of watching hollies, he knew too, strange and mysterious,
with their dark, suggestive beauty, and the yellow shimmer of their
pale dropped leaves.

Here all the Forest lived and breathed in safety, secure from muti-
lation. No terror of the axe could haunt the peace of its vast subconscious life, no terror of devastating Man afflict it with the dread of

premature death. It knew itself supreme; it spread and preened itself without concealment. It set no spires to carry warnings, for no wind brought messages of alarm as it bulged outwards to the sun and stars.

But, once its leafy portals left behind, the trees of the countryside were otherwise. The houses threatened them; they knew themselves in danger. The roads were no longer glades of silent turf, but noisy, cruel ways by which men came to attack them. They were civilised, cared for—but cared for in order that some day they might be put to death. Even in the villages, where the solemn and immemorial repose of giant chestnuts aped security, the tossing of a silver birch against their mass, impatient in the littlest wind, brought warning. Dust clogged their leaves. The inner humming of their quiet life became inaudible beneath the scream and shriek of clattering traffic. They longed and prayed to enter the great Peace of the Forest yonder, but they could not move. They knew, moreover, that the Forest with its august, deep splendour despised and pitied them. They were a thing of artificial gardens, and belonged to beds of flowers all forced to grow one way. . . .

'I'd like to know that artist fellow better,' was the thought upon which he returned at length to the things of practical life. 'I wonder if Sophia would mind him here for a bit—?' He rose with the sound of the gong, brushing the ashes from his speckled waistcoat. He pulled the waistcoat down. He was slim and spare in figure, active in his movements. In the dim light, but for that silvery moustache, he might easily have passed for a man of forty. 'I'll suggest it to her anyhow,' he decided on his way upstairs to dress. His thought really was that Sanderson could probably explain this world of things he had always felt about—trees. A man who could paint the soul of a cedar in that way must know it all.

'Why not?' she gave her verdict later over the bread-and-butter pudding; 'unless you think he'd find it dull without companions.'

'He would paint all day in the Forest, dear. I'd like to pick his brains a bit, too, if I could manage it.'

'You can manage anything, David,' was what she answered, for this elderly childless couple used an affectionate politeness long since deemed old-fashioned. The remark, however, displeased her, making her feel uneasy, and she did not notice his rejoinder, smiling his pleasure and content—'Except yourself and our bank account, my dear.' This passion of his for trees was of old a bone of contention, though very mild contention. It frightened her. That was the truth. The Bible, her Baedeker* for earth and heaven, did not mention it. Her husband, while humouring her, could never alter that instinctive dread she had. He soothed, but never changed her. She liked the woods, perhaps as spots for shade and picnics, but she could not, as he did, love them.

And after dinner, with a lamp beside the open window, he read aloud from *The Times* the evening post had brought, such fragments as he thought might interest her. The custom was invariable, except on Sundays, when, to please his wife, he dozed over Tennyson or Farrar*as their mood might be. She knitted while he read, asked gentle questions, told him his voice was a 'lovely reading voice,' and enjoyed the little discussions that occasions prompted because he always let her win them with 'Ah, Sophia, I had never thought of it quite in *that* way before; but now you mention it I must say I think there's something in it. . . .'

For David Bittacy was wise. It was long after marriage, during his months of loneliness spent with trees and forests in India, his wife writing at home in the Bungalow, that his other, deeper side had developed the strange passion that she could not understand. And after one or two serious attempts to let her share it with him, he had given up and learned to hide it from her. He learned, that is, to speak of it only casually; for since she knew it was there, to keep silence altogether would only increase her pain. So from time to time he skimmed the surface just to let her show him where he was wrong and think she won the day. It remained a debatable land of compromise. He listened with patience to her criticisms, her excursions and alarms, knowing that while it gave her satisfaction, it could not change himself. The thing lay in him too deep and true for change. But, for peace' sake, some meeting-place was desirable, and he found it thus. It was her one fault in his eyes, this religious mania carried over from her up-bringing, and it did no serious harm. Great emotion could shake it sometimes out of her. She clung to it because her father taught it her and not because she had thought it out for herself. Indeed, like many women, she never really *thought* at all, but merely reflected the images of others' thinking which she had learned to see. So, wise in his knowledge of human nature, old David Bittacy accepted the pain of being obliged to keep a portion of his inner life shut off from the woman he deeply loved. He regarded her little biblical phrases as oddities that still clung to a rather fine, big soul—like horns and little useless things some animals have not yet lost in the course of evolution while they have outgrown their use.

'My dear, what is it? You frightened me!' She asked it suddenly, sitting up so abruptly that her cap dropped sideways almost to her ear. For David Bittacy behind his crackling paper had uttered a sharp exclamation of surprise. He had lowered the sheet and was staring at her over the tops of his gold glasses.

'Listen to this, if you please,' he said, a note of eagerness in his voice, 'listen to this, my dear Sophia. It's from an address by Francis Darwin before the Royal Society.* He is president, you know, and son of the great Darwin. Listen carefully, I beg you. It is *most* significant.'

'I *am* listening, David,' she said with some astonishment, looking up. She stopped her knitting. For a second she glanced behind her. Something had suddenly changed in the room, and it made her feel wide awake, though before she had been almost dozing. Her husband's voice and manner had introduced this new thing. Her instincts rose in warning. '*Do* read it, dear.' He took a deep breath, looking first again over the rims of his glasses to make quite sure of her attention. He had evidently come across something of genuine interest, although herself she often found the passages from these 'Addresses' somewhat heavy.

In a deep, emphatic voice he read aloud:

' "It is impossible to know whether or not plants are conscious; but it is consistent with the doctrine of continuity that in all living things there is something psychic, and if we accept this point of view——" '

'*If*,' she interrupted, scenting danger.

He ignored the interruption as a thing of slight value he was accustomed to.

' "If we accept this point of view," ' he continued, ' "we must believe that in plants there exists a faint copy of *what we know as consciousness in ourselves.*" '

He laid the paper down and steadily stared at her. Their eyes met. He had italicised the last phrase.

For a minute or two his wife made no reply or comment. They stared at one another in silence. He waited for the meaning of the words to reach her understanding with full import. Then he turned and read them again in part, while she, released from that curious driving look in his eyes, instinctively again glanced over her shoulder round the room. It was almost as if she felt some one had come in to them unnoticed.

'We must believe that in plants there exists a faint copy of what we know as consciousness in ourselves.'

'*If*,' she repeated lamely, feeling before the stare of those question-ing eyes she must say something, but not yet having gathered her wits together quite.

'*Consciousness*,' he rejoined. And then he added gravely: 'That, my dear, is the statement of a scientific man of the Twentieth Century.'

Mrs Bittacy sat forward in her chair so that her silk flounces crackled louder than the newspaper. She made a characteristic little sound between sniffing and snorting. She put her shoes closely together, with her hands upon her knees.

'David,' she said quietly, 'I think these scientific men are simply losing their heads. There is nothing in the Bible that I can remember about any such thing whatsoever.'

'Nothing, Sophia, that I can remember either,' he answered patiently. Then, after a pause, he added, half to himself perhaps more than to her: 'And, now that I come to think about it, it seems that Sanderson once said something to me that was similar.'

'Then Mr Sanderson is a wise and thoughtful man, and a safe man,' she quickly took him up, '*if* he said that.'

For she thought her husband referred to her remark about the Bible, and not to her judgment of the scientific men. And he did not correct her mistake.

'And plants, you see, dear, are not the same thing as trees,' she drove her advantage home, 'not quite, that is.'

'I agree,' said David quietly; 'but both belong to the great vegetable kingdom.'

There was a moment's pause before she answered.

'Pah! the vegetable kingdom, indeed!' She tossed her pretty old head. And into the words she put a degree of contempt that, could the vegetable kingdom have heard it, might have made it feel ashamed for covering a third of the world with its wonderful tangled network of roots and branches, delicate shaking leaves, and its millions of spires that caught the sun and wind and rain. Its very right to existence seemed in question.

II

SANDERSON accordingly came down, and on the whole his short visit was a success. Why he came at all was a mystery to those who heard of it, for he never paid visits and was certainly not the kind of man to court a customer. There must have been something in Bittacy he liked.

Mrs Bittacy was glad when he left. He brought no dress-suit for one thing, not even a dinner-jacket, and he wore very low collars with big balloon ties like a Frenchman, and let his hair grow longer than was nice, she felt. Not that these things were important, but that she considered them symptoms of something a little disordered. The ties were unnecessarily flowing.

For all that he was an interesting man, and, in spite of his eccentricities of dress and so forth, a gentleman. 'Perhaps,' she reflected in her genuinely charitable heart, 'he had other uses for the twenty guineas, an invalid sister or an old mother to support!' She had no notion of the cost of brushes, frames, paints, and canvases. Also she forgave him much for the sake of his beautiful eyes and his eager enthusiasm of manner. So many men of thirty were already blasé.

Still, when the visit was over, she felt relieved. She said nothing about his coming a second time, and her husband, she was glad to notice, had likewise made no suggestion. For, truth to tell, the way the younger man engrossed the older, keeping him out for hours in the Forest, talking on the lawn in the blazing sun, and in the evenings when the damp of dusk came creeping out from the surrounding woods, all regardless of his age and usual habits, was not quite to her taste. Of course, Mr Sanderson did not know how easily those attacks of Indian fever came back, but David surely might have told him.

They talked trees from morning till night. It stirred in her the old subconscious trail of dread, a trail that led ever into the darkness of big woods; and such feelings, as her early evangelical training taught her, were temptings. To regard them in any other way was to play with danger.

Her mind, as she watched these two, was charged with curious thoughts of dread she could not understand, yet feared the more on that account. The way they studied that old mangy cedar was a trifle unnecessary, unwise, she felt. It was disregarding the sense of proportion which deity had set upon the world for men's safe guidance.

Even after dinner they smoked their cigars upon the low branches that swept down and touched the lawn, until at length she insisted on their coming in. Cedars, she had somewhere heard, were not safe after sundown; it was not wholesome to be too near them; to sleep beneath them was even dangerous, though what the precise danger was she had forgotten. The upas* was the tree she really meant.

At any rate she summoned David in, and Sanderson came presently after him.

For a long time, before deciding on this peremptory step, she had watched them surreptitiously from the drawing-room window—her husband and her guest. The dusk enveloped them with its damp veil of gauze. She saw the glowing tips of their cigars, and heard the drone of voices. Bats flitted overhead, and big, silent moths whirred softly over the rhododendron blossoms. And it came suddenly to her, while she watched, that her husband had somehow altered these last few days—since Mr Sanderson's arrival in fact. A change had come over him, though what it was she could not say. She hesitated, indeed, to search. That was the instinctive dread operating in her. Provided it passed she would rather not know. Small things, of course, she noticed; small outward signs. He had neglected *The Times* for one thing, left off his speckled waistcoats for another. He was absent-minded sometimes; showed vagueness in practical details where hitherto he showed decision. And—he had begun to talk in his sleep again.

These and a dozen other small peculiarities came suddenly upon her with the rush of a combined attack. They brought with them a faint distress that made her shiver. Momentarily her mind was startled, then confused, as her eyes picked out the shadowy figures in the dusk, the cedar covering them, the Forest close at their backs. And then, before she could think, or seek internal guidance as her habit was, this whisper, muffled and very hurried, ran across her brain: 'It's Mr Sanderson. Call David in at once!'

And she had done so. Her shrill voice crossed the lawn and died away into the Forest, quickly smothered. No echo followed it. The sound fell dead against the rampart of a thousand listening trees.

'The damp is so very penetrating, even in summer,' she murmured when they came obediently. She was half surprised at her own audacity, half repentant. They came so meekly at her call. 'And my husband is sensitive to fever from the East. No, *please* do not throw away your cigars. We can sit by the open window and enjoy the evening while you smoke.'

She was very talkative for a moment; subconscious excitement was the cause.

'It is so still—so wonderfully still,' she went on, as no one spoke, 'so peaceful, and the air so very sweet . . . and God is always near to those who need His aid.' The words slipped out before she realised quite what she was saying, yet fortunately, in time to lower her voice, for no one heard them. They were, perhaps, an instinctive expression of relief. It flustered her that she could have said the thing at all.

Sanderson brought her shawl and helped to arrange the chairs; she thanked him in her old-fashioned, gentle way, declining the lamps which he had offered to light. 'They attract the moths and insects so, I think!'

The three of them sat there in the gloaming, Mr Bittacy's white moustache and his wife's yellow shawl gleaming at either end of the little horseshoe, Sanderson with his wild black hair and shining eyes midway between them. The painter went on talking softly, continuing evidently the conversation begun with his host beneath the cedar. Mrs Bittacy, on her guard, listened—uneasily.

'For trees, you see, rather conceal themselves in daylight. They reveal themselves fully only after sunset. I never *know* a tree,' he bowed here slightly towards the lady as though to apologise for something he felt she would not quite understand or like, 'until I've seen it in the night. Your cedar, for instance,' looking towards her husband again so that Mrs Bittacy caught the gleaming of his turned eyes, 'I failed with badly at first, because I did it in the morning. You shall see to-morrow what I mean—that first sketch is upstairs in my portfolio; it's quite another tree to the one you bought. That view'—he leaned forward, lowering his voice—'I caught one morning about two o'clock in very faint moonlight and the stars. I saw the naked being of the thing.'

'You mean that you went out, Mr Sanderson, at that hour?' the old lady asked with astonishment and mild rebuke. She did not care particularly for his choice of adjectives either.

'I fear it was rather a liberty to take in another's house, perhaps,' he answered courteously. 'But, having chanced to wake, I saw the tree from my window, and made my way downstairs.'

'It's a wonder Boxer didn't bite you; he sleeps loose in the hall,' she said.

'On the contrary. The dog came out with me. I hope,' he added, 'the noise didn't disturb you, though it's rather late to say so. I feel quite guilty.' His white teeth showed in the dusk as he smiled. A smell of earth and flowers stole in through the window on a breath of wandering air.

Mrs Bittacy said nothing at the moment. 'We both sleep like tops,' put in her husband, laughing. 'You're a courageous man, though, Sanderson; and, by Jove, the picture justifies you. Few artists would have taken so much trouble, though I read once that Holman Hunt,

Rossetti, or some one of that lot, painted all night in his orchard to get an effect of moonlight that he wanted.'*

He chattered on. His wife was glad to hear his voice; it made her feel more easy in her mind. But presently the other held the floor again, and her thoughts grew darkened and afraid. Instinctively she feared the influence on her husband. The mystery and wonder that lie in woods, in forests, in great gatherings of trees everywhere, seemed so real and present while he talked.

'The Night transfigures all things in a way,' he was saying; 'but nothing so searchingly as trees. From behind a veil that sunlight hangs before them in the day they emerge and show themselves. Even buildings do that—in a measure—but trees particularly. In the day-time they sleep; at night they wake, they manifest, turn active—live. You remember,' turning politely again in the direction of his hostess, 'how dearly Henley understood that?'

'That socialist person, you mean?' asked the lady. Her tone and accent made the substantive sound criminal. It almost hissed, the way she uttered it.

'The poet, yes,' replied the artist tactfully, 'the friend of Stevenson, you remember, Stevenson who wrote those charming children's verses.'*

He quoted in a low voice the fines he meant. It was, for once, the time, the place, and the setting all together. The words floated out across the lawn towards the wall of blue darkness where the big Forest swept the little garden with its league-long curve that was like the shore-line of a sea. A wave of distant sound that was like surf accompanied his voice, as though the wind was fain to listen too:

> Not to the staring Day,
> For all the importunate questionings he pursues
> In his big, violent voice.
> Shall those mild things of bulk and multitude,
> The trees—God's sentinels . . . .
> Yield of their huge, unutterable selves.
>
> . . . .
>
> But at the word
> Of the ancient, sacerdotal Night,
> Night of the many secrets, whose effect—
> Transfiguring, hierophantic, dread—
> Themselves alone may fully apprehend,

They tremble and are changed:
In each the uncouth, individual soul
Looms forth and glooms
Essential, and, their bodily presences
Touched with inordinate significance.
Wearing the darkness like a livery
Of some mysterious and tremendous guild,
They brood—they menace—they appal.

The voice of Mrs Bittacy presently broke the silence that followed.

'I like that part about God's sentinels,' she murmured. There was no sharpness in her tone; it was hushed and quiet. The truth, so musically uttered, muted her shrill objections though it had not lessened her alarm. Her husband made no comment; his cigar, she noticed, had gone out.

'And old trees in particular,' continued the artist, as though to himself, 'have very definite personalities. You can offend, wound, please them; the moment you stand within their shade you feel whether they come out to you, or whether they withdraw.' He turned abruptly towards his host. 'You know that singular essay of Prentice Mulford's, no doubt, "God in the Trees"*—extravagant perhaps, but yet with a fine true beauty in it? You've never read it, no?' he asked.

But it was Mrs Bittacy who answered; her husband keeping his curious deep silence.

'I never did!' It fell like a drip of cold water from the face muffled in the yellow shawl; even a child could have supplied the remainder of the unspoken thought.

'Ah,' said Sanderson gently, 'but there *is* "God" in the trees, God in a very subtle aspect and sometimes—I have known the trees express it too—that which is *not* God—dark and terrible. Have you ever noticed, too, how clearly trees show what they want—choose their companions, at least? How beeches, for instance, allow no life too near them—birds or squirrels in their boughs, nor any growth beneath? The silence in the beech wood is quite terrifying often! And how pines like bilberry bushes at their feet and sometimes little oaks—all trees making a clear, deliberate choice, and holding firmly to it? Some trees obviously—it's very strange and marked—seem to prefer the human.'

The old lady sat up crackling, for this was more than she could permit. Her stiff silk dress emitted little sharp reports.

'We know,' she answered, 'that He was said to have walked in the garden in the cool of the evening*—the gulp betrayed the effort that it cost her—'but we are nowhere told that He hid in the trees, or anything like that. Trees, after all, we must remember, are only large vegetables.'

'True,' was the soft answer, 'but in everything that grows, has life, that is, there's mystery past all finding out. The wonder that lies hidden in our own souls lies also hidden, I venture to assert, in the stupidity and silence of a mere potato.'

The observation was not meant to be amusing. It was *not* amusing. No one laughed. On the contrary, the words conveyed in too literal a sense the feeling that haunted all that conversation. Each one in his own way realised—with beauty, with wonder, with alarm—that the talk had somehow brought the whole vegetable kingdom nearer to that of man. Some link had been established between the two. It was not wise, with that great Forest listening at their very doors, to speak so plainly. The Forest edged up closer while they did so.

And Mrs Bittacy, anxious to interrupt the horrid spell, broke suddenly in upon it with a matter-of-fact suggestion. She did not like her husband's prolonged silence, stillness. He seemed so negative—so changed.

'David,' she said, raising her voice, 'I think you're feeling the dampness. It's grown chilly. The fever comes so suddenly, you know, and it might be wise to take the tincture. I'll go and get it, dear, at once. It's better.' And before he could object she had left the room to bring the homoeopathic dose that she believed in, and that, to please her, he swallowed by the tumbler-full from week to week.

And the moment the door closed behind her, Sanderson began again, though now in quite a different tone. Mr Bittacy sat up in his chair. The two men obviously resumed the conversation—the real conversation interrupted beneath the cedar—and left aside the sham one which was so much dust merely thrown in the old lady's eyes.

'Trees love you, that's the fact,' he said earnestly. 'Your service to them all these years abroad has made them know you.'

'Know me?'

'Made them, yes,'—he paused a moment, then added,—'made them *aware of your presence*; aware of a force outside themselves that deliberately seeks their welfare, don't you see?'

'By Jove, Sanderson—!' This put into plain language actual sensations he had felt, yet had never dared to phrase in words before. 'They get into touch with me, as it were?' he ventured, laughing at his own sentence, yet laughing only with his lips.

'Exactly,' was the quick, emphatic reply. 'They seek to blend with something they feel instinctively to be good for them, helpful to their essential beings, encouraging to their best expression—their life.'

'Good Lord, Sir!' Bittacy heard himself saying, 'but you're putting my own thoughts into words. D'you know, I've felt something like that for years. As though—' he looked round to make sure his wife was not there, then finished the sentence—'as though the trees were after me!'

'"Amalgamate" seems the best word, perhaps,' said Sanderson slowly. 'They would draw you to themselves. Good forces, you see, always seek to merge; evil to separate; that's why Good in the end must always win the day—everywhere. The accumulation in the long run becomes overwhelming. Evil tends to separation, dissolution, death. The comradeship of trees, their instinct to run together, is a vital symbol. Trees in a mass are good; alone, you may take it generally, are—well, dangerous. Look at a monkey-puzzler, or better still, a holly. Look at it, watch it, understand it. Did you ever see more plainly an evil thought made visible? They're wicked. Beautiful too, oh yes! There's a strange, miscalculated beauty often in evil——'

'That cedar, then——?'

'Not evil, no; but alien, rather. Cedars grow in forests all together. The poor thing has drifted, that is all.'

They were getting rather deep. Sanderson, talking against time, spoke so fast. It was too condensed. Bittacy hardly followed that last bit. His mind floundered among his own less definite, less sorted thoughts, till presently another sentence from the artist startled him into attention again.

'That cedar will protect you here, though, because you both have humanised it by your thinking so lovingly of its presence. The others can't get past it, as it were.'

'Protect me!' he exclaimed. 'Protect me from their love?'

Sanderson laughed. 'We're getting rather mixed,' he said; 'we're talking of one thing in the terms of another really. But what I mean is—you see—that their love for you, their "awareness" of your personality and presence involves the idea of winning you—across the border—into themselves—into their world of living. It means, in a way, taking you over.'

The ideas the artist started in his mind ran furious wild races to and fro. It was like a maze sprung suddenly into movement. The whirling of the intricate lines bewildered him. They went so fast, leaving but half an explanation of their goal. He followed first one, then another, but a new one always dashed across to intercept before he could get anywhere.

'But India,' he said, presently in a lower voice, 'India is so far away—from this little English forest. The trees, too, are utterly different for one thing?'

The rustle of skirts warned of Mrs Bittacy's approach. This was a sentence he could turn round another way in case she came up and pressed for explanation.

'There is communion among trees all the world over,' was the strange quick reply. 'They always know.'

'They always know! You think then——?'

'The winds, you see—the great, swift carriers! They have their ancient rights of way about the world. An easterly wind, for instance, carrying on stage by stage as it were—linking dropped messages and meanings from land to land like the birds—an easterly wind——'

Mrs Bittacy swept in upon them with the tumbler—

'There, David,' she said, 'that will ward off any beginnings of attack. Just a spoonful dear. Oh, oh! not *all!*' for he had swallowed half the contents at a single gulp as usual; 'another dose before you go to bed, and the balance in the morning, first thing when you wake.'

She turned to her guest, who put the tumbler down for her upon a table at his elbow. She had heard them speak of the east wind. She emphasised the warning she had misinterpreted. The private part of the conversation came to an abrupt end.

'It is the one thing that upsets him more than any other—an east wind,' she said, 'and I am glad, Mr Sanderson, to hear you think so too.'

III

A DEEP hush followed, in the middle of which an owl was heard calling its muffled note in the forest. A big moth whirred with a soft collision against one of the windows. Mrs Bittacy started slightly, but no one spoke. Above the trees the stars were faintly visible. From the distance came the barking of a dog.

Bittacy, relighting his cigar, broke the little spell of silence that had caught all three.

'It's rather a comforting thought,' he said, throwing the match out of the window, 'that life is about us everywhere, and that there is really no dividing line between what we call organic and inorganic.'

'The universe, yes,' said Sanderson, 'is all one, really. We're puzzled by the gaps we cannot see across, but as a fact, I suppose, there are no gaps at all.'

Mrs Bittacy rustled ominously, holding her peace meanwhile. She feared long words she did not understand. Beelzebub lay hid among too many syllables.

'In trees and plants especially, there dreams an exquisite life that no one yet has proved unconscious.'

'Or conscious either, Mr Sanderson,' she neatly interjected. 'It's only man that was made after His image, not shrubberies and things. . . .'

Her husband interposed without delay.

'It is not necessary,' he explained suavely, 'to say that they're alive in the sense that we are alive. At the same time,' with an eye to his wife, 'I see no harm in holding, dear, that all created things contain some measure of His life Who made them. It's only beautiful to hold that He created nothing dead. We are not pantheists for all that!' he added soothingly.

'Oh, no! Not that, I hope!' The word alarmed her. It was worse than pope. Through her puzzled mind stole a stealthy, dangerous thing . . . like a panther.

'I like to think that even in decay there's life,' the painter murmured. 'The falling apart of rotten wood breeds sentiency; there's force and motion in the falling of a dying leaf, in the breaking up and crumbling of everything indeed. And take an inert stone: it's crammed with heat and weight and potencies of all sorts. What holds its particles together indeed? We understand it as little as gravity or why a needle always turns to the "North." Both things may be a mode of life. . . .'

'You think a compass has a soul, Mr Sanderson?' exclaimed the lady with a crackling of her silk flounces that conveyed a sense of outrage even more plainly than her tone. The artist smiled to himself in the darkness, but it was Bittacy who hastened to reply.

'Our friend merely suggests that these mysterious agencies,' he said quietly, 'may be due to some kind of life we cannot understand. Why should water only run downhill? Why should trees grow at right angles to the surface of the ground and towards the sun? Why should the worlds spin for ever on their axes? Why should fire change the form of everything it touches without really destroying them? To say these things follow the law of their being explains nothing. Mr Sanderson merely suggests—poetically, my dear, of course—that these may be manifestations of life, though life at a different stage to ours.'

'The "*breath* of life," we read, "He breathed into them." These things do not breathe.' She said it with triumph.

Then Sanderson put in a word. But he spoke rather to himself or to his host than by way of serious rejoinder to the ruffled lady.

'But plants do breathe too, you know,' he said. 'They breathe, they eat, they digest, they move about, and they adapt themselves to their environment as men and animals do. They have a nervous system too . . . at least a complex system of nuclei which have some of the qualities of nerve cells. They may have memory too. Certainly, they know definite action in response to stimulus. And though this may be physiological, no one has proved that it is only that, and not—psychological.'

He did not notice, apparently, the little gasp that was audible behind the yellow shawl. Bittacy cleared his throat, threw his extinguished cigar upon the lawn, crossed and recrossed his legs.

'And in trees,' continued the other, 'behind a great forest, for instance,' pointing towards the woods, 'may stand a rather splendid Entity that manifests through all the thousand individual trees—some huge collective life, quite as minutely and delicately organised as our own. It might merge and blend with ours under certain conditions, so that we could understand it by *being* it, for a time at least. It might even engulf human vitality into the immense whirlpool of its own vast dreaming life. The pull of a big forest on a man can be tremendous and utterly overwhelming.'

The mouth of Mrs Bittacy was heard to close with a snap. Her shawl, and particularly her crackling dress, exhaled the protest that burned within her like a pain. She was too distressed to be overawed, but at the same time too confused 'mid the litter of words and meanings half understood, to find immediate phrases she could use. Whatever the actual meaning of his language might be, however, and whatever subtle dangers lay concealed behind them meanwhile, they certainly wove a kind of gentle spell with the glimmering darkness that held all three delicately enmeshed there by that open window. The odours of dewy lawn, flowers, trees, and earth formed part of it.

'The moods,' he continued, 'that people waken in us are due to their hidden life affecting our own. Deep calls to deep. A person, for instance, joins you in an empty room: you both instantly change. The new arrival, though in silence, has caused a change of mood. May not the moods of Nature touch and stir us in virtue of a similar prerogative? The sea, the hills, the desert, wake passion, joy, terror, as the case may be; for a few, perhaps,' he glanced significantly at his host so that Mrs Bittacy again caught the turning of his eyes, 'emotions of a curious, flaming splendour that are quite nameless. Well . . . whence come these powers? Surely from nothing that is . . . dead! Does not the influence of a forest, its sway and strange ascendancy over certain minds, betray a direct manifestation of life? It lies otherwise beyond all explanation, this mysterious emanation of big woods. Some natures, of course, deliberately invite it. The authority of a host of trees,'—his voice grew almost solemn as he said the words—'is something not to be denied. One feels it here, I think, particularly.'

There was considerable tension in the air as he ceased speaking. Mr Bittacy had not intended that the talk should go so far. They had drifted. He did not wish to see his wife unhappy or afraid, and he was aware—acutely so—that her feelings were stirred to a point he did not care about. Something in her, as he put it, was 'working up' towards explosion.

He sought to generalise the conversation, diluting this accumulated emotion by spreading it.

'The sea is His and He made it,' he suggested vaguely, hoping Sanderson would take the hint, 'and with the trees it is the same. . . .'

'The whole gigantic vegetable kingdom, yes,' the artist took him up, 'all at the service of man, for food, for shelter and for a thousand purposes of his daily life. Is it not striking what a lot of the globe they cover . . . exquisitely organised life, yet stationary, always ready to our hand when we want them, never running away? But the taking them, for all that, not so easy. One man shrinks from picking flowers, another from cutting down trees. And, it's curious that most of the forest tales and legends are dark, mysterious, and somewhat ill-omened. The forest-beings are rarely gay and harmless. The forest life was felt as terrible. Tree-worship still survives today. Woodcutters . . . those who take the life of trees . . . you see, a race of haunted men. . . .'

He stopped abruptly, a singular catch in his voice. Bittacy felt something even before the sentences were over. His wife, he knew, felt it still more strongly. For it was in the middle of the heavy silence following upon these last remarks, that Mrs Bittacy, rising with a violent abruptness from her chair, drew the attention of the others to something moving towards them across the lawn. It came silently. In outline it was large and curiously spread. It rose high, too, for the sky above the shrubberies, still pale gold from the sunset, was dimmed by its passage. She declared afterwards that it moved in 'looping circles,' but what she perhaps meant to convey was 'spirals.'

She screamed faintly. 'It's come at last! And it's you that brought it!'

She turned excitedly, half afraid, half angry, to Sanderson. With a breathless sort of gasp she said it, politeness all forgotten. 'I knew it . . . if you went on. I knew it. Oh! Oh!' And she cried again, 'Your talking has brought it out!' The terror that shook her voice was rather dreadful.

But the confusion of her vehement words passed unnoticed in the first surprise they caused. For a moment nothing happened.

'What is it you think you see, my dear?' asked her husband, startled. Sanderson said nothing. All three leaned forward, the men still sitting, but Mrs Bittacy had rushed hurriedly to the window, placing herself of a purpose, as it seemed, between her husband and the lawn. She pointed. Her little hand made a silhouette against the sky, the yellow shawl hanging from the arm like a cloud.

'Beyond the cedar—between it and the lilacs.' The voice had lost its shrillness; it was thin and hushed. 'There . . . now you see it going round upon itself again—going back, thank God! . . . going back to the Forest.' It sank to a whisper, shaking. She repeated, with a great dropping sigh of relief—'Thank God! I thought . . . at first . . . it was coming here . . . to us! . . . David . . . to *you!*'

She stepped back from the window, her movements confused, feeling in the darkness for the support of a chair, and finding her husband's outstretched hand instead. Hold me, dear, hold me, please . . . tight. Do not let me go.' She was in what he called afterwards 'a regular state.' He drew her firmly down upon her chair again.

'Smoke, Sophie, my dear,' he said quickly, trying to make his voice calm and natural. 'I see it, yes. It's smoke blowing over from the gardener's cottage. . . .'

'But, David,'—and there was new horror in her whisper now—'it made a noise. It makes it still. I hear it swishing.' Some such word she used—swishing, sishing, rushing, or something of the kind. 'David, I'm very frightened. It's something awful! That man has called it out . . . !'

'Hush, hush,' whispered her husband. He stroked her trembling hand beside him.

'It is in the wind,' said Sanderson, speaking for the first time, very quietly. The expression on his face was not visible in the gloom, but his voice was soft and unafraid. At the sound of it, Mrs Bittacy started violently again. Bittacy drew his chair a little forward to obstruct her view of him. He felt bewildered himself, a little, hardly knowing quite what to say or do. It was all so very curious and sudden.

But Mrs Bittacy was badly frightened. It seemed to her that what she saw came from the enveloping forest just beyond their little garden. It emerged in a sort of secret way, moving towards them as with a purpose, stealthily, difficultly. Then something stopped it. It could not advance beyond the cedar. The cedar—this impression remained with her afterwards too—prevented, kept it back. Like a rising sea the Forest had surged a moment in their direction through the covering darkness, and this visible movement was its first wave. Thus to her mind it seemed . . . like that mysterious turn of the tide that used to frighten and mystify her in childhood on the sands. The outward surge of some enormous Power was what she felt . . . something to which every instinct in her being rose in opposition because it threatened her and hers. In that moment she realised the Personality of the Forest . . . menacing.

In the stumbling movement that she made away from the window and towards the bell she barely caught the sentence Sanderson—or was it her husband?—murmured to himself: 'It came because we talked of it; our thinking made it aware of us and brought it out. But the cedar stops it. It cannot cross the lawn, you see. . . .'

All three were standing now, and her husband's voice broke in with authority while his wife's fingers touched the bell.

'My dear, I should *not* say anything to Thompson.' The anxiety he felt was manifest in his voice, but his outward composure had returned. 'The gardener can go. . . .'

Then Sanderson cut him short. 'Allow me,' he said quickly. 'I'll see if anything's wrong. And before either of them could answer or object, he was gone, leaping out by the open window. They saw his figure vanish with a run across the lawn into the darkness.

A moment later the maid entered, in answer to the bell, and with her came the loud barking of the terrier from the hall.

'The lamps,' said her master shortly, and as she softly closed the door behind her, they heard the wind pass with a mournful sound of singing round the outer walls. A rustle of foliage from the distance passed within it.

'You see, the wind *is* rising. It *was* the wind!' He put a comforting arm about her, distressed to feel that she was trembling. But he knew that he was trembling too, though with a kind of odd elation rather than alarm. 'And it *was* smoke that you saw coming from Stride's cottage, or from the rubbish heaps he's been burning in the kitchen garden. The noise we heard was the branches rustling in the wind. Why should you be so nervous?'

A thin whispering voice answered him:

'I was afraid for *you*, dear. Something frightened me for *you*. That man makes me feel so uneasy and uncomfortable for his influence upon you. It's very foolish, I know. I think . . . I'm tired; I feel so overwrought and restless.' The words poured out in a hurried jumble and she kept turning to the window while she spoke.

'The strain of having a visitor,' he said soothingly, 'has taxed you. We're so unused to having people in the house. He goes to-morrow.' He warmed her cold hands between his own, stroking them tenderly. More, for the life of him, he could not say or do. The joy of a strange, internal excitement made his heart beat faster. He knew not what it was. He knew only, perhaps, whence it came.

She peered close into his face through the gloom, and said a curious thing. 'I thought, David, for a moment . . . you seemed . . . different. My nerves are all on edge to-night.' She made no further reference to her husband's visitor.

A sound of footsteps from the lawn warned of Sanderson's return, he answered quickly in a lowered tone—'There's no need to be afraid on my account, dear girl. There's nothing wrong with me, I assure you; I never felt so well and happy in my life.'

Thompson came in with the lamps and brightness, and scarcely had she gone again when Sanderson in turn was seen climbing through the window.

'There's nothing,' he said lightly, as he closed it behind him. 'Somebody's been burning leaves, and the smoke is drifting a little through the trees. The wind,' he added, glancing at his host a moment significantly, but in so discreet a way that Mrs Bittacy did not observe it, 'the wind, too, has begun to roar . . . in the Forest . . . further out.'

But Mrs Bittacy noticed about him two things which increased her uneasiness. She noticed the shining of his eyes, because a similar light had suddenly come into her husband's; and she noticed, too, the apparent depth of meaning he put into those simple words that 'the wind had begun to roar in the Forest . . . further out.' Her mind retained the disagreeable impression that he meant more than he said. In his tone lay quite another implication. It was not actually 'wind' he spoke of, and it would not remain 'further out' . . . rather, it was coming in. Another impression she got too—still more unwelcome—was that her husband understood his hidden meaning.

IV

'DAVID, dear,' she observed gently as soon as they were alone upstairs, 'I have a horrible uneasy feeling about that man. I cannot get rid of it.' The tremor in her voice caught all his tenderness.

He turned to look at her. 'Of what kind, my dear? You're so imaginative sometimes, aren't you?'

'I think,' she hesitated, stammering a little, confused, still frightened, 'I mean—isn't he a hypnotist, or full of those theofosical* ideas or something of the sort? You know what I mean——'

He was too accustomed to her little confused alarms to explain them away seriously as a rule, or to correct her verbal inaccuracies, but to-night he felt she needed careful tender treatment. He soothed her as best he could.

'But there's no harm in that, even if he is,' he answered quietly. 'Those are only new names for very old ideas, you know, dear.' There was no trace of impatience in his voice.

'That's what I mean,' she replied, the texts he dreaded rising in an unuttered crowd behind the words. 'He's one of those things that we are warned would come—one of those Latter-Day things.* For her mind still bristled with the bogeys of Antichrist and Prophecy, and she had only escaped the Number of the Beast, as it were, by the skin of her teeth. The Pope drew most of her fire usually, because she could understand him; the target was plain and she could shoot. But this tree-and-forest business was so vague and horrible. It terrified her. 'He makes me think,' she went on, 'of Principalities and Powers in high places, and of things that walk in darkness.* I did *not* like the way he spoke of trees getting alive in the night, and all that; it made me think of wolves in sheep's clothing. And when I saw that awful thing in the sky above the lawn——'

But he interrupted her at once, for that was something he had decided it was best to leave unmentioned. Certainly it was better not discussed.

'He only meant, I think, Sophie,' he put in gravely, yet with a little smile, 'that trees may have a measure of conscious life—rather a nice idea on the whole, surely,—something like that bit we read in the *Times* the other night, you remember—and that a big forest may possess a sort of Collective Personality. Remember, he's an artist, and poetical.'

'It's dangerous,' she said emphatically. 'I feel it's playing with fire, unwise, unsafe——'

'Yet all to the glory of God,' he urged gently. 'We must not shut our ears and eyes to knowledge—of any kind, must we?'

'With you, David, the wish is always farther than the thought,'* she rejoined. For, like the child who thought that 'suffered under Pontius Pilate' was 'suffered under a bunch of violets,' she heard her proverbs phonetically and reproduced them thus. She hoped to convey her warning in the quotation. 'And we must always try the spirits whether they be of God,' she added tentatively.

'Certainly, dear, we can always do that,' he assented, getting into bed.

But, after a little pause, during which she blew the light out, David Bittacy settling down to sleep with an excitement in his blood that was new and bewilderingly delightful, realised that perhaps he had not said quite enough to comfort her. She was lying awake by his side, still frightened. He put his head up in the darkness.

'Sophie,' he said softly, 'you must remember, too, that in any case between us and—and all that sort of thing—there is a great gulf fixed, a gulf that cannot be crossed—er—while we are still in the body.'

And hearing no reply, he satisfied himself that she was already asleep and happy. But Mrs, Bittacy was not asleep. She heard the sentence, only she said nothing because she felt her thought was better unexpressed. She was afraid to hear the words in the darkness. The Forest outside was listening. and might hear them too—the Forest that was 'roaring further out.'

And the thought was this: That gulf, of course, existed, but Sanderson had somehow bridged it.

It was much later that night when she awoke out of troubled, uneasy dreams and heard a sound that twisted her very nerves with fear. It passed immediately with full waking, for, listen as she might, there was nothing audible but the inarticulate murmur of the night. It was in her dreams she heard it, and the dreams had vanished with it. But the sound was recognisable, for it was that rushing noise that had come across the lawn; only this time closer. Just above her face while she slept had passed this murmur as of rustling branches in the very room, a sound of foliage whispering. 'A going in the tops of the mulberry trees,' ran through her mind. She had dreamed that she lay beneath a spreading tree somewhere, a tree that whispered with ten thousand soft lips of green; and the dream continued for a moment even after waking.

She sat up in bed and stared about her. The window was open at the top; she saw the stars; the door, she remembered, was locked as usual; the room, of course, was empty. The deep hush of the summer night lay over all, broken only by another sound that now issued from the shadows close beside the bed, a human sound, yet unnatural, a sound that seized the fear with which she had waked and instantly increased it. And, although it was one she recognised as familiar, at first she could not name it. Some seconds certainly passed—and, they were very long ones—before she understood that it was her husband talking in his sleep.

The direction of the voice confused and puzzled her, moreover, for it was not, as she first supposed, beside her. There was distance in it. The next minute, by the light of the sinking candle flame, she saw his white figure standing out in the middle of the room, half-way towards the window. The candlelight slowly grew. She saw him move then nearer to the window, with arms outstretched. His speech was low and mumbled, the words running together too much to be distinguishable.

And she shivered. To her, sleep-talking was uncanny to the point of horror; it was like the talking of the dead, mere parody of a living voice, unnatural.

'David!' she whispered, dreading the sound of her own voice, and half afraid to interrupt him and see his face. She could not bear the sight of the wide-opened eyes. 'David, you're walking in your sleep. Do—come back to bed, dear, *please!*' Her whisper seemed so dreadfully loud in the still darkness. At the sound of her voice he paused, then turned slowly round to face her. His widely-opened eyes stared into her own without recognition; they looked through her into something beyond; it was as though he knew the direction of the sound, yet

could not see her. They were shining, she noticed, as the eyes of
Sanderson had shone several hours ago; and his face was flushed,
distraught. Anxiety was written upon every feature. And, instantly,
recognising that the fever was upon him, she forgot her terror temporarily in practical considerations. He came back to bed without
waking. She closed his eyelids. Presently he composed himself quietly
to sleep, or rather to deeper sleep. She contrived to make him swallow
something from the tumbler beside the bed.

Then she rose very quietly to close the window, feeling the night air
blow in too fresh and keen. She put the candle where it could not
reach him. The sight of the big Baxter Bible* beside it comforted her
a little, but all through her under-being ran the warnings of a curious
alarm. And it was while in the act of fastening the catch with one hand
and pulling the string of the blind with the other, that her husband sat
up again in bed and spoke in words this time that were distinctly audible. The eyes had opened wide again. He pointed. She stood stock
still and listened, her shadow distorted on the blind. He did not come
out towards her as at first she feared.

The whispering voice was very clear, horrible, too, beyond all she
had ever known.

'They are roaring in the Forest further out . . . and I . . . must go
and see.' He stared beyond her as he said it, to the woods. 'They are
needing me. They sent for me. . . .' Then his eyes wandering back
again to things within the room, he lay down, his purpose suddenly
changed. And that change was horrible as well, more horrible, perhaps, because of its revelation of another detailed world he moved in
far away from her.

The singular phrase chilled her blood; for a moment she was
utterly terrified. That tone of the somnambulist, differing so slightly
yet so distressingly from normal, waking speech, seemed to her somehow wicked. Evil and danger lay waiting thick behind it. She leaned
against the window-sill, shaking in every limb. She had an awful feeling for a moment that something was coming in to fetch him.

'Not yet, then,' she heard in a much lower voice from the bed, 'but
later. It will be better so. . . . I shall go later. . . .'

The words expressed some fringe of these alarms that had haunted
her so long, and that the arrival and presence of Sanderson seemed to
have brought to the very edge of a climax she could not even dare to
think about. They gave it form; they brought it closer; they sent her

thoughts to her Deity in a wild, deep prayer for help and guidance. For here was a direct, unconscious betrayal of a world of inner purposes and claims her husband recognised while he kept them almost wholly to himself.

By the time she reached his side and knew the comfort of his touch, the eyes had closed again, this time of their own accord, and the head lay calmly back upon the pillows. She gently straightened the bed clothes. She watched him for some minutes, shading the candle carefully with one hand. There was a smile of strangest peace upon the face.

Then, blowing out the candle, she knelt down and prayed before getting back into bed. But no sleep came to her. She lay awake all night thinking, wondering, praying, until at length with the chorus of the birds and the glimmer or the dawn upon the green blind, she fell into a slumber of complete exhaustion.

But while she slept the wind continued roaring in the Forest further out. The sound came closer—sometimes very close indeed.

V

WITH the departure of Sanderson the significance of the curious incidents waned, because the moods that had produced them passed away. Mrs Bittacy soon afterwards came to regard them as some growth of disproportion that had been very largely, perhaps, in her own mind. It did not strike her that this change was sudden, for it came about quite naturally. For one thing her husband never spoke of the matter, and for another she remembered how many things in life that had seemed inexplicable and singular at the time turned out later to have been quite commonplace.

Most of it, certainly, she put down to the presence of the artist and to his wild, suggestive talk. With his welcome removal, the world turned ordinary again and safe. The fever, though it lasted as usual a short time only, had not allowed of her husband's getting up to say good-bye, and she had conveyed his regrets and adieux. In the morning Mr Sanderson had seemed ordinary enough. In his town hat and gloves, as she saw him go, he seemed tame and unalarming.

'After all,' she thought as she watched the pony-cart bear him off, 'he's only an artist!' What she had thought he might be otherwise her slim imagination did not venture to disclose. Her change of feeling was wholesome and refreshing. She felt a little ashamed of her behaviour. She gave him a smile—genuine because the relief she felt was genuine—as he bent over her hand and kissed it, but she did not suggest a second visit, and her husband, she noted with satisfaction and relief, had said nothing either.

The little household fell again into the normal and sleepy routine to which it was accustomed. The name of Arthur Sanderson was rarely if ever mentioned. Nor, for her part, did she mention to her husband the incident of his walking in his sleep and the wild words he used. But to forget it was equally impossible. Thus it lay buried deep within her like a centre of some unknown disease of which it was a mysterious symptom, waiting to spread at the first favourable opportunity. She prayed against it every night and morning: prayed that she might forget it—that God would keep her husband safe from harm.

For in spite of much surface foolishness that many might have read as weakness, Mrs Bittacy had balance, sanity, and a fine deep faith. She was greater than she knew. Her love for her husband and her God were somehow one, an achievement only possible to a single-hearted nobility of soul.

There followed a summer of great violence and beauty; of beauty, because the refreshing rains at night prolonged the glory of the spring and spread it all across July, keeping the foliage young and sweet; of violence, because the winds that tore about the south of England brushed the whole country into dancing movement. They swept the woods magnificently, and kept them roaring with a perpetual grand voice. Their deepest notes seemed never to leave the sky. They sang and shouted, and torn leaves raced and fluttered through the air long before their usually appointed time. Many a tree, after days of this roaring and dancing, fell exhausted to the ground. The cedar on the lawn gave up two limbs that fell upon successive days, at the same hour too—just before dusk. The wind often makes its most boisterous effort at that time, before it drops with the sun, and these two huge branches lay in dark ruin covering half the lawn. They spread across it and towards the house. They left an ugly gaping space upon the tree, so that the Lebanon looked unfinished, half destroyed, a monster shorn of its old-time comeliness and splendour. Far more of the Forest was now visible than before; it peered through the breach of the broken defences. They could see from the windows of the house now—especially from the drawing-room and bedroom windows—straight out into the glades and depths beyond.

Mrs Bittacy's niece and nephew, who were staying on a visit at the time, enjoyed themselves immensely helping the gardeners carry off the fragments. It took two days to do this, for Mr Bittacy insisted on the branches being moved entire. He would not allow them to be chopped; also, he would not consent to their use as firewood. Under his superintendence the unwieldy masses were dragged to the edge of the garden and arranged upon the frontier line between the Forest and the lawn. The children were delighted with the scheme. They entered into it with enthusiasm. At all costs this defence against the inroads of the Forest must be made secure. They caught their uncle's earnestness, felt even something of a hidden motive that he had, and the visit, usually rather dreaded, became the visit of their lives instead. It was Aunt Sophia this time who seemed discouraging and dull.

'She's got so old and funny,' opined Stephen.

But Alice, who felt in the silent displeasure of her aunt some secret thing that half alarmed her, said:

'I think she's afraid of the woods. She never comes into them with us, you see.'

'All the more reason then for making this wall impreg——all fat and thick and solid,' he concluded, unable to manage the longer word. 'Then nothing—simply *nothing*—can get through. Can't it, Uncle David?'

And Mr Bittacy, jacket discarded and working in his speckled waistcoat, went puffing to their aid, arranging the massive limb of the cedar like a hedge.

'Come on,' he said, 'whatever happens, you know, we must finish before it's dark. Already the wind is roaring in the Forest further out.' And Alice caught the phrase and instantly echoed it. 'Stevie,' she cried below her breath, 'look sharp, you lazy lump. Didn't you hear what Uncle David said? It'll come in and catch us before we've done!'

They worked like Trojans,* and, sitting beneath the wistaria tree that climbed the southern wall of the cottage, Mrs Bittacy with her knitting watched them, calling from time to time insignificant messages of counsel and advice. The messages passed, of course, unheeded. Mostly, indeed, they were unheard, for the workers were too absorbed. She warned her husband not to get too hot, Alice not to tear her dress, Stephen not to strain his back with pulling. Her mind hovered between the homoeopathic medicine-chest upstairs and her anxiety to see the business finished.

For this breaking up of the cedar had stirred again her slumbering alarms. It revived memories of the visit of Mr Sanderson that had been sinking into oblivion; she recalled his queer and odious way of talking, and many things she hoped forgotten drew their heads up from that subconscious region to which all forgetting is impossible. They looked at her and nodded. They were full of life; they had no intention of being pushed aside and buried permanently. 'Now look!' they whispered, 'didn't we tell you so?' They had been merely waiting the right moment to assert their presence. And all her former vague distress crept over her. Anxiety, uneasiness returned. That dreadful sinking of the heart came too.

This incident of the cedar's breaking up was actually so unimportant, and yet her husband's attitude towards it made it so significant. There was nothing that he said in particular, or did, or left undone that frightened her, but his general air of earnestness seemed so unwarranted. She felt that he deemed the thing important. He was so exercised about it. This evidence of sudden concern and interest, buried all the summer from her sight and knowledge, she realised now had been buried purposely; he had kept it intentionally concealed. Deeply submerged in him there ran this tide of other thoughts, desires, hopes. What were they? Whither did they lead? The accident to the tree betrayed it most unpleasantly; and, doubtless, more than he was aware.

She watched his grave and serious face as he worked there with the children, and as she watched she felt afraid. It vexed her that the children worked so eagerly. They unconsciously supported him. The thing she feared she would not even name. But it was waiting.

Moreover, as far as her puzzled mind could deal with a dread so vague and incoherent, the collapse of the cedar somehow brought it nearer. The fact that, all so ill-explained and formless, the thing yet lay in her consciousness, out of reach but moving and alive, filled her with a kind of puzzled, dreadful wonder. Its presence was so very real, its power so gripping, its partial concealment so abominable. Then, out of the dim confusion, she grasped one thought and saw it stand quite clear before her eyes. She found difficulty in clothing it in words, but its meaning perhaps was this: That cedar stood in their life for something friendly; its downfall meant disaster; a sense of some protective influence about the cottage, and about her husband in particular, was thereby weakened.

'Why do you fear the big winds so?' he had asked her several days before, after a particularly boisterous day; and the answer she gave surprised her while she gave it. One of those heads poked up unconsciously, and let slip the truth:

'Because, David, I feel they—bring the Forest with them,' she faltered. 'They blow something from the trees—into the mind—into the house.'

He looked at her keenly for a moment.

'That must be why I love them then,' he answered. 'They blow the souls of the trees about the sky like clouds.'

The conversation dropped. She had never heard him talk in quite that way before.

And another time, when he had coaxed her to go with him down one of the nearer glades, she asked why he took the small hand-axe with him, and what he wanted it for.

'To cut the ivy that clings to the trunks and takes their life away,' he said.

'But can't the verdurers do that?' she asked. 'That's what they're paid for, isn't it?'

Whereupon he explained that ivy was a parasite the trees knew not how to fight alone, and that the verdurers were careless and did not do it thoroughly. They gave a chop here and there, leaving the tree to do the rest for itself if it could.

'Besides, I like to do it for them. I love to help them and protect,' he added, the foliage rustling all about his quiet words as they went.

And these stray remarks, as his attitude towards the broken cedar, betrayed this curious, subtle change that was going forward, in his personality. Slowly and surely all the summer it had increased.

It was growing—the thought startled her horribly—just as a tree grows, the outer evidence from day to day so slight as to be unnoticeable, yet the rising tide so deep and irresistible. The alteration spread all through and over him, was in both mind and actions, sometimes almost in his face as well. Occasionally, thus, it stood up straight outside himself and frightened her. His life was somehow becoming linked so intimately with trees, and with all that trees signified. His interests became more and more their interests, his activity combined with theirs, his thoughts and feelings theirs, his purpose, hope, desire, his fate——

His fate! The darkness of some vague, enormous terror dropped its shadow on her when she thought of it. Some instinct in her heart she dreaded infinitely more than death—for death meant sweet translation for his soul—came gradually to associate the thought of him with the thought of trees, in particular with these Forest trees. Sometimes, before she could face the thing, argue it away, or pray it into silence, she found the thought of him running swiftly through her mind like a thought of the Forest itself, the two most intimately linked and joined together, each a part and complement of the other, one being.

The idea was too dim for her to see it face to face. Its mere possibility dissolved the instant she focussed it to get the truth behind it. It was too utterly elusive, mad, protæan. Under the attack of even a minute's concentration the very meaning of it vanished, melted away. The idea lay really behind any words that she could ever find, beyond the touch of definite thought. Her mind was unable to grapple with it. But, while it vanished, the trail of its approach and disappearance flickered a moment before her shaking vision. The horror certainly remained.

Reduced to the simple human statement that her temperament sought instinctively it stood perhaps at this: Her husband loved her, and he loved the trees as well; but the trees came first, claimed parts of him she did not know. *She* loved her God and him. *He* loved the trees and her.

Thus, in guise of some faint, distressing compromise, the matter shaped itself for her perplexed mind in the terms of conflict. A silent, hidden battle raged, but as yet raged far away. The breaking of the cedar was a visible outward fragment of a distant and mysterious encounter that was coming daily closer to them both. The wind, instead of roaring in the Forest further out, now came nearer, booming in fitful gusts about its edge and frontiers.

Meanwhile the summer dimmed. The autumn winds went sighing through the woods; leaves turned to golden red, and the evenings were drawing in with cosy shadows before the first sign of anything seriously untoward made its appearance. It came then with a flat, decided kind of violence that indicated mature preparation beforehand. It was not impulsive nor ill-considered. In a fashion it seemed expected, and indeed inevitable. For within a fortnight of their annual change to the little village of Seillans above St Raphael*—a change so regular for the past ten years that it was not even discussed between them—David Bittacy abruptly refused to go.

Thompson had laid the tea-table, prepared the spirit lamp beneath the urn, pulled down the blinds in that swift and silent way she had, and left the room. The lamps were still unlit. The fire-light shone on the chintz armchairs, and Boxer lay asleep on the black horse-hair rug. Upon the walls the gilt picture frames gleamed faintly, the pictures themselves indistinguishable. Mrs Bittacy had warmed the tea-pot and was in the act of pouring the water in to heat the cups when her husband, looking up from his chair across the hearth, made the abrupt announcement:

'My dear,' he said, as though following a train of thought of which she only heard this final phrase, 'it's really quite impossible for me to go.'

And so abrupt, inconsequent, it sounded that she at first misunderstood. She thought he meant go out into the garden or the woods. But her heart leaped all the same. The tone of his voice was ominous.

'Of course not,' she answered, 'it would be *most* unwise. Why should you——?' She referred to the mist that always spread on autumn nights upon the lawn; but before she finished the sentence she knew that *he* referred to something else. And her heart then gave its second horrible leap.

'David! You mean abroad?' she gasped.

'I mean abroad, dear, yes.'

It reminded her of the tone he used when saying good-bye years ago before one of those jungle expeditions she dreaded. His voice then was so serious, so final. It was serious and final now. For several moments she could think of nothing to say. She busied herself with the teapot. She had filled one cup with hot water till it overflowed, and she emptied it slowly into the slop-basin, trying with all her might not to let him see the trembling of her hand. The firelight and the dimness of the room both helped her. But in any case he would hardly have noticed it. His thoughts were far away. . . .

VI

MRS BITTACY had never liked their present home. She preferred a flat, more open country that left approaches clear. She liked to see things coming. This cottage on the very edge of the old hunting grounds of William the Conqueror* had never satisfied her ideal of a safe and pleasant place to settle down in. The sea-coast, with treeless downs behind and a clear horizon in front, as at Eastbourne, say, was her ideal of a proper home.

It was curious, this instinctive aversion she felt to being shut in—by trees especially; a kind of claustrophobia almost; probably due, as has been said, to the days in India when the trees took her husband off and surrounded him with dangers. In those weeks of solitude the feeling had matured. She had fought it in her fashion, but never conquered it. Apparently routed, it had a way of creeping back in other forms. In this particular case, yielding to his strong desire, she thought the battle won, but the terror or the trees came back before the first month had passed. They laughed in her face.

She never lost knowledge of the fact that the leagues of forest lay about their cottage like a mighty wall, a crowding, watching, listening presence that shut them in from freedom and escape. Far from morbid naturally, she did her best to deny the thought, and so simple and unartificial was her type of mind that for weeks together she would wholly lose it. Then, suddenly it would return upon her with a rush of bleak reality. It was not only in her mind; it existed apart from any mere mood; a separate fear that walked alone; it came and went, yet when it went—went only to watch her from another point of view. It was in abeyance—hidden round the corner.

The Forest never let her go completely. It was ever ready to encroach. All the branches, she sometimes fancied, stretched one way—towards their tiny cottage and garden, as though it sought to draw them in and merge them in itself. Its great, deep-breathing soul resented the mockery, the insolence, the irritation of the prim garden at its very gates. It would absorb and smother them if it could. And every wind that blew its thundering message over the huge sounding-board of the million, shaking trees conveyed the purpose that it had. They had angered its great soul. At its heart was this deep, incessant roaring.

All this she never framed in words; the subtleties of language lay far beyond her reach. But instinctively she felt it; and more besides. It troubled her profoundly. Chiefly, moreover, for her husband. Merely for herself, the nightmare might have left her cold. It was David's peculiar interest in the trees that gave the special invitation.

Jealousy, then, in its most subtle aspect came to strengthen this aversion and dislike, for it came in a form that no reasonable wife could possibly object to. Her husband's passion, she reflected, was natural and inborn. It had decided his vocation, fed his ambition, nourished his dreams, desires, hopes. All his best years of active life had been spent in the care and guardianship of trees. He knew them, understood their secret life and nature, 'managed' them intuitively as other men 'managed' dogs and horses. He could not live for long away from them without a strange, acute nostalgia that stole his peace of mind and consequently his strength of body. A forest made him happy and at peace; it nursed and fed and soothed his deepest moods. Trees influenced the sources of his life, lowered or raised the very heart-beat in him. Cut off from them he languished as a lover of the sea can droop inland, or a mountaineer may pine in the flat monotony of the plains.

This she could understand, in a fashion at least, and make allow-ances for. She had yielded gently, even sweetly, to his choice of their English home; for in the little island there is nothing that suggests the woods of wilder countries so nearly as the New Forest. It has the genuine air and mystery, the depth and splendour, the loneliness, and here and there the strong, untamable quality of old-time forests as Bittacy of the Department knew them.

In a single detail only had he yielded to her wishes. He consented to a cottage on the edge, instead of in the heart of it. And for a dozen years now they had dwelt in peace and happiness at the lips of this great spreading thing that covered so many leagues with its tangle of swamps and moors and splendid ancient trees.

Only with the last two years or so—with his own increasing age, and physical decline perhaps—had come this marked growth of pas-sionate interest in the welfare of the Forest. She had watched it grow, at first had laughed at it, then talked sympathetically so far as sincer-ity permitted, then had argued mildly, and finally come to realise that its treatment lay altogether beyond her powers, and so had come to fear it with all her heart.

The six weeks they annually spent away from their English home, each regarded very differently of course. For her husband it meant a painful exile that did his health no good; he yearned for his trees—the sight and sound and smell of them; but for herself it meant release from a haunting dread—escape. To renounce those six weeks by the sea on the sunny, shining coast of France, was almost more than this little woman, even with her unselfishness, could face.

After the first shock of the announcement, she reflected as deeply as her nature permitted, prayed, wept in secret—and made up her mind. Duty, she felt clearly, pointed to renouncement. The discipline would certainly be severe—she did not dream at the moment how severe!—but this fine, consistent little Christian saw it plain; she accepted it, too, without any sighing of the martyr, though the courage she showed was of the martyr order. Her husband should never know the cost. In all but this one passion his unselfishness was ever as great as her own. The love she had borne him all these years, like the love she bore her anthropomorphic deity, was deep and real. She loved to suffer for them both. Besides, the way her husband had put it to her was singular. It did not take the form of a mere selfish predilection. Something higher than two wills in conflict seeking compromise was in it from the beginning.

'I feel, Sophia, it would be really more than I could manage,' he said slowly, gazing into the fire over the tops of his stretched-out muddy boots. 'My duty and my happiness lie here with the Forest and with you. My life is deeply rooted in this place. Something I can't define connects my inner being with these trees, and separation would make me ill—might even kill me. My hold on life would weaken; here is my source of supply. I cannot explain it better than that.' He looked up steadily into her face across the table so that she saw the gravity of his expression and the shining of his steady eyes.

'David, you feel it as strongly as that!' she said, forgetting the tea things altogether.

'Yes,' he replied, 'I do. And it's not of the body only; I feel it in my soul.'

The reality of what he hinted at crept into that shadow-covered room like an actual Presence and stood beside them. It came not by the windows or the door, but it filled the entire space between the walls and ceiling. It took the heat from the fire before her face. She felt suddenly cold, confused a little, frightened. She almost felt the rush of foliage in the wind. It stood between them.

'There are things—some things,' she faltered, 'we are not intended to know, I think.' The words expressed her general attitude to life, not alone to this particular incident.

And after a pause of several minutes, disregarding the criticism as though he had not heard it—'I cannot explain it better than that, you see,' his grave voice answered. 'There *is* this deep, tremendous link,—some secret power they emanate that keeps me well and happy and—alive. If you cannot understand, I feel at least you may be able to—forgive.' His tone grew tender, gentle, soft.

'My selfishness, I know, must seem quite unforgivable. I cannot help it somehow; these trees, this ancient Forest, both seem knitted into all that makes me live, and if I go——'

There was a little sound of collapse in his voice. He stopped abruptly, and sank back in his chair. And, at that, a distinct lump came up into her throat which she had great difficulty in managing while she went over and put her arms about him.

'My dear,' she murmured, 'God will direct. We will accept His guidance. He has always shown the way before.'

'My selfishness afflicts me——' he began, but she would not let him finish.

'David, He will direct. Nothing shall harm you. You've never once been selfish, and I cannot bear to hear you say such things. The way will open that is best for you—for both of us.' She kissed him; she would not let him speak; her heart was in her throat, and she felt for him far more than for herself.

And then he had suggested that she should go alone perhaps for a shorter time, and stay in her brother's villa with the children, Alice and Stephen. It was always open to her as she well knew.

'You need the change,' he said, when the lamps had been lit and the servant had gone out again; 'you need it as much as I dread it. I could manage somehow till you returned, and should feel happier that way if you went. I cannot leave this Forest that I love so well. I even feel, Sophie dear'—he sat up straight and faced her as he half whispered it—'that I can *never* leave it again. My life and happiness lie here together.'

And even while scorning the idea that she could leave him alone with the Influence of the Forest all about him to have its unimpeded way, she felt the pangs of that subtle jealousy bite keen and close. He loved the Forest better than herself, for he placed it first. Behind the words, moreover, hid the unuttered thought that made her so uneasy. The terror Sanderson had brought revived and shook its wings before her very eyes. For the whole conversation, of which this was a fragment, conveyed the unutterable implication that while he could not spare the trees, they equally could not spare him. The vividness with which he managed to conceal and yet betray the fact brought a profound distress that crossed the border between presentiment and warning into positive alarm.

He clearly felt that the trees would miss him—the trees he tended, guarded, watched over, loved.

'David, I shall stay here with you. I think you need me really,—don't you?' Eagerly, with a touch of heart-felt passion, the words poured out.

'Now more than ever, dear. God bless you for your sweet unselfishness. And your sacrifice,' he added, 'is all the greater because you cannot understand the thing that makes it necessary for me to stay.'

'Perhaps in the spring instead——' she said, with a tremor in the voice.

'In the spring—perhaps,' he answered gently, almost beneath his breath. 'For they will not need me then. All the world can love them in the spring. It's in the winter that they're lonely and neglected. I wish to stay with them particularly then. I even feel I ought to—and I must.'

And in this way, without further speech, the decision was made. Mrs Bittacy, at least, asked no more questions. Yet she could not bring herself to show more sympathy than was necessary. She felt, for one thing, that if she did, it might lead him to speak freely, and to tell her things she could not possibly bear to know. And she dared not take the risk of that.

VII

THIS was at the end of summer, but the autumn followed close. The conversation really marked the threshold between the two seasons, and marked at the same time the line between her husband's negative and aggressive state. She almost felt she had done wrong to yield; he grew so bold, concealment all discarded. He went, that is, quite openly to the woods, forgetting all his duties, all his former occupations. He even sought to coax her to go with him. The hidden thing blazed out without disguise. And, while she trembled at his energy, she admired the virile passion he displayed. Her jealousy had long ago retired before her fear, accepting the second place. Her one desire now was to protect. The wife turned wholly mother.

He said so little, but—he hated to come in. From morning to night he wandered in the Forest; often he went out after dinner; his mind was charged with trees—their foliage, growth, development; their wonder, beauty, strength; their loneliness in isolation, their power in a herded mass. He knew the effect of every wind upon them; the danger from the boisterous north, the glory from the west, the eastern dryness, and the soft, moist tenderness that a south wind left upon their thinning boughs. He spoke all day of their sensations: how they drank the fading sunshine, dreamed in the moonlight, thrilled to the kiss of stars. The dew could bring them half the passion of the night, but frost sent them plunging beneath the ground to dwell with hopes of a later coming softness in their roots. They nursed the life they carried—insects, larvae, chrysalis—and when the skies above them melted, he spoke of them standing 'motionless in an ecstasy of rain,' or in the noon of sunshine 'self-poised upon their prodigy of shade.'

And once in the middle of the night she woke at the sound of his voice, and heard him—wide awake, not talking in his sleep—but talking towards the window where the shadow of the cedar fell at noon:

O art thou sighing for Lebanon
In the long breeze that streams to thy delicious East?
Sighing for Lebanon,
Dark cedar;*

and, when, half charmed, half terrified, she turned and called to him by name, he merely said—

'My dear, I felt the loneliness—suddenly realised it—the alien desolation of that tree, set here upon our little lawn in England when all her Eastern brothers call to her in sleep.' And the answer seemed so queer, so 'un-evangelical,' that she waited in silence till he slept again. The poetry passed her by. It seemed unnecessary and out of place. It made her ache with suspicion, fear, jealousy.

The fear, however, seemed somehow all lapped up and banished soon afterwards by her unwilling admiration of the rushing splendour of her husband's state. Her anxiety, at any rate, shifted from the religious to the medical. She thought he might be losing his steadiness of mind a little. How often in her prayers she offered thanks for the guidance that had made her stay with him to help and watch is impossible to say. It certainly was twice a day.

She even went so far once, when Mr Mortimer, the vicar, called, and brought with him a more or less distinguished doctor—as to tell the professional man privately some symptoms of her husband's queerness. And his answer that there was 'nothing he could prescribe for' added not a little to her sense of unholy bewilderment. No doubt Sir James had never been 'consulted' under such unorthodox conditions before. His sense of what was becoming naturally overrode his acquired instincts as a skilled instrument that might help the race.

'No fever, you think?' she asked insistently with hurry, determined to get something from him.

'Nothing that *I* can deal with, as I told you, Madam,' replied the offended allopathic Knight.*

Evidently he did not care about being invited to examine patients in this surreptitious way before a teapot on the lawn, chance of a fee most problematical. He liked to see a tongue and feel a thumping pulse; to know the pedigree and bank account of his questioner as well. It was most unusual, in abominable taste besides. Of course it was. But the drowning woman seized the only straw she could.

For now the aggressive attitude of her husband overcame her to the point where she found it difficult even to question him. Yet in the house he was so kind and gentle, doing all he could to make her sacrifice as easy as possible.

'David, you really *are* unwise to go out now. The night is damp and very chilly. The ground is soaked in dew. You'll catch your death of cold.'

His face lightened. 'Won't you come with me, dear,—just for once? I'm only going to the corner of the hollies to see the beech that stands so lonely by itself.'

She had been out with him in the short dark afternoon, and they had passed that evil group of hollies where the gipsies camped. Nothing else would grow there, but the hollies throve upon the stony soil.

'David, the beech is all right and safe.' She had learned his phraseology a little, made clever out of due season by her love, 'There's no wind to-night.'

'But it's rising,' he answered, 'rising in the east. I heard it in the bare and hungry larches. They need the sun and dew, and always cry out when the wind's upon them from the east.'

She sent a short unspoken prayer most swiftly to her deity as she heard him say it. For every time now, when he spoke in this familiar, intimate way of the life of the trees, she felt a sheet of cold fasten tight against her very skin and flesh. She shivered. How *could* he possibly know such things?

Yet, in all else, and in the relations of his daily life, he was sane and reasonable, loving, kind and tender. It was only on the subject of the trees he seemed unhinged and queer. Most curiously it seemed that, since the collapse of the cedar they both loved, though in different fashion, his departure from the normal had increased. Why else did he watch them as a man might watch a sickly child? Why did he linger especially in the dusk to catch their 'mood of night' as he called it? Why think so carefully upon them when the frost was threatening or the wind appeared to rise?

As she put it so frequently now to herself—How could he possibly *know* such things?

He went. As she closed the front door after him she heard the distant roaring in the Forest. . . .

And then it suddenly struck her: How could she know them too?

It dropped upon her like a blow that she felt at once all over, upon body, heart and mind. The discovery rushed out from its ambush to overwhelm. The truth of it, making all arguing futile, numbed her faculties. But though at first it deadened her, she soon revived, and her being rose into aggressive opposition. A wild yet calculated courage like that which animates the leaders of splendid forlorn hopes flamed in her little person—flamed grandly, and invincible. While knowing herself insignificant and weak, she knew at the same time that power at her back which moves the worlds. The faith that filled her was the weapon in her hands, and the right by which she claimed it; but the spirit of utter, selfless sacrifice that characterised her life was the means by which she mastered its immediate use. For a kind of white and faultless intuition guided her to the attack. Behind her stood her Bible and her God.

How so magnificent a divination came to her at all may well be a matter for astonishment, though some clue of explanation lies, perhaps, in the very simpleness of her nature. At any rate, she saw quite clearly certain things; saw them in moments only—after prayer, in the still silence of the night, or when left alone those long hours in the house with her knitting and her thoughts—and the guidance which then flashed into her remained, even after the manner of its coming was forgotten.

They came to her, these things she saw, formless, wordless; she could not put them into any kind of language; but by the very fact of being uncaught in sentences they retained their original clear vigour.

Hours of patient waiting brought the first, and the others followed easily afterwards, by degrees, on subsequent days, a little and a little. Her husband had been gone since early morning, and had taken his luncheon with him. She was sitting by the tea things, the cups and teapot warmed, the muffins in the fender keeping hot, all ready for his return, when she realised quite abruptly that this thing which took him off, which kept him out so many hours day after day, this thing that was against her own little will and instincts—was enormous as the sea. It was no mere prettiness of single Trees, but something massed and mountainous. About her rose the wall of its huge opposition to the sky, its scale gigantic, its power utterly prodigious. What she knew of it hitherto as green and delicate forms waving and rustling in the winds was but, as it were, the spray of foam that broke into sight upon the nearer edge of viewless depths far, far away. The trees, indeed, were sentinels set visibly about the limits of a camp that itself remained invisible. The awful hum and murmur of the main body in the distance passed into that still room about her with the firelight and hissing kettle. Out yonder—in the Forest further out—the thing that was ever roaring at the centre was dreadfully increasing.

The sense of definite battle, too—battle between herself and the Forest for his soul—came with it. Its presentment was as clear as though Thompson had come into the room and quietly told her that the cottage was surrounded. 'Please, ma'am, there are trees come up about the house,' she might have suddenly announced. And equally might have heard her own answer: 'It's all right, Thompson. The main body is still far away.'

Immediately upon its heels, then, came another truth, with a close reality that shocked her. She saw that jealousy was not confined to the human and animal world alone, but ran through all creation. The Vegetable Kingdom knew it too. So-called inanimate nature shared it with the rest. Trees felt it. This Forest just beyond the window—standing there in the silence of the autumn evening across the little lawn—this Forest understood it equally. The remorseless, branching power that sought to keep exclusively for itself the thing it loved and needed, spread like a running desire through all its million leaves and stems and roots. In humans, of course, it was consciously directed; in animals it acted with frank Instinctiveness; but in trees this jealousy rose in some blind tide of impersonal and unconscious wrath that would sweep opposition from its path as the wind sweeps powdered snow from the surface of the ice. Their number was a host with endless reinforcements, and once it realised its passion was returned the power increased. . . . Her husband loved the trees. . . . They had become aware of it. . . . They would take him from her in the end. . . .

Then, while she heard his footsteps in the hall and the closing of the front door, she saw a third thing clearly;—realised the widening of the gap between herself and him. This other love had made it. All these weeks of the summer when she felt so close to him, now especially when she had made the biggest sacrifice of her life to stay by his side and help him, he had been slowly, surely—drawing away. The estrangement was here and now—a fact accomplished. It had been all this time maturing; there yawned this broad deep space between them. Across the empty distance she saw the change in merciless perspective. It revealed his face and figure, dearly-loved, once fondly worshipped, far on the other side in shadowy distance, small, the back turned from her, and moving while she watched—moving away from her.

They had their tea in silence then. She asked no questions, he volunteered no information of his day. The heart was big within her, and the terrible loneliness of age spread through her like a rising icy mist. She watched him, filling all his wants. His hair was untidy and his boots were caked with blackish mud. He moved with a restless, swaying motion that somehow blanched her cheek and sent a miserable shivering down her back. It reminded her of trees. His eyes were very bright.

He brought in with him an odour of the earth and forest that seemed to choke her and make it difficult to breathe; and—what she noticed with a climax of almost uncontrollable alarm—upon his face beneath the lamplight shone traces of a mild, faint glory that made her think of moonlight falling upon a wood through speckled shadows. It was his new-found happiness that shone there, a happiness uncaused by her and in which she had no part.

In his coat was a spray of faded yellow beech leaves. 'I brought this from the Forest for you,' he said, with all the air that belonged to his little acts of devotion long ago. And she took the spray of leaves mechanically with a smile and a murmured 'thank you, dear,' as though he had unknowingly put into her hands the weapon for her own destruction and she had accepted it.

And when the tea was over and he left the room, he did not go to his study, or to change his clothes. She heard the front door softly shut behind him as he again went out towards the Forest.

A moment later she was in her room upstairs, kneeling beside the bed—the side he slept on—and praying wildly through a flood of tears that God would save and keep him to her. Wind brushed the window panes behind her while she knelt.

VIII

ONE sunny November morning, when the strain had reached a pitch that made repression almost unmanageable, she came to an impulsive decision, and obeyed it. Her husband had again gone out with luncheon for the day. She took adventure in her hands and followed him. The power of seeing-clear was strong upon her, forcing her up to some unnatural level of understanding. To stay indoors and wait inactive for his return seemed suddenly impossible. She meant to know what he knew, feel what he felt, put herself in his place. She would dare the fascination of the Forest—share it with him. It was greatly daring; but it would give her greater understanding how to help and save him and therefore greater Power. She went upstairs a moment first to pray.

In a thick, warm skirt, and wearing heavy boots—those walking boots she used with him upon the mountains about Seillans—she left the cottage by the back way and turned towards the Forest. She could not actually follow him, for he had started off an hour before and she knew not exactly his direction. What was so urgent in her was the wish to be with him in the woods, to walk beneath the leafless branches just as he did: to be there when he was there, even though not together. For it had come to her that she might thus share with him for once this horrible mighty life and breathing of the trees he loved. In winter, he had said, they needed him particularly; and winter now was coming. Her love *must* bring her something of what he felt himself—the huge attraction, the suction and the pull of all the trees. Thus, in some vicarious fashion, she might share, though unknown to himself, this very thing that was taking him away from her. She might thus even lessen its attack upon himself.

The impulse came to her clairvoyantly, and she obeyed without a sign of hesitation. Deeper comprehension would come to her of the whole awful puzzle. And come it did, yet not in the way she imagined and expected.

The air was very still, the sky a cold pale blue, but cloudless. The entire Forest stood silent, at attention. It knew perfectly well that she had come. It knew the moment when she entered; watched and followed her; and behind her something dropped without a sound and shut her in. Her feet upon the glades of mossy grass fell silently, as the oaks and beeches shifted past in rows and took up their positions at her back. It was not pleasant, this way they grew so dense behind her the instant she had passed. She realised that they gathered in an ever-growing army, massed, herded, trooped, between her and the cottage, shutting off escape. They let her pass so easily, but to get out again she would know them differently—thick, crowded, branches all drawn and hostile. Already their increasing numbers bewildered her. In front, they looked so sparse and scattered, with open spaces where the sunshine fell; but when she turned it seemed they stood so close together, a serried army, darkening the sunlight.

They blocked the day, collected all the shadows, stood with their leafless and forbidding rampart like the night. They swallowed down into themselves the very glade by which she came. For when she glanced behind her—rarely—the way she had come was shadowy and lost.

Yet the morning sparkled overhead, and a glance of excitement ran quivering through the entire day. It was what she always knew as 'children's weather,' so clear and harmless, without a sign of danger, nothing ominous to threaten or alarm. Steadfast in her purpose, looking back as little as she dared, Sophia Bittacy marched slowly and deliberately into the heart of the silent woods, deeper, ever deeper. . . .

And then, abruptly, in an open space where the sunshine fell unhindered, she stopped. It was one of the breathing-places of the forest. Dead, withered bracken lay in patches of unsightly grey. There were bits of heather too. All round the trees stood looking on—oak, beech, holly, ash, pine, larch, with here and there small groups of juniper. On the lips of this breathing-space of the woods she stopped to rest, disobeying her instinct for the first time. For the other instinct in her was to go on. She did not really want to rest.

This was the little act that brought it to her—the wireless message from a vast Emitter.

'I've been stopped,' she thought to herself with a horrid qualm.

She looked about her in this quiet, ancient place. Nothing stirred. There was no life nor sign or life; no birds sang; no rabbits scuttled off at her approach. The stillness was bewildering, and gravity hung down upon it like a heavy curtain. It hushed the heart in her. Could this be part of what her husband felt—this sense of thick entanglement with stems, boughs, roots, and foliage?

'This has always been as it is now,' she thought, yet not knowing why she thought it. 'Ever since the Forest grew it has been still and secret here. It has never changed.' The curtain of silence drew closer while she said it, thickening round her. 'For a thousand *years*—I'm here with a thousand years. And behind this place stand all the forests of the world!'

So foreign to her temperament were such thoughts, and so alien to all she had been taught to look for in Nature, that she strove against them. She made an effort to oppose. But they clung and haunted just the same; they refused to be dispersed. The curtain hung dense and heavy as though its texture thickened. The air with difficulty came through.

And then she thought that curtain stirred. There was movement somewhere. That obscure dim thing which ever broods behind the visible appearances of trees came nearer to her. She caught her breath and stared about her, listening intently. The trees, perhaps because she saw them more in detail now, it seemed to her had changed. A vague, faint alteration spread over them, at first so slight she scarcely would admit it, then growing steadily, though still obscurely, outwards. 'They tremble and are changed,' flashed through her mind the horrid line that Sanderson had quoted. Yet the change was graceful for all the uncouthness attendant upon the size of so vast a movement. They had turned in her direction. That was it. *They saw her.*

In this way the change expressed itself in her groping, terrified thought. Till now it had been otherwise: she had looked at them from her own point of view; now they looked at her from theirs. They stared her in the face and eyes; they stared at her all over. In some unkind, resentful, hostile way, they watched her. Hitherto in life she had watched them variously, in superficial ways, reading into them what her own mind suggested. Now they read into her the things they actually *were*, and not merely another's interpretation of them.

They seemed in their motionless silence there instinct with life, a life, moreover, that breathed about her a species of terrible soft enchantment that bewitched. It branched all through her, climbing to the brain. The Forest held her with its huge and giant fascination. In this secluded breathing-spot that the centuries had left untouched, she had stepped close against the hidden pulse of the whole collective mass of them. They were aware of her and had turned to gaze with their myriad, vast sight upon the intruder. They shouted at her in the silence. For she wanted to look back at them, but it was like staring at a crowd, and her glance merely shifted from one tree to another, hurriedly, finding in none the one she sought. They saw her so easily, each and all. The rows that stood behind her also stared. But she could not return the gaze. Her husband, she realised, could. And their steady stare shocked her as though in some sense she knew that she was naked. They saw so much of her: she saw of them—so little.

Her efforts to return their gaze were pitiful. The constant shifting increased her bewilderment. Conscious of this awful and enormous sight all over her, she let her eyes first rest upon the ground; and then she closed them altogether. She kept the lids as tight together as ever they would go.

But the sight of the trees came even into that inner darkness behind the fastened lids, for there was no escaping it. Outside, in the light, she still knew that the leaves of the hollies glittered smoothly, that the dead foliage of the oaks hung crisp in the air above her, that the needles of the little junipers were pointing all one way. The spread perception of the Forest was focussed on herself, and no mere shutting of the eyes could hide its scattered yet concentrated stare—the all-inclusive vision of great woods.

There was no wind, yet here and there a single leaf hanging by its dried-up stalk shook all alone with great rapidity—rattling. It was the sentry drawing attention to her presence. And then, again, as once long weeks before, she felt their Being as a tide about her. The tide had turned. That memory of her childhood sands came back, when the nurse said, 'The tide has turned now; we must go in,' and she saw the mass of piled-up waters, green and heaped to the horizon, and realised that it was slowly coming in. The gigantic mass of it, too vast for hurry, loaded with massive purpose, she used to feel, was moving towards herself. The fluid body of the sea was creeping along beneath the sky to the very spot upon the yellow sands where she stood and played. The sight and thought of it had always overwhelmed her with a sense of awe—as though her puny self were the object of the whole sea's advance. 'The tide has turned; we had better now go in.'

This was happening now about her—the same thing was happening in the woods—slow, sure, and steady, and its motion as little discernible as the sea's. The tide had turned. The small human presence that had ventured among its green and mountainous depths, moreover, was its objective.

That all was clear within her while she sat and waited with tight-shut lids. But the next moment she opened her eyes with a sudden realization of something more. The presence that it sought was after all not hers. It was the presence of some one other than herself. And then she understood. Her eyes had opened with a click, it seemed; but the sound, in reality, was outside herself. Across the clearing where the sunshine lay so calm and still, she saw the figure of her husband moving among the trees—a man, like a tree, walking.

With hands behind his back, and head uplifted, he moved quite slowly, as though absorbed in his own thoughts. Hardly fifty paces separated them, but he had no inkling of her presence there so near. With mind intent and senses all turned inwards, he marched past her like a figure in a dream, and like a figure in a dream she saw him go. Love, yearning, pity rose in a storm within her, but as in nightmare she found no words or movement possible. She sat and watched him go—go from her—go into the deeper reaches of the green enveloping woods. Desire to save, to bid him stop and turn, ran in a passion through her being, but there was nothing she could do. She saw him go away from her, go of his own accord and willingly beyond her; she saw the branches drop about his steps and hide him. His figure faded out among the speckled shade and sunlight. The trees covered him. The tide just took him, all unresisting and content to go. Upon the bosom of the green soft sea he floated away beyond her reach of vision. Her eyes could follow him no longer. He was gone.

And then for the first time she realised, even at that distance, that the look upon his face was one of peace and happiness—rapt, and caught away in joy, a look of youth. That expression now he never showed to her. But she *had* known it. Years ago, in the early days of their married life, she had seen it on his face. Now it no longer obeyed the summons of her presence and her love. The woods alone could call it forth; it answered to the trees; the Forest had taken every part of him—from her—his very heart and soul. . . .

Her sight that had plunged inwards to the fields of faded memory now came back to outer things again. She looked about her, and her love, returning empty-handed and unsatisfied, left her open to the invading of the bleakest terror she had ever known. That such things could be real and happen found her helpless utterly. Terror invaded the quietest corners of her heart, that had never yet known quailing. She could not—for moments at any rate—reach either her Bible or her God. Desolate in an empty world of fear she sat with eyes too dry and hot for tears, yet with a coldness as of ice upon her very flesh. She stared, unseeing, about her. That horror which stalks in the stillness of the noonday, when the glare of an artificial sunshine lights up the motionless trees, moved all about her. In front and behind she was aware of it. Beyond this stealthy silence, just within the edge of it, the things of another world were passing. But she could not know them. Her husband knew them, knew their beauty and their awe, yes, but for her they were out of reach. She might not share with him the very least of them. It seemed that behind and through the glare of this wintry noonday in the heart of the woods there brooded another universe of life and passion, for her all unexpressed. The silence veiled it, the stillness hid it; but he moved with it all and understood. His love interpreted it.

She rose to her feet, tottered feebly, and collapsed again upon the moss. Yet for herself she felt no terror; no little personal fear could touch her whose anguish and deep longing streamed all out to him whom she so bravely loved. In this time of utter self-forgetfulness, when she realised that the battle was hopeless, thinking she had lost even her God, she found Him again quite close beside her like a little Presence in this terrible heart of the hostile Forest. But at first she did not recognise that He was there; she did not know Him in that strangely unacceptable guise. For He stood so very close, so very intimate, so very sweet and comforting, and yet so hard to understand—as Resignation.

Once more she struggled to her feet, and this time turned successfully and slowly made her way along the mossy glade by which she came. And at first she marvelled, though only for a moment, at the ease with which she found the path. For a moment only, because almost at once she saw the truth. The trees were glad that she should go. They helped her on her way. The Forest did not want her.

The tide was coming in, indeed, yet not for her.

And so, in another of those flashes of clear-vision that of late had lifted life above the normal level, she saw and understood the whole terrible thing complete.

Till now, though unexpressed in thought or language, her fear had been that the woods her husband loved would somehow take him from her—to merge his life in theirs—even to kill him in some mysterious way. This time she saw her deep mistake, and so seeing, let in upon herself the fuller agony of horror. For their jealousy was not the petty jealousy of animals or humans. They wanted him because they loved him, but they did not want him dead. Full charged with his splendid life and enthusiasm they wanted him. They wanted him—alive.

It was she who stood in their way, and it was she whom they intended to remove.

This was what brought the sense of abject helplessness. She stood upon the sands against an entire ocean slowly rolling in against her. For, as all the forces of a human being combine unconsciously to eject a grain of sand that has crept beneath the skin to cause discomfort, so the entire mass of what Sanderson had called the Collective Consciousness of the Forest strove to eject this human atom that stood across the path of its desire. Loving her husband, she had crept beneath its skin. It was her they would eject and take away; it was her they would destroy, not him. Him, whom they loved and needed, they would keep alive. They meant to take him living.

She reached the house in safety, though she never remembered how she found her way. It was made all simple for her. The branches almost urged her out.

But behind her, as she left the shadowed precincts, she felt as though some towering Angel of the Woods let fall across the threshold the flaming sword of a countless multitude of leaves that formed behind her a barrier, green, shimmering, and impassable. Into the Forest she never walked again.

And she went about her daily duties with a calm and quietness that was a perpetual astonishment even to herself, for it hardly seemed of this world at all. She talked to her husband when he came in for tea—after dark. Resignation brings a curious large courage—when there is nothing more to lose. The soul takes risks, and dares. Is it a curious short-cut sometimes to the heights?

'David, I went into the Forest, too, this morning; soon after you I went. I saw you there.'

'Wasn't it wonderful?' he answered simply, inclining his head a little. There was no surprise or annoyance in his look; a mild and gentle *ennui* rather. He asked no real question. She thought of some garden tree the wind attacks too suddenly, bending it over when it does not want to bend—the mild unwillingness with which it yields. She often saw him this way now, in the terms of trees.

'It was very wonderful indeed, dear, yes,' she replied low, her voice not faltering though indistinct. 'But for me it was too—too strange and big.'

The passion of tears lay just below the quiet voice all unbetrayed. Somehow she kept them back.

There was a pause, and then he added:

'I find it more and more so every day.' His voice passed through the lamp-lit room like a murmur of the wind in branches. The look of youth and happiness she had caught upon his face out there had wholly gone, and an expression of weariness was in its place, as of a man distressed vaguely at finding himself in uncongenial surroundings where he is slightly ill at ease. It was the house he hated—coming back to rooms and walls and furniture. The ceilings and closed windows confined him. Yet, in it, no suggestion that he found *her* irksome. Her presence seemed of no account at all; indeed, he hardly noticed her. For whole long periods he lost her, did not know that she was there. He had no need of her. He lived alone. Each lived alone.

The outward signs by which she recognised that the awful battle was against her and the terms of surrender accepted were pathetic. She put the medicine-chest away upon the shelf; she gave the orders for his pocket-luncheon before he asked; she went to bed alone and early, leaving the front door unlocked, with milk and bread and butter in the hall beside the lamp—all concessions that she felt impelled to make. For more and more, unless the weather was too violent, he went out after dinner even, staying for hours in the woods. But she never slept until she heard the front door close below, and knew soon afterwards his careful step come creeping up the stairs and into the room so softly. Until she heard his regular deep breathing close beside her, she lay awake. All strength or desire to resist had gone for good. The thing against her was too huge and powerful. Capitulation was complete, a fact accomplished. She dated it from the day she followed him to the Forest.

Moreover, the time for evacuation—her own evacuation—seemed approaching. It came stealthily ever nearer, surely and slowly as the rising tide she used to dread. At the high-water mark she stood waiting calmly—waiting to be swept away. Across the lawn all those terrible days of early winter the encircling Forest watched it come, guiding its silent swell and currents towards her feet. Only she never once gave up her Bible or her praying. This complete resignation, moreover, had somehow brought to her a strange great understanding, and if she could not share her husband's horrible abandonment to powers outside himself, she could, and did, in some half-groping way grasp at shadowy meanings that might make such abandonment—possible, yes, but more than merely possible—in some extraordinary sense not evil.

Hitherto she had divided the beyond-world into two sharp halves—spirits good or spirits evil. But thoughts came to her now, on soft and very tentative feet, like the footsteps of the gods which are on wool, that besides these definite classes, there might be other Powers as well, belonging definitely to neither one nor other. Her thought stopped dead at that. But the big idea found lodgment in her little mind, and, owing to the largeness of her heart, remained there unejected. It even brought a certain solace with it.

The failure—or unwillingness, as she preferred to state it—of her God to interfere and help, that also she came in a measure to understand. For here, she found it more and more possible to imagine, was perhaps no positive evil at work, but only something that usually stands away from humankind, something alien and not commonly recognised. There *was* a gulf fixed between the two, and Mr Sanderson *had* bridged it, by his talk, his explanations, his attitude of mind. Through these her husband had found the way into it. His temperament and natural passion for the woods had prepared the soul in him, and the moment he saw the way to go he took it—the line of least resistance. Life was, of course, open to all, and her husband had the right to choose it where he would. He had chosen it—away from her, away from other men, but not necessarily away from God. This was an enormous concession that she skirted, never really faced; it was too revolutionary to face. But its possibility peeped into her bewildered mind. It might delay his progress, or it might advance it. Who could know? And why should God, who ordered all things with such magnificent detail, from the pathway of a sun to the falling of a sparrow,* object to his free choice, or interfere to hinder him and stop?

She came to realise resignation, that is, in another aspect. It gave her comfort, if not peace. She fought against all belittling of her God. It was, perhaps, enough that He—knew.

'You are not alone, dear, in the trees out there?' she ventured one night, as he crept on tiptoe into the room not far from midnight. 'God is with you?'

'Magnificently,' was the immediate answer, given with enthusiasm, 'for He is everywhere. And I only wish that you——'

But she stuffed the clothes against her ears. That invitation on his lips was more than she could bear to hear. It seemed like asking her to hurry to her own execution. She buried her face among the sheets and blankets, shaking all over like a leaf.

IX

AND so the thought that she was the one to go remained and grew. It was, perhaps, first sign of that weakening of the mind which indicated the singular manner of her going. For it was her mental opposition, the trees felt, that stood in their way. Once that was overcome, obliterated, her physical presence did not matter. She would be harmless.

Having accepted defeat, because she had come to feel that his obsession was not actually evil, she accepted at the same time the conditions of an atrocious loneliness. She stood now from her husband farther than from the moon. They had no visitors. Callers were few and far between, and less encouraged than before. The empty dark of winter was before them. Among the neighbours was none in whom, without disloyalty to her husband, she could confide. Mr Mortimer, had he been single, might have helped her in this desert of solitude that preyed upon her mind, but his wife was there the obstacle; for Mrs Mortimer wore sandals, believed that nuts were the complete food of man, and indulged in other idiosyncrasies that classed her inevitably among the 'latter signs' which Mrs Bittacy had been taught to dread as dangerous. She stood most desolately alone.

Solitude, therefore, in which the mind unhindered feeds upon its own delusions, was the assignable cause of her gradual mental disruption and collapse.

With the definite arrival of the colder weather her husband gave up his rambles after dark; evenings were spent together over the fire; he read *The Times*; they even talked about their postponed visit abroad in the coming spring. No restlessness was on him at the change; he seemed content and easy in his mind; spoke little of the trees and woods; enjoyed far better health than if there had been change of scene, and to herself was tender, kind, solicitous over trifles, as in the distant days of their first honeymoon.

But this deep calm could not deceive her; it meant, she fully understood, that he felt sure of himself, sure of her, and sure of the trees as well. It all lay buried in the depths of him, too secure and deep, too intimately established in his central being to permit of those surface fluctuations which betray disharmony within. His life was hid with trees. Even the fever, so dreaded in the damp of winter, left him free. She now knew why. The fever was due to their efforts to obtain him, his efforts to respond and go—physical results of a fierce unrest he had never understood till Sanderson came with his wicked explanations. Now it was otherwise. The bridge was made. And—he had gone.

And she, brave, loyal, and consistent soul, found herself utterly alone, even trying to make his passage easy. It seemed that she stood at the bottom of some huge ravine that opened in her mind, the walls whereof instead of rock were trees that reached enormous to the sky, engulfing her. God alone knew that she was there. He watched, permitted, even perhaps approved. At any rate—He knew.

During those quiet evenings in the house, moreover, while they sat over the fire listening to the roaming winds about the house, her husband knew continual access to the world his alien love had furnished for him. Never for a single instant was he cut off from it. She gazed at the newspaper spread before his face and knees, saw the smoke of his cheroot curl up above the edge, noticed the little hole in his evening socks, and listened to the paragraphs he read aloud as of old. But this was all a veil he spread about himself of purpose. Behind it—he escaped. It was the conjurer's trick to divert the sight to unimportant details while the essential thing went forward unobserved. He managed wonderfully; she loved him for the pains he took to spare her distress; but all the while she knew that the body lolling in that arm-chair before her eyes contained the merest fragment of his actual self. It was little better than a corpse. It was an empty shell. The essential soul of him was out yonder with the Forest—farther out near that ever-roaring heart of it.

And, with the dark, the Forest came up boldly and pressed against the very walls and windows, peering in upon them, joining hands above the slates and chimneys. The winds were always walking on the lawn and gravel paths; steps came and went and came again; some one seemed always talking in the woods, some one was in the building too. She passed them on the stairs, or running soft and muffled, very large and gentle, down the passages and landings after dusk, as though loose fragments of the Day had broken off and stayed there caught among the shadows, trying to get out. They blundered silently all about the house. They waited till she passed, then made a run for it. And her husband always knew. She saw him more than once deliberately avoid them—because *she* was there. More than once, too, she saw him stand and listen when he thought she was not near, then heard herself the long bounding stride of their approach across the silent garden. Already *he* had heard them in the windy distance of the night, far, far away. They sped, she well knew, along that glade of mossy turf by which she last came out; it cushioned their tread exactly as it had cushioned her own.

It seemed to her the trees were always in the house with him, and in their very bedroom. He welcomed them, unaware that she also knew, and trembled.

One night in their bedroom it caught her unawares. She woke out of deep sleep and it came upon her before she could gather her forces for control.

The day had been wildly boisterous, but now the wind had dropped; only its rags went fluttering through the night. The rays of the full moon fell in a shower between the branches. Overhead still raced the scud and wrack, shaped like hurrying monsters; but below the earth was quiet. Still and dripping stood the hosts of trees. Their trunks gleamed wet and sparkling where the moon caught them. There was a strong smell of mould and fallen leaves. The air was sharp—heavy with odour.

And she knew all this the instant that she woke; for it seemed to her that she had been elsewhere—following her husband—as though she had been *out*! There was no dream at all, merely this definite, haunting certainty. It dived away, lost, buried in the night. She sat upright in bed. She had come back.

The room shone pale in the moonlight reflected through the windows, for the blinds were up, and she saw her husband's form beside her, motionless in deep sleep. But what caught her unawares was the horrid thing that by this fact of sudden, unexpected waking she had surprised these other things in the room, beside the very bed, gathered close about him while he slept. It was their dreadful boldness—herself of no account as it were—that terrified her into screaming before she could collect her powers to prevent. She screamed before she realised what she did—a long, high shriek of terror that filled the room, yet made so little actual sound. For wet and shimmering presences stood grouped all round that bed. She saw their outline underneath the ceiling, the green, spread bulk of them, their vague extension over walls and furniture. They shifted to and fro, massed yet translucent, mild yet thick, moving and turning within themselves to a hushed noise of multitudinous soft rustling. In their sound was something very sweet and winning that fell into her with a spell of horrible enchantment. They were so mild, each one alone, yet so terrific in their combination. Cold seized her. The sheets against her body turned to ice.

She screamed a second time, though the sound hardly issued from her throat. The spell sank deeper, reaching to the heart; for it softened all the currents of her blood and took life from her in a stream—towards themselves. Resistance in that moment seemed impossible.

Her husband then stirred in his sleep, and woke. And, instantly, the forms drew up, erect, and gathered themselves in some amazing way together. They lessened in extent—then scattered through the air like an effect of light when shadows seek to smother it. It was tremendous, yet most exquisite. A sheet of pale-green shadow that yet had form and substance filled the room. There was a rush of silent movement, as the Presences drew past her through the air,—and they were gone.

But, clearest of all, she saw the manner of their going; for she recognised in their tumult of escape by the window open at the top, the same wide 'looping circles'—spirals it seemed—that she had seen upon the lawn those weeks ago when Sanderson had talked. The room once more was empty.

In the collapse that followed, she heard her husband's voice, as though coming from some great distance. Her own replies she heard as well. Both were so strange and unlike their normal speech, the very words unnatural:

'What is it, dear? Why do you wake me *now?*' And his voice whispered it with a sighing sound, like wind in pine boughs.

'A moment since something went past me through the air of the room. Back to the night outside it went.' Her voice, too, held the same note as of wind entangled among too many leaves.

'My dear, it *was* the wind.'

'But it called, David. It was calling you—by name!'

'The stir of the branches, dear, was what you heard. Now, sleep again, I beg you, sleep.'

'It had a crowd of eyes all through and over it—before and behind——' Her voice grew louder.

But his own in reply sank lower, far away, and oddly hushed.

'The moonlight, dear, upon the sea of twigs and boughs in the rain, was what you saw.'

'But it frightened me. I've lost my God—and you—I'm cold as death!'

'My dear, it is the cold of the early morning hours. The whole world sleeps. Now sleep again yourself.'

He whispered close to her ear. She felt his hand stroking her. His voice was soft and very soothing. But only a part of him was there; only a part of him was speaking; it was a half-emptied body that lay beside her and uttered these strange sentences, even forcing her own singular choice of words. The horrible, dim enchantment of the trees was close about them in the room—gnarled, ancient, lonely trees of winter, whispering round the human life they loved.

'And let me sleep again,' she heard him murmur as he settled down among the clothes, 'sleep back into that deep, delicious peace from which you called me. . . .'

His dreamy, happy tone, and that look of youth and joy she discerned upon his features even in the filtered moonlight, touched her again as with the spell of those shining, mild green presences. It sank down into her. She felt sleep grope for her. On the threshold of slumber one of those strange vagrant voices that loss of consciousness lets loose cried faintly in her heart—

'There is joy in the Forest over one sinner that——'*

Then sleep took her before she had time to realise even that she was vilely parodying one of her most precious texts, and that the irreverence was ghastly. . . .

And though she quickly slept again, her sleep was not as usual, dreamless. It was not woods and trees she dreamed of, but a small and curious dream that kept coming again and again upon her: that she stood upon a wee, bare rock in the sea, and that the tide was rising. The water first came to her feet, then to her knees, then to her waist. Each time the dream returned, the tide seemed higher. Once it rose to her neck, once even to her mouth, covering her lips for a moment so that she could not breathe. She did not wake between the dreams; a period of drab and dreamless slumber intervened. But, finally, the water rose above her eyes and face, completely covering her head.

And then came explanation—the sort of explanation dreams bring. She understood. For, beneath the water, she had seen the world of sea-weed rising from the bottom of the sea like a forest of dense green—long, sinuous stems, immense thick branches, millions of feelers spreading through the darkened watery depths the power of their ocean foliage. The Vegetable Kingdom was even in the sea. It was everywhere. Earth, air, and water helped it, way of escape there was none.

And even underneath the sea she heard that terrible sound of roaring—was it surf or wind or voices?—further out, yet coming steadily towards her.

And so, in the loneliness of that drab English winter, the mind of Mrs Bittacy, preying upon itself, and fed by constant dread, went lost in disproportion. Dreariness filled the weeks with dismal, sunless skies and a clinging moisture that knew no wholesome tonic of keen frosts. Alone with her thoughts, both her husband and her God with-drawn into distance, she counted the days to Spring. She groped her way, stumbling down the long dark tunnel. Through the arch at the far end lay a brilliant picture of the violet sea sparkling on the coast of France. There lay safety and escape for both of them, could she but hold on. Behind her the trees blocked up the other entrance. She never once looked back.

She drooped. Vitality passed from her, drawn out and away as by some steady suction. Immense and incessant was this sensation of her powers draining off. The taps were all turned on. Her personality, as it were, streamed steadily away, coaxed outwards by this Power that never wearied and seemed inexhaustible. It won her as the full moon wins the tide. She waned; she faded; she obeyed.

At first she watched the process, and recognised exactly what was going on. Her physical life, and that balance of the mind which depends on physical well-being, were being slowly undermined. She saw that clearly. Only the soul, dwelling like a star apart from these and independent of them, lay safe somewhere—with her distant God. That she knew—tranquilly. The spiritual love that linked her to her husband was safe from all attack. Later, in His good time, they would merge together again because of it. But, meanwhile, all of her that had kinship with the earth was slowly going. This separation was being remorselessly accomplished. Every part of her the trees could touch was being Steadily drained from her. She was being—removed.

After a time, however, even this power of realisation went, so that she no longer 'watched the process' or knew exactly what was going on. The one satisfaction she had known—the feeling that it was sweet to suffer for his sake—went with it. She stood utterly alone with this terror of the trees . . . mid the ruins of her broken and disordered mind.

She slept badly; woke in the morning with hot and tired eyes; her head ached dully; she grew confused in thought and lost the clues of daily life in the most feeble fashion. At the same time she lost sight, too, of that brilliant picture at the exit of the tunnel; it faded away into a tiny semicircle of pale light, the violet sea and the sunshine the merest point of white, remote as a star and equally inaccessible. She knew now that she could never reach it. And through the darkness that stretched behind, the power of the trees came close and caught her, twining about her feet and arms, climbing to her very lips. She woke at night, finding it difficult to breathe. There seemed wet leaves pressed against her mouth, and soft green tendrils dinging to her neck. Her feet were heavy, half rooted, as it were, in deep, thick earth. Huge creepers stretched along the whole of that black tunnel, feeling about her person for points where they might fasten well, as ivy or the giant parasites of the Vegetable Kingdom settle down on the trees themselves to sap their life and kill them.

Slowly and surely the morbid growth possessed her life and held her. She feared those very winds that ran about the wintry forest. They were in league with it. They helped it everywhere.

'Why don't you sleep, dear?' It was her husband now who played the rôle of nurse, tending her little wants with an honest care that at least aped the services of love. He was so utterly unconscious of the raging battle he had caused. 'What is it keeps you so wide awake and restless?'

'The winds,' she whispered in the dark. For hours she had lain watching the tossing of the trees through the blindless windows. 'They go walking and talking everywhere to-night, keeping me awake. And all the time they call so loudly to you.'

And his strange whispered answer appalled her for a moment until the meaning of it faded and left her in a dark confusion of the mind that was now becoming almost permanent.

'The trees excite them in the night. The winds are the great swift carriers. Go with them, dear—and not against. You'll find sleep that way if you do.'

'The storm is rising,' she began, hardly knowing what she said.

'All the more then—go with them. Don't resist. They'll take you to the trees, that's all.'

Resist! The word touched on the button of some text that once had helped her.

'Resist the devil and he will flee from you,' she heard her whispered answer, and the same second had buried her face beneath the clothes in a flood of hysterical weeping.

But her husband did not seem disturbed. Perhaps he did not hear it, for the wind ran just then against the windows with a booming shout, and the roaring of the Forest farther out came behind the blow, surging into the room. Perhaps, too, he was already asleep again. She slowly regained a sort of dull composure. Her face emerged from the tangle of sheets and blankets. With a growing terror over her—she listened. The storm was rising. It came with a sudden and impetuous rush that made all further sleep for her impossible.

Alone in a shaking world, it seemed, she lay and listened. That storm interpreted for her mind the climax. The Forest bellowed out its victory to the winds; the winds in turn proclaimed it to the Night.

The whole world knew of her complete defeat, her loss, her little human pain. This was the roar and shout of victory that she listened to.

For, unmistakably, the trees were shouting in the dark. There were sounds, too, like the flapping of great sails, a thousand at a time, and sometimes reports that resembled more than anything else the distant booming of enormous drums. The trees stood up—the whole beleaguering host of them stood up—and with the uproar of their million branches drummed the thundering message out across the night. It seemed as if they all had broken loose. Their roots swept trailing over field and hedge and roof. They tossed their bushy heads beneath the clouds with a wild, delighted shuffling of great boughs. With trunks upright they raced leaping through the sky. There was upheaval and adventure in the awful sound they made, and their cry was like the cry of a sea that has broken through its gates and poured loose upon the world. . . .

Through it all her husband slept peacefully as though he heard it not. It was, as she well knew, the deep of the semi-dead. For he was out with all that clamouring turmoil. The part of him that she had lost was there. The form that slept so calmly at her side was but the shell, half emptied. . . .

And when the winter's morning stole upon the scene at length, with a pale, washed sunshine that followed the departing tempest, the first thing she saw, as she crept to the window and looked out, was the ruined cedar lying on the lawn. Only the gaunt and crippled trunk of it remained. The single giant bough that had been left to it lay dark upon the grass, sucked endways towards the Forest by a great wind eddy. It lay there like a mass of drift-wood from a wreck, left by the ebbing of a high springtide upon the sands—remnant of some friendly, splendid vessel that once had sheltered men.

And in the distance she heard the roaring of the Forest further out. Her husband's voice was in it.

A DESCENT INTO EGYPT

I

HE was an accomplished, versatile man whom some called brilliant. Behind his talents lay a wealth of material that right selection could have lifted into genuine distinction. He did too many things, however, to excel in one, for a restless curiosity kept him ever on the move. George Isley was an able man. His short career in diplomacy proved it; yet, when he abandoned this for travel and exploration, no one thought it a pity. He would do big things in any line. He was merely finding himself.

Among the rolling stones of humanity a few acquire moss of considerable value. They are not necessarily shiftless; they travel light; the comfortable pockets in the game of life that attract the majority are too small to retain them; they are in and out again in a moment. The world says, 'What a pity! They stick to nothing!' but the fact is that, like questing wild birds, they seek the nest they need. It is a question of values. They judge swiftly, change their line of flight, are gone, not even hearing the comment that they might have 'retired with a pension.'

And to this homeless, questing type George Isley certainly belonged. He was by no means shiftless. He merely sought with insatiable yearning that soft particular nest where he could settle down in permanently. And to an accompaniment of sighs and regrets from his friends he found it; he found it, however, not in the present, but by retiring from the world 'without a pension,' unclothed with honours and distinctions. He withdrew from the present and slipped softly back into a mighty Past where he belonged. Why; how; obeying what strange instincts—this remains unknown, deep secret of an inner life that found no resting-place in modern things. Such instincts are not disclosable in twentieth-century language, nor are the details of such a journey properly describable at all. Except by the few—poets, prophets, psychiatrists and the like—such experiences are dismissed with the neat museum label—'queer.'

So, equally, must the recorder of this experience share the honour of that little label—he who by chance witnessed certain external and visible signs of this inner and spiritual journey. There remains, nevertheless, the amazing reality of the experience; and to the recorder alone was some clue of interpretation possible, perhaps, because in himself also lay the lure, though less imperative, of a similar journey. At any rate the interpretation may be offered to the handful who realise that trains and motors are not the only means of travel left to our progressive race.

In his younger days I knew George Isley intimately. I know him now. But the George Isley I knew of old, the arresting personality with whom I travelled, climbed, explored, is no longer with us. He is not here. He disappeared—gradually—into the past. There is no George Isley. And that such an individuality could vanish, while still his outer semblance walks the familiar streets, normal apparently, and not yet fifty in the number of his years, seems a tale, though difficult, well worth the telling. For I witnessed the slow submergence. It was very gradual. I cannot pretend to understand the entire significance of it. There was something questionable and sinister in the business that offered hints of astonishing possibilities. Were there a corps of spiritual police, the matter might be partially cleared up, but since none of the churches have yet organised anything effective of this sort, one can only fall back upon variants of the blessed 'Mesopotamia,'* and whisper of derangement, and the like. Such labels, of course, explain as little as most other *clichés* in life. That well-groomed, soldierly figure strolling down Piccadilly, watching the Races,* dining out—there is no derangement there. The face is not melancholy, the eye not wild; the gestures are quiet and the speech controlled. Yet the eye is empty, the face expressionless. Vacancy reigns there, provocative and significant. If not unduly noticeable, it is because the majority in life neither expect, nor offer, more.

At closer quarters you may think questioning things, or you may think—nothing; probably the latter. You may wonder why something continually expected does not make its appearance; and you may watch for the evidence of 'personality' the general presentment of the man has led you to expect. Disappointed, therefore, you may certainly be; but I defy you to discover the smallest hint of mental disorder, and of derangement or nervous affliction, absolutely nothing. Before long, perhaps, you may feel you are talking with a dummy, some well-trained automaton, a nonentity devoid of spontaneous life; and afterwards you may find that memory fades rapidly away, as though no impression of any kind has really been made at all. All this, yes; but nothing pathological. A few may be stimulated by this startling discrepancy between promise and performance, but most, accustomed to accept face values, would say, 'a pleasant fellow, but nothing in him much . . .' and an hour later forget him altogether.

For the truth is as you, perhaps, divined. You have been sitting beside no one, you have been talking to, looking at, listening to—no one. The intercourse has conveyed nothing that can waken human response in you, good, bad or indifferent. There is no George Isley. And the discovery, if you make it, will not even cause you to creep with the uncanniness of the experience, because the exterior is so wholly pleasing. George Isley to-day is a picture with no meaning in it that charms merely by the harmonious colouring of an inoffensive subject. He moves undiscovered in the little world of society to which he was born, secure in the groove first habit has made comfortably automatic for him. No one guesses; none, that is, but the few who knew him intimately in early life. And his wandering existence has scattered these; they have forgotten what he was. So perfect, indeed, is he in the manners of the commonplace fashionable man, that no woman in his 'set' is aware that he differs from the type she is accustomed to. He turns a compliment with the accepted language of her text-book, motors, golfs and gambles in the regulation manner of his particular world. He is an admirable, perfect automaton. He is nothing. He is a human shell.

II

THE name of George Isley had been before the public for some years when, after a considerable interval, we met again in a hotel in Egypt,* I for my health, he for I knew not what—at first. But I soon discovered: archaeology and excavation had taken hold of him, though he had gone so quietly about it that no one seemed to have heard. I was not sure that he was glad to see me, for he had first withdrawn, annoyed, it seemed, at being discovered, but later, as though after consideration, had made tentative advances. He welcomed me with a curious gesture of the entire body that seemed to shake himself free from something that had made him forget my identity. There was pathos somewhere in his attitude, almost as though he asked for sympathy. 'I've been out here, off and on, for the last three years,' he told me, after describing something of what he had been doing. 'I find it the most repaying hobby in the world. It leads to a reconstruction—an imaginative reconstruction, of course, I mean—of an enormous thing the world had entirely lost. A very gorgeous, stimulating hobby, believe me, and a very entic—' he quickly changed the word—'exacting one indeed.'

I remember looking him up and down with astonishment. There was a change in him, a lack; a note was missing in his enthusiasm, a colour in the voice, a quality in his manner. The ingredients were not mixed quite as of old. I did not bother him with questions, but I noted thus at the very first a subtle alteration. Another facet of the man presented itself. Something that had been independent and aggressive was replaced by a certain emptiness that invited sympathy. Even in his physical appearance the change was manifested—this odd suggestion of lessening. I looked again more closely. Lessening *was* the word. He had somehow dwindled. It was startling, vaguely unpleasant too.

The entire subject, as usual, was at his fingertips; he knew all the important men; and had spent money freely on his hobby. I laughed, reminding him of his remark that Egypt had no attractions for him, owing to the organised advertisement of its somewhat theatrical charms. Admitting his error with a gesture, he brushed the objection easily aside. His manner, and a certain glow that rose about his atmosphere as he answered, increased my first astonishment. His voice was significant and suggestive. 'Come out with me,' he said in a low tone, 'and see how little the tourists matter, how inappreciable the excavation is compared to what remains to be done, how gigantic'—he emphasised the word impressively—'the scope for discovery remains.' He made a movement with his head and shoulders that conveyed a sense of the prodigious, for he was of massive build, his cast of features stern, and his eyes, set deep into the face, shone past me with a sombre gleam in them I did not quite account for. It was the voice, however, that brought the mystery in. It vibrated somewhere below the actual sound of it. 'Egypt,' he continued—and so gravely that at first I made the mistake of thinking he chose the curious words on purpose to produce a theatrical effect—'that has enriched her blood with the pageant of so many civilisations, that has devoured Persians, Greeks and Romans, Saracens and Mamelukes,* a dozen conquests and invasions besides,—what can mere tourists or explorers matter to her? The excavators scratch their skin and dig up mummies; and as for tourists!'—he laughed contemptuously—'flies that settle for a moment on her covered face, to vanish at the first signs of heat! Egypt is not even aware of them. The real Egypt lies underground in darkness. Tourists must have light, to be seen as well as to see. And the diggers——!'

He paused, smiling with something between pity and contempt I did not quite appreciate, for, personally, I felt a great respect for the tireless excavators. And then he added, with a touch of feeling in his tone as though he had a grievance against them, and had not also 'dug' himself, 'Men who uncover the dead, restore the temples, and reconstruct a skeleton, thinking they have read its beating heart. . . .' He shrugged his great shoulders, and the rest of the sentence may have been but the protest of a man in defence of his own hobby, but that there seemed an undue earnestness and gravity about it that made me wonder more than ever. He went on to speak of the strangeness of the land as a mere ribbon of vegetation along the ancient river, the rest all ruins, desert, sun-drenched wilderness of death, yet so breakingly alive with wonder, power and a certain disquieting sense of deathlessness. There seemed, for him, a revelation of unusual spiritual kind in this land where the Past survived so potently. He spoke almost as though it obliterated the Present.

Indeed, the hint of something solemn behind his words made it difficult for me to keep up the conversation, and the pause that presently came I filled in with some word of questioning surprise, which yet, I think, was chiefly in concurrence. I was aware of some big belief in him, some enveloping emotion that escaped my grasp. Yet, though I did not understand, his great mood swept me. . . . His voice lowered, then, as he went on to mention temples, tombs and deities, details of his own discoveries and of their effect upon him, but to this I listened with half an ear, because in the unusual language he had first made use of I detected this other thing that stirred my curiosity more—stirred it uncomfortably.

'Then the spell,' I asked, remembering the effect of Egypt upon myself two years before, 'has worked upon you as upon most others, only with greater power?'

He looked hard at me a moment, signs of trouble showing themselves faintly in his rugged, interesting face. I think he wanted to say more than he could bring himself to confess. He hesitated.

'I'm only glad,' he replied after a pause, 'it didn't get hold of me earlier in life. It would have absorbed me. I should have lost all other interests. Now,'—that curious look of helplessness, of asking sympathy, flitted like a shadow through his eyes—'now that I'm on the decline . . . it matters less.'

On the decline! I cannot imagine by what blundering I missed this chance he never offered again; somehow or other the singular phrase passed unnoticed at the moment, and only came upon me with its full significance later when it was too awkward to refer to it. He tested my readiness to help, to sympathise, to share his inner life. I missed the clue. For, at the moment, a more practical consideration interested me in his language. Being of those who regretted that he had not excelled by devoting his powers to a single object, I shrugged my shoulders. He caught my meaning instantly.

Oh, he was glad to talk. He felt the possibility of my sympathy underneath, I think.

'No, no, you take me wrongly there,' he said with gravity. 'What I mean—and I ought to know if any one does!—is that while most countries give, others take away. Egypt changes you. No one can live here and remain exactly what he was before.'

This puzzled me. It startled, too, again. His manner was so earnest. 'And Egypt, you mean, is one of the countries that take away?' I asked. The strange idea unsettled my thoughts a little.

'First takes away from you,' he replied, 'but in the end takes *you* away. Some lands enrich you,' he went on, seeing that I listened, 'while others impoverish. From India, Greece, Italy, all ancient lands, you return with memories you can use. From Egypt you return with—nothing. Its splendour stupefies; it's useless. There is a change in your inmost being, an emptiness, an unaccountable yearning, but you find nothing that can fill the lack you're conscious of. Nothing comes to replace what has gone. You have been drained.'

I stared; but I nodded a general acquiescence. Of a sensitive, artistic temperament this was certainly true, though by no means the superficial and generally accepted verdict. The majority imagine that Egypt has filled them to the brim. I took his deeper reading of the facts. I was aware of an odd fascination in his idea.

'Modern Egypt,' he continued, 'is, after all, but a trick of civilisation,' and there was a kind of breathlessness in his measured tone, 'but ancient Egypt lies waiting, hiding, underneath. Though dead, she is amazingly alive. And you feel her touching you. She takes from you. She enriches herself. You return from Egypt—less than you were before.'

What came over my mind is hard to say. Some touch of visionary imagination burned its flaming path across my mind. I thought of some old Grecian hero speaking of his delicious battle with the gods—battle in which he knew he must be worsted, but yet in which he delighted because at death his spirit would join their glorious company beyond this world. I was aware, that is to say, of resignation as well as resistance in him. He already felt the effortless peace which follows upon long, unequal battling, as of a man who has fought the rapids with a strain beyond his strength, then sinks back and goes with the awful mass of water smoothly and indifferently—over the quiet fall.

Yet, it was not so much his words which clothed picturesquely an undeniable truth, as the force of conviction that drove behind them, shrouding my mind with mystery and darkness. His eyes, so steadily holding mine, were lit, I admit, yet they were calm and sane as those of a doctor discussing the symptoms of that daily battle to which we all finally succumb. This analogy occurred to me.

'There *is*'—I stammered a little, faltering in my speech—'an incalculable element in the country . . . somewhere, I confess. You put it—rather strongly, though, don't you?'

He answered quietly, moving his eyes from my face towards the window that framed the serene and exquisite sky towards the Nile.

'The real, invisible Egypt,' he murmured, 'I do find rather—strong. I find it difficult to deal with. You see,' and he turned towards me, smiling like a tired child, 'I think the truth is that Egypt deals with me.'

'It draws——' I began, then started as he interrupted me at once.

'Into the Past.' He uttered the little word in a way beyond me to describe. There came a flood of glory with it, a sense of peace and beauty, of battles over and of rest attained. No saint could have brimmed* 'Heaven' with as much passionately enticing meaning. He went willingly, prolonging the struggle merely to enjoy the greater relief and joy of the consummation.

For again he spoke as though a struggle were in progress in his being. I got the impression that he somewhere wanted help. I understood the pathetic quality I had vaguely discerned already. His character naturally was so strong and independent. It now seemed weaker, as though certain fibres had been drawn out. And I understood then that the spell of Egypt, so lightly chattered about in its sensational aspect, so rarely known in its naked power, the nameless, creeping influence that begins deep below the surface and thence sends delicate tendrils outwards, was in his blood. I, in my untaught ignorance, had felt it too; it is undeniable; one is aware of unaccountable, queer things in Egypt; even the utterly prosaic feel them. Dead Egypt is marvellously alive. . . .

I glanced past him out of the big windows where the desert glimmered in its featureless expanse of yellow leagues, two monstrous pyramids* signalling from across the Nile, and for a moment—inexplicably, it seemed to me afterwards—I lost sight of my companion's stalwart figure that was yet so close before my eyes. He had risen from his chair; he was standing near me; yet my sight missed him altogether. Something, dim as a shadow, faint as a breath of air, rose up and bore my thoughts away, obliterating vision too. I forgot for a moment who I was; identity slipped from me. Thought, sight, feeling, all sank away into the emptiness of those sun-baked sands, sank, as it were, into nothingness, caught away from the Present, enticed, absorbed. . . . And when I looked back again to answer him, or rather to ask what his curious words could mean—he was no longer there. More than surprised—for there was something of shock in the disappearance—I turned to search. I had not seen him go. He had stolen from my side so softly, slipped away silently, mysteriously, and—so easily. I remember that a faint shiver ran down my back as I realised that I was alone.

Was it that, momentarily, I had caught a reflex of his state of mind? Had my sympathy induced in myself an echo of what he experienced in full—a going backwards, a loss of present vigour, the enticing, subtle draw of those immeasurable sands that hide the living dead from the interruptions of the careless living . . .?

I sat down to reflect and, incidentally, to watch the magnificence of the sunset; and the thing he had said returned upon me with insistent power, ringing like distant bells within my mind. His talk of the tombs and temples passed, but this remained. It stimulated oddly. His talk, I remembered, had always excited curiosity in this way. Some countries give, while others take away. What did he mean precisely? What had Egypt taken away from him? And I realised more definitely that something in him *was* missing, something he possessed in former years that was now no longer there. He had grown shadowy already in my thoughts. The mind searched keenly, but in vain . . . and after some time I left my chair and moved over to another window, aware that a vague discomfort stirred within me that involved uneasiness—for him. I felt pity. But behind the pity was an eager, absorbing curiosity as well. He seemed receding curiously into misty distance, and the strong desire leaped in me to overtake, to travel with him into some vanished splendour that he had rediscovered. The feeling was a most remarkable one, for it included yearning—the yearning for some nameless, forgotten loveliness the world has lost. It was in me too.

At the approach of twilight the mind loves to harbour shadows. The room, empty of guests, was dark behind me; darkness, too, was creeping across the desert like a veil, deepening the serenity of its grim, unfeatured face. It turned pale with distance; the whole great sheet of it went rustling into night. The first stars peeped and twinkled, hanging loosely in the air as though they could be plucked like golden berries; and the sun was already below the Libyan horizon, where gold and crimson faded through violet into blue. I stood watching this mysterious Egyptian dusk, while an eerie glamour seemed to bring the incredible within uneasy reach of the half-faltering senses. . . . And suddenly the truth dropped into me. Over George Isley, over his mind and energies, over his thoughts and over his emotions too, a kind of darkness was also slowly creeping. Something in him had dimmed, yet not with age; it had gone out. Some inner night, stealing over the Present, obliterated it. And yet he looked towards the dawn. Like the Egyptian monuments his eyes turned—eastwards.

And so it came to me that what he had lost was personal ambition. He was glad, he said, that these Egyptian studies had not caught him earlier in life; the language he made use of was peculiar: 'Now I am on the decline it matters less.' A slight foundation, no doubt, to build conviction on, and yet I felt sure that I was partly right. He was fascinated, but fascinated against his will. The Present in him battled against the Past. Still fighting, he had yet lost hope. The desire *not* to change was now no longer in him. . . .

I turned away from the window so as not to see that grey, encroaching desert, for the discovery produced a certain agitation in me. Egypt seemed suddenly a living entity of enormous power. She stirred about me. She was stirring now. This flat and motionless land pretending it had no movement, was actually busy with a million gestures that came creeping round the heart. She was reducing him. Already from the complex texture of his personality she had drawn one vital thread that in its relation to the general woof was of central importance— ambition. The mind chose the simile; but in my heart where thought fluttered in singular distress, another suggested itself as truer. 'Thread' changed to 'artery.' I turned quickly and went up to my room where I could be alone. The idea was somewhere ghastly.

III

YET, while dressing for dinner, the idea exfoliated as only a living thing exfoliates. I saw in George Isley this great question mark that had not been there formerly. All have, of course, some question mark, and carry it about, though with most it rarely becomes visible until the end. With him it was plainly visible in his atmosphere at the hey-day of his life. He wore it like a fine curved scimitar above his head. So full of life, he yet seemed willingly dead. For, though imagination sought every possible explanation, I got no further than the somewhat negative result—that a certain energy, wholly unconnected with mere physical health, had been withdrawn. It was more than ambition, I think, for it included intention, desire, self-confidence as well. It was life itself. He was no longer in the Present. He was no longer *here*.

'Some countries give while others take away. . . . I find Egypt difficult to deal with. I find it . . .' and then that simple, uncomplex adjective—'strong.' In memory and experience the entire globe was mapped for him; it remained for Egypt, then, to teach him this marvellous new thing. But not Egypt of to-day; it was vanished Egypt that had robbed him of his strength. He had described it as underground, hidden, waiting. . . . I was again aware of a faint shuddering—as though something crept secretly from my inmost heart to share the experience with him, and as though my sympathy involved a willing consent that this should be so. With sympathy there must always be a shedding of the personal self; each time I felt this sympathy, it seemed that something left me. I thought in circles, arriving at no definite point where I could rest and say 'that's it; I understand.' The giving attitude of a country was easily comprehensible; but this idea of robbery, of deprivation baffled me. An obscure alarm took hold of me—for myself as well as for him.

At dinner, where he invited me to his table, the impression passed off a good deal, however, and I convicted myself of a woman's exaggeration; yet, as we talked of many a day's adventure together in other lands, it struck me that we oddly left the present out. We ignored to-day. His thoughts, as it were, went most easily backwards. And each adventure led, as by its own natural weight and impetus, towards one thing—the enormous glory of a vanished age. Ancient Egypt was 'home' in this mysterious game life played with death. The specific gravity of his being, to say nothing for the moment of my own, had shifted lower, farther off, backwards and below, or as he put it—underground. The sinking sensation I experienced was of a literal kind. . . .

And so I found myself wondering what had led him to this particular hotel. I had come out with an affected organ the specialist promised me would heal in the marvellous air of Helouan, but it was queer that my companion also should have chosen it. Its *clientèle* was mostly invalid, German and Russian invalid at that. The Management set its face against the lighter, gayer side of life that hotels in Egypt usually encourage eagerly. It was a true rest-house, a place of repose and leisure, a place where one could remain undiscovered and unknown. No English patronised it. One might easily—the idea came unbidden, suddenly—hide in it.

'Then you're doing nothing just now,' I asked, 'in the way of digging? No big expeditions or excavating at the moment?'

'I'm recuperating,' he answered carelessly. 'I've have had two years up at the Valley of the Kings, and overdid it rather. But I'm by way of working at a little thing near here across the Nile.' And he pointed in the direction of Sakkhâra, where the huge Memphian cemetery stretches underground from the Dachûr Pyramids to the Gizeh monsters,* four miles lower down. 'There's a matter of a hundred years in that alone!'

'You must have accumulated a mass of interesting material. I suppose later you'll make use of it—a book or——'

His expression stopped me—that strange look in the eyes that had stirred my first uneasiness. It was as if something struggled up a moment, looked bleakly out upon the present, then sank away again.

'More,' he answered listlessly, 'than I can ever use. It's much more likely to use me.' He said it hurriedly, looking over his shoulder as though some one might be listening, then smiled significantly, bringing his eyes back upon my own again. I told him that he was far too modest. 'If all the excavators thought like that,' I added, 'we ignorant ones should suffer.' I laughed, but the laughter was only on my lips.

He shook his head indifferently. 'They do their best; they do wonders,' he replied, making an indescribable gesture as though he withdrew willingly from the topic altogether, yet could not quite achieve it. 'I know their books; I know the writers too—of various nationalities.' He paused a moment, and his eyes turned grave. 'I cannot understand quite—how they do it,' he added half below his breath.

'The labour, you mean? The strain of the climate, and so forth?' I said this purposely, for I knew quite well he meant another thing. The way he looked into my face, however, disturbed me so that I believe I visibly started. Something very deep in me sat up alertly listening, almost on guard.

'I mean,' he replied, 'that they must have uncommon powers of resistance.'

There! He had used the very word that had been hiding in me! 'It puzzles me,' he went on, 'for, with one exception, they are not unusual men. In the way of gifts—oh yes. It's in the way of resistance and protection that I mean. Self-protection,' he added with emphasis.

It was the way he said 'resistance' and 'self-protection' that sent a touch of cold through me. I learned later that he himself had made surprising discoveries in these two years, penetrating closer to the secret life of ancient sacerdotal Egypt than any of his predecessors or colabourers—then, inexplicably, had ceased. But this was told to me afterwards and by others. At the moment I was only conscious of this odd embarrassment. I did not understand, yet felt that he touched upon something intimately personal to himself. He paused, expecting me to speak.

'Egypt, perhaps, merely pours through them,' I ventured. 'They give out mechanically, hardly realising how much they give. They report facts devoid of interpretation. Whereas with you it's the actual spirit of the past that is discovered and laid bare. You live it. You feel old Egypt and disclose her. That divining faculty was always yours—uncannily, I used to think.'

The flash of his sombre eyes betrayed that my aim was singularly good. It seemed a third had silently joined our little table in the corner. Something intruded, evoked by the power of what our conversation skirted but ever left unmentioned. It was huge and shadowy; it was also watchful. Egypt came gliding, floating up beside us. I saw her reflected in his face and gaze. The desert slipped in through walls and ceiling, rising from beneath our feet, settling about us, listening, peering, waiting. The strange obsession was sudden and complete. The gigantic scale of her swam in among the very pillars, arches, and windows of that modern dining-room. I felt against my skin the touch of chilly air that sunlight never reaches, stealing from beneath the granite monoliths. Behind it came the. stifling breath of the heated tombs, of the Serapeum,* of the chambers and corridors in the pyramids. There was a rustling as of myriad footsteps far away, and as of sand the busy winds go shifting through the ages. And in startling contrast to this impression of prodigious size, Isley himself wore suddenly an air of strangely dwindling. For a second he shrank visibly before my very eyes. He was receding. His outline seemed to retreat and lessen, as though he stood to the waist in what appeared like flowing mist, only his head and shoulders still above the ground. Far, far away I saw him.

It was a vivid inner picture that I somehow transferred objectively. It was a dramatised sensation, of course. His former phrase 'now that I am declining' flashed back upon me with sharp discomfort. Again, perhaps, his state of mind was reflected into me by some emotional telepathy. I waited, conscious of an almost sensible oppression that would not lift. It seemed an age before he spoke, and when he did there was the tremor of feeling in his voice he sought nevertheless to repress. I kept my eyes on the table for some reason. But I listened intently.

'It's you that have the divining faculty, not I,' he said, an odd note of distance even in his tone, yet a resonance as though it rose up between reverberating walls. 'There *is*, I believe, something here that resents too close inquiry, or rather that resists discovery—almost—takes offence.'

I looked up quickly, then looked down again. It was such a startling thing to hear on the lips of a modern Englishman. He spoke lightly, but the expression of his face belied the careless tone. There was no mockery in those earnest eyes, and in the hushed voice was a little creeping sound that gave me once again the touch of goose-flesh. The only word I can find is 'subterranean': all that was mental in him had sunk, so that he seemed speaking underground, head and shoulders alone visible. The effect was almost ghastly.

'Such extraordinary obstacles are put in one's way,' he went on, 'when the prying gets too close to the—reality; physical, external obstacles, I mean. Either that, or—the mind loses its assimilative faculties. One or other happens—' his voice died down into a whisper—'and discovery ceases of its own accord.'

The same minute, then, he suddenly raised himself like a man emerging from a tomb; he leaned across the table; he made an effort of some violent internal kind, on the verge, I fully believe, of a pregnant personal statement. There was confession in his attitude; I think he was about to speak of his work at Thebes and the reason for its abrupt cessation. For I had the feeling of one about to hear a weighty secret, the responsibility unwelcome. This uncomfortable emotion rose in me, as I raised my eyes to his somewhat unwillingly, only to find that I was wholly at fault. It was not me he was looking at. He was staring past me in the direction of the wide, unshuttered windows. The expression of yearning was visible in his eyes again. Something had stopped his utterance.

And instinctively I turned and saw what he saw. So far as external details were concerned, at least, I saw it.

Across the glare and glitter of the uncompromising modern dining-room, past crowded tables, and over the heads of Germans feeding unpicturesquely, I saw—the moon. Her reddish disc, hanging unreal and enormous, lifted the spread sheet of desert till it floated off the surface of the world. The great window faced the east, where the Arabian desert breaks into a ruin of gorges, cliffs, and flat-topped ridges; it looked unfriendly, ominous, with danger in it; unlike the serener sand-dunes of the Libyan desert, there lay both menace and seduction behind its flood of shadows. And the moonlight emphasised this aspect: its ghostly desolation, its cruelty, its bleak hostility, turning it murderous. For no river sweetens this Arabian desert; instead of sandy softness, it has fangs of limestone rock, sharp and aggressive. Across it, just visible in the moonlight as a thread of paler grey, the old camel-trail to Suez beckoned faintly. And it was this that he was looking at so intently.

It was, I know, a theatrical stage-like glimpse, yet in it a seductiveness most potent. 'Come out,' it seemed to whisper, 'and taste my awful beauty. Come out and lose yourself, and die. Come out and follow my moonlit trail into the Past . . . where there is peace and immobility and silence. My kingdom is unchanging underground. Come down, come softly, come through sandy corridors below this tinsel of your modern world. Come back, come down into my golden past . . .'

A poignant desire stole through my heart on moonlit feet; I was personally conscious of a keen yearning to slip away in unresisting obedience. For it was uncommonly impressive, this sudden, haunting glimpse of the world outside. The hairy foreigners, uncouthly garbed, all busily eating in full electric light, provided a sensational contrast of emphatically distressing kind. A touch of what is called unearthly hovered about that distance through the window. There was weirdness in it. Egypt looked in upon us. Egypt watched and listened, beckoning through the moonlit windows of the heart to come and find her. Mind and imagination might flounder as they pleased, but something of this kind happened undeniably, whether expression in language fails to hold the truth or not. And George Isley, aware of being seen, looked straight into the awful visage—fascinated.

Over the bronze of his skin there stole a shade of grey. My own feeling of enticement grew—the desire to go out into the moonlight, to leave my kind and wander blindly through the desert, to see the gorges in their shining silver, and taste the keenness of the cool, sharp air. Further than this with me it did not go, but that my companion felt the bigger, deeper draw behind this surface glamour, I have no reasonable doubt. For a moment, indeed, I thought he meant to leave the table; he had half risen in his chair; it seemed he struggled and resisted—and then his big frame subsided again; he sat back; he looked, in the attitude his body took, less impressive, smaller, actually shrunken into the proportions of some minuter scale. It was as though something in that second had been drawn out of him, decreasing even his physical appearance. The voice, when he spoke presently with a touch of resignation, held a lifeless quality as though deprived of virile timbre.

'It's always there,' he whispered, half collapsing back into his chair, 'it's always watching, waiting, listening. Almost like a monster of the fables, isn't it? It makes no movement of its own, you see. It's far too strong for that. It just hangs there, half in the air and half upon the earth—a gigantic web. Its prey flies into it. That's Egypt all over. D'you feel like that too, or does it seem to you just imaginative rubbish? To me it seems that she just waits her time; she gets you quicker that way; in the end you're bound to go.'

'There's power certainly,' I said after a moment's pause to collect my wits, my distress increased by the morbidness of his simile. 'For some minds there may be a kind of terror too—for weak temperaments that are all imagination.' My thoughts were scattered, and I could not readily find good words. 'There is startling grandeur in a sight like that, for instance,' and I pointed to the window. 'You feel drawn—as if you simply *had* to go.' My mind still buzzed with his curious words, 'In the end you're bound to go.' It betrayed his heart and soul. 'I suppose a fly does feel drawn,' I added, 'or a moth to the destroying flame. Or is it just unconscious on their part?'

He jerked his big head significantly. 'Well, well,' he answered, 'but the fly isn't necessarily weak, or the moth misguided. Over-adventurous, perhaps, yet both obedient to the laws of their respective beings. They get warnings too—only, when the moth wants to know too much, the fire stops it. Both flame and spider enrich themselves by understanding the natures of their prey; and fly and moth return again and again until this is accomplished.'

Yet George Isley was as sane as the head waiter who, noticing our interest in the window, came up just then and enquired whether we felt a draught and would prefer it closed. Isley, I realised, was struggling to express a passionate state of soul for which, owing to its rarity, no adequate expression lies at hand. There is a language of the mind, but there is none as yet of the spirit. I felt ill at ease. All this was so foreign to the wholesome, strenuous personality of the man as I remembered it.

'But, my dear fellow,' I stammered, 'aren't you giving poor old Egypt a bad name she hardly deserves? I feel only the amazing strength and beauty of it; awe, if you like, but none of this resentment you so mysteriously hint at.'

'You understand, for all that,' he answered quietly; and again he seemed on the verge of some significant confession that might ease his soul. My uncomfortable emotion grew. Certainly he was at high pressure somewhere. 'And, if necessary, you could help. Your sympathy, I mean, *is* a help already.' He said it half to himself and in a suddenly lowered tone again.

'A help!' I gasped. 'My sympathy! Of course, if——'

'A witness,' he murmured, not looking at me, 'some one who understands, yet does not think me mad.'

There was such appeal in his voice that I felt ready and eager to do anything to help him. Our eyes met, and my own tried to express this willingness in me; but what I said I hardly know, for a cloud of confusion was on my mind, and my speech went fumbling like a schoolboy's.

I was more than disconcerted. Through this bewilderment, then, I just caught the tail-end of another sentence in which the words 'relief it is to have . . . some one to hold to . . . when the disappearance comes . . .' sounded like voices heard in dream. But I missed the complete phrase and shrank from asking him to repeat it.

Some sympathetic answer struggled to my lips, though what it was I know not. The thing I murmured, however, seemed apparently well chosen. He leaned across and laid his big hand a moment on my own with eloquent pressure. It was cold as ice. A look of gratitude passed over his sunburned features. He sighed. And we left the table then and passed into the inner smoking-room for coffee—a room whose windows gave upon columned terraces that allowed no view of the encircling desert. He led the conversation into channels less personal and, thank heaven, less intensely emotional and mysterious. What we talked about I now forget; it was interesting but in another key altogether. His old charm and power worked; the respect I had always felt for his character and gifts returned in force, but it was the pity I now experienced that remained chiefly in my mind. For this change in him became more and more noticeable. He was less impressive, less convincing, less suggestive. His talk, though so knowledgeable, lacked that spiritual quality that drives home. He was uncannily less *real*. And I went up to bed, uneasy and disturbed, 'It is not age,' I said to myself, 'and assuredly it is not death he fears, although he spoke of disappearance. It is mental—in the deepest sense. It is what religious people would call soul. Something is happening to his soul.'

IV

AND this word 'soul' remained with me to the end. Egypt was taking his soul away into the Past. What was of value in him went willingly; the rest, some lesser aspect of his mind and character, resisted, holding to the present. A struggle, therefore, was involved. But this was being gradually obliterated too.

How I arrived gaily at this monstrous conclusion seems to me now a mystery; but the truth is that from a conversation one brings away a general idea that is larger than the words actually heard and spoken. I have reported, naturally, but a fragment of what passed between us in language, and of what was suggested—by gesture, expression, silence—merely perhaps a hint. I can only assert that this troubling verdict remained a conviction in my mind. It came upstairs with me; it watched and listened by my side. That mysterious Third evoked in our conversation was bigger than either of us separately; it might be called the spirit of ancient Egypt, or it might be called with equal generalisation, the Past. This Third, at any rate, stood by me, whispering this astounding thing. I went out on to my little balcony to smoke a pipe and enjoy the comforting presence of the stars before turning in. It came out with me. It was everywhere. I heard the barking of dogs, the monotonous beating of a distant drum towards Bedraschien,* the sing-song voices of the natives in their booths and down the dim-lit streets.

I was aware of this invisible Third, behind all these familiar sounds. The enormous night-sky, drowned in stars, conveyed it too. It was in the breath of chilly wind that whispered round the walls, and it brooded everywhere above the sleepless desert. I was alone as little as though George Isley stood beside me in person—and at that moment a moving figure caught my eye below. My window was on the sixth story, but there was no mistaking the tall and soldierly bearing of the man who was strolling past the hotel. George Isley was going slowly out into the desert.

There was actually nothing unusual in the sight. It was only ten o'clock; but for doctor's orders I might have been doing the same myself. Yet, as I leaned over the dizzy ledge and watched him, a chill struck through me, and a feeling nothing could justify, nor pages of writing describe, rose up and mastered me. His words at dinner came back with curious force. Egypt lay round him, motionless, a vast grey web. His feet were caught in it. It quivered. The silvery meshes in the moonlight announced the fact from Memphis up to Thebes, across the Nile, from underground Sakkhâra to the Valley of the Kings. A tremor ran over the entire desert, and again, as in the dining-room, the leagues of sand went rustling. It seemed to me that I caught him in the act of disappearing.

I realised in that moment the haunting power of this mysterious still atmosphere which is Egypt, and some magical emanation of its mighty past broke over me suddenly like a wave. Perhaps in that moment I felt what he himself felt; the withdrawing suction of the huge spent wave swept something out of me into the past with it. An indescribable yearning drew something living from my heart, something that longed with a kind of burning, searching sweetness for a glory of spiritual passion that was gone. The pain and happiness of it were more poignant than may be told, and my present personality—some vital portion of it, at any rate—wilted before the power of its enticement.

I stood there, motionless as stone, and stared. Erect and steady, knowing resistance vain, eager to go yet striving to remain, and half with an air of floating off the ground, he went towards the pale grey thread which was the track to Suez and the far Red Sea. There came upon me this strange, deep sense of pity, pathos, sympathy that was beyond all explanation, and mysterious as a pain in dreams. For a sense of his awful loneliness stole into me, a loneliness nothing on this earth could possibly relieve. Robbed of the Present, he sought this chimera of his soul, an unreal Past. Not even the calm majesty of this exquisite Egyptian night could soothe the dream away; the peace and silence were marvellous, the sweet perfume of the desert air intoxicating; but all these intensified it only.

And though at a loss to explain my own emotion, its poignancy was so real that a sigh escaped me and I felt that tears lay not too far away. I watched him, yet felt I had no right to watch. Softly I drew back from the window with the sensation of eavesdropping upon his privacy; but before I did so I had seen his outline melt away into the dim world of sand that began at the very walls of the hotel. He wore a cloak of green that reached down almost to his heels, and its colour blended with the silvery surface of the desert's dark sea-tint. This sheen first draped and then concealed him. It covered him with a fold of its mysterious garment that, without seam or binding, veiled Egypt for a thousand leagues. The desert took him. Egypt caught him in her web. He was gone.

Sleep for me just then seemed out of the question. The change in *him* made me feel less sure of myself. To see him thus invertebrate shocked me. I was aware that I had nerves.

For a long time I sat smoking by the window, my body weary, but my imagination irritatingly stimulated. The big sign-lights of the hotel went out; window after window closed below me; the electric standards in the streets were already extinguished; and Helouan looked like a child's white blocks scattered in ruin upon the nursery carpet. It seemed so wee upon the vast expanse. It lay in a twinkling pattern, like a cluster of glow-worms dropped into a negligible crease of the tremendous desert. It peeped up at the stars, a little frightened.

The night was very still. There hung an enormous brooding beauty everywhere, a hint of the sinister in it that only the brilliance of the blazing stars relieved. Nothing really slept. Grouped here and there at intervals about this dun-coloured world stood the everlasting watchers in solemn, tireless guardianship—the soaring Pyramids, the Sphinx, the grim Colossi,* the empty temples, the long-deserted tombs. The mind was aware of them, stationed like sentries through the night. 'This is Egypt; you are actually in Egypt,' whispered the silence. 'Eight thousand years of history lie fluttering outside your window. *She* lies there underground, sleepless, mighty, deathless, not to be trifled with. Beware! Or she will change you too!'

My imagination offered this hint: Egypt *is* difficult to realise. It remains outside the mind, a fabulous, half-legendary idea. So many enormous elements together refuse to be assimilated; the heart pauses, asking for time and breath; the senses reel a little; and in the end a mental torpor akin to stupefaction creeps upon the brain. With a sigh the struggle is abandoned and the mind surrenders to Egypt on her own terms. Alone the diggers and archaeologists, confined to definite facts, offer successful resistance. My friend's use of the words 'resistance' and 'protection' became clearer to me. While logic halted, intuition fluttered round this clue to the solution of the influences at work. George Isley realised Egypt more than most—but as she had been.

And I recalled its first effect upon myself, and how my mind had been unable to cope with the memory of it afterwards. There had come to its summons a colossal medley, a gigantic, coloured blur that merely bewildered. Only lesser points lodged comfortably in the heart. I saw a chaotic vision: sands drenched in dazzling light, vast granite aisles, stupendous figures that stared unblinking at the sun, a shining river and a shadowy desert, both endless as the sky, mountainous pyramids and gigantic monoliths, armies of heads, of paws, of faces—all set to a scale of size that was prodigious. The items stunned; the composite effect was too unwieldy to be grasped. Something that blazed with splendour rolled before the eyes, too close to be seen distinctly—at the same time very distant—unrealised.

Then, with the passing of the weeks, it slowly stirred to life. It had attacked unseen; its grip was quite tremendous; yet it could be neither told, nor painted, nor described. It flamed up unexpectedly—in the foggy London streets, at the Club, in the theatre. A sound recalled the street-cries of the Arabs, a breath of scented air brought back the heated sand beyond the palm groves. Up rose the huge Egyptian glamour, transforming common things; it had lain buried all this time in deep recesses of the heart that are inaccessible to ordinary daily life. And there hid in it something of uneasiness that was inexplicable; awe, a hint of cold eternity, a touch of something unchanging and terrific, something sublime made lovely yet unearthly with shadowy time and distance. The melancholy of the Nile and the grandeur of a hundred battered temples dropped some unutterable beauty upon the heart. Up swept the desert air, the luminous pale shadows, the naked desolation that yet brims with sharp vitality. An Arab on his donkey tripped in colour across the mind, melting off into tiny perspective, strangely vivid. A string of camels stood in silhouette against the crimson sky. Great winds, great blazing spaces, great solemn nights, great days of golden splendour rose from the pavement or the theatre-stall, and London, dim-lit England, the whole of modern life, indeed, seemed suddenly reduced to a paltry insignificance that produced an aching longing for the pageantry of those millions of vanished souls. Egypt rolled through the heart for a moment—and was gone.

I remembered that some such fantastic experience had been mine. Put it as one may, the fact remains that for certain temperaments Egypt can rob the Present of some thread of interest that was formerly there. The memory became for me an integral part of personality; something in me yearned for its curious and awful beauty. He who has drunk of the Nile shall return to drink of it again. . . . And if for myself this was possible, what might not happen to a character of George Isley's type? Some glimmer of comprehension came to me. The ancient, buried, hidden Egypt had cast her net about his soul. Grown shadowy in the Present, his life was being transferred into some golden, reconstructed Past, where it was real. Some countries give, while others take away. And George Isley was worth robbing. . . .

Disturbed by these singular reflections, I moved away from the open window, closing it. But the closing did not exclude the presence of the Third. The biting night air followed me in. I drew the mosquito curtains round the bed, but the light I left still burning; and, lying there, I jotted down upon a scrap of paper this curious impression as best I could, only to find that it escaped easily between the words. Such visionary and spiritual perceptions are too elusive to be trapped in language. Reading it over after an interval of years, it is difficult to recall with what intense meaning, what uncanny emotion, I wrote those faded lines in pencil. Their rhetoric seems cheap, their content much exaggerated; yet at the time truth burned in every syllable. Egypt, which since time began has suffered robbery with violence at the hands of all the world, now takes her vengeance, choosing her individual prey. Her time has come. Behind a modern mask she lies in wait, intensely active, sure of her hidden power. Prostitute of dead empires, she lies now at peace beneath the same old stars, her loveliness unimpaired, bejewelled with the beaten gold of ages, her breasts uncovered, and her grand limbs flashing in the sun. Her shoulders of alabaster are lifted above the sand-drifts; she surveys the little figures of to-day. She takes her choice. . . .

That night I did not dream, but neither did the whole of me lie down in sleep. During the long dark hours I was aware of that picture endlessly repeating itself, the picture of George Isley stealing out into the moonlight desert. The night so swiftly dropped her hood about him; so mysteriously he merged into the unchanging thing which cloaks the past. It lifted. Some huge shadowy hand, gloved softly yet of granite, stretched over the leagues to take him. He disappeared.

They say the desert is motionless and has no gestures! That night I saw it moving, hurrying. It went tearing after him. You understand my meaning? No! Well, when excited it produces this strange impression, and the terrible moment is—when you surrender helplessly—you desire it shall swallow you. You let it come. George Isley spoke of a web. It is, at any rate, some central power that conceals itself behind the surface glamour folk call the spell of Egypt. Its home is not apparent. It dwells with ancient Egypt—underground. Behind the stillness of hot windless days, behind the peace of calm, gigantic nights, it lurks unrealised, monstrous and irresistible. My mind grasped it as little as the fact that our solar system with all its retinue of satellites and planets rushes annually many million miles towards a star in Hercules, while yet that constellation appears no closer than it did six thousand years ago. But the clue dropped into me. George Isley, with his entire retinue of thought and life and feeling, was being similarly drawn. And I, a minor satellite, had become aware of the horrifying pull. It was magnificent. . . . And I fell asleep on the crest of this enormous wave.

V

THE next few days passed idly; weeks passed too, I think; hidden away in this cosmopolitan hotel we lived apart, unnoticed. There was the feeling that time went what pace it pleased, now fast, now slow, now standing still. The similarity of the brilliant days, set between wondrous dawns and sunsets, left the impression that it was really one long, endless day without divisions. The mind's machinery of measurement suffered dislocation. Time went backwards; dates were forgotten; the month, the time of year, the century itself went down into undifferentiated life.

The Present certainly slipped away curiously. Newspapers and politics became unimportant, news uninteresting, English life so remote as to be unreal, European affairs shadowy. The stream of life ran in another direction altogether—backwards. The names and faces of friends appeared through mist. People arrived as though dropped from the skies. They suddenly were there; one saw them in the dining-room, as though they had just slipped in from an outer world that once was real—somewhere. Of course, a steamer sailed four times a week, and the journey took five days, but these things were merely known, not realised. The fact that here it was summer, whereas over there winter reigned, helped to make the distance not quite thinkable. We looked at the desert and made plans. 'We will do this, we will do that; we must go there, we'll visit such and such a place . . .' yet nothing happened. It always was to-morrow or yesterday, and we shared the discovery of Alice that there was no real 'to-day.'* For our thinking made everything happen. That was enough. It *had* happened. It was the reality of dreams. Egypt was a dream-world that made the heart live backwards.

It came about, thus, that for the next few weeks I watched a fading life, myself alert and sympathetic, yet unable somehow to intrude and help. Noticing various little things by which George Isley betrayed the progress of the unequal struggle, I found my assistance negatived by the fact that I was in similar case myself. What he experienced in large and finally, I, too, experienced in little and for the moment. For I seemed also caught upon the fringe of the invisible web. My feelings were entangled sufficiently for me to understand. . . . And the decline of his being was terrible to watch. His character went with it; I saw his talents fade, his personality dwindle, his very soul dissolve before the insidious and invading influence. He hardly struggled. I thought of those abominable insects that paralyse the motor systems of their victims and then devour them at their leisure—alive.* The incredible adventure was literally true, but, being spiritual, may not be told in the terms of a detective story. This version must remain an individual rendering—an aspect of *one* possible version. All who know the real Egypt, that Egypt which has nothing to do with dams and Nationalists and the external welfare of the falaheen* will understand. The pilfering of her ancient dead she suffers still; she, in revenge, preys at her leisure on the living.

The occasions when he betrayed himself were ordinary enough; it was the glimpse they afforded of what was in progress beneath his calm exterior that made them interesting. Once, I remember, we had lunched together at Mena* and, after visiting certain excavations beyond the Gizeh pyramids, we made our way homewards by way of the Sphinx. It was dusk, and the main army of tourists had retired, though some few dozen sight-seers still moved about to the cries of donkey-boys and baksheesh.* The vast head and shoulders suddenly emerged, riding undrowned above the sea of sand. Dark and monstrous in the fading light, it loomed, as ever, a being of non-human lineage; no amount of familiarity could depreciate its grandeur, its impressive setting, the lost expression of the countenance that is too huge to focus as a face. A thousand visits leave its power undiminished. It has intruded upon our earth from some uncommon world. George Isley and myself both turned aside to acknowledge the presence of this alien, uncomfortable thing. We did not linger, but we slackened pace. It was the obvious, inevitable thing to do. He pointed then, with a suddenness that made me start. He indicated the tourists standing round.

'See,' he said, in a lowered tone, 'day and night you'll always find a crowd obedient to that thing. But notice their behaviour. People don't do that before any other ruin in the world I've ever seen.' He referred to the attempts of individuals to creep away alone and stare into the stupendous visage by themselves. At different points in the deep sandy basin were men and women, standing solitary, lying, crouching, apart from the main company where the dragomen* mouthed their exposition with impertinent glibness.

'The desire to be alone,' he went on, half to himself, as we paused a moment, 'the sense of worship which insists on privacy.'

It *was* significant, for no amount of advertising could dwarf the impressiveness of the inscrutable visage into whose eyes of stone the silent humans gazed. Not even the red-coat, standing inside one gigantic ear, could introduce the commonplace. But my companion's words let another thing into the spectacle, a less exalted thing, dropping a hint of horror about that sandy cup: It became easy, for a moment, to imagine these tourists worshipping—against their will; to picture the monster noticing that they were there; that it might slowly turn its awful head; that the sand might visibly trickle from a stirring paw; that, in a word, they might be taken—changed.

'Come,' he whispered in a dropping tone, interrupting my fancies as though he half divined them, 'it is getting late, and to be alone with the thing is intolerable to me just now. But you notice, don't you,' he added, as he took my arm to hurry me away, 'how little the tourists matter? Instead of injuring the effect, they increase it. It uses *them*.'

And again a slight sensation of chill, communicated possibly by his nervous touch, or possibly by his earnest way of saying these curious words, passed through me. Some part of me remained behind in that hollow trough of sand, prostrate before an immensity that symbolised the past. A curious, wild yearning caught me momentarily, an intense desire to understand exactly why that terror stood there, its actual meaning long ago to the hearts that set it waiting for the sun, what definite role it played, what souls it stirred and why, in that system of towering belief and faith whose indestructible emblem it still remained. The past stood grouped so solemnly about its menacing presentment. I was distinctly aware of this spiritual suction backwards that my companion yielded to so gladly, yet against his normal, modern self. For it made the past appear magnificently desirable, and loosened all the rivets of the present. It bodied forth three main ingredients of this deep Egyptian spell—size, mystery, and immobility.

Yet, to my relief, the cheaper aspect of this Egyptian glamour left him cold. He remained unmoved by the commonplace mysterious; he told no mummy stories, nor ever hinted at the supernatural quality that leaps to the mind of the majority. There was no play in him. The influence was grave and vital. And, although I knew he held strong views with regard to the impiety of disturbing the dead, he never in my hearing attached any possible revengeful character to the energy of an outraged past. The current tales of this description he ignored; they were for superstitious minds or children; the deities that claimed his soul were of a grander order altogether. He lived, if it may be so expressed, already in a world his heart had reconstructed or remembered; it drew him in another direction altogether; with the modern, sensational view of life his spirit held no traffic any longer; he was living backwards. I saw his figure receding mournfully, yet never sentimentally, into the spacious, golden atmosphere of recaptured days. The enormous soul of buried Egypt drew him down. The dwindling of his physical appearance was, of course, a mental interpretation of my own; but another, stranger interpretation of a spiritual kind moved parallel with it—marvellous and horrible. For, as he diminished outwardly and in his modern, present aspect, he grew within—gigantic. The size of Egypt entered into him. Huge proportions now began to accompany any presentment of his personality to my inner vision. He towered. These two qualities of the land already obsessed him—magnitude and immobility.

And that awe which modern life ignores contemptuously woke in my heart. I almost feared his presence at certain times. For one aspect of the Egyptian spell is explained by sheer size and bulk. Disdainful of mere speed to-day, the heart is still uncomfortable with magnitude; and in Egypt there is size that may easily appal, for every detail shunts it laboriously upon the mind. It elbows out the present. The desert's vastness is not made comprehensible by mileage, and the sources of the Nile are so distant that they exist less on the map than in the imagination. The effort to realise suffers paralysis; they might equally be in the moon or Saturn. The undecorated magnificence of the desert remains unknown, just as the proportions of pyramid and temple, of pylons and Colossi approach the edge of the mind yet never enter in. All stand outside, clothed in this prodigious measurement of the past. And the old beliefs not only share this titanic effect upon the consciousness, but carry it stages further. The entire scale haunts with uncomfortable immensity, so that the majority run back with relief to the measurable details of a more manageable scale. Express trains, flying machines, Atlantic liners—these produce no unpleasant stretching of the faculties compared to the influence of the Karnak pylons, the pyramids, or the interior of the Serapeum.

Close behind this magnitude, moreover, steps the monstrous. It is revealed not in sand and stone alone, in queer effects of light and shadow, of glittering sunsets and of magical dusks, but in the very aspect of the bird and animal life. The heavy-headed buffaloes betray it equally with the vultures, the myriad kites, the grotesqueness of the mouthing camels. The rude, enormous scenery has it everywhere. There is nothing lyrical in this land of passionate mirages. Uncouth immensity notes the little human fittings. The days roll by in a tide of golden splendour; one goes helplessly with the flood; but it is an irresistible flood that sweeps backwards and below. The silent-footed natives in their coloured robes move before a curtain, and behind that curtain dwells the soul of ancient Egypt—the Reality, as George Isley called it—watching, with sleepless eyes of grey infinity. Then, sometimes the curtain stirs and lifts an edge; an invisible hand creeps forth; the soul is touched. And some one disappears.

VI

THE process of disintegration must have been at work a long time before I appeared upon the scene; the changes went forward with such rapidity.

It was his third year in Egypt, two of which had been spent without interruption in company with an Egyptologist named Moleson, in the neighbourhood of Thebes. I soon discovered that this region was for him the centre of attraction, or as he put it, of the web. Not Luxor, of course, nor the images of reconstructed Karnak; but that stretch of grim, forbidding mountains where royalty, earthly and spiritual, sought eternal peace for the physical remains. There, amid surroundings of superb desolation, great priests and mighty kings had thought themselves secure from sacrilegious touch. In caverns underground they kept their faithful tryst with centuries, guarded by the silence of magnificent gloom. There they waited, communing with passing ages in their sleep, till Ra, their glad divinity, should summon them to the fulfilment of their ancient dream.* And there, in the Valley of the Tombs of the Kings, their dream was shattered, their lovely prophecies derided, and their glory dimmed by the impious desecration of the curious.

That George Isley and his companion had spent their time, not merely digging and deciphering like their practical confrères, but engaged in some strange experiments of recovery and reconstruction, was matter for open comment among the fraternity. That incredible things had happened there was the big story of two Egyptian seasons at least. I heard this later only—tales of utterly incredible kind, that the desolate vale of rock was seen repeopled on moonlit nights, that the smoke of unaccustomed fires rose to cap the flat-topped peaks, that the pageantry of some forgotten worship had been seen to issue from the openings of these hills, and that sounds of chanting, sonorous and marvellously sweet, had been heard to echo from those bleak, repellent precipices. The tales apparently were grossly exaggerated; wandering Bedouins brought them in; the guides and dragomen repeated them with mysterious additions; till they filtered down through the native servants in the hotels and reached the tourists with highly picturesque embroidery. They reached the authorities too. The only accurate fact I gathered at the time, however, was that they had abruptly ceased. George Isley and Moleson, moreover, had parted company. And Moleson, I heard, was the originator of the business. He was, at this time, unknown to me; his arresting book on 'A Modern Reconstruction of Sun-worship in Ancient Egypt' being my only link with his unusual mind. Apparently he regarded the sun as the deity of the scientific religion of the future which would replace the various anthropomorphic gods of childish creeds. He discussed the possibility of the zodiacal signs being some kind of Celestial Intelligences. Belief blazed on every page. Men's life is heat, derived solely from the sun, and men were, therefore, part of the sun in the sense that a Christian is part of his personal deity. And absorption was the end. His description of 'sun-worship ceremonials' conveyed an amazing reality and beauty. This singular book, however, was all I knew of him until he came to visit us in Helouan, though I easily discerned that his influence somehow was the original cause of the change in my companion.

At Thebes, then, was the active centre of the influence that drew my friend away from modern things. It was there, I easily guessed, that 'obstacles' had been placed in the way of these men's too close enquiry. In that haunted and oppressive valley, where profane and reverent come to actual grips, where modern curiosity is most busily organised, and even tourists are aware of a masked hostility that dogs the prying of the least imaginative mind—there, in the neighbourhood of the hundred-gated city, had Egypt set the headquarters of her irreconcilable enmity. And it was there, amid the ruins of her loveliest past, that George Isley had spent his years of magical reconstruction and met the influence that now dominated his entire life.

And though no definite avowal of the struggle betrayed itself in speech between us, I remember fragments of conversation, even at this stage, that proved his willing surrender of the present. We spoke of fear once, though with the indirectness of connection I have mentioned. I urged that the mind, once it is forewarned, can remain master of itself and prevent a thing from happening.

'But that does not make the thing unreal,' he objected.

'The mind can deny it,' I said. 'It then becomes unreal.'

He shook his head. 'One does not deny an unreality. Denial is a childish act of self-protection against something you expect to happen.' He caught my eye a moment. 'You deny what you are afraid of,' he said. 'Fear invites.' And he smiled uneasily. 'You know it must get you in the end.' And, both of us being aware secretly to what our talk referred, it seemed bold-blooded and improper; for actually we discussed the psychology of his disappearance. Yet, while I disliked it, there was a fascination about the subject that compelled attraction. . . .

'Once fear gets in,' he added presently, 'confidence is undermined, the structure of life is threatened, and you—go gladly. The foundation of everything is belief. A man is what he believes about himself; and in Egypt you can believe things that elsewhere you would not even think about. It attacks the essentials.' He sighed, yet with a curious pleasure; and a smile of resignation and relief passed over his rugged features and was gone again. The luxury of abandonment lay already in him.

'But even belief,' I protested, 'must be founded on some experience or other.' It seemed ghastly to speak of his spiritual malady behind the mask of indirect allusion. My excuse was that he so obviously talked willingly.

He agreed instantly. 'Experience of one kind or another,' he said darkly, 'there always is. Talk with the men who live out here; ask any one who thinks, or who has the imagination which divines. You'll get only one reply, phrase it how they may. Even the tourists and the little commonplace officials feel it. And it's not the climate, it's not nerves, it's not any definite tendency that they can name or lay their finger on. Nor is it mere orientalising of the mind. It's something that first takes you from your common life, and that later takes common life from you. You willingly resign an unremunerative Present. There are no half-measures either—once the gates are open.'

There was so much undeniable truth in this that I found no corrective by way of strong rejoinder. All my attempts, indeed, were futile in this way. He meant to go; my words could not stop him. He wanted a witness, he dreaded the loneliness of going—but he brooked no interference. The contradictory position involved a perplexing state of heart and mind in both of us. The atmosphere of this majestic land, to-day so trifling, yesterday so immense, most certainly induced a lifting of the spiritual horizon that revealed amazing possibilities.

VII

It was in the windless days of a perfect December that Moleson, the Egyptologist, found us out and paid a flying visit to Helouan. His duties took him up and down the land, but his time seemed largely at his own disposal. He lingered on. His coming introduced a new element I was not quite able to estimate; though, speaking generally, the effect of his presence upon my companion was to emphasise the latter's alteration. It underlined the change, and drew attention to it. The new arrival, I gathered, was not altogether welcome. 'I should never have expected to find you *here*,' laughed Moleson when they met, and whether he referred to Helouan or to the hotel was not quite clear. I got the impression he meant both; I remembered my fancy that it was a good hotel to hide in. George Isley had betrayed a slight involuntary start when the visiting card was brought to him at tea-time. I think he had wished to escape from his former co-worker. Moleson had found him out. 'I heard you had a friend with you and were contemplating further exper—work,' he added. He changed the word 'experiment' quickly to the other.

'The former, as you see, is true, but not the latter,' replied my companion dryly, and in his manner was a touch of opposition that might have been hostility. Their intimacy, I saw, was close and of old standing. In all they said and did and looked, there was an undercurrent of other meaning that just escaped me. They were up to something—they *had* been up to something; but Isley would have withdrawn if he could!

Moleson was an ambitious and energetic personality, absorbed in his profession, alive to the poetical as well as to the practical value of archaeology, and he made at first a wholly delightful impression upon me. An instinctive *flair* for his subject had early in life brought him success and a measure of fame as well. His knowledge was accurate and scholarly, his mind saturated in the lore of a vanished civilisation.

Behind an exterior that was quietly careless, I divined a passionate and complex nature, and I watched him with interest as the man for whom the olden sun-worship of unscientific days held some beauty of reality and truth. Much in his strange book that had bewildered me now seemed intelligible when I saw the author. I cannot explain this more closely. Something about him somehow made it possible. Though modern to the finger-tips and thoroughly equipped with all the tendencies of the day, there seemed to hide in him another self that held aloof with a dignified detachment from the interests in which his 'educated' mind was centred. He read living secrets beneath museum labels, I might put it. He stepped out of the days of the Pharaohs if ever man did, and I realised early in our acquaintance that this was the man who had exceptional powers of 'resistance and self-protection,' and was, in his particular branch of work, 'unusual.' In manner he was light and gay, his sense of humour strong, with a way of treating everything as though laughter was the sanest attitude towards life. There is, however, the laughter that hides—other things. Moleson, as I gathered from many clues of talk and manner and silence, was a deep and singular being. His experiences in Egypt, if any, he had survived admirably. There were at least two Molesons. I felt him more than double——multiple.

In appearance tall, thin, and fleshless, with a dried-up skin and features withered as a mummy's, he said laughingly that Nature had picked him physically for his 'job'; and, indeed, one could see him worming his way down narrow tunnels into the sandy tombs, and writhing along sunless passages of suffocating heat without too much personal inconvenience. Something sinuous, almost fluid in his mind expressed itself in his body too. He might go in any direction without causing surprise. He might go backwards or forwards. He might go in two directions at once.

And my first impression of the man deepened before many days were past. There was irresponsibility in him, insincerity somewhere, almost want of heart. His morality was certainly not to-day's, and the mind in him was slippery. I think the modern world, to which he was unattached, confused and irritated him. A sense of insecurity came with him. His interest in George Isley was the interest in a psychological 'specimen.' I remembered how in his book he described the selection of individuals for certain functions of that marvellous worship, and the odd idea flashed through me—well, that Isley exactly suited some purpose of his re-creating energies. The man was keenly observant from top to toe, but not with his sight alone; he seemed to be aware of motives and emotions before he noticed the acts or gestures that these caused. I felt that he took me in as well. Certainly he eyed me up and down by means of this inner observation that seemed automatic with him.

Moleson was not staying in our hotel; he had chosen one where social life was more abundant; but he came up frequently to lunch and dine, and sometimes spent the evening in Isley's rooms, amusing us with his skill upon the piano, singing Arab songs, and chanting phrases from the ancient Egyptian rituals to rhythms of his own invention. The old Egyptian music, both in harmony and melody, was far more developed than I had realised, the use of sound having been of radical importance in their ceremonies. The chanting in particular he did with extraordinary effect, though whether its success lay in his sonorous voice, his peculiar increasing of the vowel sounds, or in anything deeper, I cannot pretend to say. The result at any rate was of a unique description. It brought buried Egypt to the surface; the gigantic Presence entered sensibly into the room. It came, huge and gorgeous, rolling upon the mind the instant he began, and something in it was both terrible and oppressive. The repose of eternity lay in the sound. Invariably, after a few moments of that transforming music, I saw the Valley of the Kings, the deserted temples, titanic faces of stone, great effigies coifed with zodiacal signs, but above all—the twin Colossi.

I mentioned this latter detail.

'Curious *you* should feel that too—curious you should say it, I mean,' Moleson replied, not looking at me, yet with an air as if I had said something he expected. 'To me the Memnon figures express Egypt better than all the other monuments put together. Like the desert, they are featureless. They sum her up, as it were, yet leave the message unuttered. For, you see, they cannot.' He laughed a little in his throat. 'They have neither eyes nor lips nor nose; their features are gone.'

'Yet they tell the secret—to those who care to listen,' put in Isley in a scarcely noticeable voice. 'Just because they have no words. They still sing at dawn,' he added in a louder, almost a challenging tone. It startled me.

Moleson turned round at him, opened his lips to speak, hesitated, stopped. He said nothing for a moment. I cannot describe what it was in the lightning glance they exchanged that put me on the alert for something other than was obvious. My nerves quivered suddenly, and a breath of colder air stole in among us. Moleson swung round to me again. 'I almost think,' he said, laughing when I complimented him upon the music, 'that I must have been a priest of Aton-Ra in an earlier existence, for all this comes to my finger-tips as if it were instinctive knowledge. Plotinus, remember, lived a few miles away at Alexandria with his great idea that knowledge is recollection,'* said, with a kind of cynical amusement. 'In those days, at any rate,' he added more significantly, 'worship was real and ceremonials actually expressed great ideas and teaching. There was power in them.' Two of the Molesons spoke in that contradictory utterance.

I saw that Isley was fidgeting where he sat, betraying by certain gestures that uneasiness was in him. He hid his face a moment in his hands; he sighed; he made a movement—as though to prevent something coming. But Moleson resisted his attempt to change the conversation, though the key shifted a little of its own accord. There were numerous occasions like this when I was aware that both men skirted something that had happened, something that Moleson wished to resume, but that Isley seemed anxious to postpone.

I found myself studying Moleson's personality, yet never getting beyond a certain point. Shrewd, subtle, with an acute rather than a large intelligence, he was cynical as well as insincere, and yet I cannot describe by what means I arrived at two other conclusions as well about him: first, that this insincerity and want of heart had not been so always; and, secondly, that he sought social diversion with deliberate and un-ordinary purpose. I could well believe that the first was Egypt's mark upon him, and the second an effort at resistance and self-protection.

'If it wasn't for the gaiety,' he remarked once in a flippant way that thinly hid significance, 'a man out here would go under in a year. Social life gets rather reckless—exaggerated—people do things they would never dream of doing at home. Perhaps you've noticed it,' he added, looking suddenly at me; 'Cairo and the rest—they plunge at it as though driven—a sort of excess about it somewhere.' I nodded agreement. The way he said it was unpleasant rather. 'It's an antidote,' he said, a sub-acid flavour in his tone. 'I used to loathe society myself. But now I find gaiety—a certain irresponsible excitement—of importance. Egypt gets on the nerves after a bit. The moral fibre fails.

The will grows weak.' And he glanced covertly at Isley as with a desire to point his meaning. 'It's the clash between the ugly present and the majestic past, perhaps.' He smiled.

Isley shrugged his shoulders, making no reply; and the other went on to tell stories of friends and acquaintances whom Egypt had adversely affected: Barton, the Oxford man, school teacher, who had insisted in living in a tent until the Government relieved him of his job. He took to his tent, roamed the desert, drawn irresistibly, practical considerations of the present of no avail. This yearning took him, though he could never define the exact attraction. In the end his mental balance was disturbed. 'But now he's all right again; I saw him in London only this year; he can't say what he felt or why he did it. Only—he's different.' Of John Lattin, too, he spoke, whom agarophobia caught so terribly in Upper Egypt; of Malahide,* upon whom some fascination of the Nile induced suicidal mania and attempts at drowning; of Jim Moleson, a cousin (who had camped at Thebes with himself and Isley), whom megalomania of a most singular type attacked suddenly in a sandy waste—all radically cured as soon as they left Egypt, yet, one and all, changed and made otherwise in their very souls.

He talked in a loose, disjointed way, and though much he said was fantastic, as if meant to challenge opposition, there was impressiveness about it somewhere, due, I think, to a kind of cumulative emotion he produced.

'The monuments do not impress merely by their bulk, but by their majestic symmetry,' I remember him saying. 'Look at the choice of form alone—the Pyramids, for instance. No other shape was possible: dome, square, spires, all would have been hideously inadequate. The wedge-shaped mass, immense foundations and pointed apex were the *mot juste* in outline. Do you think people without greatness in themselves chose that form? There was no unbalance in the minds that conceived the harmonious and magnificent structures of the temples. There was stately grandeur in their consciousness that could only be born of truth and knowledge. The power in their images is a direct expression of eternal and essential things they knew.'

We listened in silence. He was off upon his hobby. But behind the careless tone and laughing questions there was this lurking passionateness that made me feel uncomfortable. He was edging up, I felt, towards some climax that meant life and death to himself and Isley.

I could not fathom it. My sympathy let me in a little, yet not enough to understand completely. Isley, I saw, was also uneasy, though for reasons that equally evaded me.

'One can almost believe,' he continued, 'that something still hangs about in the atmosphere from those olden times.' He half closed his eyes, but I caught the gleam in them. 'It affects the mind through the imagination. With some it changes the point of view. It takes the soul back with it to former, quite different, conditions, that must have been almost another kind of consciousness.'

He paused an instant and looked up at us. 'The *intensity* of belief in those days,' he resumed, since neither of us accepted the challenge, 'was amazing—something quite unknown anywhere in the world to-day. It was so sure, so positive; no mere speculative theories, I mean;—as though something in the climate, the exact position beneath the stars, the "attitude" of this particular stretch of earth in relation to the sun—thinned the veil between humanity—and other things. Their hierarchies of gods, you know, were not mere idols; animals, birds, monsters, and what-not, all typified spiritual forces and powers that influenced their daily life. But the strong thing is—they *knew*. People who were scientific as they were did not swallow foolish superstitions. They made colours that could last six thousand years, even in the open air; and without instruments they measured accurately—an enormously difficult and involved calculation—the precession of the equinoxes. You've been to Denderah?'—he suddenly glanced again at me. 'No! Well, the minds that realised the zodiacal signs could hardly believe, you know, that Hathor was a cow!'*

Isley coughed. He was about to interrupt, but before he could find words, Moleson was off again, some new quality in his tone and manner that was almost aggressive. The hints he offered seemed more than hints. There was a strange conviction in his heart. I think he was skirting a bigger thing that he and his companion knew, yet that his real object was to see in how far I was open to attack—how far my sympathy might be with them. I became aware that he and George Isley shared this bigger thing. It was based, I felt, on some certain knowledge that experiment had brought them.

'Think of the grand teaching of Aknahton,* that young Pharaoh who regenerated the entire land and brought it to its immense prosperity. He taught the worship of the sun, but not of the visible sun.

The deity had neither form nor shape. The great disk of glory was but the manifestation, each beneficent ray ending in a hand that blessed the world. It was a god of everlasting energy, love and power, yet men could know it at first hand in their daily lives, worshipping it at dawn and sunset with passionate devotion. No anthropomorphic idol masqueraded in *that!*'

An extraordinary glow was about him as he said it. The same minute he lowered his voice, shifting the key perceptibly. He kept looking up at me through half-closed eyelids.

'And another thing they wonderfully knew,' he almost whispered, 'was that, with the precession of their deity across the equinoctial changes, there came new powers down into the world of men. Each cycle—each zodiacal sign—brought its special powers which they quickly typified in the monstrous effigies we label to-day in our dull museums. Each sign took some two thousand years to traverse. Each sign, moreover, involved a change in human consciousness. There was this relation between the heavens and the human heart. All that they knew. While the sun crawled through the sign of Taurus, it was the Bull they worshipped; with Aries, it was the ram that coifed their granite symbols. Then came, as you remember, with Pisces the great New Arrival, when already they sank from their grand zenith, and the Fish was taken as the emblem of the changing powers which the Christ embodied. For the human soul, they held, echoed the changes in the immense journey of the original deity, who is its source, across the Zodiac, and the truth of "As above, so Below" remains the key to all manifested life. And to-day the sun, just entering Aquarius, new powers are close upon the world. The old—that which has been for two thousand years—again is crumbling, passing, dying. New powers and a new consciousness are knocking at our doors. It is a time of change. It is also'—he leaned forward so that his eyes came close before me—'the time to make the change. The soul can choose its own conditions. It can——'

A sudden crash smothered the rest of the sentence. A chair had fallen with a clatter upon the wooden floor where the carpet left it bare. Whether Isley in rising had stumbled against it, or whether he had purposely knocked it over, I could not say. I only knew that he had abruptly risen and as abruptly sat down again. A curious feeling came to me that the sign was somehow prearranged. It was so sudden. His voice, too, was forced, I thought.

'Yes, but we can do without all that, Moleson,' he interrupted with acute abruptness. 'Suppose we have a tune instead.'

VIII

It was after dinner in his private room, and he had sat very silent in his corner until this sudden outburst. Moleson got up quietly without a word and moved over to the piano. I saw—or was it imagination merely?—a new expression slide upon his withered face. He meant mischief somewhere.

From that instant—from the moment he rose and walked over the thick carpet—he fascinated me. The atmosphere his talk and stories had brought remained. His lean fingers ran over the keys, and at first he played fragments from popular musical comedies that were pleasant enough, but made no demand upon the attention. I heard them without listening. I was thinking of another thing—his walk. For the way he moved across those few feet of carpet had power in it. He looked different; he seemed another man; he was changed. I saw him curiously—as I sometimes now saw Isley too—bigger. In some manner that was both enchanting and oppressive, his presence from that moment drew my imagination as by an air of authority it held.

I left my seat in the far corner and dropped into a chair beside the window, nearer to the piano. Isley, I then noticed, had also turned to watch him. But it was George Isley not quite as he was now. I felt rather than saw the change. Both men had subtly altered. They seemed extended, their outlines shadowy.

Isley, alert and anxious, glanced up at the player, his mind of earlier years—for the expression of his face was plain—following the light music, yet with difficulty that involved effort, almost struggle. 'Play that again, will you?' I heard him say from time to time. He was trying to take hold of it, to climb back to a condition where that music had linked him to the present, to seize a mental structure that was gone, to grip hold tightly of it—only to find that it was too far forgotten and too fragile. It would not bear him. I am sure of it, and I can swear I divined his mood. He fought to realise himself as he had been, but in vain. In his dim corner opposite I watched him closely. The big black Blüthner* blocked itself between us. Above it swayed the outline, lean and half shadowy, of Moleson as he played. A faint whisper floated through the room. 'You are in Egypt.' Nowhere else could this queer feeling of presentiment, of anticipation, have gained a footing so easily. I was aware of intense emotion in all three of us. The least reminder of To-day seemed ugly. I longed for some ancient forgotten splendour that was lost.

The scene fixed my attention very steadily, for I was aware of something deliberate and calculated on Moleson's part. The thing was well considered in his mind, intention only half concealed. It was Egypt he interpreted by sound, expressing what in him was true, then observing its effect, as he led us cleverly towards—the past. Beginning with the present, he played persuasively, with penetration, with insistent meaning too. He had that touch which conjured up real atmosphere, and, at first, that atmosphere termed modern. He rendered vividly the note of London, passing from the jingles of musical comedy, nervous rag-times and sensuous Tango dances, into the higher strains of concert rooms and 'cultured' circles. Yet not too abruptly. Most dexterously he shifted the level, and with it our emotion. I recognised, as in a parody, various ultramodern thrills: the tumult of Strauss, the pagan sweetness of primitive Debussy, the weirdness and ecstasy of metaphysical Scriabin.* The composite note of To-day in both extremes, he brought into this private sitting-room of the desert hotel, while George Isley, listening keenly, fidgeted in his chair.

' "Après-midi d'un Faune," ' said Moleson dreamily, answering the question as to what he played. 'Debussy's, you know. And the thing before it was from "Til Eulenspiegel"—Strauss, of course.'

He drawled, swaying slowly with the rhythm, and leaving pauses between the words. His attention was not wholly on his listener, and in the voice was a quality that increased my uneasy apprehension. I felt distress for Isley somewhere. Something, it seemed, was coming; Moleson brought it. Unconsciously in his walk, it now appeared consciously in his music; and it came from what was underground in him. A charm, a subtle change, stole oddly over the room. It stole over my heart as well. Some power of estimating left me, as though my mind were slipping backwards and losing familiar, common standards.

'The true modern note in it, isn't there?' he drawled; 'cleverness, I think—intellectual—surface ingenuity—no depth or permanence—just the sensational brilliance of To-day.' He turned and stared at me fixedly an instant. 'Nothing *everlasting*,' he added impressively. 'It tells everything it knows—because it's small enough——'

And the room turned pettier as he said it; another, bigger shadow draped its little walls. Through the open windows came a stealthy gesture of eternity. The atmosphere stretched visibly. Moleson was playing a marvellous fragment from Scriabin's 'Prometheus.' It sounded thin and shallow. This modern music, all of it, was out of place and trivial. It was almost ridiculous. The scale of our emotion changed insensibly into a deeper thing that has no name in dictionaries, being of another age. And I glanced at the windows where stone columns framed dim sections of great Egypt listening outside. There was no moon; only deep draughts of stars blazed, hanging in the sky. I thought with awe of the mysterious knowledge that vanished people had of these stars, and of the Sun's huge journey through the Zodiac. . . .

And, with astonishing suddenness as of dream, there rose a pictured image against that starlit sky. Lifted into the air, between heaven and earth, I saw float swiftly past a panorama of the stately temples, led by Denderah, Edfu, Abou Simbel.* It paused, it hovered, it disappeared. Leaving incalculable solemnity behind it in the air, it vanished, and to see so vast a thing move at that easy yet unhasting speed unhinged some sense of measurement in me. It was, of course, I assured myself, mere memory objectified owing to something that the music summoned, yet the apprehension rose in me that the whole of Egypt presently would stream past in similar fashion—Egypt as she was in the zenith of her unrecoverable past. Behind the tinkling of the modern piano passed the rustling of a multitude, the tramping of countless feet on sand. . . . It was singularly vivid. It arrested in me something that normally went flowing. . . . And when I turned my head towards the room to call attention to my strange experience, the eyes of Moleson, I saw, were laid upon my own. He stared at me. The light in them transfixed me, and I understood that the illusion was due in some manner to his evocation. Isley rose at the same moment from his chair. The thing I had vaguely been expecting had shifted closer. And the same moment the musician abruptly changed his key.

'You may like this better,' he murmured, half to himself, but in tones he somehow made echoing. 'It's more suited to the place.' There was a resonance in the voice as though it emerged from hollows underground. 'The other seems almost sacrilegious—here.' And his voice drawled off in the rhythm of slower modulations that he played. It had grown muffled. There was an impression, too, that he did not strike the piano, but that the music issued from himself.

'Place! What place?' asked Isley quickly. His head turned sharply as he spoke. His tone, in its remoteness, made me tremble.

The musician laughed to himself. 'I meant that this hotel seems really an impertinence,' he murmured, leaning down upon the notes he played upon so softly and so well; 'and that it's but the thinnest kind of pretence—when you come to think of it. We are in the desert really. The Colossi are outside, and all the emptied temples. Or ought to be,' he added, raising his tone abruptly with a glance at me.

He straightened up and stared out into the starry sky past George Isley's shoulders.

'That,' he exclaimed with betraying vehemence, 'is where we are and what we play to!' His voice suddenly increased; there was a roar in it. 'That,' he repeated, 'is the thing that takes our hearts away.' The volume of intonation was astonishing.

For the way he uttered the monosyllable suddenly revealed the man beneath the outer sheath of cynicism and laughter, explained his heartlessness, his secret stream of life. He, too, was soul and body in the past. 'That' revealed more than pages of descriptive phrases. His heart lived in the temple aisles, his mind unearthed forgotten knowledge; his soul had clothed itself anew in the seductive glory of antiquity: he dwelt with a quickening magic of existence in the reconstructed splendour of what most term only ruins. He and George Isley together had revivified a power that enticed them backwards; but whereas the latter struggled still, the former had already made his permanent home there. The faculty in me that saw the vision of streaming temples saw also this—remorselessly definite. Moleson himself sat naked at that piano. I saw him clearly then. He no longer masqueraded behind his sneers and laughter. He, too, had long ago surrendered, lost himself, gone out, and from the place his soul now dwelt in he watched George Isley sinking down to join him. He lived in ancient, subterranean Egypt. This great hotel stood precariously on the merest upper crust of desert. A thousand tombs, a hundred temples lay outside, within reach almost of our very voices. Moleson was merged with 'that.'

This intuition flashed upon me like the picture in the sky; and both were true.

And, meanwhile, this other thing he played had a surge of power in it impossible to describe. It was sombre, huge and solemn. It conveyed the power that his walk conveyed. There was distance in it, but a distance not of space alone. A remoteness of time breathed through it with that strange sadness and melancholy yearning that enormous interval brings. It marched, but very far away; it held refrains that assumed the rhythms of a multitude the centuries muted; it sang, but the singing was underground in passages that fine sand muffled. Lost, wandering winds sighed through it, booming. The contrast, after the modern, cheaper music, was dislocating. Yet the change had been quite naturally effected.

'It would sound empty and monotonous elsewhere—in London, for instance,' I heard Moleson drawling, as he swayed to and fro, 'but here it is big and splendid—true. You hear what I mean,' he added gravely. 'You understand?'

'What is it?' asked Isley thickly, before I could say a word. 'I forget exactly. It has tears in it—more than I can bear.' The end of his sentence died away in his throat.

Moleson did not look at him as he answered. He looked at me.

'You surely ought to know,' he replied, the voice rising and falling as though the rhythm forced it. 'You have heard it all before—that chant from the ritual we——'

Isley sprang up and stopped him. I did not hear the sentence complete. An extraordinary thought blazed into me that the voices of both men were not quite their own. I fancied—wild, impossible as it sounds—that I heard the twin Colossi singing to each other in the dawn. Stupendous ideas sprang past me, leaping. It seemed as though eternal symbols of the cosmos, discovered and worshipped in this ancient land, leaped into awful life. My consciousness became enveloping. I had the distressing feeling that ages slipped out of place and took me with them; they dominated me; they rushed me off my feet like water. I was drawn backwards. I, too, was changing—being changed.

'I remember,' said Isley softly, a reverence of worship in his voice. But there was anguish in it too, and pity; he let the present go completely from him; the last strands severed with a wrench of pain. I imagined I heard his soul pass weeping far away—below.

'I'll sing it,' murmured Moleson, 'for the voice is necessary. The sound and rhythm are utterly divine!'

IX

AND forthwith his voice began a series of long-drawn cadences that seemed somehow the root sounds of every tongue that ever was.

A spell came over me I could touch and feel. A web encompassed me; my arms and feet became entangled; a veil of fine threads wove across my eyes. The enthralling power of the rhythm produced some magical movement in the soul. I was aware of life everywhere about me, far and near, in the dwellings of the dead, as also in the corridors of the iron hills. Thebes stood erect, and Memphis teemed upon the river banks. For the modern world fell, swaying, at this sound that restored the past, and in this past both men before me lived and had their being. The storm of present life passed o'er their heads, while they dwelt underground, obliterated, gone. Upon the wave of sound they went down into their recovered kingdom.

I shivered, moved vigorously, half rose up, then instantly sank back again, resigned and helpless. For I entered by their side, it seemed, the conditions of their strange captivity. My thoughts, my feelings, my point of view were transplanted to another centre. Consciousness shifted in me. I saw things from another's point of view—antiquity's.

The present forgotten but the past supreme, I lost Reality. Our room became a pin-point picture seen in a drop of water, while this subterranean world, replacing it, turned immense. My heart took on the gigantic, leisured stride of what had been. Proportions grew; size captured me; and magnitude, turned monstrous, swept mere measurement away. Some hand of golden sunshine picked me up and set me in the quivering web beside those other two. I heard the rustle of the settling threads; I heard the shuffling of the feet in sand; I heard the whispers in the dwellings of the dead. Behind the monotony of this sacerdotal music I heard them in their dim carved chambers. The ancient galleries were awake. The Life of unremembered ages stirred in multitudes about me.

The reality of so incredible an experience evaporates through the stream of language. I can only affirm this singular proof—that the deepest, most satisfying knowledge the Present could offer seemed insignificant beside some stalwart majesty of the Past that utterly usurped it. This modern room, holding a piano and two figures of To-day, appeared as a paltry miniature pinned against a vast transparent curtain, whose foreground was thick with symbols of temple, sphinx and pyramid, but whose background of stupendous hanging grey slid off towards a splendour where the cities of the Dead shook off their sand and thronged space to its ultimate horizons. . . . The stars, the entire universe, vibrating and alive, became involved in it. Long periods of time slipped past me. I seemed living ages ago. . . . I was living backwards. . . .

The size and eternity of Egypt took me easily. There was an overwhelming grandeur in it that elbowed out all present standards. The whole place towered and stood up. The desert reared, the very horizons lifted; majestic figures of granite rose above the hotel, great faces hovered and drove past; huge arms reached up to pluck the stars and set them in the ceilings of the labyrinthine tombs. The colossal meaning of the ancient land emerged through all its ruined details . . . reconstructed—burningly alive. . . .

It became at length unbearable. I longed for the droning sounds to cease, for the rhythm to lessen its prodigious sweep. My heart cried out for the gold of the sunlight on the desert, for the sweet air by the river's banks, for the violet lights upon the hills at dawn. And I resisted, I made an effort to return.

'Your chant is horrible. For God's sake, let's have an Arab song—or the music of To-day!'

The effort was intense, the result was—nothing. I swear I used these words. I heard the actual sound of my voice, if no one else did, for I remember that it was pitiful in the way great space devoured it, making of its appreciable volume the merest whisper as of some bird or insect cry. But the figure that I took for Moleson, instead of answer or acknowledgment, merely grew and grew as things grow in a fairy tale. I hardly know; I certainly cannot say. That dwindling part of me which offered comments on the entire occurrence noted this extraordinary effect as though it happened naturally—that Moleson himself was marvellously increasing.

The entire spell became operative all at once. I experienced both the delight of complete abandonment and the terror of letting go what *had* seemed real. I understood Moleson's sham laughter, and the subtle resignation of George Isley. And an amazing thought flashed birdlike across my changing consciousness—that this resurrection into the Past, this rebirth of the spirit which they sought, involved taking upon themselves the guise of these ancient symbols each in turn. As the embryo assumes each evolutionary stage below it before the human semblance is attained,* so the souls of those two adventurers took upon themselves the various emblems of that intense belief. The devout worshipper takes on the qualities of his deity. They wore the entire series of the old-world gods so potently that I perceived them, and even objectified them by my senses. The present was their pre-natal stage; to enter the past they were being born again.

But it was not Moleson's semblance alone that took on this awful change. Both faces, scaled to the measure of Egypt's outstanding quality of size, became in this little modern room distressingly immense. Distorting mirrors can suggest no simile, for the symmetry of proportion was not injured. I lost their human physiognomies. I saw their thoughts, their feelings, their augmented, altered hearts, the thing that Egypt put there while she stole their love from modern life. There grew an awful stateliness upon them that was huge, mysterious, and motionless as stone.

For Moleson's narrow face at first turned hawk-like in the semblance of the sinister deity, Horus,* only stretched to tower above the toy-scaled piano; it was keen and sly and monstrous after prey, while a swiftness of the sunrise leaped from both the brilliant eyes. George Isley, equally immense of outline, was in general presentment more magnificent, a breadth of the Sphinx about his spreading shoulders, and in his countenance an inscrutable power of calm temple images. These were the first signs of obsession; but others followed. In rapid series, like lantern-slides upon a screen, the ancient symbols flashed one after another across these two extended human faces and were gone. Disentanglement became impossible. The successive signatures seemed almost superimposed as in a composite photograph, each appearing and vanished before recognition was even possible, while I interpreted the inner alchemy by means of outer tokens familiar to my senses. Egypt, possessing them, expressed herself thus marvellously in their physical aspect, using the symbols of her intense, regenerative power. . . .

The changes merged with such swiftness into one another that I did not seize the half of them—till, finally, the procession culminated in a single one that remained fixed awfully upon them both. The entire series merged. I was aware of this single masterful image which summed up all the others in sublime repose. The gigantic thing rose up in this incredible statue form. The spirit of Egypt synthesised in this monstrous symbol, obliterated them both. I saw the seated figures of the grim Colossi, dipped in sand, night over them, waiting for the dawn. . . .

X

I MADE a violent effort, then, at self-assertion—an effort to focus my mind upon the present. And, searching for Moleson and George

Isley, its nearest details, I was aware that I could not find them. The familiar figures of my two companions were not discoverable.

I saw it as plainly as I also saw that ludicrous, wee piano—for a moment. But the moment remained; the Eternity of Egypt stayed. For that lonely and terrific pair had stooped their shoulders and bowed their awful heads. They were in the room. They imaged forth the power of the everlasting Past through the little structures of two human worshippers. Room, walls, and ceiling fled away. Sand and the open sky replaced them.

The two of them rose side by side before my bursting eyes. I knew not where to look. Like some child who confronts its giants upon the nursery floor, I turned to stone, unable to think or move. I stared. Sight wrenched itself to find the men familiar to it, but found instead this symbolising vision. I could not see them properly. Their faces were spread with hugeness, their features lost in some uncommon magnitude, their shoulders, necks, and arms grown vast upon the air. As with the desert, there was physiognomy yet no personal expression, the human thing all drowned within the mass of battered stone. I discovered neither cheeks nor mouth nor jaw, but ruined eyes and lips of broken granite. Huge, motionless, mysterious, Egypt informed them and took them to herself. And between us, curiously presented in some false perspective, I saw the little symbol of To-day—the Blüthner piano. It was appalling. I knew a second of majestic horror. I blenched. Hot and cold gushed through me. Strength left me, power of speech and movement too, as in a moment of complete paralysis.

The spell, moreover, was not within the room alone; it was outside and everywhere. The Past stood massed about the very walls of the hotel. Distance, as well as time, stepped nearer. That chanting summoned the gigantic items in all their ancient splendour. The shadowy concourse grouped itself upon the sand about us, and I was aware that the great army shifted noiselessly into place; that pyramids soared and towered; that deities of stone stood by; that temples ranged themselves in reconstructed beauty, grave as the night of time whence they emerged; and that the outline of the Sphinx, motionless but aggressive, piled its dim bulk upon the atmosphere. Immensity answered to immensity. . . . There were vast intervals of time and there were reaches of enormous distance, yet all happened in a moment, and all happened within a little space. It was now and here. Eternity whispered in every second as in every grain of sand. Yet, while aware of so many stupendous details all at once, I was really aware of one thing only—that the spirit of ancient Egypt faced me in these two terrific figures, and that my consciousness, stretched painfully yet gloriously, included all, as She also unquestionably included them—and me.

For it seemed I shared the likeness of my two companions. Some lesser symbol, though of similar kind, obsessed me too. I tried to move, but my feet were set in stone; my arms lay fixed; my body was embedded in the rock. Sand beat sharply upon my outer surface, urged upwards in little flurries by a chilly wind. There was nothing felt: I *heard* the rattle of the scattering grains against my hardened body. . . .

And we waited for the dawn; for the resurrection of that unchanging deity who was the source and inspiration of all our glorious life. . . . The air grew keen and fresh. In the distance a line of sky turned from pink to violet and gold; a delicate rose next flushed the desert; a few pale stars hung fainting overhead; and the wind that brought the sunrise was already stirring. The whole land paused upon the coming of its mighty God. . . .

Into the pause there rose a curious sound for which we had been waiting. For it came familiarly, as though expected. I could have sworn at first that it was George Isley who sang, answering his companion. There beat behind its great volume the same note and rhythm, only so prodigiously increased that, while Moleson's chant had waked it, it now was independent and apart. The resonant vibrations of what he sang had reached down into the places where it slept. *They* uttered synchronously. Egypt spoke. There was in it the deep muttering as of a thousand drums, as though the desert uttered in prodigious syllables. I listened while my heart of stone stood still. There were two voices in the sky. *They* spoke tremendously with each other in the dawn:

'So easily we still remain possessors of the land. . . . While the centuries roar past us and are gone.'

Soft with power the syllables rolled forth, yet with a booming depth as though caverns underground produced them.

'Our silence is disturbed. Pass on with the multitude towards the East. . . . Still in the dawn we sing the old-world wisdom. . . . They shall hear our speech, yet shall not hear it with their ears of flesh. At dawn our words go forth, searching the distances of sand and time across the sunlight. . . . At dusk they return, as upon eagles' wings, entering again our lips of stone. . . . Each century one syllable, yet no sentence yet complete. While our lips are broken with the utterance. . . .'

It seemed that hours and months and years went past me while I listened in my sandy bed. The fragments died far away, then sounded very close again. It was as though mountain peaks sang to one another above clouds. Wind caught the muffled roar away. Wind brought it back. . . . Then, in a hollow pause that lasted years, conveying marvellously the passage of long periods, I heard the utterance more clearly. The leisured roll of the great voice swept through me like a flood:

'We wait and watch and listen in our loneliness. We do not close our eyes. The moon and stars sail past us, and our river finds the sea. We bring Eternity upon your broken lives. . . . We see you build your little lines of steel across our territory behind the thin white smoke. We hear the whistle of your messengers of iron through the air. . . . The nations rise and pass. The empires flutter westwards and are gone. . . . The sun grows older and the stars turn pale. . . . Winds shift the line of the horizons, and our River moves its bed. But we, everlasting and unchangeable, remain. Of water, sand and fire is our essential being, yet built within the universal air. . . . There is no pause in life, there is no break in death. The changes bring no end. The sun returns. . . . There is eternal resurrection. . . . But our kingdom is underground in shadow, unrealised of your little day. . . . Come, come! The temples still are crowded, and our Desert blesses you. Our River takes your feet. Our sand shall purify, and the fire of our God shall burn you sweetly into wisdom. . . . Come, then, and worship, for the time draws near. It is the dawn. . . .'

The voices died down into depths that the sand of ages muffled, while the flaming dawn of the East rushed up the sky. Sunrise, the great symbol of life's endless resurrection, was at hand. About me, in immense but shadowy array, stood the whole of ancient Egypt, hanging breathlessly upon the moment of adoration. No longer stern and terrible in the splendour of their long neglect, the effigies rose erect with passionate glory, a forest of stately stone. Their granite lips were parted and their ancient eyes were wide. All faced the east. And the sun drew nearer to the rim of the attentive Desert.

XI

EMOTION there seemed none, in the sense that *I* knew feeling. I knew, if anything, the ultimate secrets of two primitive sensations—joy and awe. . . . The dawn grew swiftly brighter. There was gold, as though the sands of Nubia spilt their brilliance on each shining detail; there was glory, as though the retreating tide of stars spilt their light foam upon the world; and there was passion, as though the beliefs of all the ages floated back with abandonment into the—Sun. Ruined Egypt merged into a single temple of elemental vastness whose floor was the empty desert, but whose walls rose to the stars.

Abruptly, then, chanting and rhythm ceased; they dipped below. Sand muffled them. And the Sun looked down upon its ancient world. . . .

A radiant warmth poured through me. I found that I could move my limbs again. A sense of triumphant life ran through my stony frame. For one passing second I heard the shower of gritty particles upon my surface like sand blown upwards by a gust of wind, but this time I could *feel* the sting of it upon my skin. It passed. The drenching heat bathed me from head to foot, while stony insensibility gave place with returning consciousness to flesh and blood. The sun had risen. . . . I was alive, but I was—changed.

It seemed I opened my eyes. An immense relief was in me. I turned; I drew a deep, refreshing breath; I stretched one leg upon a thick, green carpet. Something had left me; another thing had returned. I sat up, conscious of welcome release, of freedom, of escape.

There was some violent, disorganising break. I found myself; I found Moleson; I found George Isley too. He had got shifted in that room without my being aware of it. Isley had risen. He came upon me like a blow. I saw him move his arms. Fire flashed from below his hands; and I realised then that he was turning on the electric lights. They emerged from different points along the walls, in the alcove, beneath the ceiling, by the writing-table; and one had just that minute blazed into my eyes from a bracket close above me. I was back again in the Present among modern things.

But, while most of the details presented themselves gradually to my recovered senses, Isley returned with this curious effect of speed and distance—like a blow upon the mind. From great height and from prodigious size—he dropped. I seemed to find him rushing at me. Moleson was simply 'there'; there was no speed or sudden change in him as with the other. Motionless at the piano, his long thin hands lay down upon the keys yet did not strike them. But Isley came back like lightning into the little room, signs of the monstrous obsession still about his altering features. There was battle and worship mingled in his deep-set eyes. His mouth, though set, was smiling. With a shudder

I positively saw the vastness slipping from his face as shadows from a stretch of broken cliff. There was this awful mingling of proportions. The colossal power that had resumed his being drew slowly inwards. There was collapse in him. And upon the sunburned cheek of his rugged face I saw a tear.

Poignant revulsion caught me then for a moment. The present showed itself in rags. The reduction of scale was painful. I yearned for the splendour that was gone, yet still seemed so hauntingly almost within reach. The cheapness of the hotel room, the glaring ugliness of its tinsel decoration, the baseness of ideals where utility instead of beauty, gain instead of worship, governed life—this, with the dwindled aspect of my companions to the insignificance of marionettes, brought a hungry pain that was at first intolerable. In the glare of light I noticed the small round face of the portable clock upon the mantelpiece, showing half-past eleven. Moleson had been two hours at the piano. And this measuring faculty of my mind completed the disillusionment. I was, indeed, back among present things. The mechanical spirit of To-day imprisoned me again.

For a considerable interval we neither moved nor spoke; the sudden change left the emotions in confusion; we had leaped from a height, from the top of the pyramid, from a star—and the crash of landing scattered thought. I stole a glance at Isley, wondering vaguely why he was there at all; the look of resignation had replaced the power in his face; the tear was brushed away. There was no struggle in him now, no sign of resistance; there was abandonment only; he seemed insignificant. The real George Isley was elsewhere: he himself had not returned.

By jerks, as it were, and by awkward stages, then, we all three came back to common things again. I found that we were talking ordinarily, asking each other questions, answering, lighting cigarettes, and all the rest. Moleson played some commonplace chords upon the piano, while he leaned back listlessly in his chair, putting in sentences now and again and chatting idly to whichever of us would listen. And Isley came slowly across the room towards me, holding out cigarettes. His dark brown face had shadows on it. He looked exhausted, worn, like some soldier broken in the wars.

'You liked it?' I heard his thin voice asking. There was no interest, no expression; it was not the real Isley who spoke; it was the little part of him that had come back. He smiled like a marvellous automaton.

Mechanically I took the cigarette he offered me, thinking confusedly what answer I could make.

'It's irresistible,' I murmured; 'I understand that it's easier to go.'

'Sweeter as well,' he whispered with a sigh, 'and very wonderful!'

XII

THE hand that lit my cigarette, I saw, was trembling. A desire to do something violent woke in me suddenly—to move energetically, to push or drive something away.

'What was it?' I asked abruptly, in a louder, half-challenging voice, intended for the man at the piano, 'Such a performance—upon *others*—without first asking their permission—seems to me unpermissible—it's——'

And it was Moleson who replied. He ignored the end of my sentence as though he had not heard it. He strolled over to our side, taking a cigarette and pressing it carefully into shape between his long thin fingers.

'You may well ask,' he answered quietly; 'but it's not so easy to tell. We discovered it'—he nodded towards Isley—'two years ago in the "Valley." It lay beside a Priest, a very important personage, apparently, and was part of the Ritual he used in the worship of the sun. In the Museum now—you can see it any day at the Boulak—it is simply labelled "Hymn to Ra." The period was Aknahton's.'*

'The words, yes,' put in Isley, who was listening closely.

'The words?' repeated Moleson in a curious tone. 'There *are* no words. It's all really a manipulation of the vowel sounds. And the rhythm, or chanting, or whatever you like to call it, I—I invented myself. The Egyptians did not write their music, you see.' He suddenly searched my face a moment with questioning eyes, 'Any words you heard,' he said, 'or thought you heard, were merely your own interpretation.'

I stared at him, making no rejoinder.

'They made use of what they called a "root-language" in their rituals,' he went on, 'and it consisted entirely of vowel sounds. There were no consonants. For vowel sounds, you see, run on for ever without end or beginning, whereas consonants interrupt their flow and break it up and limit it. A consonant has no sound of its own at all. Real language is continuous.'

We stood a moment, smoking in silence. I understood then that this thing Moleson had done was based on definite knowledge. He had rendered some fragment of an ancient Ritual he and Isley had unearthed together, and while he knew its effect upon the latter, he chanced it on myself. Not otherwise, I feel, could it have influenced me in the extraordinary way it did. In the faith and poetry of a nation lies its soul-life, and the gigantic faith of Egypt blazed behind the rhythm of that long, monotonous chant. There were blood and heart and nerves in it. Millions had heard it sung; millions had wept and prayed and yearned; it was ensouled by the passion of that marvellous civilisation that loved the godhead of the Sun, and that now hid, waiting but still alive, below the ground. The majestic faith of ancient Egypt poured up with it—that tremendous, burning elaboration of the after-life and of Eternity that was the pivot of those spacious days. For centuries vast multitudes, led by their royal priests, had uttered this very form and ritual—believed it, lived it, felt it. The rising of the sun remained its climax. Its spiritual power still clung to the great ruined symbols. The faith of a buried civilisation had burned back into the present and into our hearts as well.

And a curious respect for the man who was able to produce this effect upon two modern minds crept over me, and mingled with the repulsion that I felt. I looked furtively at his withered, dried-up features. He wore some vague and shadowy impress still of what had just been in him. There was a stony appearance in his shrunken cheeks. He looked smaller. I saw him lessened. I thought of him as he had been so short a time before, imprisoned in his great stone captors that had obsessed him. . . .

'There's tremendous power in it,—an awful power,' I stammered, more to break the oppressive pause than for any desire in me to speak with him. 'It brings back Egypt in some extraordinary way—ancient Egypt, I mean—brings it close—into the heart.' My words ran on of their own accord almost. I spoke with a hush, unwittingly. There was awe in me. Isley had moved away towards the window, leaving me face to face with this strange incarnation of another age.

'It must,' he replied, deep light still glowing in his eyes, 'for the soul of the old days is in it. No one, I think, can hear it and remain the same. It expresses, you see, the essential passion and beauty of that gorgeous worship, that splendid faith, that reasonable and intelligent worship of the sun, the only scientific belief the world has ever known.

Its popular form, of course, was largely superstitious, but the sacer-dotal form—the form used by the priests, that is—who understood the relationship between colour, sound and symbol, was——'

He broke off suddenly, as though he had been speaking to himself. We sat down. George Isley leaned out of the window with his back to us, watching the desert in the moonless night.

'You have tried its effect before upon—others?' I asked point-blank.

'Upon myself,' he answered shortly.

'Upon others?' I insisted.

He hesitated an instant.

'Upon one other—yes,' he admitted.

'Intentionally?' And something quivered in me as I asked it.

He shrugged his shoulders slightly. 'I'm merely a speculative archaeologist,' he smiled, 'and—and an imaginative Egyptologist. My bounden duty is to reconstruct the past so that it lives for others.'

An impulse rose in me to take him by the throat. 'You know per-fectly well, of course, the magical effect it's sure—likely at least—to have?'

He stared steadily at me through the cigarette smoke. To this day I cannot think exactly what it was in this man that made me shudder.

'I'm sure of nothing,' he replied smoothly, 'but I consider it quite legitimate to try. Magical—the word you used—has no meaning for me. If such a thing exists, it is merely scientific—undiscovered or forgotten knowledge.' An insolent, aggressive light shone in his eyes as he spoke; his manner was almost truculent. 'You refer, I take it, to—our friend—rather than to yourself?'

And with difficulty I met his singular stare. From his whole person something still emanated that was forbidding, yet overmasteringly persuasive. It brought back the notion of that invisible Web, that dim gauze curtain, that motionless Influence lying waiting at the centre for its prey, those monstrous and mysterious Items standing, alert and watchful, through the centuries. 'You mean,' he added lower, 'his altered attitude to life—his going?'

To hear him use the words, the very phrase, struck me with sudden chill. Before I could answer, however, and certainly before I could master the touch of horror that rushed over me, I heard him continu-ing in a whisper. It seemed again that he spoke to himself as much as he spoke to me.

'The soul, I suppose, has the right to choose its own conditions and surroundings. To pass elsewhere involves translation, not extinction.' He smoked a moment in silence, then said another curious thing, looking up into my face with an expression of intense earnestness. Something genuine in him again replaced the pose of cynicism. 'The soul is eternal and can take its place anywhere, regardless of mere duration. What is there in the vulgar and superficial Present that should hold it so exclusively; and where can it find to-day the belief, the faith, the beauty that are the very essence of its life—where in the rush and scatter of this tawdry age can it make its home? Shall it flutter for ever in a valley of dry bones, when a living Past lies ready and waiting with loveliness, strength, and glory?' He moved closer; he touched my arm; I felt his breath upon my face. 'Come with us,' he whispered awfully; 'come back with us! Withdraw your life from the rubbish of this futile ugliness! Come back and worship with us in the spirit of the Past. Take up the old, old splendour, the glory, the immense conceptions, the wondrous certainty, the ineffable knowledge of essentials. It all lies about you still; it's calling, ever calling; it's very close; it draws you day and night—calling, calling, calling. . . .'

His voice died off curiously into distance on the word; I can hear it to this day, and the soft, droning quality in the intense yet fading tone: 'Calling, calling, calling.' But his eyes turned wicked. I felt the sinister power of the man. I was aware of madness in his thought and mind. The Past he sought to glorify I saw black as with the forbidding Egyptian darkness of a plague.* It was not beauty but Death that I heard calling, calling, calling.

'It's real,' he went on, hardly aware that I shrank, 'and not a dream. These ruined symbols still remain in touch with that which was. They are potent to-day as they were six thousand years ago. The amazing life of those days brims behind them. They are not mere masses of oppressive stone; they express in visible form great powers that still are—*knowable*.' He lowered his head, peered up into my face, and whispered. Something secret passed into his eyes.

'I saw you change,' came the words below his breath, 'as you saw the change in us. But only worship can produce that change. The soul assumes the qualities of the deity it worships. The powers of its deity possess it and transform it into its own likeness. You also felt it. *You* also were possessed. I saw the stone-faced deity upon your own.'

I seemed to shake myself as a dog shakes water from its body. I stood up. I remember that I stretched my hands out as though to push him from me and expel some creeping influence from my mind. I remember another thing as well. But for the reality of the sequel, and but for the matter-of-fact result still facing me to-day in the disappearance of George Isley—the loss to the present time of all George Isley *was*—I might have found subject for laughter in what I saw. Comedy was in it certainly. Yet it was both ghastly and terrific. Deep horror crept below the aspect of the ludicrous, for the apparent mimicry cloaked truth. It was appalling because it was real.

In the large mirror that reflected the room behind me I saw myself and Moleson; I saw Isley too in the background by the open window. And the attitude of all three was the attitude of hieroglyphics come to life. My arms indeed were stretched, but not stretched, as I had thought, in mere self-defence. They were stretched—unnaturally. The forearms made those strange obtuse angles that the old carved granite wears, the palms of the hands held upwards, the heads thrown back, the legs advanced, the bodies stiffened into postures that expressed forgotten, ancient minds. The physical conformation of all three was monstrous; and yet reverence and truth dictated even the uncouthness of the gestures. Something in all three of us inspired the forms our bodies had assumed. Our attitudes expressed buried yearnings, emotions, tendencies—whatever they may be termed—that the spirit of the Past evoked.

I saw the reflected picture but for a moment. I dropped my arms, aware of foolishness in my way of standing. Moleson moved forward with his long, significant stride, and at the same instant Isley came up quickly and joined us from his place by the open window. We looked into each other's faces without a word. There was this little pause that lasted perhaps ten seconds. But in that pause I felt the entire world slide past me. I heard the centuries rush by at headlong speed. The present dipped away. Existence was no longer in a line that stretched two ways; it was a circle in which ourselves, together with Past and Future, stood motionless at the centre, all details equally accessible at once. The three of us were falling, falling backwards. . . .

'Come!' said the voice of Moleson solemnly, but with the sweetness as of a child anticipating joy. 'Come! Let us go together, for the boat of Ra has crossed the Underworld.* The darkness has been conquered. Let us go out together and find the dawn. Listen! It is calling, calling, calling. . . .'

XIII

I WAS aware of rushing, but it was the soul in me that rushed. It experienced dizzy, unutterable alterations. Thousands of emotions, intense and varied, poured through me at lightning speed, each satisfyingly known, yet gone before its name appeared. The life of many centuries tore headlong back with me, and, as in drowning, this epitome of existence shot in a few seconds the steep slopes the Past had so laboriously built up. The changes flashed and passed. I wept and prayed and worshipped; I loved and suffered; I battled, lost and won. Down the gigantic scale of ages that telescoped thus into a few brief moments, the soul in me went sliding backwards towards a motionless, reposeful Past.

I remember foolish details that interrupted the immense descent—I put on coat and hat; I remember some one's words, strangely sounding as when some bird wakes up and sings at midnight—'We'll take the little door; the front one's locked by now'; and I have a vague recollection of the outline of the great hotel, with its colonnades and terraces, fading behind me through the air. But these details merely flickered and disappeared, as though I fell earthwards from a star and passed feathers or blown leaves upon the way. There was no friction as my soul dropped backwards into time; the flight was easy and silent as a dream. I felt myself sucked down into gulfs whose emptiness offered no resistance . . . until at last the appalling speed decreased of its own accord, and the dizzy flight became a kind of gentle floating. It changed imperceptibly into a gliding motion, as though the angle altered. My feet, quite naturally, were on the ground, moving through something soft that clung to them and rustled while it clung.

I looked up and saw the bright armies of the stars. In front of me I recognised the flat-topped, shadowy ridges; on both sides lay the open expanses of familiar wilderness; and beside me, one on either hand, moved two figures who were my companions. We were in the desert, but it was the desert of thousands of years ago. My companions, moreover, though familiar to some part of me, seemed strangers or half known. Their names I strove in vain to capture; Mosely, Ilson, sounded in my head, mingled together falsely. And when I stole a glance at them, I saw dark lines of mannikins unfilled with substance, and was aware of the grotesque gestures of living hieroglyphics. It seemed for an instant that their arms were bound behind their backs impossibly, and that their heads turned sharply across their lineal shoulders.

But for a moment only; for at a second glance I saw them solid and compact; their names came back to me; our arms were linked together as we walked. We had already covered a great distance, for my limbs were aching and my breath was short. The air was cold, the silence absolute. It seemed, in this faint light, that the desert flowed beneath our feet, rather than that we advanced by taking steps. Cliffs with hooded tops moved past us, boulders glided, mounds of sand slid by. And then I heard a voice upon my left that was surely Moleson speaking:

'Towards Enet our feet are set,' he half sang, half murmured, 'towards Enet-te-ntōrē.* There, in the House of Birth, we shall dedicate our hearts and lives anew.'

And the language, no less than the musical intonation of his voice, enraptured me. For I understood he spoke of Denderah, in whose majestic temple recent hands had painted with deathless colours the symbols of our cosmic relationships with the zodiacal signs. And Denderah was our great seat of worship of the goddess Hathor, the Egyptian Aphrodite, bringer of love and joy. The falcon-headed Horus was her husband, from whom, in his home at Edfu, we imbibed swift kinds of power. And—it was the time of the New Year, the great feast when the forces of the living earth turn upwards into happy growth.

We were on foot across the desert towards Denderah, and this sand we trod was the sand of thousands of years ago.

The paralysis of time and distance involved some amazing lightness of the spirit that, I suppose, touched ecstasy. There was intoxication in the soul. I was not divided from the stars, nor separate from this desert that rushed with us. The unhampered wind blew freshly from my nerves and skin, and the Nile, glimmering faintly on our right, lay with its lapping waves in both my hands. I knew the life of Egypt, for it was in me, over me, round me. I was a part of it. We went happily, like birds to meet the sunrise. There were no pits of measured time and interval that could detain us. We flowed, yet were at rest; we were endlessly alive; present and future alike were inconceivable; we were in the Kingdom of the Past.

The Pyramids were just a-building, and the army of Obelisks looked about them, proud of their first balance; Thebes swung her hundred gates upon the world. New, shining Memphis glittered with myriad reflections into waters that the tears of Isis sweetened, and the cliffs of Abou Simbel were still innocent of their gigantic progeny. Alone, the Sphinx, linking timelessness with time, brooded unguessed and underived upon an alien world. We marched within antiquity towards Denderah. . . .

How long we marched, how fast, how far we went, I can remember as little as the marvellous speech that passed across me while my two companions spoke together. I only remember that suddenly a wave of pain disturbed my wondrous happiness and caused my calm, which had seemed beyond all reach of break, to fall away. I heard their voices abruptly with a kind of terror. A sensation of fear, of loss, of nightmare bewilderment came over me like cold wind. What *they* lived naturally, true to their inmost hearts, *I* lived merely by means of a temperamental sympathy. And the stage had come at which my powers failed. Exhaustion overtook me. I wilted. The strain—the abnormal backwards stretch of consciousness that was put upon me by another—gave way and broke. I heard their voices faint and horrible. My joy was extinguished. A glare of horror fell upon the desert and the stars seemed evil. An anguishing desire for the safe and wholesome Present usurped all this mad yearning to obtain the Past. My feet fell out of step. The rushing of the desert paused. I unlinked my arms. We stopped all three.

The actual spot is to this day well known to me. I found it afterwards, I even photographed it. It lies actually not far from Helouan— a few miles at most beyond the Solitary Palm, where slopes of undulating sand mark the opening of a strange, enticing valley called the Wadi Gerraui. And it is enticing because it beckons and leads on. Here, amid torn gorges of a limestone wilderness, there is suddenly soft yellow sand that flows and draws the feet onward. It slips away with one too easily; always the next ridge and basin must be seen, each time a little farther. It has the quality of decoying. The cliffs say, No; but this streaming sand invites. In its flowing curves of gold there is enchantment.

And it was here upon its very lips we stopped, the rhythm of our steps broken, our hearts no longer one. My temporary rapture vanished. I was aware of fear. For the Present rushed upon me with attack in it, and I felt that my mind was arrested close upon the edge of madness. Something cleared and lifted in my brain.

The soul, indeed, could 'choose its dwelling-place'; but to live else-where completely was the choice of madness, and to live divorced from all the sweet wholesome business of To-day involved an exile that was worse than madness. It was death. My heart burned for George Isley. I remembered the tear upon his cheek. The agony of his struggle I shared suddenly with him. Yet with him was the reality, with me a sympathetic reflection merely. *He* was already too far gone to fight. . . .

I shall never forget the desolation of that strange scene beneath the morning stars. The desert lay down and watched us. We stood upon the brink of a little broken ridge, looking into the valley of golden sand. This sand gleamed soft and wonderful in the starlight some twenty feet below. The descent was easy—but I would not move. I refused to advance another step. I saw my companions in the mys-terious half-light beside me peering over the edge, Moleson in front a little.

And I turned to him, sure of the part I meant to play, yet conscious painfully of my helplessness. My personality seemed a straw in mid-stream that spun in a futile effort to arrest the flood that bore it. There was vivid human conflict in the moment's silence. It was an eddy that paused in the great body of the tide. And then I spoke. Oh, I was ashamed of the insignificance of my voice and the weakness of my little personality.

'Moleson, we go no farther with you. We have already come too far. We now turn back.'

Behind my words were a paltry thirty years. His answer drove sixty centuries against me. For his voice was like the wind that passed whis-pering down the stream of yellow sand below us. He smiled.

'Our feet are set towards Ēnet-te-ntōrē. There is no turning back. Listen! It is calling, calling, calling!'

'We will go home,' I cried, in a tone I vainly strove to make imperative.

'Our home is there,' he sang, pointing with one long thin arm towards the brightening east, 'for the Temple calls us and the River takes our feet. We shall be in the House of Birth to meet the sunrise——'

'You lie,' I cried again, 'you speak the lies of madness, and this Past you seek is the House of Death. It is the kingdom of the underworld.'

The words tore wildly, impotently out of me. I seized George Isley's arm.

'Come back with me,' I pleaded vehemently, my heart aching with a nameless pain for him. 'We'll retrace our steps. Come home with me! Come back! Listen! The Present calls you sweetly!'

His arm slipped horribly out of my grasp that had seemed to hold it so tightly. Moleson, already below us in the yellow sand, looked small with distance. He was gliding rapidly farther with uncanny swiftness. The diminution of his form was ghastly. It was like a doll's. And his voice rose up, faint as with the distance of great gulfs of space.

'Calling . . . calling. . . . You hear it for ever calling . . .'

It died away with the wind along that sandy valley, and the Past swept in a flood across the brightening sky. I swayed as though a storm was at my back. I reeled. Almost I went too—over the crumbling edge into the sand.

'Come back with me! Come home!' I cried more faintly. 'The Present alone is real. There is work, ambition, duty. There is beauty too—the beauty of good living! And there is love! There is—a woman . . . calling, calling . . . !'

That other voice took up the word below me. I heard the faint refrain sing down the sandy walls. The wild, sweet pang in it was marvellous.

'Our feet are set for Enet-te-ntōrē. It is calling, calling . . . !'

My voice fell into nothingness. George Isley was below me now, his outline tiny against the sheet of yellow sand. And the sand was moving. The desert rushed again. The human figures receded swiftly into the Past they had reconstructed with the creative yearning of their souls.

I stood alone upon the edge of crumbling limestone, helplessly watching them. It was amazing what I witnessed, while the shafts of crimson dawn rose up the sky. The enormous desert turned alive to the horizon with gold and blue and silver. The purple shadows melted into grey. The flat-topped ridges shone. Huge messengers of light flashed everywhere at once. The radiance of sunrise dazzled my outer sight.

But if my eyes were blinded, my inner sight was focused the more clearly upon what followed. I witnessed the disappearance of George Isley. There was a dreadful magic in the picture. The pair of them, small and distant below me in that little sandy hollow, stood out sharply defined as in a miniature. I saw their outlines neat and terrible like some ghastly inset against the enormous scenery. Though so close to me in actual space, they were centuries away in time. And a dim, vast shadow was about them that was not mere shadow of the ridges. It encompassed them; it moved, crawling over the sand, obliterating them. Within it, like insects lost in amber, they became visibly imprisoned, dwindled in size, borne deep away, absorbed.

And then I recognised the outline. Once more, but this time recumbent and spread flat upon the desert's face, I knew the monstrous shapes of the twin obsessing symbols. The spirit of ancient Egypt lay over all the land, tremendous in the dawn. The sunrise summoned her. She lay prostrate before the deity. The shadows of the towering Colossi lay prostrate too. The little humans, with their worshipping and conquered hearts, lay deep within them. George Isley I saw clearest. The distinctness, the reality were appalling. He was naked, robbed, undressed. I saw him a skeleton, picked clean to the very bones as by an acid. His life lay hid in the being of that mighty Past. Egypt had absorbed him. He was gone. . . .

I closed my eyes, but I could not keep them closed. They opened of their own accord. The three of us were nearing the great hotel that rose yellow, with shuttered windows, in the early sunshine. A wind blew briskly from the north across the Mokattam Hills. There were soft cannon-ball clouds dotted about the sky, and across the Nile, where the mist lay in a line of white, I saw the tops of the Pyramids gleaming like mountain peaks of gold. A string of camels, laden with white stone, went past us. I heard the crying of the natives in the streets of Helouan, and as we went up the steps the donkeys arrived and camped in the sandy road beside their *bersim** till the tourists claimed them.

'Good morning,' cried Abdullah, the man who owned them. 'You all go Sakkhara to-day, or Memphis? Beat'ful day to-day, and vair good donkeys!'

Moleson went up to his room without a word, and Isley did the same. I thought he staggered a moment as he turned the passage corner from my sight. His face wore a look of vacancy that some call peace. There was radiance in it. It made me shudder. Aching in mind and body, and no word spoken, I followed their example. I went upstairs to bed, and slept a dreamless sleep till after sunset. . . .

XIV

AND I woke with a lost, unhappy feeling that a withdrawing tide had left me on the shore, alone and desolate. My first instinct was for my friend, George Isley. And I noticed a square, white envelope with my name upon it in his writing.

Before I opened it I knew quite well what words would be inside:

'We are going up to Thebes,' the note informed me simply. 'We leave by the night train. If you care to——' But the last four words were scratched out again, though not so thickly that I could not read them. Then came the address of the Egyptologist's house and the signature, very firmly traced, 'Yours ever, GEORGE ISLEY.' I glanced at my watch and saw that it was after seven o'clock. The night train left at half-past six. They had already started. . . .

The pain of feeling forsaken, left behind, was deep and bitter, for myself; but what I felt for him, old friend and comrade, was even more intense, since it was hopeless. Fear and conventional emotion had stopped me at the very gates of an amazing possibility—some state of consciousness that, *realising* the Past, might doff the Present, and by slipping out of Time, experience Eternity. That was the seduction I had escaped by the uninspired resistance of my pettier soul. Yet, he, my friend, yielding in order to conquer, had obtained an awful prize—ah, I understood the picture's other side as well, with an unutterable poignancy of pity—the prize of immobility which is sheer stagnation, the imagined bliss which is a false escape, the dream of finding beauty away from present things. From that dream the awakening must be rude indeed. Clutching at vanished stars, he had clutched the oldest illusion in the world. To me it seemed the negation of life that had betrayed him. The pity of it burned me like a flame.

But I did not 'care to follow' him and his companion. I waited at Helouan for his return, filling the empty days with yet emptier explanations. I felt as a man who sees what he loves sinking down into clear, deep water, still within visible reach, yet gone beyond recovery. Moleson had taken him back to Thebes; and Egypt, monstrous effigy of the Past, had caught her prey.

The rest, moreover, is easily told. Moleson I never saw again. To this day I have never seen him, though his subsequent books are known to me, with the banal fact that he is numbered with those energetic and deluded enthusiasts who start a new religion, obtain notoriety, a few hysterical followers and—oblivion.

George Isley, however, returned to Helouan after a fortnight's absence. I saw him, knew him, talked and had my meals with him. We even did slight expeditions together. He was gentle and delightful as a woman who has loved a wonderful ideal and attained to it—in memory. All roughness was gone out of him; he was smooth and polished as a crystal surface that reflects whatever is near enough to ask a picture. Yet his appearance shocked me inexpressibly: there was nothing in him—*nothing*. It was the representation of George Isley that came back from Thebes; the outer simulacra; the shell that walks the London streets to-day. I met no vestige of the man I used to know. George Isley had disappeared.

With this marvellous automaton I lived another month. The horror of him kept me company in the hotel where he moved among the cosmopolitan humanity as a ghost that visits the sunlight yet has its home elsewhere.

This empty image of George Isley lived with me in our Helouan hotel until the winds of early March informed his physical frame that discomfort was in the air, and that he might as well move elsewhere—elsewhere happening to be northwards.

And he left just as he stayed—automatically. His brain obeyed the conventional stimuli to which his nerves, and consequently his muscles, were accustomed. It sounds so foolish. But he took his ticket automatically; he gave the natural and adequate reasons automatically; he chose his ship and landing-place in the same way that ordinary people chose these things; he said good-bye like any other man who leaves casual acquaintances and 'hopes' to meet them again; he lived, that is to say, entirely in his brain. His heart, his emotions, his temperament and personality, that nameless sum total for which the great sympathetic nervous system is accountable—all this, his soul, had gone elsewhere. This once vigorous, gifted being had become a normal, comfortable man that everybody could understand—a commonplace nonentity. He was precisely what the majority expected him to be—ordinary; a good fellow; a man of the world; he was 'delightful.' He merely reflected daily life without partaking of it. To the majority it was hardly noticeable; 'very pleasant' was a general verdict. His ambition, his restlessness, his zeal had gone; that tireless zest whose driving power is yearning had taken flight, leaving behind it physical energy without spiritual desire. His soul had found its nest and flown to it. He lived in the chimera of the Past, serene, indifferent, detached. I saw him immense, a shadowy, majestic figure, standing— ah, not moving!—in a repose that was satisfying because it *could* not change. The size, the mystery, the immobility that caged him in seemed to me—terrible. For I dared not intrude upon his awful privacy, and intimacy between us there was none. Of his experiences at Thebes I asked no single question—it was somehow not possible or legitimate; he, equally, vouchsafed no word of explanation—it was uncommunicable to a dweller in the Present. Between us was this barrier we both respected. He peered at modern life, incurious, listless, apathetic, through a dim, gauze curtain. He was behind it.

People round us were going to Sakkhâra and the Pyramids, to see the Sphinx by moonlight, to dream at Edfu and at Denderah. Others described their journeys to Assouan, Khartoum and Abou Simbel, and gave details of their encampments in the desert. Wind, wind, wind! The winds of Egypt blew and sang and sighed. From the White Nile came the travellers, and from the Blue Nile, from the Fayum,* and from nameless excavations without end. They talked and wrote their books. They had the magpie knowledge of the present. The Egyptologists, big and little, read the writing on the wall and put the hieroglyphs and papyri into modern language. Alone George Isley *knew* the secret. He lived it.

And the high passionate calm, the lofty beauty, the glamour and enchantment that are the spell of this thrice-haunted land, were in *my* soul as well—sufficiently for me to interpret his condition. I could not leave, yet having left I could not stay away. I yearned for the Egypt that he knew. No word I uttered; speech could not approach it. We wandered by the Nile together, and through the groves of palms that once were Memphis. The sandy wastes beyond the Pyramids knew our footsteps; the Mokattam Ridges, purple at evening and golden in the dawn, held our passing shadows as we silently went by. At no single dawn or sunset was he to be found indoors, and it became my habit to accompany him—the joy of worship in his soul was marvellous. The great, still skies of Egypt watched us, the hanging stars, the gigantic dome of blue; we felt together that burning southern wind; the golden sweetness of the sun lay in our blood as we saw the great boats take the northern breeze upstream. Immensity was everywhere and this golden magic of the sun. . . .

But it was in the Desert especially, where only sun and wind observe the faint signalling of Time, where space is nothing because it is not divided, and where no detail reminds the heart that the world is called To-Day—it was in the desert this curtain hung most visibly between us, he on that side, I on this. It was transparent. He was with a multitude no man can number. Towering to the moon, yet spreading backwards towards his burning source of life, drawn out by the sun and by the crystal air into some vast interior magnitude, the spirit of George Isley hung beside me, close yet far away, in the haze of olden days.

And, sometimes, he moved. I was aware of gestures. His head was raised to listen. One arm swung shadowy across the sea of broken ridges. From leagues away a line of sand rose slowly. There was a rustling. Another—an enormous—arm emerged to meet his own, and two stupendous figures drew together. Poised above Time, yet throned upon the centuries, They knew eternity. So easily they remained possessors of the land. Facing the east, they waited for the dawn. And their marvellously forgotten singing poured across the world. . . .

ONANONANON

CERTAIN things had made a deep impression in his childhood days; among these was the incident of the barking dog.

It barked during his convalescence from something that involved scarlet and a peeling skin;* his early mind associated bright colour and peeling skin with the distress of illness. The tiresome barking of a dog accompanied it. In later years this sound always brought back the childhood visualization: across his mind would flit a streak of vivid colour, a peeling skin, a noisy dog, all set against a background of emotional discomfort and physical distress.

'It's barking at *me*!' he complained to his old nurse, whose explanation that it was 'Carlo with his rheumatics in the stables' brought no relief. He spoke to his mother later: 'It never, never stops. It goes on and on and on on purpose—onanonanon!'

How queer the words sounded! He had got them wrong somewhere—onanonanon. Or was it a name, the name of the barking animal—Onan Onan Onanonanon?

His mother's words were more comforting; 'Carlo's barking because you're ill, darling; he wants you to get well.' And she added: 'Soon I'll bring him in to see you. You shall ride on his back again.'

'Would he peel if I stroked him?' he enquired, a trifle frightened. 'Is the skin shiny like mine?'

She shook her head and smiled. 'I'll explain to him,' she went on, 'and then he'll understand. He won't bark any more.' She brought the picture-book of natural history that included all creatures in Ark and Zoo and Jungle. He picked out the brightly-coloured tiger.

'A *tiger* doesn't bark, does it?' he asked, and her reply added slightly to his knowledge, but much to his imagination. 'But does it ever *bark?*' he persisted. 'That's really what I asked.'

'Growls and snarls,' said a deep voice from the doorway. He started; but it was only his father, who then came in and amused him by imitating the sound a tiger makes, until Carlo's naughtiness was forgotten, and the world went on turning smoothly as before.

After that the barking ceased; the rheumatic creature sniffed the air and nosed the metal biscuit tray in silence. He understood apparently. It had been rather dreadful, this noise he made. The sharp sound had broken the morning stillness for many days; no one but the boy was awake at that early hour; the boy and the dog had the dawn entirely to themselves. He used to lie in bed, counting the number of barks. They seemed endless, they jarred, they never stopped. They came singly, then in groups of three and four at a time, then in a longer series, then singly again. These single barks often had a sound of finality about them, the creature's breath was giving out, it was tired; it was the full-stop sound. But the true full-stop, the final bark, never came—and the boy had complained.

He loved old Carlo, loved riding on his burly back that wobbled from side to side, as they moved forward very slowly; in particular he loved stroking the thick curly hair; it tickled his fingers and felt nice on his palm. He was relieved to know it would not peel. Yet he wondered impatiently why the creature he loved to play with should go on making such a dreadful noise. 'Doesn't he know? Can't he wait till I'm ready?' There were moments when he doubted if it really was Carlo, when he almost hated the beast, when he asked himself, 'Is this Carlo, or is it Onanonanon . . .?' The idea alarmed him rather. Onanonanon was not quite friendly, not quite safe.

At the age of fifty he found himself serving his King during the Great War* in a neutral country whose police regarded him with disfavour, and would have instantly arrested and clapped him into gaol, had he made a slip. He did not make this slip, though incessant caution had to be his watchword. He belonged to that service which runs risks yet dare claim no credit. He passed under another name than his own, and his *alias* sometimes did things his true self would not do. This *alter ego* developed oddly. He projected temporarily, as it were, a secondary personality—which he disliked, often despised, and sometimes even feared. His sense of humour, however, made light of the split involved. When he was followed, he used to chuckle: 'I wonder if the sleuths know which of the two they're tracking down—myself or my *alias*?'

It was in the melancholy season between autumn and winter, snow on the heights and fog upon the lower levels, when he was suddenly laid low by the plague that milked the world.* The Spanish influenza caught him. He went to bed; he had a doctor and a nurse; no one else in the hotel came near his room; the police forgot him, and he forgot the police. His hated *alias*, Baker* also was forgotten, or perhaps merged back into the parent self. . . . Outside his quarters on the first floor the plane-trees shed their heavy, rain-soaked leaves, letting them fall with an audible plop upon the gravel path; he heard the waves of the sullen lake in the distance; the crunching of passing feet he heard much closer. The heating was indifferent, the light too weak to read by. It was a lonely, dismal time. On the floor above two people died, three on the one below, the French officer next door was carried out. The hotel, like many others, became a hospital.

In due course, the fever passed, the intolerable aching ceased, he forgot the times when he had thought he was going to die. He lay, half convalescent, remembering the recent past, then the remoter past, and so slipped back to dim childhood scenes when the cross but faithful old nurse had tended him. He smelt the burning leaves in the kitchen-garden, and heard the blackbird whistle beyond the summer-house. The odour of moist earth in the tool-house stole back, with the fragrance of sweet apples in the forbidden loft. These earliest layers of memory fluttered their ghostly pictures like a cinema before his receptive mind. There were eyes long closed, voices long silent, the touch of hands long dead and gone. The rose-garden on a sultry August afternoon was vivid, with the smell of the rain-washed petals, as the sun blazed over them after a heavy shower. The soaked lawn emitted warm little bubbles like a soft squeezed sponge, audibly; even the gravel steamed. He remembered Carlo, with his rheumatism, his awkward gambol, his squashy dog-biscuit beside the kennel and— his bark.

In the state of semi-unconsciousness he lay, weary, weak, depressed and very lonely. The nurse, on her rare visits, afflicted him, the hotel guests did not ask after him. To the Service at home he was on the sick-list, useless. The morning newspaper and the hurried, perfunctory visits of the doctor were his only interest. It seemed a pity he had not died. The mental depression after influenza can be extremely devastating. He looked forward to nothing.

Then, suddenly, the dog began its barking.

He heard it first at six o'clock when, waking, hot and thirsty in a bed that had lost its comfort, he wondered vaguely if the day was going to be fine or wet. His window opened on to the lake. He watched the shadows melt across the dreary room. The late dawn came softly, its hint of beauty ever unfulfilled. Would it be gold or grey behind the mountains? The dog went on barking.

He dozed, counting the barks without being aware that he did so. He felt hot and uncomfortable, and turned over in bed, counting automatically as he did so: 'fifteen, sixteen, seventeen'—pause—'eighteen, nineteen'—another pause, then with great rapidity, 'twenty, twenty-one, twenty-two, twenty-three.' He opened his eyes wide and cursed aloud. The barking stopped.

The wind came softly off the lake, entering the room. He heard the last big leaf of the plane-trees rattle to the gravel path. As it touched the ground the barking began again, his counting—now conscious counting—began with it.

'Curse the brute!' he muttered, and turned over once more to try and sleep. The rasping, harsh, staccato sound reached his ears piercingly through sheets and blankets; not even the thick *duvet* could muffle it. Would no one stop it? Did no one care? He felt furious, but helpless, dreadfully helpless.

It barked, stopped, then barked again. There were solitary, isolated barks, followed by a rapid series, short and hurried. A shower of barks came next. Pauses were frequent, but they were worse than the actual sound. It continued, it went on, the dog barked without ceasing. It barked and barked. He had lost all count. It barked and barked and barked. It stopped.

'At last!' he groaned. 'My God! Another minute, and I——!'

His whole body, as he turned over, knew an immense, deep relaxation. His jangled nerves were utterly exhausted. A great sigh of relief escaped him. The silence was delicious. It was real silence. He rested at last. Sleep, warm and intoxicating, stole gently back. He dozed. Forgetfulness swam over him. He lay in down, in cotton-wool. Police, *alias*, nurse and loneliness were all obliterated, when, suddenly, across the blissful peace, cracked out that sharp, explosive sound again—the bark.

But the dog barked differently this time; the sound was much nearer. At first this puzzled him. Then he guessed the truth; the animal had come into the hotel and up the stairs; it was outside in the passage. He opened his eyes and sat up in bed. The door, to his surprise, was being cautiously pushed ajar. He was just in time to see who pushed it with such gentle, careful pressure. Standing on the landing in the early twilight was Baker, his other self, his *alias*, the personality he disliked and sometimes dreaded. Baker put his head round the corner, glanced at him, nodded familiarly, and withdrew, closing the door instantly, making no slightest sound. But, before it closed, and before he had time even to feel astonishment, the dog had been let in. And the dog, he saw at once, was old Carlo!

Having expected a little stranger dog, this big, shaggy, familiar beast caused him to feel a sense of curious wonder and bewilderment.

'But were *you* the dog down there that barked?' he asked aloud, as the friendly creature came waddling up to the bedside. 'And have you come to say you're sorry?'

It blinked its rheumy eyes and wagged its stumpy tail. He put out his hand and stroked its familiar, wobbly back. His fingers buried themselves in the stiff crinkly hair. Its dim old eyes turned affectionately up at him. It smiled its silly, happy smile. He went on rubbing. 'Carlo, good old Carlo!" he mumbled; 'well, I'm blessed! I'll get on your back in a minute and ride——'

He stopped rubbing. '*Why* did you come in?' he asked abruptly, and repeated the question, a touch of anxiety in his voice. 'How did you manage it, really? Tell me, Carlo?'

The old beast shifted its position a little, making a side-ways motion that he did not like. It seemed to move its hind legs only. Its muzzle now rested on the bed. Its eyes, seen full, looked not quite so kind and friendly. They cleared a little. But its tail still wagged. Only, now that he saw it better, the tail seemed longer than it ought to have been. There was something unpleasant about the dog—a faint inexplicable shade of difference. He stared a moment straight into its face. It no longer blinked in the silly, affectionate way as at first. The rheum was less. There was a light, a gleam, in the eyes, almost a flash.

'*Are* you—Carlo?' he asked sharply, uneasily, 'or are you— Onanonanon?'

It rose abruptly on its hind legs, laying the front paws on the counterpane of faded yellow. The legs made dark streaks against this yellow.

He had begun stroking the old back again. He now stopped. He withdrew his hand. The hair was coming out. It came off beneath his fingers, and each stroke he made left a line of lighter skin behind it. This skin was yellowish, with a slight tinge, he thought, of scarlet.

The dog—he could almost swear to it—had altered; it was still altering. Before his very eyes, it grew, became curiously enlarged. It now towered over him. It was longer, thinner, leaner than before, its tail came lashing round its hollow, yellowing flanks, the eyes shone brilliantly, its tongue was a horrid red. The brute straightened its front paws. It was huge. Its open mouth grinned down at him.

He was petrified with terror. He tried to scream, but the only sound that came were little innocent words of childhood days. He almost lisped them, simpering with horror: 'I'd get on your back—if I was allowed out of bed. You'd carry me. I'd ride.'

It was a desperate attempt to pacify the beast, to persuade it, even in this terrible moment, to be friendly, a feeble, hopeless attempt to convince *himself* that it was—Carlo. The Monster was twelve feet from head to tail, of dull yellow striped with black. The great jaws, wide open, dripped upon his face. He saw the pointed teeth, the stiff, quivering whiskers of white wire. He felt the hot breath upon his cheeks and lips. It was foetid. He tasted it.

He was on the point of fainting when a step sounded outside the door. Someone was coming.

'Saved!' he gasped.

The suspense and relief were almost intolerable. The touch of a hand feeling cautiously, stealthily, over the door was audible. The handle rattled faintly.

'Saved!' his heart repeated, as the great brute turned its giant head to listen.

He knew that touch. It was Baker, his hated *alias*, come in the nick of time to rescue him. Yet the door did not open. Instead, the monster lashed its tail, it stiffened horribly, it turned its head back from watching the door, and lowered itself appallingly. The key turned in the lock, a bolt was shot. He was locked in alone with a tiger. He closed his eyes.

His recurrent nightmare had ruined sleep again, and outside, in the dreary autumn dawn, a little dog was yapping fiendishly on and on and on and on.

THE LAND OF GREEN GINGER*

IN his luxurious service flat* the elderly Mr Adam sat before the fire with a frown upon his face, a frown not of anger or annoyance but of perplexity. It was the cosy time between tea and dinner; about his armchair lay scattered a number of opened and unopened letters; he was scanning a brief typewritten note, wondering how he should deal with it, and this wonder was the cause of his frown.

'These newspaper symposiums,'* he grumbled to himself, 'are a nuisance!' His secretary had gone home, taking away with her the dictated chapters of his book, his twentieth novel—his twentieth *successful* novel, he remembered with a smile that momentarily displaced the frown. '"How I started,"' he read the typed sentence before him. '"What made me first begin to write?"' The frown came back. Thought ran off into the mists of years ago. . . . He remembered quite well what made him first begin to write. 'But no one would believe me. . . .' His face grew quite puckered. . . . He finally decided he would dictate in the morning a few commonplace paragraphs, giving facts, of course, yet not this queer incident that had first discovered his gift to himself. It had been due to a shock, this discovery; and a shock, some say, can bring out latent possibilities in the mind hitherto ignored. Circumstances, that is, are necessary for their appearance; unless life produces them, the possibilities remain unknown, inactive.

He remembered the shock in his own case, the queer experience it produced, and the first hint of his imaginative gift that appeared as a result. 'But they'd think I was romancing!' His pencil, meanwhile, scribbled a few words on the blank part of the letter. . . .

'It is interesting,' he paused a moment to reflect, 'how every important detail of the experience was due to something in my mind at the time. All the ingredients were in me. Something just used them, dramatized them. That's the imaginative gift, I suppose. . . . It shapes the raw material.'

He could see it all as though it were yesterday . . . instead of thirty years ago. . . .

The shock, in his case, had been the sudden total loss of the comfortable fortune he had been brought up to expect. The trustee, his guardian, had played ducks and drakes with it, and at twenty, an orphan, just down from Oxford with a prospect of £2,000 a year, he found himself instead with £50, perhaps less. Two details only bear importantly upon the story: his intense bitterness against the swindling guardian, whom he knew personally, and the question of what he could do to earn his living. These two, had he written the truth for the symposium, Mr Adam would have stressed. For it was with these two, this thought and this feeling burning intensely in his mind, that he had gone for a walk to think things over. . . .

To him, at the age of twenty, the situation seemed intensely tragic; no one in the world before had ever been so overwhelmed by fate; his anger against the psalm-singing guardian was of that bitter kind that could have killed. The young man was stirred to an intense anger and hatred. He could have murdered Mr Holyoake. The swindler deserved it. And Adam, dwelling upon the years of dishonest speculation that had left him penniless, meant this precisely. Not that he actually wanted to commit murder, but that he realized the possibility lay in him. He still remembered—with a smile to-day—how he finally dismissed the idea from his mind: 'What's the use?' he had reflected bitterly. 'Even if I did murder him, the State would only murder me in return. I should be hanged. Who murders is murdered in his turn.'

In this way the notion was—as he believed—dismissed from his mind.

The other 'important detail' concerned his immediate future. What could he do to earn his living? He dwelt upon it with eager concentration. He reviewed a dozen futures: the stage, journalism, the motor trade, then in its infancy; insurance, emigrating—he thought of many fields and callings, but realized he was trained for none. The choice of work, of something that he *could* do, troubled him obsessingly. There were a hundred, a thousand, possible futures open to a fellow, he discovered. It was the choice that he found impossible. At a given moment in anybody's life, he reflected, a number of possible things lie waiting—he can take only one, but the multiple choice is there.

He had been walking for some time, and in a circle apparently, for he now found himself wandering toward the water-front of the ancient port that was his home town. It was after six o'clock on a summer evening, a Saturday, and few people were about. The sunshine fell slanting down the tangle of deserted alleyways. There was a smell of the sea, of tarred ropes, rigging, fish, and these brought back the idea of emigrating. He thought of a cousin who had just gone to some job or other in China. . . . One notion chased another; his mind was a seething mass of wild ideas, with bitter, turbulent emotion behind them. Then, glancing up, his eye caught suddenly five little words, whose faded black letters shone in a patch of sunshine on the dull brick wall above his head. They were rather romantic little words, and they snatched at something in his mind. He stood and stared. It was merely the name of the alley, of course, yet thought took a new turn. A kind of enchantment stole over him, for the words, as the poet puts it, walked up and down in his heart. . . . There rose before him a picture of forgotten days when the old port traded with Southern isles, when dark-bearded sailors gabbling foreign tongues thronged these narrow alleyways, and the high romance of gallant sailing-ships was in the air. . . . The five little words were almost a line of poetry.

'The Land of Green Ginger,' was what he read.

Mr Adam, the young one of thirty years ago, paused, his eyes fastened on the faded lettering in the yellow sunlight. Then he stared down the twisting alley, whose high walls now housed nothing more romantic than offices of ship-brokers, notaries, typists, packers, and commissioners of oaths, until his eyes noted suddenly an exception—an old-furniture shop, with its queer wares overflowing on to the narrow pavement. They were a heterogeneous collection apparently. A circular mirror standing on a three-legged pedestal nearly six feet high reflected his figure as he moved idly toward the shop a few yards lower down. He saw himself reflected, not without satisfaction, his smart flannel suit, his eyeglass, his straw hat with its Oxford colours.* He also saw a bent, thin little old man with a skull-cap on his head standing among the shadows a few feet inside beyond the dingy doorway.

This figure now moved slowly toward him, scenting perhaps a possible customer.

'A fine piece,' said the wheezy voice. 'A perfect bit of glass, me lord! Cheap, too!' He rubbed his hands, nodding his ancient head in the direction of the article. 'It come from Chiney thirty year ago!'

Adam realized that he had been examining his own reflection for some minutes. He entered the shop, as an escape from troubling thoughts more than anything else, and as he did so the old man, bowing and scraping, moved, too, backing away before him. The interior was dark, and much larger than the small entrance promised. A single oil-lamp revealed a series of deep, narrow rooms, cluttered up with stuff, among which the bent figure now set down the mirror carefully, for he had carried it in with him.

In the dimness the young man found his own reflection more attractive than before: it was softened, more effective, he decided. The wheezy voice was mentioning a price, rather a trumpery price, considered Mr Adam, a few shillings only. He did not want to buy it, but anything was better than being alone with his tormenting thoughts, and he went closer to examine it. He bent down, noticing an inscription cut deeply into the dark wood of the framework. It was in Chinese characters. He ran his finger over them, then looked up to ask.

'*Who looks in me,*' translated the wheezy voice, '*murders—and is murdered.*' And, carrying the mirror with him, the old man retreated a little further into the shadow of the room beyond.

The young man was startled. He felt his body give an imperceptible twitch he was unable to suppress. His mind likewise gave a twitch. Was it uneasiness? It was, at any rate, surprise, while at the same time he was aware that something drew him, so that, almost involuntarily, he found himself following the retreating figure, who now, still carrying the mirror with him, was on the threshold of the next long room. It was the third extension of the premises, and it was considerably darker than the first two rooms. A chilliness hung in the fusty atmosphere. The place seemed lonely suddenly.

Aware of a faint tremor in him, though not yet of anything more than that, he spoke in a brusque, almost an aggressive, voice.

'And what may such rubbish mean?' he inquired sharply.

'Precisely what it says, me lord,' came the wheezy voice, much lower than before. There was an unpleasant hush in it. And there came a look into the face that hardly invited merriment, which was, perhaps, the very reason why Mr Adam chose the moment for an audible guffaw. It betrayed him, he realized, when it was too late. He felt nervous. More of a chuckle than an actual laugh, it sounded unnatural among this piled-up paraphernalia from foreign lands that gave back no single echo. It sounded dead.

'Does it hold good?' Mr Adam challenged, the tone of his voice again betraying him—to himself at least. For the tremor crept somehow from the body into the sound. 'If I buy the thing, for instance, d'you mean to tell me that *I*—that *you* already before me——?'

He could not finish the sentence. A shudder stopped his breath, and the voice died on his lips. While speaking he had been looking, not into the old man's face, but into the mirror, where he still saw his own reflection. But it was not this that stopped his speech and froze his blood. It was something else he saw. With one wrinkled hand the old shopman still clutched the pedestal; in the other was an unsheathed knife.

'So far, me lord, it has held good,' came his whisper down the long, dim room, and as he spoke he tilted the mirror to a slightly different angle. The young man saw himself in the glass as before, but he now saw something else behind him, too. It lay stretched upon the floor, motionless, crumpled dreadfully, its position not quite natural. One arm was twisted about the face at an angle not possible to life. In the narrow fairway of the room behind him, the room he had already passed, this pitiful, repulsive body lay. To stand where he now stood, the young man realized, he must actually have stepped over it.

'*You*—did—that?' he gasped, in a voice that emitted hardly any sound.

'He looked in the mirror,' came the whispered answer. 'What d'you expect?'

'And before that—*he* in turn——?'

'It works that way,' the other gave with an awful grin.

Adam felt his body stiffen; yet the blood began to flow in tumult. He felt his fists clench tightly. With his eye fixed on the shop-man and not leaving him for a single instant, he saw that the old man, letting go of the mirror, had begun to dodge. Light-footed he was, amazingly agile, quick, his movements convulsive, horribly alert. He dodged sideways, backwards, swift as a shadow round his customer, who watched the hideous dance with arrested muscles and with spell-bound eyes. The knife gleamed and flashed.

Adam made an effort that seemed to wrench his heart—and the muscles began to function again. Instinctively he picked up a heavy iron mace from a teak-wood table close beside him. With a strain he could just lift it.

'It's up to *me* then, now—is it?' he cried, his own feet shifting quickly.

'I can defend meself!' shrieked the shopman, dodging with incredible rapidity. 'If *that's* any good to you, me lord!' he yelled, shooting across the floor as an arrow flies, and brandishing the knife.

Moved by a sudden power that surprised himself, the young man leaped toward the pirouetting horror. He made one bound. He swung his heavy mace. The great weapon crashed down upon the ancient skull, driving the cap deep into the split bone. The figure stopped abruptly, uttered a tiny squeak, crumpled, and lay like a great mutilated insect where it fell. It did not move again.

'Murders and *is* murdered!' the other tried to scream, his voice, as in extreme nightmare agony, making no sound upon the air. 'I've done *you* in, at any rate. Then it's *my* turn next, is it——?'

He turned swiftly, with the feeling that someone watched him from behind.

A tall figure, sure enough, darkened the distant door into the street, the outline of a stranger who bent a little to examine something that stood upon the pavement just outside. The young man stared and stared. Though in semi-darkness himself, the outline was clearly defined in the evening light. But was it a stranger? He wore a smart flannel suit, a straw hat with Oxford colours. As he straightened up, an eyeglass became visible.

Mr Adam shot round and stared at the crumpled heap upon the floor at his feet. It was *not* the shopman. What he stared down at wore a neat flannel suit, a straw hat with Oxford colours.

He shrieked. He raced headlong down the room. He darted at top speed along the next narrow room as well, straight toward the street door, toward the stranger with the tall outline. And this tall outline now came gliding to meet him, very swiftly gliding, silently too, making no sound upon the boarded floor, just as he had seen his own reflected image gliding toward himself in the mirror before. Closer it came and closer, something oddly, dreadfully familiar about it, something that he almost recognized. It came remorselessly nearer, he could not have stopped it if he tried, while, curiously, he felt that he did not want to, even *must* not, stop it. Like Fate—his own fate—he must meet it; he could not avoid it—because he somehow welcomed it.

He did not pause himself; he even moved faster, till there was but a foot between them. Terrified he was, yet at the same time his courage rose. They met, they slipped into one another, they emerged, and instantaneously though this came about, he had time to recognize— himself . . . and that same second to find himself standing on the pavement outside, gazing at a mirror on a high three-legged pedestal, while a little, thin, bent old man faced him, wearing a skull-cap and rubbing his hands. It was the shopman evidently, scenting a possible customer.

'A fine piece,' the old man wheezed. His eyes pierced like gimlets. 'And cheap, too. It come from Chiney thirty year ago.'

A wave of pleasant, even delightful, emotion fluttered through the young man's heart as he bent to read an inscription carved in Chinese characters upon the wooden frame. He ran his finger over them, then looked up to ask.

'*To each*,' the wheezy voice translated, '*ten thousand futures. Yet each must choose*,' and went on to explain how a learned gentleman had once kindly deciphered the words for him—only the young man was no longer listening. He was staring intently at the upper part of the frame.

'But—the frame's empty!' he cried aloud. 'There *is* no mirror!' And again that marvellous emotion passed fluttering across his heart.

'It got broke,' he heard the wheezy voice explaining, 'got broke on the vige over. But it's easy put in again, me lord. A fine old piece.' He mentioned a trumpery price, a few shillings merely.

Young Mr Adam bought it and took it home with him. . . . In due course he entered his cousin's insurance office as a clerk, and one evening he scribbled an account of his adventure in the Land of Green Ginger. Later, he wrote other, longer adventures, too. He had inside him, it seems, some queer gift of scribbling imaginary, possibly imaginative, adventures. . . . A shock had brought it to the surface.

Next morning the elderly Mr Adam dictated to his secretary a few commonplace paragraphs about 'How I started to write.' They began: 'At the age of twenty I entered an insurance office as a clerk. . . .' They were extremely dull. 'Send it to the editor,' he told his secretary, 'with a line to say I hope it is what he wants; he need not use it otherwise, of course.' And as he dictated the paragraphs his eye wandered from a long shelf, holding some twenty adventure books, to a mirror on a high three-legged pedestal which, oddly, had no glass, and which, the elderly Mr Adam knew, had never had one, nor ever would.

THE DOLL

SOME nights are merely dark, others are dark in a suggestive way as though something ominous, mysterious, is going to happen. In certain remote outlying suburbs, at any rate, this seems true, where great spaces between the lamps go dead at night, where little happens, where a ring at the door is a summons almost, and people cry 'Let's go to town!' In the villa gardens the mangey cedars sigh in the wind, but the hedges stiffen, there is a muffling of spontaneous activity.

On this particular November night a moist breeze barely stirred the silver pine in the narrow drive leading to the 'Laurels' where Colonel Masters lived, Colonel Hymber Masters, late of an Indian regiment, with many distinguished letters after his name. The house-maid in the limited staff being out, it was the cook who answered the bell when it rang with a sudden, sharp clang soon after ten o'clock—and gave an audible gasp half of surprise, half of fear. The bell's sudden clangour was an unpleasant and unwelcome sound. Monica, the Colonel's adored yet rather neglected child, was asleep upstairs, but the cook was not frightened lest Monica be disturbed, nor because it seemed a bit late for the bell to ring so violently; she was frightened because when she opened the door to let the fine rain drive in she saw a black man standing on the steps. There, in the wind and the rain, stood a tall, slim nigger holding a parcel.

Dark-skinned, at any rate, he was, she reflected afterwards, whether negro, hindu or arab; the word 'nigger' describing any man not really white. Wearing a stained yellow macintosh and dirty slouch hat, and 'looking like a devil, so help me God,' he shoved the little parcel at her out of the gloom, the light from the hall flaring red into his gleaming eyes. 'For Colonel Masters,' he whispered rapidly, 'and very special into his own personal touch and no one else.' And he melted away into the night with his 'strange foreign accent, his eyes of fire, and his nasty hissing voice.'

He was gone, swallowed up in the wind and rain.

'But I saw his eyes,' swore the cook the next morning to the house-maid, 'his fiery eyes, and his nasty look, and his black hands and long thin fingers, and his nails all shiny pink, and he looked to me—if you know wot I mean—he looked like—death. . . .'

Thus the cook, so far as she was intelligently articulate next day, but standing now against the closed door with the small brown paper parcel in her hands, impressed by the orders that it was to be given into his personal touch, she was relieved by the fact that Colonel Masters never returned till after midnight and that she need not act at once. The reflection brought a certain comfort that restored her equanimity a little though she still stood there, holding the parcel gingerly in her grimy hands, reluctant, hesitating, uneasy. A parcel, even brought by a mysterious dark stranger, was not in itself frightening, yet frightened she certainly felt. Instinct and superstition worked perhaps; the wind, the rain, the fact of being alone in the house, the unexpected black man, these also contributed to her discomfort. A vague sense of horror touched her, her Irish blood stirred ancient dreams, so that she began to shake a little, as though the parcel contained something alive, explosive, poisonous, unholy almost as though it moved, and, her fingers loosening their hold, the parcel—dropped. It fell on the tiled floor with a queer, sharp clack, but it lay motionless. She eyed it closely, cautiously, but, thank God, it did not move, an inert, brown-paper parcel. Brought by an errand boy in daylight, it might have been groceries, tobacco, even a mended shirt. She peeped and tinkered, that sharp clack puzzled her. Then, after a few minutes, remembering her duty, she picked it up gingerly even while she shivered. It was to be handed into the Colonel's 'personal touch.' She compromised, deciding to place it on his desk and to tell him about it in the morning; only Colonel Masters, with those mysterious years in the East behind him, his temper and his tyrannical orders, was not easy of direct approach at the best of times, in the morning least of all.

The cook left it at that—that is, she left it on the desk in his study, but left out all explanations about its arrival. She had decided to be vague about such unimportant details, for Mrs O'Reilly was afraid of Colonel Masters, and only his professed love of Monica made her believe that he was quite human. He paid her well, oh yes, and sometimes he smiled, and he was a handsome man, if a bit too dark for her fancy, yet he also paid her an occasional compliment about her curry, and that soothed her for the moment. They suited one another, at any rate, and she stayed, robbing him comfortably, if cautiously.

'It ain't no good,' she assured the housemaid next day, 'wot with that "personal touch into his hands, and no one else," and that black man's eyes and that crack when it came away in my hands and fell on the floor. It ain't no good, not to us nor anybody. No man as black as he was means lucky stars to anybody. A parcel indeed—with those devil's eyes——'

'What did you do with it?' enquired the housemaid.

The cook looked her up and down 'Put it in the fire o' course,' she replied. 'On the stove if you want to know exact.'

It was the housemaid's turn to look the cook up and down.

'I don't think,' she remarked.

The cook reflected, probably because she found no immediate answer. 'Well,' she puffed out presently, 'D'you know wot *I* think? You don't. So I'll tell you. It was something the master's afraid of, that's wot it was. He's afraid of something—ever since I been here I've known that. And that's wot it was. He done somebody wrong in India long ago and that lanky nigger brought wot's coming to him, and that's why I says I put it on the stove—see?' She dropped her voice. 'It was a bloody idol,' she whispered, 'that's wot it was, that parcel, and he—why, he's a bloody secret worshipper.' And she crossed herself 'That's why I said I put it on the stove—see?'

The housemaid stared and gasped.

'And you mark my words, young Jane!' added the cook, turning to her dough.

And there the matter rested for a period, for the cook, being Irish, had more laughter in her than tears, and beyond admitting to the scared housemaid that she had not really burnt the parcel but had left it on the study table, she almost forgot the incident. It was not her job, in any case, to answer the front door. She had 'delivered' the parcel. Her conscience was quite clear.

Thus, nobody 'marked her words' apparently, for nothing untoward happened, as the way is in remote Suburbia, and Monica in her lonely play was happy, and Colonel Masters as tyrannical and grim as ever. The moist wintry wind blew through the silver pine, the rain beat against the bow window, and no one called. For a week this lasted, a longish time in uneventful Suburbia.

But suddenly one morning Colonel Masters rang his study bell and, the housemaid being upstairs, it was the cook who answered. He held a brown paper parcel in his hands, half opened, the string dangling.

'I found this on my desk. I haven't been in my room for a week. Who brought it? And when did it come?' His face, yellow as usual, held a fiery tinge.

Mrs O'Reilly replied, post-dating the arrival vaguely.

'I asked *who* brought it?' he insisted sharply.

'A stranger,' she fumbled. 'Not any one,' she added nervously, 'from hereabouts. No one I ever seen before. It was a man.'

'What did he look like?' The question came like a bullet.

Mrs O'Reilly was rather taken by surprise. 'D-darkish,' she stumbled, 'Very darkish,' she added, 'if I saw him right. Only he came and went so quick I didn't get his face proper like, and . . .'

'Any message?' the Colonel cut her short.

She hesitated. 'There was no answer,' she began remembering former occasions.

'Any *message*, I asked you?' he thundered.

'No message, sir, none at all. And he was gone before I could get his name and address, sir, but I think it was a sort of black man, or it may have been the darkness of the night—I couldn't reely say, sir . . .'

In another minute she would have burst into tears or dropped to the floor in a faint, such was her terror of her employer especially when she was lying blind. The Colonel, however, saved her both disasters by abruptly holding out the half opened parcel towards her. He neither cross-examined nor cursed her as she had expected. He spoke with the curtness that betrayed anger and anxiety, almost it occurred to her, distress.

'Take it away and burn it,' he ordered in his army voice, passing it into her outstretched hands. 'Burn it,' he repeated it, 'or chuck the damned thing away.' He almost flung it at her as though he did not want to touch it. 'If the man comes back,' he ordered in a voice of steel, 'tell him it's been destroyed—and say it *didn't reach me*,' laying tremendous emphasis on the final words. 'You understand?' He almost chucked it at her.

'Yes, sir. Exactly, sir,' and she turned and stumbled out, holding the parcel gingerly in her arms rather than in her hands and fingers, as though it contained something that might bite or sting.

Yet her fear had somehow lessened, for if he, Colonel Masters, could treat the parcel so contemptuously, why should she feel afraid of it. And, once alone in her kitchen among her household gods, she opened it. Turning back the thick paper wrappings, she started, and to her rather disappointed amazement, she found herself staring at nothing but a fair, waxen faced doll that could be bought in any toyshop for one shilling and sixpence. A commonplace little cheap doll!

Its face was pallid, white, expressionless, its flaxen hair was dirty, its tiny ill-shaped hands and fingers lay motionless by its side, its mouth was closed, though somehow grinning, no teeth visible, its eyelashes ridiculously like a worn toothbrush, its entire presentment in its flimsy skirt, contemptible, harmless, even ugly.

A doll! She giggled to herself, all fear evaporated.

'Gawd!' she thought. 'The master must have a conscience like the floor of a parrot's cage! And worse than that!' She was too afraid of him to despise him, her feeling was probably more like pity. 'At any rate,' she reflected, 'he had the wind up pretty bad. It was something else he expected—not a two-penny halfpenny doll!' Her warm heart felt almost sorry for him.

Instead of 'chucking the damned thing away or burning it,' however,—for it was quite a nice looking doll, she presented it to Monica, and Monica, having few new toys, instantly adored it, promising faithfully, as gravely warned by Mrs O'Reilly, that she would never, *never* let her father know she had it.

Her father, Colonel Hymber Masters, was, it seems, what's called a 'disappointed' man, a man whose fate forced him to live in surroundings he detested, disappointed in his career probably, possibly in love as well, Monica a love-child doubtless, and limited by his pension to face daily conditions that he loathed.

He was a silent, bitter sort of fellow, no more than that, and not so much disliked in the neighbourhood, as misunderstood. A sombre man they reckoned him, with his dark, furrowed face and silent ways. Yet 'dark' in the suburbs meant mysterious, and 'silent' invited female fantasy to fill the vacuum. It's the frank, corn-haired man who invites sympathy and generous comment. He enjoyed his Bridge, however, and was accepted as a first-class player. Thus, he went out nightly, and rarely came back before midnight. He was welcome among the gamblers evidently, while the fact that he had an adored child at home softened the picture of this 'mysterious' man. Monica, though rarely seen, appealed to the women of the neighbourhood, and 'whatever her origin' said the gossips, 'he loves her.'

To Monica, meanwhile, in her rather play-less, toy-less life, the doll, her new treasure, was a spot of gold. The fact that it was a 'secret' present from her father, added to its value. Many other presents had come to her like that; she thought nothing of it; only, he had never given her a doll before, and it spelt rapture. Never, never, would she betray her pleasure and delight; it should remain her secret and his; and that made her love it all the more. She loved her father too, his taciturn silence was something she vaguely respected and adored. 'That's just like father,' she always said, when a strange new present came, and she knew instinctively that she must never say *Thank you* for it, for that was part of the lovely game between them. But this doll was exceptionally marvellous.

'It's much more real and alive than my teddy-bears,' she told the cook, after examining it critically. 'What ever made him think of it? Why, it even talks to me!' and she cuddled and fondled the half mis-shapened toy. 'It's my baby,' she cried taking it against her cheek.

For no teddy-bear could really be a child; cuddly bears were not offspring, whereas a doll was a potential baby. It brought sweetness, as both cook and governess realized, into a rather grim house, hope and tenderness, a maternal flavour almost, something anyhow that no young bear could possibly bring. A child, a human baby! And yet both cook and governess—for both were present at the actual delivery—recalled later that Monica opened the parcel and recognised the doll with a yell of wild delight that seemed almost a scream of pain. There was this too high note of delirious exultation as though some instinctive horror of revulsion were instantly smothered and obliterated in a whirl of overmastering joy. It was Madame Jodzka who recalled—long afterwards—this singular contradiction.

'I did think she shrieked at it a bit, now you ask me,' admitted Mrs O'Reilly later, though at the actual moment all she said was 'Oh, lovely, darling, ain't it a pet!' While all Madame Jodzka said was a caution-ary 'If you squash its mouth like that, Monica, it won't be able to breathe!'

While Monica, paying no attention to either of them, fell to cud-dling the doll with ecstasy.

A cheap little flaxen-haired, waxen-faced doll.

That so strange a case should come to us at second hand is, admit-tedly, a pity; that so much of the information should reach us largely through a cook and housemaid and through a foreigner of question-able validity, is equally unfortunate. Where precisely the reported facts creep across the feathery frontier into the incredible and thence into the fantastic would need the spider's thread of the big telescopes* to define. With the eye to the telescope, the thread of that New Zealand spider seems thick as a rope; but with the eye examining second-hand reports the thread becomes elusive gossamer.

The Polish governess, Madame Jodzka, left the house rather abruptly. Though adored by Monica and accepted by Colonel Masters, she left not long after the arrival of the doll. She was a comely, youngish widow of birth and breeding, tactful, discreet, understanding. She adored Monica, and Monica was happy with her; she feared her employer, yet perhaps secretly admired him as the strong, silent, dominating Englishman. He gave her great freedom, she never took liberties, everything went smoothly. The pay was good and she needed it. Then, suddenly, she left. In the suddenness of her departure, as in the odd reason she gave for leaving, lie doubtless the first hints of this remarkable affair, creeping across that 'feathery frontier' into the incredible and fantastic. An understandable reason she gave for leaving was that she was too frightened to stay in the house another night. She left at twenty-four hours' notice. Her reason was absurd, even if understandable, because any woman might find herself so frightened in a certain building that it has become intolerable to her nerves. Foolish or otherwise, this is understandable. An *idée fixe*, an obsession, once lodged in the mind of a superstitious, therefore hysterically-favoured woman, cannot be dislodged by argument. It may be absurd, yet it is 'understandable.'

The story behind the reason for Madame Jodzka's sudden terror is another matter, and it is best given quite simply. It relates to the doll. She swears by all her gods that she saw the doll 'walking by itself.' It was walking in a disjointed, hoppity, hideous fashion across the bed in which Monica lay sleeping.

In the gleam of the night-light, Madame Jodzka swears she saw this happen. She was half inside the opened door, peeping in, as her habit and duty decreed, to see if all was well with the child before going up to bed herself. The light, if faint, was clear. A jerky movement on the counterpane first caught her attention, for a smallish object seemed blundering awkwardly across its slippery silken surface. Something rolling, possibly, some object Monica had left outside on falling asleep rolling mechanically as the child shifted or turned over.

After staring for some seconds, she then saw that it was not merely an 'object,' since it had a living outline, nor was it rolling mechanically, or sliding, as she had first imagined. It was horribly taking steps, small but quite deliberate steps as though alive. It had a tiny, dreadful face, it had an expressionless tiny face, and the face had eyes—small, brightly shining eyes, and the eyes looked straight at Madame Jodzka.

She watched for a few seconds thunderstruck, and then suddenly realised with a shock of utter horror that this small, purposive monster was the doll, Monica's doll! And this doll was moving towards her across the tumbled surface of the counterpane. It was coming in her direction—straight at her.

Madame Jodzka gripped herself, physically and mentally, making a great effort, it seems, to deny the abnormal, the incredible. She denied the ice in her veins and down her spine. She prayed. She thought frantically of her priest in Warsaw. Making no audible sound, she screamed in her mind. But the doll, quickening its pace, came hobbling straight towards her, its glassy eyes fixed hard upon her own.

Then Madame Jodzka fainted.

That she was, in some ways, a remarkable woman, with a sense of values, is clear from the fact that she realised this story 'wouldn't wash,' for she confided it only to the cook in cautious whispers, while giving her employer some more 'washable' tale about a family death that obliged her to hurry home to Warsaw. Nor was there the slightest attempt at embroidery, for on recovering consciousness she had recovered her courage, too—and done a remarkable thing: she had compelled herself to investigate. Aided and fortified by her religion, she compelled herself to make an examination. She had tiptoed further into the room, had made sure that Monica was sleeping peacefully, and that the doll lay—motionless—half way down the counterpane. She gave it a long, concentrated look. Its lidless eyes, fringed by hideously ridiculous black lashes, were fixed on space. Its expression was not so much innocent, as blankly stupid, idiotic, a mask of death that aped cheaply a pretence of life, where life could never be. Not ugly merely, it was revolting.

Madame Jodzka however, did more than study this visage with concentration, for with admirable pluck she forced herself to touch the little horror. She actually picked it up. Her faith, her deep religious conviction denied the former evidence of her senses. She had *not* seen movement. It was incredible, impossible. The fault lay somewhere in herself. This persuasion, at any rate, lasted long enough to enable her to touch the repulsive little toy, to pick it up, to lift it. She placed it steadily on the table near the bed between the bowl of flowers and the night-light, where it lay on its back helpless, innocent, yet horrible, and only then on shaking legs did she leave the room and go up to her own bed. That her fingers remained ice-cold until eventually she fell asleep can be explained, of course, too easily and naturally to claim examination.

Whether imagined or actual, it must have been, none the less, a horrifying spectacle—a mechanical outline from a commercial factory walking like a living thing with a purpose. It holds the nightmare touch. To Madame Jodzka, protected since youth within cast-iron tenets, it came as a shock. And a shock dislocates. The sight smashed everything she knew as possible and real. The flow of her blood was interrupted, it froze, there came icy terror into her heart, her normal mechanism failed for a moment, she fainted. And fainting seemed a natural result. Yet it was the shock of the incredible masquerade that gave her the courage to act. She loved Monica, apart from any consideration of paid duty. The sight of this tiny monstrosity strutting across the counterpane not far from the child's sleeping face and folded hands—it was this that enabled her to pick it up with naked fingers and set it out of reach. . . .

For hours, before falling asleep, she reviewed the incredible thing, alternately denying the facts, then accepting them, yet taking into sleep finally the assured conviction that her senses had not deceived her. There seems little, indeed, that in a court of law could have been advanced against her character for reliability, for sincerity, for the logic of her detailed account.

'I'm sorry,' said Colonel Masters quietly, referring to her bereavement. He looked searchingly at her. 'And Monica will miss you,' he added with one of his rare smiles. 'She needs you.' Then just as she turned away, he suddenly extended his hand. 'If perhaps later you can come back—do let me know. Your influence is—so helpful—and good.'

She mumbled some phrase with a promise in it, yet she left with a queer, deep impression that it was not merely, not chiefly perhaps, Monica who needed her. She wished he had not used quite those words. A sense of shame lay in her, almost as though she were running away from duty, or at least from a chance to help God had put in her way. 'Your influence is—so good.'

Already in the train and on the boat conscience attacked her, biting, scratching, gnawing. She had deserted a child she loved, a child who needed her. because she was scared out of her wits. No, that was a one-sided statement. She had left a house because the Devil had come into it. No, that was only partially true. When a hysterical temperament, engrained since early childhood in fixed dogmas, begins to sift facts and analyse reactions, logic and common sense themselves become confused. Thought led one way, emotion another, and no honest conclusion dawned on her mind.

She hurried on to Warsaw, to a stepfather, a retired General whose gay life had no place for her and who would not welcome her return. It was a derogatory prospect for this youngish widow who had taken a job in order to escape from his vulgar activities to return now empty-handed. Yet it was easier, perhaps, to face a stepfather selfish anger than to go and tell Colonel Masters her real reason for leaving his service. Her conscience, too, troubled her on another score as thoughts and memories travelled backwards and half-forgotten details emerged.

Those spots of blood, for instance, mentioned by Mrs O'Reilly, the superstitious Irish cook. She had made it a rule to ignore Mrs O'Reilly's silly fairy tales, yet now she recalled suddenly those ridiculous discussions about the laundry list and the foolish remarks that the cook and housemaid had let fall.

'But there ain't no paint in a doll, I tell you. It's all sawdust and wax and muck,' from the housemaid. 'I know red paint when I sees it, and that ain't paint, it's blood.' And from Mrs O'Reilly later: 'Mother o' God! Another red blob! She's biting her finger-nails—and that's not *my* job . . . !'

The red stains on sheets and pillow cases were puzzling certainly, but Madame Jodzka, hearing these remarks by chance as it were, had paid no particular attention to them at the moment. The laundry lists were hardly her affair. These ridiculous servants anyhow . . . ! And yet, now in the train, those spots of red, be they paint or blood, crept back to trouble her.

Another thing, oddly enough, also troubled her—the ill-defined feeling that she was deserting a man who needed help, help that she could give. It was too vague to put into words. Was it based on his remark that her influence was 'good' perhaps? She could not say. It was an intuition, and few intuitions bear analysis. Supporting it, however, was a conviction she had felt since first she entered the service of Colonel Masters, the conviction, namely, that he had a Past that frightened him. There was something he had done, something he regretted and was probably ashamed of, something at any rate, for which he feared retribution. A retribution, moreover, he expected; a punishment that would come like a thief in the night and seize him by the throat.

It was against this dreaded vengeance that her influence was 'good,' a protective influence possibly that her religion supplied, something on the side of the angels, in any case, that her personality provided.

Her mind worked thus, it seems; and whether a concealed admiration for this sombre and mysterious man, an admiration and protective instinct never admitted even to her inmost self, existed below the surface, hidden yet urgent, remains the secret of her own heart.

It was naturally and according to human nature, at any rate, that after a few weeks of her stepfather's outrageous behaviour in the house, his cruelty too, she decided to return. She prayed to her gods incessantly, also she found oppressive her sense of neglected duty and failure of self-respect. She returned to the soulless suburban villa. It was understandable; the welcome from Monica was also understandable, the relief and pleasure of Colonel Masters still more so. It was expressed, this latter, in a courteous message only, tactfully worded, as though she had merely left for brief necessity, for it was some days before she actually saw him to speak to. From cook and housemaid the welcome was voluble and—disquieting. There were no more inexplicable 'spots of red,' but there were other unaccountable happenings even more distressing.

'She's missed you something terrible,' said Mrs O'Reilly, 'though she's found something else to keep her quiet—if you like to put it that way.' And she made the sign of the cross.

'The doll?' asked Madame Jodzka with a start of shocked horror, forcing herself to come straight to the point and forcing herself also to speak lightly, casually.

'That's it, Madame. The bleeding doll.'

The governess had heard the strange adjective many times already, but did not know whether to take it figuratively or not. She chose the latter.

'Blood?' she asked in a lowered voice.

The cook's body gave an odd jerk. 'Well,' she explained 'I meant more the way it goes on. Like a thing of flesh and blood, if you get me. And the way *she* treats it and plays with it,' and her voice, while loud, had a hush of fear in it somewhere. She held her arms before her in a protective, shielding way, as though to ward off aggression.

'Scratches ain't proof of nothing,' interjected the housemaid scornfully.

'You mean,' asked Madame Jodzka gravely, 'there's a question of—of injury—to someone?' She suppressed an involuntary gasp, but paid no attention to the maid's interruption otherwise.

Mrs O'Reilly seemed to mis-manage her breath for a moment.

'It ain't Miss Monica it's after,' she announced in a defiant whisper as soon as she recovered herself, 'it's someone else. *That's* what I mean. And no man as black as *he* was,' she let herself go, 'ever brought no good into a house, not since I was born.'

'Someone else——?' repeated Madame Jodzka almost to herself, seizing the vital words.

'You and yer black man!' interjected the housemaid. 'Get along with yer! Thank God I ain't a Christian or anything like that! But I did 'ear them sort of jerky shuffling footsteps one night, I admit, and the doll did look bigger,—swollen like—when I peeked in and looked——'

'Stop it!' cried Mrs O'Reilly, 'for you ain't saying what's true or what you reely know.'

She turned to the governess.

'There's more talk what means nothing about this doll,' she said by way of apology, 'than all the fairy tales I was brought up with as a child in Mayo, and I—I wouldn't be believing anything of it.'

Turning her back contemptuously on the chattering housemaid, she came close to Madame Jodzka.

'There's no harm coming to Miss Monica, Madame,' she whispered vehemently, 'you can be quite sure about *her*. Any trouble there may be is for someone else.' And again she crossed herself.

Madame Jodzka, in the privacy of her room, reflected between her prayers. She felt a deep, a dreadful uneasiness.

A doll! A cheap, tawdry little toy made in factories by the hundred, by the thousand, a manufactured article of commerce for children to play with . . . But . . .

'The way she treats it and plays with it . . .' rang on in her disturbed mind.

A doll! But for the maternal suggestion, a doll was a pathetic, even horrible plaything, yet to watch a child busy with it involved deep reflections, since here the future mother prophesied. The child fondles and caresses her doll with passionate love, cares for it, seeks its welfare, yet stuffs it down into the perambulator, its head and neck twisted, its limbs broken and contorted, leaving it atrociously upside down so that blood and breathing cannot possibly function, while she runs to the window to see if the rain has stopped or the sun has come out. A blind and hideous automatism dictated by the Race, provided nothing of more immediate interest interferes, yet a herd-instinct that overcomes all obstacles, its vitality insuperable. The maternity instinct defies, even denies death. The doll, whether left upside down on the floor with broken teeth and ruined eyes, or lovingly arranged to be overlaid in the night, squashed, tortured, mutilated, survives all cruelties and disasters, and asserts finally its immortal qualities. It is unkillable. It is beyond death.

A child with her doll, reflected Madame Jodzka, is an epitome of nature's remorseless and unconquerable passion, of her dominant purpose—the survival of the race. . . .

Such thoughts, influenced perhaps by her bitter subconscious grievance against nature for depriving her of a child of her own, were unable to hold that level for long; they soon dropped back to the concrete case that perplexed and frightened her—Monica and her flaxen haired, sightless, idiotic doll. In the middle of her prayers, falling asleep incontinently, she did not even dream of it, and she woke refreshed and vigorous, facing the fact that sooner or later, sooner probably, she would have to speak to her employer.

She watched and listened. She watched Monica; she watched the doll. All seemed as normal as in a thousand other homes. Her mind reviewed the position, and where mind and superstition clashed, the former held its own easily. During her evening off she enjoyed the local cinema, leaving the heated building with the conviction that coloured fantasy benumbed the faculties, and that ordinary life was in itself prosaic. Yet before she had covered the half-mile to the house, her deep, unaccountable uneasiness returned with overmastering power.

Mrs O'Reilly had seen Monica to bed for her, and it was Mrs O'Reilly who let her in. Her face was like the dead.

It's been talking,' whispered the cook, even before she closed the door. She was white about the gills.

'Talking! *Who's* been talking? What do you mean?'

Mrs O'Reilly closed the door softly. 'Both,' she stated with dramatic emphasis, then sat down and wiped her face. She looked distraught with fear.

Madame took command, if only a command based on dreadful insecurity.

'Both?' she repeated, in a voice deliberately loud so as to counteract the other's whisper. 'What are you talking about?'

'They've *both* been talking—talking together,' stated the cook.

The governess kept silent for a moment, fighting to deny a shrinking heart.

'You've heard them talking together, you mean?' she asked presently in a shaking voice that tried to be ordinary.

Mrs O'Reilly nodded looking over her shoulder as she did so. Her nerves were, obviously, in rags. 'I thought you'd *never* come back,' she whimpered. 'I could hardly stay in the house.'

Madame looked intently into her frightened eyes.

'You *heard* . . .?' she asked quietly.

'I listened at the door. There were two voices. Different voices.'

Madame Jodzka did not insist or cross-examine, as though acute fear helped her to a greater wisdom.

'You mean, Mrs O'Reilly,' she said in flat, quiet tones, 'that you heard Miss Monica talking to her doll as she always does, and herself inventing the doll's answers in a changed voice? Isn't that what you mean you heard?'

But Mrs O'Reilly was not to be shaken. By way of answer she crossed herself and shook her head.

She spoke in a low whisper. 'Come up now and listen with me, Madame, and judge for yourself.'

Thus, soon after midnight, and Monica long since asleep, these two, the cook and governess in a suburban villa, took up their places in the dark corridor outside a child's bedroom door. It was a quiet windless night; Colonel Masters, whom they both feared, doubtless long since gone to his room in another corner of the ungainly villa. It must have been a long dreary wait before sounds in the child's bedroom first became audible—the low quiet sound of voices talking audibly—two voices. A hushed, secretive, unpleasant sound in the room where Monica slept peacefully with her beloved doll beside her. Yet two voices, assuredly, it was.

Both women sat erect, both crossed themselves involuntarily, exchanging glances. Both were bewildered, terrified. Both sat aghast.

What lay in Mrs O'Reilly's superstitious mind, only the gods of 'ould Oireland' can tell, but what the Polish woman's contained was clear as a bell: it was not two voices talking, it was only one. Her ear was pressed against the crack in the door. She listened intently; shaking to the bone, she listened. Voices in sleep-talking, she remembered, changed oddly.

'The child's talking to herself in sleep,' she whispered firmly, 'and that's all it is, Mrs O'Reilly. She's just talking in her sleep,' she repeated with emphasis to the woman crowding against her shoulder as though in need of support. 'Can't you hear it,' she added loudly, half angrily, 'isn't it the same voice always? Listen carefully and you'll see I'm right.'

She listened herself more closely than before.

'Listen! Hark . . . !' she repeated in a breathless whisper, concentrating her mind upon the curious sound, 'isn't that the same voice—answering itself?'

Yet, as she listened, another sound disturbed her concentration, and this time it seemed a sound behind her—a faint, rustling, shuffling sound rather like footsteps hurrying away on tiptoe. She turned her head sharply and found that she had been whispering to no one. There was no one beside her. She was alone in the darkened corridor. Mrs O'Reilly was gone. From the well of the house below a voice came up in a smothered cry beneath the darkened stairs: 'Mother o' God and all the Saints . . .' and more besides.

A gasp of surprise and alarm escaped her doubtless at finding herself deserted and alone but in the same instant, exactly as in the story books, came another sound that caught her breath still more aghast—the rattle of a key in the front door below. Colonel Masters, after all, had not yet come in and gone to bed as expected: he was coming in now. Would Mrs O'Reilly have time to slip across the hall before he caught her? More—and worse—would he come up and peep into Monica's bedroom on his way up to bed, as he rarely did? Madame Jodzka listened, her nerves in rags. She heard him fling down his coat. He was a man quick in such actions. The stick or umbrella was banged down noisily, hastily. The same instant his step sounded on the stairs. He was coming up. Another minute and he would start into the passage where she crouched against Monica's door.

He was mounting rapidly, two stairs at a time.

She, too, was quick in action and decision. She thought in a flash. To be caught crouching outside the door was ludicrous, but to be caught inside the door would be natural and explicable. She acted at once.

With a palpitating heart, she opened the bedroom door and stepped inside. A second later she hear Colonel Masters' tread, as he stumped along the corridor up to bed. He passed the door. He went on. She heard this with intense relief.

Now, inside the room, the door closed behind her, she saw the picture clearly.

Monica, sound asleep, was playing with her beloved doll, but in her sleep. She was indubitably in deep slumber. Her fingers, however, were roughing the doll this way and that, as though some dream perplexed her. The child was mumbling in her sleep, though no words were distinguishable. Muffled sighs and groans issued from her lips. Yet another sound there certainly was, though it could not have issued from the child's mouth. Whence, then, did it come?

Madame Jodzka paused, holding her breath, her heart panting. She watched and listened intently. She heard squeaks and grunts, but a moment's examination convinced her whence these noises came. They did not come from Monica's lips. They issued indubitably from the doll she clutched and twisted in her dream. The joints, as Monica twisted them, emitted these odd sounds, as though the sawdust in knees and elbows wheezed and squeaked against the unnatural rubbing. Monica obviously was wholly unconscious of these noises. As the doll's neck screwed round, the material—wax, thread, sawdust—produced this curious grating sound that was almost like syllables of a word or words.

Madame Jodzka stared and listened. She felt icy cold. Seeking for a natural explanation she found none. Prayer and terror raced in her helter-skelter. Her skin began to sweat.

Then, suddenly Monica, her expression peaceful and composed, turned over in her sleep, and the dreadful doll, released from the dream-clutch, fell to one side on the bed and lay apparently lifeless and inert. In which moment, to Madame Jodzka's unbelieving yet horrified ears, it continued to squeak and utter. It went on mouthing by itself. Worse than that, the next instant it stood abruptly upright, rising on its twisted legs. It started moving. It began to move, walking crookedly, across the counterpane. Its glassy, sightless eyes, seemed to look straight at her. It presented an inhuman and appalling picture, a picture of the utterly incredible. With a queer, hoppity motion of its broken legs and joints, it came fumbling and tumbling across the rough unevenness of the slippery counterpane towards her. Its appearance was deliberate and aggressive. The sounds, as of syllables, came with it—strange, meaningless syllables that yet managed to convey anger. It stumbled towards her like a living thing. Its whole presentment conveyed attack.

Once again, this effect of a mere child's toy, aping the life of some awful monstrosity with purpose and passion in its hideous tiny outline, brought collapse to the plucky Polish governess. The rush of blood without control drained her heart, and a moment of unconsciousness supervened so that everything, as it were, turned black.

This time, however, the moment of dark unconsciousness passed instantly: it came and went, almost like a moment of forgetfulness in passion. Passionate it certainly was, for the reaction came upon her like a storm. With recovered consciousness a sudden rage rushed into her woman heart—perhaps a coward's rage, an exaggerated fury against her own weakness? It rushed, in any case, to help her. She staggered, caught her breath, clutched violently at the cupboard next her, and—recovered her self-control. A fury of resentment blazed through her, fury against this utterly incredible exhibition of a wax doll walking and squawking as though it were something intelligently alive that could utter syllables. Syllables, she felt convinced, in a language she did not know.

If the monstrous can paralyse, it also can affront. The sight and sound of this cheap factory toy behaving with a will and heart of its own stung her into an act of violence that became inperative. For it was more than she could stand. Irresistibly, she rushed forward. She hurled herself against it, her only available weapon the high-heeled shoe her foot kicked loose on the instant, determined to smash down the frightful apparition into fragments and annihilate it. Hysterical, no doubt, she was at the moment, and yet logical: the godless horror must be blotted out of visible existence. This one thing obsessed her—to destroy beyond all possibility of survival. It must be smashed into fragments, into dust.

They stood close, face to face, the glassy eyes staring into her own, her hand held high for the destruction she craved—but the hand did not fall. A stinging pain, sharp as a serpent's bite, darted suddenly through her fingers, wrist and arm, her grip was broken, the shoe spun sideways across the room, and in the flickering light of the candle, it seemed to her, the whole room quivered. Paralysed and helpless, she stood utterly aghast. What gods or saints could come to aid her? None. Her own will alone could help her. Some effort, at any rate, she made, trembling, on the edge of collapse: 'My God!' she heard her half whispering, strangled voice cry out. 'It is not true! You are a lie! My God denies you! I call upon my God . . . !'

Whereupon, to her added horror, the dreadful little doll, waving a broken arm, squawked back at her, as though in definite answer, the strange disjointed syllables she could not understand, syllables as though in another tongue. The same instant it collapsed abruptly on the counterpane like a toy balloon that had been pricked. It shrank down in a mutilated mess before her eyes, while Monica—added touch of horror—stirred uneasily in her sleep, turning over and stretching out her hands as though feeling blindly for something that she missed. And this sight of the innocently sleeping child fumbling instinctively towards an incomprehensibly evil and dangerous something that attracted her proved again too strong for the Polish woman to control.

The blackness intervened a second time.

It was undoubtedly a blur in memory that followed, emotion and superstition proving too much for common-sense to deal with. She just remembers violent, unreasoned action on her part before she came back to clearer consciousness in her own room, praying volubly on her knees against her own bed. The interval of transit down the corridor and upstairs remained a blank. Yet her shoe was with her, clutched tightly in her hand. And she remembered also having clutched an inert, waxen doll with frantic fingers, clutched and crushed and crumpled its awful little frame till the sawdust came spurting from its broken joints and its tiny body was mutilated beyond recognition, if not annihilated . . . then stuffing it down ruthlessly on a table far out of Monica's reach, Monica lying peacefully in deepest sleep. She remembered that. She also saw the clear picture of the small monster lying upside down, grossly untidy, an obscene attitude in the disorder of its flimsy dress and exposed limbs, lying motionless, its eyes crookedly aglint, motionless, yet alive still, alive moreover with intense and malignant purpose.

No duration or intensity of prayer could obliterate the picture.

She knew now that a plain, face to face talk with her employer was essential; her conscience, her peace of mind, her sanity, her sense of duty all demanded this. Deliberately, and she was sure, rightly, she had never once risked a word with the child herself. Danger lay that way, the danger of emphasizing something in the child's mind that was best left ignored. But with Colonel Masters, who paid her for her services, believed in her integrity, trusted her, with him there must be an immediate explanation.

An interview was absurdly difficult; in the first place because he loathed and avoided such occasions; secondly because he was so exceedingly impervious to approach, being so rarely even visible at all. At night he came home late, in the mornings no one dared go near him. He expected the little household, once its routine established, to run itself. The only inmate who dared beard him was Mrs O'Reilly, who periodically, once every six months, walked straight into his study, gave notice, received an addition to her wages, and then left him alone for another six months.

Madame Jodzka, knowing his habits, waylaid him in the hall next morning while Monica was lying down before lunch, as usual. He was on his way out and she had been watching from the upper landing. She had hardly set eyes on him since her return from Warsaw. His lean, upright figure, his dark, emotionless face, she thought magnificent. He was the perfect expression of the soldier. Her heart fluttered as she raced downstairs. Her carefully prepared sentences, however, evaporated when he stopped and looked at her, a jumble of wild words pouring from her in confused English instead. He cut her rigmarole short, though he listened politely enough at first.

'I'm so glad you were able to come back to us, as I told you. Monica missed you very much——'

'She has something now she plays with——'

'The very thing,' he interrupted. 'No doubt the kind of toy she needs . . . Your excellent judgment . . . Please tell me if there's anything else you think . . .' and he half turned as though to move away.

'But I didn't get it. It's a horrible,—*horrible*——' Colonel Masters uttered one of his rare laughs.

'Of course, all children's toys are horrible, but if she's pleased with it . . . I haven't seen it, I'm no judge . . . If you can buy something better——' and he shrugged his shoulders.

'I didn't buy it,' she cried desperately. 'It was brought. It makes sounds by itself—syllables. I've seen it move—move by itself. It's a doll.'

He turned from the front door which he had just reached as though he had been shot; the skin held a sudden pallor beneath the flush and something contradicted the blazing eyes, something that seemed to shrink.

'A doll,' he repeated in a very quiet voice. 'You said—a doll?'

But his eyes and face disconcerted her, so that she merely gave a fumbling account of a parcel that had been brought. His question about a parcel he had ordered strictly to be destroyed added to her confusion.

'Wasn't it?' he asked in a rasping whisper, as though a disobeyed order seemed incredible.

'It was thrown away, I believe,' she prevaricated, unable to meet his eyes, anxious to protect the cook as well. 'I think Monica—perhaps found it.' She despised her lack of courage, but his intensity scattered her wits; she was conscious, moreover, of a strange desire not to give him pain, as though his safety and happiness, not Monica's, were at stake. 'It—talks!—as well as *moves*,' she cried desperately, forcing herself at last to look at him.

Colonel Masters seemed to stiffen; his breath caught oddly.

'You say Monica has it? Plays with it? You've seen movement and heard sounds like syllables?' He asked the questions in a low voice, almost as though talking to himself. 'You've—listened?' he whispered.

Unable to find convincing words, she bowed her head, while some terror in him came across to her like a blast of icy wind. The man was afraid in his heart. Instead, however, of some explosive reply by way of blame or criticism, he spoke quietly, even calmly: 'You did right to come and tell me this—quite right,' adding then in so low a tone that she barely caught the ominous words, 'for I have been expecting something of the sort . . . sooner or later . . . it was bound to come . . .' the voice dying away into the handkerchief he put to his face.

And abruptly then, as though aware of an appeal for sympathy, an emotional reaction swept her fear away. Stepping closer, she looked her employer straight in the eyes.

'See the child for yourself,' she said with sudden firmness. 'Come and listen with me. Come into the bedroom.'

She saw him stagger. For a moment he said nothing.

'Who,' he then asked, the low voice unsteady, 'who brought that parcel?'

'A man, I believe.'

There was a pause that seemed like minutes before his next question.

'White,' he asked, 'or—black?'

'Dark,' she told him, 'very dark.'

He was shaking like a leaf, the skin of his face blanched; he leaned against the door, wilted, limp; unless she somehow took command there threatened a collapse she did not wish to witness.

'You shall come with me tonight,' she said firmly, 'and we shall listen together. Wait till I return now. I go for brandy,' and a minute later as she came back breathless and watched him gulp down half a tumbler full, she knew that she had done right in telling him. His obedience proved it, though it seemed strange that cowardice should borrow from its like to produce courage.

'Tonight,' she repeated, 'tonight after your Bridge. We meet in the corridor outside the bedroom. I shall be there. At half-past twelve.'

He pulled himself into an upright position, staring at her fixedly, making a movement of his head, half bow, half nod.

'Twelve thirty,' he muttered, 'in the passage outside the bedroom door,' and using his stick heavily rather, he opened the door and passed out into the drive. She watched him go, aware that her fear had changed to pity, aware also that she watched the stumbling gait of a man too conscience-stricken to know a moment's peace, too frightened even to think of God.

Madame Jodzka kept the appointment; she had eaten no supper, but had stayed in her room—praying. She had first put Monica to bed.

'My doll,' the child pleaded, good as gold, after being tucked up. 'I must have my doll or else I'll never get to sleep,' and Madame Jodzka had brought it with reluctant fingers, placing it on the night-table beside the bed.

'She'll sleep quite comfortably here, Monica, darling. Why not leave her outside the sheets?' It had been carefully mended, she noticed, patched together with pins and stitches.

The child grabbed at it. 'I want her in bed beside me, close against me,' she said with a happy smile. 'We tell each other stories. If she's too far away I can't hear what she says.' And she seized it with a cuddling pleasure that made the woman's heart turn cold.

'Of course, darling—if it helps you to fall asleep quickly, you shall have it,' and Monica did not see the trembling fingers, not notice the horror in the face and voice. Indeed, hardly was the doll against her cheek on the pillow, her fingers half stroking the flaxen hair and pink wax cheeks, than her eyes closed, a sigh of deep content breathed out, and Monica was asleep.

Madame Jodzka, fearful of looking behind her, tiptoed to the door, and left the room. In the passage she wiped a cold sweat from her forehead. 'God bless her and protect her,' her heart murmured, 'and may God forgive me if I've sinned.'

She kept the appointment; she knew Colonel Masters would keep it, too.

It had been a long wait from eight o'clock till after midnight. With great determination she had kept away from the bedroom door, fearful lest she might hear a sound that would necessitate action on her part: she went to her room and stayed there. But praying exhausted itself, for it both excited and betrayed her. If her God could help, a brief request alone was needed. To go on praying for help hour by hour was not only an insult to her deity, but it also wore her out physically. She stopped, therefore, and read some pages of a Polish saint which she did not understand. Later she fell into a state of horrified nervous drowse. In due course, she slept . . .

A noise awoke her—steps going softly past her door. A glance at her watch showed eleven o'clock. The steps, though stealthy, were familiar. Mrs O'Reilly was waddling up to bed. The sounds died away. Madame Jodzka, a trifle ashamed, though she hardly knew why, returned to her Polish saint, yet determined to keep her ears open. Then slept again . . .

What woke her a second time she could not tell. She was startled. She listened. The night was unpleasantly still, the house quiet as the grave. No casual traffic passed. No wind stirred the gloomy evergreens in the drive. The world outside was silent. And then, as she saw by her watch that it was some minutes after midnight, a sharp click became audible that acted like a pistol shot to her keyed-up nerves. It was the front door closing softly. Steps followed across the hall below, then up the stairs, unsteadily a little. Colonel Masters had come in. He was coming up slowly, unwillingly she felt, to keep the appointment. Madame Jodzka started from her chair, looked in the glass, mumbled a quick confused prayer, and opened her door into the dark passage.

She stiffened, physically and mentally. 'Now, he'll hear and perhaps see—for himself,' she thought. 'And God help him!'

She marched along the passage and reached the door of Monica's bedroom, listening with such intentness that she seemed to hear only the confused running murmur of her own blood. Having reached the appointed spot, she stood stock still and waited while his steps approached. A moment later his bulk blocked the passage, shown up as a dark shadow by the light in the hall below. This bulk came nearer, came right up to her. She believed she said 'Good evening,' and that he mumbled something about 'I said I'd come . . . damned nonsense . . .' or words to that effect, whereupon the couple stood side by side in the darkened silence of the corridor, remote from the rest of the house, and waited without further words. They stood shoulder to shoulder outside the door of Monica's bedroom. Her heart was knocking against her side.

She heard his breathing, there came a whiff of spirits, of stale tobacco, smoke, his outline seemed to shift against the wall unsteadily, he moved his feet; and a sudden, extraordinary wave of emotion swept over her, half of protective maternal yearning, half almost of sexual desire, so that for a passing instant she burned to take him in her arms and kiss him savagely, and at the same time shield him from some appalling danger his blunt ignorance laid him open to. With revulsion, pity, and a sense of sin and passion, she acknowledged this odd sudden weakness in herself, but the face of the Warsaw priest flashed across her fuddled mind the next instant. There was evil in the air. This meant the Devil. She felt herself trembling dreadfully, shaking in her shoes, losing her balance, her whole body leaning over, but leaning in his direction. A moment more and she must have fallen towards him, dropped into his arms.

A sound broke the silence, and she drew up just in time. It came from beyond the door, from inside the bedroom.

'Hark!' she whispered, her hand upon his arm, and while he made no movement, spoke no word, she saw his head and shoulders bend down toward the panel of the closed door. There was a noise, upon the other side, there were noises, Monica's voice distinctly recognizable, another slighter, shriller sound accompanying it, breaking in upon it, answering it. Two voices.

'Listen,' she repeated in a whisper scarcely audible, and felt his warm hand grip her own so fiercely that it hurt her.

No words were distinguishable at first, just these odd broken sounds of two separate voices in that dark corridor of the silent house—the voice of a child, and the other a strange faint, hardly a human sound, while yet a voice.

'*Que le bon Dieu*——'* she began, then faltered, breath failing her, for she saw Colonel Masters stoop down suddenly and do the last thing that would have occurred to her as likely: he put his eye to the key-hole and kept it there steadily, for the best part of a minute, his hand still gripping her own firmly. He knelt on one knee to keep his balance.

The sounds had ceased, no movement now stirred inside the room. The night-light, she knew, would show him clearly the pillows of the bed, Monica's head, the doll in her arms. Colonel Masters must see clearly anything there was to see, and he yet gave no sign that he saw anything. She experienced a queer sensation for a few seconds—almost as though she had perhaps imagined everything and proved herself a consummate, idiotic, hysterical fool. For a few seconds this ghastly thought flashed over her, the odd silence emphasizing it. Had she been after all, just a crazy lunatic? Had her senses all deceived her? Why should he see nothing, make no sign? Why had the voice, the voices, ceased? Not a murmur of any sort was audible in the room.

Then Colonel Masters, suddenly releasing his grip of her hand, shuffled on to both feet and stood up straight, while in the same instant she herself stiffened, trying to prepare for the angry scorn, the contemptuous abuse he was about to pour upon her. Protecting herself against this attack, expecting it, she was the more amazed at what she did hear:

'I saw it,' came in a strangled whisper. 'I saw it walk!'

She stood paralysed.

'It's watching me,' he added, scarcely audible. '*Me!*'

The revulsion of feeling at first left her speechless; it was the sheer terror in his strangled whisper that restored a measure of self possession to her. Yet it was he who found words first, awful whispered words, words spoken to himself, it seemed, more than to her.

'It's what I've always feared—I knew it must come some day—yet not like this. Not this way.'

Then immediately the voice in the room became audible, and it was a sweet and gentle voice, sincere and natural, with feeling in it—Monica's childish voice, pleading:

'Don't go, don't leave me! Come back into bed—please.'

An incomprehensible sound followed, as though by way of answer. There were syllables in that faint, creaky tone Madame Jodzka recognised, but syllables she could not comprehend. They seemed to enter her like points of ice. She froze. And facing her stood the motionless, inanimate bulk of him, his outline, then leaned over towards her, his lips so close to her own face that, as he spoke, she felt the breath upon her cheek.

'*Buth laga . . .*' she heard him repeat the syllables to himself again and again. '*Revenge . . .* in Hindustani* . . . !' He drew a long, anguished breath. The sounds sank into her like drops of poison, the syllables she had heard several times already but had not understood. At last she understood their meaning. Revenge!

'I must go in, go in,' he was mumbling to himself. 'I must go in and face it.' Her intuition was justified: the danger was not for Monica but for himself. Her sudden protective maternal instinct found its explanation too. The lethal power concentrated in that hideous puppet was aimed at *him*. He began to edge impetuously past her.

'No!' she cried, 'I'll go! Let me go in!' pushing him aside with all her strength. But his hand was already on the knob and the next instant the door was open and he was inside the room. On the threshold they stood still a second side by side, though she was slightly behind, struggling to shove past him and stand protectively in front.

She stared across his shoulder, her eyes so wide open that the intense strain to note everything at once threatened to defeat its own end. Sight, none the less, worked normally; she saw all there was to see, and that was—nothing; nothing unusual, that is, nothing abnormal, nothing terrifying, so that this second time the threat of anti-climax rose to her mind. Had she worked herself up to this peak of horror merely to behold Monica lying sound asleep in a safe and quiet room? The flickering night-light revealed no more than a child in natural slumber without a toy of any sort against her pillow. There stood the glass of water beside the flowers in their saucer, the picture-book on the sill of the window within reach, the window opened a little at the bottom, and there also lay the calm face of Monica with eyes tight shut upon the pillow. Her breathing was deep and regular, no sign of disquiet anywhere, no hint of disturbance that might have accompanied that pleading sentence of two minutes ago, except that the bedclothes were perhaps somewhat tumbled. The counterpane humped itself in folds towards the foot of the bed, she noticed, as though Monica, finding it too warm, had tossed it away in sleep. No more than that.

In that first moment Colonel Masters and the governess took in this whole pretty picture complete. The room was so still that the child's breathing was distinctly audible. Their eyes roved all over. Nothing was anywhere in movement. Yet the same instant Madame Jodzka became aware that there was movement. Something stirred. The report came, perhaps, through her skin, for no sense announced it. It was undeniable; in that still, silent room there was movement somewhere, and with that unreported movement there was danger.

Certain, rightly or wrongly, that she herself was safe, also that the quietly sleeping child was safe, she was equally certain that Colonel Masters was the one in danger. She knew in that her very bones.

'Wait here by the door,' she said almost peremptorily, as she felt him pushing past her further into the quiet room. 'You saw it watching you. It's somewhere—Take care!'

She clutched at him, but he was already beyond her.

'Damned nonsense,' he muttered and strode forward.

Never before in her whole life had she admired a man more than in this instant when she saw him moving towards what she knew to be physical and spiritual danger—never before, and never again, was such a hideous and dreadful sight to be repeatable in a woman's life. Pity and horror drowned her in a sea of passionate, futile longing. A man going to meet his fate, it flashed over her, was something none, without power to help, should witness. No human power can stay the courses of the stars.

Her eye rested, as it were by chance, on the crumpled ridges and hollows of the discarded counterpane. These lay by the foot of the bed in shadow, confused a little in their contours and their masses. Had Monica not moved, they must have lain thus till morning. But Monica did move. At this particular moment she turned over in her sleep. She stretched her little legs before settling down in the new position, and this stretching squeezed and twisted the contours of the heavy counterpane at the foot of the bed. The tiny landscape altered thus a fraction, its immediate detail shifted. And an outline—a very small outline-emerged. Hitherto, it had lain concealed among the shadows. It emerged now with disconcerting rapidity, as though a spring released it. Out of its nest of darkness it seemed almost to leap forward. Fast it came, supernaturally fast, its velocity actually shocking, for a shock came with it. It was exceedingly small, it was exceedingly dreadful, its head erect and venomous and the movement of its legs and arms, as of its bitter, glittering eyes, aping humanity. Malignant evil, personified and aggressive, shaped itself in this otherwise ridiculous outline.

It was the doll.

Racing with incredible security across the slippery surface of the crumpled silk counterpane, it dived and climbed and shot forward with an appearance of complete control and deliberate purpose. That it had a definite aim was overwhelmingly obvious. Its fixed, glassy eyes were concentrated upon a point beyond and behind the terrified governess, the point precisely where Colonel Masters, her employer, stood against her shoulder.

A frantic, half protective movement on her part, seemed lost in the air. . . .

She turned instinctively, putting an arm about his shoulders, which he instantly flung off.

'Let the bloody thing come,' he cried. 'I'll deal with it . . . !' He thrust her violently aside.

The doll came at him. The hinges of its diminutive broken arms and its jointed legs emitted a thin, creaking sound as it came darting— the syllables Madame Jodzka had already heard more than once. Syllables she had heard without understanding—'*buth laga*'—but syllables now packed with awful meaning: *Revenge.*

The sounds hissed and squeaked, yet clear as a bell as the beast advanced at this miraculous speed.

Before Colonel Masters could move an inch backwards or forwards in self protection, before he could command himself to any sort of action, or contrive the smallest measure of self defence, it was off the bed and at him. It settled. Savagely, its little jaws of tiny make-believe were bitten deep into Colonel Masters' throat, fastened tightly.

In a flash this happened, in a flash it was over. In Madame Jodzka's memory it remained like the impression of a lightning flash, simultaneously etched in black and white. It had happened in the present as though it had no past. It came and was gone again. Her faculties, as after a vivid lightning flash, were momentarily paralysed, without past or present. She had witnessed these awful things, but had not realized them. It was this lack of realization that struck her motionless and dumb.

Colonel Masters, on the other hand, stood beside her quietly as though nothing unusual had happened, wholly master of himself, calm, collected. At the moment of attack no sound had left his lips, there had been no gesture even of defence. Whatever had come, he had apparently accepted. The words that now fell from his lips were, thus, all the more dreadful in their appalling commonplaceness.

'Hadn't you better put that counterpane straight a bit . . . Perhaps?'

Common sense, as always, enables the gas of hysteria to escape. Madame Jodzka gasped, but she obeyed. Automatically she moved across to do his bidding, yet aware, even as she thus moved, that he flicked something from his neck, as though a wasp, a mosquito, or some poisonous insect, had tried to sting him. She remembered no more than that, for he, in his calmness, had contributed nothing else.

Fumbling with the folds of slippery counterpane she tried to straighten out, she was startled to find that Monica was sitting up in bed, awake.

'Oh, Doska—you here!' the child exclaimed innocently, straight out of sleep and using the affectionate nickname. 'And Daddy, too! Oh, my goodness . . . !'

'Sm-moothing your bed, darling,' she stammered, hardly aware of what she said. 'You ought to be asleep. I just looked in to see . . .' She mumbled a few other automatic words.

'And Daddy with you!' repeated the child excitedly, sleep still about her, wondering what it all meant. 'Ooh! Ooh!' holding out her arms.

This brief exchange of spoken words, though it takes a minute to describe, occurred simultaneously with the action—perhaps ten seconds all told, for while the governess fumbled with the counterpane, Colonel Masters was in the act of brushing something from his neck. Nothing else was audible, nothing but his quick gasp and sudden intake of breath: but something else—she swears it on her Warsaw priest—was visible.

Madame Jodzka maintains by all her gods she saw this other thing.

In moment of paralysing stress it is not the senses that act less speedily nor with less precision; their action, on the contrary, is intensified and speeded up: what takes longer is the registration of their reports. The numbed brain causes the apparent delay; realization is slowed down.

Madame Jodzka thus only realized a fraction of a second later what her eyes had indubitably witnessed; a dark-skinned arm slanting in through the open window by the bed and snatching at a small object that lay on the floor after dropping from Colonel Masters' throat, then withdrawing again at lightning speed into the darkness of the night outside.

No one but herself, apparently, had seen this—it was almost supernaturally swift.

'And now you'll be asleep again in two minutes, lucky Monica,' Colonel Masters was whispering over by the bed. 'I just peeped in to see that you were all right . . .' His voice was thin, dreadfully soundless.

Madame Jodzka, against the door, frozen, terrified, looked on and listened.

'Are you quite well, Daddy? Sure? I had a dream, but it's gone now.'

'Splendid. Never better in my life. But better still if I saw you sound asleep. Come now, I'll blow out this silly night-light, for that's what woke you up, I'll be bound.'

He blew it out, he and the child blew it out together, the latter with sleepy laughter that then hushed. And Colonel Masters tiptoed to join Madame Jodzka at the door. 'A lot of damned fuss about nothing,' she heard him muttering in that same thin dreadful voice, and then, as they closed the door and stood a moment in the darkened passage, he did suddenly an unexpected thing. He took the Polish woman in his arms, held her fiercely to him for a second, kissed her vehemently, and flung her away.

'Bless you and thank you,' he said in a low, angry voice. 'You did your best. You made a great fight. But I got what I deserved. I've been waiting years for it.' And he was off down the stairs to his own quarters. Half way down he stopped and looked up to where she stood against the rails. 'Tell the doctor,' he whispered hoarsely, 'that I took a sleeping draught—an overdose.' And he was gone.

And this was, roughly, what she did tell the doctor next morning when a hurried telephone summons brought him to the bed whereon a dead man lay with a swollen, blackened tongue. She told the same tale at the inquest too and an emptied bottle of a powerful sleeping-draught supported her . . .

And Monica, too young to realize grief beyond its trumpery meaning of a selfishly felt loss, never once—oddly enough—referred to the absence of her lovely doll that had comforted so many hours, proved such an intimate companion day and night in a life that held no other playmates. It seemed forgotten, expunged utterly from her memory, as though it had ever existed at all. She stared blankly, stupidly, when a doll was mentioned: she preferred her worn-out teddy-bears. The slate of memory in this particular, was wiped clean.

'They're so warm and comfy,' she described her bears, 'and they cuddle without tickling. Besides,' she added innocently, 'they don't squeak and try to slip away . . .'

Thus in the suburbs, where great spaces between the lamps go dead at night, where the moist wind comes whispering through the mournful branches of the silver-pines, where nothing happens and people cry 'Let's go to town!' there are occasional stirrings among the dead dry bones that hide behind respectable villa walls. . . .

EXPLANATORY NOTES

ABBREVIATIONS

Ashley	Mike Ashley, *Starlight Man* (2019)
Dutton	Algernon Blackwood, Introduction to *The Tales of Algernon Blackwood* (1938, 1965)
EBT	*Episodes before Thirty* (1924)
EH	*The Empty House and Other Ghost Stories* (1906)
FE	*The Face of the Earth and Other Imaginings* (2015)
IA	*Incredible Adventures* (1914)
JS	*John Silence—Physician Extraordinary* (1912)
L	*The Listener and Other Stories* (1907)
LV	*The Lost Valley and Other Stories* (1910)
PG	*Pan's Garden: A Volume of Nature Stories* (1912)
TMS	*Ten Minute Stories* (1914)
WG	*The Wolves of God and Other Fey Stories* (1921)

A HAUNTED ISLAND

One of Blackwood's earliest published stories, 'A Haunted Island' first appeared in the *Pall Mall Magazine* (April 1899); reprinted in *EH* (from which it is reproduced here). Written sometime after Blackwood's first sojourn on Lake Rosseau in Ontario, Canada (May–September 1892); Ashley suggests late 1896 as a probable time of composition.

3 *a small island . . . a large Canadian lake*: this has been identified as Bohemia Island in Lake Rosseau, Ontario. Blackwood would later describe this 'fairyland of peace and loveliness': '[o]ur island, one of many in Lake Rosseau, was about ten acres in extent, irregularly shaped, overgrown with pines, its western end running out to a sharp ridge we called Sunset Point, its eastern end facing the dawn in a high rocky bluff . . . The three big lakes—Rosseau, Muskoka and Joseph—form the letter Y, our island being where the three strokes joined' (*EBT*, 84).

'reading': i.e. an intensive course of study, often used in the context of legal training (particularly, as here, cramming after 'foolishly neglecting' one's studies).

maskinonge: a large pike, *Esox masquinongy*; *maskinongé* is the Canadian French approximation of the Algonquin *maskinunga*; the more usual common name in English is 'muskellunge'.

12 *pneumatic tube*: refers to the networks of pipes, primarily in use in the later nineteenth and early twentieth centuries, which used air pressure to propel cylindrical containers; one can easily imagine Blackwood becoming accustomed to the sound of cylinders whooshing their way through

the tubes of the *New York Times* building during his tenure as reporter there.

THE EMPTY HOUSE

First published in *EH* and often anthologized since, 'The Empty House' is, for Blackwood, a relatively conventional contribution to the haunted house subgenre. The story has its origins in Blackwood's association with the Society for Psychical Research (SPR), founded in the 1880s for the pursuit of scholarly research into apparently paranormal phenomena. Though never himself a member, Blackwood joined author and leading SPR member Frank Podmore (1856–1910) and others in several investigations of haunted houses. 'The Empty House' is based on a visit to a house in Brunswick Square, Hove, probably in 1888 or 1889—a visit made not with an 'elderly spinster aunt' (as in the story) but, as he admitted in a 1943 letter, with 'a misguided, but charming lady, who had persuaded herself that I should make a good husband, though such a thought had never even entered my head' (Ashley, 59).

19 *Shorthouse . . . the town*: this is one of four stories—'A Case of Eavesdropping', 'The Strange Adventures of a Private Secretary in New York', 'The Empty House', and 'With Intent to Steal'—to feature early Blackwood stand-in Jim Shorthouse. Shorthouse is also something of a prototype for Blackwood's occult detective John Silence (whose initials he shares). The seaside town is Hove, today part of the city of Brighton and Hove.

psychical research: see headnote.

bathing-machine: bathing machines were wheeled, cabin-like aids to propriety in use throughout the nineteenth century; Shorthouse is pretending to believe that he has been summoned to Hove, then as now a popular resort town, for a simple seaside holiday.

the haunted house in the square: see headnote.

27 *'physical mediums'*: those able to facilitate physical manifestations from the spirit world such as table rappings and bell ringing, as opposed to 'mental mediums' who receive messages or perceive other-worldly phenomena.

THE LISTENER

Written in 1899 but not published until 1907, as the title story in *L*; Blackwood later wrote, 'such are the tricks of memory, I can still see the grave expression on the faces of [publisher] Eveleigh Nash and his gifted "reader", Maude ffoulkes, while we discussed together whether a large Ear might be printed on the cover (picture-jackets had not yet come in), and whether the title-story was not perhaps of too pathogenic a character to be included' (Dutton, 10).

33 *P——Place*: presumably Portland Place, in Marylebone; being within 'a stone's throw' of here would also correspond with the narrator's subsequent account of his walks 'through Regent's Park, into Kensington

Gardens, or farther afield to Hampstead Heath' and his regular afternoon visits to 'the reading-room of the British Museum, where [he has] a reader's ticket'.

H——shire: Hampshire.

34 *All the morning . . . the struggle of life*: as with a number of details within the story, this catalogue of projects reflects Blackwood's own writing life during this period: he produced a number of (published) articles and (unpublished) poems; Ashley suggests that the novel may have been *A Flying Boy* (later published as *Jimbo*) and the children's book a never-published manuscript called *The Children's Secret Society*, with the 'honest record of [his] soul's advance or retreat' probably referring to the notes which would later be used in composing *EBT*.

36 *an 'A.B.C.' shop*: chain of tea rooms operated by the Aerated Bread Company.

38 *Cimabue and Raphael*: important Italian Renaissance painters, whose 'real' works would be quite valuable.

Trinity Hall: one of Cambridge University's oldest colleges, founded in 1350; Blackwood's older brother Arthur Stevenson went to Trinity for two years before joining Algernon at Edinburgh University in 1888.

41 *Greek Street, Soho . . . able to keep*: locations and episodes from Thomas De Quincey's autobiographical *Confessions of an English Opium-Eater*, first published in the *London Magazine* in 1820 and subsequently revised and expanded. De Quincey was one of Blackwood's most treasured authors; he brought the *Confessions* with him to Canada; later, in New York, Blackwood lent it to his friend Dr Otto Huebner, himself an addict who administered small doses of morphine to Blackwood.

46 *Earl's Court Road*: runs through Earl's Court, a district in the Royal Borough of Kensington and Chelsea.

57 *he was a leper*: although the causative agent of leprosy, a bacterial skin infection, had been identified in 1873 by the Norwegian physician Gerhard Henrik Armauer Hansen, effective treatments would not be found until the 1940s.

THE WILLOWS

'The Willows', first published in *L*, is Blackwood's most frequently anthologized story, and the one most frequently adduced by critics as his masterpiece. In his influential essay 'Supernatural Horror in Literature', H. P. Lovecraft, naming Blackwood as one of four 'Modern Masters' (with Arthur Machen, M. R. James, and Lord Dunsany), wrote, 'Foremost of all' among Blackwood's tales 'must be reckoned *The Willows*, in which the nameless presences on a desolate Danube island are horribly felt and recognised by a pair of idle voyagers. Here art and restraint in narrative reach their very highest development, and impression of lasting poignancy is produced without a single strained passage or a single false note.' Blackwood here combines elements of two (possibly more) separate voyages, later recalling both 'a journey down the Danube in a Canadian canoe, and how my friend and I camped on one of the countless lonely islands below Pressburg (Bratislava) and the willows seemed to suffocate us in spite of the gale blowing, and how a year or two later, making the same trip in a barge, we found a dead body caught by a root, its decayed mass dangling against the sandy shore of the very same island my story describes. A coincidence, of course!' (Dutton, 10).

58 *gipsy tent*: probably the more familiar long, low tent, though the term was also used in reference to a beehive-shaped tent associated with the Romany in England. In any case, Blackwood sang its praises in the essay 'Down the Danube in a Canadian Canoe': 'We pegged the tent inside and out. All night the wind tore at it, howling; but a gipsy-tent never comes down. The wind sweeps over it, and finding an ever lessening angle of resistance, only drives it more firmly into the ground' (*FE*, 143).

59 *Orth . . . Hungary*: compare with Blackwood's description in 'Down the Danube': 'For two days at racing speed we journeyed through wild and lonely country towards the frontiers of Hungary. The river was like a wide lake. . . . We passed signs of Roman days and Turkish occupancy strangely mingled, where Marcus Aurelius is said to have written much of his philosophy; Theben on a spur of the little Carpathians, with its rock-perched fortress destroyed by the Turks. . . . At its very feet the March (the boundary between Austria and Hungary) comes sedately in, and the Danube received a new impetus as we passed below its shadow and into Hungary at last' (*FE*, 148).

bioscope pictures: movies, i.e. a cinematic 'cut'. Blackwood used the same metaphor in 'Down the Danube': 'The river communicated something of its hurry to ourselves, and in my mind the journey now presents itself something in the form of a series of brilliant cinematographs' (*FE*, 142).

60 *Donaueschingen*: Blackwood wrote of this place in 'Down the Danube': 'Donaueschingen is an old-fashioned little town on the southern end of the Schwarzwald plateau, and the railway that runs through it brings it apparently no nearer to the world. It breathes a spirit of remoteness and tranquillity born of the forests that encircle it, and that fill the air with pleasant odours and gentle murmurings' (*FE*, 131).

61 *like Brer Fox*: Br'er Fox, a trickster figure from the series of African American folk tales compiled and adapted by Joel Chandler Harris (1848–1908).

a whole army of Undines: elemental water spirits or nymphs, an originally alchemical conceit made famous by Friedrich de la Motte Fouqué in his fairy-tale novel *Undine* (1811), which E. T. A. Hoffmann set as an opera in 1816 (it also influenced Antonín Dvořák's better-known opera *Rusalka* of 1901).

70 *The psychology of places*: the title of an essay by Blackwood, in which he warns against pitching one's tent on 'borderland' regions—'[f]or a threshold is ever the critical frontier that invites adventure and therefore possible

disaster' (*FE*, 155). A relevant maxim, no doubt, for the protagonists of 'The Willows'.

86 *the fourth dimension*: a subject in which Blackwood had long been interested; one of his favourite books was *The Fourth Dimension* (1904) by British mathematician Charles H. Hinton (1852–1907).

87 *Komorn or Gran*: German names for Komárno and Komárom, today divided between Hungary and Slovakia, and Esztergom, in Hungary; in 'Down the Danube' Blackwood writes of 'la[ying] in provisions' in Komorn and of being 'charm[ed]' by the 'quaint little town' of Gran (*FE*, 150–1).

92 *as the Americans say*: while there are several uses of the verb 'to locate' associated with North American origins, this particular sense of pinpointing an exact location does not appear to be one of them; perhaps Blackwood simply encountered it more frequently while living in America.

SECRET WORSHIP

First published in *JS* (as 'Case IV'), though probably written some time earlier, the story and its setting have their origin in the year 1885–6, which a 16-year-old Blackwood had spent at the Moravian school in Königsfeld im Schwarzwald, Germany (the Moravians are the 'small Protestant community (which it is unnecessary to specify)' described in the second paragraph). Of the town and school Blackwood would write a few years later, in a magazine article titled 'About the Moravians', 'To the visitor axious [*sic*] to see a Moravian settlement to its best advantage, no place offers greater attractions than Königsfeld. Remote from the world, it is a perfect model for its earnest, active life and at the same time its perfect peacefulness. . . . Nothing was more conspicuous in this school, as in all their other ones, than the beautiful spirit of gentleness and merciful justice, tempered by true brotherly loyalty, with which the boys of as many temperaments as nationalities were taught to live' (*Methodist Magazine* (Jan. 1890), 169–70).

104 *Mittagessen*: lunch (literally 'midday meal').

Speisesaal: dining room.

Waschkammer: washroom.

his violin studies: Blackwood played the violin, apparently well, throughout his life, though he deprecated his own ability.

108 *Heimweh*: homesickness.

109 *Unsinn!*: Nonsense!

110 *'Gruss Got'*: 'Grüß Gott'—'Good day', akin to 'God bless you'; more common in southern Germany (where the story is set) and Austria.

Gasthof der Brüdergemeinde: 'Inn of the Brotherhood'; in his article 'About the Moravians' Blackwood noted that 'Even the inn [of Königsfeld] is the property of the Brotherhood, who give to a salaried man the charge of the house and guests' (170).

111 *Bruderstube*: literally 'brother room'.

113 *"zweite Geige"*: second violin.

114 *Wie so, denn?*: How so, then?

 Es ist doch selbstverständlich: Of course, it goes without saying.

116 *Es ist wirklich merkwürdig*: It's really quite strange.

117 *Schlafzimmer*: bedroom.

118 *his Amati*: violin made by the celebrated Amati family of Cremona.

120 *tausendmal*: a thousand times.

124 *Asmodelius*: the name is suggestive of Asmodeus, the King of Demons in Judaic legend.

 The import of the word 'Opfer' flashed upon his soul: Harris suddenly grasps the significance of *Opfer*—it means 'sacrifice, victim, prey'.

125 *Hauptbruder*: head-brother.

131 *Rosicrucian*: supposed esoteric society whose symbol is the 'Rosy Cross', and from which a number of actual societies claimed descent or kinship, including the famous Hermetic Order of the Golden Dawn, to which Blackwood belonged.

 Jacob wrestling with an angel: see Genesis 32:22–32.

ANCIENT SORCERIES

One of Blackwood's three or four most popular stories, this tale of witchcraft and feline transformation was an inspiration, though not a direct source, for the 1942 movie *Cat People*. Blackwood recalled the origins of the story in an unplanned stop in a town in Picardy, remembering 'that old French town of "Ancient Sorceries", where the slinking inhabitants behaved as cats behave, sidling along the pavement with slanting gestures, twitching their sleeky ears and snakey tails, their sharp eyes glinting, all alert and concentrated upon some hidden, secret life of their own while they feigned attention to tourists like ourselves—ourselves just back from climbing in the Dolomites and finding the train so boring on its way from Basle to Boulogne that we hopped out at Laon and spent two days in this witch-ridden atmosphere. The "Auberge de la Hure" was the name of the Inn, and it was not Angoulême, as some fancied . . . nor elsewhere as variously attributed, but Laon, a lovely old haunted town where the Cathedral towers stand up against the sunset like cats' ears, the paws running down the dusky streets, the feline body crouched just below the hill. Yet who should guess that so much magic lay within a kilometre of its dull, desolate railway station, or that from my little bedroom window I should presently stand enthralled as I looked across the moonlit tiles and towers, jotting down on the backs of envelopes an experience that kept sleep away till dawn?' (Dutton, 10). 'Ancient Sorceries', while possibly (like 'Secret Worship') written some time earlier, first appeared in *JS*, (as 'Case II').

136 *Surbiton*: neighbourhood in south-west London, functioning here, no doubt, as a symbol of stolid, unimaginative suburban life, in contrast to the experience Vezin is about to have.

137 *The little town . . . summit*: the town is based on Laon in the Picardy region, which Blackwood had visited 'probably in 1903 or 1904' (Ashley, 176) (see headnote). The present Laon Cathedral, whose construction dates from the twelfth and early thirteenth centuries, was damaged but not 'ruined' during the Franco-Prussian War of 1870. It stands some 100 metres above the Picardy plain.

138 *Dundreary whiskers*: long, drooping sideburns popular in the nineteenth century, named after a character in the popular 1858 comedy *Our American Cousin* by Tom Taylor (1817–80).

141 *an Æolian harp*: stringed instrument played by currents of air.

147 *the old church of St Martin*: the twelfth-century church originally associated with Laon's abbey of Saint-Martin (dissolved during the French Revolution).

152 *'Ah, Ma'mselle est de retour!'*: 'Ah, Mademoiselle (i.e. Miss Ilsé) is back!'

156 *soupe à l'oignon*: onion soup made with beef broth and caramelized onions, often topped with toasted bread and/or cheese, is a traditional French dish.

158 *the witches had been burnt by the score*: Laon was the epicentre of a region where 'the witch craze raged most fiercely' in the sixteenth century (Alfred Soman, 'The Parlement of Paris and the Great Witch Hunt (1565–1640)', *Sixteenth Century Journal*, 9/2 (July 1978), 37). The town was also famous for a public exorcism in 1566 of the demonically possessed Nicole Aubrey or Obry.

165 *'Enfin! . . . contente'*: 'At last, Monsieur has made his decision, and a good thing too. I am glad of it.'

'On pourrait . . . vite!': 'We might take a few turns about together, yes? We'll be going there tonight and you'll need a little practice first. Ilse, Ilse, come in here, quickly!'

vervain: *Verbena officinalis*, a flowering plant long associated with magic and enchantment (as is rue, which we will shortly see in Ilsé's hair as well).

169 *The salve . . . come!*: witches were supposed to use a 'flying ointment' to effect transformation; it has long been speculated that toxic ingredients including belladonna might have induced hallucinations in users.

175 *the stigmata of the religieuses*: reference to marks of the Crucifixion appearing on nuns (French *religieuses*).

THE KIT-BAG

First published in the December 1908 number of the *Pall Mall Magazine* and resurrected some eight decades later by Richard Dalby in the anthology *Ghosts for Christmas* (1988) and Mike Ashley in his collection of 'lost' Blackwood stories, *The Magic Mirror* (1989). The original (1908) appearance has been used here.

177 *[title]*: the large canvas 'kit-bag', better known today as a duffel bag, would be immortalized during the First World War in the popular 1915 marching song, 'Pack Up Your Troubles in Your Old Kit-Bag, and Smile, Smile, Smile'.

K.C.: King's Counsel, a prestigious title conferred upon senior barristers (trial lawyers).

skate and ski in the Alps: Blackwood, himself an excellent skier, is perhaps anticipating the coming winter (1908–9) which he is about to spend in the Swiss Alps; he would return there nearly every year thereafter.

179 *puttees*: from *paṭṭī*, Hindi for 'bandage'; cloth leg wrappings then worn by British Commonwealth soldiers as well as skiers and other sportsmen and -women (one 1920 advertisement urges readers to 'Wear Fox's Puttees at the winter sports. You can choose from joyous bright art shades, or, if you wish, from colours more restrained . . . [a]nd you assure your legs of utmost comfort—warmth, support, protection').

181 *snow-glasses*: tinted glasses to protect against snow blindness.

183 *the Old Bailey*: the Central Criminal Court of London. Its history goes back to the sixteenth century; the present building, constructed in 1902, would have been relatively new at the time of the story.

THE MAN WHO FOUND OUT

First published in *Lady's Realm* (June 1909); reprinted in *WG* (the version reproduced here).

188 *F.R.S.*: Fellow of the Royal Society; i.e. a highly distinguished man of science.

190 *Scrutator*: presumably a stand-in for the weekly magazine *The Spectator*.

199 *the great hypnotic doctor*: Blackwood had a deep and long-standing interest in hypnosis; as a student at Edinburgh he had known a 'Dr H——who used hypnotism in his practice, taught me various methods of using it, and often admitted me to private experiments in his study' (*EBT*, 59); according to Ashley this may have been a Dr Robert Howden or a Dr David Hepburn (61).

202 *Bath brick*: a brick-shaped scouring block made from gritty riverbed silt (like the Tablets of the Gods, Bath bricks, too, often bore inscriptions—of their manufacturer's name).

THE FACE OF THE EARTH

The story seems to have first appeared in the weekly newspaper *The Leader* (Melbourne, Victoria) on 26 June 1909 (the version consulted here). It was not collected in book form until 2015, in *FE*.

203 *Bismarck*: the Prussian statesman Otto von Bismarck (1815–98), instrumental in the Unification of Germany and subsequent formation of the German Empire.

Spinrobin: Blackwood also used the name for the protagonist (Robert Spinrobin) of his novel *The Human Chord*, published the following year.

Novalis and Schlegel: Georg Philipp Friedrich von Hardenberg (1772–1801) and Friedrich Schlegel (1772–1829), key figures in early German Romanticism; Novalis in particular was a favourite author of Blackwood's.

204 *Wer weisst?*: 'Who knows?'

205 *Fechner*: Gustav Theodor Fechner (1801–87), experimental psychologist and philosopher; in this latter (and here, more relevant) capacity, Fechner was an animist and panpsychist, believing non-human, even inanimate, entities to possess minds or souls. In his books *Nanna, oder über das Seelenleben der Pflanzen* ('Nanna, or the Soul-Life of Plants', 1848) and *Zend-Avesta, oder über die Dinge des Himmels und des Jenseits* ('Zend-Avesta, or on the Things of Heaven and the Hereafter', 1851), Fechner attributed consciousness to plants and planets respectively, calling the earth 'an angel, an angel so rich and fresh and flower-like, and yet going her round in the skies so firmly and so at one with herself, turning her whole living face to Heaven . . . that I asked myself how the opinions of men could have ever so spun themselves away from life so far as to deem the earth only a dry clod' (quoted in William James, 'Concerning Fechner', in *Essays in Radical Empiricism and A Pluralistic Universe* (Gloucester, MA, 1967), 165). The influence of Fechner is central to Blackwood's novel *The Centaur*; his conception of plant consciousness is important to 'The Man Whom the Trees Loved' as well.

Blake: English Romantic poet and artist William Blake (1757–1827).

206 *music of the spheres*: the conceit, first advanced by the Greek philosopher Pythagoras (*c*.570–*c*.495 BC), of a 'universal music' (*musica universalis*) produced by the movements of the heavenly bodies through space. This idea has had a profound influence on Western art, philosophy, and science since antiquity (William Blake, to give one example, begins the preface to his 1794 *Europe: A Prophecy*: 'Five windows light the cavern'd Man: thro' one he breathes the air; | Thro' one hears music of the spheres . . .').

Donnenwetter!: literally 'thunder weather', i.e. 'thunderstorm'—German expression of admiration and/or astonishment.

THE WENDIGO

Written in November of either 1908 or 1909 in Champéry, Switzerland (Ashley, 200); first appeared in *LV*.

212 *[title]*: the Windigo or Wendigo is a monstrous forest spirit-creature in Algonquian legend (see Introduction, pp. xxiii–xxix).

Nimrods: mighty hunters, here used facetiously (Nimrod is a legendary biblical king, called 'a mighty hunter before the Lord').

212 'Wee Kirk': in 1843 there was a schism in the Church ('Kirk') of Scotland; the breakaway group, the Free Kirk of Scotland, which had congregants but no buildings to worship in, was taunted with the doggerel verse, 'The Free Kirk, the Wee Kirk, the Kirk without the Steeple'. There is a later, more complicated contention as well *between* two factions called the 'Wee Kirk' and 'Free Kirk', but the most likely meaning here is simply the United Free Church of Scotland, formed in 1900 by the merging of most of the original Free Church with the United Presbyterian Church of Scotland.

Défago: Blackwood takes the name from a prominent family in the Champéry municipality of Switzerland, where he had travelled.

Rat Portage . . . a-building: Rat Portage, today Kenora, is a city located on the traditional territory of the Ojibway; it was connected with the railway in 1886. In 1887, Blackwood had visited Canada with his father who, in his capacity as a Post Office official, was surveying the newly completed Canadian Pacific Railway line from Montreal to Vancouver.

voyageur songs: folk-songs sung by French-Canadian *voyageurs* ('travellers'), who transported furs by canoe during the North American fur trade of the eighteenth and nineteenth centuries. The fur trader Edward Ermatinger (1797–1876) collected and recorded a number of these while working for the Hudson's Bay Company.

214 *Garden Lake*: Blackwood described this Ontario lake in his essay "Mid the Haunts of the Moose': 'Garden lake stretched its lonely bays and arms over an immense surface, dotted with wooded islands, on one of which the Indians had built their annual crop of birch-bark canoes. . . . It was just sunset when we reached the shores of Garden Lake and saw the expanse of still water, with dark patches in all directions showing the islands . . . before we were half-way across this arm of Garden Lake the moon rose over the ridge of forest and silvered a picture of fairy-like enchantment such as I have never seen equalled' (*FE*, 122–4).

portage over: carry overland between navigable waters.

funked: showed fear.

219 *Titan*: in Greek mythology, race of huge, powerful older gods predating the Olympians.

'*blaze*': mark a trail by chipping bark from trees.

252 '*How terrible . . . that——*': seems to combine references to 'the great and terrible wilderness' in Deuteronomy 1:19 and 8:15 with the verse in Isaiah 52:7 which begins, 'How beautiful upon the mountains are the feet of him that bringeth good tidings'.

THE MAN WHOM THE TREES LOVED

Written in 1911 and published in the *London Magazine* (March 1912) and as the first story in *PG*, whose working title was *The Man Whom the Trees Loved*.

In October 1911, Blackwood wrote to Macmillan's of the proposed book, 'Although composed of separate pieces, varying from 26,000 words to 2,000 words it is a coherent whole, the same idea running throughout, and it illustrates that characteristic belief, present in all my work, that there exists a definite relationship between Human Beings and Nature. I have been steadily adding to this book for some years, taking in turn different aspects of Nature—Sea, Mountains, Snow, Fire etc.' (Ashley, 223–4). (*PG* has been consulted here.)

256 *Sanderson*: modelled after Blackwood's friend, the painter Walford Graham Robertson (1866–1948), who also provided illustrations for *PG*.

C.B., late of the Woods and Forests: Bittacy is a Companion of the Order of the Bath, which in the nineteenth century was opened to civil as well as military appointments. (Blackwood's own father, a Post Office official, was made a CB in 1880 and a Knight Commander of the Bath (KCB) in 1887.) Presumably Bittacy has been so recognized for his service in the Imperial Forest Service (today the Indian Forest Service), established in 1867. (Possibly his surname was suggested by Bittacy Hill in Mill Hill, on the outskirts of London.)

257 *an evangelical clergyman*: recalls Blackwood's own upbringing in a strict religious household. His father, while not a clergyman, was highly active in evangelical Christian circles.

260 *New Forest*: vast protected forest in southern England, extending over portions of Hampshire, Wiltshire, and Dorset. It is mentioned in the Domesday Book of 1086.

262 *Baedeker*: series of popular travel guides published by German firm founded by Karl Baedeker (1801–59).

Tennyson or Farrar: Poet Laureate Alfred, Lord Tennyson (1809–92), whose poem *Maud* is quoted later in the story, and Frederic William Farrar (1831–1903), clergyman and writer; both men are certainly examples of what Sophia Bittacy would consider 'safe' authors.

263 *Francis Darwin . . . Royal Society*: Sir Francis Darwin (1848–1925), botanist and author (with his father Charles Darwin) of *The Power of Movement in Plants* (1880); he was made a Fellow of the Royal Society in 1882.

265 *upas*: *Antiaris toxicaria*, whose toxic properties, while real, are often exaggerated. In his poem *The Loves of the Plants*, Erasmus Darwin calls it 'Fell Upas . . . the Hydra-Tree of death' (*The Botanic Garden* (London, 1825), 168).

268 *Holman Hunt . . . effect of moonlight that he wanted*: Victorian painters William Holman Hunt (1827–1910) and Dante Gabriel Rossetti (1828–82), who with John Everett Millais formed the Pre-Raphaelite Brotherhood in 1848. The anecdote refers to Holman Hunt and his painting *The Light of the World* (1851–3), one of the religious canvases which brought him fame.

Henley . . . Stevenson . . . children's verses: poet and critic William Ernest Henley (1849–1903) was a friend and collaborator of Robert Louis Stevenson (1850–94) (and certainly no 'socialist', as Mrs Bittacy seems to think); Long John Silver in *Treasure Island* may have been modelled after Henley, whose left leg was amputated at the knee after he contracted tuberculosis of the bone as a youth. Stevenson's book of poetry is *A Child's Garden of Verses* (1885); the poem by Henley which Sanderson is discussing here, and will presently quote, is 'Not to the Staring Day'.

269 *Prentice Mulford's . . . "God in the Trees"*: Mulford (1834–91) was an American author closely involved with the 'New Thought' spiritual movement; 'God in the Trees or the Infinite Mind in Nature' is contained in his *Your Forces and How To Use Them* (1888).

270 *He was said . . . evening*: see Genesis 3:8 (this is one of several echoes of Genesis in this part of the story).

279 *theofosical*: garbled reference to Theosophy, the occult religion chiefly associated with mystic and writer Helena Blavatsky (1831–91).

Latter-Day things: signs of the Last Days, as prophesied in the Book of Revelation and Johannine epistles, including the Antichrist, the False Prophet, and the Number of the Beast (all mentioned in the next sentence).

Principalities . . . darkness: mingles language from Ephesians 8:12 with, most likely, Psalm 91:6 ('the pestilence that walketh in darkness').

280 *farther than the thought*: Sophia Bittacy's phonetically generated malapropism for 'the wish is father to the thought', e.g. our desires drive our beliefs; originally from Shakespeare's *Henry IV, Part II*.

282 *Baxter Bible*: popular large quarto Bible, with commentary and engravings, published by Surrey-born printer John Baxter (1781–1858) in 1811.

285 *Trojans*: the inhabitants of Troy, as depicted by classical authors, were proverbially industrious.

289 *Seillans above St Raphael*: Seillans is a Provençal village and holiday destination, about 43 kilometres away from the resort town of Saint-Raphaël on the coast.

290 *William the Conqueror*: the New Forest was originally the royal hunting ground of William I (*c.*1028–87).

295 *O art thou . . . Dark cedar*: from Part I of *Maud* (1855) by Alfred, Lord Tennyson.

296 *allopathic Knight*: allopathy is modern, science-based medicine, in contradistinction to 'the homeopathic dose that she [Mrs Bittacy] believed in' and that she administers to her husband.

308 *the falling of a sparrow*: see Matthew 10:29.

313 *'There is joy . . . one sinner that——'*: see Luke 15:7.

A DESCENT INTO EGYPT

Published in *IA*. In January 1912, Blackwood travelled to Helwan, Egypt, the health resort town (today part of Greater Cairo) where his friend Baron Johann

Knoop had established a sanitarium and hotel. It was the first of many visits there, and his Egyptian experiences are reflected in a number of essays and stories, as well as a novel, *The Wave* (1916). Of his Egyptian tales, the most compelling (and by far the longest) are 'Sand' (completed in March 1912 and appearing in *PG*) and 'A Descent into Egypt'. Both are substantial novellas set in Helwan, near the ancient capital of Memphis, and inspired by Blackwood's confrontation with the daunting antiquity of Egypt; as he wrote in his essay, 'Egypt: An Impression': 'Egypt is endless and inexhaustible; some hint of eternity lies there. . . . There *is* a sense of deathlessness about the ancient Nile, about the grim Sphinx and Pyramids, in the very colonnades of Karnak, whose pylons now once more stand upright after a sleep of forty centuries on their backs; above all, in the appealing strength of the floating, rustling sand—something that defies time and repudiates change in death' (*Country Life*, 34/879 (8 November 1913), 626).

319 *one can only . . . blessed 'Mesopotamia'*: in other words, one can only have recourse to hifalutin theories that explain nothing; Blackwood is invoking the phrase 'The true Mesopotamian ring', once applied to 'something high-sounding and pleasing, but wholly past comprehension. The allusion is to the story of the old woman who told her pastor that she "found great support in the blessed word Mesopotamia"' (E. Cobham Brewer, *Dictionary of Phrase and Fable* (London, 1870), 572). (The association of the word 'Mesopotamia' with euphonious delivery derives ultimately from an anecdote about the eighteenth-century Methodist preacher George Whitefield.)

watching the Races: the racing-grounds at Ascot had long been a place for fashionable society to see and be seen; the Welsh sporting writer 'Nimrod' (Charles James Apperley) wrote that 'the charms of Ascot, to those not interested in the horses, consist in the promenade on the course between the various races, where the highest fashion, in its best garb, mingles with the crowd, and gives a brilliant effect to the passing scene' ('Nimrod', *The Chace, the Turf, and the Road* (London, 1852), 105).

320 *a hotel in Egypt*: while 'Sand' takes place at the Tewfik Palace Hotel, where Blackwood had stayed on his first visit to Helwan, the reference here to Isley's health, and later to the hotel's '*clientèle* [of] German and Russian invalid[s]' ('No English patronised it', notes the narrator), point to Johann Knoop's own establishment, the Al-Hayat (which, according to a 1906 guide, *Helouan: An Egyptian Health Resort and How to Reach It*, was 'chiefly patronised by Germans').

321 *Persians, Greeks and Romans, Saracens and Mamelukes*: after two and a half millennia of rule by (primarily) native pharaohs, Egypt fell under the yoke of a succession of foreign powers: the Persian Empire under Cambyses in 525 BC, the Macedonian conqueror Alexander the Great in 332 BC, the Roman Empire in 30 BC, and Muslim invaders ('Saracens', to medieval Christendom) in the seventh century AD. The Mamluks were a knightly class (originally slaves—the meaning of 'Mamluk' in Arabic) who ruled in Egypt from AD 1250 until the Ottoman conquest in 1517.

324 *brimmed*: filled to the brim.

325 *two monstrous pyramids*: the famous Giza pyramids of Khufu and Khaphre
(then more usually called the Great Pyramid of Kheops and the Second
Pyramid), visible from Helwan, some 24 kilometres away (the third Giza
pyramid, that of Menkaure, looks far less 'monstrous' alongside its
neighbours).

328 *the Valley of the Kings . . . Gizeh monsters*: Isley has 'overdone it' in the
region of Thebes, the greatest of Egypt's ancient capitals (though
Memphis, across the Nile from Helwan, was its first) which functions in
Blackwood's story as the mystic centre of the Egyptian 'web'. More specifically, he and Moleson were excavating in the Valley of Kings, a renowned
complex of royal tombs cut into the rock of cliffs in a valley across the Nile
from Thebes. Though far to the south, Thebes is counter-intuitively 'up'
from Memphis ('Lower Egypt' is so called because it is nearer sea level:
the Nile runs 'down'—northward—to the Mediterranean). The vast,
ancient necropolis of Memphis comprises multiple cemeteries including
Dahshur, Saqqara, and Giza.

330 *the Serapeum*: a temple complex in Saqqara, near the catacombs of bulls sacred
to the Egyptian god Ptah (Serapis in his Graeco-Egyptian incarnation).

335 *Bedraschien*: Badrashin, 6 kilometres west of Helwan.

337 *the Sphinx . . . Colossi*: the Sphinx in question is of course the iconic limestone statue at Giza; the colossi (colossal statues) are of Rameses II
(Rameses the Great), in Memphis.

340 *the discovery of Alice that there was no real 'to-day'*: cf. chapter 5 of Lewis
Carroll's *Through the Looking-Glass*, in which the White Queen proposes to
employ Alice, with 'twopence a week, and jam every other day' for wages:

> Alice couldn't help laughing, as she said, 'I don't want you to hire
> *me*—and I don't care for jam.'
> 'It's very good jam,' said the Queen.
> 'Well, I don't want any *to-day*, at any rate.'
> 'You couldn't have it if you *did* want it', the Queen said. 'The rule is,
> jam to-morrow and jam yesterday—but never jam *to-day*.'
> 'It *must* come sometimes to "jam to-day,"' Alice objected.
> 'No, it ca'n't,' said the Queen. 'It's jam every *other* day: to-day isn't any
> *other* day, you know.'
> 'I don't understand you,' said Alice. 'It's dreadfully confusing!'
> 'That's the effect of living backwards,' the Queen said kindly: 'it always
> makes one a little giddy at first——'
> 'Living backwards!' Alice repeated in great astonishment. 'I never
> heard of such a thing!'

It is, of course, precisely the danger of 'living backwards' that Egypt represents to the European visitor in Blackwood's tale.

341 *those abominable insects . . . alive*: Blackwood probably has some type of
parasitic wasp in mind, such as the ichneumon wasp, of which Charles

Darwin wrote: 'I cannot persuade myself that a beneficent and omnipotent God would have designedly created the Ichneumonidae with the express intention of their feeding within the living bodies of Caterpillars'. *The Life and Letters of Charles Darwin*, Vol. II (London, 1888), 312.

dams . . . falaheen: references to the Egypt of the present day, in contrast with its 'eternal' past: the Great Nile Dam of Assuân (today called the 'Old Aswan Dam' or 'Aswan Low Dam') was a major engineering project undertaken by the British in 1898 and completed in 1902; early Egyptian nationalists sought to end the British occupation dating from 1882; the term 'fellahin' refers to the Egyptian peasant or farmer class, the improvement of whose condition was a subject of discussion among English reformers.

Mena: the Mena House Hotel outside Cairo, named after Egypt's half-legendary King Menes; contemporary guidebooks recommend that day-travellers to the Giza pyramids lunch at the Mena House's restaurant.

baksheesh: a tip or bribe. Here, *Baedeker* cautions the Western tourist against a too-liberal treatment of the natives: 'The average Oriental regards the European traveller as a Crœsus . . . [and] therefore looks upon him as fair game . . . pressing upon him with a perpetual demand for bak-shish (*bakshîsh*), which simply means "a gift" . . . Bakshish should never be given except for services rendered, or to the aged and crippled' (p. xxiii).

dragomen: a dragoman is a guide and interpreter conversant in Arabic, Persian, and Turkish ('dragomans' is the preferred plural form in English). Here, too, *Baedeker* strongly recommends firmness: 'The dragomans are inclined to assume a patronizing manner towards their employers . . . [t]he sooner this impertinence is checked, the more satisfactory will be the traveller's subsequent relations with his guide. Above all, travellers should never permit their dragoman to "explain" the monuments. These men are without exception quite uneducated' (pp. xxiv–xxv).

344 *till Ra . . . ancient dream*: Ra, the great sun god of ancient Egyptian mythology, with whom the pharaohs were expected to become one after death.

350 *Plotinus . . . recollection*: third-century AD philosopher Plotinus, the founder of Neoplatonism.

351 *Malahide*: Blackwood would use the name again in his story 'Malahide and Forden', appearing in the 1924 collection *Tongues of Fire and Other Sketches*.

352 *Denderah . . . Hathor was a cow*: references to the Dendera Temple complex, dominated by the Temple of Hathor, an Egyptian sky-goddess associated by the Greeks with Aphrodite, and often depicted as a cow or cow-headed goddess. The Dendera zodiac, a depiction of the sky in bas-relief, has been in the Louvre since 1922.

Aknahton: the 'heretic pharaoh' of the Eighteenth Dynasty who attempted to scrub all deities from Egypt's culture save one, Aton or Aten, in whose honour he had a new capital built, Akhetaton.

354 *Blüthner*: celebrated German piano-manufacturing company, founded by Julius Blüthner in 1853.

355 *Strauss ... Debussy ... Scriabin*: composers Richard Strauss (1864–1949), Claude Debussy (1862–1918), and Alexander Scriabin (1872–1915), whose respective tone poems—Moleson moves from Strauss's *Till Eulenspiegels lustige Streiche* (1894–5) to Debussy's *Prélude à l'après-midi d'un faune* (1894) to Scriabin's *Prometheus: The Poem of Fire* (1910)—here symbolise different flavours of 'ultra-modern' music.

356 *Edfu, Abou Simbel*: Edfu is the site of the Temple of Horus, begun by Ptolemy III in 237 BC; Abu Simbel, to the extreme south of Egypt near Nubia, contains rock-cut temples to Ramesses II and his queen, Nefertari; according to *Baedeker*, '[t]he two temples of Abu Simbel, built by Rameses II, are among the most stupendous monuments of ancient Egyptian architecture and challenge comparison with the gigantic edifices situated in Egypt proper' (394). In 1968 the Abu Simbel temples were relocated to avoid being flooded during the construction of the Aswan High Dam.

360 *As the embryo ... attained*: refers to the intuitively appealing but deeply flawed theory of recapitulation in evolutionary biology, captured in Ernst Haeckel's famous phrase 'ontogeny recapitulates phylogeny', i.e. the development of an individual embryo belonging to a particular species 'replays' in miniature the evolutionary history of the species itself.

361 *Horus*: falcon-headed sky god; one of the greater gods of ancient Egypt.

367 *the Museum ... Aknahton's*: the Egyptian Museum, the present version of which was established in 1858 in Boulaq, a district of Cairo; the hymn-poem which Moleson and Isley have discovered seems to be akin to the famous, monotheistic 'Great Hymn to the Aten' composed by or under Aknahton, now part of the Egyptian Museum's collections.

370 *Egyptian darkness of a plague*: cf. Exodus 10:21–3: 'Then the LORD said to Moses, "Stretch out your hand toward the sky so that darkness will spread over Egypt—darkness that can be felt." So Moses stretched out his hand toward the sky, and total darkness covered all Egypt for three days. No one could see anyone else or leave his place for three days.'

371 *the boat of Ra has crossed the Underworld*: by day, the sun god was supposed to cross the sky in a solar barque; night-time on earth meant that he was passing through the underworld below.

373 *Enet-te-ntōrē*: ancient name for Dendera.

377 *bersim*: berseem or Egyptian clover (*Trifolium alexandrinum*).

380 *the White Nile ... Blue Nile ... Fayum*: the Blue Nile and White Nile (the two great tributaries of the Nile River) and the Faiyum oasis region were much frequented by European 'travellers' of different kinds.

ONANONANON

Published in the *English Review* (March 1921), and not reprinted until 1989, in the posthumous collection *The Magic Mirror: Lost Supernatural and Mystery Stories*. One of a number of stories written by Blackwood in the aftermath of the

First World War, 'Onanonanon' more specifically grows from his stint as a British secret agent in Switzerland. He disliked this form of service, writing: 'It was a beastly job. I hated pretending to be someone else; telephoning "meet me at Monday at noon", which actually meant "on Tuesday at 6.00"; changing my tram at intervals to make sure I was not being followed, and a dozen other schoolboy tricks' (Ashley, 285). The original periodical appearance has been used here.

382 *his convalescence . . . peeling skin*: presumably scarlet fever.

383 *At the age of fifty . . . the Great War*: reflects Blackwood's own experience; see headnote (the 'neutral country' is Switzerland).

the plague that milked the world: in the sense of 'milked dry', depleted or depopulated. The 1918 influenza pandemic, known popularly as 'Spanish flu', raged for two years and claimed many millions of lives globally (estimates vary widely). By this time, Blackwood had resigned from the secret service and was working for the Red Cross in Rouen, France, where the epidemic arrived in the spring of 1918; he may well have caught the flu himself, though there is no evidence of this.

His hated alias, Baker: this was also Blackwood's hated alias during his own stint as a secret agent.

THE LAND OF GREEN GINGER

First published in the Christmas issue of the BBC magazine *Radio Times* (23 Dec. 1927), and subsequently reprinted in two collections: *Short Stories of To-day and Yesterday* (1930) and *Shocks* (1935). (The story has here been set using the 1930 collection; the original 1927 magazine has also been consulted.) 'The Land of Green Ginger' is one of several later stories by Blackwood involving such topics as time, 'higher space', and multidimensionality (others include 'The Pikestaffe Case', 'The Man Who Was Milligan', and 'The Man Who Lived Backwards') influenced or inspired by the metaphysical speculations of thinkers including his friend, the engineer-philosopher J. W. Dunne (author of *An Experiment with Time*, which explored the idea of 'serial time'), as well as the philosopher-mystic George Gurdjieff and the esoteric writer P. D. Ouspensky.

388 *[title]*: the Land of Green Ginger is a winding, cobblestoned street in the port city of Hull (presumably 'the ancient port' in which the story is set). The origin of the name is obscure; Blackwood's narrator here connects it with China and Chinese trade.

service flat: a flat whose rent also covers such hotel-like services as cleaning, catering, and valet service.

newspaper symposiums: a type of feature first appearing in the 1920s, 'The newspaper symposium [was] a series of brief interviews commenting on a subject of current news interest', or alternatively comprising short 'interviews with famous persons on a selected topic' (Nancy Barr Mavity, *The Modern Newspaper* (New York, 1930), 174, 205). Adam, a well-known author, has apparently been asked to contribute to a symposium of the second variety, in response to the prompt, 'How I started'.

390 *Oxford colours*: i.e. a boater hat with a ribbon of, probably, blue and white (Oxford University's colour was and is blue, but particular crews' ribbon schemes could vary by college).

THE DOLL

First published by August Derleth's Arkham Press in *The Doll and One Other* (1946), along with 'The Trod'; both stories appear to have been written in or shortly before January 1939 (Ashley, 387).

400 *the spider's thread of the big telescopes*: refers to the use of spider-web strands for cross-hairs in the eyepieces of telescopes and microscopes.

417 *Que le bon dieu*: (French) 'May God . . .' e.g. hear my prayer, bless you, give me strength.

418 *'Buth laga' . . . Revenge in Hindustani*: the lingua franca of North India, today referred to as 'Hindi' or 'Urdu' depending on (upon other factors) the script used, was commonly called 'Hindustani' well into the twentieth century. 'Buth laga' does not, however, mean 'revenge' (or anything else) in that language, but is conceivably a corrupted, misspelled version of *badlā legā*, *legā* being the singular third-person masculine future form of *lenā*, 'he shall take revenge' (I am indebted to Hajnalka Kovacs for this surmise).

A SELECTION OF   **OXFORD WORLD'S CLASSICS**

An Anthology of Elizabethan Prose
Fiction

Early Modern Women's Writing

Three Early Modern Utopias (Utopia;
New Atlantis; The Isle of Pines)

FRANCIS BACON   Essays
The Major Works

APHRA BEHN   Oroonoko and Other Writings
The Rover and Other Plays

JOHN BUNYAN   Grace Abounding
The Pilgrim's Progress

JOHN DONNE   The Major Works
Selected Poetry

JOHN FOXE   Book of Martyrs

BEN JONSON   The Alchemist and Other Plays
The Devil is an Ass and Other Plays
Five Plays

JOHN MILTON   The Major Works
Paradise Lost
Selected Poetry

EARL OF ROCHESTER   Selected Poems

SIR PHILIP SIDNEY   The Old Arcadia
The Major Works

SIR PHILIP and   The Sidney Psalter
MARY SIDNEY

IZAAK WALTON   The Compleat Angler

A SELECTION OF   **OXFORD WORLD'S CLASSICS**

	Late Victorian Gothic Tales
	Literature and Science in the Nineteenth Century
JANE AUSTEN	Emma
	Mansfield Park
	Persuasion
	Pride and Prejudice
	Selected Letters
	Sense and Sensibility
MRS BEETON	Book of Household Management
MARY ELIZABETH BRADDON	Lady Audley's Secret
ANNE BRONTË	The Tenant of Wildfell Hall
CHARLOTTE BRONTË	Jane Eyre
	Shirley
	Villette
EMILY BRONTË	Wuthering Heights
ROBERT BROWNING	The Major Works
JOHN CLARE	The Major Works
SAMUEL TAYLOR COLERIDGE	The Major Works
WILKIE COLLINS	The Moonstone
	No Name
	The Woman in White
CHARLES DARWIN	The Origin of Species
THOMAS DE QUINCEY	The Confessions of an English Opium-Eater
	On Murder
CHARLES DICKENS	The Adventures of Oliver Twist
	Barnaby Rudge
	Bleak House
	David Copperfield
	Great Expectations
	Nicholas Nickleby

A SELECTION OF   **OXFORD WORLD'S CLASSICS**

CHARLES DICKENS	**The Old Curiosity Shop**
	Our Mutual Friend
	The Pickwick Papers
GEORGE DU MAURIER	**Trilby**
MARIA EDGEWORTH	**Castle Rackrent**
GEORGE ELIOT	**Daniel Deronda**
	The Lifted Veil and Brother Jacob
	Middlemarch
	The Mill on the Floss
	Silas Marner
EDWARD FITZGERALD	**The Rubáiyát of Omar Khayyám**
ELIZABETH GASKELL	**Cranford**
	The Life of Charlotte Brontë
	Mary Barton
	North and South
	Wives and Daughters
GEORGE GISSING	**New Grub Street**
	The Nether World
	The Odd Women
EDMUND GOSSE	**Father and Son**
THOMAS HARDY	**Far from the Madding Crowd**
	Jude the Obscure
	The Mayor of Casterbridge
	The Return of the Native
	Tess of the d'Urbervilles
	The Woodlanders
JAMES HOGG	**The Private Memoirs and Confessions of a Justified Sinner**
JOHN KEATS	**The Major Works**
	Selected Letters
CHARLES MATURIN	**Melmoth the Wanderer**
HENRY MAYHEW	**London Labour and the London Poor**

A SELECTION OF   **OXFORD WORLD'S CLASSICS**

WILLIAM MORRIS   **News from Nowhere**

JOHN RUSKIN   **Praeterita**
    Selected Writings

WALTER SCOTT   **Ivanhoe**
    Rob Roy
    Waverley

MARY SHELLEY   **Frankenstein**
    The Last Man

ROBERT LOUIS STEVENSON   **Strange Case of Dr Jekyll and Mr Hyde**
    and Other Tales
    Treasure Island

BRAM STOKER   **Dracula**

W. M. THACKERAY   **Vanity Fair**

FRANCES TROLLOPE   **Domestic Manners of the Americans**

OSCAR WILDE   **The Importance of Being Earnest**
    and Other Plays
    The Major Works
    The Picture of Dorian Gray

ELLEN WOOD   **East Lynne**

DOROTHY WORDSWORTH   **The Grasmere and Alfoxden Journals**

WILLIAM WORDSWORTH   **The Major Works**

WORDSWORTH and   **Lyrical Ballads**
COLERIDGE

A SELECTION OF   **OXFORD WORLD'S CLASSICS**

HENRY ADAMS	The Education of Henry Adams
LOUISA MAY ALCOTT	Little Women
SHERWOOD ANDERSON	Winesburg, Ohio
EDWARD BELLAMY	Looking Backward 2000–1887
CHARLES BROCKDEN BROWN	Wieland; or The Transformation and Memoirs of Carwin, The Biloquist
WILLA CATHER	My Ántonia O Pioneers!
KATE CHOPIN	The Awakening and Other Stories
JAMES FENIMORE COOPER	The Last of the Mohicans
STEPHEN CRANE	The Red Badge of Courage
J. HECTOR ST. JEAN DE CRÈVECŒUR	Letters from an American Farmer
FREDERICK DOUGLASS	Narrative of the Life of Frederick Douglass, an American Slave
THEODORE DREISER	Sister Carrie
F. SCOTT FITZGERALD	The Great Gatsby The Beautiful and Damned Tales of the Jazz Age This Side of Paradise
BENJAMIN FRANKLIN	Autobiography and Other Writings
CHARLOTTE PERKINS GILMAN	The Yellow Wall-Paper and Other Stories
ZANE GREY	Riders of the Purple Sage
NATHANIEL HAWTHORNE	The Blithedale Romance The House of the Seven Gables The Marble Faun The Scarlet Letter Young Goodman Brown and Other Tales

A SELECTION OF | **OXFORD WORLD'S CLASSICS**

WASHINGTON IRVING | **The Sketch-Book of Geoffrey Crayon, Gent**

HENRY JAMES | **The Ambassadors**
The American
The Aspern Papers and Other Stories
The Awkward Age
The Bostonians
Daisy Miller and Other Stories
The Europeans
The Golden Bowl
The Portrait of a Lady
The Spoils of Poynton
The Turn of the Screw and Other Stories
Washington Square
What Maisie Knew
The Wings of the Dove

JACK LONDON | **The Call of the Wild, White Fang and Other Stories**
John Barleycorn
The Sea-Wolf

HERMAN MELVILLE | **Billy Budd, Sailor and Selected Tales**
The Confidence-Man
Moby-Dick

FRANK NORRIS | **McTeague**

FRANCIS PARKMAN | **The Oregon Trail**

EDGAR ALLAN POE | **The Narrative of Arthur Gordon Pym of Nantucket and Related Tales**
Selected Tales

HARRIET BEECHER STOWE | **Uncle Tom's Cabin**

HENRY DAVID THOREAU | **Walden**

A SELECTION OF   **OXFORD WORLD'S CLASSICS**

MARK TWAIN   **Adventures of Huckleberry Finn**
                     The Adventures of Tom Sawyer
                     A Connecticut Yankee in King Arthur's
                       Court
                     Pudd'nhead Wilson

THORSTEIN VEBLEN   **The Theory of the Leisure Class**

BOOKER T. WASHINGTON **Up from Slavery**

EDITH WHARTON   **The Age of Innocence**
                     The Custom of the Country
                     Ethan Frome
                     The House of Mirth

WALT WHITMAN   **Leaves of Grass**

OWEN WISTER   **The Virginian**

A SELECTION OF **OXFORD WORLD'S CLASSICS**

ANTON CHEKHOV **About Love and Other Stories**
Early Stories
Five Plays
The Princess and Other Stories
The Russian Master and Other Stories
The Steppe and Other Stories
Twelve Plays
Ward Number Six and Other Stories

FYODOR DOSTOEVSKY **Crime and Punishment**
Devils
A Gentle Creature and Other Stories
The Idiot
The Karamazov Brothers
Memoirs from the House of the Dead
**Notes from the Underground and
The Gambler**

NIKOLAI GOGOL **Dead Souls**
Plays and Petersburg Tales

MIKHAIL LERMONTOV **A Hero of Our Time**

ALEXANDER PUSHKIN **Boris Godunov**
Eugene Onegin
The Queen of Spades and Other Stories

LEO TOLSTOY **Anna Karenina**
The Kreutzer Sonata and Other Stories
The Raid and Other Stories
Resurrection
War and Peace

IVAN TURGENEV **Fathers and Sons**
First Love and Other Stories
A Month in the Country

A SELECTION OF   **OXFORD WORLD'S CLASSICS**

LUDOVICO ARIOSTO	**Orlando Furioso**
GIOVANNI BOCCACCIO	**The Decameron**
LUÍS VAZ DE CAMÕES	**The Lusíads**
MIGUEL DE CERVANTES	**Don Quixote de la Mancha** **Exemplary Stories**
CARLO COLLODI	**The Adventures of Pinocchio**
DANTE ALIGHIERI	**The Divine Comedy** **Vita Nuova**
GALILEO	**Selected Writings**
J. W. VON GOETHE	**Faust: Part One and Part Two**
FRANZ KAFKA	**The Metamorphosis and Other Stories** **The Trial**
LEONARDO DA VINCI	**Selections from the Notebooks**
LOPE DE VEGA	**Three Major Plays**
FEDERICO GARCIA LORCA	**Four Major Plays** **Selected Poems**
NICCOLÒ MACHIAVELLI	**Discourses on Livy** **The Prince**
MICHELANGELO	**Life, Letters, and Poetry**
PETRARCH	**Selections from the Canzoniere and** **Other Works**
LUIGI PIRANDELLO	**Three Plays**
RAINER MARIA RILKE	**Selected Poems**
GIORGIO VASARI	**The Lives of the Artists**

TROLLOPE IN   **OXFORD WORLD'S CLASSICS**

ANTHONY TROLLOPE   **The American Senator**
                      An Autobiography
                      Barchester Towers
                      Can You Forgive Her?
                      Cousin Henry
                      Doctor Thorne
                      The Duke's Children
                      The Eustace Diamonds
                      Framley Parsonage
                      He Knew He Was Right
                      Lady Anna
                      The Last Chronicle of Barset
                      Orley Farm
                      Phineas Finn
                      Phineas Redux
                      The Prime Minister
                      Rachel Ray
                      The Small House at Allington
                      The Warden
                      The Way We Live Now

A SELECTION OF   OXFORD WORLD'S CLASSICS

HORACE	The Complete Odes and Epodes
JUVENAL	The Satires
LIVY	The Dawn of the Roman Empire
	Hannibal's War
	The Rise of Rome
MARCUS AURELIUS	The Meditations
OVID	The Love Poems
	Metamorphoses
PETRONIUS	The Satyricon
PLATO	Defence of Socrates, Euthyphro, and Crito
	Gorgias
	Meno and Other Dialogues
	Phaedo
	Republic
	Symposium
PLAUTUS	Four Comedies
PLUTARCH	Greek Lives
	Roman Lives
	Selected Essays and Dialogues
PROPERTIUS	The Poems
SOPHOCLES	Antigone, Oedipus the King, and Electra
SUETONIUS	Lives of the Caesars
TACITUS	The Annals
	The Histories
THUCYDIDES	The Peloponnesian War
VIRGIL	The Aeneid
	The Eclogues and Georgics
XENOPHON	The Expedition of Cyrus

	Classical Literary Criticism
	The First Philosophers: The Presocratics and the Sophists
	Greek Lyric Poetry
	Myths from Mesopotamia
APOLLODORUS	**The Library of Greek Mythology**
APOLLONIUS OF RHODES	**Jason and the Golden Fleece**
APULEIUS	**The Golden Ass**
ARISTOPHANES	**Birds and Other Plays**
ARISTOTLE	**The Nicomachean Ethics**
	Politics
ARRIAN	**Alexander the Great**
BOETHIUS	**The Consolation of Philosophy**
CAESAR	**The Civil War**
	The Gallic War
CATULLUS	**The Poems of Catullus**
CICERO	**Defence Speeches**
	The Nature of the Gods
	On Obligations
	Political Speeches
	The Republic and The Laws
EURIPIDES	**Bacchae and Other Plays**
	Heracles and Other Plays
	Medea and Other Plays
	Orestes and Other Plays
	The Trojan Women and Other Plays
HERODOTUS	**The Histories**
HOMER	**The Iliad**
	The Odyssey